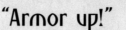

"Armor up!"

I squeezed into a waiting Mark 10 hanging on the rack, sealed it off, and accepted a helmet from Thomason. "Thanks, Staff Sergeant," I told him. "What's going down?"

"Some of our people are on the ice," he said. "Trapped . . . by one of those *things*."

Wiseman handed me a Mk. 30 carbine. I checked the safety, wondering if a half-megajoule laser pulse would even register in a cuttlewhale's consciousness. I might have better luck throwing snowballs at the things.

"Open the hatch!" Hancock called. The dim reddish light of Abyssworld spilled into the lock as the ramp lowered in front of us.

Haldane had touched down on the ice perhaps a kilometer away from the spot where the cuttlewhale had lunged up through the ice. Thirty Marines and two Corpsmen were out here, converging on the ship as quickly as possible. I could see several of them using their meta-thrusters to make low, bounding leaps across the pressure ridges, their combat-armor nano-flage making them almost invisible in the dim light. In the distance, the snaky silhouette of a cuttlewhale weaved against the swollen red face of the sun.

"Perimeter defense!" Hancock called. "Dalton! Set up your weapon to put fire on that thing!"

We spread out, creating a broad circle around the grounded *Haldane*. Visibility sucked. The wind from the west had picked up, and we were staring into a layer of blowing ice crystals and freezing fog perhaps two meters deep. I dropped to the ice alongside Bob Dalton, helping him unship his M4-A2 plasma weapon.

ABYSS DEEP

STAR CORPSMAN
BOOK TWO

IAN DOUGLAS

HARPER
Voyager

Harper*Voyager*
77–85 Fulham Palace Road,
Hammersmith, London W6 8JB

www.harpervoyagerbooks.com

Published by Harper*Voyager*
An imprint of HarperCollins*Publishers* 2014

A catalogue record for this book
is available from the British Library

ISBN: 978-0-00-748904-6

Cover art by Fred Gambino

MIX
Paper from
responsible sources

FSC www.fsc.org **FSC™ C007454**

For Dave Plottel, who first introduced me to the wonders of Godel numbers many years ago . . .

and, as always, to my beloved Brea.

ABYSS DEEP

Chapter One

THERE'S AN OLD, OLD EXPRESSION IN THE MILITARY, ONE THAT CAN probably be traced back to some platoon sergeant in the army of Sargon the Great: *hurry up and wait.*

In fact, it's been said that 99 percent of military life ranges from tedium to unbearable boredom, with the remaining 1 percent consisting of stark, abject terror. A lot of that tedium comes with the waiting . . . especially if what you're waiting for is that few moments of crisp, cold terror.

"Doc Carlyle!" the gunnery sergeant's voice called on my private channel. "You okay?"

"Yeah, Gunny. No problems."

"Remember to breathe, okay?"

I swallowed, trying to center myself into a calm acceptance of whatever was to be. "Aye, aye, Gunnery Sergeant." As the platoon's Corpsman, I was supposed to be monitoring all of the Marines inside the tin can . . . but Gunnery Sergeant Hancock had been watching my readouts, and noted the increase in pulse and the unevenness of my respiration.

I was packed in with the forty-one Marines of 2nd Platoon, Bravo Company, inside the cargo deck of a shotgun Katy. That's the Marines' name for the KT-54 orbital cargo transporter, a big, chunky tug with meta-thrusters on one end and a blunt-ended cylinder on the other. We were in full armor—a KT's cargo can isn't pressurized—strapped upright to ranks of backboards . . . and waiting. They hadn't opened the can yet, so we were in near total darkness. A maddeningly calm voice inside my head, an extremely sexy *woman's* voice, said, "Five mikes."

"Ah, copy that," another voice said. "Crack 'er open and let's see what we got."

In front of me, beyond the lined-up helmet backs of nine Marines, the end cap of the Katy split in two and began to swing open. If we'd been riding in the throat of an alligator, that's what we would have seen when he yawned. Light blasted in from a slender horizon to my right, silhouetting the closely packed Marines and illuminating the utilitarian interior of the can.

"Four minutes. Brace for course correction in three . . . two . . . one . . . fire."

I felt a short, sharp kick along my back. The Katy's AI pilot had just fired the engines, giving us a slight bump up in velocity and making a micro correction to our course. I wondered if the bad guys at Capricorn Zeta had noted the course change, and were getting ready to welcome us.

"Okay, platoon." That was our platoon CO, Second Lieutenant Paul Singer. "Unship your harnesses."

I used a thoughtclick to unsnap the harness holding me against the rigid backboard. God knows we didn't have room in there to fumble with snaps and fasteners with our gauntleted hands. I glanced up and felt claustrophobic. The Marines of 2nd Platoon were lined up on the canister's bulkheads in four ranks of ten each, plus two extras—Singer and Staff Sergeant Thomason. The helmets of three of them were less than a meter from my own, coming in from either side and one seemingly suspended head-down directly above me.

There *is* no "up" or "down" in zero-G, of course. From Corporal Gobel's vantage point, *I* was the one hanging upside down.

"Three minutes." Damn, but that AI's voice sounded sexy. "Two hundred kilometers."

The seconds trickled away as we continued waiting in ranks. Two hundred kilometers to the target was a long way, too far for us to see the objective yet. But it was out there, probably well above the gleaming curve of the Earth. Then I noticed a bright star directly ahead, and queried my in-head. Was that the objective? The platoon AI responded by putting a red box around the star, together with a fast dwindling set of numerals just to one side. Approaching in a lower, higher-speed orbit, we were closing with the target at just over two kilometers per second. According to the opplan, the shotgun would fire when we were ten kilometers from our objective.

"Okay, Marines," Lieutenant Singer said, "Listen up. We do this by the book, and we'll come through this alive."

Well, most of us, I thought. *Maybe . . .*

If we were very, very lucky. . . .

"Remember to steer for the rock end of the facility," Singer went on. "The doughnut will navigate itself to the main control hab, and that's where we'll make the breach. We don't know what kind of defenses the tangos might have in there, so stay sharp, and keep an eye on your CT2 displays. Got it?"

"Ooh-rah!" a number of the Marines chorused back, their centuries-old battle cry.

I wondered how the CT2W could sort new fear from what was there already.

Oh, I knew how it worked in theory. The Cognitive Technology Threat Warning System has been around in one form or another since the early twenty-first century. It picks up P300 brainwaves, which are linked to stimulus evaluation and categorization. Back in the 2020s, this was handled by a smart helmet equipped with scalp sensors. For the last century or so, though, it's been a program running within a soldier's cerebral implants. The idea is that we can detect a threat subconsciously, well *before* it actually manifests as a bad guy with a weapon. It sounds wild, using brainwaves to detect subconsciously perceived threats, but tests show Marines pick up about 47 percent of hidden threats with just their eyes or standard optics . . . compared with 90-plus percent when they're running a CT2WS.

"Two minutes."

"Weapons check," Staff Sergeant Thomason called. "Lock and load!"

I looked at my own weapon, a Mk. 30 Sunbeam-Sony carbine packing a half-megajoule-pulse in a mass of just four kilos. My sidearm was the usual Browning Five, a stubby, mag-accelerator handgun that could hurl a five-millimeter bit of steel-jacketed depleted uranium at a thousand meters per second. Both weapons were charged, hot-linked to my in-head, and safed.

There's an old myth that says Navy Hospital Corpsmen don't go into combat armed. That might have been true once, back when the Geneva Convention dictated the rules for civilized warfare. Unfortunately, any nonhuman bad guys we happened to run into weren't going to be signatories of those documents . . . and that was definitely true of the human hijackers we were facing now.

"Hey, Gunny," Sergeant Woznowiec called. "Any intel yet on how many tangos are waiting for us in there?"

"Negative on that, Woz," Hancock replied. "When I know, you'll know."

"Comm silence," Singer warned. "Stay the hell off the TC."

Shit. The tactical channel was shielded and short-ranged. There was no way the bad guys could be listening in. Singer was an asshole . . . worse, a *wannabe* asshole fresh out of the Naval Academy.

"One minute."

"We're getting a warn-off from Zeta station," Thomason said. "They've seen us."

There was a lot of traffic in low-Earth orbit. The idea had

been to slip in close like an innocent cargo tug. Unfortunately, that deception couldn't provide us with cover indefinitely. The station's radar would have been tracking us for long minutes already, and collision avoidance alarms might be going off over there already.

"Twenty seconds," Thomason added. "Dropping the backrests."

Those rigid boards behind our backs, shaped to fit our armor backpacks and meta tanks with snug precision, were grown from the canister's internal nanomatrix, just like made-to-order chairs and tables grown from the floor. At an electronic command from our AI, they dissolved back into the deck, leaving each of us moving with the Katy. I felt my boots leaving the deck, just by a few millimeters, as the sexy AI voice sounded off the final countdown.

"Cargo launch in five . . . four . . . three . . . two . . . one . . . *initiate*."

The Katy fired its forward maneuvering thrusters. From our point of view, the walls of the cargo canister abruptly slid backward, and the entire platoon emerged suddenly into open, empty space. The vast, eye-watering blue and mottled white of Earth filled half of the sky with aching beauty. The sun was squarely at our backs; the sunset terminator stretched along the curve of the horizon ahead.

The Marine version of a KT-54 was called a shotgun Katy for a reason. By decelerating sharply, the vessel's armored human cargo hurtled from the wide-open bow, moving at the same speed as the tug until it slowed. Now it was dropping away behind us, empty, and 2nd Platoon kept moving at a constant velocity toward our objective. For all intents and purposes, it was as though we'd just been fired into space like a cloud of pellets from an enormous shotgun.

"Platoon, shift to Formation One," Singer ordered. "*Deploy!*"

Our Mk. 10 suits were locked into standard M287 dorsal

jumpjet packs. On the ground they let us bound across the landscape in twenty-meter jumps. In open space, they turned each of us, in effect, into a small, independent spacecraft. They were fueled by cryo-stabilized $N-He_{64}$, an exotic fuel commonly called meta that was far denser in terms of available energy than conventional propellants. The thrusters were controlled by our in-head software; I told mine that I wanted to move into Formation One, and my backpack gave a gentle kick to my right.

The Marine formation was opening up, creating a more dispersed target in case the bad guys started taking shots at us. The shift also cleared the way for our doughnut, which was accelerating now on its own, moving up the center of the formation and into the distance ahead, homing on the bright star of Capricorn Zeta.

My jumpjet pack bumped again, halting my outward drift. Around me, the Marines appeared to be unmoving, hanging motionless in space relative to me and to one another. The surface of the Earth, however, drifted past at a steady pace. We were coming up on the west coast of Baja at the moment; north, I saw the cloudless ocher expanses of the Arizona and New Mexico deserts; southeast, bright stars strung in a vertical line stretching up into the sky flashed with a steady wink-wink-wink that marked the space elevator over Cayambe, a thread otherwise made invisible by distance.

And moment by moment, the Zeta facility grew brighter, taking on shape and form—an awkward collection of cylinders dazzling in the sunlight, connected at one end to a black rock a kilometer across.

We'd been thoroughly briefed on the Zeta situation, of course, complete with in-head downloads showing every detail of the five-hundred-meter facility. Asteroid mining was a particular target of the neo-Ludd movement, of course, so Zeta had offered them some highly visible propaganda for the watching global netizens back on Earth.

That small and wrinkled-looking nickel-iron asteroid, listed as Atun 3840, was only a kilometer across, but it contained an estimated 2 trillion dollars' worth of platinum, 2 trillion in iron and nickel, and perhaps 1.5 trillion dollars' worth of cobalt . . . a total of more than 5 trillion dollars of commercial metals.

The first asteroid mining had commenced early in the twenty-first century, with robots that extracted precious metals on-site and slingshotted them back to circum-Earth space where they were captured. There, one-ton slugs of solar-purified metal were injected with inert gas, molded into lightweight glider wings, sheathed in cheap, refractory heat shielding, and sent on down for recovery in the ocean . . . a cheap and highly efficient system still used to this day. The very first of Humankind's trillionaires made their fortunes with the various space mining start-ups of the 2020s, paid for our expansion out into the Solar System, helped us survive the return of the Ice Age, and ultimately funded the first starships.

Later, it proved more cost effective to nudge target asteroids out of their original orbits and swing them into Earth orbit. Decelerating one large mass, it turned out, was a lot easier than trying it with millions . . . and safer as well. *That* fact was abundantly demonstrated when the catchers missed a slug of iridium in 2094 and it slammed into the Lunar farside.

For a century and a half, now, more or less, we've been bringing whole asteroids into Earth orbit and dismantling them there, using a couple of close Lunar passes to decelerate them. The AIs managing their vectors are *good* . . . and the meta-thrusters used for precision adjustments are reliable enough that even if something—unthinkable!—goes wrong, they can sling the rock into a higher and safer orbit. Hell, they *have* to be good just to shift the orbit periodically to avoid cutting the space elevator.

But the neo-Ludds are less accepting of the claims and

promises of technology. They're probably best known for their opposition to cerebral implants and the global Net, but orbital mining is a popular target too. This time, they'd made it a literal target by boarding Capricorn Zeta and threatening to drop Atun 3840 on Earth.

The rock wasn't a dinosaur-killer, but it would make a hell of a mess if it hit. An ocean strike meant tidal scouring continents for hundreds of kilometers inland; a land strike could annihilate a dozen cities and raise a global dust cloud that would wreck our ongoing attempts to beat back the new ice age, and might even knock us all the way into a "Snowball Earth" scenario. These guys were *nuts*.

And so the president had given the order: the Marines *would* take back Capricorn Zeta. Negotiations had been going on for a week already, but had been going nowhere. And then a few hours ago a hostage had been shoved out an airlock. The terrorists' key and nonnegotiable demand— that humans abandon space industrialization—simply wasn't going to happen.

The kicker was that there were still fifty-four people on board Capricorn Zeta, not counting an estimated twenty tangos. There reportedly also were two M'nangat on board . . . and that made it an interstellar incident. Our orders were distressingly precise. Our first priority was to secure Atun 3840—which meant capturing the facility's meta-thruster controls. Second was to make certain the two visiting M'nangat were safe. Saving the miners and corporate officials in the facility came in only at number three.

My tactical in-head showed the doughnut was almost there. A steady countdown was silently running against my field of view. We were twenty seconds now from touching down.

Thirty meters away, Lance Corporal Stalzar's armor lit up, a dazzling flare of light consuming the torso of his suit. We all heard the shriek . . .

"Sniper!" Thomason called. "Marine down!"

I was already checking Stalzar's readouts on my in-head. There was nothing . . . *nothing* I could do. . . .

A second star appeared close to the asteroid's horizon, opposite the mining station, growing brilliant, then fading. We had countersnipers both up on Geosynch Center, halfway up the space elevator, and on board a Marine transport a few thousand kilometers above and behind us. They'd seen the pulse of the tango's laser when he'd shot Stalzar, and vaporized the chunk of asteroid terrain where he'd been hiding.

Ten seconds. What had been a bright star, then a gleaming toy in the sunlight, was expanding now into something much larger. Another silent flare of light on the asteroid marked a second countersniper shot. Maybe they'd spotted a tango's heat signature against the rock.

Five seconds. The rock drifted off to my right. Directly ahead, the silvery smooth surface of the mining facility's Hab One now filled my forward view. I could see the alphanumerics painted on the hull, and a corporate logo— Skye Metals—sandblasted by orbiting grit. The doughnut was affixed to the hull high and a little to my left. I shifted my vector slightly, aiming for a flat surface nearby. I gave an in-head order, and my AI flipped me end-for-end. My feet were aimed at the station as my thrusters cut in, slowing me. I hit the hull two seconds later, flexing my knees to absorb the impact. Around me, Marines were raining out of the sky, touching down on the hull, then moving toward the doughnut.

I let the Marines go first, of course. As the platoon's Corpsman—the "Doc"—I was expected to keep up but not to engage in combat. That was the contract U.S. Navy Corpsmen had shared with the Marine Corp for the past three centuries or so: they do the fighting, and we patch 'em up.

The waiting was over. The first Marine fireteam was plunging into the doughnut, headfirst.

The VBSS Mobile Nano-utility Lock is indispensible for

Visit Board Search and Seizure ops in hard vacuum, especially when the visit is being resisted by an armed enemy. It really is a doughnut wheel some three meters across, with what looks like a black sheet stretched taut across the hole. It hits the hull of a target vessel or base, and nanodisassemblers on the business side chew through metal, plastic, and active nano sheathing with ease. The black sheet is a nanomatrix pressure shield just a few molecules thick; it holds in the target vessel's air, but molds close to a boarder's armor, letting him pass through without venting atmosphere.

"Rogers! Jorgenson!" Thomason snapped over the platoon channel. "Hold up!"

The next two Marines in line waited, clinging to handholds on the doughnut. Thomason was watching what was happening inside by means of cameras mounted on the helmets of the first four-man fireteam.

"Okay!" Thomason said. "Fireteam two! Go!"

Rogers and Jorgenson slipped through the lock, followed by Beaudet and Tomacek. They were followed by the next fireteam . . . and the next. I wasn't tapped in to the visual channels, but I could hear the radio calls of the Marines already inside.

"Watch it! Watch it! Tango at oh-one-five!"

"Moving! Firing!"

"Rogers! Morrisey! To your right!"

"Got him! Tango down!"

"Sobiesky! You and Marshall secure the hatch! The rest of you, with me!"

More and more of the platoon's Marines vanished through the doughnut, until it was my turn. I grabbed the handholds and pulled myself forward. I could feel the nanoseal closing around me, clinging to me, sliding down my torso as I moved . . . and then I was through.

The interior was a large compartment some ten meters across, dark except for emergency lights spaced around the bulkheads. Directly ahead, my helmet light illuminated a massive tangle of pipes and conduits—the business end of the nano-D mining equipment eating its way into the heart of Atun 3840. A dead tango floated in the air nearby, wearing what looked like a Chinese space suit without the helmet. A MAW drifted nearby.

Magnetic accelerator weapons aren't a real good choice for close combat inside a pressurized environment. I wondered how well trained these idiots were.

A Marine fireteam on the far end of the hab module used an applicator gun to smear a two-meter circle of nano-D against the bulkhead, and then one of them gave the smoking ring a hard kick. Gunfire cracked and clanged as magnetic rounds snapped through the opening and punched through bulkheads, a cacophony of noise after the silence of our passage through vacuum. Corporal Tom Morrisey screamed, and I saw a flash of incoming data on my med channel.

"Corpsman!" Thomason yelled. "Marine down!"

I was also getting environmental warnings, and a station Klaxon began sounding an alert. Some of the rounds that had missed Morrisey had punched through the facility's outer hull. The station's external nanomatrix would seal the holes, but that would take a few moments, and the air pressure was dropping precipitously in the meantime.

That wouldn't hurt us, of course, but it put the station's crew in danger.

I kicked off the bulkhead and glided across the compartment to Morrisey. His right arm was missing below the elbow, the armor there was a tangled mess, and blood was spurting from the wreckage in a bright orange-red arterial stream that was breaking off into darker gobbets as it spiraled with his rotation. I collided with him and stabilized his spin, then jacked into his armor for a direct readout.

The magnetically accelerated slug had sliced through his elbow with kinetic energy enough to shred armor and amputate the lower arm. Normally, Marine armor will guillotine shut above a serious leg or arm wound, stopping the bleeding and, more important, stopping the suit from venting its air into vacuum. That last might be a problem in another few minutes, but right now the cabin pressure was high enough that the armor's slice-and-seal function hadn't triggered. Morrisey's brachial artery was pumping out blood fast; he would be dead in a few minutes if I didn't stop the bleeding.

I did a quick scan to make certain he didn't have any head trauma—it looked like it was just his arm that had been hit, but you never know—then thoughtclicked a key directing Morrisey's suit to autoinject a jolt of anodynic recep blockers into his carotid artery. Heart rate 155 . . . BP 149 over 90, respiration 36 and gasping, rapidly elevating levels of both adrenalin and noradrenalin.

Morrisey stopped screaming as the nanoanadynes started shutting down the doloric receptors in his thalamus and the insular cortex, blocking the pain signals as they reached his brain. "Jesus, Doc!" he said. "I can still feel it! It feels . . . *weird*!"

"That's because your pressure receptors are still firing. Don't worry. You're going to be fine."

I hoped. His extremities were already starting to cool, which meant he was already shocky. I ordered his suit to clamp down on his upper arm to reduce the brachial artery flow, then raise its internal temp slightly and relax the external pressure on the arteries leading to his head to interrupt the shock response.

I had to make a quick decision, though. The armor clamp would slow the bleeding, but wouldn't stop it by itself. I could cram a packet of skinseal into the injury, and let that seal off the wound . . . or I could order his suit to slice off what was left of his arm well above the bleeding stump. The guillotine at his elbow, obviously, was smashed; the next working blade was eight centimeters up, midway up his humerus. The nanonarcs would block the pain, or most of it, but he would still *feel* it, and that would increase the risk of shock.

Shock or not, I elected to cut. Skinseal is great stuff, but it's better for minor bleeding. And if the mining station's outer hull didn't seal off the leaks, Morrisey would have other problems in a moment if he started losing air.

I again checked his nananodyne levels, then thought-clicked through the link to trigger the suit's chopper. Another chunk of his arm came off, a squat cylinder encased in black armor, but the bleeding stopped at once.

"God," he said. "I'm gonna be sick. . . ."

"No," I told him. "You're not."

Vomiting inside a space suit is *very* serious business, and can lead to drowning. Morrisey's armor was already firing antiemetic 'bots into his carotid artery, but it wasn't enough.

The vomiting reflex is triggered in the *area postrema*, a tiny nub on the floor of the brain's fluid-filled fourth ventricle snugged up against the cerebellum. There are a number of different chemical pathways leading to emeses triggers, but most involve a neuropeptide called substance P, or SP, which is found in both the brain and the spinal cord and which is associated with inflammation, pain, and shock.

I pulled my N-prog from my M-7 medical kit and thought a quick series of commands into it. The device, in turn, reprogrammed some of the nananodyne bots now circulating through Morrisey's brain, ordering them to block out the SP . . . and also to shut down the cholinergic receptor input from his inner ears, since his vestibular system—reacting to zero-G—was also screaming at him. The reprogrammed 'bots would add to the suit's antiemetic response, helping to stifle Morrisey's nausea before he vomited inside his helmet.

"Yeah," Morrisey said. "Yeah . . . that's . . . that's better, Doc. Thanks."

I gave his readouts a final check. His BP was stabilizing at 125 over 70, and his respiration was a bit slower now. "You'll be fine," I told him. "Some time in sick bay, and we'll grow you a new arm, better than the old."

He nodded inside his helmet. "I know."

I sent him back to the doughnut to await a medevac. Now that we had our foothold on board Zeta, more Marines were on the way in, along with support vessels and transports to haul away the wounded. I made my way toward the second breach in the bulkhead, slipping through and into the compartment on the other side. The fighting appeared to be over—here, at least. There was a seething mob of people in brown utilities, more spacesuited bodies, Marines, and a lot more drifting globules of blood, a tangle too confused for me to count. Marines were moving among the rescued hostages, cuffing their hands with zipstrips. Until we were absolutely sure of who was a tango and who was a hostage, we handled them *all* as potential terrorists. There was a bank of link-in controls along one bulkhead. I saw one deeply padded seat with a dead tango strapped into it, his hands still on the palmpads on the chair's arms. He'd probably been the terrorist commander, running the station's defenses by jacking in at this secondary control center, but the ugly crater in his spacesuit's chest showed that a Marine had taken him out with a laser rifle.

"Corpsman, front!"

I homed on this new call, pushing my way through the milling civilians and Marines. Gunny Hancock was waving to me from an open hatch in the bulkhead beyond. "In here, Doc! On the double!"

Drifting through the opening, I entered a small and bare compartment—probably a storage locker. There were two M'nangat drifting inside, and one of them looked like it was hurt. Another dead tango floated near the overhead, a MAW pistol still clutched his hand.

I drifted over to the alien. "What happened?" I asked.

"That guy shot him," Hancock said, "just as we came through the door. Is it bad?"

"It's not good."

The M'nangat are surprisingly like us biologically—

carbon-based oxygen breathers, with metal-chelated tetra-pyroles pumped through an enclosed circulatory system by a pair of two-chambered hearts working in synch. They even use DNA for genetic coding rather than one of several other xenobiological possibilities, but that's where the similarities stop. The being was a couple of meters long, resembling a pale, blue-green pillar of thick, tightly twisted tentacles like a tree's trunk, which then spread out from the creature's base like the roots of a tree. At the top end was what looked like a half-meter cluster of grapes—though each grape was the size of an orange—translucent, and shot through with flecks of red and gold. The wounded one had a savage puncture in one side of its leathery trunk, and blue-green liquid was jetting in spurts from the wound with enough force to paint one bulkhead and drive the being into the other like a small rocket. Slits beneath the grape cluster representing mouths and breathing apertures gaped and pulsed, and the being ut-tered a startlingly human-sounding groan.

"You'll be okay, fella," I said. The reassurance was au-tomatic; I didn't expect the creature to answer. But a link switched on within my in-head, and the words "Thank you" wrote themselves out on an inner window.

I'd not realized that the M'nangat shared something else with us besides our body chemistries, that they had CNS prostheses that, among other things, could connect with an AI residing within their internal hardware and communi-cate with other software in the area . . . such as a translator program.

And as soon as I thought about that, something clicked into place . . . something I'd just seen and not thought about, but which represented a terrible danger to the sta-tion and to us.

"Gunny!" I yelled, turning. "That dead tango in the seat out there . . ."

"What about him, Doc?"

"If he has an AI—"

I saw Hancock's eyes widen behind his helmet visor. It had clicked for him too. He turned to duck out of the small compartment, but in that same instant I felt a solid jolt, and the sensation of weight tugged at me with a terrifying insistence. It wasn't much—maybe a tenth of a gravity, but it was terrifying in its implications.

The massive meta-fueled thrusters mounted to the surface of Atun 3840 had just fired. The one-kilometer asteroid and its attached mining station were decelerating . . . which meant we were now beginning to fall out of orbit and toward the Earth's surface.

And if we hit we were going to leave one hell of a big crater.

Chapter Two

WE WERE FALLING OUT OF THE SKY.

I knew immediately what had happened . . . and kicked myself for not picking up on it as soon as I'd seen that dead tango in the control seat. The guy might have been a neo-Ludd . . . but if he was running the control software for Capricorn Zeta—that's the only reason he would have been strapped into that chair with his hands on the palm interfaces—then he *must* have had a resident AI inside his in-head hardware, his cerebral implant. I have one; all Marines do as well, and most civilians have them too. It's how we can interface with all of the thousands of computers and control systems around us every day, from operating devices like my N-prog to pulling down in-head data feeds and scans and communication to telling the deck to grow a chair.

And a person doesn't have to be alive for the AI to keep working.

Whoever had helped the neo-Ludds take over Capricorn Zeta had had some high-powered technology behind them, and that would include AIs carefully programmed to help carry out their mission. That meant there would have been some sort of backup electronic deadman's switch; the man controlling the station dies, and his software tells the station to destroy itself . . . taking out a big part of the planet as it does so.

I heard Thomason's shouts outside. *"Get his hands off of there! Get him out of that fucking seat!"* But moment followed moment and the deceleration continued. The neo-Ludd software must have had run-if-interrupted code sequences. Someone would have to regain control of the system to stop those rockets.

That wasn't my immediate problem, however. The Marines had people who could regain control of the falling asteroid. I had a patient to worry about. If we re-entered Earth's atmosphere he would die—as would I—but he would die anyway even if we regained a stable orbit and I didn't patch him up.

There are certain priorities in treating a wounded patient no matter what his, her, or its species might be. The M'nangat was losing blood fast, and that was my immediate priority. M'nangat blood is cupriglobin, copper-based, rather than iron-based as with human hemoglobin. That's why the blue-green color of the blood. But the different blood chemistry wouldn't affect skinseal. These guys had a similar body temperature, and their skin, though thicker than in humans, was made up of the same sorts of carbon-based keratinocytes, keratin proteins, and lipids.

I pulled a packet of skinseal from my M-7 kit, thumbed it open, and pressed the whole pack, powder-side-down, over the wound. Skinseal includes both absorbents and binding nanoagents that would work on a variety of more or less similar body building blocks.

As it worked, I pulled down the species EG data from the Orbital Net.

**Encyclopedia Galactica/Xenospecies Profile
Entry: Sentient Galactic Species 14566
"M'nangat"**

M'nangat, "M'naggies," "Broccolis," "Brocs," "Stalks"
Civilization type: 1.042 G

TL 19: FTL, Genetic Prostheses, Cerebral Prostheses
Societal code: AQCB
Dominant: loose associative/scavenger/defensive/sexual
Cultural library: 4.11×10^{16} bits
Data Storage/Transmission DS/T: 3.07×10^{11}s
Biological code: 156.872.119
Genome: 3.8×10^9 bits; Coding/non-coding: 0.028.
Biology: C, N, O, S, H_2O, PO_4
    DNA
    Cupric metal-chelated tetrapyroles in aqueous circu-
      latory fluid.
    Mobile heterotrophs, omnivores, O_2 respiration.
    Upright tentacular locomotion.
    Mildly gregarious, Polyspecific [1 genera, 12 spe-
      cies]; trisexual.
Communication: modulated sound at 150 to 300 Hz.
Neural connection equivalence NCE = 1.1×10^{14}
T = ~260° to 300° K; **M** = 0.9×10^5 g; **L**: ~2.5×10^9s
Vision: ~200 nanometers to 720 nanometers; **Hearing**:
    12 Hz to 18,000 Hz
Member: Galactic Polylogue
    Receipt galactic nested code: 3.86×10^{10} s ago
    Locally initiated contact 0.11×10^9 s ago
    Star G1V; Planet: Fourth; "M'gat"
    a = 1.669×10^{11}m; M = 8.5×10^{27}g; R = 7.2×10^6m;
      p = 3.6×10^7s
    P_d = 2.3×10^5s, G = 10.9 m/s² Atm: O_2 20.1, N_2 79.6,
      CO_2 0.3;
    P_{atm} 0.97×10^5 Pa
Librarian's note: First direct human contact occurred in
    2119 C.E., the very first extraterrestrial space-faring
    civilization encountered by Humankind. Threat
    level—8.

I let the numbers cascade through my brain, watching
for anything that was so far out of the ordinary that it would

put up a red flag. *Ordinary* when discussing alien biochemistry takes in a huge chunk of territory, of course, but there were some basic rules to play by if the patient was a carbon-based oxygen breather. Hell, compared to some of the critters we've encountered out there, methane-breathers and gas giant floaters and fluoro-silicate crystal autotrophs, these guys were practically next of kin.

We'd known the Brocs for over a century, now . . . since just after the discovery of the local Encyclopedia Galactica Node at Sirius. They were our first ET encounter, face-to . . . whatever it is they have in place of a face. Once we established contact with them, they helped us figure out how to extract the oceans upon oceans of data in the EG, which helped us begin to make some small bit of sense out of the bewildering forest of intelligent life we were encountering as we moved out into the Galaxy. In fact, we were reading parts of the EG only twelve or thirteen years after we logged in; that we were doing so in *only* thirteen years was due almost entirely to Broc help. They've taught us five, so far, of the major Galactic *linguae francae*, as well as giving us the inside scoop on the slow-motion collapse of the R'agch'lgh Collective in toward the Core. In many ways, they've been Humankind's friendly native guides in our first tentative explorations into the Galaxy jungle at large.

A few have been allowed to come to the Sol System as consultants—so long as they didn't have astrogation devices that might give away Earth's most closely guarded secret . . . exactly *where* Sol was among the four hundred billion stars of our Galaxy. It pays to be *damned* cautious in a star wilderness filled with roving predarians and the wreckage of a collapsing galactic empire. These two, according to our pre-mission briefing, had been at Capricorn Zeta to advise us on in-orbit mining techniques.

Unfortunately, they'd been at the wrong place at the wrong time when a Chinese tug declared an emergency and docked alongside. Twenty armed tangos had been hiding on board. As soon as the tug docked, they'd come swarming out of the tug's cargo compartment and into the mining station.

PLEASE HELP HERM. The words printed themselves out in my in-head as the second, uninjured, M'nangat leaned closer.

Herm. The M'nangat had three sexes, I saw—male, female, and a third that received the fertilized embryo from the female and carried it to term. The wounded one, apparently, was one of those.

They were called life carriers.

I hesitated. I'd already done everything I could for the wounded Broccoli . . . everything I could, that is, without firing nano into its circulatory system to give me a look from the inside. Putting *anything* foreign into an alien body was risky, especially if you didn't know about possible antibody or immune-system responses. The nanobots I carried in my M-7 kit were designed to neatly bypass the human immune response . . . but how would that play out inside an alien circulatory system?

I pulled out a biochem analyzer and pressed its business end against my patient's tough, ropy hide. After a moment, I shifted the analyzer to a splatter of blue-green blood near the wound. The readouts downloaded straight into my in-head, giving me a more detailed understanding of the being's biochemistry than was available on the Net. In particular, I had my AI leapfrog through the incoming data to pinpoint those biochemistries associated with the alien's immune response.

The immune system for any species is an enormous set of chemistries—varied, complex, and efficient. Even bacteria have their own simple immune system—secreted enzymes that protect the cell against bacteriophage infections. Life forms as complicated as humans have many, many layers of physical and biochemical defenses . . . and quite a few of those are changing all the time to react to specific threats. I couldn't expect the M'nangat to be any different.

Our databases on M'nangat physiology weren't extensive—at least not the ones available to me over the Fleet channels—but I could have my AI run a series of simulations: what would happen if I shot my green patient full of nanobots? The answer came back in a few seconds. There was a solid 86 percent chance that my nano would *not* trigger an immune response.

Nanobots are designed and programmed with immune responses in mind, of course. They're coated with buckyweave carbon shells with the active molecular machinery hidden away inside a non-reactive sheath. Still, there was always a small chance—in this case 14 percent—that my nanobots might hit a biochemical trigger and sensitize the organism, telling it in effect that invaders were entering the body and it was time to call out the troops. Those percentages applied to the entire dose of 'bots, of course, and not to each nanobot individually. Otherwise, with a few hundred million foreign particles entering the alien system, sensitization would have been guaranteed.

I looked again at the wound, and decided I would have to accept those odds. The Broc had an entry wound but no exit cavity. The projectile must still be inside.

I felt a shudder through the deck, and then zero-gravity resumed. The meta rockets had switched off. Had the Marines gotten to the controls in time? Or had we just deorbited?

I couldn't tell, and I was too busy at the moment to link in and query the network. If we hit atmosphere, my work on the alien would be wasted, but if we didn't burn up on reentry or slam into the Earth I preferred to have a live patient to a dead one. I kept working.

I used the injector from my M-7 kit to fire a full dose of nanobots into the alien's hide. As I waited for them to be assimilated, I wondered why we used terms like "Broccoli" or "Stalk" with aliens like the M'nangat. I understood why Marines dehumanized their enemies—especially the human ones—but the M'nangat, as far as we could tell, had been benevolent and helpful galactic neighbors.

The answer, I suppose, was psychological. Friendly the M'nangat may be, but they were still *alien*, meaning we could never really get inside their heads—or what passes for heads—and understand them nearly as well as, say, a human living in San Antonio can understand a human living in Kyoto. They had their own agenda—all intelligent beings do—and we had no idea what that agenda might be and probably never would. That's why we were careful not to let them learn where Sol was, why trading and diplomatic exchanges took place at neutral meeting spots like Sirius, just in case.

And that was fair enough, since we had no idea where they hailed from either, other than that their homeworld was the fourth planet of a star only slightly brighter than Sol. In a galaxy of four hundred billion stars, you can't tell much from that.

But maybe we called the weirdly stalked and tentacled beings Broccoli or Brocs or Stalks to make them seem a little more . . . comprehensible. *Familiar.* I glanced up at the sensory cluster, that cluster of orange-sized luminous eyes at one end of the body. Those quivering jelly-globe eyes had no pupils, so I couldn't tell if it was looking at me, but then, that sphere of light-gathering organs was designed to look in every direction at once.

What kind of brain can see through 360 degrees and straight up at all times? I wondered. What did that suggest about M'nangat psychology?

D'DNAH CARRIES MY BUDS, the uninjured M'nangat said, the translated words typing themselves across my in-head screen. PLEASE . . .

"I'll do what I can," I replied aloud, letting my AI handle the translation and transmission. "I'm just checking to see if your partner is okay on the inside."

The being floating next to me and my patient was showing no emotion that I could recognize, but the words on my in-head sounded like human pain. Buds . . . that would be a clutch of young. According to the downloading xeno data, fertilized eggs from the female took root inside the life carrier and grew as buds that eventually tuned into young and chewed their way to freedom.

I tried not to think about that part. M'nangat reproduction was messy, violent, and painful . . . and the carrier usually didn't survive. And how did *that* color their psychology?

The nanobots were clustering now around the wounded being's internal organs. I used my N-prog to program them to transmit an overlay.

An overlay is a translucent image of a being's internal structure projected over the image from my unaugmented eyes. I could see the Broc in front of me, but could also see its internal structure in remarkable depth and detail, picked out by hundreds of millions of cell-sized nanobots adhering to every internal surface and transmitting their relative positions to my N-prog. The Broc's body appeared to fade away, and I could see the muscular system and, just underneath, the criss-crossing weave of cartilage running from tentacles to eyes. They didn't have true internal skeletons, but the muscles of the body were attached to flexible, cartilaginous scaffolding that doubled as protection for the inner organs. By concentrating, I could let my viewpoint sink deeper. I linked in to the medical data feed from the Net; my AI identified various organs and threw names in so I could tell what I was looking at.

Right away, I could see that my patient was in serious trouble. A ragged cavity extended from the wound into the central core of its body, and a pale, diffuse cloud showed massive internal bleeding. The cartilage had been torn open and several organs damaged, but what really worried me was the bullet.

My nanobots had carefully picked it out: a glittering metal slug now resting immediately above the pulsing two-chambered muscle that was the M'nangat's upper heart, tucked in beside the artery that corresponded to the aorta in humans. My AI identified the thing from the 'bots' transmissions. It was an M550ND mag-accelerated nano-D round, and for some reason the thing had not gone off.

And that made it *extremely* dangerous.

I drew a deep breath, thinking fast. Nanodisassembler rounds are designed to explode on impact, flooding the target with nanobots programmed to dissolve molecular bonds—in essence reducing it to its component atoms. If the nano in that bullet was omnivorous, programmed to dissolve all bonds, it would have been an insanely dangerous round to use inside a space station. More likely, the nano had been programmed to focus on carbon bonds only: deadly for organic chemistries and most plastics, but inert if they slammed into a metal bulkhead.

Which kind were these? I wanted to believe that the tangos hadn't been *that* crazy . . . crazy enough to fire omnivorous nano-D rounds inside Zeta Capricorn's hull . . . but their record so far didn't exactly inspire confidence in their rationality. They'd threatened to drop a one-kilometer rock onto Earth from orbit, for God's sake . . . and when the Marines came on board, they'd set the deadly machinery in motion. When Atun 3840 touched down, the impact quite possibly could kill *billions*.

WHAT DO YOU SEE? the uninjured M'nangat asked. He . . . no, she—my data link provided that correction—wasn't linked into my download feed, but could tell that I was peering closely at something inside her friend. She sounded as worried as any human might be.

"Just taking a look . . ." I said. I opened a private channel to Hancock. "Hey, Gunny? Can you send someone to get this Broc out of my hair?"

"On the way, Doc." There was a pause. "How's it going in there? We have two more wounded Marines out here."

Damn! "Sorry. I've got a . . . a situation here, and it can't wait. Put 'em on suit med-support."

Marine Mark 10 MMCA combat armor can provide some extremely sophisticated first aid to the wearer, including nanobot auto-injections for both pain and hemorrhage control. Trouble was, my orders for this mission said that our M'nangat guests had first claim on my professional attentions. I guess the brass was afraid of an interstellar incident if one of them bled to death.

"Already done, Doc," Hancock said. "But one of 'em's in a bad way. We've already captured her, just in case."

"Acknowledged."

And I *really* didn't want to think about *that*. CAPTR stands for cerebral access polytomographic reconstruction, and refers to technology that can record a living brain's neural states and chemistries, synaptic pathways, and even its quantum spin states to provide a digital picture of brain activity. If a person suffers serious brain trauma, we can often repair the brain, then download the backup CAPTR data. I'd had it happen to me during the Gliese 581 deployment six months earlier.

The question was . . . was I still me? Or was I a copy of me with all the same memories, so that "I," the *new* "I," didn't know the difference?

Marines have a name for people brought back by CAPTR technology: *zombies*.

The tangled philosophies involved made my head hurt, and I hated inflicting the same emotional issues on anyone else. But orders were orders . . .

And I had a patient to save.

Pulling a bullet out of someone isn't that hard. In the old days, you took a forceps and a probe and fished around in the wound until you could grab the thing and drag it out . . . though if you weren't careful you could do more damage with the fishing than the original shot had caused. I had a better means at my disposal . . . but the danger was that if I managed to release the bullet's charge of nano-D, I would kill the patient. I could leave the round where it was, and I seriously considered that option . . . but it was lodged in a bad place, smack between the M'nangat's upper heart and the underside of the brain. If it shifted while we were transporting the Broc, it could kill him.

There was also a chance that the round had a timer or a contact switch in it, set to go off when someone like me was trying to pull it out. Tangos had been known to booby-trap their victims that way sometimes.

Wonderful. Just fricking wonderful.

I linked in through my N-prog and began giving commands.

Nanobots are tiny, about one micron in length . . . one-fifth the width of a human red blood cell. A human hair is anywhere from 40 to 120 times thicker. They propel themselves through blood or interstitial fluid using local magnetic fields—in this case, that of the Earth itself—and can also link themselves together magnetically in order to apply force enough to, say, set a broken bone. Could they generate enough unified force to drag a bullet out of the patient without setting it off?

I was about to find out.

I COULDN'T KNOW IT AT THE TIME, OF COURSE, BUT AS I STUDIED MY patient, Earth was entering a paroxysm of recriminations, verbal assaults, and counterassaults that were bringing us to the brink of a very nasty war. The Terran Commonwealth doesn't speak for all of Earth's teeming billions, not by a damned sight. The North Chinese Socialist Cooperative is an independent nation, for instance, as is Brazil and most of what used to be called India. Most of the Islamic states from Morocco to Indonesia are independents, as is the vast sprawl of Islamic Central Asia.

Even the supposedly happily united nation-states of the Commonwealth have their share of rebellions, popular insurrections, and independence movements, and the neo-Ludd movement, as much religious as political, has roots in every technic society on the planet. We knew the tangos who had attacked Capricorn Zeta were neo-Ludd, but the neo-Ludds don't have spacecraft. We knew they'd hitched a ride from the space elevator to the mining station on a Chinese tug, but that didn't prove that North China was behind the attack. In fact, the Chinese tug argued against Beijing's involvement. The Chinese weren't stupid, and they knew that endangering the entire planet was certain to call down upon themselves the wrath of almighty God in the form of Commonwealth assault forces, aerospace attacks, and a barrage of orbital railgun strikes.

Logic . . . but at the moment no one on Earth was feeling like indulging in *logic*. The president of Germany had just announced that the terror attack on Capricorn Zeta—and its subsequent deorbit burn—was tantamount to a declaration of war by North China. South China had launched a similar verbal assault; Canton wanted full admission to the Commonwealth, and this gave them an opportunity to settle old scores.

And everything was happening so *fast*. In a global network where mind could speak to mind in an instant, news items more than fifteen minutes old were ancient history, and governments could threaten, be counterthreatened, and war be declared in the space of an hour or less.

Below the hurtling mass of the asteroid and its attendant structures, armies were mobilizing, and everywhere, *everywhere*, people were waiting to see just exactly where Atun 3840 was going to fall.

THE BULLET WAS MOVING. ENCASED IN A SHEATH OF TIGHTLY PACKED nanobots, it was sliding slowly up through the M'nangat's cardiac envelope, moving back the way it had come because that path was already open. At each point where the bullet had ripped open tissue, I detailed a few tens of thousands of 'bots to stay behind and begin repairs, closing up torn tissue and, especially, closing open blood vessels. Most of them, though, kept pushing and pulling at the projectile to ease it back up the wound cavity.

Zero-gravity made the task easier. I was holding my breath. The bullet showed no sign of being live . . . but if it exploded now my patient was dead. Nano-D works *fast*, eating the target from the inside out. It burns out quickly, but the nano in a half-centimeter disassembler round would create a spherical cavity inside the M'nangat a tenth of a meter across, filled with a hot chemical goo of dissociated atoms and a *lot* of suddenly released energy.

I considered the possibility of using my own 'bots to encase any emerging nano-D if things did go bad, containing the release. They were packed in closely now, sealing the bullet off from its surroundings like a glistening coat of paint. Unfortunately, any nano-D inside the M550 round would be programmed to target the bonds between carbon atoms, and my 'bots were coated in nothing *but* carbon.

And the energy released from broken molecular bonds . . . I didn't have the exact figures, but the explosion would rip the wounded being in half, and might breach my own armor.

Five centimeters to go. On a human scale—if my 'bots had been humans—that was only another one hundred kilometers. I had a momentary, surreal mental image of hundreds of millions of Egyptian laborers hauling one of the stone blocks destined for a pyramid with sledges and ropes . . . except that the bullet in this case would have been a completed pyramid one kilometer high.

With smooth surfaces unreactive to the surrounding tissue, however, the 'bots squeezed the bullet along as if it were a watermelon seed, gathering behind it, opening the path ahead, sliding it through glistening wet tissue. I had it clear of the heart and brain, finally, but if the round detonated it would still kill my patient.

Easy . . . easy . . .

Dimly, I was aware of Corporal Lewis coming up behind

me and saying something to the other M'nangat, something about needing her help with a report. Good. I don't like an audience when I work, even if the audience can't see what the hell I'm doing.

Three more centimeters. Through my N-prog, I'd programmed the 'bots to work together as a single organism, contracting, and then expanding as it moved, clawing against the local magnetic field. I was approaching now the part of the wound that I'd already covered with skinseal. I didn't want to disturb the congealing powder, and would have to route my microscopic parade around that region. *That* way, I decided, just beneath the M'nangat's tough, outer layer of skin.

I would have to slice through the skin to remove the bullet, just *there*, two centimeters to one side of the skin-sealed wound.

"I'm going to have to make a small cut in your skin," I said, allowing my AI to translate for me. I touched her side. "Right about here. But I don't have anything to keep it from hurting."

IT . . . HURTS . . . NOW, was the reply.

I hated working without anesthetic, but the way a species transmits signals through its central nervous system—pain, temperature, pressure, or the more esoteric impulses for emotions or thoughts—is as unique as the way it deals with immune responses. I can block pain in a human patient easily enough because we understand how human pain works through the doloric receptors inside the thalamus and the insular cortex of the brain, but we have no idea how the analogous system works in the M'nangat. We just don't understand their biochemistry well enough yet.

"Okay," I said, slipping a laser scalpel from my M-7 pack and snapping it on. "Brace yourself."

I made a single quick, short incision, trying to slice through just the tough and gnarled outer integument without touching the nano-clad bullet just underneath. The M'nangat tensed, and its tentacles whiplashed for an instant, threatening to put us both into a microgravity tumble.

"Steady," I told herm. "Hold on now . . ."

Several tentacles flicked up and wrapped themselves around my legs, gripping me tightly. That hadn't been what I'd meant by "hold on," but it seemed to serve as the Broc equivalent of biting the bullet. Green blood emerged from the cut in a dense, expanding cloud . . . and the nano-D round came with it.

I let the bullet float free as I released the scalpel and snatched another bag of skinseal, thumbing it open. Right about then, I felt another shudder and weight returned . . . again, about a tenth of a gravity.

The meta thrusters were firing again.

Chapter Three

For a terrifying moment I was way too busy for only two hands, but I slapped the sealant in place, then pulled out a glass specimen container for the M550 round, which was now drifting toward the bulkhead at a bit less than a meter per second, reached out, and scooped it up just before it hit the wall. As I sealed the cap, the bullet abruptly dissolved, filling the vial with an inky black syrup. My breath caught in my throat; if the stuff was programmed to disassemble everything, the vial would dissolve in less than a second, and then we would have a cloud of charged nano-D floating into the interior of Capricorn Zeta.

But . . . no. The glass contained the ink, and I let out a deep and fervent breath of relief. The stuff must have been programmed to go after carbon, and the silica molecules—silicon dioxide—of the glass were beyond its scope. The scalpel and the N-prog both hit the bulkhead and clung there, and a second later my patient and I thumped against the wall as well.

What . . . is . . . happening?

"I'm hoping the Marines managed to hack into the station's drive," I told herm, "and are boosting us back into a stable orbit. Um . . . can you let go of my legs now?" The largest of those tentacles, as thick as my thigh and a couple of meters long, were *strong*.

Obligingly, they unfurled, then coiled up again into a tight ball. I picked up the N-prog and used it to call up a scan of the being's internal systems, ordering the nanobots still inside to spread out and give me a full-body image.

The major bleeders, I noted, had been sealed off. Good. Both hearts were throbbing in lockstep with each other, first one, then the other, and both appeared to be beating steadily. My downloaded medical data suggested that the M'nangat's temperature, respiration, and heart rate all were more or less within normal ranges. That was a damned good thing, too, since I didn't have the nano programming or drugs to change them if they were off.

Down near the creature's base I saw three small shadows. *Buds.* The growing young that in all probability would kill the M'nangat at parturition.

The shudder of the base's engines cut off, and once again, we were in microgravity. I completed my examination. What I could understand appeared to be working okay; I just wished I understood more.

"Okay, Gunny?" I called. "I've got the patient stabilized. We need a medevac, though, to someplace that understands Broc physiology."

"We have a couple of medevacs inbound, Doc." Hancock replied. "Your friend'll be heading down to San Antone."

"Excellent."

The San Antonio Military Medical Center—usually abbreviated as "SAMMC" and pronounced "Sam-sea"—was an enormous installation located at Fort Sam Houston on the northeast edge of San Antonio, Texas. It was where I'd had my Navy Hospital Corps training and where I'd gone to Advanced Medical Technology School a few months later. The naval hospital there is our biggest and best, and if any human facility could handle M'nangat physiology, they could.

"How about our wounded?" I asked.

"Sergeant Rutherford is doing okay," Hancock replied. "Private Donohue is tech-dead."

"How long?"

"Six . . . six and a half mikes."

Fuck.

The human brain starts to break down the moment blood stops flowing through it. After three minutes, it might just be possible to bring a person back with little or no brain damage. Longer than that, though, and the damage from oxygen starvation is irreversible. The person is "tech-dead," technically dead, and is going to need extensive stem-cell grafts and transplants for the brain to be brought back on-line again.

And that's why we use CAPTR technology to try to put the patient's mind back in his brain after we've repaired it. It doesn't always work. More often than not it doesn't. If there's been too much damage and neuron replacement, the CAPTR download won't take.

And if it does, the Marine becomes a "zombie," shunned or worse by other Marines. They're usually redeployed to a different unit after they recover, to avoid being ostracized by superstitious nonsense.

Caryl Donohue had been brain dead too long for me to be able to pull her back.

Would it have made a difference if I'd been able to treat her within a minute or two of being hit? There was no way to tell. Everything depended on the severity of the wound.

But I did know that she would have had a better chance if I'd been there, if I hadn't been trying to gentle that nano-D round out of the M'nangat carrier's chest.

And that made me feel . . . guilty, somehow. Like I'd not been doing my job. Like I'd let down another member of the platoon.

I didn't want to think about that. "What's the situation, Gunny?" I asked, changing the topic. In any case, I wanted to know if the mission had succeeded . . . or if it had all been for nothing.

"We're in good shape," Hancock replied. "The bastards

planted a blocker virus in the thruster control system, but First Platoon touched down on the rock and took direct control of the thrusters. They hardwired a new control system into the jets, and that let us stabilize the rock's orbit."

So, the bad guys had sabotaged Capricorn Zeta's controls so that no matter what we'd done, the station and a one-kilometer asteroid would have burned into Earth's atmosphere and impacted somewhere on the surface moments later. First Platoon had been on an approach vector above and behind us, with the goal of landing on the asteroid itself and securing the thruster complex. Evidently, the plan had worked.

"We were thirty-five minutes from re-entry," Hancock added, "and about forty from impact."

"Where?"

"Somewhere just south of Japan."

In many ways, an ocean impact is far worse for the planet than having an asteroid come down on solid ground. Billions of tons of water flashed into vapor . . . a thick cloud ceiling over most of the planet reflecting the heat of the sun back into space . . . and, oh yes, titanic tidal waves racing across the ocean at the speed of sound. The western coast of the Americas would have been hard hit.

But it would have been a hell of a lot worse for Japan and both Chinas. Again, it didn't seem logical that the North Chinese were behind the terror attack on Capricorn Zeta. They would have been vulnerable to an impact anywhere in the Pacific basin—a bull's-eye covering one-third of the planet. But if *not* them, who?

That, however, was for the politicians to argue about. Right now, it was our job to finish securing the mining station, making sure the black hats hadn't planted any bombs or otherwise compromised the base. We also had to process the rescued hostages, still floating around with their hands zip-tied behind them. This meant interviewing each one, comparing their story with both station computer records and records off the Net, checking their DNA to make sure each man or woman was who he or she claimed to be, and evacuating the wounded shoreside. The Marines were taking care of that part of the evolution.

My job was to prep our wounded for evac . . . and to pull suit recordings on the Marines who'd been hit. Marine combat armor has simple-minded AIs resident within the electronics that keep a log of events in a battle. What a Marine does wrong during a firefight can be helpful as a basis for Marine training sims, a means of keeping other Marines from making the same mistakes.

Second Platoon had suffered three wounded and one dead—not a bad casualty ratio, actually, for space combat, where even minor damage to vacuum armor can very easily mean a fast and unpleasant death. We'd lost Lance Corporal Stalzar going in; the others we'd been able to treat or stabilize. We still didn't know about Private Donohue . . . *wouldn't* know about her until we could get her to a proper med facility. I didn't have a report yet from 1st Platoon. I tagged HM2 Michael C. Dubois, the 1st Platoon Corpsman, over the company Net. If he needed help out there on the rock's surface, he could yell for me.

"Carlyle!" Lieutenant Singer called. "What are you doing?"

"Grabbing suit recordings, sir," I replied.

"That can wait. I need you sweeping the station for goo threats."

I sighed. No rest for the Wiccans . . .

"Aye, aye, sir."

"That includes the prisoners. *Especially* the prisoners. We can't allow the medevacs in until the mining station is declared clean."

Shit. "I'm on it, sir."

I wondered whether that order was coming down from Washington, or if it represented the technoparanoia of the local brass—at a battalion or company level, or even of Second Lieutenant Singer himself.

No matter. Orders *were* orders. I pulled out my N-prog and began resetting it.

GRAY GOO. THAT WAS THE OLD AND FEAR-ENTANGLED TERM IN-vented by Eric Drexler, one of the twentieth-century fathers of nanotechnology—though he'd later said he wished he'd never come up with the phrase. Back in those early days, before the first molecular disassemblers had even been brought on-line, there'd been a widespread concern about nanomachines programmed to take apart raw materials and create more of themselves. Since human beings are as good as sources of raw materials as an ancient landfill, the fear was that nano-D would keep on eating and eating until the entire planet was converted to so-called gray goo.

It couldn't happen, of course. *Run until the raw material is used up* is a piss-poor way to program molecular machines, first off. They also require energy, a lot of it, to break molecular bonds, and are generally fairly limited in range. Nanodisassemblers are designed to reach an end point and quit. They're also easily shut down by an ultraviolet radiation bath, or by transmission of a seek-kill signal in their immediate vicinity.

But Humankind has had a love-hate relationship with nano since the beginning. Medical nano has effectively tripled our expected life span, ended the tyranny of pain, overturned the death sentences of cancer and heart disease, and even holds out the eventual promise of . . . if not immortality, then the next best thing: lifetimes measured by millennia rather than years. Some people with full-course nananagathics in their systems have been around for well over a century, now, and still look like they're in their thirties. Not only that, nanotechnology has completely transformed the way we control and interact with our material

surroundings, allowing us to grow everything from a siz-
zling steak to a house, and pull what we need from the
background matrix—furniture, workstations, nanufactories,
anything that can be stored in digital AI memory and re-
trieved by a thoughtclick.

But the term *gray goo* remains a bugaboo, a terror
phrase for anyone nervous about the ever-increasing pace
of our technology. Washington in particular was afraid of
what would happen if terrorists got hold of so-called black
nano, which when released would proceed to chow down on
Earth's ecosphere.

Ecophagia—devouring the ecosphere.

Machines—even very tiny ones—only did what humans
told them to do.

But then, humans were always the weak part of the equation, capable of the most incredibly stupid or irresponsible
of acts.

I STARTED SCANNING THE COMPARTMENT WITH MY N-PROG, LOOK-
ing for the telltale electronic signature of nanobots. The
trouble was, there were 'bots everywhere. When my N-prog
detected active nano, it transmitted the data to my in-head,
which painted green pinpoints against my vision, marking
objects that otherwise would have been invisibly small. I
looked at the station bulkhead in front of me, gray-painted
and consisting entirely of massive pipes running from deck
to overhead. The biggest, I knew, were sorting pipes, carrying the component elements of Atun 3840 into storage
and assembly bays. The thinner tubes were nano-D feed-
ers, sending microscopic disassemblers into the depths of
the captive asteroid. The pipes were silent at the moment,
the mining process shut down. But they showed as solid
masses of green, each packed with trillions upon un-
countable trillions of live nanobots—motionless, but still
powered and on standby. Most of the Marines around me
showed diffuse green masses within the outlines of their

bodies—the medical nano we all carried to improve our combat efficiency, react to wounds, and keep us healthy.

There was loose nano drifting in the air too. The damned things are so tiny that there's always leakage, and any environment with active nano running will have escapees. I pointed my N-prog at several, interrogating them; a lot of the floaters actually were disassemblers— leftovers from the rounds the tangos had used. They'd shut down but were still broadcasting. Damn, they were *everywhere*.

This was freaking *hopeless*.

"Lieutenant Singer?"

"Go ahead."

"We've got nano soup in here. It appears inert, but there's so much it's overloading my readings. I recommend a UV bath. The whole station, top to bottom."

Facilities like Capricorn Zeta were required by law to have ultraviolet lights installed in every compartment, a means of turning off any loose nano that leaked into the environment or came inside on workers' spacesuits. It was the simplest solution, and the only one we had time for.

"Very well," Singer said. "But check out the tangos. One of them might be a carrier."

"Aye, aye, sir."

The prisoners were being held in the next compartment out from the rock, a common area that served as lounge and mess hall for the miners. One entire bulkhead was transplas, looking down on the cloud tops hugging the Earth. We were crossing the terminator into night, and the clouds were red and flaming orange. The planet looked fragile and terribly vulnerable.

Sergeant Aguirre and a couple of privates had the tangos under guard—five of them. They'd been yanked out of their spacesuits, stripped naked, and tied hand and foot. We were taking no chances with these animals.

They watched with large, dark, and angry eyes as I

scanned the first one with my N-prog. No RFID tag, no edentity. "Name?" I asked him.

He spat at me, the shimmering glob of saliva drifting past my helmet in microgravity to splat against the transparent bulkhead at my back. I shrugged and kept scanning. There was, of course, nothing.

Neo-Ludds. They've been with us forever, I think. When Tharg the caveman first discovered fire, there were probably members of the tribe who wanted to make the stuff illegal, a clear and present danger to the community. The original Luddites had been early-nineteenth-century textile workers who'd sabotaged the machinery introduced by the Industrial Revolution, machinery that was putting them out of work. Toward the end of the twentieth century neo-Luddism had arisen—a rejection of those technologies perceived as having a negative impact on both individuals and communities.

Nanotechnology was at the top of the neo-Ludds' hit list, of course, not only because of the whole "gray goo" scenario, but because it was changing the very meaning of what it meant to be human. Nano-chelated circuitry grown inside the human brain, control contacts in the palms of our hands, genetic reconfiguration . . . sure, we might have cured cancer with the stuff, but was it *safe*?

I would have been extremely surprised if any of these people had nanobots in them, or any of the nanotech extensions—cerebral implants, neural circuitry, or other internal hardware.

For neo-Ludds, asteroid mining came right behind nanotech as a key target—especially when that industry involved moving asteroids into Earth orbit. Proponents suggested that the technology, with massively redundant backups, was failsafe. The neo-Ludds pointed out that sooner or later technology *always* fails, and that Earth could not risk even a single such failure.

But did it make sense, I wondered, for them to protest the

technology by bringing about the very disaster they feared? That simply wasn't rational.

But then, I had trouble thinking of neo-Ludds as *rational*.

I went down the line, scanning each man in turn. All of them were clean—no active nano circulating inside their bodies. Curious, I put the N-prog away and pulled out a DNA tester. Approaching the first man, I touched it to his upper arm. He yelped when it bit him, and cut loose with a torrent of invective in a language I didn't understand.

"You understand any of that, Sarge?" I asked Aguirre.

"Negative, Doc," he replied. "The station translators aren't programmed for it, whatever it is."

Figured. The station AI could translate between us and the Brocs, but we couldn't understand this group of humans. I studied them as my analyzer churned away. They weren't Chinese, certainly. No epicanthic folds. Their skin was swarthy; Middle Eastern, possibly.

I took samples from the rest of them, eliciting reactions that ran the gamut from bored indifference to angry hostility.

A few minutes later, my analyzer started to send back data, scrolling it down through my in-head in a sudden cascade of alphanumerics. I couldn't follow it all; genetics is not my specialty. But I caught a couple of key indicators as they flicked by: macro-haplogroup K . . . paragroup L . . . haplogroups R1a1 and R2 . . . mutation M198 . . .

The analyzer popped up a series of possible answers: a 65 percent probability of Central Asia, 22 percent South Asia, lesser percentages for portions of western China, Siberia, the Middle East, and Eastern Europe.

I looked at the first man, who was still scowling at me. "Kazakh?" I asked.

His nostrils flared, and he barked at me in the same unknown harsh and vehement language. The others looked frightened.

"We know they speak English," Aguirre told me. "Some of 'em, anyway."

"Betcha that's Turkic," I told him. "Kazakh. Kyrgyz, Uzbek—one of those."

"Damned Cackies," Aguirre said.

I looked at the sullen prisoners. "We don't *know* it's the Caliphate, Sarge."

"Aw, c'mon, Doc! Who the fuck else would it be?"

He had a point. The Central Asian Caliphate—the western name usually shortened to "CAC" and pronounced "cack"—was the Islamic theocracy sprawling from Azerbaijan to Sinkiang, notoriously volatile, notoriously anti-Western, notoriously anti-technology. They were known to sponsor neo-Ludd terror all over the world. Allah, after all, hates anything not found in the holy Qur'an, including nanomedical life extension, educational downloads, and anything at all that changes the eternal heavens.

I opened a channel to operations HQ back at Synchorbit. They had access to more complete haplogroup records than I did through the Net, and would be able to confirm the results. As the results came back down then link, a call came through my in-head from Major Lansky, the Battalion CO. "This is . . . who? Carlyle?"

"HM2 Elliot Carlyle, sir," I said. "Second Platoon Corpsman."

"What's this stuff you're uploading?"

"DNA readouts from five prisoners, sir. They would appear to be Central Asian."

"Shit. You're sure of that?"

"About sixty-five percent, sir."

"Okay. I—" The transmission cut off in mid-sentence.

I waited, wondering what was going on up-El. Abruptly, a sign popped up in my in-head: SECURITY BREACH: CONVERSATION TERMINATED.

What the fuck? And then something queried my AI.

Normally my in-head software handles routine e-queries, everything from sales pitches for masculine enhancement genetic prosthetics to calls from home. It's got a fairly comprehensive response list that lets it act as my personal secretary. It can even imitate me—audio and video—if need be, and most incoming traffic is either flagged for my attention or spam-slammed.

The thing is, nothing should have queried my personal AI while I was in the middle of a mission. Bad operational security, that. The only things that should be able to get through are military traffic or . . .

I slapped a trace on the query. I didn't catch it . . . but I did get an ID.

GNN.

The Global News Network would have a particular interest in this mission, I imagined. Though we certainly hadn't told them we were going in—why tip off the tangos who had access to GNN feeds on Capricorn Zeta?—the newsies knew about the station's takeover, of course, and would have been flooding local virtual space with netbots and snoopers. There were reporters embedded with the unit, I knew, and—shit. They were up-El, up in Synchorbit with Major Lansky.

I felt a sinking feeling in my gut, something like a realization of impending doom.

"Carlyle!"

It was Singer. "Yes, sir."

"What the fuck are you doing?"

"I'm with the prisoners, sir. They're clean. I, ah, went ahead and pulled a DNA analysis on them. They're Central Asian . . . probably CAC."

There was a long pause. "I ordered you to sweep them for nanobots, Carlyle, not play geneticist!"

"Yes, sir, but—"

"No buts. Get your ass in here!"

I looked at Aguirre. He wouldn't have heard the conversation going on in my head, but the glazed look in my eyes would have told him I was talking with someone. "Gotta go," I told him.

"Keep your ass covered, Doc," he said. I wondered how he knew, or if that was just a lucky guess.

"In here" turned out to be Capricorn Zeta's primary command center, two levels farther out from the rock. It was cramped and high tech, filled with microgravity consoles, bulkhead vidscreens, and couches with palmlinks on the armrests, so that mining personnel could connect directly with the facility's computers and operational controls. A smaller version of the transplas window on the lounge deck looked down on Earth's nightside. Glowing cities drifted past as the station orbited above them. A soft-glowing mass of cloud flickered and pulsed with lightning deep inside.

Singer was floating beside the main console, talking with a man in corporate utilities bearing the rank tabs of a senior administrator. A couple of command staff people floated nearby, obviously just released.

I thumped the side of the hatch. "HM2 Carlyle reporting as ordered, sir."

Singer ignored me for a long moment, continuing his conversation. Then the admin guy nodded, said, "You're the boss," and pushed off for the hatch, followed by his staff. Singer turned then, glaring.

"Why did you link through to Synchorbit?" he demanded.

"I needed access to a better DNA library," I told him. "The ones we have in-head aren't that comprehensive."

"What the hell were you doing running a DNA scan? That's a job for our S-2."

I started to reply, then stopped myself. Singer was furious, and if I said anything, anything at all, I was just going to make things worse.

"Yes, sir. I'm sorry, sir."

"Sorry doesn't cut it, Doc! You broke SCP and got tagged by a fucking newsie!"

It was worse than I'd imagined. Secure Communications Protocol is like radio silence, but more flexible. It allows us to talk to others on our command Net, and query local, secure subnets, but not link in to unsecured networks or AIs. Breaking SCP during combat was serious, a potential court-martial offense.

"Sir, I thought Ops Command was secure."

Singer started to give a sharp retort, then softened a bit. The scowl didn't leave his face, though. "Normally it would be, Doc. But those damned embeds are up there now, following the hijacking. And they obviously had netbots on the prowl. You understand? You bypassed the chain of command, you idiot, and you told Major Lansky we had CAC prisoners on an open channel. Don't you think GNN would be all over that?"

"Yes, sir."

I could just imagine. As soon as the neo-Ludd ultimatum had hit the GNN newsfeeds hours before, the whole world would have been wondering who was behind it, what government. Neo-Ludds couldn't get to orbit without help. *Who had helped them?*

There were probably netbots—electronic agents on the Net programmed to listen for certain key words and phrases. Hijack. Marines. Terrorists. DNA. That kind of thing. When they picked up something of interest, they would start probing, looking for more information. That tag I'd sensed had been a netbot shooting down the open radio channel and into my in-head, copying my personal contact data, and slipping away again. With my name, rate, rank, and number, they would be able to figure out who I was, know I was with Deep Recon 7, the Black Wizards . . . 2nd Platoon, Bravo Company, 1st Battalion, 1MARDIV, and that was *news*. It would be all over the Net; hell, it was probably all over the Net already.

And Deep Recon really hates that kind of publicity.

In short, I was now in a world of shit.

Chapter Four

At least I wasn't under arrest, or even restricted to base. Twenty-four hours later I was up-El, 35,800 kilometers above Earth's equator at the Cayambe Space Elevator's Geosynch Center. The place is a bustling hive of space industry, communications, orbital hotels, and offices. From the Universe View of the sprawling Hilton Orbital Wheel, I could look down at the shrunken Earth with the nearby elevator cable vanishing with perspective into the blue planet's center. She was a little past full at the moment, spanning just twenty degrees. If I held up both hands side by side at arm's length with fingers outstretched, I could just about block half of her from view. Off to one side, several of the big, free-orbiting solar reflector mirrors and microwave antenna arrays hung in open space, angled to reflect sunlight onto Earth's northern hemisphere. Bit by bit, in tiny steps, we were winning against the grinding southward advance of the ice sheets.

At least that's what the newsnets told us. Sometimes I wasn't sure I believed them. A good third of the planet's northern hemisphere was locked in ice, gleaming in the glare of daylight. I stifled a small, cold shudder.

"What is it, E-Car?" Leighton asked, looking at me askance. "You okay?"

Sergeant Joy Leighton, U.S. Marines, was a friend . . . a very *dear* friend. Military regulations frowned on enlisted

personnel becoming sexually involved, but military regulations rarely acknowledged that personnel are *human*, not
machines. Joy and I had been in combat together, out on
Bloodworld, and that counts for a lot. I'd patched her up and
dragged her ass out of a firefight. That counted for more.
And as long as we didn't go around flaunting the relationship, rubbing it in the brass's collective face, no one was
going to say a word.

"I'm fine, No-Joy," I told her, lying through my teeth.
"Just fine."

"I think they're going to let that whole security-breach
thing drop," she said, knowing I was lying, but misunderstanding the reason for it. "Everything is too public now.
They don't want to be seen as punishing a genu-wine hero."

I didn't answer right away, watching the Earth instead.
The Hilton's viewing lounge counter-rotated to the rest of
the habitat, providing a half-G of spin gravity but cancel-
ling the dizzying spin of the rest of the universe.

"What hero?" I asked after a moment. "Taking down
Capricorn Zeta? We all did that."

"Actually, I was thinking about the Hero of Bloodworld,
the doc who brokered peace with the Qesh. You're still a
highly newsworthy commodity, you know. GNN probably
had a whole army of newsbots programmed to follow you,
sniff you out as soon as you popped onto an unsecure channel. In any case . . ." She leaned over and kissed me. "You're
still *my* hero."

"Ooh-rah," I said quietly, a lackluster rendition of the old
Marine battle cry.

"That's not what's bugging you, is it?" she asked. "It's
Paula again."

No-Joy is sharp. Paula Barton was the woman I almost
married back in 'forty-four when I was still in Hospital
Corps training . . . until she had a stroke while we were
in a robot-skippered day sailer off the Maine Glacier. The
boat's first-aid suite didn't include a CAPTR device—most

civilians don't have access to that technology on a routine basis—and by the time the EMTs got to her, I'd lost her.

I always thought of her when I looked down the North American ice sheet like that. Paula's death and the ice—the two were inextricably locked together for me now. I *hated* the ice now, as if it were a living, despicable thing.

"I suppose it is," I admitted. "Damn it, I just felt so fucking *helpless.*"

I don't think Joy resented Paula, the fact of her. I'd been able to talk to her about what had happened off the Maine coast, about what I still felt.

Or *didn't* feel. Often all I felt was numb, even yet, three years later.

"There was nothing you could have done, Elliot." She'd only said those words a few thousand times since I'd met her.

"I know. I know." I managed a grin. "It'll be better when they finally manage to melt the damned ice."

The New Ice Age got its official start in the late twenty-first century as a result of—of all things—what used to be called global *warming.* Rising temperatures all over the planet—but especially in the polar regions—began melting the polar ice caps, especially the one that covered the Arctic Ocean. Cold, fresh water poured out through the Davis Strait into the North Atlantic, short-circuiting the Atlantic Conveyor—that part of the globe-circulating currents that brought warm water north from the tropics, keeping New England and Northern Europe livable.

The last time that happened was twelve thousand years ago. The planet was warming, the ice sheets of the Pleistocene were retreating, and suddenly the ice collapsed—quite possibly as the result of a small asteroid impact—and fresh water poured into the Atlantic. The Earth plunged back into a short-lived ice age known today as the Younger Dryas. The megafauna of North America—mammoth and mastodon and short-faced bear and countless other species—abruptly went extinct. Human communities known as the Clovis people, who'd crossed in skin boats along the edge of the ice from Europe hunting seals, were wiped out as well, or forced to migrate to the American Southwest. The renewed cold and drought may well have stimulated the growth of agriculture in the near East when climactic change led to starvation among hunter-gatherer cultures.

The same thing was happening today. This time, however, instead of Clovis spear points and skin boats, we had the space elevator and orbital solar arrays. The North Hemisphere Reclamation Project had been reflecting sunlight and beaming high-energy microwaves onto the ice for well over a century now, but *carefully*. The Commonwealth didn't want to eliminate the ice entirely; that would toss us back into the bad old days of the pre-ice twenty-first century, when cities like Miami, D.C., New York, and London all were in danger of being swallowed up entirely or in part by the rising sea levels. The idea was to gradually increase the temperatures of both the ice sheets and the cold North Atlantic until a comfortable balance was struck, a balance that could be indefinitely maintained by the Commonwealth's NHRP and applied global climate engineering. It was the biggest-scale piece of applied engineering ever attempted, and the one that promises to affect a larger percentage of Earth's population than any other by far.

And there's just a chance that it killed Paula.

Oh, the theory is largely discredited now after some four centuries of study—the idea that high-frequency microwaves can cause everything from cancer and Alzheimer's to high blood pressure and stroke. There's never been a provable link, but the neo-Ludds and other anti-space groups often trot out various statistics that show increases in those conditions when they started beaming microwaves down from Geosynch along with reflected visible light. Paula and I were out on the fringes of the beam, which should have been diffuse enough not to cause a problem.

Still, sometimes I wonder how much I have in common with some of the neo-Luddite crazies. It would be *so* easy to blame the NHRP and its synchorbital microwave arrays for my pain.

"You know, *Doc*," Joy said gently, emphasizing the title, "there's stuff you can do for that. Nanomeds and neuroengineering and all of that."

I nodded, but said nothing. Of *course* there's stuff that can be done, just as we can block the doloric receptors in the brain and switch off physical pain. Grief is just chemicals in the system, same as love and anger and any other emotion you care to name. You lose a loved one, and the pituitary gland at the base of the brain secretes adrenocorticotrophin hormone—ACTH—which is part of the fight-or-flight response. Among other things, ACTH acts on the adrenal glands, perched on top of the kidneys, to release a cascade of reactions that lead to the production of a steroid hormone called cortisone.

Normally, cortisone switches off the production of ACTH, but if the stress, the grief, continues, cortisone levels rise . . . and rise . . . and *rise*, eventually reaching ten or twenty times their normal levels.

And that does all sorts of nasty things, among them shutting down our thalamus and switching off the production of leukocytes. No white blood cells, no way to fight bacteria, viruses, and even precancerous cells.

There's also CRF—corticotrophin releasing factor. That is a stress-related neurotransmitter and peptide hormone that shoots sky high with the loss of a loved one. It stimulates the production of ACTH, and can lead to a number of truly nasty conditions, including major depression. You find elevated levels of CRFs in the spinal fluid of most suicides.

I'd gone through therapy after Paula's death—been *required* to do it, I should say. They'd given me the option of nanomeds—including CRF nanoblockers—to kill the emotional pain associated with my memories of Paula. Problem was, I didn't want to lose Paula. I know it sounds crazy, but the memories, and the emotional pain connected with them, were all I had left, and I didn't want to give them up.

So I went on a nanomed routine aimed at boosting my immune response, circulatory support, and anticarcinogen 'bots. Treating the symptoms rather than the cause, yeah, but at least I wouldn't die of grief, as a lot of other people still do. As for the grief itself, well, lots of other people were able to get through it, had been getting through it since long before nanomeds and thalamic receptor blocking. I would get over it. Eventually.

In the meantime, I had my career in the Hospital Corps, and I had Joy, and if I occasionally felt overwhelmed by grief or by those nightmare memories of helplessness when Paula had her stroke, well, that was all part of the territory, as my father likes to say. He's senior VP of research and development for General Nanodynamics, and he's the one who suggested I go into the Hospital Corps in the first place. Out on the frontier, interacting with newfound cultures and civilizations, that's where Humankind will learn new technologies, develop new nanopharmaceuticals, and make new fortunes.

That was the original idea, anyway. I'd long since given up on making fortunes—you *don't* enter military service with *that* as your goal—but I think Spencer Carlyle still had hopes for his Navy med-tech son.

Too bad. I hadn't been home since shortly after Paula's death.

"C'mon," Joy said, grabbing my arm and tugging me closer to her. "We're here to have *fun*."

Yeah . . . fun. Specifically, losing ourselves for a few hours in the Hilton's Free Fall . . . a combination restaurant and microgravity swimming sphere that's a bit on the pricey side, but well worth it. We managed to go there once every few months, for celebrations, as often as the budget allowed. And this *was* a celebration. We'd survived the assault on

Capricorn Zeta . . . and while I was under an official cloud, I hadn't been court-martialed.

At least, not yet.

We'd been to the Free Fall before. Hell, the first time Joy and I had had sex with each other had been up there, in that shimmering blue sphere of water suspended in microgravity.

We weren't here for swimming this time. We entered the rotating sphere at one pole, in zero-gravity, the interior rotating around us. A human hostess met us, and led us down along the curving deck through exotic tropical foliage to a table between sky and water, with every step taking us into a higher G level until we reached our table near the equator.

Directly overhead, the big, ten-meter hydrosphere flashed and rippled blue-green in the constantly shifting beams of sunlight, hovering at the center of the fifty-meter hollow globe rotating around it. Where we sat, the turning of the main hab sphere generated four-tenths of a gravity, about the same as on Mars, and a transplas viewall section in the deck showed the stars and Earth sliding past beneath, making a complete circuit once every twenty-some seconds.

A human waitress arrived to take our drink orders. That's one reason the place is so expensive, of course—human waitstaff instead of robots. In keeping with the jungle theme of the place, they wore either skin nano or animated tattoos—I couldn't tell which—that gave their skin constantly shifting dapplings of sunlight and shadow.

"So . . . what do you think of the latest from Earthside?" Joy asked after she'd left.

"I haven't been paying attention," I told her, truthfully enough. I'd told my AI secretary to put a block on all of my auto news alerts and downloads. "At this point I'm afraid to download anything. What *is* the latest?"

"Oh, come *on*, e-Car!" She laughed. "Get with the program!"

"I've had other stuff on my mind," I said. "Like maybe getting court-martialed and ending up in Atlantica for ten years?" Atlantica was a seafloor colony off the coast of Florida, mostly a civilian facility with a scientific research community, but which included a Commonwealth submarine base and a high-security naval prison.

"Well, there *is* that. Don't worry, though. If you go to Atlantica, I'll bake you a cake with nano-D in the flour."

"Thanks so much. I'll have to remember to practice holding my breath before I use it, though."

"Seriously, Elliot. If they were going to lock you away, or even send you for deep neurophysiological rehab, you would *not* be walking around free now. They might decide to kick you out of the Navy just to be rid of you, but nothing more. Okay?"

I shrugged. "I'm sure you're right." What I didn't add was that getting booted out of the Navy would be as bad as having my brain rewired. I'd found a home here, a place of my own, a meaningful career.

Not to mention Joy. We were still deep in the initial rampant lust phase of our relationship, but I could see it moving beyond sex and pleasant companionship to something more permanent. Maybe.

If I could just shake off Paula's ghost, and put her to rest at last.

The waitress returned with our drinks—a Cosmic Dehibitor for Joy, a Metafuel Thruster for me. I paid her by linking through to the restaurant's e-pay AI, and included a generous tip for her. She thanked me, then took our orders for dinner. Meat from Earthside has to be shipped up-El and is expensive, but there are some locally nanufactured proteins indistinguishable from nature. *Real* cow meat from the Amazon prairies is just for status; the stuff built up molecule by molecule really can't be distinguished from the real thing. We both ordered local cultures, mine in the form of lobster tail, hers looking and tasting like steak.

"So what's the news?" I asked when we were alone again.

"War, of course. At least there's serious talk of war.

The Commonwealth is blaming the CAC for hijacking that mining station . . . and for trying to drop an asteroid into the ocean. That's an act of war in anyone's manual."

I shook my head. "I have trouble believing that the CAC government would be openly behind something like that. Some extremist Islamic sect, maybe . . . or a rogue para-military group operating in the shadows. But the people, the ruling council in Dushanbe, they aren't crazy."

"They *are* neo-Ludd," Joy pointed out. "Or strongly sup-portive of the movement. And a tidal wave in the Pacific wouldn't touch them."

"No, but the outraged survivors of the rest of the world would."

"True. But maybe they didn't count on you figuring out where those tangos hailed from."

A shrill squeal sounded from overhead and we both looked up. A couple had managed to propel themselves clear of the hydrosphere and had landed in the nearly in-visible netting surrounding the water in case of just such an eventuality. Laughing, naked and glistening wet, they half-scrambled and half-flew across the netting toward the sphere's zero-gravity poles to re-enter the water. I half ex-pected some of the flying spray to reach us . . . but subtly directed air jets were in place to whisk away any stray flying droplets and keep the diners below from getting rained on. The illusion of dining in a rain forest *did* have reasonable limits, after all.

"I don't buy it," I told her, as the squeals died away again. "Those men had to know that someone would pull a DNA analysis on them if they were killed or captured."

"Maybe they just didn't count on the U.S. Marines coming in and spoiling their party," she said. "Either they would have their demands met . . . or they would all be in-cinerated on impact. Either way, no DNA left to sample."

"I suppose."

But I wasn't convinced.

The terrorists who'd seized Capricorn Zeta had clearly had a neo-Ludd agenda. Their demands had been that all asteroid mining be stopped—not only in Earth orbit, which was a song they'd been singing for a long time, but out in trans-lunar space as well.

They needed high-tech help. The Chinese were out, because if something had gone wrong and the asteroid had come down anywhere in the Pacific, the tidal waves would have washed them away. The CACs had the ideology, yeah, and they were far inland, but why use their own people in the attack, inviting military retaliation? It seemed likelier to me that those Central Asians we'd captured had been mercenaries, hirelings being used by someone else, possibly with an eye to calling attention to Dushanbe and away from the *real* masterminds.

Who would profit, I wondered, from having asteroid mining stopped? Or from having a one-kilometer asteroid fall out of the sky, killing a few hundred million people or more?

And with their plan for extortion blocked, what would they do next?

An inner ping alerted me to an incoming call request. I glanced at it, saw that it was another GNN e-comm request, and dismissed it. I'd become a pretty popular guy, it seemed. "A highly newsworthy commodity," like Joy had said. Reporters, both on Earth and embedded at HQ, wanted to talk to me.

Well, I didn't want to talk to *them*. I felt used and ambushed, and I wouldn't have opened the channel even if Gunny Hancock hadn't told me he would skin me alive and hang me out an airlock to dry if I did.

"Let's change the subject," I told Joy. "I don't really want to discuss work when the most gorgeous U.S. Marine in the Galaxy is sitting here right across from me."

"Flatterer."

"I like the utilities."

She dimpled. "Thank you. I put *so* much work into it."

In fact, she was wearing ordinary ship utilities, a black skinsuit that clung to her like paint. She'd stroked the top away, though, to give her the currently fashionable Minoan Princess look, proudly bare breasted. She'd programmed the remaining nanofabric to give it an illusion of depth, scattered through and through with gleaming stars.

She was radiantly beautiful.

"Elliot, someone is pinging our ID."

The voice wasn't Joy's. It was my AI secretary, a smart bit of AI software that normally resided silently within my in-head hardware without making its presence known. That it was speaking now, interrupting my conversation with Joy, meant that it had detected a close-in attempt to physically locate me by homing in on my personal electronics. Normally that stuff is pretty heavily firewalled, with name and rank *only* out there for public access, but I'd opened it wider in order to pay for the drinks and the meal.

Or maybe the name and rank had been enough. *Damn it!*

"Where is he?" I asked my secretary.

"Highlighting. To your left."

I looked, and saw a conservatively dressed man coming through the restaurant entrance, about forty meters away, painted with a green nimbus by my in-head. He stopped, looked around . . . and our eyes met. He smiled and started walking toward us. His pace was slow, shuffling, and a bit awkward; I pegged him as a groundpounder, someone who hadn't been in space much and wasn't used to walking in low-G.

"What's the matter?" Joy asked. She must have seen the blank look on my face while I talked with my secretary.

"We've got company," I told her. "Wait here."

I got up and walked over to meet the guy. I pinged his ID as I approached, and got a readout: Christpher Ivarson, Global Net News. By the time I reached him, three-quarters of the way up the curve of the sphere, I was at a slow simmer but well on my way to coming to a boil.

"Petty Officer Carlyle—"

"What the fuck are you doing, following me around?" I demanded. "Can't a guy have any privacy?"

"You've been blocking our newsbots, sir, and we *really* would like to have you answer a few questions."

"Maybe there's a reason I've been blocking you," I told him. "Such as . . . I don't want to answer your questions."

"This will only take a moment, really."

"No. This ends now. I'm having dinner with a friend and I will not have it spoiled by the likes of you!"

"Now, don't be like that, Elliot! If the Central Asian Caliphate was behind the hijacking of that asteroid, the public has a right to know! And after all, the Hero of Bloodworld will have a unique perspective on the attack! You might not know it, but Elliot Carlyle is big news right now! First Bloodworld and the Qesh, and now you're charging a terrorist stronghold with the U.S. Marines! Great stuff!"

"Oh . . . you want a . . . what did you say? A unique perspective?"

"Absolutely! If you could just—"

"Here you go," I told him, reaching out with both hands and grabbing the lapels of his stylish maroon tunic. Bending my knees, I shoved upward . . . *hard*.

As noted, the spin gravity at the Free Fall's equator was around four-tenths of a G. Three-quarters of the way to the sphere's pole, which was at zero-G, the gravity was a lot lower . . . maybe a tenth of a G, or even a bit less. The GNN reporter probably massed eighty kilos, but he only *weighed* about eight here . . . about as much as a large cat, so once I got him moving he *kept* moving, moving hard. My shove sent him sailing up into the air, arms and legs thrashing . . . and he yelled bloody murder when he realized he wasn't coming down again.

Gravity inside rotating systems like the Free Fall is tricky. Ignoring things like air resistance, he technically was in zero-gravity as soon as he left the deck, but the Coriolis effect caused his straight-line path to curve alarmingly against the hab module's spin. For a moment I thought I'd misjudged, that he was going to miss.

Then one thrashing arm snagged the safety net surrounding the central sphere of water thirty meters above the restaurant's deck. He screamed again and grabbed hold with both arms and both legs, dangling far overhead.

Of course, the net was turning with the rest of the module, so hanging on up there he probably felt a spin gravity of something like fifteen hundredths of a gravity . . . maybe twelve kilos. If he let go, he'd drift back to the sphere's inner surface with a tangential velocity of, oh, a few meters per second, and if he didn't fall into some diner's salad, he'd be just fine.

But for someone born and raised on Earth, the possibility of that thirty-meter drop between the outside of the safety net and the restaurant floor was terrifying. The net enclosed the water sphere from pole to pole; it was designed to catch people falling out of the water and keep them from dropping onto the restaurant clientele. Ivarson only needed to clamber along the outside of the net until he reached one of the access tubes at the sphere's axis.

But panic had set in, and all he could do was cling to the outside of the net and howl.

I returned to Joy, who was watching the spectacle overhead. "What in the world . . . ?"

"*Out* of the world, I'm afraid."

"Why did you—"

"Reporter," I told her. "The bastards have been dogging me electronically ever since Zeta Capricorn, and now it looks like they're siccing humans on me."

"Excuse me, Petty Officer Carlyle?"

I turned and found myself facing a polite but stern Free Fall employee. I didn't know they had bouncers in places like that.

"Yes?"

"I'm afraid I'm going to have to ask you to leave."

I looked up at Ivarson, whose shouts and screams by now had become the focus of attention for every patron in the Free Fall. A couple of men in work utilities were making their way across the net to reach him.

"He's a reporter," I said. "Gross invasion of privacy."

"I quite understand, sir. Still, our guests have a right to enjoy their meals without . . . spectacles of this nature. I can ask you to leave, or I can summon the shore patrol."

"No need," I said. "Joy? You can stay and enjoy your meal, if you like. . . ."

"What, and miss a date with a man who can throw an asshole thirty meters? You've got to be kidding!"

So we left. We never did get our homegrown steak and lobster.

But it turned out to be a spectacular evening nonetheless.

Chapter Five

I GOT THE CALL NEXT MORNING TO REPORT TO SECOND LIEUTENANT Singer's office on board the *Clymer*, up-El at Starport.

The Commonwealth's Starport One Naval Base occupies the five-kilometer asteroid suspended at the high end of the space elevator, the stone spun at the end of a whirling string that keeps the string nice and taut. The docking facility is on the asteroid's far side; centrifugal force at that distance, 70,000 kilometers from Earth, amounts to just about one six-hundredth of a gravity. Ships departing the docks get a small but measurable nudge of delta-V when they release.

As her designation "APA" declared, the *George Clymer* was an attack transport, and she carried on board a battalion-strength MEU, a Marine Expeditionary Unit, consisting of 1,200 Marines, an aerospace strike force, heavy weapons, and vehicles, plus logistics and command elements. The *Clymer*'s habitation module was a fifty-meter rotating ring amidships, spinning two and a half times per minute to provide four-tenths of a gravity, roughly the same as on Mars. Singer's office was in the ring's outer level, right under the skin.

"HM2 Carlyle, reporting as ordered, sir."

Singer glanced up from his holographic computer display. "Stand at ease, Doc. Hang on a sec."

I waited as he completed whatever holowork he was doing—reports, probably, that were easier to read on an external screen than in-head. Fred Singer had come aboard just four months ago, after our last CO, Earnest Baumgartner, had gotten himself bumped up the pole to full lieutenant and transferred to Mars. I hadn't formed any real opinions of the new CO yet, beyond his essential assholitude. He was meticulous, a bit on the prissy side, and, like all second lieutenants fresh out of the Academy, he was inexperienced. Capricorn Zeta, I'd heard, had been his first time in combat.

That by itself is no crime, of course. The fact that he'd been tasked with taking his platoon in on a direct assault against Capricorn Zeta suggested that his superiors thought he could do the job. But for the enlisted pukes under him, both Marine and Navy, there was going to be a trial period when we were all keeping a wary eye on the guy. Would he be a prima donna? A perfectionist? A martinet? Or a decent Marine who listened to his NCOs and looked after his people?

"Okay, Doc," Singer said after a moment, switching off the holographic screen. "Thanks for coming."

"You wanted to see me, sir." Any maybe ream me a brand-new asshole.

"Thought you'd like to hear," he said. "You are officially off the hook."

I blinked. "Sir?"

"Headquarters has chosen to see your actions at Capricorn Zeta—in particular your unauthorized sampling of the prisoners' DNA—as 'an appropriate display of initiative in a combat situation.'"

"That's . . . uh . . . good news, sir." Singer seemed a little too cheerful, and I was waiting for the other combat boot to land.

"We will ignore the fact that you went over my head and failed to ask my permission to take those samples . . . *and* your failure to observe established protocol in the handling of prisoners . . . *and* your use of a comm channel compromised by newsbots. *This time!*"

The sheer threat wrapped into those last two words was like a blow. "Yes, sir."

"There's also the small matter of your assaulting a civilian at the Free Fall last night. I can *not* overlook that."

"It was a reporter, sir. He tracked me to the Free Fall! All I did was . . . push him a little. Sir."

"You pushed him. Witnesses say you threw him thirty meters! What were you on, G-Boost?"

"No, sir!" G-Boost is an artificial protein that bonds with the respirocytes all FMF personnel carry in their bloodstreams. It temporarily makes us stronger, faster, more alert, with better endurance. It's also tightly controlled, and you do *not* use it casually. The Freitas respirocytes in my blood had boosted my strength a little, of course, by improving the efficiency of my oxygen metabolism. But no, I'd not been Boosting.

"You're sure?"

"Absolutely, sir! It will not happen again, sir."

"It had damned well better not!" He gave me a sour look. "Okay, you have a choice. Accept my NJP here and now . . . or you can request to see Captain Reichert."

Shit. I hadn't realized I was in that much trouble. NJP meant non-judicial punishment. The Marines called it being NJP'd, while the Navy referred to is as captain's mast, and military slang called it being booked. Lieutenant Singer, as my immediate CO, could impose any of several punishments on me. Reichert was the Bravo Company commanding officer, and next up the command ladder from Singer. If I asked to see *him*, he might throw it out—fat chance—or he could give me more and worse than a mere second lieutenant could hand out, including, if he thought it serious enough, a court-martial, and that's when things got *really* serious.

It wasn't a real choice. Getting NJP'd was definitely preferable to a court, and having Second Lieutenant Singer come down on me was better than the company commander.

"Sir, I will accept whatever punishment you think fit. Sir."

"You have any excuses for your behavior? Extenuating circumstances?"

They drilled the correct and acceptable reply to *that* question into your head in boot camp. "No excuses, sir."

Yeah, the more I thought about it, the more I knew I'd screwed up big-time. It hadn't seemed that way at the time . . . but laying hands on a civilian like that, tossing him across the compartment? If he'd missed the net he might have gone on to hit the rotating deck hard enough to hurt himself, especially since he obviously wasn't experienced with low-G.

"Okay, Doc. I understand your problem with the newsies, so I'll go easy on you. Fourteen days' restriction, fourteen days' extra duty."

This was going easy on me? Singer had hit me with just about the hardest punishment he could manage as a lowly O-2 imposing Article 15 punishment.

But then, if he'd chosen to hand me company-grade punishment, I could have lost seven days of base pay, taken a reduction in grade, from HM2 back to HM3, and had a written reprimand put into my personnel folder. And if I'd gone up in front of the Old Man, I could have been slapped with restriction and extra duty for forty-five days, forfeiture of half my pay for two months, reduction in grade, a written reprimand—hell, even bread and water for three days if he was feeling *real* generous.

So maybe I was getting off light after all.

"Yes, sir. Thank you, sir."

"I also want a written letter of apology to Mr. Ivarson on my desk by oh eight thirty tomorrow."

I started to bristle, and I almost said something like "I'm

so sorry you're an asshole, Mr. Ivarson," but bit my tongue. This wasn't the time to try to win points with insulting comments that could only make things worse.

"Aye, aye, sir." I hesitated. "Uh . . . will this be going on my record, sir?"

"Do a good job, keep your nose clean . . . and no. No it won't."

I sagged with relief. A downgrudge letter in your file will pursue you to the end of your naval career. "Thank you, sir."

"Okay. That takes care of you and your reporter friend. Back to what happened at Zeta Capricorn. Damn it, Doc, do you have *any* idea what kind of a firestorm you've released around here?"

"I wasn't aware of any firestorm, sir."

"Jesus, Doc! Where's your head, up your ass? To start with, we just might be looking at a shooting war, and all because you released information about the ethnic and political identity of our prisoners onto the open Net! Half the world wants to nuke or railgun Dushanbe into a kilometer-deep crater right now. And Dushanbe claims we're lying, that we set the whole thing up to discredit them, to create a *causus bellum*."

Well, they would *claim something like that*, I thought. But I didn't say so out loud.

"Captain Reichert has been ragging my ass, asking me how I plan to tighten my operational security in my platoon. What the hell am I going to tell him?"

"Sir. You can tell him that the man responsible has learned his lesson and promises not to open channels directly to the HQ Net again."

"Why'd you do it, Doc?" The anger evaporated, and he seemed friendly again . . . a bit puzzled, perhaps, at why I'd been so careless. Or maybe the anger had all been a put-on, a bit of drama designed to show me he cared.

"I saw a chance to gather some useful intel, sir. This *is* Deep Recon, after all."

I didn't think he could fault me there. "Deep Recon" is the designation used for elite Marine units normally operating in deep space on interstellar deployments. They're supposed to be the first ones in, usually, to scout out the terrain and the ecology, determine what and where the enemy is, and, if necessary, pin that enemy until heavier forces can be deployed. Our primary business is gathering intelligence.

That doesn't mean we're not occasionally tapped for other missions—like taking down a bunch of terrorists holed up in an orbital mining facility. We'd been the closest available assault force when the bad guys stormed the mining facility the other day. We *are* FMF—Fleet Marine Force—and we go where we're told. But above all else we're trained to gather intelligence, *any* intelligence that may be of use to someone farther up the chain of command.

And the Black Wizards, Deep Recon 7 of the One MarDiv, were the *best*.

When Singer didn't respond right away, I added, "Sir, I really didn't know the channel had been compromised. How the hell was I *supposed* to know?"

"Ahh . . . you couldn't know, Doc. Hell, I didn't know either. The damned newsies slipped their netbots in to spy on the operation. I should have known they'd be keeping an eye on you, especially."

"I'm nothing special, sir."

"Maybe. But they know your name, and they have your ID tagged so they can track you on the Net. They remember you from the Bloodworld affair, so the second you go on-line with a query or a message, they're going to be swarming all over you. You been getting harassed by the sons-of-bitches at all?"

"My secretary tells me I've had a lot of calls, requests for interviews, requests for bios and backgrounds, that sort of thing." I managed a grin. "I haven't been answering them. In fact, that's why Ivarson came looking for me."

"Good. And in another couple of days, they won't be able to find you."

That made my blood run cold for a moment. "Sir? You're shipping me out?"

"That we are, Doc. Your new orders just came through."

"Yes, sir."

"Between you and me, I think General Craig just wants to be rid of you."

Major General William Craig was the commander of One MarDiv. Shit. It's *never* a good idea for a lowly enlisted man to attract the attention of a general.

"Yes, sir." I desperately wanted to ask where they were sending me, but knew better than to appear anxious. He would tell me, but he'd tell me in his own time.

He must have read the worried expression on my face. "Don't worry, Doc. You're not going alone."

"I'm pleased to hear it."

"You'll be deploying on the *Haldane* with a Marine scout-recon element. Five Corpsmen, pulled from the company as science-tech staff, plus a couple of xeno experts. One of the other docs will be your buddy Dubois. Net media has been after him as well."

"They have?" It was news to me. "Why Doob?"

Singer shrugged. "Maybe one doc is as good as another, to them. He was at Bloodworld too. *And* he's your buddy."

"Not for long. The guy's gonna kill me." HM2 Michael C. Dubois had a snug and happy billet for himself in Alpha Company. He had an under-the-counter deal with the lab to use their assemblers to manufacture paint stripper . . . ah, ethanol, rather, and he was *the* original cumshaw artist. He wasn't going to appreciate being yanked out of his comfortable little world because he associated with the likes of me.

"The seven of you will be the expedition's scientific survey team."

That caught my attention. "What are we surveying?"

"Ever hear of a place called Abyss Deep?"

I refrained from pulling down the data off the ship's Net. "No, sir."

"It's not much. GJ 1214 I. A lot like Bloodworld, so you ought to feel right at home. Just be sure you pack your long flannel undies. It's a hundreds-of-kilometers-deep ocean covered over by ice. Doc, this place is *cold*."

Great, I thought. Just what I *really* like. Ice . . .

As soon as I left Singer's office and got back to my quarters, I downloaded the Net information available on GJ 1214.

I had a strong sense of déjà vu as the data scrolled through my in-head window. GJ 1214 was another red dwarf, one even smaller and cooler than the primary of Bloodworld we'd visited the year before. I suppose I shouldn't have been surprised at that. In all the Galaxy, out of 400 billion stars, something like 80 percent are class-M red dwarfs, at least out in our general stellar neighborhood. Red dwarfs range from something like half the mass of our sun down to cool, red stars of only .075 solar masses—the cut-off line. Any smaller and they're not stars anymore, but brown dwarfs.

In our galactic neighborhood, twenty of the thirty nearest stars are red dwarfs, but they're so small and dim that we can't see any of them with the naked eye. The closest star to us outside of the Sol System, Proxima Centauri, is a Type M5 red dwarf, and you need a pretty powerful telescope to see it from Earth at all.

Proxima's partners in the cosmic dance, Alpha Centauri A and B, are very much like our sun . . . and, damn it, someday I'd like to be deployed to an Earthlike world of that kind of star, instead of another of these dim, cool, blood-red misers.

This time, though, I was stuck with another tide-locked split-personality planet: half ice, half steam. The readout wasn't pretty at all.

Download
Commonwealth Planetary Ephemeris
Entry: GJ 1214 I
"Abyssworld"

Star: GJ 1214

Type: M4.5V

M = .157 Sol; **R** = 0.206 Sol; **L** = .0033 Sol; **T** = 3000°K

Coordinates: RA 17_h 15_m 19_s; Dec +04° 57' 50"; D = 42 ly

Planet I

Name: GJ 1214 I; Gliese 1214b, Abyssworld, Abyss Deep

Type: Terrestrial/rocky core, ocean planet; "super-Earth"

Mean orbital radius: 0.0143 AU; **Orbital period**: 1_d 13_h 55_m 47_s

Inclination: 0.0°; Rotational period: 1_d 13_h 55_m 47_s (tide-locked with primary)

Mass: 3.914×10^{28} g = 6.55 Earth; **Equatorial diameter**: 34,160 km = 2.678 Earth

Mean planetary density: 1.87 g/cc = 0.34 Earth

Surface gravity: 0.91 G

Surface temperature range: ~ -120°C [nightside] to 220°C [dayside]

Surface atmospheric pressure: ~0.47×10^3 kPa [0.47 Earth average]

Percentage composition (mean): H_2 54.3, CO_2 20.3, H_2O 11.2, CH_4 9.3, CO 4.2, NH_3 3.1, Ar 0.5; others < 500 ppm

Age: 6 billion years

Biology: H_2O (exotic ices), C, N, O, H_2O, S, PO_4: mobile submarine heterotrophs in reducing aquatic medium in presumed symbiosis with unknown deep marine auto- or chemotrophs.

Human presence: The Murdock Expedition of 2238 established the existence of large deep-marine organisms known as cuttlewhales. Subsequent

research at the colony designated Murdock Base
demonstrated possible intelligent activity, and attempts were made to establish communications in
2244. Contact with the colony abruptly ended in
early 2247, and there has been no futher contact
since. . . .

The Commonwealth government had decided that word
from the research colony on the ice out there on Abyssworld
was too long overdue, and they were dispatching a small
Navy task force and some Marines to find out what had
happened. The Marines were volunteers drawn from First,
Second, and Third Platoons, plus the headquarters platoon
of Bravo Company, forty-two men and women in all, and
all of them blooded both by combat and by experience on
extrasolar worlds. Lieutenant Lyssa Kemmerer, Captain
Reichert's exec, would be leading us.

The five Navy Corpsmen, however, were not volunteers.
Where the Marines went, we would go as well.

The company's senior Corpsman was Chief Richard
R. Garner, an old hand with gold hash marks running
halfway up his dress uniform sleeve, each stripe showing
four years of good-conduct duty. He was a bluff, craggy,
no-nonsense sort, and when he barked at you he meant
business.

Garner called us to a briefing the next morning. There
were four of us sitting in the lounge in front of Garner—me
and Dubois, plus HM1 Charlie "Machine" McKean and
HM2 Kari Harris.

There was another man present as well, a Navy lieutenant
commander with the gold caduceus at his throat indicating
he was Medical Corps.

"Good morning, people," Garner began. "We've been
tapped as tech support for an important mission, and it's important to get this off on the right foot. We'll be transferring
to the USRS *Haldane* tomorrow. There's a download wait-

ing for each of you giving billeting information and duty schedules."

DuBoise and McKean both groaned. Harris remained impassive.

"Knock it off," Garner said. "First off, it is my pleasure to introduce Dr. Lyman Kirchner, fresh up-El from Sam-Sea. He will be our department head on this expedition."

I looked at Kirchner with curiosity. He was a small older man with an intense gaze that made me uncomfortable. If he was from SAMMC, though, he would be good. I wondered about his age, though. His white hair was thickly interspersed with black, and his face, with deep-set wrinkles, was an odd mixture of weathered skin and baby-pink new.

Anagathic treatments. He was under treatment for that most deadly of the diseases to afflict Humankind—old age.

"Dr. Kirchner," Garner continued, "was chief of the xenopathology department at Sam-Sea, so he will be our expedition xenologist as well as ship's doctor. We're very lucky to have him on board."

And *that* was a relief. I'd been wondering since Singer had told me I was being assigned to this mission whether we'd have a medical officer on board. I knew that Garner was IDC, but none of the rest of us were.

Independent-duty Corpsmen were *the* medical department on ships or bases too small to have a ship's doctor, and that was a hellacious responsibility. Oh, we operated independently in the field as often as not . . . but it was always good to have a real doctor backing you up.

You know, even today, we still hear the story of an independent-duty Corpsman during the Second World War—we were called Pharmacy Mates in those days—who successfully performed an appendectomy while on board a submarine, the USS *Seadragon*, while she was on her fourth war patrol, in 1942. He was twenty-three-year-old PhM1/c Wheeler B. Lipes—a first class, like McKean.

In fact, though it's not well known, there were *three* emergency appendectomies carried out by Pharmacy Mates on board Navy submarines during that war, this when the only commonly available antibiotics were powdered sulfanilamide and phenol, and the only anesthetic was ether. My God! The responsibility those guys faced was staggering! But, damn it, when there were no qualified surgeons within a thousand miles, you did what you had to do. . . .

Kirchner stood and acknowledged Garner's introduction. "Thank you, Chief." He glared at us. "No speeches, people. I know you're well trained, I know you're experienced, and I know you're going to do your jobs competently and well. With pre-screening of the ship's complement, we shouldn't have any major health issues, and *Haldane*'s medical department will be able to focus on the tech support at GJ 1214. So do your jobs, do what you're told, and we'll all get along just fine. Chief Garner?"

"Thank you, sir." Garner turned to face us again. "Okay, I want all of you to pull down the Abyss Deep docuinteractive from the *Clymer*'s library. On your own time."

"Aw, Chief," Dubois said. "What for? The place is nothing but a freaking ice ball." He'd been angry ever since his orders had come down telling him he was deploying to Abyss Deep, and he didn't mind letting everyone else within range know it.

"Can the gripeload, Doobie. That goddamn bleak ball of ice can kill you faster and in more ways than a Qesh Daitya platform."

McKean and Harris both grumbled a bit, too, and, I have to admit, I did as well. Sailors *hate* having official shit intrude on their precious downtime, and I already had the extra duty tagged onto my daily schedule by my NJP. But as the ancient adage has it, a griping sailor is a happy sailor. Garner had scored a point by bringing up the Daityas, heavy-weapons platforms named for a class of giant or demon in Hindu mythology. We'd faced Qesh Daityas out on Bloodworld, and had a healthy respect for the things.

"Okay," Garner went on, "we're slated to board the *Haldane* tomorrow evening. Our civilian . . . *guests* will be joining us on board. They are Dr. Carla Montgomery and Dr. Raúl Ortega. Montgomery is an expert on exobiology. Ortega is an expert on planets and environments with extreme temperatures or other exotic conditions.

"We have absolutely no idea what happened to Murdock Base. None. The last report from there, via robot courier, mentioned sightings of the autochthones, the native life, but no contact . . . and no danger. The next courier was due from them four days later. It's been three weeks, now, with no word from them whatsoever. We must assume that the base has suffered some significant problem. It may be as minor as a failure in the AIs they use to launch and transmit to the couriers. Or it may be more serious. A *lot* more serious.

"So they're sending in the Marines. And us."

More download information flooded through our inheads, a schematic view of a multilevel dome equipped with living quarters, common areas, airlocks, and a large central laboratory space.

"The base," Garner went on, "is a standard nano-grown all-climate dome, with several outlying structures . . . but only the main dome is pressurized. The colony consists of eighty-five men and women—mostly science staff, but including admin and support—plus twelve M'nangat in four family triads. The M'nangat are there to liaise with the EG, if need be, in order to conduct deep research on any locals that they might manage to contact."

The Brocs had become more and more important as we researched the labyrinth of data that was the Encyclopedia Galactica. Our best guess right now is that we have been able to access something less than one hundredth of 1 percent of the EG data that's out there, and we wouldn't have been able to tap that much if not for M'nangat help. If the organisms discovered on GJ 1214 I were intelligent—and that was by no means certain yet—there ought to be a listing and a lot more data available on the local EG nodes.

As yet we could find nothing, but that didn't mean it wasn't there. There are an estimated 50 to 100 million intelligent species scattered through our Galaxy, and perhaps a thousand times that number that have existed during the past billion years, but which now are extinct. Many, though by no means all, of these have entries in the EG. Technic species that discover the EG and learn how to tap in, sometimes, though not always, list themselves. Atechnic species— marine organisms that have never discovered fire and metal smelting, for instance—or the more inwardly focused species who have turned their backs on space travel are often described by others who encounter them.

For a billion years—as long as multicellular life has existed on Earth—the Encyclopedia Galactica has grown in both size and complexity, with millions of separate channels, nested frequencies, and deep-heterodyned polylogues. Lots of channels we can't even access yet; we're certain there are neutrino channels, for instance, but we don't know how to read them. When we discovered the local node at Sirius, just 8.6 light years from Earth, we swiftly decided that we needed friendly native guides to lead us through the data jungles.

We would have copies of small parts of the EG with us at GJ 1214, as much as could be accommodated by the *Haldane*'s sizeable quantum computer storage. We're still working out how the EG is organized, but we think it includes data on all nearby stars in the direction of the constellation Ophiuchus, which is where GJ 1214 is located in the night sky. With luck, we'd scooped up the still-hidden entry on Abyssworld along with known nearby stars in that region—70 and 36 Ophiuchi, Sabik, Raselhague, and others—and our AIs could be hacking through the jungle while we worked.

Eventually the briefing ended—a lot of talk with no surprises—and I went back to work. I was working in the *Clymer*'s main sick bay that week, which meant the usual shipboard morning routine of sick call, screening Marines and naval personnel who were showing up with problems ranging from colds to an eye infection to a full-blown case of pneumonia. The pneumonia actually was easier to treat than the colds. Despite our much-vaunted advances in medical technology over the past couple of centuries, the collection of minor infections and immune-system failures known as "the common cold" is still tough to treat other than purely symptomatically. Rather than being a single malady, the complaint we call a cold can be caused by any of some two hundred different viruses. The rhinovirus associated with the majority of colds alone has ninety-nine serotypes. That makes it tough to program an injection of nanobots to go in and kill the viruses, and the preferred treatment remains taking care of the symptoms rather than the cause.

There were an unusual number of colds this morning, though, so I pulled some nasopharyngeal samples and sent them up to the lab for a full serotypal workup. We often had these little micro epidemics running their course of the ship when we were in port. Sailors and Marines went ashore on liberty, of course—even taking the elevator down-El to Earth—and they were exposed to bugs they wouldn't have otherwise encountered if they'd stayed on board. If we could identify a specific strain of virus, we could whip up a nanobot to attack it. In the meantime, though, I'd stick with the old-fashioned treatment—acetaminophen, chlorpheniramine maleate, phenylephrine hydrochloride, and dextromethorphan, plus lots of water. The pain reliever, the antihistamine, the decongestant, and the cough suppressant would do everything a round of nanobots would, and—heresy!—might even do it better.

At a few past 1700 hours I checked out of sick bay and reported to Chief Garner, who was in charge of handing out my extra-duty hours each evening. He just grinned at me and said, "You *have* your duty assignment, Carlyle. Go bone up on Abyss Deep."

So after a quick sonoshower back in my quarters, I prepared to climb into my rack-tube to take the sim. Just as I slipped inside, though, a call came through from Doob, suggesting that we rack out together in the ship's lounge. I told him I'd meet him there.

"E-Car!" he called as I entered the lounge. "Let's get this fucking sim out of the way, okay? I have a hot date tonight and I'm damned if I'm going to miss it."

"Who is it, Doob? Carla again?" HM3 Carla Harper was a lab assistant whom Dubois had bedded . . . a *lot*. There was a pool running among some of the platoon Corpsmen as to whether or not he would pop the question, and when.

"Nah. Someone new."

"Someone *new*? My God, it's the end of life as we know it!"

"Knock it off."

"Who is it?"

"None of your damned business!" He scowled at me. "What I wanna know is how come you get in trouble, but I get to share in the punishment!"

"Welcome to the Navy," I told him. "At least you didn't get two weeks' restriction."

"What restriction? We boost for Abyssworld day after tomorrow, we'll be gone a couple of months at least, and all you miss is a couple of liberties!"

That stopped me. I hadn't thought about that. Restriction means you stay in your quarters *except* when you're going about your normal day-to-day duties, or eating in the mess hall, or doing whatever your CO tells you to do . . . so Doob was right. Maybe I *had* gotten off light.

"Okay, Doobie," I told him. "You wanna tag the 'interactive together? It'll go faster that way, and you can be off to your mystery date."

"My thought exactly, E-Car."

I thoughtclicked an internal control. "Compartment, two chairs, downloungers with full link capability. Here and here."

The active nanomatrix in the deck obediently shaped two areas into egg-shaped chairs, both almost completely enclosed except for the oval front openings, and with deeply padded interiors that let you stretch out and back in fair comfort. I backed into one, brought my palm contacts down on the link board, and ordered a library download of the required docuinteractive.

Dubois dropped into the second seat. "I hate these things."

"I kind of like 'em," I replied. "Just like being there, but you don't get eaten by the bug-eyed monster."

"That's the problem. You get used to ignoring dangers in a sim, they could bite you for real when you're actually there."

"So? Don't be complacent. The idea is that we can step into another world and learn about it experientially. No surprises when you step into the world for real."

"So, what did the chief call it? 'That goddamn bleak ball of ice?' No fun at all, man!"

"I didn't realize we were going out there to have fun!" I nestled back into the yielding foam of the seat and put my palm on the contact pad.

There was a burst of in-head static, and then I was standing on the surface of Abyssworld.

My God, I thought. *"Goddamn bleak" doesn't even begin to cover it. . . .*

Chapter Six

A BIT OF BACKGROUND CAME DOWN THE LINK FIRST.

The formal name of the place is GJ 1214 I, but most people call it either Abyssworld or Abyss Deep. The data we were simming had been sent back to Earth just five years ago, but in fact the world has been known since the early twenty-first century. It was discovered by the MEarth Project, which was searching for extrasolar planets by watching for minute dips in the brightness of some thousands of red dwarfs, an indicator of a planet transiting the star's face. They used red dwarfs because it was easier to record light fluctuations against a dimmer light source, and because planets circling red dwarfs tended to be tucked in a *lot* closer to their parent suns, and therefore had orbital periods measured in days as opposed to months or years. In 2009, the planet named—by the astronomical convention of the day—GJ 1214b was first detected, and subsequent observations showed that it was a so-called super-Earth, with more than six and a half times Earth's mass and over two and a half times Earth's diameter.

The real surprise came when they did the math and determined that the new planet had a density of just one-third of Earth's, which meant that the huge world had a quite small rocky core covered by either ice or liquid water.

It was, in fact, the first true ocean exoplanet discovered;

the side of the world eternally locked beneath a small sun just 2 million and some kilometers away was *hot*, well above the boiling point of water. At first it was assumed that the surface of any world so close to its parent would have to be well above habitable temperatures. The measured equilibrium temperatures, however, turned out to be from dayside cloud decks; the nightside was cold enough that the global ocean was half covered by a permanent ice cap, with the entire night hemisphere locked in ice.

The extreme differences in temperature between the day and night hemispheres, though, resulted in some absolutely incredible storms.

If Dubois and I had *really* been standing on the edge of the Abyss Deep icepack in nothing but our shipboard utilities, we would have been dead in moments. The environment was nothing short of hellish, balanced precariously between frigid ice and scalding steam, with a poisonous pea-soup-fog atmosphere and a wind thundering in from the day with tornadic force. The docuinteracive wasn't recreating all of the possible physical sensations, though. I could see water spray and surface clouds whipping past me, hear the deafening roar of moving air, but the wind didn't sweep me off my feet. The two of us could stand there, at the very edge of the ice, and take in the view.

And the view was . . . spectacular.

Despite both high-altitude cloud decks and the scud whipping across the surface of water and ice, I could see the star on the knife-edge horizon across the purple-red ocean, a swollen, deep ruby dome mottled by vast, ragged sunspots. Clouds—black, green, and purple—banked hugely to either side in an emerald sky; lightning played along the horizon. As I watched, fast-moving clouds filled the momentary crack in the sky that had revealed the star, blotting it out.

In the opposite direction, the sky grew darker still and heavy with snow. Ice, undulating and raw, ran off into the distance in a barren white desert, punctuated here and there by upthrusts—slabs, pillars, daggers, and tumbled blocks of ice, some of them hundreds of meters across. A hundred meters away, a low, bright orange dome added a spot of color to the endless white—the colony's main dome. Smaller domes and Quonset-style huts were scattered about nearby, and I could see a large, bright yellow quantum spin-floater grounded outside the main entrance to the base.

The colony was obscured by a sudden gust of spray and windblown snow. It made me shiver just looking at it, though I couldn't feel the actual cold.

"The place is a lot like Bloodworld," Dubois said, turning to look back out to sea. We were standing at the edge of the icepack, though waves and spray made it a little difficult to tell exactly where the sea ended, and the ice began. "Hurricanes, high winds, hellacious storms . . ."

"It's worse," a voice told us. We turned and faced the program's interactive agent, an older man with the look of a college professor. "I'm Dr. Murdock. I'll be your guide to Abyss Deep this evening."

Well, it wasn't the *real* Dr. Murdock, of course, since the Abyssworld Expedition's science team leader was currently on the planet some forty-two light years away . . . assuming he was even alive now. Based on the real James Eric Murdock, the man in a civilian tunic and dark slacks was a computer-generated image, data seamlessly woven together inside our heads by *Clymer*'s library AI. This simulation component was the whole point of a docuinteractive; we could ask the program questions, and it could take us through the landscape as if we were really there. The AI running the show was programmed to incorporate the voice, mannerisms, and recorded thoughts of the real Murdock, and present them as though we were actually there.

The simulated Murdock held out his hand, palm up, and a small globe representing the planet came up between us. He rotated it in front of us.

"We call the main atmospheric disturbance *Abysstorm*," he said. "It's generated by the heat of the star, and serves to transfer that heat across the planet."

On the globe, Abyss Deep's dayside was blanketed by a perpetual hurricane many thousands of kilometers across, pinned in place by the glare of the star directly over its eye. It showed vast, far-reaching spirals of cloud that reached across half the planet. The nightside was completely covered by ice.

"Hang on a sec," Dubois said, pointing. "Something's wrong. Hurricanes are caused by the spin of the planet. Coriolis effect, right? Abyss Deep doesn't rotate, so the winds ought to blow straight back from dayside to night."

The simulated Dr. Murdock gave him a sharp look. "Idiot. Why do you say the planet doesn't rotate? Of course it does."

"Hey!" Doob said. Evidently he wasn't used to *personality* coming through in a sim along with basic information. Murdock reminded me of an acid, acerbic professor of A and P—anatomy and physiology—I remembered from my training in San Antonio. He'd called students "idiot," and worse, as well.

"*'Tidally locked* means the planet rotates once in its year," I put in.

"Precisely," Murdock said. "GJ 1214 I *does* spin, and does so fairly quickly, quickly enough that it generates its own magnetic field, which is a damned good thing considering the background radiation flux from the star. It makes one rotation in just over a day and a half as it moves around its star, its day perfectly matching its year.

"The storm dynamics are quite complex, with smaller storms constantly spinning off of the one big one and following gently curved tracks around the planet and into the night. The atmosphere is fairly thin, about half of Earth's atmospheric pressure at the surface, so a lot of the heat dissipates before it reaches the nightside. The world-ocean traps a lot of it. Most of the dissipation, however, appears to be through molecular escape. The star turns water into steam, which rises high in the atmosphere above the Abysstorm. Solar radiation then blasts a lot of that water completely away from the planet. See?"

The model of Abyss Deep floating above Murdock's hand developed a faint, ghostly tail streaming away from the daylight side. "In many ways," he continued, "Abyssworld is similar to a comet . . . a very *large* comet with a tail of hot gasses blowing away from the local star."

"That can't be a stable configuration," I said. "It's losing so much mass that the whole planet is going to boil away."

"Correct. We believe Abyssworld formed much farther out in the planetary system, then migrated inward as a result of gravitational interactions with the two outer gas giants. We don't have a solid dating system with which to work, but it's possible that the planet began losing significant mass as much as five billion years ago, when it would have been perhaps six times the diameter it is now.

"Abyssworld is now losing mass, which has the advantage of bleeding away excess heat. Within another billion years, though, this ongoing loss of mass will significantly reduce the planet's size, until the entire world ocean has boiled away. At that point, Abyssworld will be dead."

"There's life here now?" Dubois asked. He looked around the encircling landscape, wind-blasted waves and spray in one direction, and in the other an endless plain of undulating white ice beneath black and lightning-shot clouds.

"Of course," Murdock told him. "The cuttlewhales."

Murdock turned, sweeping the ocean panorama with his arm. In the distance, halfway to the horizon, something sinuous emerged from the sea.

The thing wasn't close enough to get a decent look at it. It was large, obviously, perhaps fifty meters or more in length, and a good half of that was arcing high above the wind-whipped surface of the ocean. It was also obviously alive, twisting and arcing and writhing as it plowed ahead through the water, tantalizing in its mist-shrouded obscurity. It put me in mind of a mythical Earthly sea serpent, and I wanted to see it up close.

"Can we get out there?" I asked. "Or bring that thing in close? I can't see through the spray."

"Sorry, no," Murdock told me. "This is the best data we had prior to sending the last courier to Earth."

I had to remind myself that the information I was seeing was five years out of date. Had the colony managed to make contact since then?

Had something gone wrong with that meeting . . . something that had ended with the colony's destruction?

That was what we were going to try to find out.

"Some of our people saw one close up," Murdock continued, "but they didn't get any images. They said the head is something like the head of a terrestrial squid or cuttlefish . . . and that it could change the coloration on its body in pretty complex patterns. Dr. Samuelson believes they may use their chromataphores to communicate fairly complex ideas . . . which is why he reported that they may be intelligent."

A number of species on Earth could change the color and patterning and even the apparent texture of their skin by controlling their chromataphores, which are pigment-containing organelles in their skin. That didn't make them intelligent, however. They used it for camouflage or to display emotion rather than for more complex communication. Sure, an octopus flashes dark red when it's angry and white if it's afraid, which is pretty complex when you think about it, but that doesn't make them starship builders, either.

I found it interesting that one of the toughest jobs in xenobiology is determining whether a given species is intelligent in the first place. The jury was still out on these Abyss cuttlewhales. Hell, we still aren't sure what intelligence *is*, though we know there are many different kinds, and that it includes things like problem-solving skills, curiosity, and self-awareness. Wegener, the guy who made first contact with the Brocs, is supposed to have said, "I don't know what intelligence is, but I know it when I see it."

The trouble is that often we *don't* know it when we see it . . . or we find we've been looking for all the wrong things. The Europan Medusea are a case in point. Are they intelligent? Beats me. And we may well never know, simply because we don't have enough in common with them to even begin to communicate with them on a meaningful level.

"Come on," Murdock said. "I'll show you the base."

Two hours later, we'd been through the dome top to bottom, and met a number of the researchers there. They seemed like nice people, most of them, and that left me with a nagging depression. It was entirely possible, even likely, that every one of them was already dead, that I was speaking, in a way, to their digitized ghosts.

But the ordeal ended at last, and I emerged back in the lounge area on board the *Clymer*.

"That's it, E-Car," Doobie said. "I'm outta here!"

"Have fun," I told him.

And I resolved to have chow in the mess hall, then retire to my quarters for a quiet evening alone.

Supper was a mystery-meat culture that was actually pretty tasty if you dialed up the habanero sauce. It was well past the main mess period, and the place was nearly empty. I finished up, then went back to my quarters.

"Elliot?" It was Joy. My secretary had orders to always route her calls through. I was surprised to find she was standing right outside my compartment. "Can I come in?"

I thoughtclicked the hatch open and she stepped inside. She palmed the touchpoint on her shipboard utilities just below the throat and they evaporated as she came into my arms, gloriously nude. "I *had* to see you," she said. "I . . . I volunteered for the *Haldane* expedition, but they wouldn't take me!"

"I know. I looked up the personnel manifest." They were only taking twenty-four Marines, after all, out of a company numbering almost two hundred people. *Someone* had to stay behind.

"I was trying to swap assignments with Gibbs, but he wouldn't agree to it." She looked disgusted. "The idiot *wants* to go."

"Well, apparently, so do you."

"Because I want to be with *you*."

I reached up for my own touchpoint and clicked my uniform away. By that time, I didn't even need to go to my in-head menu and turn on my CC-PDE5 inhibitors. I was *ready. . . .*

But of course Sergeant Tomacek chose that moment to come through the door.

Bruce Tomacek was one of the three Second Platoon Marines with whom I shared a berthing compartment, a nice enough guy, but with a nasty tendency to tease newbies unmercifully.

"What the fuck?" he asked when he saw our embrace. "Hey, E-Car, if you're on restriction you're not supposed to *enjoy* it!"

"Do you mind?" I asked. "We're saying good-bye."

"Nope," he said, grinning as he dropped into the chair at the compartment's small desk. "I don't mind at all!"

Privacy was always tough to come by on board a Navy vessel, but we did have an answer. The compartment's rack-tube hatches occupied the bulkhead to the left of the door, four circular openings that cold be sealed shut with a thoughtclick. At just a meter wide, they were a bit on the claustrophobic side for two, but it could be done. I helped Joy into mine, gave the leering Tomacek a dirty look, then skinnied in next to her. I thoughtclicked the hatch shut, and we were alone.

Each rack-tube had internal lighting, Net connection pads, environment controls, and a flow of fresh air from hidden vents. The padding was warm and soft, as was Joy. I took her in my arms and we snuggled close.

"Just like the *hoteru*," she said, smiling into my face.

"Well, except for the gravity, yeah."

Rabu Hoteru was the Japanese honeymoon hotel in Geosynch. Joy and I had spent a couple of nights there on liberty once, just after we'd come back from Bloodworld. Zero-gravity sex is a lot of fun, but it helps if you and your partner are . . . *restrained*, somewhat. In microgravity, every movement has an equal and opposite reaction, and what is euphemistically called "the docking maneuver"—and *staying* docked—can be a bit tricky.

The answer was softly padded tubes in the honeymoon suites, where you and your partner could get plenty of purchase for your more energetic acrobatics. The ends were left open, so you could look toward the head end of your tube and see the endlessly wondrous spectacle of Earth hanging in star-clotted space.

I pulled up my in-head menu, made a selection, and clicked it; a view of the shrunken Earth, taken by external cams on the Earth-side of the Starport asteroid, appeared on the head-end of the tube.

"I can't do anything about the gravity," I said. Well, not without convincing the ship's skipper to shut down the hab module rotation—like *that* was ever going to happen. "But I can provide us with a room with a view."

"I think the best view was that time at Yellowstone," she told me. That had been last fall. We'd taken a few days of leave, rented an e-Car at San Antonio, and driven up to Montana. The weather had been bitter cold and snowy— we'd been way too close to the Canadian ice sheet for my peace of mind—but the view from the hotel in Jackson had been spectacular.

"The best view," I told her, "is you."

I was having some trouble with the docking maneuver. Damn it, thinking about ice always did that to me. I'd been ready enough a few moments ago, but having Tomacek barge in, and then remembering the ice sheet . . .

This time, I *did* switch on my CC-PDE5 inhibitors. Phosphodiesterase type 5 is a natural enzyme found within the corpus cavernosum, the smooth muscle responsible for the guy's part in the proceedings. Certain drugs and appropriately programmed nanobots can act as PDE5 inhibitors, which relax the smooth muscles *preventing* erection.

No good. The ice was winning.

Well, not the ice, specifically . . . but the thoughts of Paula that I associated with glaciers, with sailboats, with cold, with loneliness . . . with *anything* that took me back to that afternoon off the chill coast of ice-locked Maine when Paula had died in my arms—those were circling in my brain, now, relentless and anxious. Damn it, why couldn't I put that crap away?

"It's okay," Joy whispered. "Just hold me."

And that only made it worse, somehow.

At some point during the night, however, ice and loneliness gave way to soft warmth and caresses, and thoughts of Paula were submerged in rising passion.

At least for a time.

I REPORTED ABOARD THE USRS *J. B. S. HALDANE* LATE THE NEXT day, along with the rest of the Marine Special Expeditionary Platoon, now dubbed MSEP-Alpha. One of the Commonwealth's Scientist-class research ships, the *Haldane* was a no-frills ride, a minnow to the *Clymer*'s whale when she docked alongside for the payload transfer. She was named for the twentieth-century British geneticist and evolutionary biologist who'd famously said, "[T]he universe is not only queerer than we suppose, but queerer than we *can* suppose."

And that had been long before we started meeting extraterrestrial species, or visiting the worlds they lived on.

The *Haldane* was only eighty-one meters long and thirty

broad, and the trip out to GJ 1214 was going to be a bit on the cramped side. Technically, she was a civilian research vessel, but Commander Janice Summerlee was a Navy officer, and most of her crew personnel were Navy as well. *Haldane* was listed on the rolls as a research ship, which meant she served a wide range of roles. One of her most important missions, though, was transporting personnel and supplies to the far-flung science colonies across near interstellar space.

I floated out of the boarding tube and into her quarterdeck compartment, where I saluted the officer of the deck. "Permission to come aboard, sir."

"Granted," the man growled. You don't go through the military formalities on a civilian vessel, but if the *Haldane* was being pressed into military duties, the niceties of tradition were maintained. "Pre-screen records?"

I thoughtclicked the appropriate icon in my in-head, giving him access to the results of the med scan I'd gone through a few hours earlier. Purely routine stuff, that. *Haldane* would be out and on its own for at least a couple of months, and it wouldn't do for anyone on board to come down with something nasty while we were in deep space . . . *especially* something that might contaminate the entire crew.

That sort of screening is anything but simple, and it takes a pretty powerful AI to carry it out. The human body is host to thousands of species of bacteria, but in terms of sheer numbers, our bacterial hangers-on are overwhelming. The typical person has about 10 trillion cells in his or her body . . . and *ten times* that number of bacteria in their gut alone. Something like 3 percent of our body mass consists of microbiota: bacteria, archaea, and fungi. All of these actively help us and keep us healthy, in a symbiotic relationship with their human host. We couldn't digest stuff like carbohydrates without them, and for that reason they're known as the "forgotten organ."

Generally, when we get sick it's because our immune system has been compromised in some way—generally by stress of one sort or another—and that allows some otherwise innocuous organism that was there all along to get out of hand. So a screening for pathogens doesn't mean spotting *Eschericia coli* in the colon, for example, but determining whether the population of *E. Coli* is out of balance with all the rest, whether the patient's immune system is functioning properly, and whether normal body cells in the area are showing signs of inflammation are all part of the process. Picking up problems caused by viruses can be even tougher.

So the screening process concentrates on whether or not the person is showing an immunological response or not. It doesn't rule out the possibility of an infection breaking out later, but it helps spot trouble before it gets out of hand.

My scans had come up clean.

The OOD downloaded the scan results, then recorded my ID data on his e-pad. "Carlyle," he said. "Welcome aboard. I'm Lieutenant Walthers, the ship's exec." He jerked his thumb over his shoulder. "Says here somebody wants to see you. Mess bay."

Curious, I followed the thumb down a short passageway, swimming through the corridor in microgravity. There was technically a faint echo of spin gravity here. Starport was on the out-most end of the space elevator, and as the asteroid whirled about Earth on the end of its 70,000-kilometer tether, it created a six-hundredth of a gravity . . . scarcely enough to feel. Drop something, and it would "fall" a bit less than a centimeter in the first second.

The mess bay was the *Haldane*'s common area, which served as mess deck, recreation lounge, briefing room, and social space for the small ship. Three Brocs were floating in front of the big viewall, which was set to look past the swell of the *Clymer* close alongside, and off along the line of other naval vessels entangled within a forest of docking ramps, boarding gantries, and connector cables, the business end of Starport.

My personal ID was pinged, checking my name and rank. Obviously, the M'nangat had as much trouble telling humans apart as we had with them.

YOU ARE DOCTOR CARLYLE. The translation flowed across my in-head. I could only tell which one was speaking by the almost spastic twitch of its tentacles. YOU SAVED D'DNAH. YOU SAVED OUR BUDS.

"Not 'Doctor,' " I said. "I'm a Navy Corpsman. They just call me Doc."

DOC CARLYLE, THEN. WE WISHED TO THANK YOU FOR SAVING OUR BUDS.

"All in the line of duty," I said. The Broc in the middle of the three was D'dnah. I could tell by the patch of skinseal still glistening on herm's side. "How are you feeling, D'dnah?" I asked.

I AM WELL, the M'nangat said. YOUR PEOPLE TRANSPORTED ME TO THE NAVAL HOSPITAL IN SAN ANTONIO. WE WERE TOLD THAT YOU HAD DONE EVERYTHING NECESSARY, THAT NO FURTHER TREATMENT, SURGERY, OR NANOTECHNIC INTERVENTION WAS NECESSARY.

"Sometimes we get lucky," I said. "I'm glad to hear you're okay."

I'd not done anything for the M'nangat life carrier beyond pretty basic emergency first aid. Sure, I'd pulled the unexploded nano-D bullet out of herm's torso, which was something usually best left to well-equipped operating rooms, but there'd not been a lot of choice, there, and no leeway if I'd guessed wrong. Apparently, the nanobots I'd put into D'dnah's body had managed to seal off all of the internal bleeding, and the skinseal had taken care of surface bleeding. The M'nangat, evidently, had fairly robust biological repair and recovery systems. I'd slapped the equivalent of a bandage on D'dnah's wound, and the M'nangat's physiology had taken care of the rest.

Even so, it had only been three days since the battle on board Capricorn Zeta. "I'm surprised they released you so soon," I added. "I would have thought that they'd want to keep an eye on you for a few days, just to make sure you were healing okay."

THEY DID, the Broc on the right said. THEY STATED A DESIRE TO KEEP HERM UNDER OBSERVATION. OUR CONSULATE MISSION WAS ABLE TO CONVINCE THEM THAT THERE WAS NO NEED.

Well, the M'nangat would understand their own emergency medical needs better than we did.

I felt a bit awkward. Two of the M'nangat I'd met on Capricorn Zeta, of course, but the third had been on Earth during the attack. I recognized D'Dnah, but I had no idea which of the other two was which. I wondered how to ask for an introduction.

"So, D'dnah," I said. "I take it this is your triad?" It was a lame ploy, but it worked.

I AM D'DREVAH, the one on the left said. I AM EGG BEARER.

I AM D'DEEN, said the one on the right. I AM LIFE DONOR. FORGIVE US IF WE MISUSE YOUR PROTOCOLS OF SOCIAL INTERACTION. THEY ARE . . . AS YET UNFAMILIAR TO US.

"Not at all," I said. "You're doing great."

WE WERE DIRECTED TO COME TO EARTH AS POLITICAL LIAISONS, D'drevah told me, AND TO ASSIST YOUR PEOPLE WITH YOUR ACCESS TO THE DEEP TIME EPHEMERIS— WHAT YOU CALL THE ENCYCLOPEDIA GALACTICA. I WAS, UNFORTUNATELY, INVOLVED IN WORK AT OUR CONSULATE ON EARTH WHEN OUR LIFE BEARER WAS INJURED. BUT D'DEEN TOLD ME WHAT YOU DID ON THE MINING STATION, ABOUT HOW YOU SAVED OUR BUDS.

"I was glad to be able to help," I told them. If I'd felt awkward before, I was downright uncomfortable now. The introduction seemed to have released an avalanche of personal information, as if we'd passed some sort of privacy threshold to enter a new level of intimacy. More than that,

I was increasingly aware that the male and female of the triad, D'drevah and D'deen, seemed *much* more concerned about the safety of their offspring than they were about their bearer, D'dnah.

Well, that's the thing about aliens. They're *alien* . . . different to the point of incomprehensibility.

In Corps School, when they were teaching us about alien cultures and social norms, they spent a lot of time hammering home the idea that just because a particular cultural belief set is *different*, it's not wrong. I've never necessarily subscribed to that notion, not wholeheartedly. I mean . . . look at radical fundamentalist Islam as practiced a couple of centuries ago during the Troubles . . . or even today in places like the Central Asian Caliphate that recognize only Sharia law. Ask the inhabitants of what once was Tel Aviv about the morality—or the validity—of a god who glories in murder, vengeance, and genocide.

But the rule is that alien environments, alien physiologies, alien psychologies produce worldviews that are fundamentally different from ours. The M'nangat would have developed ways of thinking, patterns of beliefs, that fit their particular evolutionary backgrounds.

And according to the xenosoc downloads I'd taken in school, it was wrong to judge them for simply being what they were.

"So . . ." I said, "was that what you wanted to see me about?"

To thank you, yes, D'deen told me, and to make a specific request.

"Oh?"

The three of us have been assigned to this mission, D'drevah said. We are to help your scientists with access to portions of the Ephemeris during this expedition to the place you call Abyssworld.

There'd been M'nangat in the Murdock colony, too, I remembered. The chances were good that they were also there to look after their own.

D'DNAH IS DUE TO RELEASE OUR BUDS IN ANOTHER THREE OF YOUR WEEKS, D'deen said. WE WILL REQUIRE MEDICAL ASSISTANCE. WE WISH FOR YOU TO PROVIDE THAT ASSISTANCE.

I gaped at them. They wanted me to deliver their young.

And from what I'd learned so far of M'nangat physiology, that would mean allowing D'dnah, the being whose life I'd saved, to die.

Chapter Seven

I'D HOPED FOR A LAST CHANCE TO SAY GOOD-BYE TO JOY, BUT IT didn't happen. I was still on restriction, which now meant I couldn't leave the *Haldane*, and security had been stepped up and no one was allowed to come on board who wasn't part of her assigned crew or an appropriately tagged member of the Starport work crew. War fever—the worsening situation in the Caliphate—had everyone on edge, and the CAC's views on scientific research were well known. Privacy would have been an issue on board the cramped science vessel in any case. We had a final in-head conversation late at night. "Damn it, you come back to me, Elliot," she told me. "That's a goddamn fucking order."

"You don't outrank me, Sergeant," I said, grinning into the darkness. A Marine sergeant and a Navy second class both were E-5, the same rank. "But I'll be back for you. Promise . . ."

We departed from Starport at 0700 the next morning.

Our immediate destination, though, was not the world of GJ 1214 I, some forty-two light years distant. Instead, we used our Plottel Drive to tack on the sun's magnetic field out-system to Jupiter, making the passage of 9 AUs in eight and a half days.

During the outbound passage, I pulled down the ephemeral data. I'd actually been scheduled to deploy to Europa at the end of my FMF training, but the deployment to Blood-world had intervened.

Commonwealth Planetary Ephemeris
Entry: Europa, Jupiter II

Star: Sol

Planet: Sol V, Jupiter

Satellite: Sol Vf, Jupiter-f

Name: Europa

Type: Ice-covered world ocean, kept liquid by tidal heating; rocky core

Mean orbital radius: 670.900 km; **Orbital period**: 3_d 13_h 13_m 42_s

Orbital eccentricity: 0.009; **Inclination**: 0.47°

Rotational period: 3_d 13_h 13_m (tide-locked with primary)

Mass: 4.7988 x 10^{25} g = 0.008 Earth; **Equatorial diameter**: 3,121.6 km = 0.245 Earth

Mean planetary density: 3.01 g/cc = .545 Earth; **Surface gravity**: 0.134 G

Surface temperature range: ~ -160° C to -220° C

Surface atmospheric pressure: 0.1 υPa, or 10^{-13} bar [0.000000000001 Earth average]; **Percentage composition**: O_2 100 [Molecular oxygen]

Age: 4.6 billion years

Biology: Diverse marine forms; no surface forms present

Human presence: Conamara Chaos research colony, established 2110. Fifty scientists, xenobiologists, and technicians in residence as of 2247. The base is an inverted cone hanging from the underside of the ice cap, at the bottom end of a 600-meter access tube from the surface. Further human presence in Europa is prohibited pending additional study of Europan biosphere, and in particular of the Medusae, which show evidence of being sapient. . . .

Well, that's the sort of information you can download from the ship's library to your in-head memory. But how do you convey the sense of an entire, living *world* . . . even one as small, as bleak, and as ice bound as Europa? Like many moons and tide-locked planetary bodies of this type, the world has a very slight eccentricity to its orbit—0.009 in this case. When Europa is closest to Jupiter, it's stretched slightly by Jove's massive gravitational grip. A little less than two days later, at its farthest point from the gas giant, the squeezing relaxes. This constant stretch-relax cycle through every three and a half Earth days creates internal heat, kneading the core like a lump of clay in a potter's hands.

There's a second set of tidal forces at work too—Europa's resonances with both Io and Ganymede. Europa circles Jupiter once for every two orbits of Io, and twice for every one orbit of Ganymede. These Laplace resonances, as they are called, help pump up Europa's interior temperature by ultimately stealing energy from Jupiter's rotation through the tidal interactions between the planet and Io.

The combined effects are strong enough that even though the surface temperature is a frigid two hundred below zero, it turns out that there's a liquid ocean between ice and the rocky mantle a hundred kilometers down.

And liquid water always means there's a good potential for life.

During the last few hours of the approach, I watched the banded, slightly flattened disk of Jupiter swelling on the viewall in the mess bay. Three stars were visible to either side of the giant planet—two to the left and one on the right—three of the four classic Galilean satellites. First glimpsed through his primitive telescope by Galileo Galilei in 1610, those four moons shuttling around *Jupiter* rather than around a geocentric Earth had sounded the death knell of Aristotelian Cosmology. Four centuries later, the discovery of an induced magnetic field around one of those moons, Europa—a discovery made by a spacecraft named

Galileo—had demonstrated for the first time that an actual liquid saltwater ocean existed somewhere other than on the planet Earth. In 2107, the Olympus Expedition to Jupiter had drilled down through the ice and discovered the Medusae. Three years later, exactly half a millennium after Galileo's observations, the base beneath Conamara Chaos had been built, primarily to study them.

I was interested to see in the ephemeris data that "Jupiter II" is an alternate name for Europa. Until the mid-nineteenth century, only the four Galilean satellites were known. Europa was the second out from Jupiter after Io, and was followed by Ganymede and Callisto, Jupiter I through IV. Not counting Jupiter's dark and mostly invisible ring system, though, we now know there are five moons closer to Jupiter than Europa; hence, "Jupiter f."

The *Haldane* continued decelerating as we dropped deeper and deeper into Jupiter's titanic gravity well. The missing moon of the quartet turned out to be Io, which eventually appeared as a tiny red disk visible against the backdrop of the Jovian cloud decks closely paced by the black dot of its own shadow. Hour by hour, the view slid off to the left as the turbulent colored bands of Jupiter's upper atmosphere filled the viewall. The mess bay was filled now with Marines and off-duty naval personnel who'd wandered in to see the show.

Eventually, though, Jupiter drifted out of frame, and we were bearing down on the inner of the two stars to the left. Another hour, and Europa resolved as a gleaming blue-white sphere, as smooth faced as a billiard ball, and thickly webbed by darker, brownish streaks and lines. Those lines, properly called *lineae*, reminded me of the supposed "canals" once thought to have crisscrossed the deserts of Mars, thanks to a nineteenth-century English mistranslation of the Italian word for "channels," *canali*.

One crater on that icy surface stood out more brightly than any other—a 26-kilometer-wide hole called Pwyll, looking like the starred impact of a hammer against a sphere of glass crystal. A thousand kilometers to the north, two particularly dark *lineae* crossed in a giant X, and just below was a tangle of broken and jumbled ice terrain darker than the surrounding areas. This was the Conamara Chaos, and the location of Humankind's sole outpost within the vast Europan ocean.

It takes some getting used to . . . the idea of an ocean more than a hundred kilometers deep covering the entire Jovian satellite. Europa is slightly smaller than Earth's moon, with a diameter of just over three thousand kilometers. Between its rocky, silicate mantle below and its shell of ice above lies that ocean of liquid water, but because of its depth, it's an ocean that actually and surprisingly holds more than twice the volume of water of all of the oceans on Earth.

Europa's ice varies considerably in thickness. South, where Pwyll Crater punched deep into the surface in the recent past, the crust is more than fifty kilometers thick. Elsewhere, though, as at Conamara Chaos, the ice is much thinner—in places only a few hundred meters thick. There's evidence that the ice doesn't rotate at the same speed, quite, as the moon's central core . . . and even that the entire shell has shifted, rotating independently of that core by as much as eighty degrees, many times throughout its history.

The base itself was invisible from space. Europa's disk filled the viewall, continuing to expand as the *Haldane* zeroed in on the navigation broadcasts from the colony's surface facility.

The Conamara Chaos *looks* chaotic from above—a vast, sprawling tumble of ice blocks and floes, all frozen together now, but quite obviously the product of some major melting and jostling at some point in the not-so-distant past. We think there's a collection of hot vents opening from the rocky core a hundred kilometers down, that major eruptions in the past actually broke through the ice cap at this point, and that continuing upwellings of hot water keep the ice at

Conamara relatively thin. That's what they were looking for when they began probing beneath Europa's icy roof, of course—thin ice.

And they found it, here amid ten-kilometer floes and bergs that looked like they'd been jumbled together, spun about, and even flipped upside down before being refrozen, broken, and refrozen yet again. The dark reds and browns mixed in with the ice were organic chemicals from the sea below, organics that had worked their way up and onto the surface each time the ice cracked all the way through, a clue both to the presence of life and to the richness of that life down in that chill, lightless void.

Eventually, we were close enough to see a kind of navigational marker, a vast, twin plume or cloud hovering above its shadow. The Europan surface is *cold*—about minus 160 degrees Celsius near the equator, and much lower, minus 220°C, at the poles. Conamara Base is heavily insulated to avoid damage to the local environment, and that means they need to dispose of excess heat as efficiently as possible, venting it as sterile plumes of steam from a pair of hundred-meter stacks north of the facility. The steam cools high above the surface, crystallizing as ice that eventually falls back across the chaotic terrain as a blanket of fresh, white snow.

The landing zone was well south of the plume, a flattened-out rectangle a kilometer across with a couple of other spacecraft resting there in the open. Nearby was a surface blockhouse, heavily insulated, and the array of dish antennas that maintained communications—through a satellite network orbiting Jupiter—with Earth.

Conamara Chaos is about a quarter of the way east around the moon from the sub-Jovian point; Jupiter at half-phase dominated the bleak, ice-block tumble of the western horizon, an enormous dome with pale red and pink, brown, white, gray, and salmon-hued stripes running up and down, with detail enough at this distance to see the swirls, eddies, and storm spots within the various fast-rotating cloud bands. I looked for the Great Red Spot, the south hemisphere super-storm two to three times as broad as Earth herself, but didn't see it. I did see the small, flattened oval of Io's shadow, though, close to the planet's limb, and above, a tiny red disk that was Io itself.

We settled to ground, and the elevator tube rose up out of the ice to meet us. The expedition's five Corpsmen, as technical staff, plus our two civilian passengers, the ship's skipper, and Lieutenant Kemmerer would make the journey down to the base. Dr. Kirchner had been invited, I under-stood, but had opted to stay in his office on *Haldane*.

The radiation at Europa's surface is fierce—about 540 rem per day, enough to kill an unprotected human in fairly short order. *Haldane*'s rad shielding had protected us down to the surface; from there on, the ice itself would keep us safe from being fried by Jupiter's intense radiation belts.

I felt a spring in my step as I entered the elevator. We'd been accelerating at one gravity for a week, now, but the surface gravity on Europa was only a bit more than a tenth of that. Drop something and it will fall half a meter in the first second, so there *is* a clear up and down, unlike on the tethered asteroid at Starport, but you need to watch your re-flexes. Jump, and you could bang your noggin against the overhead.

"Welcome to Chaos," a voice said from a hidden speaker as we gathered within the elevator. "We're bringing you all the way down to Level Three. Please hang on to the hand-rails beside you. Enjoy the ride!"

The elevator ride was a long one—well over half a ki-lometer straight down. The warning about handrails was a good one. With a surface gravity of only 1.314 meters per second squared, our downward acceleration through that tunnel more than canceled our weight. I don't know how fast we were going, but we were in zero-G for most of the descent. The trip was also *boring*, with nothing to see but the gray metal of the shaft sliding up around us through the clear transplas of the car.

But then the elevator emerged at the bottom level, we stepped out onto the main deck, and I gasped at the view.

Okay, so I'm easily impressed. But the others were speechless, too, even the usually unflappable Dubois, who said, "Fuck me," the words spoken very, very softly. Nearby, Dr. Ortega muttered something that sounded like, "Sweet holy Mother of God."

Conamara Base is upside down, as humans think of things, literally growing down from the underside of the ice ceiling overhead. Level One, with the hab quarters, is at the top, then Level Two with the lab spaces, with Level Three and the command center at the bottom, a broad, circular compartment fifty meters wide with instrument consoles and deck-to-overhead viewalls looking out into the abyss. The walls leaned out at a sharp angle, giving a clear view almost straight down.

Down . . .

The ocean here was just over a hundred kilometers deep. Lights on the outside of the base illuminated the water around us, as well as the eerily inverted icescape ceiling hanging above our heads. The light faded away swiftly with distance, however, and below, there yawned only a vast and empty night.

And yet, there were stars in that night. . . .

The year before, during the Bloodworld op, I'd spent some time on a gas giant moon—Niffelheim-e—my first experience with a hydrosubglacean world like Europa. On Niffelheim-e, the moon circling gas giant Gliese 581 VI, I'd linked in to a teleoperated submersible, cruising beneath the ice and encountering a variety of life forms there. Like abyssal forms in Earth's oceans, many created their own light; one titanic species, the five-kilometer-wide *Luciderm gigans*, had looked like the night view of a city seen from the air.

There were lights here as well, clouds of soft-glowing phosphorescence speckled by thousands of harder points, like stars, shining yellow and green. All were in motion, the whole giving an irresistible impression of vibrant, thriving life.

We now suspect that the majority of life across the Galaxy may live in environments like this one, locked in the eternal darkness of an ocean between rock and ice. Life, it seems, appears anywhere the conditions are at all favorable—and that frequently means liquid water. There are far more ice-locked moons and worlds in the Galaxy, possibly on the order of thousands to every one, than there are temperate, habitable-zone planets like Earth. Humans and Brocs are the exceptions, not the rules.

"Welcome aboard, folks," a civilian in white utilities said. "I'm Dr. Selby. I see you like the view."

"Spectacular," Lieutenant Kemmerer said. "And here I thought it would be boring, not having Jupiter in the sky all the time."

"You *do* get used to it after a while. But we keep discovering new species out there, and that keeps us on our toes."

"What's the outside temperature here?" Dr. Montgomery wanted to know.

"About five Celsius. That's actually pretty warm. We have some major convection currents rising beneath us at this point."

"The warmest water is in the deeps, am I right?" Ortega said.

"Exactly. The interior of Europa's core and deep mantle are still molten, and tidal interactions with Jupiter keep the mantle fairly plastic. The water near the mantle's surface is close to five hundred degrees, most places, but the pressure a hundred kilometers down is so high the water stays liquid, and can't turn to steam."

"And convection currents heat the entire ocean, keep it liquid," Ortega said, nodding.

"Correct. If Europa was a bit closer to Jupiter, she'd be like Io—kneaded and squeezed so hard by old Jove that the surface would be covered by volcanoes and flows of molten sulfur, and with all of the water driven off long ago. But out here the heating is just enough to maintain a liquid ocean."

"And Ganymede's mantle is all ice?" Ortega said.

"Right: ice, and a kind of warm ice slush down deep, above the inner silicate mantle. We have robots exploring Ganymede, looking for enclosed pockets of subsurface water like the deep lakes in Antarctica, and those might have evolved life as well, but so far at least, Europa is where all the biology is happening out here."

"Well, Europa," Montgomery said, "*and* the Jovian atmosphere."

Selby grimaced, and looked uncomfortable. "Of course."

We know precious little about life within Jupiter's atmosphere, and that still made exobiologists like Selby uncomfortable. Collector robots skimming through Jupiter's upper cloud layers have picked up organic molecules and what appear to be something like single-celled algae, the Jovian aeoleaprotistae. There was just a hint from these in their biochemistry that there might be more complex life existing deeper within the Jovian atmosphere, but at temperatures and pressures that made it unlikely that we'd be meeting it face to face anytime soon.

What it all added up to was the indisputable fact that life is incredibly resilient, amazingly adaptive, and as common as dirt throughout the cosmos.

"Europan life," Lieutenant Kemmerer said, "they're all heat eaters?"

Selby laughed. "Thermovores. Well, a lot of it is. We've been studying the Europan biome for almost a century and a half, and we've almost *literally* just scratched the surface. Most of the life forms we've catalogued so far appear to be thermovores, yes. We believe that there are chemovores in the great deeps, mainly because Europan life is based on sulfur, rather than carbon. We think they started off metabolizing chemical emissions around hot vents at the mantle, like the sulfur-metabolizing microbes around deep-ocean hydrothermal vents on Earth."

"But the Medusae are different, aren't they?" Dr. Montgomery said. "Not thermovores, but . . . what's the word? Kymovores?"

"Exactly."

"What the hell is a kymovore?" Garner wanted to know.

"They eat chemicals, of course," McKean said, mistaking the pronunciation for *chemovore*.

"Uh-uh. *Kymovores*," Selby said, stressing the *y* as more of an "oo" sound. "From *kym*, the Greek word for 'waves.' They get energy directly from the energy of waves in the water."

McKean reddened slightly, but didn't say anything. He didn't like being caught in the wrong.

"Besides tidal flexing," Selby went on, "there's a second force acting on Europa's ocean, keeping it warm. Europa has a very slight axial tilt—less than a tenth of a degree—but it's enough to respond to Jupiter's tide action and generate waves that pass through the ocean. They're called Rossby waves. They travel quite slowly, only a few kilometers per day, but they release a *lot* of energy into the water—maybe two hundred times what Europa gets from tidal forces alone, and some species in the Europan ocean use that energy directly for metabolism. That includes the Medusae."

As the conversation continued, I walked over to one of the big windows and looked down. The water was filled with small, drifting bits of white matter illuminated by the colony's external lights. The underside of the ice cap was covered by branching, whitish growths called *Europafitoformes*—Europan plant forms—and debris from the stuff constantly drifted down into Europa's ocean depths like snow. A lot of the biology down there depended on that organic rain.

I saw something rising out of the darkness.

It was large, it was round—a kind of flattened umbrella shape—and it looked as though it was manufactured out of spun glass. I was reminded of certain terrestrial jellyfish, and recognized the Europan Medusa from downloads I'd taken on Earth a year ago.

At the translucent core of the thing's body, there was a cluster of organic lights, and these were winking on and off in an obvious pattern as it rose. One light . . . two . . . four . . . eight . . . sixteen. Then they all winked off and the pattern began again: one, two, four, eight, sixteen. The Medusan Count, it was called, and it was the main reason xenosophontologists thought that the organism was intelligent.

"Dr. Selby?" I said. "Looks like you have someone trying to talk to you out here."

Selby joined me at the window. "Hah! Looks like. They come up and blink at us every so often. I think they're just saying 'Hi, there.' Or else they might just be reacting to our lights."

I noticed from the light showing in the water above the window that the station was flashing something in response. "You have a bank of lights on the outside of the building, sir?" I asked.

"That's right. We've been trying to respond to them."

"Responding how?" Kemmerer asked.

"By continuing the series," Selby replied. "We repeat the Medusa's pattern, then add thirty-two, sixty-four, and one hundred twenty-eight."

"Does it work?"

"Not really," Selby explained. "Or rather, not yet. We try to respond every time they signal. Unfortunately, all either we or the Medusae can learn from the exchange is that the other guy knows how to count in geometric series. There's no other exchange of information, no way to *encode* information. None that we've been able to discover, anyway."

"You've tried longer sequences?" McKean asked.

"We have," Selby said. "But the Medusae seem to only

have those sixteen light-producing organs in their bodies, so that's apparently all the higher they can count. If the blinking lights are a conversation, we don't know how to continue it with them, and apparently neither do they."

"Do they even have brains?" Chief Garner asked. "That thing out there looks like a goddamn jellyfish."

"We think they have a kind of a nerve net, similar to terrestrial sea jellies. There's also a node of tissue in there among the light organs that may be a brain of sorts. They have what appear to be fairly sophisticated ocelli, sixteen of them around the rim of the bell, so they can see. How well, we're not sure."

"They might not really be counting," Montgomery said. "The lights could be coming on as a kind of autonomous reflex, with more lights coming on successively as more and more neuron bundles fire."

"Quite a few xenosophontologists have come to that exact same conclusion," Selby told her. "Right now, we're at a complete impasse. We here at Chaos Base think the Medusae might be intelligent, but we have no way to prove it."

And that, I thought, was a hell of a note. We think we know what *human* intelligence is, but we still have trouble defining exactly what that is. And in a nonhuman species . . . well, if they build spaceships like the Brocs or the Qesh, and have a language we're able to translate, we have to assume that they are. But something like the Medusae are so damned different we may not have anything whatsoever in common . . .

. . . and we may never know for certain that they can *think.*

Outside, the solitary Medusa was going through some unusual acrobatics, the skirts of its bell coming up on all sides . . . and then the top appeared to split open, exposing a forest of furiously beating tendrils, like the cilia of a protozoan. The thing looked like it was trying to turn itself inside out.

"Chow time," Selby said. Indeed, the organism was rising closer to the ice ceiling outside. It appeared to be inhaling large quantities of the drifting organic snow.

"Wait, I thought you said it got metabolic energy from Rossby waves," Kari Harris said. "That thing is *eating*."

Selby smiled. "With our kind of life . . . okay, we ingest food, and breaking that food down—metabolism—provides us with the energy we need for life. The Medusae get their energy from waves passing through their bodies . . . but they still need to ingest food to get the raw material they need for growth . . . to add to their own mass, don't you see? It's actually an efficient way to do things, here. In an environment like this one, life would be *very* limited if it depended on chemical metabolism alone. The amount of energy in that organic snow out there just isn't enough . . . we say the energy is low density. It would take more energy than that material can provide in order to get energy out of it. So our Medusan friends have learned to get the energy they need another way, and just use solid food for growth, physiological repair, and reproduction."

"A grazer," Ortega said. "It seems an unlikely candidate for a sapient species, don't you think?"

"Maybe the question we should be asking," Montgomery said, thoughtful, "is why an organism like that would *need* intelligence in the first place."

It was, I thought, a damned good question. The thing drifted in the dark, absorbed waves moving through the cold water, fed on the local equivalent of plankton, and its slow movements suggested that it didn't have any major predators . . . none that it would be required to run from or outwit, at any rate. No spaceships, no buildings, not even any knowledge of the universe beyond the ice above. If the Medusae *were* intelligent, it would mean lives of unimaginable boredom.

Or did it simply mean that their mental lives, their imaginations, perhaps, their view of the world around them all were so alien, so inexpressibly different from those of humans, that we could not begin to understand them?

We watched the creature a moment more, and then Selby turned from the window. "So, you good people came by to pick up the *Walsh*?"

"An EDD Mark V, Doctor," Kemmerer said. "Yes. I gather you have spares."

"A few. Earth didn't give me any details when they lasered the orders last week. I take it you have some deep diving to do?"

"We don't know yet," Kemmerer replied, "but we want to be ready, just in case." She looked out the window. "What's the water pressure here?"

"Not too bad, actually," Selby replied. "Six hundred sixty meters . . . but at only point one three four of a G. And ice is only nine-tenths the density of water. Make it the equivalent of eighty meters on Earth . . . or about eight atmospheres. I gather you're going deeper than that?"

"Yes," Lieutenant Kemmerer said, her voice taking on a grim note. "A *lot* deeper . . ."

Chapter Eight

I WATCHED FROM THE MESS DECK AS A ROBOT CARGO TRACTOR hauled the *Walsh* out to the landing area on the surface of Europa. Jupiter remained on the western horizon, huge and banded seemingly just beyond the horizon of tumbled blocks of ice. "You think we're even going to use that thing?" Charlie McKean asked.

"Don't know, Machine," I replied. "I imagine the skipper wants to have it on board just in case."

HM1 McKean was known by the nickname Machine at least in part from his meticulous nature. One of the stories about him was that he'd raced high-speed e-Cars for a living, back before he'd joined the Navy. It might be true. I think he was the guy who hung the "E-Car" moniker on me, though ever since FMF training I'd been trying to be accepted as "Hawkeye."

It had turned out to be a losing battle.

Moving slowly, the robot crawler positioned the EDDV beneath the *Haldane*, and then lifted it up into the research vessel's broad, flat storage bay. Captain Summerlee had given orders to shift the dynamic nanomatrix of the *Haldane*'s cargo compartment to better accommodate the deep diver, which was over a quarter of the starship's length.

The *Walsh* was a research submersible designed to operate under extremes of temperature and pressure. A black compressed-matter cigar just twenty-two meters long, it massed almost 2,500 tons. CM explorers were relatively new, but they'd given us a powerful tool for investigating places like the upper atmospheres of Jupiter and Saturn, and the broiling, ninety-atmosphere surface of Venus.

Almost three centuries ago, in 1958, the U.S. Navy had purchased a bathyscaph, an Italian-made submersible named *Trieste*, and used her for a series of deep exploratory test dives. The series had culminated on January 23, 1960, when the *Trieste* reached the bottom of the Challenger Deep in the Marianas Trench, just less than eleven kilometers down, the deepest point of Earth's world ocean. On board, crammed into the bathyscaph's tiny pressure sphere, were two men—Jacques Piccard, the son of the craft's designer, and Lieutenant Don Walsh of the U.S. Navy. The pressure at that depth was about one and an eighth metric tons per square centimeter. The eighteen-meter-long float chamber above the pressure sphere was filled with gasoline—less dense than water, which made it buoyant, but incompressible, which meant that the float chamber didn't need steel walls 12.7 centimeters thick like the crew compartment. Nine tons of magnetic iron pellets served as ballast; at those pressures, the *Trieste* could not possibly have emptied ballast tanks like a conventional submarine.

Of particular interest was the fact that Piccard and Walsh spotted a sole or flounder swimming slowly along the floor of the trench. Though the sighting was controversial for many years after, with some biologists insisting that the creature must instead have been a sea cucumber, it ultimately was proof that vertebrate life could withstand and even thrive under the intense pressure at the bottom of the Challenger Deep. Life, it seemed, was unimaginably adaptable, resilient, and tough, a realization that would lead ultimately to the discovery of life within the ice-locked oceans of Europa and Enceladus, adrift in the

Jovian and Venerean cloud tops, buried beneath the Martian permafrost, and swimming in lakes of ethane and methane on Titan.

And now, a vessel named for Lieutenant Walsh was being used within the Europan ocean.

But the *Walsh* now being jockied into *Haldane*'s belly was a far cry from a twentieth-century bathyscaph. Where the original *Trieste* had had an estimated crush depth of over eighteen kilometers, the *Walsh* technically could not *be* crushed . . . at least, that was the theory.

CM—collapsed matter—is a special form of exotic, artificial material. It occurs naturally in neutron stars when the gravitational collapse of a dying sun of between 1.4 and 3.2 solar masses forces electrons to combine with protons, creating a neutron star, a fast-spinning sphere composed of degenerate matter so compact that a teaspoonful contains the mass of Mount Everest.

A century ago, materials engineers figured out how to artificially collapse matter down to a state just short of neutron star material, using the quantum dynamics of vacuum energy to remove a large fraction of the empty space among atoms. The result was artificial matter normally incompressible, so much so that even with inner compartments at standard surface atmospheric pressure, bulkheads constructed of this material remained rigidly inert even under pressures of tens of thousands of atmospheres.

At least, that was the theory. I wasn't sure I wanted to trust my life that completely to the materials engineers just yet, however. According to Dr. Shelby, the *Walsh*, or its sister vessels, had descended to depths of around fifty kilometers within the Europan ocean, going about halfway down toward the mantle, a depth that in Europa's scant gravity corresponded to a pressure of 690 atmospheres, or about a tenth of a ton per square centimeter. At a depth of ten thousand kilometers within Abyssworld, and in Abyssworld's gravity, the pressure would be considerably greater:

900,000 atmospheres, or almost a *thousand* tons per square centimeter.

I'm all for modern technology, yeah . . . and I was relying on modern materials engineering *now* to keep me alive in Europa's near-vacuum atmosphere, with a radiation flux outside the *Haldane*'s hull that would have killed me in a few days. But CM-hulled ships had never been tested under such insane conditions, and I wasn't sure that I wanted to be the guinea pig.

Still, Lieutenant Kemmerer said we were only taking the *Walsh* along as a precaution, just in case our search for the missing research colony took us into the Abyssworld's deeps. Besides, I'd teleoperated a deep-sea high-pressure probe on Niffelheim-e. I assumed that we would be pulling the same trick with the *Walsh*.

At least I hoped that would be the case.

HALF A EUROPAN DAY AFTER OUR ARRIVAL AT EUROPA, *HALDANE* lifted into the tenuous atmosphere, hesitated a moment as though getting her bearings, and then began to accelerate. That atmosphere, I'd been surprised to learn, was molecular oxygen, O_2, though at a pressure so low as to seem like hard vacuum to an Earth-evolved air breather. Rather than having an organic source, as oxygen did on Earth, the O_2 sputtered off the ice as incoming solar radiation plus high-energy particles from Jupiter's magnetosphere hit the surface and dissociated the oxygen from the hydrogen. The lighter hydrogen vanished into space; the oxygen was just heavy enough to hang around, though its pressure at the surface was just 10^{-12} of the surface atmospheric pressure on Earth: 1 trillionth of a bar.

Jupiter, the opposite hemisphere now in sunlight, hung off our port side . . . and this time I could make out the deep salmon pink of the Great Red Spot, just south of the equator and close to the dawn terminator. Minute points of lightning flashed and pulsed across the planet's nightside.

Then we accelerated, and Europa—and then Jupiter—dwindled away, a single bright star falling into the glare of the distant sun.

Harris, Dubois, and McKean were with me in the mess bay. "So why the hell wasn't Kirchner with us when we went down to the base?" Dubois asked.

"Don't know," I said. "He didn't see fit to fill me in."

"Ah," McKean said, shrugging. "The poor bastard's ghost-ridden."

"So?" Dubois said, sounding skeptical. "Dr. Francis on the *Clymer* handles his ghosts okay. Most doctors do."

Ghost-ridden, in Corps parlance, referred to doctors and some other personnel who were permanently linked through their implants to Net expert systems. *No* one, not the best doctor in the world, can keep everything in his head that he needs to know—about chemistry, pharmacology, anatomy, bacteriology, pathology, biochemistry, nanotechnic programming, holistics, medical imaging, cybernetics, psychology, and the gods of medicine know what all else. Most doctors had a kind of glassy, faraway stare, and usually that was because they were listening to the voices in their heads.

"Well, sure," McKean said. "Most doctors can handle it. But Kirchner, he's kind of old, y'know? Maybe it's starting to wear him down."

"How old *is* he, anyway?" Kari Harris wanted to know.

"One hundred twelve," I told them. "This is his second round of anagathic treatments."

"How the hell do you know *that*?" McKean demanded.

I shrugged. "I looked up the Sam-Sea records on-line the day before we left Earth," I told them. You weren't supposed to do that, of course. Personnel records were *private*, accessible by others only with specific authorization, and peeking at an officer's records was a definite no-no.

But there are always ways around the safeguards. Mine was a bit of software residing in my cerebral implants called

Lockpick, courtesy of my father and General Nanodynamics. I wasn't going to tell them about *that*, however.

But there was something about the way Kirchner had looked at us that morning at the briefing with Chief Garner that had given me hot-and-cold running willies, and that's when I'd decided to check him out.

"I rest my case," McKean said. "Paranoia . . . schizophrenia . . . the ghosts'll do that to you."

"Bullshit," I told him. "His records also say he had a brilliant career at SMMC, teaching path, *materia medica*, and A and P. I never had him myself, but he's got commendations in his jacket."

"I *did* have him," McKean said, his expression sour. "Officious, picky, OCD bastard. Cost me my four-oh a couple of times. I was lucky to graduate."

"Well *there's* your problem," Harris said, grinning. "You just don't like the guy!"

"Hell no, I don't like him. They need to retire his ass . . . or promote him out of the classroom."

"He's only a lieutenant commander," Dubois said. "At a hundred and twelve? He must have pissed someone off."

"Yeah," McKean said. "Maybe he got caught fucking an admiral's daughter."

"He's only been a Navy physician for fifteen years," I told them. "This is his second career . . . third if you count his being Medical Corps as separate from being a civilian doctor."

With life extension, people could expect to live to be two or three centuries old, assuming they had the money to swing the treatments. Most people didn't. Those who did were expected to switch careers five or six times through a long life span.

I say *expected* because we've only been able to carry out major anagathic treatments for the last century or so. Hell, we didn't pick up the trick of telemeric engineering from the X'ghr until just thirty-five years ago. The oldest person alive right now is only somewhere in his mid-hundreds—150, 160, something like that.

But people like Dr. Kirchner got tired of the same job decade after decade. According to the records I'd seen, Lyman Kirchner had started off as a nanotechnics program designer, and switched to medical nanotechnics in 2188. He went from there to med school at Bethesda Medical Center in 2195, about the time he received his first anagathic treatment at age sixty. He'd had his second overhaul at age ninety, joined the Navy Medical Corps in 2232 at ninety-seven, and been a Navy doctor ever since.

Oh . . . yeah. The guy had made a fortune in the nanotech boom. That was how he'd been able to afford the tune-ups. I didn't share that much with the others, though. I guess I was feeling guilty for having peeked.

"He probably didn't show up at Europa because he already knows everything!" Harris said.

"That's certainly the way he acted when he was teaching pathology at Sam-Sea," McKean said with considerable feeling. "Damn him!"

Machine McKean's vehemence surprised me . . . and it worried me a bit, too. Any expedition to a new world, into an alien environment, required that the members work smoothly with one another, and they had to *trust* their department heads. Normally, Machine was pretty laid-back, though he could be intensely focused when he needed to be. I'd never known him to be this angry.

From the little I'd seen of Kirchner, he wasn't making himself easy to trust . . . but he certainly deserved the benefit of the doubt.

Haldane accelerated out-system at one gravity, using her Plottel Drive to crawl up the sun's far-flung magnetic field, seeking that region, a billion and a half kilometers out, where the gravitational metric of spacetime was flat enough to make the transition to FTL. Eventually, shortly after evening mess, the warning came down from the bridge. "Now hear this, now hear this. Zero-gravity in thirty seconds. I say again, zero-gravity in thirty seconds. Stand by to engage the Alcubierre Drive."

Half a minute later, as promised, weight vanished. In another moment, the *Haldane* gathered up her figurative skirts—if by "skirts" you mean the intangible field of space-time within which she was moving—and dropped into her very own pocket universe.

Mexican physicist Miguel Alcubierre had worked out what became known as the Alcubierre metric in 1994, though it had taken over a century to work out how to transform theory into fact. In particular, it had taken the Vacuum Energy Tap to liberate enough power to create a warp bubble, continually contracting the space ahead of a ship and expanding it behind. The vessel within the warp bubble was in free fall, and motionless in relation to the pocket of space within which it rested, while the bubble holding that pocket traveled at many times the speed of light. The laws of physics still prohibited both matter and energy from moving faster than light . . . but there was nothing at all in those laws prohibiting *space* from doing so. Indeed, current inflationary models of the big bang *demanded* that the expansion of space had vastly exceeded the speed of light in the first instants after Creation itself.

"Now hear this, now hear this. Stand by to initiate spin gravity." There was a measured pause, as if for dramatic effect, and I knew what was coming. "All hands commence attitude adjustment. Spin gravity will initiate in ten minutes."

Like most ships, *Haldane*'s habitation modules were mounted within a carousel, rotating to create an out-is-down spin gravity. Long stretches of microgravity could cause some nasty physiological problems for the crew . . . and if you were a Marine arriving on a hostile world after weeks of zero-gravity, your lack of muscle tone could ruin your whole day. There were drugs and exercises to lessen the effects of weightlessness, of course, but the simplest solution was for the transport to tailor-make its own gravity.

The real problem in starship design lay in what was humorously known as "attitude adjustment." When your ship is tooling along under acceleration, "down" is toward the rear of the ship, while "up" is toward the nose, along the direction of travel. With spin gravity, though, "up" is generally at right angles to the direction of travel, toward the ship's spine, while "down" is out, toward the deck of a rotating wheel, a wheel thirty meters across in *Haldane*'s case. Her hab module rotated at a pretty fair clip—just over five rotations per minute, to generate a half G of spin gravity in her outer deck. The higher up inside the carousel you went, the lower the gravity, until you were at zero-G near the ship's spine, just like in the Free Fall Restaurant back at the El.

But that meant that crew compartments had to be reconfigured each time the vessel shifted between acceleration gravity and spin gravity. Decks became bulkheads, and God help us if the *Haldane*'s designers had gotten the plumbing wrong. I had the duty in Sick Bay that morning when the conversion order came through. Most of the change was automatic, handled by *Haldane*'s on-board AI, but I interfaced with the compartment controls to handle the details, dissolving the examination table into the deck there, and regrowing it from the bulkhead over *there*. Decks, bulkheads, and overheads were nanomatrix substrates, and things like viewalls and furniture could be pulled from the matrix pretty much at will. Certain pieces of heavy equipment—the full body scanner, for instance—had to be rotated in place, and the sink, toilet, and shower in the small head had to be twisted around and remounted on the ends of highly flexible piping.

I had the sixteen-to-midnight watch that evening, so it was up to me to complete the rearrangement of the sick bay, the four-bed hospital ward, and the heads in plenty of time, then swim over to the closed door of Dr. Kirchner's office, where he was working late. I palmed the contact to chime an announcement, then called, "Dr. Kirchner? Do you need a hand in there making the conversion?"

I heard a muffled and unintelligible sound from the other side of the door.

"Dr. Kirchner? Are you okay?"

"Go away," he growled.

"Is there anything you need, sir?"

"No! Leave me alone!"

I shrugged and returned to my desk. A moment later, the final announcement came through. "All hands, commence spin gravity. That is, commence spin gravity."

I pulled myself into the chair I'd grown on one bulkhead, and after a moment I could feel weight slowly beginning to pull me down into the padding. It took a couple of minutes to spin the hab modules up to a full half-gravity, but then the transition was complete. The doors to the ward, the head, the passageway outside, and to Dr. Kirchner's office all completed their ninety-degree crawls. The shift took a bit of getting used to, and could be disorienting.

I stood up, flexing my knees a bit to test the half-G pull, and walked over to the bulkhead coffee mess to pour myself a cup. It took a sharp eye and steady hand; the hab module was spinning rapidly enough that the Coriolis effect could bend the stream of coffee from the carafe enough to make it miss the cup.

"Duty Corpsman to A-Deck, Hab Compartment 2/4! Corpsman to Hab A-2/4! Emergency!"

Damn! I set the cup aside, snatched my M-7 med kit off the bulkhead, and raced through the newly repositioned door to sick bay, stepping across the hatchway combing and breaking into a dead run down the main passageway. I banged past a couple of surprised Marines and kept going. Hab 2/4 was a Marine billet space a third of the way spinward around the carousel. I was already on A-Deck, the outermost level of the wheel, and it only took me a couple of minutes to reach the compartment.

A Marine was on his back on the deck, a puddle of blood under his head and a glassy look in his eyes. Six other Marines were gathered around him, and I had to shove to get through. "Gangway!" I bellowed. "Let me through!"

"Doc coming through!" Sergeant Tomacek yelled. "Make a hole!"

I kneeled next to the downed man, but didn't touch him, not yet. He had a head injury, obviously, but there might be more. "What happened?" I demanded, pulling out my N-prog and a nanobot autoinjector.

"Ricky fell," one Marine said.

"I can *see* that. From where? What was he doing?"

"He was skylarking around on the overhead, Doc," Sergeant Randy Gibbs said, "when the gravity came back on."

There was more to it than that, I knew. The compartment was three meters high, but he wouldn't have simply fallen when the carousel started to spin. Either he'd been hit by a bulkhead when it began moving toward him, or he'd somehow managed to land on his head, and the moving deck had caused the head injury somehow.

I fired a load of nanobots into his carotid, at the angle of the jaw, and used my N-prog to send them into and around his skull. His electronic ID said he was Private Jeremy Pollard; his medical readout gave a pulse of 50, a blood pressure of 120 over 72, a respiration of 28, rapid and shallow. His eyes shifted to look at me, and I could see some alertness returning. "How are you doing, Private?" I asked.

"O-okay, Doc," he said.

"Do you hurt anywhere?"

"Yeah. My head . . . back of my head."

"Well, you gave yourself a hell of a bump. No . . . don't move. Stay put for a moment. Okay?"

Mentally, I ticked off his mental state as "A" on the AVPU scale, meaning he was alert, responsive to my questions, and reacting simultaneously to stimuli.

There was a bit of blood in his left ear, and when I checked his pupils, the left side was dilated wide open, the right closed down small. I pulled a small LED light from my

M-7 and shone it in first one eye, then the other. No response there. Classic signs of head trauma, most likely a fractured skull. I'd know more when the nanobots moving around his skull began reporting in.

There . . . that was good. Some millions of robots, each a fifth the length of a human blood cell, were migrating through the space between muscle and bone just beneath the skin of Pollard's head, transmitting their positions to my N-prog, which in turn began building up an image inside my own skull. In effect, the image was overlaying my normal view of Pollard's head, making it look like his skin and flesh were fading away and leaving behind only the bone. By adjusting the focus of my eyes, I could look through his skull to the back side. Sure enough, there was a crack and a slight flattening at the occiput, the very back of Pollard's skull. As some of the nanobots began seeping through the crack in the skull, I began to see what was inside as well.

Yeah. I'd been afraid of that. Blood was filling a space between bone and gray matter, too, the first blush of a nasty epidural hematoma that would be putting pressure on Pollard's brain.

In-head, I snapped off a request for a stretcher. We were going to have to be careful moving this guy. "Okay, you hurt anywhere else?"

"Nah. I'm a little dizzy, though."

"Wiggle the fingers on your right hand for me." I watched him do it. "Now the left hand."

He seemed to have some trouble with that one. "Try moving your right foot. Okay . . . now the left."

That worried me. He could move his left arm and leg, but awkwardly, as though that side of his body was weaker. I pinched his left hand. "You feel this?"

"Yeah . . . sorta . . ."

I don't know why, but it never works out exactly as the textbooks and sims and med downloads say it should. *Never.* Pollard had a serious head injury—that much was obvious.

An epidural hematoma—a pocket of blood forming between the dura (the protective outer layer of his central nervous system) and the inside of his skull—was potentially deadly, and needed immediate attention. But what I wasn't sure about was whether or not he might have a spinal injury as well.

A clear sign of a broken back would have been paralysis below the level of the break. A typical broken neck, for example, would have left him paralyzed from the neck down. He still had sensation all the way to his feet, though, so if there was an injury to his spinal cord, it wasn't a complete break. It seemed as though there was some nerve damage affecting the left side of his body, but that could have been due to a spinal injury—with bone pressing against the spinal cord itself—or it could have been a result of the head trauma instead.

Carefully, I reached under Pollard's back, palpating. "Does that hurt?"

"Nah."

I shifted up a bit, toward the base of his neck. "How about this?"

"A little . . ."

"Hey, Doc," a Marine said, leaning over us. "Is Polly gonna be okay?"

"He will be if you let me do my job. Back off! All of you!" Why the hell do people always crowd around to gawk at something like this?

My first order of business was to stabilize that epidural hematoma. As more and more blood seeped into the space between bone and dura mater, more and more pressure would build up against the brain. It happened in something like 3 percent of all head injuries, and it was 15 to 20 percent fatal if the injury was untreated.

His systole was up to 140, now, while his diastole had stayed at 82.

Interfacing directly with my N-prog, I began delivering

instructions to my fleet of microscopic nanobots. Leaving half to continue to send me an image of what was happening, I directed the rest to begin seeking out tears in the web of blood vessels both outside the skull and within, sending some through the crack in Pollard's occipit to explore for damage in the blood vessels over the dura mater.

Normally, if a patient was bleeding I would zap the wound with hemostatin foam. The stuff turned hard, like plastic, when it contacted blood, creating an instant clot that would seal off anything from torn capillaries to a major artery. I couldn't use the stuff here, though, because *anything* that put additional pressure on Pollard's brain could be fatal.

What I could do, though, was have my nanobots begin to physically grab hold of the walls of blood vessels at the breaks, then connect with one another, more and more of them pulling together to create a tough micro-suture bridging the tear, then contracting to pull the edges of the break together. The hematoma was still small, smaller than the tip of my little finger, so it hadn't done much damage yet. There was still time.

But I needed to get Pollard back to sick bay, stat. I wanted to give him a full soft-tissue scan to make absolutely certain his spine wasn't injured, and I wanted to put a drain into the hematoma itself to take the pressure down.

I was also working right on the edge of my own experience and expertise. I wanted Dr. Kirchner to see the patient as quickly as possible.

Chapter Nine

THE STRETCHER TEAM ARRIVED AND TOGETHER WE LOG-ROLLED POL-lard onto his side, taking care to keep his back and his neck as straight as possible, then slid the stretcher under his back and lowered him into place, centering him on a metamaterial sheet over the bed. The stretcher was a standard spin-floater, which meant it had controls that let me grow bracing around Pollard's head and neck. I strapped him down, taking care to secure his hands as well, then engaged the spin-repulsor motor to lift Pollard off the deck.

Quantum spin-floater technology would have let me guide the stretcher to sick bay one-handed, but the two-man stretcher team was on hand, so I decided to use them. I pointed at two of the Marines—including the one who'd been asking whether Pollard was going to make it. "I need two volunteers: you and you. Go ahead of the stretcher and clear the passageway."

"Right, Doc!"

That would keep us from bumping into curious Marines or naval personnel, and it would also let those two feel useful. I brought up the rear, using the time to send a call down to Kirchner's office.

"What is it?" he demanded.

"Marine, twenty-year-old male, head injury, possible spinal injury as well. Beginnings of an epidural hematoma, copious occipital bleeding, BP . . . BP is now 152 over 80 with rising systole, respiration shallow and rapid. Unequal pupils and no left-side pupillary response. Patient is a conscious and alert . . . with severe head pain, tenderness at about C7-T1, and weakness on his left side . . ."

I went on down the list of signs and symptoms, and described what I'd done already. Kirchner told me to get the patient on oxygen as soon as we got him to sick bay, and to put him in Rack One on the ward.

"Sir," I said, "I'd really like to run an STS on him first. If he has a spine injury—"

"Are you telling me my business, Petty Officer Carlyle?" Kirchner demanded. "Rack One! That's an order!"

Haldane's tiny hospital ward had four beds—"racks" in Navy parlance—and Rack One was the critical care unit. You could hook up the patient to provide constant monitoring with or without nanobots, immobilize any and all parts of the body, provide oxygen, put nutrients in, pull wastes out, and even take simple X-ray shots.

But I *really* wanted to pull an STS on Pollard first. "STS" stands for "soft-tissue scan," a technique derived from various earlier MRI technologies. Magnetic resonance imaging used magnetic fields to detect the precession of certain atomic nuclei—notably those of the hydrogen atoms in water molecules—to get information about soft body tissue. Nowadays, though, you can't use traditional MRI techniques, because nearly everyone has a load of metal inside their skulls, the palms of their hands, and along certain key neural networks. The metals, including gold, iron, and copper, are chelated into place by standard nanotechnic processes, growing our cerebral implants, the cybernetic prostheses that give us our in-head imaging and RAM, access to the local NET, and even control over everything from coffeemakers and doors to e-Cars and starships. There's enough ferrous metal in our heads to make real trouble if we enter a powerful magnetic field, like the ones used by early MRIs.

Modern soft-tissue scanning units, though, are a lot more sensitive, and they use a number of different sensory inputs, combined and interpreted by powerful medical AIs. They employ background radiation, background magnetic fields, injected nanobots, and tightly focused sound to build up a detailed image of what's going on inside the body.

So why not use Rack One's X-ray unit? Well . . . I might have been okay with that if the unit could have handled computed tomography—a CT scan . . . what used to be called a CAT scan in the old days. But a simple X-ray? Too risky for my money. X-ray images miss something like 20 percent of all fractures—in particular hairline fractures, which can be all but invisible, especially on a wet reading. Pollard's symptoms had already told me he didn't have a *complete* break in his spine—not if he could still wiggle his fingers and toes.

So when we reached sick bay, I told them to put Pollard on the full-body scanner.

I chimed Dr. Kirchner's office, but didn't get an answer. What the hell? He would have heard the emergency call when it came through, and I'd been talking to him just a moment ago. Where the hell was he?

I shrugged it off and went to supervise moving Pollard onto the table. That was tricky—getting him off the stretcher and onto the table without further injuring his skull or letting his spine go crooked. If his back was broken—even a hairline fracture—we could cause some truly serious problems for the guy if we weren't damned careful.

There was that sheet of metacomposite nanocloth on the stretcher beneath his back, though—a soft fabric weave that becomes rigid when you put stress on it. When we grabbed the corners of the sheet and tugged in opposite directions, it became as unyielding as a hard plastic board, and we used that to shift Pollard onto the table, where the cloth went limp once again.

"Thank you, gentlemen," I told the Marines. I flicked on the STS scanner. "If you guys could stand by for a sec, I'll ask you to help me move him to the ward when we're done here."

I brought up a viewall image showing Pollard's body, as a bright bar of light switched on above his head, then slowly moved down to below his feet. An expert AI took the data and created a three-dimensional image on the viewall, which allowed me to see inside Pollard's body from any angle, to any depth. Linking in through my in-head, I could zoom in, rotate the image, even remove layers of tissue for a clear view.

I was still looking at the skull fracture—hadn't even gotten to his back yet—when Kirchner came through the door from the passageway outside and exploded all over me.

"What the fuck are you doing, Carlyle! I distinctly ordered you to put the patient on Rack One!"

"Sir . . . I thought it best to do a full-body STS. There's a chance—"

"You thought! You *thought*? You're supposed to follow the orders of the doctor-in-charge, not *think*!"

"But sir—"

"This man has a serious skull injury! You're risking his life by doing an additional transfer! A *needless* patient transfer, since we can x-ray him in the rack!"

"I thought there was a chance—"

"Thinking again! My God . . . save me from enlisted men *thinking*!" He drew a deep breath. "*You're on report!*"

His fury took me aback. It even startled the Marines standing there in the sick bay, and they were used to getting chewed on by angry D.I.s in boot camp, and by gunnery sergeants and other deities once they became full-fledged Marines.

"The scan is completed, sir . . ."

"Delete it!"

"Sir?"

"I said *delete* it!" Before I could thoughtclick the controls, though, he did it for me. The image on the viewall winked out.

"Get the hell out of my sick bay, mister! You're confined to your quarters until further notice!"

"Aye, aye, sir." There was nothing else I could say or do. I turned on my heel and walked out of the compartment, making my way back to my berthing compartment.

I was in a pretty foul mood by the time I got there. The sheer . . . *injustice* of it all was mind-numbing. And here I was on report for the second time in less than two weeks. This was going to look like hell on my personnel record.

"Hey, E-Car?" It was Dubois, calling on my in-head. Less than an hour had passed since Kirchner had thrown me out of sick bay. "What gives? I just heard some scuttle-butt . . ."

Scuttlebutt—shipboard rumor. A form of faster-than-light travel that actually surpasses the theoretical top velocity of the Alcubierre Drive by a factor of at least ten.

"You heard right," I told him.

"What the hell happened?"

I told him.

"Well that sucks," he said. "For what it's worth, I think you did the right thing."

I sighed. "At this point, Doob, right and wrong don't count for a hell of a lot. How's Pollard?"

"In the CC rack, wired up the wazoo. Head elevated to help drain the excess fluid out of his skull. I think they're going to put in a microtube and draw it out."

"What about his spine?"

"We did an x-ray on the rack. Nothing."

I sagged inside. It wasn't that I'd *wanted* them to find a fractured vertebrae . . . but it might have justified my decision.

The hell of it was, I knew that Kirchner was right about one thing. Every time you move a patient—from deck to

stretcher back in the berthing compartment, from stretcher
to STS table, from table back to stretcher, from stretcher to
Rack One—you add to the risk, and the less you have to
move him the better. The skull fracture was bad enough; a
bad jostle at any point in the evolution could have further
injured Pollard's brain.

And if his back *had* been broken—even just a hairline
fracture—a bit of awkwardness in any one of the patient
transfers could have pulled his spine apart and torn the
spinal cord. We *can* reconnect major nerves, of course, but
it's not something you want to have to do, especially in a
small exploration vessel with limited medical resources.
That sort of surgery is best carried out in a major med facility, like Bethesda or San Antonio.

"Don't worry, E-Car," Doob told me. "It'll work out okay."

I wasn't so sure of that. "Listen, Doob, watch out for
Kirchner. He's . . . hell, I don't know what his problem is,
but he's not acting rational."

"So what else is new? He's been on all our cases. Machine is about ready to jump ship, I think. Shit . . . they're
calling me. Gotta go."

The connection cut off.

I checked the time—just before 2100. I wondered what
Doob and Machine were doing in sick bay when they didn't
have the duty . . . then decided that Kirchner must have
called one of them in to cover for me.

Fuck it. They would sort it out without me.

But what was Kirchner's problem, anyway? Was he just a
class-A asshole . . . or was he under some kind of stress? In
the Navy—even in the Medical Corps, which is its own, private little navy of its own—you don't often think about what
sort of pressure your department heads or senior officers
might be under. An ancient adage has it that shit rolls downhill . . . which means that when the captain is unhappy, he
makes his exec unhappy, who makes the department heads
unhappy, and eventually all of that unhappiness makes it all

the way down to the enlisted guy pushing the broom. We don't have push brooms any longer, not when we have robots for keeping things tidy and filters to keep out the dust, but you get the idea.

Who was dumping enough shit on Kirchner that he felt it necessary to send some my way?

Well, maybe that was just life in the Navy, a natural consequence of rank and responsibility. It would have been nice, though, if I'd had someone to kick.

I turned in early, and crawled out of my tube at reveille. Bruce Tomacek was nice enough to bring me a plate of breakfast up from the mess hall. It sounded as though my disagreement with the ship's doctor was now the chief topic of discussion on board the ship.

"We're with you on this one, Doc," he said. "We know you were looking out for Polly."

"Well, win a few, lose a few," I replied, shrugging. "Sometimes we screw up."

One difficulty with medicine is that there very rarely is a clear-cut right or wrong. Oh, sure, you can be wrong with a diagnosis or read a blood type wrong, or you can do something so blindingly *right* that everyone thinks you're working miracles. It happens.

But nine times out of ten, whatever symptoms your patient is showing are *not* going to be textbook. Okay, so you spotted the broken leg right off . . . but maybe his pain was masking *another* pain where his rib punctured his spleen. Or you treat the skull fracture but miss the broken neck. Or—and this is the one I *really* hate—you're confronted by a half dozen minor symptoms that let you know something is definitely wrong, but those symptoms could point to damn near anything. Allergic reaction, poisoning, AIDS or a similar autoimmune breakdown, lyme disease, varicella-zoster virus, erythema, roseola, angioedema, lupus, or just a bad rash—all of them and many others can show the same collection of vague symptoms, especially early on.

"Bullshit, Doc," Tomacek said. "Kirchner is nuts. You see that look in his eyes?"

I decided it was best if I didn't let myself get drawn into that sort of talk. "Kirchner knows his shit," I said. "He's been a doctor for longer than I've been alive. But thanks, man. I appreciate the vote of confidence."

I got a call from Captain Summerlee's office a couple of hours later, telling me to report for mast.

Janice Summerlee's rank was commander, but she was skipper of the *Haldane* and her title always was *Captain*. I'd wondered at first if I would be going up in front of Lieutenant Kemmerer. She was the CO of the Marines, and technically in charge of all Fleet Marine Force personnel on board, which included us.

A Marine lieutenant, though, is lower in rank than a Navy lieutenant; it's the equivalent of a Navy lieutenant junior grade, or "JG," which isn't normally a command rank. Kirchner outranked Kemmerer by two grades, but *he* couldn't hold mast for me because he was the one filing the report.

Ultimately, though, the ship's captain is the one to adjudicate all legal problems, and she outranked Kirchner. So I chimed her door, heard her say "Come," and walked in.

Kirchner wasn't there. That surprised me. I'd figured he would be there to put the boot in, as it were. "HM2 Carlyle, reporting for mast, as ordered, ma'am."

"Stand at ease, Carlyle." She gave me a sharp look up and down. "You seem to be making a habit of coming to captain's mast."

"That certainly was not my intent, ma'am."

"I suppose not. Dr. Kirchner says you disobeyed explicit orders in the handling of a patient last night. What do you have to say about that?"

Well, what *could* I say? Dr. Kirchner was an officer and a doctor and I was a mere petty officer second class . . . the equivalent of a sergeant in the Marines or Army. If it came down to his word against mine in an argument over medical procedure or diagnosis, guess who was going to win?

And if I criticized Kirchner in any way, or tried to point out that he'd been acting strangely since he'd come aboard, or called him an asshole or even just said something snarky about how I didn't know what his problem was, it was certain to rebound back against me. I would be the one with the attitude problem . . . or the one who thought he knew it all.

"I don't know what to say, Captain," I replied. "I *did* disobey an order, but I was worried about missing a spinal fracture. I was trained to . . . well, if a guy falls on his head, you *always* check for spinal injury along with the obvious head trauma."

"And Dr. Kirchner didn't do this?"

I grimaced. "You can use the CC rack to get X-rays of the patient, ma'am. But there's a chance of missing something. You have a much better chance of seeing it on the soft-tissue scan."

"So you were second-guessing the doctor."

I could see which way this was going. "Yes, ma'am. No excuse, ma'am."

"Why?"

"Ma'am . . . when a patient has a serious head injury— *especially* if he falls on his head, or is in a serious accident— you always assume there's a C-spine injury as well, until you can rule it out. Always."

"But as I understand it, Dr. Kirchner *was* making that assumption. He didn't want you risking that additional patient transfer onto the scan table, and then from there to the critical-care rack, which did have the diagnostic equipment required to determine if Pollard had a spinal injury."

There are very rarely clear-cut situations in emergency medicine.

"That's . . . that's correct, ma'am."

What, I wondered, was Summerlee going to do to me? I

was already confined to quarters—which essentially meant
the ship. She might extend the extra duty, which was pretty
much a joke to begin with since I didn't have much else
to do. Or she might write me up with a recommendation
for further disciplinary action when we got back to Earth.
Or . . .

Her office door chimed. "What is it? I'm busy!"

The door opened and Chief Garner came in. "Captain?
I've got something you ought to see."

"About this case?"

"Yes, ma'am. May I?"

She nodded, and Garner looked at the captain's viewall,
which switched on with his thoughtclick. Pollard's three-D
STS image came up on the bulkhead, eerily translucent, rotating in space.

"Those images were deleted!" I said. "I watched Kirchner do it!"

"*Doctor* Kirchner," Summerlee said, stressing the title.

"Yes, ma'am."

"The doctor deleted the images from the table," Garner
said, "but there's *always* a record with the AI that runs the
medical-imaging systems."

True. But it was also true that to get at those records,
you needed special authorization. Kirchner—sorry, *Dr.*
Kirchner—could have given it, though that hardly seemed
likely. Captain Summerlee could have ordered it, but she
obviously was as surprised by Garner's arrival as I was.
Fleet Command or a medical review board could have
given the necessary authorization . . . but they were light
years away, now, and even if there was such a thing as
faster-than-light radio, we were wrapped up inside our Alcubierre warp bubble, in effect barricaded inside our own
private universe.

Garner was steering the viewpoint on the image in toward
the side of Pollard's neck, which grew so huge against the
viewall that all we could see were his cervical vertebrae,

neatly interlocked and protecting the all-important spinal cord within. The image continued to expand until we were looking at a pair of vertebrae, one atop the other, now stretching across three meters of space and still expanding slowly.

"There," Garner said. "You see it, ma'am?"

"I'm not sure what I'm looking at."

"C6, the sixth cervical vertebra down from the spine." He touched the back of his neck, right above his shoulders. "Just about here." A hair-thin line appeared in the bone, highlighted by the imaging program. "That is a hairline compression fracture, ma'am. And if you'll notice, the entire vertebra is very slightly out of line with the one above, with C5. See how it's pushed forward a bit? The medical term is *spondylolisthesis*, the forward slippage of one vertebra over another."

The bone faded away, revealing a slender trunk of tissue hidden inside, with branches extending out and down.

"No damage to the spinal cord, thank God," Garner said. "But the slippage was putting some pressure on the nerves just about here. See the swelling? *Any* movement at all and that fracture could have split and shifted."

"And that would have killed him?"

"That, or it would have left him paralyzed from the neck down. *That* we could have fixed, once we got him back to a big hospital Earthside. But, yeah, it could also have killed him, at least temporarily. Pollard had a CAPTR program on file—all of the Marines do—so we could have downloaded his backup once we repaired his body, but, well—"

"But it's not the same. I know."

Summerlee didn't say it, but I could feel her thinking the unpleasant word. *Zombie.*

The bone faded back into view on the screen, the minute fracture again visible. "So, would this have shown up on X-rays?"

"It did not, ma'am. I couldn't see it, at any rate."

"What about the . . . what did you call it? The slippage?"

"Spondylolisthesis, ma'am. That depends on the exact angle of the X-ray shot. I missed it when I saw the X-rays last night. If you know exactly what to look for, you can maybe see that the one vertebra is very slightly out of line, but it's not obvious."

"I see. So you are challenging Dr. Kirchner's handling of the case?"

"Challenging? No, ma'am. Not really. Medicine is not an exact science, whatever they say. It's an *art*, and success in medicine depends on luck and skill and training and *really* good instincts. Private Pollard was very, very lucky, ma'am. And Carlyle here had some excellent instincts going for him."

"Has Dr. Kirchner seen these images?"

"No, ma'am. I just pulled them down from the sick bay AI."

"Uh-huh." I wondered if she was going to call Garner on his unauthorized tapping of sealed medical records. "And how's the patient?"

"Doing well, ma'am. His condition is stable and improving. The swelling inside his skull is down, now that we have it drained, and the intracranial bleeding has stopped. His head and neck are immobilized, of course, but we've applied a very slight traction to his head, which let the surrounding soft tissue push the misalignment back into place. Now we have nanobots beginning to reconnect the bone. We're applying low-intensity pulsed ultrasound to accelerate bone growth. The prognosis for a full recovery is excellent."

"In how long?"

"Two, maybe three weeks."

"I see." Summerlee looked at me. "So, Carlyle, it seems that you have . . . good instincts."

I said nothing. It seemed the safest course of action.

"However," she went on, "those instincts have left us with a rather serious problem."

"Yes, ma'am," Garner said. He didn't look happy.

"I cannot relieve Doctor Kirchner of his responsibilities as expedition medical officer, nor can I challenge his fitness as a physician. That would require a medical board back on Earth. And if Petty Officer Carlyle goes back to working in sick bay, it will raise . . . issues."

She was dead right there. I'd just been wondering how the hell I was going to fit back into shipboard routine after this little . . . misunderstanding.

"We all make mistakes, ma'am," Garner said.

"Indeed. But when doctors make mistakes, people die. I can't sideline him. I can't even write him up for a reprimand, because I don't have the medical training to sit in judgment on his decisions."

"If I could make a suggestion, ma'am?"

"By all means, Chief. I would love to hear it."

"Nurses and Corpsmen are used to . . . let's call it *managing* doctors."

"How do you mean?"

"Look, doctors are busy, okay? In a hospital, they sweep into a patient's room, half the time in conversation with an expert AI so they're not really there. They look at the test results, prescribe a round of treatment, and they're gone, usually muttering to themselves. It's the nursing staff that's with the patient all the time, including the patient-care AI that's supervising everything."

"So?"

Garner's expression said he didn't really want to go into the details. "Don't get me wrong. There are good doctors out there, *really* good ones. But there always are a few bad apples, and nursing staffs know how to take up the slack and look after the patients' best interests."

"That's horrifying."

Garner shrugged. "It's the way things are. The medical community—other doctors, mostly—tend to close ranks and protect the bad ones. Sometimes it's tough to tell which ones are genuinely *bad*, and which ones are just having a bad day."

"Is Dr. Kirchner . . . a bad doctor?"

"Ma'am . . . I don't know. I don't even want to guess. It's not my place to say."

"Take a shot at it."

"Ma'am, he *must* know his stuff. He taught medicine at SMMC, and that's not a billet for mediocrity. But since he's come aboard, he's been abrupt, short-tempered, rude, and making snap decisions that . . . aren't always the best. He doesn't *listen*—"

"None of which makes him incompetent. He sounds like he's a little shy on people skills."

"Yes, ma'am."

I'd been wondering if they'd forgotten I was in the room, but now the captain looked at me.

"What do you think, Carlyle?"

"I don't think Dr. Kirchner is incompetent, ma'am. He's been acting like . . . I don't know. Like he has personal problems, maybe? Stress at home . . . or maybe he didn't want to come on this expedition."

"Mm. Point. How do you feel about going back to work with him?"

Damn, what was I supposed to say to that? "I'm not exactly looking forward to it, ma'am . . . but I'll do what I'm told to do."

"What do you have to say about the idea of protecting patients from the man?"

"Well . . . Chief Garner is right. That sort of thing does happen. Not very often, thank God, but sometimes a doctor gets assigned to a duty station, and you wonder how he ever got through medical school. The nursing staff has to follow his orders . . . but they know when the physician in charge makes a bad call. And . . . well, I don't expect that there'll be mass casualties on the *Haldane*, ma'am. The crew and the Marine complement on board are all healthy. All we're likely to have are minor complaints and the odd case of accidental trauma, like Pollard."

"You're saying Dr. Kirchner can't do that much damage."

"I guess so, ma'am."

"And when we get to Abyssworld?"

That stopped me. As senior medical officer, Dr. Kirchner would be responsible for everyone on *Haldane* operating in a highly dangerous, extremely unforgiving environment . . . *and* he would be the biochemistry expert backing up our civilian specialists, Drs. Montgomery and Ortega.

"You know, Captain," Garner put in, "that if the cuttlewhales turn out to be intelligent . . . Dr. Kirchner might be lacking people skills, but the cuttlewhales aren't *people*."

It was a lame attempt at humor, and no one laughed.

"Okay," Summerlee said, arriving at a decision. "I'll have a private word with Dr. Kirchner about his . . . attitude. Carlyle . . . I'm dropping all charges against you."

The relief I felt was palpable, a warm flush from the head down. "Thank you, ma'am."

"I'm assigning you to First Section, where you'll serve as resident Corpsman. Understand?" The MSEP was divided into two sections, First and Second, with twenty-four Marines in each.

"Yes, ma'am." She was essentially pulling me out of sick bay and sticking me in with the Marines full-time. I wouldn't have a lot to do, but it would keep me out of Kirchner's sight.

"Chief? That means the other Corpsmen will be standing a watch-in-three. Is that okay?"

One of us always had to be in the sick bay, in case there was an emergency, like last night. Garner didn't stand watches, which meant the remaining four of us split up two night watches—1600 to 2400, and 2400 to 0800. That meant that we got a full night's sleep every other night. Taking a watch-in-three meant that the other Corpsmen would have to cover for me, basically working two nights, and getting off the third.

"Not a problem, Captain. I can stand watch in the sick bay, and we'll keep it simple."

"Very well. Anything else to discuss?"

"No, ma'am," Garner said.

"No, ma'am. Thank you."

"Don't thank me, Carlyle. If I have to invoke Article Ninety-two, I'm coming to you for validation. Understand me?"

"Yes, ma'am." I understood very well. Article 92 was the military regulation covering dereliction of duty, or of gross negligence or incompetence, requiring that someone be relieved of duty. If she had to relieve Dr. Kirchner, she would have me making a statement . . . and testifying later at his court-martial. It's *never* a good thing when an enlisted man has to give testimony against an officer, and that sort of thing can follow you throughout the rest of your career. *There goes the guy who ruined Dr. Kirchner's medical career. . . .*

Not good. Even if Kirchner got what he deserved, not good at all.

As with medicine, things were rarely clear-cut or obvious in legal military issues either, not when it was one guy's word against another's.

But then . . . well . . . maybe Kirchner was just having a bad day. Maybe his wife had left him . . . or he really, *really* hadn't wanted to leave Earth. Maybe the skipper would have that talk with him, and everything would get straightened out.

Yeah . . . maybe . . .

And maybe I was going to get promoted to admiral.

Chapter Ten

THREE DAYS LATER, I WAS IN THE MESS HALL WITH KARI HARRIS. THE viewalls were set to show a spring day on Earth, complete with mountain peaks reflected in a lake, a scene that seemed calculated to raise issues of nostalgia and homesickness. Outside, of course, there was still not a thing to see, as the bubble of tightly wrapped space containing the *Haldane* continued its faster-than-light slide into deep interstellar space.

There were no relativistic effects, of course; *we* weren't moving faster than light—just the volume of space within which *Haldane* was resting, and if that sounds counterintuitive to you, well, welcome to the club. How long the forty-two-light-year journey would last depended entirely on how much energy we put into the warp bubble. Theoretically, the amount of energy inside each cubic centimeter of hard vacuum was, if not infinite, then enough to *seem* infinite for all practical purposes. But there were engineering issues involved, not least of which was accurately calculating when it would be time to release the warp bubble and re-emerge in normal space—and that meant that the trip was going to take a couple of weeks.

Still, two weeks for forty-two light years? Three light years a day? That wasn't bad. Not bad at *all*.

"Kirchner," Kari told me, "is crazy."

"Is that an official diagnosis?" I asked, grinning.

She missed the sarcasm. "No, of course not. But he's acting . . . strange."

"Doing what?"

She frowned. "Well, he never leaves his office."

"He sleeps in there?"

She shrugged. "I don't know. He might go back to his quarters for a few hours some nights. But I know he's been there, locked in his office all night, each time I had the twenty-four to oh-eight-hundred watch. It kind of creeped me out, y'know?"

"Where does he eat?"

"He's got a small food nanufactory in there."

"Okay, maybe he's simply behind on his record keeping. Catching up on the backlog, y'know?" Still, acute insomnia could be an important symptom—a problem with the thalamus, perhaps.

"Elliot, I really think something is wrong with the guy. The way he rants about you . . . it's really scary."

"About *me*!"

"Yeah. He goes on about how enlisted people shouldn't question a doctor's decisions . . . how you were committing mutiny by disobeying orders, that kind of stuff."

I felt a bit of a chill at that. It's never good to attract the unswerving attention of the brass, especially when that attention is negative.

But I really didn't want to get drawn into the discussion. The truth was, I didn't want to believe that there was something *mentally* wrong with Kirchner. In some ways, I think we're still in the Dark Ages when it comes to psychological pathology. I mean, we can reach inside the brain and switch off the pain receptors. We can image the *zona fasciculate* of the human adrenal glands and actually watch it cranking out cortisol in response to emotional stress. But we're damned near helpless when the patient starts hearing voices or screaming that he's being chased by alien demons with big black eyes who are working for the government.

Was there anything I should do about it? Was there anything I *could* do?

The easiest, of course, was simply to stay out of the man's way.

The next afternoon, though, I was in the Marine squad bay, hanging out with a number of the Marines. The ship was packed with them, of course. Worse, though, it was packed with *bored* Marines. You could only link in to training or entertainment sims for so many hours each day, and after that the principle form of recreation became an age-old art form devised by and for enlisted personnel—the bull session.

"Hell, *I* know what Kirchner's problem is," Corporal Benjamin Hutchison declared. "He's a back-to-Earth neo-Ludd and he's afraid of pissing off the Qesh!"

"How do you figure neo-Ludd? Sergeant Tomacek said. "He's a fuckin' *doctor* fer Chrissakes! They're all about high tech!"

Predictably, I suppose, the principle topic of conversation and scuttlebutt was Dr. Kirchner, after I'd been assigned to spend my duty hours with the Marines in their natural habitat. How they knew what they knew about the situation was beyond me; *I* hadn't said anything about it, other than admit that the captain had let me off after a . . . *misunderstanding* with the good doctor. Either one of the other Corpsmen had blabbed, or the Marines were simply demonstrating the reality of psychic powers and reading someone's mind—mine, Chief Garner's, or the skipper's.

Whatever it was, every one of them knew what had happened—and *almost* happened—to Pollard. The four Marines who'd helped me get Pollard back to sick bay would have told the others about my being put on report, of course, and why. But unless Chief Garner or the captain had said something about Kirchner's apparent incompetence—and that was starkly and absolutely unthinkable—they were guessing, or they were reading between the lines.

They'd tried to draw me out, of course, but so far I'd gotten away with declaring ignorance—or suggesting that it was best that I not say.

That didn't stop the speculation, however.

"Sure," Private Wiseman said. "The back-to-Earthers say we have no business being in space, but not all of them are neo-Ludd. I think most of 'em are just afraid of the Qesh . . . or the Raggies."

"Fuck, the Jackers are our bosom buddies now," Sergeant Dalton growled. He grinned at me. "Ain't that right, Doc?"

"So they say," I replied. *Jacker* was Marine slang for the Qesh, drawn from their societal code of JKRS on their entry in the Encyclopedia Galactica.

"Hell, *I* don't trust 'em," Staff Sergeant Thomason said. "Or the Raggies either, for that matter."

The Brocs had told us about the broader political picture in our Galaxy when we'd first met them, and we'd learned more from the Encyclopedia Galactica. We knew that the Galactic Empire—more properly the R'agch'lgh Collective, though that was a *lot* harder to pronounce—had been in the process of falling apart for at least the past twenty thousand years.

Twenty thousand years? Gods, all of human civilization fit neatly into less than half of that span!

The R'agch'lgh Collective, the "Raggies," had been running things in the Galaxy for a long, long time. A million years? More? We're still not sure. We haven't found an EG entry for them, though we've looked. But we do know that about fifty thousand years ago, they made contact with some seven-legged armored centaurs known as the Qesh and collectivized them, brought them into their empire, making them one of their sources of military muscle. When things began turning pear-shaped for the Collective, though, somewhere along about the time that the last major ice age was ending on Earth, the Qesh appear to have cast off the imperial yoke and set up in business for themselves.

Predarians, the news nets called them back home, meaning a predator species wandering the Galaxy looking for easy pickings.

We first encountered the Qesh sixty-one years ago at a star called Gamma Ophiuchi, eighty-four light years away, where they figured we were up next on their easy pickings list. Last year, we fought them to a standstill at Bloodstar, and hashed out a treaty of sorts: we promise not to be a nuisance to them, and they promise not to strip-mine our worlds down to bedrock.

No one knew how long that treaty was going to hold. Most likely, it would last just about exactly as long as it was convenient for the Qesh *not* to step on us. They were centuries ahead of us in technology; if and when they decided that we were in their way, it probably wouldn't take all that much effort on their part to correct matters. We'd seen them destroy planets by slamming rocks into them at close to the speed of light.

Dalton had directed his snide remark at me because I'd had a hand in making that treaty possible. During a Marine reconnaissance of Bloodworld—Gliese 581 IV—I'd saved the life of one of the Jacker warriors, and that had turned out to be a big deal in their warrior-oriented culture.

Glad I could help, fellas. . . . but it was a good deed thin enough that we couldn't count on it to make the agreement last. Nor could we count on Qesh good will. Especially now, since the red dwarf star known as GJ 1214 was located in the constellation in Earth's sky known as Ophiuchus.

The same constellation that held two other stars—Gamma and Eta Ophiuchi.

Did the Qesh consider that part of the sky to be their sovereign territory? Hell if I knew. All of our encounters with them had been in that general part of the sky—Gamma Oph, Psi Serpentis, Eta Ophiuchi, HD 147513 in Scorpio, and Gliese 581 in Libra. The presumption was that they'd been coming out of that corner of the sky, each strike closer to us than the one before. Gliese 581 was only twenty light years from Sol, practically chiming our front door by Galactic standards.

"Okay, so it's like Wiseman here says," Hutchison went on. "Maybe Kirchner isn't neo-Ludd, but he could be scared shitless that we're gonna bump into the Qesh out here. GJ 1214 isn't all that far from Eta Oph."

"Yeah," Thomason said, "but you're forgetting that the Qesh aren't at Eta Oph anymore. They travel about as a fleet."

"Right," I said. "Last we saw, the Predarian fleet was at Bloodstar. That's a long, long way from here. No way they're going to notice little ole us."

"Yeah?" Wiseman said. "And how do we know what they can do?"

"Bullshit," Dalton said. "Spotting us out here is like spotting one particular grain of sand somewhere along a twenty-kilometer beach."

"It's worse than that," Thomason added. "With us tucked into our own private little universe right now, it's spotting one particular grain of sand *that isn't there.*"

"We have to come out of our hole and play sometime," Hutchison pointed out. "What then?"

"I think the real question," I said, "is what happened to Murdock Base? Was it knocked out by the local natives, whatever they are? Or was it the Qesh?"

"If it was the Qesh," Corporal Masserotti said, "then they're not traveling in a single fleet anymore."

Lance Corporal Gerald Colby said, "We know the Qesh send out scouting parties, raiders, that sort of thing. They could have left someone at Abyssworld, easy."

"Yeah," Wiseman said. "Yeah, that makes sense. Maybe Kirchner is afraid that we're going to run into the Qesh at Abyssworld."

"So what if we do?" Thomason said. "We've had a research station on Abyssworld for . . . what? Nine years, now.

Even the Qesh wouldn't have a problem with us visiting our own outpost, for God's sake."

"There you go, assuming that they're going to think like us," Hutchison said.

"Yeah," Wiseman said. "If they're alien, they're not going to think like we do. That's what the word means, right? It's like they're insane!"

"What do you think, Doc?" Thomason asked. "*You're* the expert on aliens!"

"I think that even the most alien life form we run into is going to act in a way that is logical for *it*. It'll be a logic based on its evolutionary history, its psychology, its physiology, and the way it looks at the universe around it. We may not understand that logic at first, but there *will* be logic."

"Well, that's just what I said, right?" Wiseman said. "If we don't understand the logic, they're gonna be acting crazy . . . at least so far as we're concerned."

"Doesn't mean we *can't* understand them," I pointed out. "But it's never going to be easy."

In fact, there's a whole science devoted to how aliens think—xenoepistemology, the study of how nonhuman intelligences obtain and organize knowledge. There were expert AI systems, including one called Ludwig, resident in *Haldane*'s Net, designed to figure out just what an alien means when it says, "Good morning." We had a long way to go in the field, though. We still didn't always understand the Brocs, and we'd been communicating with them for 128 years.

Eventually the conversation shifted, as it always did in this kind of free-wheeling bull session, to other topics—to women and sex, to hot liberty ports, to no-shit-there-I-was stories, to what each of them planned on doing when they got out of the service.

I got up and left the group, sending a call to Chief Garner in sick bay. It was almost 1700. "Hey, Chief. It's Carlyle. You have some extra duty for me?"

"That's a negative, Carlyle. You're off the hook."

In fact, he hadn't assigned me anything since I'd moved in with the Marines. "How are things with Dr. Kirchner?"

"No problems." His mental voice sounded a bit tight, though. I wondered if things were as smooth down in sick bay as he was making them out to be. Hell, if there *was* a problem, Garner wouldn't tell me about it, not and risk adding to the scuttlebutt flying through the ship.

"Okay, Chief. Thanks. I'll check in tomorrow."

"Tell you what, E-Car," he said. "We're going to record it that you've done your time, okay?"

"Fine with me. What gives?"

"Let's just say . . . let's just say that we don't want to have you hanging around in sick bay where Dr. Kirchner will see you. He's still bent out of shape about you disobeying orders, and he thinks you got let off too light. Out of sight, out of mind, okay?"

"Okay, Chief. Thanks."

It sounded as though Chief Garner was struggling to . . . to *control* Kirchner, to contain him, and that was serious stuff. It also sounded like Kirchner was spending an unhealthy percentage of his time in sick bay. He was at least spending his evenings there, times when I would have been down there pulling my extra-duty shifts.

I began then to seriously consider the possibility that what we were witnessing in Kirchner was some kind of pathology. He wasn't just an asshole; there was something *wrong* with him.

But what? There were no other doctors on board, certainly no one who could intervene with Kirchner, challenge his behavior, or get a solid diagnosis. Even if we had a diagnosis, it would take an act of God—meaning Captain Summerlee—to remove him from duty and force him to accept treatment.

Besides, both the military and the medical hierarchies are weighted heavily in favor of officers and doctors over enlisted personnel and nursing staff. There's an old saying that you can't fight city hall. Turns out you can't fight the medical old-boy network either, *or* Commonwealth Military Command.

I considered linking in to the medical AI that ran sick bay. Its name was Andries, short for Andries van Wesel . . . a physician and anatomist back in the sixteenth century better known by the Latin version of his name, Andreas Vesalius. Andries would have a complete program subset for diagnosing psychiatric problems. Military units, after all, had more problems with psychological conditions—depression, anxiety disorders, PTSD, suicidal ideation—than they did with sprains, strains, and broken bones.

But . . . no. Andries worked for the medical department, and out here that meant Dr. Kirchner. I wouldn't want him to see a report from Andries that suggested that I was checking up on his mental health. Besides, Andries was where Chief Garner had gone to find the deleted STS data. If I or he ended up in front of a court-martial board, a record of my rummaging around in the sick bay AI's files looking for psychiatric symptoms in my department head would look uncomfortably like mutiny.

That was what we were looking at here, right? *Mutiny* . . . a damned ugly word.

There was an alternative, though, another source of information on human psychiatric disorders.

Its name was Ludwig.

Ludwig was named for Ludwig Wittgenstein, an early twentieth-century philosopher who'd done important work on the philosophy of language and how it intersected with the philosophy of *mind*—mental functions, mental properties, and consciousness itself. Language, and how we use it, affects the way we think. We take that for granted today, but it was pretty revolutionary three hundred years ago. And the idea that language affects how we think becomes vitally important when trying to establish meaningful communication with a totally alien species.

I knew that Ludwig had a *lot* of data stored on human psychological or psychiatric conditions. Wiseman had been right about one thing, though he'd been having trouble expressing it: nonhumans think differently from humans, and those differences can make them seem crazy. Ludwig had to know about *human* mental problems in order to understand how an alien might be thinking.

I grew a chair for myself near the viewall, dropped into it, and opened the channel, passing up-link my authorization code as I did so. "Ludwig? I need a fast consult."

"What is the nature of your question?"

"Somebody on board is acting strange. I need to assess his psychological condition."

"Why not consult with Andreis? This would be his specialty, rather than mine."

"My reasons are private."

"Understood. Select the behaviors that are troubling you."

A list of symptoms ran through my in-head. Most I easily discarded. But a few . . .

Difficulty conforming to social norms: In this case, "social norms" might mean military protocol and common courtesy.

Acting impulsively; failing to consider the consequences of impulsive actions: Well, he'd decided not to give Pollard an STS, and hadn't listened to my reasons for giving him one.

Display of aggressiveness and irritability, possibly leading to physical assault: Okay, Kirchner hadn't attacked anybody, but it sure felt like he was out to get me.

Difficulty feeling empathy for others; an inability to consider the thoughts, feelings, or motivations of other people, sometimes leading to a disregard for others: Bingo.

Displays no remorse for behavior that harms others: That and the lack of empathy together were beginning to sound like sociopathy, but the diagnosis Ludwig was working toward turned out to be something else—antisocial personality disorder.

Some of the signs and symptoms were bang on. Others were borderline; Pollard's case had resolved well, with no physical harm to him, so it was tough to judge whether Kirchner had shown any remorse or not. There simply wasn't enough solid evidence for a diagnosis. That was the hell of psychological profiles like this one. Every person is different, and *every single symptom* can show up in a healthy individual. Psychiatric pathology, it turns out, is often a matter of degree.

And if Kirchner could be clinically diagnosed as suffering from APD, it turned out there wasn't a lot that could be done about it. Very few people with the condition ever sought treatment on their own; most ended getting treatment after some sort of altercation with the legal system. The only recognized treatment was something called cognitive-behavioral therapy, which involved teaching the person to find insights into his own behavior and to change those behaviors and thought patterns that were socially maladaptive. It took a long time—years, often—and if the person wasn't personally convinced that he was having trouble in social situations and that he was the cause, all the therapy in the world wouldn't help him.

Sure, I could just see it. *Excuse me, Doctor, but your bedside manner sucks and you're making impulsive decisions without thinking through the results. I think you need to seek professional counseling. . . .*

That would go over *real* well.

So . . . was it even my business at all? I mean . . . some people, some *doctors* are simply just assholes, and it's not up to me to fix any of them. I was no longer on the case, in a manner of speaking; I was under orders to stay out of Kirchner's way. Fixing him was not my job.

But there was another side to the issue. Navy Corspmen are responsible for the health of everyone on board ship, and that includes their mental health. Much more than on Earth or at a Commonwealth Navy base somewhere, the tight little community of men and women that make up a starship's crew and passengers depends on the medical department to keep everyone's mental health on an even keel . . . and that means watching out for developing problems before they reach critical and someone gets killed in a fight or as a result of bad judgment.

I couldn't do anything, but Chief Garner was the senior medical department petty officer. Maybe he could.

I thanked Ludwig for its help, then composed a written message in my head.

HEY, CHIEF,

I'M NOT TRYING TO SECOND-GUESS YOU OR DR. KIRCH-NER, BUT I'VE NOTICED SOME DISTURBING BEHAVIORS AND I THOUGHT I SHOULD PASS THEM ON TO YOU. YOU MIGHT BE IN A BETTER POSITION TO JUDGE, SINCE YOU'RE SEEING HIM EVERY DAY.

THANKS MUCH.

ELLIOT CARLYLE, HM2

I appended a link to the list of signs and symptoms I'd observed, and sent it off. I used a written message partly because I didn't want to get into an argument with Garner, but mostly because I wanted him to see the whole list of signs and symptoms before he told me to shut the hell up.

On the downside, it established a records-trail that would be most useful for the prosecution if they decided to give me a court-martial.

I didn't care, though. I hadn't done anything actionable—not yet—and I really was concerned about Kirchner and the effect he might have on shipboard morale.

I addressed it to Garner, marking it to his attention only, hesitated for a long moment, and then finally hit the SEND icon.

Then I tried to get back to work, which meant going over the health records of the Marines in MSEP-Alpha, making sure immunizations were up to date and that nanobot counts were within acceptable limits.

And I tried to forget about the damnable fact that, at that moment, Kirchner was the only physician within something like thirty light years.

My note to Chief Garner turned out to be something of a mistake. He came up to the squad bay the next day, furious, and reamed me a new one for sticking my nose in where it wasn't wanted.

"*Damn* it, E-Car," he growled, while a number of the Marines looked on in amused silence, "can't you just leave well enough alone? I've got all I can handle juggling . . . problems in sick bay, hassles with the skipper, and Dr. Kirchner on the rampage. I do not need you trying to be helpful!"

"I understand, Chief."

"No, I don't think you do! Are you an expert in psychological pathology? Have you been trained in psychiatric medicine? Taken downloads teaching you intervention techniques in social path cases?"

"No, Chief, but—"

" 'No, Chief,' " he mimicked, then glared at me. "But me no buts, E-Car. You wouldn't know antisocial personality disorder if it jumped out and bit you. And linking in to a psychiatric subroutine won't cut it."

"I'm sorry, Chief. I was worried and trying to help."

"You'll help best by staying here, staying out of the doctor's sight, and staying the hell out of my hair!"

"Aye, aye, Chief."

There was more . . . but eventually Garner ran down and stalked off, leaving me with a bunch of grinning Marines. "Don't take it too hard, Doc," Colby told me. "Chiefs and gunnery sergeants—they think they're God."

"Uh-uh, Colby," Sergeant Tomacek said, shaking his head. "Captains *think* they're God. Chiefs and gunnery sergeants *know* they're God. Basic law of the universe, that."

A week and a couple of days later, we dropped out of Alcubierre Drive. GJ 1214 is a pipsqueak even compared to a red dwarf like Gliese 581. It's sixteen-hundredths of the Sun's mass—about half of Bloodstar's, and our navigational program popped us into normal space less than half an AU out.

And almost immediately, we realized that we were not alone in the system.

Someone else had gotten there first, and was already in orbit around the planet.

Chapter Eleven

KARI AND I STOOD SILENT ON THE MESS DECK, WATCHING THE FINAL
approach to the star and its watery world. A couple of dozen
Marines were there as well, uncharacteristically silent. From
a scant 2 million kilometers away, the star GJ 1214 spanned
eight degrees, sixteen times the width of Sol in Earth's sky,
sullen red, glowering, a good 20 percent of its face blotched
and pocked by black starspots. I could see the granulation
of the photosphere, the roil and churn of the deep stellar atmosphere, the ghostly reach of prominences along far-flung
lines of magnetic force.

And the world . . . was it world or titanic comet? As
the digital avatar of Dr. James Eric Murdock had showed
us in the docuinteractive briefing two weeks before, the
planet called Abyssworld had a misty white tail streaming
out from its nightside, stretching far out into the darkness
away from that cool red ember of a sun. Abyssworld's dayside showed as a deep violet ocean beneath the hurricane
swirl of clouds that covered most of the hemisphere. The
nightside was made dimly visible by light reflecting from
the cometary tail, and by the pale ring of aurorae around
the planet's north pole. What we could see of Abyssworld's
nightside reminded me forcibly of Europa—ice from pole to
pole, streaked and webbed and crisscrossed by filamentous
networks of dark lines.

A world divided, half ice locked and frigid, half boiling, storm-tortured ocean.

And an ocean, I reminded myself, that was ten thousand kilometers deep.

What a world, I thought. *What* a world!

Haldane's instruments picked up the presence of the alien ship long before we were close enough to see it with our naked eyes, of course. The bridge threw an inset window up on the viewall showing the vessel, a gnarled and organic-looking shape, vaguely like an egg but with blisters and twisted surfaces that made you dizzy if you tried to follow them with your eye. The color overall was black or a very dark slate gray with sky-blue highlights or detailing; the color was a bit uncertain because we were seeing it by the ruby light of GJ 1214.

"Do we know who builds ships like that?" I asked.

"Maybe *Haldane*'s AI knows," Gunnery Sergeant Hancock said.

I linked through. Dozens of others were asking exactly the same question.

"The design," the AI's voice replied, "is similar to Gykr vessels encountered at Xi Serpentis in 2201. I estimate the probability of identity at eighty-five percent."

In the 128 years since we'd made our first ET contact with the Brocs, Humankind has directly met perhaps twenty alien species, though we know of hundreds more through the Encyclopedia Galactica. I remembered something about a short war with these guys, but not the details.

"Tell me about the Gykr," I said. And the data cascaded through my mind.

**Encyclopedia Galactica/Xenospecies Profile
Entry: Sentient Galactic Species 12190
"Gykr"**

Gykr, "Guckers," "Gucks"
Civilization type: 1.026 G

TL 19: FTL, Genetic/cybernetic Prostheses, Advanced
    nanotechnology
Societal code: VTRB
    Dominant: close associative/predatory/pro-active—
        invasive/sexual
    Cultural library: 4.024 x 10^{16} bits
    Data Storage/Transmission DS/T: 4.01 x 10_{11}s
Biological code: 045.422.836
    Genome: 5.1 x 10^{10} bits; Coding/non-coding: 0.622.
Biology: C, H, N, O, Cu, Mg, As, H_2O, PO_4, Fe
    GNA – Glycol Nucleic Acid
    Cupric hemocyanin free-floating in hemolymph as
        circulatory fluid.
    Mobile heterotrophs, carnivores, O_2 respiration.
    Upright jointed-limb locomotion.
    Highly gregarious, Polyspecific [1 genera, 10 species];
        asexual.
    Communication: modulated sound at 100 to 1000 Hz.
    Neural connection equivalence NCE = 9.3 x 10^{13}
    T = ~240° to ~290° K; M = ~7.6 x 10^4 g; L: ~4.7 x 10^8s
Vision: ~600 nm to 1200 nm; **Hearing:** 12 Hz to 7000 Hz
Member: Galactic Polylogue
    Receipt galactic nested code: 7.22 x 10^9 s ago
    Locally initiated contact 0.11 x 10^9 s ago
Star: Unknown.
    M = 6.2 x 10^{27}g; R = 5.5 x 10^6m; G = 8.4 m/s^2
    Atm: O_2 10.2, N_2 53.0, CO_2 33.9, NH_3 2.6; P_{atm} 0.67 x 10^5 Pa
Librarian's note: EG data suggests possibility of a Step-
    penwolf planet. First direct human contact occurred
    in 2201 C.E. at Xi Serpentis. Immediate hostile re-
    sponse/reflex led to three-month "Guck War," fol-
    lowed by the Treaty of Tanis in 2202, with no contact
    since. Threat level—9.

I had to ask for the definition of "Steppenwolf planet."
Back at the beginning of the exoplanetary discovery

period, astronomers and cosmologists began learning just how chancy the process of planetary formation truly was. Early in a planetary system's history, newly formed planets tended to migrate in or out. Gas giants formed in the system's cold outer reaches might find themselves as "hot Jupiters," circling their parent sun in a matter of days, or shifting back and forth in response to orbital resonances with other worlds. In Earth's solar system 4 billion years ago, orbital resonances moved Saturn farther out, and actually caused Uranus and Neptune to switch places. Most planetary scientists believe that the late heavy bombardment that cratered worlds throughout the inner system was generated as the gas giants shifted in or out, disturbing the orbits of countless asteroids and comets.

One consequence of this game of planetary billiards was that some planets would be ejected from the system entirely. Deprived of their sun, they would wander the frigid wastes among the stars, orphans lost within the vast and empty night. The term "Steppenwolf planet" had been coined a couple of centuries ago by planetary scientists who described such a world as "like a lone wolf wandering the Galactic steppes." Others had suggested that such rogue planets were simply "born to be wild," which seems to have been a cultural reference of the period, long since lost.

The first rogue planet ever discovered—and confirmed not to be a brown dwarf—was a world with the ungainly designation CFBDSIR 2149-0403, discovered by an infrared survey back in 2012. Current estimates suggested that there might be twice as many rogue planets as there were stars in the Galaxy, as many as 800 billion.

What had not been expected was that some of these worlds, at least, might be abodes of life. Several mechanisms for this outlandish possibility had been proposed. All required that the planet begin with an ocean of liquid water. In one, radioactive minerals deep in the planet's crust might keep the oceans liquid beneath a kilometer-thick crust of solid ice. Another possibility suggested that extensive volcanism could pump large amounts of carbon dioxide into the atmosphere, where it would freeze, fall as CO_2 snow, and ultimately blanket the oceans in insulating dry ice long before they could freeze. Enough volcanic activity might create underground caverns warmed by lava flows, as well as heating the oceans enough to keep them liquid. Calculations suggested that such worlds might maintain heat enough within their cores to keep their oceans liquid for as long as 5 billion years.

If such a world had already evolved life at the time when it was ejected from its star system, that life could be expected to adapt to slowly changing, cooling conditions. Whether that life could develop intelligence or, even more unlikely given the nature of the environment, technology, remained a hotly contested question.

But the fact that certain key planetary stats weren't listed in the Gykr entry in the Encylopedia Galactica—no orbital radius or length of year—suggested either that the Gykr had somehow managed to delete those from the record, for whatever reason, or that those data were not relevant—that the world didn't *have* a star.

If the Gucks had evolved within a rogue planet, they most likely would be a *very* different form of life. The supposition was that they did develop a technical civilization, possibly by developing metallurgy and advanced chemistry among the fiery volcanic vents in deep underground caverns; a purely marine civilization could never discover fire, could never smelt metals, could never venture into space . . . at least as we understand the processes of cultural and technic evolution and development.

"One thing's certain," Hancock said, scowling, "those little bastards mean trouble."

"We haven't even seen them since the Guck War," Lance Corporal Brady said. She shook her head. "Maybe they learned their lesson?"

"Not fucking likely," Hancock replied. "My daddy told me about them. They'd sooner shoot than say howdy."

"Fight-or-fight response," I added. "It's built into their genetic structure."

The Guck War had only lasted three months, and basically consisted of two battles: the first at Xi Serpentis, the second at Tanis, where the Fifth Fleet came down on a Gucky supply depot like a hypernova. The Treaty of Tanis was established by laser com, and the two parties never met each other. All we knew about Gykr physiology came from dead and often mangled bodies found inside space armor, plus what was listed in their entry in the Encylcopedia Galactica when we finally dug it out.

Someone in that war had described the Gykr as "overgrown fleas," and they had that insect's overall look—a hunched-over body plated with natural armor, like overlapping strips of leather, long and spindly legs, bristly sensor hairs emerging everywhere—from legs, between body segments, and from the center of what might have been a face.

They weren't actually insects, of course, but the product of a very different, very alien evolution. They had internal skeletons, breathed with triple lungs, and the body armor was not chitin, but a kind of tough, plastic skin. The more I looked at the computer-modeled images of Gucks in our library database, the less they looked like terrestrial fleas, and the more they looked like something horribly else— hive-minded nightmares so different that the human mind struggled to find any point of contact, any overlap with the known and the familiar simply to make sense of the things.

The most disturbing aspect of the Gykr, though, was not their appearance, but that "fight-or-fight" response I'd mentioned. *Any* perceived threat was attacked, immediately and violently . . . and we never did learn exactly what it was that even constituted a threat from their point of view.

It surprised the hell out of us, then, when the lone Gykr starship suddenly accelerated, breaking orbit with a burst of gamma rays, X-rays, and high-energy neutrons, and streaking off into the outer system under high-G. After our experiences with them at Xi Serpentis and Tanis, we weren't sure the little bastards *could* run away. Scuttlebutt had it, though, that there were Gykr vehicles still on the surface of the planet—worse, that they were down in the vicinity of where Murdock Base had been established. Either the Gykr ship had abandoned its landing force . . .

. . . or they were coming back soon with help.

And that was not a pleasant thought at all.

"This," Lieutenant Kemmerer said over our cerebral links, "will be strictly a volunteer operation. We want twelve Marines."

In our heads, we saw a schematic diagram of the *Haldane* dropping into planetary orbit, then releasing a small, manta-ray-shaped shuttle.

"They'll be deploying in a Misty Junior," she continued, as the schematic focused in on the manta-ray landing craft as it flew down to the edge of the ice. "Their orders will be to investigate the colony site on planet, investigate the Gykr presence, and report by laser com back to *Haldane*. They are not, repeat, *not* to initiate hostilities, but they will defend themselves if attacked, and hold the LZ until *Haldane* and the rest of the MSEP can arrive.

"Since this will be a potential first-contact situation, I want two Corpsman volunteers as well . . . that does *not* include you, Chief Garner. I want you to manage the technical end of the op here on the *Haldane*, along with Dr. Montgomery and Dr. Ortega. Understand?"

"Aye, aye, Skipper," Garner's voice replied over the link. He didn't sound at all happy about it, though.

The "Misty Junior" the skipper had mentioned was one of *Haldane*'s two onboard D/MST-28 TMVs. Like the Marine's larger MST-22 Misties, the Misty Juniors were trans-media vehicles that could operate in hard vacuum, in atmosphere, and both on and under the water. Each was designed to carry a full section—twenty-four Marines. *Haldane* was configured to allow her to land on a planet, as she'd done at the base on Europa, but the Misties allowed her to deploy just a few Marines as a scout/recon force without endangering the entire ship and all of the expedition's MSEP Marines.

As Lieutenant Kemmerer continued to describe the mission, I thought about whether or not I should volunteer to go in with the recon group. I was damned tired of the ship by that time, and of being restricted from sick bay for fear that I would bump into Kirchner.

Well . . . why not? That was why I was here, to go down to the surface of Abyssworld and investigate the disappearance of our research colony there. There was no sense in putting it off. The downside was that the situation was complicated by the Guckers, but that would have been a problem whether I went in with the first recon force or arrived later on the *Haldane*. Kirchner, certainly, would be staying with the ship. So, too, was Garner, and he'd been riding me pretty hard these past couple of weeks.

So . . . yeah. I volunteered.

There's an old saying in the military: never volunteer for *anything*. But I was amused to find out that every Marine and every Corpsman had volunteered to go down on the Misty Junior—even Dubois, who consistently maintained a pretty cynical attitude about sticking your neck out. Just my luck, I suppose, that of the four available Corpsmen, they picked me. Kari Harris was the other one.

The Marines would be Gunnery Sergeant Hancock, Staff Sergeant Darlene Callahan, plus Tomacek, Gibbs, Dalton, Hutchison, Masserotti, Colby, Aguirre, Wiseman, Gonzalez, and Woznowiec. Good people, all of them. I'd served with most of them at the Bloodstar, and all of them had been part of the Capricorn Zeta op. I wondered if the decision process had been guided by the fact that these Marines *were* combat veterans, and that they'd all worked with one another before.

Two hours later, we glided into orbit around Abyssworld, passing first over the day-lit side and its titanic swirl of storm clouds. Radio messages beamed on several frequencies to survivors of the human base went unanswered; messages deliberately beamed to the Gykrs in an attempt to open communications likewise were ignored. After several orbits, we made our way to the embarkation deck and began filing through the narrow connector rings into the Misty Junior. Both of the landing craft were actually mounted externally to *Haldane*; once aboard, we strapped ourselves down, sealed off the entrance, and broke the magnetic docking ring locks.

We fell toward the planet above the nightside, with the night-cloaked ice below a dark, blue-gray blur. The comet's tail arced above us like a vast, faint, dome of silver mist. The mechanism was simple enough. Water vapor—steam from a boiling ocean—rising high on the dayside above the storm, was snatched away by the solar wind at the edge of space and whipped back around the planet. A couple of thousand kilometers above the nightside, the water cooled enough to turn to microscopic flecks of ice, a cloud reflecting the star's light like the huge solar reflectors in Earth's Synchorbit.

The ride became bumpy as we entered the upper atmosphere. Abyssworld's air is mostly hydrogen, with a large dollop of carbon dioxide. The hydrogen comes from the dissociation of water molecules by the intense radiation from the sun. Oxygen is created by this means, too, of course, but free oxygen must recombine with hydrogen as quickly as it appears; we're not sure why so much more hydrogen remains, especially when the lighter hydrogen should more easily escape Abyssworld's gravity. Theories presented by the sub-zero base suggest that most of the free oxygen mixes with methane to create CO_2 and more free hydrogen.

Where does the methane come from? Good question. There's a hell of *lot* of methane—CH_4—dissolved in Abyssworld's enormous planetary ocean, but whether that comes from volcanism eleven thousand kilometers down or from the local ecosystem is unknown.

I was following the entry and approach on my in-head. Light glared from the viewall of the cargo deck as the swollen red sun edged above the horizon. When I opened my eyes, I saw that the interior of the cargo bay had switched to red as well.

"So, what do you think, Gunny?" Hutchison asked as we bumped deeper into the atmosphere. "Did the Gucks wipe out our colony?"

"That's what we're here to find out, Hutch," Hancock replied. "Everybody check your armor and your weapons! We hit the LZ in eight minutes!"

All of us were wrapped up in standard Mk. 10 MMCA combat armor with nanomatrix camouflage skins. We sported M287 jumpjet packs on our backs that would give us limited flight capability in Abyssworld's nine-tenths-G surface gravity. Most of the Marines carried standard Corps-issue Mk. 24 laser rifles, while Sergeants Dalton and Tomacek each were lugging a man-portable M4-A2 plasma weapon. My own weapon was a lightweight Sunbeam-Sony half-megajoule-pulse Mk. 30 laser carbine, with a holstered Browning Five slug thrower as my backup.

We just hoped that we weren't going to need to use any of that hardware. There were only the twelve of us—the TMV was piloted by an AI—and when I linked in through my in-head again, I saw a *lot* of Gucks already on the ice. At least a couple of dozen of squat, armored shapes were scattered across the ice down there as we banked over the site of the research colony. I could also see two heavy vehicles that appeared to be picking their way across the ice on a number of jointed mechanical legs, and a dark gray egg-shaped landing craft propped up on landing legs close by.

"Two minutes," Hancock said. "Hang on!"

"They're not shooting at us," Colby said. "*That's* encouraging."

The Misty TMV jolted hard. "Fuck! You spoke too soon!" Aguirre yelled.

"Negative, negative," Callahan said. "They're cold." That meant that our sensors had not picked up the heat of weapons discharging. Still, on the in-head display I could see turrets atop the legged vehicles and on the Gykr landing craft pivoting to follow us as we banked sharply left.

"The wind is something awful," Hancock said.

"Why *aren't* the Guckers shooting?" Tomacek wanted to know. "I thought those ugly little bastards shot at everything that moved!"

"Quiet down, people," Callahan said. Her voice was tense, sharp edged. "Clear the channel."

"Listen up, people!" Hancock called a moment later. "We are at Delta-Romeo Two, repeat, two."

Delta-Romeo Two. That stood for "Defense Readiness, condition two . . . meaning just short of actual hostilities. The only thing hotter was condition one, an actual, all-out firefight.

"We'll be touching down well back from the edge of the ice, about two klicks," Hancock continued. "I want you to deploy fast, slick, and by the numbers. I want to see *blurs* going down that debarkation ramp! Set up a full perimeter, and do not fire until and unless I give the order. I'm unlocking your weapons . . . *now*, but you *will* observe fire discipline on the ground. You hear me?"

"*Ooh-rah!*" chorused back from thirteen throats, the centuries-old Marine battle cry. I checked my carbine again, and saw that it was hot. Circuitry built into our combat armor could lock our weapons until the person in charge unlocked them, but Gunny Hancock didn't believe in crippling the Marines in his command that way, not when an instant's decision might mean life or death. He trusted us . . . and every one of us would have followed him into hell for that reason.

I glanced at the frigid icescape below through the cockpit feed. There were plenty of cultures on Earth that pictured hell as a frozen wasteland just like the one we were looking at.

"Marines! Stand up!"

In two columns, we stood, facing the TMV's rear door, which was already beginning to grind open. I managed to snatch a glance back at the cargo bay's viewall, and noticed that we had gotten well clear of the Guck landing area, and were coming down now on our own.

There was no sign of the Sub-zero base. What the hell had happened to it? I did see a large circular patch, like a shallow crater, lying in the ice between the alien LZ and ours, and there were some structures of some sort—small buildings, possibly—just outside the crater rim. It appeared that a perfectly circular section of the ice cap had simply vaporized, and if that was where the base had been, that would explain why it wasn't there any longer.

Was that what had happened? Had the Gykrs blown the whole base up? A kinetic-kill projectile would have punched through the ice like that . . . or a fusion beam. Damn it, Sub-zero had been a *research* station, strictly peaceful! The more I thought about it, the angrier I got.

I clutched my carbine a bit tighter.

The Misty flared out just above the ice, engaging its quantum-spin repulsors and settling down with a thump in a white swirl of glittering ice particles. Then the ramp was down, we were surging forward in twin columns, and Gunny Hancock was screaming over the tac channel, *"Move! Move! Move!"*

I emerged from the TMV's red-lit cargo bay into an equally red-lit world of ice, deep purple sky, and a stiff breeze coming in off the distant ocean to the west. The local star peeked above that horizon, a swollen, blotch-faced red dome frozen in perpetual sunset visible through a thick violet haze. The sky overhead was dark enough that stars shone overhead, crisp, hard, and bright.

The Marines broke left and right, moving out and around to create a perimeter fifty meters across, with the grounded Misty at the center. Our armor had a nanoreactive coating that mimicked our surroundings, picking up the gray-white of the ice below, the violet of the sky above, and causing the armored men and women to fade to camouflaged invisibility.

I trailed after Tomacek, who was lugging his plasma gun toward the west side of the perimeter, and threw myself down alongside him in the snow. At our backs, the Misty Junior TMV faded out as well, as the cloak came on. We don't have effective invisibility yet, but we can use a nanomatrix skin to serve as a metamaterial, channeling light around a large object like a ship instead of scattering it off. The trick was good enough to fade the craft into the background, as the plasma gun turret pivoted around to present its twin weapons to the west.

"Harris! Carlyle!" Hancock called. "I need one of you docs on point for F.C."

"I'll go," Kari said, an instant before I could respond.

"No, me," I said. "I'm already in position."

"You're it, Harris," Hancock said, and I bit off a muttered curse.

Okay, so I'm an unrepentant romantic. I don't believe in sending a woman out to face what just might be a suicide op. F.C.—First Contact—was always a damned tricky proposition. This time it was worse, because we had already had first contact with the Gykrs—an encounter that had led to a short but incredibly brutal little interstellar war.

Of course, my old-fashioned attitudes had no place in the modern military. Women had been fully integrated into the service for a couple of centuries, now, and I certainly accepted that. But my father and *his* father both had been old-fashioned enough to pass on an ethical view of the universe that . . . well, I tended to keep it well hidden. Such beliefs could get me into trouble nowadays.

So I lay in the snow and watched as HM2 Harris walked past my position and off toward that bloody, bloated sun on the horizon. She had the same weapons I did; for a moment I was afraid Hancock would order her to go unarmed . . . but he didn't, thank the gods.

I couldn't see what the Gucks were doing. We were too far away.

"We're transmitting 'parlay' in Galactic Three on all channels," Hancock's voice said over the platoon link. "No response so far."

"Galactic Three," usually abbreviated to "Gal3," was an artificial language, one of the five interstellar *linguae francae* taught to us by the Brocs and used in the Encyclopedia Galactica. We'd used it at Tanis to stop the fighting with the Gucks. The Treaty of Tanis had been composed in Galactic Three. My understanding was that it had been designed by AIs, that it was all ones and zeros, which made it explicit, precise, and utterly devoid of emotional nuance. You would never write romantic poetry in Gal3. But we knew they would be able to understand us.

"Still transmitting," Hancock's voice said. "Stop where you are, Harris. We're getting movement out there."

"Copy, Gunnery Sergeant."

Kari was a hundred meters away from the perimeter now, a very, very tiny figure silhouetted against the light of the western sky, vulnerable and alone. She'd switched off her armor's nanoflage to demonstrate that she wasn't trying to sneak up on the Gucks.

I hoped they appreciated the gesture. Hell, I hoped they *understood* it.

"Okay!" Hancock called. "We just got an 'acknowledged' from the other side. Galactic Three."

Acknowledged, not *we agree to talk*. But it was something at least.

There are a lot of races across the Galaxy like the Gykr. Long before a species evolves sentience, it is likely to find a distinct survival value in aggression . . . in particular in attacking anything else that might pose even a potential threat. Xenosophontologists back home pontificate about how this actually becomes self-limiting. Once such a species achieves intelligence and a global civilization, shooting first and asking questions later becomes decidedly contra-survival. We've discovered a number of once-inhabited planets just in our own galactic neighborhood covered in the wreckage of civilizations that have committed suicide.

Self-limiting or not, there must still be some survival value in fight-or-fight. The Gykr aren't the only genocidal sociopaths out there.

"A strider is coming toward me," Kari said. "I'm transmitting from my helmet camera now. Are you getting this?"

"Roger," Hancock told her. "We have it in sight."

I linked into the channel, and could now see what Kari saw: a huge, spidery shape against the sunset. It very vaguely looked like it had been modeled on Gykr physiology, with a curving, hunch-backed body covered by strips of armor. It stood on six legs, the hind legs longer than the forelegs so that it moved in an ungainly head-down position.

And it stood four meters tall.

I switched back to my own point of view, and used my helmet optics to magnify the image. The strider had moved to within perhaps ten meters of Kari's position, hulking above her, a pair of weapons turrets angled in her direction on either side of the forward end of that dark torso, like mandibles. Its aft-end dipped, imbedding in the ice, and a hatchway opened. Two armored figures emerged.

"Translation circuits open," Kari's voice said. "Communication desirable. Negative threat . . ."

She was speaking in the terse, tightly structured format of Gal3, the words coming to us in English, to the aliens in their own speech. She raised one hand, palm out . . .

There was a flash, and Kari was pitched backward. The

two armored Gykr rushed forward out from under the loom of the ice strider, gathering her up.

"Fire!" Hancock yelled. "Commence fire! Aim for the strider's legs!"

Beside me, Tomacek triggered his plasma weapon, slamming bolts of super-heated plasma into the war machine's dark armor. A pair of bolts snapped from the TMV behind us, searing through the air above our heads. I saw a hit on the strider . . . and then another. . . .

But the armored Gucks were already dragging Kari Harris inside the machine, and in another moment, it had turned and was picking its way across the icescape, moving back toward the Gykr encampment.

A few seconds had passed . . . and we were now at Delta-Romeo One.

Chapter Twelve

So just why is it that Navy Corpsmen are expected to take point in First Contact situations with the Marines? I suppose it's the technical focus. Time was, a few centuries ago, when Corpsmen were the medics for both the U.S. Marines and the Navy—the *water* Navy, before we got into space in a big way. Corpsmen were the natural ones to become the technical assistants when the Marines deployed to an alien world, taking care of the environmental scans and exobiological workups so that the Marines could concentrate on what they were best at—*combat*. They're fiercely proud of the old saying, Every Marine a rifleman.

So wherever the Marines go, the Navy Hospital Corps goes, too, providing medical support, handling the planetary environmental studies, and, for the past century or so, doing First Contact work as well.

Normally, First Contact was the job of highly trained specialists—folks like Dr. Montgomery and Dr. Ortega—but the reality of the matter was that specialists like that rarely are in the right place at the right time. A Marine combat team pulling a recon on an alien planet was a lot more likely to encounter local intelligent life than the xenosophontological personnel and linguistic experts on a research starship.

So . . . okay, I understood the why. I still wished Montgomery and Ortega were here.

"Ship!" Hancock yelled. "Block them! Don't let that strider rejoin the others!" Behind us, the TMV stirred, then lifted into the air. "Marines! By squads, low-level overleap, Squad One, *now!*"

We were going after Kari. Good enough. The Marines *never* leave anyone behind. But we were badly outnumbered, and this was one time when those proud words just might not be possible.

The TMV contingent had been broken into two squads—each with six Marines plus a Corpsman—and I was in First Squad. I triggered my M287 meta-thrusters, sailing into the violet sky in a long, low leap.

Controlling those damned things in flight is *hard*. You have to hold your body just so to keep your center of mass centered, and to avoid going into a nasty airborne tumble. I left the details to my armor's AI, which juggled microbursts from my backpack to keep me on course, and warned me to shift my legs under me as I started to come down. I hit the ice with a jolt, but the M287 had already fired again, sending me off on another long, low-altitude flight. Around me, the rest of First Squad sailed through the thin air like manic, oversized locusts, closing on the fleeing Gykr ice strider.

The Misty Junior accelerated, passing overhead after the alien combat machine. Another bound . . . and another. We could see the strider ahead as the Misty overflew it, spun about, then drifted toward the ice, its dorsal turret snapping off shots at the Gykr machine. The strider took a direct hit forward and staggered back a step, taking the shock by flexing its jointed legs.

I took a final leap, cutting in my meta-thrusters for an extra boost that carried me in an arc that came down squarely on the strider's back. I hit, bounced, and slid . . . scrabbling to maintain my balance and my hold on the curving, segmented dorsal armor of the thing. The entire body was only perhaps five meters long, the aft end curving down to point at the snow below. I grabbed hold of one of the starboard leg joints with one hand, using the other to swing my carbine around and aim the muzzle at the joint pointblank. The armor—some kind of extremely tough plastic, I thought, rather than metal—absorbed the laser pulse and didn't even seem to get warm.

"Outta the way, Doc!" Masserotti said, crouching beside me. "Let the professionals do the job!"

Masserotti slapped a small nano-D charge against a starboard-side leg joint. Aguirre landed on the torso next, slapping down a second charge. The strider lurched then, taking another step, and I lost my balance. I fell three meters and landed in the snow with a jolt hard enough to hurt.

The Misty Junior had ceased its frantic barrage from ahead as armored Marines descended now on the back of the lurching Gykr machine. The strider opened up at the TMV with a triplet of bolts from its jutting mandibles, scoring two direct hits. The Misty drifted unsteadily toward the ice, smoke billowing from a hole in its flank. "Shit!" Hutchison yelled over the tactical channel. "That's our ride home!"

"I'm monitoring the ship telemetry!" Hancock yelled. "It's repairable! Keep on that strider!"

I opened fire with my carbine, but my half-megajoule pulses didn't appear to be doing much good. Lasers do damage in two ways—through sheer heat, cutting molecular bonds, and through thermal shock, causing the target to explode as it heats suddenly and unevenly. Whatever the material that was sheathing that six-legged walker actually was, it appeared to be good at sucking in heat and distributing it evenly and efficiently, essentially drinking incoming coherent light and rendering it harmless.

Nano-D, though, was different. The charges planted against the leg joints went off along the strider's starboard side in unison, each releasing a small black cloud of soot that clung to the machine's side and leg mechanisms, clung and *gnawed* hungrily, dissolving armor, exposing inner workings . . . and then each of the three starboard legs began collapsing one by one. The strider tried taking another step, found no support as the last starboard leg snapped loose in a spray of parts and fragments.

"Ooh-*rah*! Take that you ugly sucker!" Tomacek yelled, as the machine arced over, falling forward and to the side, hitting with a thud against the ice and sending the Marines on its back tumbling. Hancock bounded up to the exposed underbelly of the thing, waving to me. "Carlyle! Get your PC over here!"

I triggered my thrusters for a short jump, landing next to him as I pulled my hand plasma cutter from my equipment belt. The device was just big enough to fit in my gauntleted hand, and was designed to free people trapped inside tangled wreckage. I pressed the back-spray shield against the smooth surface of the strider's belly and triggered it. That armor might dissipate the heat from a laser pulse—but where a laser could flash-heat the target to a few thousand degrees, a plasma torch achieved *and held* a temperature of almost fifty thousand degrees. If we'd been in vacuum, I would have had to use a tank of inert gas to do the actual cutting, but the Mk. 80 plasma cutter could work with local atmosphere just fine, thank you. The small, attached tank of pressurized liquid O_2 would feed the fire for the necessary few minutes.

And as I dragged the shield across the armor, a white-hot crevice opened in its track.

It wasn't quite like cutting through butter, but I kept at it, lengthening the gash that was opening slowly in the heavy armor. Then, abruptly, the hatch popped open, the hatch through which the bastards had dragged Kari a few moments before. I jumped back as a massively armored *thing* leaped out of the opening.

I had a blurred impression of dark gray armor, of a

hunched-over torso shorter and squatter than I was, of a stubby looking weapon swinging up to aim at my chest . . .

. . . and then three Marines with lasers plus Tomacek and his plasma gun were all firing together from near point-blank range, slamming energy bolts into the alien as it twisted and jittered in the crossfire. A second alien appeared behind the first, blundering into it from behind and going down in a thrashing tangle of limbs.

I saw a joint in the second alien's torso armor flashing red in my in-head imaging. The AIs resident within the Marines' armor were analyzing the enemy's strengths and weaknesses and painting their in-heads with targeting suggestions. I raised my carbine to take a shot, but Hancock put a laser bolt through the joint in the Gykr's before I could react.

A third Gykr was scrambling out of a hatch in the strider's head; Colby and Hutchison took care of that one. I was already going through the rear hatch calling for Kari.

"Kari! Kari, do you copy?"

The interior of the strider was pitch-black, though there was low-level illumination at IR wavelengths. I remembered the EG entry, which suggested that they could see into the near infrared. The interior compartment was more like a tunnel than anything else, narrow and insanely twisted. I had the unsettling feeling of crawling up into the intestinal tract of a giant dead spider.

I didn't have far to go, fortunately. Kari was lying just behind the entry hatch, partly covered by one of the massively armored Gykr bodies. She'd been peeled open like an orange.

I gagged inside my helmet, struggling to keep the vomit down. Gods . . . what had they *done* to her in the few moments since her abduction? There was so much blood. . . .

The Gykr had used something—possibly their version of a cutting torch—to slice open Kari's combat armor, though I saw no signs of burning or charring. Maybe they'd just been trying to remove her armor, but they'd gouged out chunks of her torso as well, and her right arm had been sliced off. I felt hot red fury rising with my gorge; *the filthy Guck bastards* . . .

"Is she okay?" Hancock asked from somewhere behind me. I was blocking his view in the narrow tunnel. "I'm not getting a readout."

"She's p-dead," I told him. It was hard even to speak. "We need an S-tube, stat!"

P-dead—provisionally dead. One step shy of the real thing. Her body was a hacked-open mess and she'd lost a hell of a lot of blood, but if I could stabilize her brain there was still a chance, a small one, that we would have something to resuss later. I fired a shot of nano into her open torso, then began spraying in layer upon layer of skinseal. The sealant foam would harden to a rubbery consistency that would hold her exposed internal organs in place as well as close off leaking blood vessels. The damage was too massive for me to do much about it here, but if I could keep her condition from deteriorating any more, we had a slender chance. The nano I sent to her brain, with N-prog orders to begin stabilizing it and to make certain she stayed unconscious. That was one mercy; she appeared to have been unconscious, and hadn't seen, hadn't *felt* what the monsters had been doing to her.

"The *Haldane* is inbound," Hancock told me. "Ten minutes."

"Right."

Another mercy. There were S-tubes on board the *Haldane*, and we wouldn't need to risk transporting Kari up to orbit on a shuttle. With serious combat medical casualties, *everything* depends on how quickly you can get the patient into an operating room . . . and how well you can manage their condition while you're getting them there.

Stabilizing canisters—we called them S-tubes—were designed to hold really serious casualties in medical stasis for as long as was necessary. Swarms of medical nanobots kept the patient in a deep coma, kept the circulatory system working, and repaired critical injuries in the brain or heart. It would boost the performance of her respirocytes too.

Freitas respiroctes are artificial blood cells—specialized nanobots designed to carry oxygen through the body and remove waste products, just like natural red cells. They're one micron across and extremely efficient, each carrying 236 times as much oxygen as an organic red cell, and delivering it to straight to where it's most needed—to heart muscle or the brain. All Marines carry several million of them circulating through their circulatory systems; with Freitas cells doing the heavy lifting, you can hold your breath for ten minutes or run a marathon without getting winded. Completely replace someone's blood cells with the things, and that person could hold their breath for over an hour, or run at top speed for fifteen minutes without ever taking a breath.

And what's most critical in serious battlefield trauma is protecting the brain. If the blood flow stops—as Kari's had—you've got about four or five minutes before the brain becomes starved for oxygen, and individual neurons start to die. Kari's brain functioning had been CAPTRed before the mission . . . but that wouldn't do a damn thing if her brain had deteriorated to the point that it couldn't receive a polytomographic download.

I used my N-prog to tell the newly injected nano to hook up with her respirocytes and increase their functional efficiency. I checked on her pain levels—there were some receptors firing, but she wasn't feeling any of it, which was what was important. And I took a chance and dialed down her reticular activating system, her RAS, located in her brainstem. That would take Kari into a deeper coma . . . and make certain that she stayed there.

After that I applied more sealant to close off the remaining breaks in her armor—around her abdomen and her right shoulder. We weren't in vacuum, thank God, so there'd been no explosive decompression. The planet's atmosphere was about at half a bar, and composed mostly of hydrogen, carbon dioxide, and water vapor. I would need to be careful if I decided to boost her oxygen levels at all, and the CO_2 hadn't done her any favors in the time she'd been exposed to it, but there was nothing immediately corrosive in the gas mix to cause her serious harm. Her blood oxygen saturation level, as reported by the nano inside her body, was at 91 percent, a little on the low side, but nothing to worry about immediately. I would have to keep monitoring it. Blood pressure was 80 over 30, heart rate at 110. That was more worrying, a result of her having lost so much blood. I directed a few thousand nanobots already in her brainstem to increase her blood pressure by increasing her heart rate. That was another risk, but a calculated one. Her heart was already in tachycardia; having it pump faster was dangerous, but necessary to get her falling BP under control.

And after that all I could do was sit back on my heels and watch her . . . that and hate the monstrous little aliens who'd callously sliced her open like this. What had they been doing . . . a quick vivisection to learn about human anatomy? Or just curiosity about what we looked like and carelessness with a cutting tool? *Jesus!*

"Ship's coming in," Hancock warned.

I wiggled back out of the narrow tunnel, blinking in the glare of sunlight that was as dim and red as a sunset on Earth, but which seemed bright after the infrared dimness of the strider's interior. Hancock and Masserotti gaped at me; the arms of my suit were coated in blood.

"She's in bad shape," I told them. "The bastards tried to cut her out of her armor, and didn't do a very neat job of it. If we can get her into an S-tube, though, she has a chance."

"Good job, Doc," Hancock said.

"Don't congratulate me until we know she's going to make it," I said. The words came out more harshly than I'd intended, but I was bitter and mad. I was also frustrated to the point of screaming. Outside of a few supportive things, there was nothing I could *do* for her. Gods, how long was it going to take to get the stabilizer canister here?

I could see the *Haldane* in the distance, slowly drifting our way. It appeared to be engaged in a running battle, however, its weapons turrets laying down a heavy fire across the distant ice. Research vessels like the *Haldane* were not heavily armed, but they did have weapons—a couple of side-mounted plasma cannon turrets, and a good thing, too. There was at least one other Guck strider, I remembered, as well as a number of ground troops still out there.

Burn them, I thought with a white-hot anger. *Burn them all!*

Two small, black delta shapes circled, dipped, and swooped around the larger research vessel—Marine A/S-40 Star Raiders that had been mounted on the ship's hull aft of the TMAs. I didn't know if there were any Marine pilots in the contingent on board *Haldane*, and it was possible that those two were operating under AI control. It was comforting, though, to know they were up there.

After a few more moments, the *Haldane* drifted closer, lowering its bulk gently onto the ice. A ramp came down, and more Marines emerged. Two of them double-timed it toward the downed strider, lugging an S-tube between them. I had to go back inside the alien machine and use my plasma cutter to get Kari out from under the body of one alien and, yeah, I took a certain amount of vicious pleasure doing that. Then, as carefully as I could, I pulled her body back out through the hatch and lowered it to the ice.

"My God," one of the Marines said as he positioned the S-tube next to her. "What happened to him?"

"*Her*," I said, correcting him. I didn't bother answering his question. With the open part of her armor filled with solidified foam packing, she didn't look as gruesome as she had a moment ago, but there was still a hell of a lot of blood on her armor. Gently, I scooped her up and laid her in the open tube. Later, we would need to open it up and remove the armor and her utilities, make some tube insertions, and package her up once more, but I wasn't going to do that out here.

The two Marines picked up the tube and started back toward the *Haldane*. I followed alongside, keeping track of Kari's blood pressure and respirocyte function.

I'd been so busy for the past half hour that I'd scarcely taken note of my surroundings. The surface of GJ 1214 I looked identical to the ice cap growing over Earth's northern Atlantic, between New England and Greenland. The sky overhead was a deep violet and clear, save for isolated clouds scudding past at a fairly high rate of speed. In the west, the bloated red sun was only just visible through and above a pall of violet and orange mist. I'd expected to see the edge of the permanent storm from here, but decided that the thunderheads must be below the horizon. I could certainly feel the effects, however, in the savage wind blowing in off the dayside ocean. We had to lean into the teeth of the wind to make any progress at all. I estimated that it was blowing a full gale, with surface winds of sixty or seventy kilometers per hour. We struggled into the lee of the grounded *Haldane* and the going became easier. We made it up the ship's ramp and headed straight for sick bay.

Kirchner was there. "*You*," he said, and I couldn't tell if the emotion behind that single word was anger or disdain.

"HM2 Harris is in a bad way, sir," I told him.

I'd spent a fair part of the outbound voyage wondering if Kirchner was any good as a doctor.

Now I was praying that he was.

THE SECOND STRIDER HAD BEEN DESTROYED BY THE TWO MARINE Star Raiders, but most of the remaining Gucks had escaped . . . into a submersible, if Dubois was to be believed.

"C'mon, Doob," I said, shortly after I'd delivered Kari to Dr. Kirchner. We were in the mess hall. "Pull the other one. A fucking *submarine*?"

"That's what it looked like," he told me. "A small one, maybe twenty-five meters long, fifteen wide. Kind of egg-shaped, like that ship of theirs we scared off. It surfaced right through the ice, close to the edge of the water, where the ice was real thin, and the Guckers just swarmed on in."

"How many?"

"Ten or twelve. Must've been damned crowded on the sub."

"That's also only about half of what we saw coming in. The others must have scattered across the ice." *That* was going to be a nasty security problem while we were here.

"I understand the skipper has robots out on patrol, looking for stragglers. If they're out there, we'll find them."

"We'd fucking better." I was feeling grim, angry, and vindictive as hell. What had the Gucks done to the research scientists at the base . . . dissected them? Hell, what had they done to the *base*? Except for those few outlying storage sheds we'd seen from the air, not a trace was left of the main dome beyond a hundred-meter circular patch of very thin, recently refrozen ice.

But then I began wondering . . . a submarine? What were the Gucks looking for under the water, anyway?

We know so damned little about them. We assume they're from a sunless rogue planet, and that suggests they prefer darkness. Their homeworld might be an ice-covered abyss, like Europa or Abyssworld itself, but we're not sure.

I opened a mental channel to Chief Garner. "Hey, Chief?"

"What's up, E-Car?"

"There are a couple of Guck bodies outside. It occurs to me that if we do a post, it might answer some questions about what they are, what they want."

"Way ahead of you, son. We brought in a couple of bodies thirty minutes ago. You want in on the p.m.?"

"Absolutely, if you can get the authorization for me. Otherwise, I'd like to be present VR." Normally, a post mortem—an autopsy—would be performed by a doctor, ideally by a pathologist, but we didn't have one of those available closer than forty-two light years at the moment. If Kirchner was going to do the post, he might not want to have me on hand.

But if that was a problem, I should be able to look over the doctor's shoulder, as it were, by linking in through virtual reality—VR—and watching the procedure in three-D realtime.

"Not a problem," Garner told me. "The doctor's already delegated it to me. You can assist."

"Excellent! Thanks, Chief!"

While a doctor would normally wield the scalpel in a post mortem, it was not unknown for the task to be delegated to competent personnel, especially when the procedure could be overseen and guided by an expert system AI.

I was really looking forward to this.

The dissection took place in the OR suite, which was a small complex of compartments opening up off the sick bay. The morgue was there in an adjoining compartment, which incuded storage for S-tubes, and I was painfully aware that Kari was behind one of those cold, circular hatches in the bulkhead. Chief Garner was there getting set up when I entered, already wearing a biocontainment suit and helmet. On the big steel table lay a Guck, still wrapped up inside its armor. The precisely placed hole at one of the joints over the torso suggested that it might have been the one Gunny Hancock nailed, but I couldn't be sure. Our AIs would have been guiding the sighting pictures for all of the Marines.

I picked up a biosuit pack and slapped it against my chest, activating the nanomatrix, which flowed out over my body, covering everything except my head. A filtration system went on my back rather than a standard life-support system, and a goldfish bowl sealed with the suit when I settled it over my head. The chances of an alien life form—especially one as alien as a Gykr—carrying biological agents that could harm us was vanishingly small, but we would take no chances. The opening in the alien's armor, I saw, had already been plugged with a sterile sealant so that the being could be brought inside. In addition, the temperature inside the morgue had been dropped to about 5°C, low enough to inhibit most microorganisms, and the entire OR and morgue areas were sealed off to protect the rest of the ship.

"Ready, E-Car?" Garner asked.

I nodded inside my helmet, and we began.

The dissection took three hours . . . and at that it was a quick-and-dirty one, something to give us a rough overview of Gykr physiology, not a detailed anatomical study. We were hampered by not knowing what we were doing *or* what we were looking at. We'd seen living Gykrs at Tanis, and there might have been a gross examination of some bodies, but I wasn't aware of any formal studies or dissections. We recorded this one, of course, through the sick bay AI, start to finish.

And I'm pleased to say I didn't even come close to throwing up.

Chapter Thirteen

OF COURSE, WE RAN INTO TROUBLE ALMOST FROM THE BEGINNING. The damned alien armor wasn't designed to come off.

The stuff was definitely organic—long-chain molecules of carbon and hydrogen—and appeared to have emerged from or grown out of the Gykr's outer calcareous layers of natural armor. Did they actually breed some members of the species to have built-in space suits or combat armor? Or was the stuff grafted or even welded on somehow, and removed later using some sort of organic solvent?

That also raised questions about what they'd been doing when they'd peeled off Kari's armor, and taken body parts with it. Had they really been trying to skin her alive? Or . . . as seemed plausible now, had they possessed only limited experience with humans, knowing that we put armor on and took it off almost as easily as we did clothing, *but they didn't know where to draw the line*?

In any case, we'd used a drill to try to sample the atmosphere inside the Guck's outer suit, but couldn't find an airspace. We did succeed in getting blood and tissue samples for analyses. As described by the Gykr entry in the Encylopedia Galactica, they used glycol nucleic acid to pass on genetic information, rather than deoxyribonucleic acid, and used cupric hemocyanin in hemolymph as their oxygen-bearing circulatory fluid.

Humans use hemoglobin—a porphyrin ring containing an iron atom—to transfer oxygen through their circulatory systems, and use red blood cells drifting through the blood plasma to do so. Most terrestrial mollusks, plus a few arthropods like the horseshoe crab, use an entirely different ogygenation system—metalloproteins containing two copper atoms suspended directly in hemolymph, which is similar to plasma or interstitial fluid. It works as well as red blood cells do, pretty much, though it's less efficient as a transport system in what we would consider normal pressures and temperatures . . . but it's far more efficient than blood at high pressures, low O_2 levels, and cold temperatures. It has one extra advantage, too. The stuff can carry certain nucleating agents that turn the hemolymph into a kind of antifreeze. That made sense if they'd evolved beneath an ice cap, on a world heated not by a star, but solely by internal geology.

"I think we need to bring in Bob," Garner told me.

"Coming right up." I patched a thought through to the sick bay AI, and powered up Bob.

"Bob" was our nickname for the lab's ROBERT unit—that's RObotic Biological Examination and Remote Teleoperation, a rather contrived acronym referring to using a machine run either by AI or by a linked-in human working in a room next door to avoid the risk of biological contamination. He came through the morgue airlock from the lab a moment later, wheeled, bulky, and sporting an impressive array of scalpels, laser cutters, syringes, and similar weapons of either healing or destruction, depending upon how he was programmed. He had the advantage of allowing an operator to see through his eyes, which could magnify down to the sub-micron level. Usually, he worked with a human teleoperator, but he was smart enough to do simple dissections on his own.

Garner took control of Bob, and began using the machine's pinchers—far more accurate and much stronger than human fingers—to peel back the Gykr's armor. We were really operating in the dark, here. I became more convinced than ever that they'd cut up Kari out of ignorance, unable to tell the difference between Marine armor, her skinsuit utilities, and her skin.

Eventually, we managed to peel off the outer layers of the Guck's armor, and then began investigating the organism's gross physiology and anatomy. Depending on how you counted, the Gykr had three, four, or five pairs of legs, the longest at the rear of the torso, the shortest up by what passed for a head. Apparently, a Gykr normally walked four- or six-legged, with the head end lower than the abdomen, its ass up in the air; the remaining four sets of clawed appendages could do double duty, as legs or as arms, though the uppermost set was tiny, only ten centimeters long, and probably reserved for eating or facial grooming. The hindmost legs were too long and slender for the Guck to use in order to stand upright, but they definitely were for walking, not swimming. One of my biggest questions about Gykr physiology was whether they had evolved originally as marine life forms—either as swimmers or as bottom crawlers—or whether they'd evolved on land, possibly in magma-warmed underground caverns. Knowing the answer to that might give us some hints about their psychology—about how they saw the universe around them, and how they thought.

The gross anatomy reminded both Chief Garner and myself most of terrestrial isopods. Most people are familiar with what are variously known as wood lice or pill bugs, those little silvery, many-legged critters you find underneath an overturned rock in temperate climates that curl up in a ball if you disturb them. What most people don't know is that there are marine versions of the animal, and some of those grow to enormous size—as much as forty centimeters and massing almost two kilos. They've been around for a long time—more than160 million years—and evidently have changed not at all in all that time. The biggest are found at truly impressive ocean depths—as much as two thousand meters down or more—where they eat pretty much anything they can find and sink their claws into, living or dead.

The Gykr were air-breathers, though we'd known that. Their atmosphere contains oxygen—though at a lower percentage than we favor—so like us they employ an oxygen-based metabolism. However, their lung—singular—seemed to have been adapted from a swim bladder. These guys had been marine organisms not too far back in their evolutionary history.

But the kicker came when I peeled off the last of the artificially grown armor around the creature's tail. There, tucked in on the soft underbelly beneath the overlapping dorsal strips of natural armor, were four paired structures that definitely weren't legs, but they weren't really fins, either. They reminded me of the swimmerets on terrestrial shrimp or lobster—the technical term is *pleopods*—which serve as swimming legs, as support structures for gills, and in some species as sex organs.

It looked to us as though the Gykrs *had* been marine organisms in the very recent evolutionary past, quite possibly as recent as just a few hundred thousand years ago.

Or—like giant marine isopods living in Earth's oceans—they might have been in this exact form, unchanging, for hundreds of millions of years. One theory popular among evolutionary biologists suggested that organisms living and breeding in darkness tended to change only very slowly, over long geological eras of time.

The Gykr appeared designed for a life . . . not in total darkness, perhaps, but certainly in low levels of light. They possessed a single large compound eye, arranged as a complete ring or circle around the head and below the puckered, rasping mouth, startlingly gold against the blue-gray skin. There were two simple eyes mounted far apart, large and dark—all pupil—looking out to either side, plus a couple of pits or indentations underneath that made me think of the infrared sensors of certain poisonous terrestrial snakes.

"Ugly sucker, isn't he?" Garner asked as I pulled the front part of the body back to reveal what passed as a face.

"What are those giant bugs on Madagascar?" I asked. "They look like this thing."

"Madagascar hissing cockroaches," Garner said.

"Yeah, right, I replied. "This is cockroach city."

"Okay, let's open him up. I want a look at his brain."

"Where is it?" I asked. The segments holding the face were pretty narrow, without much room.

"About here," Garner said, beginning the incision with a laser scalpel at just beneath the eyes and slicing down across the abdomen. "At least we think so. This is the first time anyone's had a chance to actually dissect one of these things. All of what we know about their anatomy comes from nanoscans of some rather badly smashed up bodies at Tanis. Ah! Here it is . . . you see? Just like a squid."

I saw what he meant. The brain turned out to be a mass of whitish tissue compacted into a doughnut shape completely encircling the esophagus about where the human throat would be. Squid in Earth's ocean had a similar arrangement, though their brains are a lot smaller in proportion to the animal's mass. It wasn't encased within a protective skull like ours, but seemed to rely on the external carapace and layers of antifreeze-saturated fat for protection.

"Fire a charge of nano into the brain," Garner told me. "I want an estimate on size and function."

I used an injector to squirt some millions of nanobots into the brain tissue from various angles, then used an N-prog to tell them what to do. Brain function can be very roughly estimated by the number of neurological connections—the gaps between individual neurons jumped by chemical sparks when we have a thought or give our body a command.

As expected from the Gykr entry in the Encyclopedia Galactica, this one had an NCE—a neural connection equivalence—of 8.981796×10^{13}, or nearly 90 trillion synaptic gaps. That was an interesting number, actually, because the average human NCE is around 10^{14}, or 100 trillion. Now, there's some flexibility built into those numbers; humans don't have *exactly* 100 trillion synapses, but a range that can run 10 percent or more in either direction. The Encyclopedia Galactica gave the Gykr a slightly lower NCE of 9.3×10^{13}.

But what it did suggest was that, on average, the Gykr had a bit less processing power, a bit less mental flexibility, than did humans. That wasn't necessarily a cause for celebration. I suppose you could say that if the average human IQ was 100, the average Gykr IQ was 93, but, damn it, things are *never* that simplistic. First off, intelligence is not purely a function of synaptic connections . . . and that assumes that we even know what the thing we call "intelligence" is. Gykr brains might be more efficient than ours in some ways.

We're pretty sure that they rely more on instinct than we do, for example; that fight-or-fight thing they have going for themselves, for instance, might be an autonomic response that bypasses the brain completely. They also appear to have a close relationship with their community. It doesn't appear to be a hive mind like that postulated for termites or bees on Earth, nor is it simply a tight, centralized government. The EG gives them a societal code that translates as "V," representing a "close associative." We're not entirely sure what that means; the best guess is that Gykr society is like a close family group . . . a family numbering in the billions.

The family reunions must be hell.

I was also interested in the fact that the Gykr were radially symmetrical in their recent evolutionary history. It was logical in an evolutionary sense, I suppose, if the animal's marine ancestor had been a radially symmetrical cylinder with a mouth at one end and an anus at the other, connected by the tube of a digestive tract. Gykr weren't radially symmetrical now, of course, but it looked like their ancestors had been. Its hearts, for example—there were five of them interconnected in a chain around the esophagus farther down, just below the brain. It turns out that there are a hell of a lot of ways to put together a life form in this Galaxy, quite apart from what we know and understand on Earth.

I was almost surprised to see the Gykr skeleton as Garner opened up the wet torso, though I'd known they did have one. The creature looked so much like an oversized bug that I still expected it to have a chitinous exoskeleton. Science fiction recsims are fond of threatening their human characters with giant insects, bugs the size of e-Cars or worse. Utter nonsense, of course. A real insect can't be larger than about the size of your fist. But the Gykrs did a good job of looking like giant cockroaches or pill bugs without violating basic physics. The internal skeleton turned out to be cartilaginous, lightweight, strong, and flexible, more like the skeletons of sharks or rays, rather than rigid, articulated bones. A kind of central support beam, like flexible plastic, ran down the middle of the body cavity, with rubbery loops alternating side to side that appeared to support the internal organs.

By the time we completed the dissection, we had a somewhat better picture of Gykr evolutionary anatomy. They definitely had evolved in deep, cold, ice-capped water—likely an environment very much like Europa or the deeps of Abyssworld. They'd emerged, though, into a moist but air-filled environment . . . caves, possibly, or hollowed-out pockets inside the ice. Somehow, they'd learned how to smelt metals, and that almost certainly meant in air rather than underwater. It's damned tough pulling iron out of ferrous ores if you can't build a fire. Garner wasn't so sure, and suggested that they might have learned some smelting skills working around hot volcanic vents or lava flows underwater. Even so, you need to *know* about stars, know they exist, before you can try to reach them.

For that kind of information, we were going to have to question a living Gucker, and that might prove difficult. There were some, evidently, hiding out among the ridges and blocks of the ice cap, and there was that submarine Doob had mentioned, somewhere underneath us.

That stirred some deep-down fear, the more I thought about it. "Chief?"

"Yeah?"

"Doobie was telling me a bunch of Gucks escaped on board some sort of submersible."

"Yup. We saw it from the air as we were coming in. Managed to submerge before we could target it, though."

"So . . . what does that mean for us? Could they attack the *Haldane* through the ice?" I wasn't entirely sure what I was suggesting, what it was that had me worried . . . some kind of torpedo, maybe. Perhaps a torpedo with a nuclear warhead, fired at the underside of the ice.

"It's possible. The LT has ordered some Marines to go out and put hydrophones and sonar transponders down through the ice—at the edge of the ice cap, and also through the thin ice where the research base used to be."

That made sense. Sonar meant sending sound waves down into the ocean, and when they hit something solid, like an alien submarine, the reflected sound waves picked up on the hydrophones would tell us where the sub was, how deep, and how fast it might be moving.

At the same time, though, I knew that Gykr technology wasn't all that well understood. If they had torpedoes, how powerful were they? What was their range? So many unknowns, so much that was *alien* and not understood . . .

And what about the native life forms the researchers had reported on this frozen ice ball, the cuttlewhales? It was beginning to look like it had been the Gykr, not the cuttlewhales, that were responsible for destroying our base. But we couldn't be sure of that, either. We couldn't be sure of *anything*.

"We're also going to be setting up the dome," Garner went on. "Once we have that, *Haldane* can go back into orbit . . . just in case."

He didn't add, of course, that *Haldane*'s safety in orbit didn't guarantee *our* safety on the ice. But at least we would still have a way to get home if we survived our time on the surface.

We were still cleaning up after ourselves in the morgue when that guarantee became a lot more slender. The ship lurched, hard, as though a titanic hammerblow had struck us from underneath. In the next moment, the deck took on a distinct tilt; we were listing, perhaps ten degrees, to starboard.

Garner and I stared at each other across the morgue table. A moment later, the voice of Lieutenant Walthers, the ship's exec, sounded through our in-heads. "All hands! Brace for immediate liftoff! We are under attack . . . repeat, we are under attack!"

We both grabbed hold of the stainless-steel table as the ship lurched again, and we felt momentarily heavier as we accelerated straight up. Captain Summerlee had engaged the ship's quantum-spin fields, lifting us up off the ice. By juggling the spin-states on *Haldane*'s belly, we could push against the electron spin of the ice below and even Abyssworld's magnetic field, turning us into a giant quantum-state floater.

The ship's AI, I saw, was transmitting a situation update; we were already at red alert, of course, ever since we'd arrived on planet, but the information coming down from the bridge said that we were under attack. How . . . whether from the alien submarine beneath the surface, or by individual Gykr out on top of the ice, we didn't know.

And almost before we'd absorbed the fact that we were being attacked, the automated voice of our AI came through our in-heads. "Emergency! Corpsman to the bridge! Emergency! Corpsman to the bridge . . . !"

"Go," Garner told me. "I'll finish up here."

I checked through the sick bay AI. Dubois was outside . . . shit, and so was McKean. That left me and Garner on board the *Haldane* to take care of whatever was going down.

I grabbed an M-7 on my way up to the bridge. I queried the ship's AI, asking about what had happened, but I didn't get an immediate reply. Well, of course not. The ship's AI is good for information about the ship's condition, and where a particular person might be on board, but not so much about things like medical emergencies. Sensors on the bridge would have detected something out of the ordinary— someone had a heart attack or had stopped breathing—and summoned me with the AI voice in my head.

All I knew for sure was that someone up there had been hurt by the attack.

I wondered who it had been.

It was the skipper.

"What happened?" I asked as I entered the bridge and hurried across to the woman sprawled on the deck.

"She got thrown from her chair," Lieutenant Walthers said. He pointed at a hard plastic console. "Hit her head there."

There were eight other officers on the bridge, plus two civilians, Ortega and Montgomery. The bridge was a broad dome-shaped compartment extending above *Haldane*'s dorsal side, and with deck-to-overhead viewwalls around all sides, giving a 360-degree view horizontally, and a 180 vertically, creating the startling illusion that the bridge was a circular pit completely open to the sky. The captain's station was raised above and behind a crescent-shaped bank of instrumentation and high-tech link couches on a low dais; Captain Summerlee evidently had pitched forward off the dais and hit her head on a helm workstation. A couple of naval ratings were kneeling on the deck next to her. The rest were still at their stations.

"We didn't think we should move her," one of the ratings said.

I nodded at her. "Absolutely right. You have to be careful with head injuries. Someone call for a stretcher team."

I was already bringing the business end of my nanobot injector up under the angle of Summerlee's jaw, sending a few tens of millions of micron-sized nanobots into her carotid artery. She was unconscious, with a five-centimeter gash high on the side of her head, a few centimeters above her left ear. Pulling her hair aside, I could see the beginnings of an ugly, bruised lump. She was bleeding, too, as only scalp wounds can bleed. I thought about Private Pollard, and prayed there was no hematoma *inside* the skull. She obviously had one on the outside, and at least a mild concussion.

It took only seconds for the 'bots to diffuse through her brain and down her spine. I checked the image coming through on my N-prog. No injury to the neck or thoracic spine, thank the gods, none that showed up here. I would want to do a full soft-tissue scan in sick bay, of course. No sign of the epidural hematoma Pollard had suffered . . . and no sign of a skull fracture. I peeled back her eyelids, checking the pupils. They were both the same size, and both responded to a flash from my mini light.

Blood pressure 120 over 70. Normal. Heart rate at 85 . . . a bit elevated.

Okay. So far so good.

Along about then her eyes fluttered and she started to move. "What the hell was that?" she asked.

"Please don't move, Captain," I told her. "You fell, hit the side of your head. I'm checking you out."

"Go ahead and check me out all you want," she said. "But we're *not* going to have a date. . . ."

If she could joke, she was doing well.

I went ahead and put skin sealant on the cut, closing it off, and used some nanobots to double-check to make sure there wasn't a major bleeder in there. I reprogrammed some of them, putting them on hemostat duty—closing off any torn blood vessels and capillaries that hadn't been reached by the foam. Two Marines with a stretcher arrived, and I supervised getting her onto it.

"Damn it, no," she said. "We're under attack!"

"I've assumed command, Skipper," Walthers told her. "There's been no sign of further attack since that first shock. I suggest you go with the nice Corpsman and behave yourself, ma'am."

"We have people out on the surface," she said.

"I know, Captain. I'm in communication with them now. The situation is under control."

"If it was that Gykr submersible . . ."

"The situation is under control, Captain. Please don't worry so much!"

"It's my fucking *job* to worry!" But she relaxed then, lying back on the stretcher and closing her eyes.

"Anybody else hurt up here?" I asked.

"No," Walthers said. "Freak accident. We were hit just as she was starting to stand up, and she got thrown forward. No reports of other injuries on the ship . . . nothing but a few bumps and bruises."

"Okay. I'm taking her down to sick bay. Let Chief Garner know if anybody else needs help."

"Right."

I wondered what had hit us. Something fired from that sub? Or artillery from the Gykrs on the surface? The people on *Haldane*'s bridge would tell us, I assumed, when they were ready. Presumably that meant when *they* knew what it was.

"Jacobs," Walthers said. "Give us one-eighty down on the bridge view."

"One-eighty down, aye, sir."

I was starting to follow the stretcher off the bridge when the image projected on the dome overhead shifted. The ship hadn't changed attitude, but the image had been flipped to show the ice directly underneath the ship. For a moment, I felt like I was hanging vertiginously upside down. I looked up . . . at an expanse of smashed and broken ice. And there was something coming up out of the ice toward us. . . .

"My God!" someone yelled. "What the hell is *that*?"

It looked like a titanic black flower, myriad short tentacles, several longer arms uncoiling, six stalked, black eyes spaced evenly around a gaping, central maw . . .

And with the inverted display it appeared to be lunging *down* toward the open bridge.

The thing appeared to reach for us, tentacles weaving, then settled back into the frothing roil of ice chunks and black water.

"Cuttlewhale!" I said. I didn't know if the *Haldane*'s bridge crew had been briefed on the things or not. I'd assumed they knew. There was, of course, an enormous gulf between seeing those graceful, far-off serpentine forms on the horizon on the images sent back from the research base and looking down the throat of a monster that must have been nearly as wide as *Haldane* herself was long. I felt weak inside. This was the mysterious life form that *might* be intelligent . . . a creature that Commonwealth Naval HQ had sent us across forty-two light years in the hope that we might learn to communicate with it. I looked at the two civilians, Montgomery and Ortega, seated at the rear of the bridge. They were staring up into the horror above us with expressions that could only translate as dismay.

Yeah, good luck with that xenocommunication thing, I thought. Damn, those two *did* have their work cut out for them. How do you talk to a monster sixty or seventy meters wide and the gods alone knew how long?

I hurried out the bridge entryway after Captain Summerlee.

Chief Garner was waiting for us in sick bay . . . as was Kirchner.

"Let's get her on the scanner," Garner told me.

"The Captain!" Kirchner said, eyes widening. "*Madre de Dios!*"

Kirchner looked . . . bad. His hair looked like Einstein's on a bad day, his face looked hollow and starved, and his eyes were bugging out like a Gyrkr's. There was something terrifying about that wild expression.

"Doctor," I said, hesitating. "Are you all right?"

Those eyes were piercing. "Of course I'm all right! Why does everyone insist on asking me that?"

"You're looking—"

"Just get the patient on the table, damn it!"

I caught Garner's glance, and he gave a little shake of his head. I shut up and helped him move the Captain off the stretcher and onto the STS table. At least Kirchner wasn't inclined to argue about whether or not she needed the scan. "I'm okay," she said.

"No, Captain, you are not," Kirchner told her. He was studying the scan results closely as they came off the machine. "Tell me, Captain," he said after a moment. "Can you access the ship's AI?"

She closed her eyes . . . then opened them again, looking startled and slightly afraid. "I can't! I can't reach the ship's AI!"

Kirchner nodded. "You have a slight concussion . . . but the shock appears to have severed much of the microcurcuitry wiring to your parietal lobe. It's not serious . . . but you are going to be off-line for a while."

"*No . . . !*"

The look of fear deepened to terror. I put my hand on her arm. "Take it easy, Captain," I told her. "It'll be okay. . . ."

"*I can't feel the ship!*"

It must have been horrible for her. Most people nowadays—and anyone with a career in a technical, scientific, or military field, had cerebral implants, allowing direct connections to local AIs, including those resident within their own heads. We joked about how many medical personalities and expert systems were running inside a typical doctor's head . . . but it was almost as bad for a ship's captain, who had to link in with her vessel's computer Net in order to run the ship. Being cut off like that would feel like being lobotomized.

In a sense, that's exactly what had happened to Summerlee. The parietal lobe of the brain—located above and ahead of the occipital lobe, at the back of the head, and behind the frontal lobe up at the front—primarily integrates sensory information coming from many different sources . . . especially data involving our spatial sense, navigation, vision, touch, hearing, tactile sensations, and somatosensation, our awareness of where the different parts of our body are at any given moment. The parietal lobe is divided in two, left and right, like most other parts of the brain. The left hemisphere is involved with symbolic functions, including language and mathematics, while the right side predominantly handles spatial relationships, including images, navigation, and understanding maps.

Janice Summerlee's organic brain was undamaged, according to the scan, but in-head circuitry feeds language and math from the implanted processors into the left parietal lobe. That's how we can hear the voice of an AI or someone we're e-comming inside our heads, and when we talk to someone in-head, the signals go out from the same region for processing and transmission. When a person suffers a concussion, what has happened essentially is that the brain, adrift in its cushion of cerebrospinal fluid, has been slammed against the inside of the skull. When Captain Summerlee hit that console, she'd done so hard enough to slam her brain to one side, and break the nano-chelated wiring in her left parietal lobe—wires that were a micron or less in thickness.

"I need to get back to the bridge," she said, trying to rise from the table.

"Sedation!" Kirchner snapped.

"Aye, sir," Garner said. He used the table controls to signal the nanobots inside the Captain's head, sending them to the hippocampus and prefrontal cortex to bind with her NMDA receptors, sending her into a drowsy, half-awake state of relaxation.

"S'feels good . . . m'okay. . . ." she said.

"*Deep* sedation!" Kirchner said.

I really didn't like Kirchner's expression . . . the quint-essential mad doctor, wild eyes, wild hair. Something was seriously wrong. . . .

Garner hesitated, then made the adjustment. Summer-lee's eyes, still wide open, went glassy as she drifted into a deep coma.

"You two pack her into one of the storage tubes," Kirch-ner said, stepping back from the table. "I've got to get up to the bridge."

"Why, Doctor?" Garner asked. "I'm sure they have things—"

"For the simple reason, Chief Garner, that I am now the ranking officer on board this ship! I am taking command!"

"Sir!" I said, shocked. "That's not right! You're not line! Lieutenant Walthers—"

"*I am in command of this ship and this expedition!*" Kirchner screamed. "*And I can have you tossed out of an airlock for insubordination!*"

I saw Kirchner's eyes, and knew in that moment that I really was staring into complete, utter, and horrific mad-ness. . . .

Chapter Fourteen

"Easy, now, Doctor," Garner said, making gentle calmdown motions with his hands. "We need to talk this out. . . ."

"*There is nothing to talk about!*" If anything, his voice went up a notch in pitch and in decibels. "I am a lieutenant commander, and that idiot Walthers is a *lieutenant*! A mere *lieutenant*! The ship is in grave danger, and I'm in command!"

The ship chose that moment to give another lurch, and it felt as though *Haldane* was turning, rotating swiftly on her z-axis. There was a sensation of rapid descent, like going down in an elevator, and then a heavy jolt. Kirchner stumbled back a step, bracing himself against a bulkhead, and both Garner and I had to grab the scanner table to keep from falling. It felt as though we'd just rapidly come down out of the sky and grounded again on the ice.

"Doctor," Garner said, his voice the calm and studied monotone of a harried parent trying to reason with a small child, "only line officers can command a ship. You're not line, you're a medical officer. You are not in the line of command."

Kirchner turned away for a moment, palming open a storage locker in a bulkhead. When he turned back, he held a nasty, snub-muzzled little laser pistol in his fist. "*And I say I am!*" he shrieked. "*Get the hell out of my way!*"

Kirchner was out-and-out nut case now—a technical

term. I didn't see anything I could do to stop him . . . or . . .
maybe . . .

"Put the gun down, please," Garner said, still speaking
to a child . . . a child throwing a particularly shrill tantrum.
"You . . . you're not well. . . ."

"I am perfectly cuttled!" He paused, drawing a deep
breath. "We need to get us now before the ice sculpts and
whale all see commanding . . . !"

Shit. Word salad. His condition was going downhill fast.
In schizophrenia, certain kinds of dementia, and a few other
mental conditions, the patient's language can devolve into
an incoherent babble. That babble might be grammatical,
but the meaning is always confused to the point of being
unintelligible. Sometimes, it can sound like stream-of-
consciousness rambling, with one word or phrase triggering
a new word or thought, with the meaning hopelessly scrambled. Medical people called the babble word salad.

Kirchner hadn't shown that symptom before. I'd been
listening for it, because I'd suspected schizophrenia. But
the rapidly escalating situation, the Gykr attack, and now the
cuttlewhale outside, could easily have pushed him over the
edge.

I'd spent the last few seconds linking in through the sick
bay AI and transferring the nanobot programming now
running in Summerlee's skull to Bob, the lab robot now pa-
tiently standing against the far bulkhead. One of the ROB-
ERT's arms ended in a nanobot pressure injector, designed
to fire a few hundred million micron-sized nanobots right
through the skin and into an artery.

The question was whether I could put my plan to work
in time. . . .

"Give me the gun, Doctor," Garner said, taking a cautious step forward. "You need—"

Kirchner shifted his hand slightly and squeezed the
trigger. There was a snap and a stink of burning flesh, and
Garner clutched at his shoulder with a grimace of pain.

I sent a command to Bob, then shouted *"Doctor Kirchner!"*

Kirchner spun, facing me, the laser raised, his hand trembling. "Summerlee after Captain *ice* shambles!" he screamed. "Down the back in never was!" His back now was to Bob, who glided forward silently and with astonishing speed and precision.

I lunged to my right. I'd thought of dropping behind the table, but I didn't want him hitting the captain accidentally. He pivoted and fired again, and I heard glassware shatter behind me.

Then the ROBERT's arms closed around Kirchner's, and the pressure gun slipped smoothly around and up against the angle of his jaw. I heard the hiss. . . .

Kirchner's eyes, still wild and staring, lost some of the intensity of focus . . . and then he sagged into Bob's mechanical arms, the laser dropping from a nerveless hand. I moved to Garner's side. "You okay, Chief?"

"Not bad. Been better . . ."

His voice shook, and the burnt-meat smell was strong. The bolt, I saw, had melted through his utilities and charred an area the size of my fist right at the joint of his right shoulder.

"Better sit down," I told him.

"What about Kirchner?"

I glanced at the doctor, slumped unconscious against the ROBERT. "He'll keep. I put him into deep coma."

"We'll need to put him in a tube and keep him that way," Garner said, "until we can get him back to Earth."

"What, you don't want a madman running around the ship? Imagine that." I had my M-7 kit open and was applying burn-repair nano.

"Duty Corpsman to Airlock One," a voice called through our in-heads. "Duty Corpsman to Airlock One . . ."

"Go ahead, Carlyle," Garner told me. "You take it. I'll handle things here."

I glanced again at Kirchner. There really wasn't anything we could do for him here. His insanity might be treatable, but we would need to get him to a full-facility psych unit Earthside before we could even begin to guess what had gone wrong.

"You sure you can—"

"Of course I can!" He snatched the burn spray unit from my hand. "*Go!*"

"Aye, aye, Chief."

On my way down to the Number One airlock, I patched through to the bridge and told Walthers about what had happened to Kirchner and to the chief.

"Shit," he said. "Do we need to keep you on board?"

"Chief Garner should be okay," I told him, "and he's putting Kirchner on ice for the rest of the expedition. But why do you need a shore party? What's going down?"

"Some of our people are on the ice," he said. "Trapped . . . by one of those *things*."

And a Marine shore party was being detailed to go rescue them. Right. It never rains but it pours and sometimes it pours liquid nitrogen, or worse.

I reached the airlock, where a party of Marines was already suited up, checking weapons, and getting ready to go outside. "Hey, Doc!" Thomacek called. "About fucking time! Armor up!"

I squeezed into a waiting Mark 10 hanging on the rack, sealed it off, and accepted a helmet from Thomason. "Thanks, Staff Sergeant," I told him.

Wiseman handed me a Mk. 30 carbine. I checked the safety, wondering if a half-megajoule laser pulse would even register in a cuttlewhale's consciousness. I might have better luck throwing snowballs at the things.

"Open the hatch!" Gunny Hancock called. The dim reddish light of Abyssworld spilled into the lock as the ramp lowered in front of us. "Move out! *Move-move-move!*"

Haldane had touched down on the ice perhaps a kilome-

ter away from the spot where the cuttlewhale had lunged up
through the ice. Thirty Marines and two Corpsmen were out
here, converging on the ship as quickly as possible. I could
see several of them using their meta-thrusters to make low,
bounding leaps across the pressure ridges, their combat-
armor nanoflage making them almost invisible in the dim
light. In the distance, the snaky silhouette of a cuttlewhale
weaved against the swollen red face of the sun.

"Perimeter defense!" Hancock called. "Dalton! Set up
your weapon to put fire on that thing!"

We spread out, creating a broad circle around the
grounded *Haldane*. Visibility sucked. The wind from the
west had picked up, and we were staring into a layer of blowing ice crystals and freezing fog perhaps two meters deep. I
dropped to the ice alongside Bob Dalton, helping him unship
his M4-A2 plasma weapon. I was wondering, though, who
we were fighting—the cuttlewhales or the Gykrs. The mission on GJ 1314 I's icy surface had just become *very* complicated.

I got my answer in the next couple of moments, when a
chunk of ice a hundred meters off to my left erupted in a
flash and a plume of steam, followed by a rain of fist-sized
chunks of ice. A second explosion rocked us, closer. That
was portable artillery, not native life forms, and they were
looking for our range.

"Combat Command, Marine Red-One!" Hancock's
voice called. "We have incoming HP at coordinates . . ."

Hancock rattled off a string of alphanumerics, locating
the explosions even as a third blast slammed into the ice
somewhere behind us.

"Copy Red-One," came the reply from *Haldane*. "We are
tracking."

A fourth explosion cracked in the sky. It had taken *Haldane* a moment to set up her radar net, but now they had
it up and running and were tracking any round coming in
toward the ship or our perimeter. *Haldane*'s dorsal laser

turret began methodically swatting the incoming out of the cloud-wracked purple sky.

Thunder boomed, and our two A/S-40 Star Raiders flashed low overhead with a sound like tearing cloth. They were in their atmospheric flight configuration, blunt-nosed deltas with drooping wingtips, and they were being vectored in by the combat command center on board *Haldane*. A moment later, a savage blast beyond a jagged line of pressure ridges to the south lit up the sky, and we felt the shock wave slam at our armor through the ice. Several Marines cheered.

But we had another problem close on the heels of the first. The last of the Marines left out on the ice were crossing our perimeter now, emerging from the ground fog like racing ghosts . . . and very close behind came a scattering of hunchbacked, massive shapes, a dozen Gykrs in dark gray combat armor. Dalton twisted around with his weapon, snapping off a rapid-fire string of plasma bolts that tore through one of the armored Guckers and shredded the upper half in molten gobbets. The Gykrs carried long and complicated-looking weapons, like two-meter lances with rods and serrations that might have been purely decorative or ceremonial . . . but which were a lot more likely to be part of what made them deadly. There was a swift, brutal exchange at point-blank range fifty meters from my position; the Guckers appeared to be coming up out of the ice, materializing from the fog; how the hell were they doing that?

Twenty meters short of the Marine perimeter, one of our people staggered and went down. "Marine down! Corpsman . . . !"

But I was already moving. My in-head marked the fallen Marine even though I couldn't see him in the murk. "Cover me, Bob!" I shouted at Dalton, and I kicked in my M287 and sailed across the intervening distance in a long, flat trajectory. I landed short, but scrambled the last few meters on hands and knees, keenly aware of energy bolts hissing and cracking through the air around me. The Marines were

using infrared for targeting, and I hoped my armor's IFF—
Identification Friend or Foe—was working as advertised.

It was Lance Corporal Enrique Gonzalez. Whatever had
hit him had taken off his right arm at the shoulder, and he
was writhing about on the ice in agony, his severed arm still
encased in white armor a couple of meters away.

"Easy, buddy," I told him. You're gonna be okay!"

His armor had operated as programmed, sealing off his
shoulder joint and the bleeding with a guillotine blade that
kept him from losing atmosphere. It had also automatically
fired a jolt of nananodynes into his carotid artery; the nanobots were already starting to shut down the pain receptors
both in his shoulder and in his brain, and his twisting strug-
gles grew less exaggerated as the pain receded.

"I'm hit, Doc! I'm *hit*!"

I heard the panic in his voice. With the pain turning
off, a lot of his reaction would be due simply to the shock
and fear of having seen his arm torn off. I jacked into his
armor and coded for more nananodynes . . . and added a
sedative effect.

"*Doc! Watch it!*"

That was Dalton's voice, from fifty meters behind me.
I looked up and saw the hulking mass of a Gykr, its armor
shifting from a mottled off-white to gray as it rose from the
ice. It was bringing its lance-weapon around to aim at the
two of us. . . .

I rolled over onto Gonzalez's body, grabbing him with one
arm as I brought my M30 carbine off my shoulder with the
other. I triggered the weapon one-handed, trying to aim for
that vulnerable patch on the front-underside. I don't know if I
hit it or not; as soon as I'd dropped out of the way, Dalton was
able to trigger a burst from his plasma weapon, and the Gykr
exploded three meters in front of me. The Guckers might not
have had blood like we do, but the effect of cupric hemolymph
splattering across the ice was remarkably similar, in shades of
blue-green instead of scarlet. I rolled off of Gonzalez, picked

him up in a fireman's carry, and started moving toward the Marine perimeter.

I left his right arm on the ice. If he made it back to an OR, he'd be able to grow a new one.

I had to engage my suit's power-assist to manage that carry. Gonzalez plus his combat armor massed about 120 kilos, though in the weaker gravity of Abyssworld he only *weighed* about 109. That was still a considerable load, too much for just me by myself. Fortunately, Mk. 10 armor could serve as a powered exoskeletal unit, giving the wearer superhuman strength—strength enough, at least, to hoist Gonzalez across my shoulders and stagger unsteadily toward the Marine lines. A couple of Marines ran out to meet me as I approached, and helped carry Gonzalez the last few meters. "Get him aboard the ship!" I yelled, releasing my load. There wasn't a lot more we could do for him, save get him out of the armor and get him stable. His blood pressure had dropped in the last few moments, a sign he was going into shock. I instructed some of the nanobots in his brain to handle that, then turned back to the perimeter.

The Gykr attack appeared to have broken off. A number of smoking bodies lay scattered across the ice. I didn't know if we'd gotten them all, or if survivors had retreated; hell, I didn't know if Gykrs *could* retreat, the way their brain wiring worked. It was possible that they were like soldier termites or ants, that they would just keep coming, keep attacking until a threat was neutralized.

Or maybe . . .

From the frying pan to the fire. Off to the west, a couple of cuttlewhales were making their ponderous way across the ice.

The wind-whipped fog was thicker off toward the horizon, so we *heard* them before we saw them . . . a steady, grinding crack and pop as those incredibly massive bodies ground their way over shattering ice. A dark blur slowly resolved into an enormous, sinuous body. As it grew closer, its head lifted above the ice, questing, the weaving tentacles surrounding that maw giving it a top-heavy, shaggy look in silhouette. It was so ponderously massive, it was hard to imagine how it could possibly move over solid ice . . . how it could possibly rear its questing head that far into the air.

An age or two ago, on a vacation visit to the newly minted glaciers of Vancouver, I had seen elephant seals, bloated and nearly immobile on the beach. Those beasts had seemed barely able to move, and yet the cuttlewhales, millions of times heavier, forged ahead faster than a man could walk. Their physiological structure must have been awesomely strong. . . .

"Hold your fire!" Hancock told us. "We're supposed to *talk* with these critters. . . ."

He didn't sound very sure of himself. The nearest cuttlewhale was still a couple of hundred meters away, but it was rearing off the ice to the height of a three-story building. The mouth of the thing reminded me of a terrestrial lamprey—circular, lined with gray-silver teeth. It was puckered at first . . . almost closed, but then the opening dilated, rolling back on itself to reveal a cavern almost as wide as the entire creature, lined with blades. Six stalked eyes surrounded the head, moving independently of one another; between each pair of eye stalks was a slender, in-curving blade or tusk longer than any of the teeth.

Could this monster possibly be intelligent? One of the basic rules of xenobiology is that intelligence requires manipulatory organs of some sort—articulated claws or tentacles or hands with fingers . . . something with which to grasp and hold and interact with its environment. Those six, curving tusks *might* fit the bill . . . I could all too vividly imagine the beast plucking a Marine from the perimeter like massive chopsticks picking up a single grain of rice, but they didn't appear able to manipulate small objects, other than, possibly, to swallow them.

And *still* the beast crawled closer with vast, sinuous

weavings of a seemingly endless body, becoming more and more clear and sharp as it emerged from the wind-blown fog and frozen sea spray. Something moved in front of it . . . a Gykr suddenly flushed from hiding. That massive, shaggy head ducked suddenly, with surprising speed, snatching up the fleeing Gykr with astonishing precision and dexterity between twenty-meter tusks.

I didn't see what happened to the alien. I think my eyes were squeezed shut. They opened when the cuttlewhale's head fell forward and dropped into the ice.

It was coming straight toward us . . . with a second just emerging from the fog in the distance.

"Marines!" That was Lieutenant Lyssa Kemmerer, back in *Haldane*'s Combat Command Center. "Commence fire! I say again . . . commence fire!"

Clearly, both we and the ship were in danger. Laser and plasma-gun fire opened up along the Marine line, and *Haldane* joined in with her turreted lasers. I hesitated. A laser carbine against *that*?

Then I steadied down, brought my weapon to my shoulder, and opened fire. I don't know that I did any damage to the enormous thing at all, but the full weight of a Marine combat platoon seemed to be getting through to the beast. The Star Raiders flashed overhead as well, and a bright flash against the creature's body seemed to spray a cloud of chunks and steaming liquid off to the side.

The cuttlewhale jerked and writhed at that onslaught, its advance halted for the moment. "Cease fire! Cease fire!" Kemmerer ordered. I saw what she was doing: initiating a conversation that basically ran something like, "Halt, or we keep hurting you!"

The cuttlewhale began moving forward once more, slower now.

"Commence fire! Commence fire!"

Again chunks were blasted from the hide of the beast, and I wondered how thick the hide was, how heavily armored it might be. Something that big might have an integument—a skin—so thick that even the ship's lasers would have trouble drilling through it.

But a lot of the damage caused by both lasers and plasma weapons is generated by thermal shock. My helmet's infra-red scanners were showing the monster to be about the same temperature as the air outside—just below zero centigrade. When a laser bolt hit the monster's skin, the sudden spike in local temperature was enough to cause a fair-sized ex-plosion, especially if that skin contained a fair amount of moisture.

Damn . . . what was the cuttlewhale *made* of?

"Everyone fall back to the ship," Kemmerer's voice or-dered. "We'll cover you . . ."

Made sense. As near as I could see, our weapons weren't making a dent in the monsters. Only the turret weapons on *Haldane* and the two Star Raiders were hurting it at all. De-spite the fire, the nearest beast continued advancing, sliding now slowly across broken and uneven ice, its titanic body slowly undulating, the hissing roar and crackling thunder of its approach growing louder.

How the hell were they able to move? One of those mon-sters must have weighed as much as a small mountain. . . .

We started moving back toward the ship, now lost in the ground fog somewhere in *that* direction. There was nothing more we could do out here. The mission, so far as I could tell, was a shambles now. No sign of the research station . . . and if we were communicating with the cuttlewhales, I didn't much like the direction in which the conversation was going.

The ground—the ice—was shaking. I felt a shock through my boots, and a tremor so violent I nearly fell. Ice was buckling and cracking off to my left. A third cuttle-whale was breaking through from underneath. Ice shattered and sprayed into the sky . . . and a gray-white wall rose pre-cipitously just thirty meters away, the shaggy head weaving uncertainly far above our heads.

The wall began falling toward us. . . .

"Move . . . *move*!" I screamed. I triggered my jumpjet and catapulted through hurtling chips of ice as the wall fell, meters behind me. Visibility was zilch. Had everyone made it clear? I couldn't tell.

"Corpsman!"

Shit! Where was he? I superimposed tactical data over my normal vision, trying to see through the nearly opaque, wind-whipped murk around me. *There . . . !*

Dalton was down, his leg pinned under an overturned block of ice. I dropped in next to him, trying to lever the ice off of him, but it wouldn't budge. That block must have weighed half a ton.

His plasma weapon was lying next to him. I snatched it up, cleared it, then opened fire at point-blank range, slamming bolts of ionized plasma into the upper half of the boulder.

Thermal shock. The explosion knocked me back a step. What was left of the boulder I could probably move . . . but as I reached for it, movement tugged at my awareness. An *eye* . . . shiny black, stalked, and a couple of meters across, was coming at me out of the fog. Behind it and stretching far above it, tentacles writhed . . . and an obscenely puckered mouth peeled itself open. The side of the thing was wet and . . . and shifting, almost as though it were unraveling . . . melting . . . coming apart . . . what *was* that stuff?

I shouldered Dalton's plasma weapon and mashed down on the trigger, firing at the eye . . . at the mouth . . . at the looming cliff of a head covered in snaking, twisting tendrils. More thermal shock, and chunks of broken monster sprayed us both.

But the head reared back and up off the ice, vanishing into fog. I dropped the weapon, grabbed Dalton's suit two-handed, and triggered my jumpjets. The load was too much for a clear flight, but it kicked us hard across the ice. I took a second to pull up an electronic overlay marking the ship, corrected my vector, and jumped—or half-jumped—again, an ungainly leap that dropped both of us back to the ice in a tumble. Thunder boomed behind me . . . all around me . . . and as the fog ahead cleared I could see the *Haldane* already hovering just above the ice ten meters away, its ramp still down, as a couple of Marines at the entryway waved me on.

The wind from dayside shrieked around me, the blowing snow threatening to shut down my vision again.

"*Doc!*" Someone yelled. "*Move your fucking ass!*"

Another Marine—it was Hancock—landed next to me, grabbed hold of Dalton's harness, and the two of us dragged him the rest of the way to the ship. I looked back over my shoulder in time to see that yawning, tooth-and-tendril-lined maw gaping as it loomed above us.

The Star Raiders shrieked low overhead, and a blast caught all of us as we struggled in the open. I staggered, then fell off the ramp to the ice a meter below.

"*Doc . . . !*"

"I'm okay!" I shouted back. Standing, I looked around the cuttlewhale. Much of the head had been torn open by particle beams from the Raiders, and chunks of pale pink-gray flesh lay steaming in a huge splash out from the body.

Had we killed it? The body was still twitching spasmodically, a vast and ragged cliff stretching twenty meters up into the sky. The surface looked . . . odd. Fuzzy . . . almost *fluffy*, and like it was melting.

"Doc! Get your ass back on board!"

"Hold on a sec!" I wanted a sample. A piece of cuttlewhale half a meter wide lay nearby. Stooping, I hoisted it up in front of me and lugged it back toward *Haldane*'s ramp. The thing was *heavy*, a good fifty kilos at least, and I was glad my armor had that exoskeleton capability. I wouldn't have been able to stagger back onto the ship otherwise.

"What the fuck, Doc?" Hancock said, his voice acid. "Out getting your last-minute shopping done?"

"Collecting specimens, Gunny. *Know your enemy.*"

I was still struggling up the ramp as the *Haldane* lifted higher, clearing the ice.

One of the other monsters reached for us, neck stretching impossibly high.

It missed. Its body stretched upright—I couldn't see its tail—and then it began to sink, falling back to the ice, which was obscured by the wind-lashed ground fog.

Spray burst up through the fog. I realized that I could no longer see any of the cuttlewhales. Had they broken back through the ice, and into the ocean beneath?

We were accelerating . . . boosting back to orbit. The two Star Raiders followed us up, pulling victory rolls as they boosted. They would dock with us in orbit.

And the rest of us would consider the failure of the mission . . . and what we could do about it.

Chapter Fifteen

HALDANE FELL INTO ORBIT AROUND THE PLANET. I DROPPED MY UN-gainly specimen into a sealer unit in the main airlock, then got some Marine help and a quantum spin-floater to haul it up to the lab. I followed as soon as I got out of my armor.

I quite literally wanted to know what a cuttlewhale was made of.

Two hours later, we remained on red alert. All of us were all too aware that the Gykr ship we'd spooked on our arrival might be back at any moment . . . and likely with friends. We thought that Guck technology was pretty close to ours, but technological development between two space-faring species is never identical and is never parallel. They had picked up tricks we didn't know. It worked the other way around, too, of course, but right now we were worried about what they could do that we couldn't. A very small difference in faster-than-light drives might mean that they could jump a thousand parsecs in a few hours, while we'd taken a leisurely couple of weeks to make it across forty-two light years.

In other words, we knew the Gykr would be back. We just didn't know *when* . . . or how many of them there would be when they arrived.

Walthers had called for an after-action debrief on *Haldane*'s mess deck, which had been transformed into an ad hoc briefing room. There were twelve of us physically present, including the ship's department heads and the four most senior Marines—Lieutenant Kemmerer and Second Lieutenant Tom Regan, plus Gunny Hancock and Staff Sergeant Thomason. I was there representing the science/technical department as well as the medical department. Both Ortega and Montgomery were present, as mission specialists.

There were electronic presences as well. Chief Garner was linked in from sick bay, as department head, and both Machine McKean and Doob were there electronically. So were our three nonhuman passengers, the Broc family, D'dnah, D'drevah, and D'deen. Brocs like things a bit on the chilly side, compared to humans. A pleasant twenty degrees is sweltering to them. Our three tended to stay to themselves, in a compartment on board *Haldane* that could be kept at a comfortable zero to ten Celsius.

The discussion had been going on for several minutes, and so far the consensus appeared to be that we should declare defeat and go home.

"Why do we even need to stay here?" Lieutenant Walthers asked with a shrug. He was the ship's skipper now, with Summerlee still recovering in sick bay, and I think the safety of both ship and crew was weighing on him heavily. "We've confirmed that Murdock Base is gone. And those . . . those *things* down there are going to make it damned hard for us to look around."

Lieutenant Kemmerer agreed. "Between the Gykr and the cuttlewhales, we've had three Marines killed," she said. "A Corpsman may not recover, and Sergeant Dalton has a broken leg. There's a Gykr submersible still loose in the ocean, and there may still be Gykr stragglers on the surface. We need a bigger force to deal with the threat."

"But we *can't* go back!" Dr. Ortega sounded shocked. "Not yet!"

"You can't believe we actually have a chance of communicating with the goddamn cuttlewhales, do you?" Walthers asked.

"Maybe not the cuttlewhales," Dr. Montgomery said. "But there's Sierra Five to consider."

Before the cuttlewhales had made their precipitous appearance, the Marines on the surface, along with McKean and Dubois, had drilled through the ice in three places and dropped in SNR-12 units—remote autonomous sonar transponders intended to paint us a picture of what was going on beneath the ice. The results had been . . . surprising.

The three-dimensional image was projected on a mess deck viewall—an empty blue abyss with several targets showing as bright white points of light. One—identified as Sierra One, for the first sonar contact—was a hard, bright target nearly two hundred meters down and twelve kilometers away from the transponders. Three more, Sierras Two through Four, looked softer—fuzzier around the edges. They were deeper, much, much longer than they were wide, like thread-slender worms, and were almost certainly the three cuttlewhales that had attacked us on the surface.

Sierra Five was a hard target, almost directly below the transponder positions, but it was deep . . . *very* deep. Exact triangulation was something of a problem, since the three transponders were relatively close to one another and didn't provide much in the way of a baseline, but the best estimate suggested that the target was something like a thousand kilometers almost straight down.

Not meters down. *Kilometers*.

The water pressure at that depth would be . . . horrific. A hundred times the depth of the Challenger Deep on Earth, or more, something like a hundred thousand atmospheres. Even at that, a thousand kilometers is still only about 10 percent of the distance from Abyssworld's icecap to the ocean floor.

The range was too great to tell what we were looking at, but it was pretty large . . . as large, perhaps, as the *Haldane*.

"We need to consider the possibility," Montgomery went on, "that Sierra Five is an artificial structure of some sort.

If it's artificial, then it was manufactured by intelligence. It might well be an intelligence native to Abyssworld."

"And it might also be a submerged Gykr ship," Walthers pointed out. "Or just another very big native life form, like the cuttlewhales. It might even be another cuttlewhale, though I'll admit that the sonar return looks a lot different."

"At that depth," Garner said, "we might expect cuttlewhales to look different. Harder. Firmer. More metallic, even. Carlyle here has something to say about *that*."

"Ah, yes," Ortega said. "Our young hero!"

"What the hell were you thinking, Carlyle?" Kemmerer said. "Running back outside to collect a piece of that thing."

"I wasn't exactly *thinking*," I said, and when several of the others at the table laughed, I shook my head and kept talking. "I mean . . . I fell off the ramp, okay? And a piece of a cuttlewhale was right there. I just saw an opportunity—"

"Carlyle's actions may help us actually make sense of the biology on this planet," Garner said. "I've seen the results. This is important."

"So what did you learn?" Montgomery wanted to know. "You analyzed that piece of flesh?"

"Yes, ma'am," I said. "I'm not sure we can call it *flesh*, though. . . ."

"What is it, then?" Kemmerer demanded.

"Ice," I told them. When that single word elicited a confused babble of voices and protests, I added, "Specifically, Ice Seven."

The sample I'd collected had been taken to the lab, where it had gone into the bio-secure compartment for Bob to do remote analyses on it. Since we didn't know what might be in that chunk of cuttlewhale I'd brought back, I'd coated it with sealant in the *Haldane*'s airlock to avoid exposing the crew to any possible microorganisms, opening it up again only when it was safely inside the secure biological containment compartment in the lab. Through Bob, I'd run a standard spectrographic analysis first . . . then done a chem series. The whole process had taken me perhaps twenty minutes.

"What the devil," Second Lieutenant Regan said, "is Ice Seven?"

"It is, sir, a very, very special kind of water ice. . . ."

Dr. Montgomery nodded. "That would explain a lot."

"It's created under extremely high pressure," I went on. "Here, I pulled this down off the *Haldane*'s Net." I showed them the chart I'd been studying before the meeting.

We're all familiar with ordinary ice, of course . . . water that freezes at zero degrees Celsius, becoming a solid. But it turns out that, depending on the temperature and on the pressure, water can freeze in a great many different ways— fifteen that we know of for sure, plus several variants, and there are almost certainly others.

Ordinary ice, which forms as hexagonal crystals, is known in exotic chemistry as Ice I_h. All the ice found within Earth's biosphere is Ice I_h, with the exception of a small amount in the upper atmosphere that occurs as a cubic crystal called Ice I_c.

But compress Ice I_h at temperatures of sixty to eighty degrees below zero and it forms a rhombohedral crystal with a tightly ordered structure known as Ice II. Heat Ice II to minus twenty-three degrees . . . or cool water to that temperature at something just over thirty atmospheres, and it becomes Ice III.

And so it goes, running up the list of exotic ices all the way to Ice XV, which forms at pressures of over 10,000 atmospheres and at temperatures of around 100 degrees Kelvin—or minus 173 degrees Celsius.

Still with me?

On Earth, the deepest point in the ocean is in the Marianas Trench, the Challenger Deep, which reaches 11 kilometers down and has a pressure of 1,100 atmospheres . . . which translates to just over one ton per square centimeter. We wouldn't hit 10,000 atmospheres until we were ten times deeper—an impossible 100 to 110 kilometers down, assuming there was a terrestrial ocean that deep.

Using the download, I gave the assembled personnel a quick overview of exotic ice chemistry. I'm not an expert, by any means, but I was drawing on research downloads from the sick bay AI, which pretty much covered the basics. I had to explain to the non-technical people present that temperatures were given in degrees Kelvin, meaning degrees Celsius above absolute zero, with 273°K marking the freezing point of water. Pressure was given in pascals, or in millions of pascals—MPa—or in billions of pascals—GPa. One atmosphere of pressure was equal to 101,325 pascals.

Download
Chemical Breakdown of Exotic Ices

Ice I$_h$: Normal crystalline ice, formed in hexagonal crystals. Formed from water at normal pressures cooled to 273°K [0°C.] Nearly all ice within Earth's biosphere is I$_h$.

Ice I$_c$: Metastable variant of I$_h$ with a cubic crystalline structure, and its oxygen atoms arranged in a diamond pattern. Produced at temperatures between 130° and 220°K, but is stable up to 240°K. It is sometimes found in Earth's upper atmosphere.

Amorphous ice: Ordinary ice lacking a crystal structure. Formed in low-, high-, and very-high-density variants, depending on pressure and temperature. Commonly found on comets, outer-planet moons, or elsewhere in space.

Ice II: Formed from ice I$_h$ when it undergoes pressure at 190° to 210°K. Rhombohedral crystalline structure.

Ice III: Formed from Ice II when heated, or by cooling water to 250°K at a pressure of 300 MPa [very approximately, 3,000 standard atmospheres]. Tetragonal crystalline structure. Denser than water, but the least dense of all high-pressure ice phases.

Ice IV: Metastable rhombohedral crystalline phase, formed by heating high-density amorphous ice at a pressure of 810 MPa [8,100 atm].

Ice V: Most complex of all exotic ice phases, with a monoclinic crystalline structure, formed by cooling water to 253°K at 500 MPa [5,000 atm].

Ice VI: A tetragonal crystalline phase formed by cooling water to 290°K at 500 MPa. Exhibits dielectric changes [Debye relaxation] in the presence of an alternating electrical field.

Ice VII: Cubic crystalline structure with disordered hydrogen atoms, exhibiting Debye relaxation.

Ice VIII: A more ordered cubic crystalline form with fixed hydrogen atoms, formed by cooling Ice VII to temperatures below 278°K

Ice IX: A tetragonal crystalline phase formed by cooling Ice III to temperatures between 208°K and 165°K. Remains stable at temperatures below 140°K and at pressures between 200 MPa and 400 MPa [2,000 to 4,000 atm].

Ice X: Highly symmetrical ice with ordered protons, formed at 70 GPa [700,000 atm].

Ice XI: A low-temperature form of hexagonal ice, formed at 240°K and with an orthorhombic structure, sometimes considered to be the most stable form of ice I_h. It forms very slowly, and has been found within Antarctic ice up to 10,000 years old.

Ice XII: Dense, metastable, tetragonal crystalline phase formed by heating high-density amorphous ice to temperatures between 77°K and 183°K at 810 MPa.

Ice XIII: A proton-ordered form of monoclinic crystalline ice V, formed by cooling water to temperatures below 130°K at 500 MPa.

Ice XIV: The proton-ordered form of ice XII, formed

below 118°K at 1.2 GPa [120,000 atm], with an orthorhombic crystalline structure.

Ice XV: The proton-ordered form of ice VI, formed by
cooling water to temperatures between 80°K and
108°K at a pressure of 1.1 GPa [110,000 atm].

"'Hexagonal crystals,' I think I understand," Ortega said
with grim humor. "Some of this is pretty thick. But 'proton-
ordered'?"

"Let's just say that ice comes in a lot of different forms,"
I said, "and those forms can have different chemical, electrical, and even nuclear effects. Here, maybe you should just
see the biostats I got in the lab."

I pulled the worksheet down from the lab AI and spread
it out for their in-head inspection. "This," I told them, "is the
biochemistry of a cuttlewhale."

I then proceeded to explain . . . and hoped to hell that I
wasn't making their eyes glaze over. I was afraid I'd already
done that with the exotic ice table.

It turns out that some exotic ices are pretty weird, and
appear only under extreme conditions. Ice IX, for instance,
forms at pressures of around 3,000 atmospheres and temperatures around 165 degrees Kelvin. Ice X doesn't form
until pressures hit 700,000 atmospheres. We're not certain, but we think that at pressures of around one and a
half terapascals—that's almost 15 million atmospheres, or
more than 15,500 tons per square centimeter—water actually becomes a metal. We've never worked with that kind
of pressure directly. Even at the core of the Earth, pressures
are estimated to reach "only" 3.5 million atmospheres; Jupiter's core may hit around seven terapascals—or 70 million
atmospheres—enough to create metallic hydrogen.

But what we had in the lab was a sample of Ice VII, and
compared to some of the exotic ices we knew, it was pretty
tame. The stuff forms at about a thousand atmospheres, and
at surprisingly high temperatures—around minus 3 degrees

Centigrade. Odd things happen to the water's hydrogen molecules at that pressure, and the hydrogen bonds actually form interpenetrating lattices. That means there are unusual electrical effects in the material, though we don't understand yet what those might be.

"Electrical effects?" *Haldane*'s chief engineering officer, Lieutenant Mikao Ishihara, sounded skeptical. "What electrical effects?"

"I don't know," I admitted. "I'm not an electrical engineer . . . and so far as I could find through *Haldane*'s databases, we haven't studied natural electricity in exotic ice at all. It's an entirely new field.

"But there's more," I went on. "That ice sample I collected is not pure. Take a closer look at the biostat imagery." I showed them photomicrographs of the ice . . . backlit white sheets through which darker chains and blobs appeared. A lot of it was diffuse, almost not there at all, like wisps of gray smoke caught frozen in solid ice.

"You can see here . . . and here. That spectrographic analysis I ran picked up substantial amounts of sulfur, iron, copper, carbon, potassium, manganese . . . a whole soup of elements strung through the ice matrix almost like . . . nerves? Blood vessels?"

"Speculation, Mr. Carlyle," Chief Garner's voice said over the conference link. "We don't *know* . . ."

"No, Chief, I don't. But it's highly suggestive."

"But what you haven't explained," Walthers said, "is how a creature made of ice could be that . . . that flexible. Those things were like giant snakes! Ice would shatter if it moved like that!"

"Not necessarily," I said. "I wondered about that too . . . but it turns out that there are different ways that ice can freeze, quite apart from the fifteen different forms of exotic ice we've been talking about. The variants are called *amorphous ice*. The ice we're familiar with on Earth has a rigid, crystalline structure, but that's actually rare out in space. In places like comets or in the subsurface ice of places like Europa or Pluto—throughout the universe, in fact—amorphous ice is the rule.

"There are different types of amorphous ice. They generally require low temperatures with very sudden freezing, like ice cream. If you freeze ice cream too slowly, you get conventional ice crystals. Pressure is also important.

"One type of amorphous ice—it's called LDA, for low-density amorphous—has a melting point of around one hundred twenty or one hundred forty degrees Kelvin—that's around minus one hundred fifty Celsius. Above that temperature, it's actually an extremely viscous form of water. You might get that effect by manipulating the pressure in various ways too. A sudden lowering of pressure will cause sudden cooling, for instance."

"Actually, that problem is trivial," Ortega said. "You don't need LDAs. We've had pumpable ice technology for centuries, now, with tiny ice particles suspended as a slurry in brine or refrigerants. The ice flows like jelly."

"A gigantic worm made of ice," Montgomery said, staring off into space. "With viscous-water-jelly muscles . . ."

"Maybe," I said. "This is all still guesswork. But there's also *this*. . . ."

I showed them more test results, these from samples of strands running through the Ice VII that also appeared to be water ice . . . but they were different.

"These structures appear to be a different type of exotic ice," I told them. "Specifically, Ice XI, running everywhere through the main body of the sample. We've found Ice XI on Earth—inside the Antarctic ice sheet. It's actually a stable form of Ice I_h, with an orthorhombic structure and—here's the important part—it's ferroelectric."

That meant that the polarization of its atoms could be reversed by an external electrical field, that it could actually store electricity like a natural capacitor, and that it could carry an electrical current.

You could actually use such a system to store electronic data.

"We used to use ferroelectric RAM in some computers on Earth, and for memory in RFID chips," Chief Garner pointed out. "It's old tech, but it works. You can also use ferroelectric effects in memory materials—in a matrix that has one shape when an electrical current is running through it, and a different shape when the current is switched off."

I nodded. "I think that the cuttlewhales are gigantic electrical motors, using organic electricity to generate movement in their analog of musculature. I think they have a kind of built-in computer RAM, probably billions upon billions of bytes of it, probably distributed throughout their bodies. And I have the distinct feeling that a cuttlewhale isn't so much a life form as it is a . . . a *machine*. Something created by, *manufactured* by . . . something else."

Consternation broke out around the table, and in the in-head connection as well. "Wait a second, Carlyle," Walthers said. "You're saying the cuttlewhales are *machines*?"

"Robots!" Hancock said. "They're fucking *robots*!"

"Something like that," I admitted. I held up a cautioning hand. "Look, I'm not saying they're *not* the product of natural evolution. They may well be. But we shouldn't discount the possibility that somebody else designed and assembled them. It would be *very* hard to explain how various ices could come together by chance in a way that worked so elegantly . . . complete with distributed natural data processing based on old AI models."

"Be careful, Mr. Carlyle," Ortega told me. "That's the argument used by the so-called Creationists of a few hundred years ago . . . that life on Earth was too complex to have been brought about by accidental, natural processes. Given enough time, natural processes can manufacture some *wonderful* things."

"Of course, sir," I said. "But . . . there's something else you all should consider."

"What's that?"

"Sunlight, sir. On Earth, it only penetrates about one hundred fifty meters into the ocean. Actually, most light goes no deeper than the top ten meters . . . but by the time you reach one hundred fifty meters, it's completely dark. Here, with the red sunlight, it's probably less . . . and under the ice, on the nightside of the planet . . . well, there's no light entering the ocean at all."

"So?" Walthers demanded. "What are you getting at?"

"*Eyes*," I replied. "The cuttlewhales have *eyes*. Six of them. If they evolved far enough down that they developed under high pressures, why do they have *eyes*?"

"Those might not be eyes," Ortega said, but he sounded unsure. "I wish you could have picked one of them up and brought it along. We might know more. . . ."

"Sorry, sir, but I wasn't going to wait around out there on the ice any longer than I absolutely had to. But . . . I wonder. If the cuttlewhales were designed, if they were manufactured somehow by another intelligence . . . maybe they were given eyes in order to explore the surface remotely."

"Huh," Garner said. "Like our remote probes."

"That is an enormous leap, Carlyle," Walthers said. "Kind of a leap of faith, isn't it?"

"I suppose so, sir. But it's something to think about."

"Over a long-enough period of time," Ortega said, thoughtful, "a deep-benthic life form might move to the surface and evolve vision . . . then migrate back to the depths. . . ."

I shrugged and spread my hands. "Look, all of this is pure speculation at this point. I'm just suggesting that we should keep in mind the *possibility* that the cuttlewhales are . . . artificial. That would certainly have an effect on our mission, wouldn't it?"

"To say the least," Montgomery said. She still looked like she was in shock. "Just where would they have evolved in Abyssworld's ocean? Or . . . where would they have been created, if that's the right term? How far down?"

I shook my head. I had numbers, but no proof, nothing solid. "Well, you need a water pressure of around a thousand atmospheres to turn ordinary water into Ice VII. That's not too extreme, as exotic ices go. You find that at a depth of ten thousand meters on Earth . . . or about eleven thousand meters on Abyssworld. Eleven kilometers down . . ."

"That's only a thousandth of the way to the sea floor," Walthers pointed out.

"My God. What are the pressures like at the bottom of Abyssworld's ocean?" Ortega asked.

"I was wondering about that myself, sir," I replied, "and I did some simple calcs. On Earth, water pressure increases by one atmosphere—that's over a hundred thousand Pascals— for every ten meters you descend. Abyssworld's gravity is only ninety-one percent of Earth's, and there's a direct one-to-one correlation between the weight of the water and the pressure it exerts, so call it nine hundred ten thousand atmospheres.

"That's a skull-crushing thousand *tons* or so pressing down on every square centimeter."

"What happens to water ice at that depth?" Garner asked.

"I don't know," I said. "Nobody does. One possibility is that the bottom of Abyssworld's ocean—maybe even the bottom three or four or five thousand kilometers of it—isn't liquid water anymore. It might be a highly compressed slurry or ice-slush composed of several exotic ices, kind of like the jelly Dr. Ortega mentioned. Heat from the planet's core might create convection currents, so it would be constantly circulating. It certainly would be a very strange environment. We don't know enough, though, to know *how* strange."

"What kind of life might we find down *there*?" Montgomery asked.

It was a rhetorical question, I knew, but I couldn't resist answering. I'd been wondering a lot about the same thing.

"Just about anything is possible, ma'am," I told her. "With heat from the planet's core, with water and various nutrients, salts, metals, stuff like that from sea-floor vents, there's no telling what might have evolved down there."

For the first time in our discussion, one of the Brocs chimed in, its words written out by the ship's AI within our in-heads. IT IS VITAL THAT YOU REMEMBER, D'drevah wrote, THAT MOST LIFE IN THE UNIVERSE LIVES IN PLACES LIKE ABYSSWORLD'S DEPTHS, AND NOT NAKEDLY EXPOSED ON THE ROCKY SURFACES OF PLANETS LIKE M'GAT OR EARTH.

I thought again about the Medusae of Europa.

"Okay," Walthers said. "That's all well and good, but I don't see how it will affect us. We don't have the technology to explore such depths."

"We might be able to probe those depths with sonar," Montgomery suggested.

"I submit, madam," Garner's voice replied, "that it was sonar that attracted the cuttlewhales in the first place. They appeared almost immediately after the Marines began using high-power, low-frequency sonar through the ice. It's possible that Murdock Base was destroyed when they tried the same thing. Perhaps we should leave well enough alone."

"I have a question," Ortega said. "If the cuttlewhales were formed at a pressure of a thousand atmospheres, why don't they explode on the surface? You know, like deep-sea fish brought up from extreme depths?"

"Actually, sir, the ones we encountered on the surface were beginning to degrade," I told him. "I don't think they can survive very long at surface temperatures and pressures. But those fish you mention explode because gas in their swim bladders expands as they're brought to the surface— expands a *lot*. I think the cuttlewhales must have some sort of internal mechanism that keeps their internal pressure balanced with what's outside. We know they have a gullet . . . but that might close completely at high pressure. And we don't know what they use for a heart. Not a conventional pump like ours, certainly. They're too big. They may rely on seawater diffusing throughout their bodies."

"Solid-state bodies, then," Ortega mused.

"Essentially, yes."

"Robots," Hancock said.

"At the surface, or in warm temperatures," I went on, "Ice VII starts to . . . *unravel* is the best word I can think of. It requires high pressure to keep the ice crystals in that configuration, with the interpenetrating lattices . . . but when the pressure goes away, it doesn't explode. It just kind of oozes into the new state."

"The question remains," Walthers said, "as to whether any of this helps us at all. Can we even hope to talk to these things? Or to . . . to their manufacturers?"

"A suggestion, sir?"

"Go ahead."

"The cuttlewhales are . . . electrical in nature. So are we, of course, but not in the same way. Humans generate what is essentially weak electrical currents through chemistry— through exchanges of positive or negative ions at neural synapses or in muscle fibers, for instance. That's what we're reading with an EEG or an EKG.

"But cuttlewhales seem to work because of actual electrical currents—moving electrons—throughout their bodies. I don't know how that would work, but the ferroelectric effect of the Ice IX strands would support a fairly high voltage."

"Great," Hancock said. "Not only can they crush us, they can electrocute us! Is that what you're saying?"

"Probably not *that* much voltage, Gunny. But enough to create a pretty strong electrical field in the water. Especially in saltwater. I haven't analyzed it yet, but I suspect that Abyssworld's ocean is pretty salty."

Salts, I thought, would be spewed into that ocean through volcanic vents. The minerals I'd detected inside the cuttle- whale sample—the sulfur and all the rest—proved that there were a *lot* of other elements in the ocean, even though there was so much of it.

"What's your point, Carlyle?" Walthers asked.

"Our most important senses," I replied, "are vision and hearing, okay? Cuttlewhales live in absolute darkness. They probably rely on sound—I like your idea about them being attracted by the sonar pulses, by the way, sir—but they might also rely on the electrical sense."

"Electrical sense?" Walthers asked. "What's that?"

"Some animals on Earth can sense electrical fields," Ortega explained. "Or they can passively sense other animals moving through them. Electric eels can do this, for instance. Sharks and rays. Certain dolphins. Even a funny little animal called the platypus. It's called *electroreception*, and it's as important to those animals as any of our senses are to us."

"If cuttlewhales can detect electrical fields," I added, "maybe that's how they communicate. Not by sound . . . or not entirely, but by modulating electrical signals in the water."

"That," Montgomery said with feeling, "is *brilliant*!"

"I wonder if Selby and his people on Europa have thought of that," Ortega said. He laughed. "You need to write that up in a paper, Carlyle. Publish it in the *Journal of Exobiology*. I think you're onto something big here. . . ."

"Well, we need to detect those signals first," I said. The sudden burst of attention from the two scientists was a bit embarrassing.

"Easy enough to do," Ortega said. "We have a submarine . . . a means of approaching a cuttlewhale in its own environment."

"Dr. Ortega, you have got to be crazy!" Walthers exclaimed. "You saw what they did on the surface. . . ."

"Our entire reason for making this journey," Ortega said, "was threefold. We were to look for Sub-zero survivors, to rescue them if necessary, and we were to attempt communication with any intelligent Abyssworld inhabitants. At this point, I submit, we are still oh for three. Young Carlyle, here, has shown us a means of improving our score."

"It seems unlikely at this point that we will find survivors from the base," Walthers pointed out. "And I have the safety of the ship and passengers to consider."

"Ortega's right," Garner's voice said over the electronic link. "I thought Marines were supposed to *fight* . . . not turn tail and run!"

"I object to that, Chief," Kemmerer said. "We are here to provide security for the operation, not involve ourselves in pointless bloodshed."

" 'Visit exotic, distant worlds,' " Garner said, " 'meet strange, alien life forms . . .' " He laughed, a chilling sound.

Visit exotic, distant worlds, meet strange alien life forms, and kill them. . . .

I decided that the chief's arm was hurting him. It was a joke dating back in a slightly different form to pre-spaceflight days. It did an injustice to the Corps, I thought, maintaining the ancient and vicious fiction that Marines were only interested in killing.

It's true that they are very, very good at killing, certainly. But another ancient adage referring to the Marines holds that while there are no worse enemies, there are no better friends.

"Lieutenant Kemmerer?" Walthers said. "What do you think about returning to the surface? Or trying to contact cuttlewhales?"

She shrugged. "The Marines will go where you send us, *Captain*," she said. She emphasized Walther's position as ship captain, rather than his rank of lieutenant. Until Summerlee returned to duty, *he* was the one with the final say. Not the Marines, not the doctors, and not the science and technical staff.

"D'deen? D'nah?" Walthers called, raising his voice. "You are the closest we have to xenosapient experts on board. What's your opinion?"

THE GYKR ARE A ROGUE INTELLIGENCE, D'deen wrote, from a rogue world between the stars. THEY DO NOT

FOLLOW . . . YOU WOULD CALL THEM . . . THE RULES. THEY
MAY HAVE THEIR OWN MOTIVES FOR ATTEMPTING CONTACT
WITH THE NATIVE ABYSSAL LIFE. WE SUBMIT THAT YOU
MAY WISH TO ESTABLISH SUCH CONTACT FIRST.

"I'm more concerned about the Gykr as a military force,"
Walthers said slowly, "than I am about talking with the
native life. They *will* be back. The question is when. What
do we do about that?"

"Not really a major problem, sir," Garner said. "If we
land at a different area . . . build a nanomatrix habitat, then
we could keep *Haldane* in orbit. With nanoflage on the outer
surface of the base, the Guckers shouldn't see us if they do
show up . . . and it *is* a damned big planet. If they show
up, *Haldane* could run for Earth, maybe come back with
reinforcements. And we stay on the planet and try to talk to
Carlyle's electric whales."

My electric whales.

But most at the table agreed then, that trying to communicate with the beasts was vitally important. The Gykrs had
turned it into a race.

We would stay.

And we would try to make contact with the locals.

Chapter Sixteen

HALDANE TOUCHED DOWN ONCE AGAIN ON THE ICECAP ABOUT twelve kilometers from the former site of Murdock Base. We used robotic vehicles to unload about forty tons of rawmat onto the ice and spread it out in a thin layer. Rawmat—raw materials for nanotechnic construction—is a balanced mix of basic elements: iron, aluminum, silicon, copper, gold, carbon, tungsten, and a dozen other elements in powder form to give it the greatest possible surface area. The most critical problem was keeping all of that fine-grained powder from being blown away by the blustery winds gusting out of the west. We managed that by mixing the stuff with water as it came out of the robots' hoppers. The water froze and nailed the rawmat down in a thin, black carpet over the ice. Nanobots don't care if their raw materials are loose, or frozen inside solid water.

Once the powders were down, we released a few trillion nanobots programmed for materials construction, beamed them an architectural plan, and in about two hours they'd grown our new base from the component atoms. On Earth, we build four-kilometer-tall towers of spun glasstic or ferrocrete from the carbon, hydrogen, silica, and metals right there in the dirt and rock of the construction site. The only native raw materials here, though, were the oxygen and hydrogen of the water ice, plus some traces of carbon and nitrogen from the CO_2, CH_4, and NH_3 in the atmosphere or trapped within the ice. When the main dome was up, though, we used drilling bots inside to tunnel down through the ice to reach the seawater below, and were able to reach quite a few more elements dissolved in the water.

We began manufacturing the base's interior gas mix then. The oxygen came from the water, of course . . . but the nitrogen was tougher, since the only source we had for N_2 was the ammonia that made up about 3 percent of the planetary atmosphere. We grew the atmosphere processing machinery for that, and seasoned the mix with three hundred parts per million of CO_2. As counter-intuitive as it seems, too little carbon dioxide in the blood—a medical condition called *hypocapnia*—can be as bad as too much.

We continued to wear breathing masks inside the base for a time, however, just to be on the safe side. There was a danger, a small one, that toxins or organic molecules had been mixed in with the surface ice, and we were taking no chances with toxic fumes or anaphylaxis. The base atmospheric regulators would continue to scrub the gas mix until we were sure there was no chance of contamination.

While some of us worked on making the new facility habitable, another team from the *Haldane* melted a hundred-meter-wide hole in the ice outside, extending it to connect with the open water beyond the edge of the icecap. *Haldane* lifted on her spin-floaters and slowly lowered the *Walsh* from her cargo bay and into the dark water. *Walsh*, with her compressed-matter construction, was designed to fly through the water, rather than control her depth with ballast tanks. To keep her from sinking as soon as they dropped her into the water, *Haldane*'s people had rigged her with quantum floaters that were kept running continually, holding the *Walsh* steady at her moorings.

By that time, we were putting the finishing touches on the base—one large dome with four smaller subsidiary domes evenly spaced around the perimeter. After laying down an airlock cylinder extending some distance from the main hab dome, *Haldane* was able to pull up several million liters of water and dump it over the outside of the facility, letting it freeze in uneven masses to disguise the regular and artificial look of the place. A molecule-thin film of specially programmed nanoflage went over that, breaking up the outlines and bending incoming light in order to create the illusion of completely natural pressure ridge.

If the Gykr came by now, they wouldn't be able to see us.

We spent another five hours transferring tons more rawmat off of the *Haldane* and into both the hab modules and the submarine. This was mostly carbon, raw material for the nanufactories on the sub and in the base. Combined with hydrogen, oxygen, nitrogen, and numerous trace elements taken from the sea and atmosphere, this would become our food supply for the next several months. If *Haldane* had to abandon us, we would be on our own for at least a month before she could return with reinforcements.

Quite apart from that, however, it would take time to descend into the depths. Sierra Five was at a depth of around a thousand kilometers. With a maximum descent rate of around ten meters per second, it would take us a bit less than thirty hours to reach Sierra Five. If we wanted to venture into the *real* depths of Abyssworld, though, it was going to take a while—more than twelve days to descend eleven thousand kilometers, and longer to come back up.

The chances were good that we would not be going that deep . . . and the experts weren't even certain that *Walsh* would survive such a dive. But we would need to take plenty of food along just to be on the safe side. Fortunately, air and water were easily enough pulled from the surrounding ocean.

The *Walsh* was large enough to carry seven people—ten or twelve if they were *very* friendly. How many of us would actually be descending into the abyss was yet to be determined.

And that was the purpose of our final meeting on *Haldane*'s mess deck, a few hours before we would be ready to make the descent. Eleven of us were in physical attendance this time, and quite a few more were virtually present, listening in over the ship's computer Net. The three Brocs were on-line . . . and so was Chief Garner, who was still recovering from his burn in sick bay.

"Doc! How is the captain doing?" Walthers asked with no preamble.

"We're bringing her up out of deep sedation," I told him. "That'll take a couple more hours. Aside from that, she's fine . . . but we don't have the medical tech on board *Haldane* to deal with her prosthesis failure."

"You mean we have to get her back to Earth."

I nodded. "We could give her a rough-and-ready implant, the sort of thing we'd do for someone who'd lost all connectivity with a bad accident or something like a severe stroke. But for full function, she'll need to have her implant traced almost molecule by molecule, and a lot of it will have to be dissolved, then rechelated as new circuitry."

That kind of work was incredibly delicate and fussy, not the sort of thing you want to try in the field at all. Fortunately, there was no need. I knew Walthers was uncomfortable being in command, but he could run the ship until we got the captain back home.

He sighed. "Okay. I guess I'm it. What about Kirchner?"

That was a tougher question. Kirchner had been worrying me more than anything else in the department. Before his final break, I'd been doing more private research, trying to plug in psychiatric symptoms. For a while, there, I'd begun wondering about Asperger's disorder, and the AI had been throwing that out as well. I'd doubted that diagnosis, however. Asperger's is part of the autism spectrum, tends to have a gradual onset, and is characterized not only by problems with social interaction but by restricted patterns of interests or behavior as well. And though we don't know yet what causes Asperger's, it appears to be a developmental problem, probably with genetic roots. You're not likely to develop it at 108.

Which had brought me back to schizophrenia. That diagnosis had been looking unlikely as well. He had the problems with social responsiveness and interpersonal dysfunction, but there'd been no sign of the usual disorganized thinking or speech. And we couldn't get inside his head to tell if he was delusional, truly paranoid, or suffering from auditory hallucinations . . . the "voices in the head" so characteristic of the disease. Besides, classic schizophrenia usually begins manifesting before the age of 30, not in old age.

But then he'd gone and pulled a gun, used the gun, and started spewing word salad.

That pretty much confirmed the schizophrenia diagnosis . . . but not completely. Damn it, we were still so *helpless* in the face of psychiatric pathology. Broken legs, epidural hematomas, even a spinal fracture . . . that stuff is child's play compared to figuring out what's gone wrong inside a person's mind.

"The doctor," I said, "is in a tube down in Medical. We'll be keeping him in a deep coma until we can get him back to Earth for proper treatment."

"Yes, but what's wrong with him?"

"Our provisional diagnosis is paranoid schizophrenia . . . but I need to emphasize that that's *provisional*, meaning we're really not sure. His genome shows none of the usual markers predicting that disease, he has no family history or personal record of either schizophrenia or schizoid personality disorder, and those diseases are just not that likely to come out of nowhere."

"Does it make a difference?"

"In his treatment, yes. Of course it does."

"But not in how we care for him until we get him home."

"No, sir."

No, the difference it made had to do with me and my

mind, not Kirchner's. I was still kicking myself for not having picked up on his illness sooner. Dammit, I hated that kind of responsibility . . . having the training to spot something like that and failing to pick up on the clues that were there. The real problem was that diseases—especially mental illness—simply didn't present a one, two, three listing of signs and symptoms. The human body and, even more, the human mind, were incredibly complex, and they steadfastly resisted being shoved into narrow little boxes with labels on them.

And just maybe that's why I wanted to leave the relative safety of the *Haldane* for the uncertain but deadly darkness of Abyssworld's deeps. While I'd be there in case someone got hurt, of course, my real purpose would be as a science technician, taking readings, running the nano programming, and just maybe getting to meet a new intelligence in the deeps.

"So," Walthers said, "we need to make some final decisions on sending the Walsh into the Abyss."

"Why do we need to send *anybody*?" Gunny Hancock demanded of the group. "We have Double-R-Ess twelves. We can teleoperate them from here."

It was a valid point, at least within limits. On Niffelheim-e, I'd helped teleoperate a small submarine into the depths of that ice world's ocean . . . and lived to tell about it when something the size of a city flattened the robot against the underside of the ice. The RRS-12 was a basketball-sized teleoperated submarine—the alphabet soup stood for remote reconnaissance submersible—running on the end of a hair-thin fiber-optic cable.

"Yes," Montgomery said, "we can. But if we have the opportunity to actually meet the whales . . . or whatever is behind them, don't you think we should do it in person?"

"But what's the point?" Chief Garner asked. "I mean . . . seriously. If the person making contact is locked up inside a twenty-meter CM cigar, he's not exactly going to be able to step outside and shake hands or tentacles or whatever, right? Not at those depths."

"There's another issue too," I pointed out. "A practical one. I think the maximum cable length on an RRS is . . . what? Something like fifty kilometers? Beyond that, we wouldn't be able to control them."

Radio signals do not propagate more than a few meters through water before they're absorbed and lost. Blue-green lasers can penetrate perhaps a hundred meters of crystal-clear water before they're lost. Sonar can be used to tele-operate remotes, but it doesn't pack anywhere near the information density of electromagnetic radiation—radio or light. Besides, there was the possibility that the cuttlewhales were angered by our sonar.

Remotes like the one I'd piloted beneath the ice on Niffelheim-e were tethered to their base by fiber-optic cables transmitting laser light, signals carrying electronic commands from the base to the probe, and returning sensory data. They worked quite well . . . but even cables as thin as a human hair were limited in how long they could be grown before they broke under their own weight. Sierra Five was more than a thousand kilometers down, well beyond range of a cable-directed remote.

"He's right," Ortega said. "If we're going to go down there at all, it *has* to be in person."

"We could take along a small fleet of Double-R-esses," Lieutenant Kemmerer suggested. "Remote-operate them from the *Walsh*."

"*If* we can do that without compromising the *Walsh*'s hull integrity," Lieutenant Ishihara observed. "Under tons of pressure per square centimeter, the slightest weakness in the hull would be fatal."

"So how many of us are going?" Lieutenant Kemmerer asked. "The *Walsh* is big enough for eight—maybe ten—-people."

"We could manage fifteen or twenty if we're *very* friendly,"

Montgomery said. "Food, water, and air supplies won't be a concern, since we'll be making our own as we go."

"But do we need that many?" Walthers said. He shook his head. "I'm with Gunny Hancock. I'm still skeptical about this whole idea."

"Right!" Garner's voice said over our in-heads. "Paying a personal visit may be a luxury we can't afford."

"What *luxury*?"

"A suicide mission, of course. How many lives can we afford to throw away?"

"It won't be suicide," Montgomery told him. "And there are way too many opportunities for misunderstanding if we try to make contact long distance."

"Perhaps. But I'm . . . concerned. The *Walsh* is not armed, and we still have a hostile submersible down there someplace . . . plus some very large creatures that have already attacked us."

"*I* am going," Montgomery said, and the tone of her voice blocked any thought of argument. "It's why I came on this godforsaken mission in the first place!"

"Me too," Ortega said. "We're still guessing about conditions more than a few kilometers down. This will be an unprecedented opportunity."

"I would suggest two Marines," Kemmerer said. "Myself and one other, preferably a pilot. Plus a couple of Corpsmen as technical staff."

"Why Marines?" Walthers wanted to know. "They won't be able to shoot, can't threaten the bad guys or scare off the Gucks. Nobody will be able to board the *Walsh* without opening her up, and under those pressures, that would instantly kill everyone on board. In fact, they won't be able to do anything but take up space."

"Point," Kemmerer said. She sounded disappointed.

ONE OF US SHOULD BE THERE, D'deen, one of the M'nangats, printed out in our in-heads. IF THERE IS INDEED ANOTHER INTELLIGENCE BEHIND THE CUTTLEWHALES, IT

LIKELY WOULD BE EXTREMELY ADVANCED. YOU WILL WANT
AN EXPERT ON GALACTIC CULTURE AND LANGUAGE ALONG.

"Just one of you?" Montgomery asked. "Or all three of
you?"

ONE SHOULD BE ENOUGH, AND I ADVANCE MYSELF AS
THE LOGICAL AND EXPENDABLE CHOICE.

That seemed a cold-blooded way to look at the situation.
But then, D'deen, I remembered, was the life donor of the
triad . . . the equivalent of a male in human reproduction. For
millennia in human society it had been the male who risked
his life in warfare, with the idea of protecting women—the
egg bearers and life bearers—back home. It wasn't that different with the Brocs.

"We still need a mission commander," Kemmerer said.
"A military commander."

"Why *military*, for God's sake?" Montgomery said. Her
face wrinkled in what I swear was disgust. "Like Mr. Walthers said, you won't be able to shoot anything down there
. . . or threaten it. This is a civilian research operation. . . ."

"A civilian research operation under the aegis of a
military mission," Kemmerer said firmly, "and one, I will
remind you, facing hostile military forces. We need someone down there capable of making key military judgments
and command decisions."

"*Jesus!*" Garner exclaimed over the link. "What the fuck
will it matter?"

"Chief Garner is right," Walthers said. "You won't be
able to give orders to the Marines from up here. If anything
goes wrong down there, we won't even know about it."

"Not quite true, Captain," Kemmerer told him. "*Walsh*
has a bail-out sphere, right?"

"Well . . . yes . . ." Walthers said with obvious reluctance.

"If the *Walsh* is destroyed, even if she's completely
crushed, the bail-out sphere will break free and pop to the
surface. And it can carry a complete log recording of everything that happens down there."

The bail-out sphere, in essence, was a one-man escape capsule, a sphere of ultradense collapsed matter with space enough inside for one or, just possibly, two, embedded within the submersible's hull just aft of her crew compartment. It would still be a long shot, of course. If the sphere popped up underneath the ice—a good chance of that—the people at the surface base or on board *Haldane* might never hear its emergency transmissions.

I pulled down a set of engineering stats to check. Okay . . . the sphere *did* have through-ice capability. If it was trapped beneath an ice ceiling, it could release nano from an external unit that would chew through the ice in order to send up a radio antenna . . . but there *were* limits. The ice would have to be less than about a kilometer in thickness for that to have a chance of working.

Most of the ice on Abyssworld's nightside was between ten and a hundred kilometers thick.

"I think you will all agree that this *is* a military situation," Kemmerer went on, "and that it may require trained military judgment. If whatever we encounter down there is, in my judgment, a military threat, I will be able to communicate that to the surface, even if the Walsh is destroyed."

"With respect, ma'am," Gunny Hancock told her, "your place will be here with the rest of the Marines, not gallivanting off on your own with the civilians."

"Command prerogative, Gunny."

"There's no such thing, ma'am. Your responsibility is to the entire unit . . . and to the mission."

"Then who do you suggest?"

He grinned at her. "Why, me, Lieutenant. Who else?"

"He does have FO experience, ma'am," Thomason pointed out. FO—Forward Observer—was a military specialty involving sneaking in close to an enemy and passing information back to the artillery, air, or space units that could actually do something about it.

And in any case, that's the way of it in the military. Any

officer worth the cost of his or her training knows you rely on the experience, the training, and the judgment of your noncommissioned officers—NCOs like Gunny Hancock or Staff Sergeant Thomason or Chief Garner. The gunny could assess any military threat we encountered in the abyss and make suggestions as well as a lieutenant could, and probably a hell of a lot better. The lieutenant would be in a better position to evaluate the threat from her office in the base topside, or on board *Haldane*, and give the appropriate orders to the Marines under her command.

The various naval officers didn't count. Walthers was needed topside to command the ship, and the other officers under his command all were specialists, each running his or her own department. They were needed topside as well . . . and none had the type of combat experience necessary to make command judgments of the sort Kemmerer and Hancock were talking about.

"Very well," Kemmerer said. "You've made your point. But we still need a pilot."

"The AI will serve that function," Walthers said.

"I'd like a *human* pilot if we can . . . a drone driver for preference."

"How about ET2 Lloyd?"

I didn't know the name. I looked it up on my in-head, from *Haldane*'s personnel roster, and found her quickly enough. Gina Lloyd. She was a Navy ET, an Electronics Tech Second Class in *Haldane*'s flight squadron. She wasn't a fighter pilot like the Marines flying the two Star Raiders, but was part of the research vessel's flight control staff who teleoperated various recon drones, fueling remotes, and robotic vessels from the *Haldane*'s combat command center.

"Is she linked in?" Kemmerer asked.

"I'm here, ma'am," a woman's voice said.

"Do you want in on this craziness? It's volunteers only."

"Wouldn't miss it, ma'am."

"Okay," Kemmerer said. "Last but not least, which Corpsmen?"

"I think only one, ma'am," Hancock told her, "not two. With Harris in cold storage and Chief Garner hurt—"

"I'm not hurt bad. I could—"

" . . . and Garner needed up here to run tech-support and sick bay," Hancock continued, ignoring him. "That leaves—"

"I'll go," I said, cutting in. "I have some experience with deep diving."

There was no objection from either Dubois or McKean. I wondered why there wasn't an objection from *me*.

"Carlyle would be my first choice, Lieutenant," Hancock said. "He's piloted a submersible . . . *and* he's been in first-contact situations before."

I wasn't sure my stint of duty running a tether-teleoperated remote beneath the ice of Gliese 581 VI-e would count for something like this, but I *did* carry a lot of data in my in-head RAM on pressure and exotic high-pressure chemistry. I guess that counted for something. And apparently, so did talking to a wounded Qesh pilot on Gliese 581 IV.

But in any case, wasn't this why I'd signed on with the Corps? Not just giving first aid to wounded Marines in the field, but learning new wrinkles in exobiology and alien bio-chemistries.

And we couldn't get a whole lot more alien than a hundred kilometers down.

In any case, it was first-contact work that I loved the most.

"Damn it, I outrank E-Car," McKean said. "I should go!"

"They're both nuts, Gunny," Dubois said. "If you want expendable . . ."

"It's Carlyle," Hancock said, with a tone of *that's final* in his voice.

"Young Carlyle's understanding of cuttlewhale biology," Ortega said, "and *especially* insights into the possibility that there is another intelligence behind the cuttlewhales . . . that alone recommends him."

Hancock grinned at me. "You should've kept your big mouth shut, E-Car."

"Hell . . . getting to look at exotic high-pressure ice?" I said. "How could I pass up an opportunity like that?"

I was suddenly remembering just how much I hated ice.

But then . . . in the oceanic abyss of this watery world, I'd actually be about as far from the surface ice as it was possible to get.

"Very well," Lieutenant Walthers said. "Drs. Montgomery and Ortega as mission specialists. D'deen as Galactic cultural liaison. HM2 Carlyle as technical specialist. ET2 Lloyd as pilot. And Gunnery Sergeant Hancock as operational CO and military liaison and forward observer. That's six. Are we missing anything?"

"I think," Hancock said, "that we're good to go."

"YOU BE CAREFUL DOWN THERE, HERO," MCKEAN TOLD ME. WE WERE standing on the ice, clad in our Mk. 10s, as the dayside wind hissed and whined around us.

"Yeah," Dubois added. "What's the matter with you, anyway? Didn't anyone tell you never to volunteer?"

"I'm a slow learner, I guess."

"Well, watch your tail down there."

"At least you won't have to worry about Kirchner," I told him. I hesitated, then added, "You have the records I sent you?"

"Yeah. You know you could get in a *lot* of trouble doing that."

"Doing what?"

"An enlisted guy prying into the medical records of an officer?" McKean said, shaking his head. "Checking up on him . . . keeping covert records of his behavior? That's heavy shit, my friend."

I'd already started worrying about a court-martial once I got home. Oh, there was no question that Kirchner was totally batshit—another of those technical medical terms—

but a court of inquiry likely would be taking a very close look at what I'd done in the time leading up to his mental break.

"The only way to prove schizophrenia," I told him, "is by keeping records of the patient's behavior over time . . . and putting that together with whatever he cares to tell you. At least in the absence of a brain scan. They'll need those records to legally order a deep brain scan when we get him home."

"Carlyle," McKean said, "they're going to hang, draw, and quarter you, and then hang you out to dry."

"And *then* they'll keelhaul your sorry ass," Dubois added.

"Getting keelhauled on a starship sounds pretty serious," I told them. "I think I'll take my chances a thousand kilometers down."

"Good luck, E-Car," Dubois said.

"Yeah," McKean said. "Remember you're still needed back up here to play midwife to a stalk of broccoli."

"How could I forget?" In fact, I *had* forgotten. The pregnant M'nangat, D'dnah, and its consorts still wanted me to deliver its buds . . . probably within the next couple of weeks.

I still wasn't looking forward to that.

A boarding gangway had been lowered between the ice and the deck of the Walsh. I was about to step onto it when Dubois added, over a private channel, "Hey, E-Car?"

"Yeah?"

"Do me a favor?"

"If I can do it a thousand kilometers underwater, sure."

"Keep a close eye on Gina, would you?"

"Gina Lloyd?" I stared at him through my visor for a second, and then realization dawned. Maybe I am slow. . . . "Not you and—"

"Yeah. Me and Gina."

"So *she's* your secret girlfriend?"

"Fuck. Why do you think I volunteered to come on this wild goose chase? And if you hadn't beaten me to the punch during the meeting earlier . . ."

"From the sound of it," I told him, "she doesn't need anybody taking care of her. Certainly not me!"

"Yeah, but I'd like her to come back topside, y'know?"

I thought of Joy Leighton, waiting for me forty-two light years away.

"I know. Don't sweat it, Doob. We'll be back. All of us."

I almost believed that.

I clung to the safety railing as I made my way across the submersible's deck, gripping it tightly in the teeth of that unrelenting wind. *Walsh* was a simple, blunt-ended cigar shape—no conning tower, no control surfaces, and with only a very low swell of her dorsal surface visible above the choppy dark water. She was slightly flattened, however, with a lateral bulge that included the active nanomatrix part of her hull that allowed her to maneuver underwater. Her airlock hatch was open on the flattened portion of her deck's dorsal surface. Once I descended the ladder to her interior, the airlock wouldn't simply close, but would be completely filled in with compressed matter. As *Haldane*'s chief engineer had pointed out, even the slightest weakness in *Walsh*'s hull would be deadly.

The interior of the submersible was cozy, an oval space just eight meters long, three wide, and two high. They'd grown enough seats out of the deck for the six of us, including all the linkages we would need to communicate with *Walsh*'s AI and direct the craft. The entire curved forward surface of the compartment was a permanent viewall, though the other surfaces could project images of our surroundings as well. There was nothing so primitive on board as *portholes*, of course. Even the strongest, thickest glasstic would shatter under the pressures we were about to encounter.

This was definitely a no-frills cruise. We would sleep in our chairs. There was a tiny compartment aft, next to the entrance to the bail-out sphere, that would absorb our wastes right through the deck, and which would serve as a sonoshower. Privacy? What's that? I wondered how Dr. Montgomery and ET2 Lloyd felt about being crammed into a narrow sewer pipe with three guys and a Broc for as long as this mission would require.

Thirty hours—over a day—to reach the mysterious Sierra Five.

And then what?

After removing our suits, we settled down in our seats and let them partially enclose us, the palms of our hands on the palmpads on either arm. D'deen, I saw, was positioned in a special seat individually programmed for him, a flat, padded board rising at a slant from a round bucket. He nestled his tentacles into the bucket and leaned back against the upright, which gently closed around his narrow torso. "Are you going to be okay there?" I asked. I was concerned about the cabin being too warm for him.

I AM QUITE CONTENT, the Broc replied. THE DIFFICULT PART WAS REPROGRAMMING YOUR NANOTECHNIC MATRICES TO GROW M'NANGAT FURNISHINGS.

The others completed securing themselves within the remaining, human-shaped couches. Gina Lloyd was in the left-front seat, right ahead of me, and I admired her competence as she brought up the sonar display on the main viewwall, and an instrument display on the screen across her lap. "*Walsh* ready in all respects for departure," she said aloud.

"You're clear for departure, *Walsh*," Kemmerer's voice said in our heads. "Good luck, people."

The sonar display winked out, replaced by a camera view looking forward from the submarine's nose. The camera was already under water, but I could see the dance of light from the opening in which we were floating, and the darker shapes of the surrounding ice.

"Gunny?" Lloyd asked. "Give the word."

"Word," Hancock said. "Let's see what this baby'll do."

"Submerging," Lloyd said, and the broken, jagged patterns of red-gold light rose, replaced by a darkness so profound I almost immediately regretted my decision to volunteer. Doob was right. *Never* volunteer. . . .

But we were dropping rapidly. "Descent rate at ten meters per second," Lloyd told us.

And our destination was waiting a mere thirty hours below. . . .

Chapter Seventeen

THE DARKNESS WAS ABSOLUTE, AN ENVELOPING AND MUFFLING cloak, and Gina Lloyd soon switched back to the sonar imaging, turning deck, overhead, and both sides to viewall displays along with directly forward. We were deliberately pinging the surrounding waters at low power, low enough, we hoped, to not invoke the wrath of the cuttlewhales again. As a result, we were picking up targets, but they were faint. Sierra Five wasn't much more than a pinpoint directly below us, while Sierra One cruised slowly off to port and occasionally emitted sonar pings of its own.

The Gykr submarine, almost certainly, tracking us.

A small eternity passed as we dropped steadily into the depths, minute dragging after minute. After a time, Lloyd had our AI overlay the optical and sonar imaging, but the darkness was so complete we could see nothing. Even when Lloyd switched on external lighting, our external nano illuminating the surrounding gulf, there was no sign of life save for those two somewhat uncommunicative sonar targets. No fish, or whatever Abyssworld might have evolved that were like fish . . . no invertebrates . . . not even any organic "snow" sifting down from the upper layers as it did on Earth. If not for the obvious exception of the cuttlewhales, I would have guessed that this world was lifeless.

"Sixteen minutes," Lloyd said from her control seat. "Passing the ten-kilometer mark."

"Ten thousand meters," I said. "That's almost as deep as the deepest spot in Earth's ocean."

"And here we've scarcely begun the descent," Ortega said.

In a sense, we were flying through the water, angled nose-down about ten degrees, our flattened hull giving us some lift in order to control the descent. Eleven kilometers . . .

Twelve . . .

"Is that target closing on us?" Hancock wanted to know.

"Contact Sierra One is at a range of three kilometers," the voice of *Walsh*'s AI said in our heads, "and is closing obliquely at a rate of fifteen kilometers per hour."

"Convergent course," Lloyd told us. "I think they're trying to sneak in closer."

"I wonder if they have weapons?" Ortega said.

"Unlikely," Hancock told him. "The only reason to have a submarine on this planet would be to explore the extreme depths . . . and torpedoes or antiship lasers would mean weaknesses built into the hull. I don't think they'd risk it."

It was a good point, I thought. I'd been assuming that the Gykr vessel had some sort of weapon—whatever it had been that had destroyed the research station—but the outside pressure now was somewhere around a ton on every square centimeter of our hull. Hatches or torpedo tubes would have been an invitation to disaster. Our external nano-coating could produce outside light, of course, or pick up and trans-mit external images, but the signals were passed through our CM hull by electrical induction—no openings, no wires, no weakness at any point.

"I hope you're right, Gunny," Lloyd said. "Because that Guck boat just turned and accelerated to close the gap. It looks an awful lot like an attack run."

On the starboard bulkhead, the patch of light represent-ing Sierra One had just sharply narrowed, as though we were seeing it now bow-on. "Range now two point five kilometers," the AI told us, "and closing at thirty kph."

Thirty kph—half a kilometer per minute.

"Target Sierra One is accelerating," the AI added. "Closing now at seventy kilometers per hour."

"What are they using for motive power?" Hancock asked.

"Sierra One almost certainly is employing a magnetic drive," the AI replied, "powered by a small quantum tap or equivalent technology."

"Looks like the same setup we have, Gunny," Lloyd added.

We were moving through the water under a variant of the Plottel Drive used for interplanetary travel, working against the local magnetic field in order to accelerate and maneuver. I wasn't certain what our top speed was, but it certainly was in excess of seventy kph.

"Target Sierra One now closing at ninety kilometers per hour," the AI said. "I am detecting signs of supercavitation."

Supercavitation happens when an object is moving through a fluid so quickly that a bubble of gas forms around the object, greatly reducing the friction of its passage through the liquid and allowing it to reach extremely high speeds.

"Hang on!" Lloyd called. "This could get nasty!"

Walsh's deck tilted suddenly, nose down, and I could sense our acceleration deeper into the ocean depths. To either side, visible by our external lighting, the flattened bulges in the sub's hull were pulling in and contracting, reducing our lift in the water, letting us descend faster. We weren't flying now so much as we were *plunging*, arrowing down past the fifteen kilometer mark. Our view into the surrounding darkness became misted over as we began supercavitating as well.

"Sonar target Sierra One is in pursuit," the AI told us. Its voice was calm and rational enough for it to have been commenting on the weather. "Range one point one kilometer, closing at one hundred kph."

Closing at that speed . . . which meant it was that much faster than we were. The thing must be pushing two hundred kilometers per hour.

"Can't this thing go any faster?" Montgomery asked.

"I've got it flat out now, ma'am," Lloyd replied. "This thing is a civilian explorer, not a fighter."

Which begged the question, was the Gykr machine designed for combat rather than for exploration? Or did they simply build *everything* to military specs, or with a military attitude? From the little we knew about them, the second option seemed more likely.

"Range four hundred meters, closing at one hundred fifteen kph. . . ."

We could hear it now, a high-pitched whine transmitted through water and the compressed matter of our hull, a whine edged with a warbling, stuttering thunder that spoke of tremendous energies released in a small volume of space. Thirty-two meters per second . . . four hundred meters . . . twelve and a half seconds . . . The numbers cascaded unbidden through my in-head as I turned in my seat to look at the fast approaching vehicle.

It came in from the starboard side aft, angled down, and it flashed past so close that I could see our external lights gleaming from dark metal and tortured water. Its shape, an echo of the *Walsh*, was enveloped in a translucent haze, the visual equivalent of a supersonic aircraft's shock wave as it rocketed past.

That shock wave struck us broadside and jolted us hard. If our seats hadn't been gripping us, we all would have been hurled against the bulkhead; for a terrifying second, we hung on our beam, wondering if we were going to flip completely over.

Then *Walsh* righted herself, at least partway, her sides flaring out under Lloyd's direction to grab the shock wave and ride it. We turned sharply away from the Gykr vessel's wake, grabbing for open water. Ahead and below, the Gykr submarine was turning, making a broad, open half circle as it slowed . . . then began accelerating again.

In space, you're moving through hard vacuum, which means the limit to your maneuvering is the amount of acceleration the crew can stand. In a fluid medium—in air or, even more, underwater—you use control surfaces to react against that medium in order to maneuver . . . and the slower combatant often has the advantage in any attempt to outmaneuver the enemy. It took long seconds for the Gykr machine to complete its turn, and the radius of that turn must have been five kilometers or more.

Under Gina Lloyd's skillful guidance, the *Walsh* twisted around sharply, killing our forward momentum against the water, then nosing over on our side into another dive. *Shit!* Lloyd was turning *into* the attacker.

"What the hell are you doing, pilot?" Ortega screamed. "You're going *toward* them!"

Lloyd didn't answer. From the seat behind hers, I could see her head turning to face the Guck vehicle, her eyes closed as she focused on her electronic in-head feed. *Walsh* continued her turn, her flanks folding back up as we picked up velocity once more, and now we were adding our speed to that of the oncoming, climbing Gykr submarine.

"Additional sonar contacts approaching," the AI reported. "Six targets, various bearings, to all sides, closing slowly."

I glanced up and saw several widely spaced targets, white stars scattered across our black sky, but I had no idea what they might be.

And there was no time to worry about them at the moment. The Guck sub was climbing to meet us. For a horrified moment, I thought we were going to collide bow-to-bow, but Lloyd swerved at the last moment, rolling to port as the enemy passed to starboard. The shock of their wake smashed against our hull, and this time we *did* roll through a complete and stomach-wrenching three-sixty. An alarm shrilled, and my hands clenched at my seat's rests.

"Kill that noise!" Hancock ordered.

"Aye, aye, Gunny," Lloyd replied, and the racket ceased.

"What was that?" Montgomery wanted to know.

"Hull stress warning," Lloyd said.

How much, I wondered, could the compressed-matter hull take? It could handle incredible pressure, yes, but it was possible that a hard enough shock could crack it. If that happened, at a ton per square centimeter, we literally would never know what hit us. *Walsh*'s interior spaces would flood in an instant, or else the hull itself would collapse under millions of tons of pressure, an implosion completed so quickly that our nerves simply would not have time to react.

"Damn it, woman!" Ortega snapped at Lloyd, "you're going to kill us!"

"Leave her alone, Doctor," Hancock told him. "She knows what she's doing."

"Ten additional sonar targets," our AI announced, "various bearings and ranges, closing slowly."

More stars were gathering around us in the black distance. The nearest, I saw, appeared to be long and slender . . . cuttlewhales, almost certainly. Our combat with the Gykr sub appeared to have attracted an audience.

Again, the Gykr boat approached from astern, following our wake as we hurtled almost vertically into greater and yet greater depths. I linked in with the AI through my in-head, intending to learn about the expected crush depth for the Walsh, and found that the channel was already occupied. *Walsh*'s AI was a micro version of the far more complex and advanced artificial intelligences on the *Haldane*, and evidently it couldn't handle more than one or, possibly, a very few conversations with humans at the same time. I was able to catch a bit on the fringes of the exchange; Lloyd was interrogating the system on the same topic about which I wanted to know . . . *just how much stress can the vessel's hull take*?

I couldn't hear the answer, if there was one.

"Sonar target Sierra One bearing directly astern," the AI announced over the public channel, "range five hundred meters, closing at ninety kilometers per hour."

Slower! Had we hurt them with that last pass? Or were they just moving a little more cautiously now? I turned in my seat, looking aft . . . but the aft bulkhead wasn't set to show us our surroundings. I could see D'deen in his bucket-seat, apparently unperturbed by the danger . . . though how the hell could you read the emotional state of a two-meter stalk of broccoli? The rest of us were feeling very human emotions at the moment . . . terror chief among them. I found myself bracing internally against the collapse of the surrounding bulkheads, even though I knew that if they failed, I would neither feel it nor be able to hold them back as they snapped shut on extremely frail flesh and bone.

"Where are they?" Ortega demanded. "*Where are they . . . ?*"

"Coming down on us from directly astern," Lloyd told him. "I think they want to nudge us with a kick in the ass."

Made sense. If they could put us into a tumble, we'd be helpless until we could regain control.

"Sierra One closing directly astern at eighty kph," the AI said, "range two hundred meters."

Seconds dragged past . . . and then without warning, *Walsh* slewed violently to starboard. At almost the same instant, the Gykr submarine appeared directly to port, only a few meters from our hull. The turbulence of the mingling wakes set up a hellish vibration that rattled our teeth, the roar filling the cabin with rushing, pounding thunder.

Just as abruptly, *Walsh* slewed back to port, turning sharply and slamming nose-first into the Gykr hull.

The impact slammed me forward against my seat restraint and for a terrifying moment the interior lights winked out. That alarm was shrieking again, and when the lights came back on they were dimmer than before. The viewall projections, however, didn't come up again. We were surrounded by the blank, gray, curving bulkheads of the cabin.

Lloyd killed the alarm, and the silence was as profound as the chaotic roar a moment before. The vibration was gone . . . as was any sensation of movement. I reached for the AI through my link and heard only silence.

"The AI is dead!" Ortega yelled.

"So's the boat," Lloyd said. "Power tap is down, drive down, life support . . . *shit*. Life support and environmental systems down too."

I could feel her helpless despair.

"Yeah, but I don't hear the other guy either," I pointed out. "Maybe you got him, Gina."

We all listened to the silence for a long moment. The whine of the other vessel's high-speed passage through the water, a sound we'd heard clearly while it was still almost half a kilometer away, was blessedly absent.

"And our hull's still intact," Hancock said, looking up at the overhead.

"It . . . it feels like we're sinking, though," Montgomery said. "Do you feel it?"

I thought I could feel what she meant, a drifting, sinking sensation. It was tough to tell; Abyssworld's gravity, nine-tenth's of Earth's, might be fooling us, but it did feel like we were descending, more or less on an even keel, but with a slight rocking motion from side to side.

"I'm sorry, guys," Lloyd said. "I . . . I thought that might be our only chance. . . ."

"You did absolutely right," Hancock told her. "That bastard was bound and determined to smash us. And he might have succeeded if he'd hit us a time or two more."

"We don't *know* she got him," Ortega said. He was staring at the overhead as well, as if he could penetrate the CM hull with the sheer intensity of his gaze.

"I'll take the silence as a vote of confidence," Montgomery said. "I don't hear anything. . . ."

"No."

"Including the air," Montgomery added. "How long can we last without air?"

"Lots of time," Hancock told her. "Hours . . . Doc?"

I nodded. "Our problem will be the build-up of carbon dioxide. If we stay calm, we should have two or three hours before the air gets unpleasantly stale."

But that was a WAG—a wild-assed guess. The air already felt uncomfortably close, though that could have been my anxiety speaking . . . and possibly the stink of fear as well. I was certainly more aware of the smell of human sweat, and there was an odd, cinnamon-like aroma as well that might have been D'deen.

There was another, stronger odor as well. "Is . . . is the washroom working?" Ortega asked.

"*Nothing* is working," Lloyd told him. "Nothing except for the emergency lights."

"You'll have to hold it, Doctor."

Ortega scowled. "Too late . . ."

"Oh, shit," Hancock said, chuckling.

Ortega refused to rise to the bait. "So what the hell do we do now?" he asked.

"What we're doing, Doctor," Lloyd told him. "Be patient. I'm trying to restart the AI now."

"But if the power is out," Montgomery said. "How? . . ."

"The AI can run off just a trickle of power, ma'am," I said. "At least *part* of it can . . . enough to bootstrap the other systems back on-line. It doesn't take much. . . ."

And a few seconds later, we all felt an internal click and rising hum as *Walsh*'s AI came back on-line. "Rebooting," its voice announced. Then, "Systems check . . . restoring from cache in safe mode . . . initiating damage control functions. . . ."

Static hissed across our internal windows, then cleared. . . . IS HAPPENING? appeared on my in-head. D'deen, evidently, had been silenced by the AI's temporary downtime.

I glanced back at the M'nangat, which appeared agitated, the tips of its tentacles flickering rapidly along the edge of its bucket and turning bright lime-green. "It's okay, D'deen," I told it. "We lost power in the collision, but we're working to restore it."

THANK YOU. I WAS CONCERNED.

"So were we all," Hancock said, but he grinned. "With the AI working again, we'll have full repairs under way in no time."

"Damage report," the AI said, implacable and calm. "Power tap nonfunctioning. Magnetic drive nonfunctioning. Life support—"

"Damn it, we *know*!" Lloyd snapped. She sounded close to breaking. "Tell us something we *don't* know . . . like maybe some good news for a change!"

"Request task hierarchy for power allocation."

"Life support," Hancock said. "That's first."

"Routing all available internal nanobots to life-support functions."

The interior of *Walsh*'s cabin was coated with engineering-grade nanobots, including the ones that had grown our couches out of the deck matrix, and they would be swarming now through our life-support units beneath our feet, trying to bring them back on-line. They drew their motive power from the emergency batteries that were running our lights, now, and took their orders directly from the AI.

"Quantum power tap distributor node identified as source of electrical failure," the AI told us. "Rerouting eighty percent of available internal nanobots to quantum power tap distribution systems."

Most vehicles nowadays use quantum power taps— paired sub-microscopic artificial singularities orbiting one another—to pull energy from the seething foam of virtual particles appearing and vanishing at the so-called base-state of reality. If the power tap had broken down, we would have been well and totally screwed, since repairs generally meant a long stretch in spacedock for starships, and an expensive replacement unit for vehicles of *Walsh*'s size. Our AI had identified our problem, however, as a fault within the bundle of wires transmitting that energy to all of the vessel's systems, not in the power plant itself. The violence of the impact, apparently, had jarred something loose.

"How long to effect repairs?" Lloyd asked it.

"One moment . . . one moment . . . current time to completion estimated at twenty-three minutes."

That seemed like a hell of a long time, but it did take longer to nanotechnically repair gross structures like wiring, fiber-optic cable, and power-shunt transmitters than it did to call forth programmed shapes from a prepared nanomatrix.

"Twenty-three minutes!" Montgomery said.

"We should be okay for that long," Hancock reassured her. He didn't sound completely certain, however. Privately, I wondered if he was more concerned about CO_2 levels in the compartment, or the fetid odor that seemed to be growing steadily stronger.

And we, meanwhile, continued to sink.

"Power distribution node repairs complete," the AI said after what seemed like forever. "Testing. . . . Test satisfactory. Restoring power to all systems in sequence. . . ."

In fact, according to my in-head, only eleven minutes had passed. The lighting came up to full, and we heard again the gentle hiss of fresh air coming up through the deck. I could also feel my in-head link with the AI being fully restored, and that was a hell of a relief. I'm not as bad as some people are when it comes to losing their cybernetic connections to the local Net, but I certainly didn't like it. I felt helpless, cut off, and vulnerable.

"Is the damned bathroom working yet?" Ortega demanded.

"Affirmative."

"Excuse me." His seat released him and he got up and made his way aft. The close, foul stench filling the small compartment was already clearing rapidly.

"Through-hull connectivity restored," the AI said. "Hull matrix control systems, lighting, sonar, and imaging systems have been restored but not engaged. Awaiting pilot command."

"No outside lights yet!" Hancock said, his voice sharp. "Let's have a look around first."

If the Gykr were still out there, alive and kicking, we didn't want them to know that we were alive as well. At least, not yet.

"Good idea, Gunny," Lloyd said. The bulkheads and overhead switched over to black.

Completely black. I'd forgotten just how dark it was down here. We appeared to be alone in a lightless void.

Gunny stared into the blackness a moment, as though trying to see what lay out there. "Okay," he said after a moment. "I don't like it . . . but let's bring the outside lights up. Slowly. Don't switch them on full yet."

"Aye, aye, Gunny."

Our outer hull began to glow, the light very gradually intensifying. . . .

And then we saw the Gykr submarine.

"My God," Montgomery said. "They were disabled by the collision too!"

The Gykr vessel was a little longer than we were— perhaps twenty-five meters stem to stern—but slightly bulkier and more egg-shaped. The surface, dimly reflecting our light, had the matte-gray finish of compressed matter, and seemed partially lost in shadow.

Well, it would have to be a CM hull, wouldn't it? "How deep are we, Gina?" I asked.

"Two hundred ninety kilometers," she replied.

The figure startled me. We must have been diving at quite a clip during the battle, to have gotten this deep in this short a time."The pressure on our hull," she went on, "is roughly twenty-seven tons per square centimeter."

I looked again at the Gykr sub. It was hanging more or less motionless in relationship to us. I noticed that there were some small fragments drifting in a thin, glittering cloud around it. Not paint, certainly. Tiny flecks of outer CM hull?

I also noticed that the Gykr vessel was not on an even keel. The broad end of the egg shape was hanging lower than the other, at an angle of more than forty-five degrees.

"Are we moving?" I asked.

"We're descending at approximately five meters per second."

So that uneasy, queasy feeling of descending in the pit of my stomach wasn't due to the planet's lower gravity after all.

"The thing is," Hancock said after a long moment of watching the thing, "what if they're busy getting their systems back on-line too?"

IF SO, D'deen wrote, WE MAY HAVE BUT SCANT MOMENTS BEFORE THAT VESSEL WAKES UP AND ATTACKS US AGAIN.

"Lloyd?" Hancock said. "Can you ram them again? Maybe one more good nudge would do it."

"Gunny!" she cried. "I can't do that!"

"Do I have to make it an order?"

"But if they're crippled, that would be like murder!"

THE GYKR, D'deen said, WOULD NOT HESITATE TO DE-STROY US.

"I don't like it either, Lloyd," Hancock said. "But it's them or us."

"Well there's nothing I can do about it just yet anyway," she told him. "We still don't have maneuvering or power to the mag drive."

"When we do," Hancock told her, "I'm going to want you to hit them as hard as you can . . . at least, as hard as you can without sinking us as well."

"What's this about the Gykr destroying us?" Ortega said. He'd just stepped naked from the washroom. "Uh . . . where? . . ."

"Fresh uniforms in the aft stowage locker," Hancock told him. "By the galley."

"Thanks." He opened a storage compartment, removed a utilities egg, and slapped it against his bare chest. The material activated, running out in a thin, opaque film across his body, growing him a new set of skintight shipboard utilities in a few seconds. "That feels better!"

"Smells better, too, Raúl," Montgomery told him with a twinkle.

"Yes, well, I'm sorry about that. My God . . . is that the Guck submarine?"

"It is, Doctor," Hancock told him. "Apparently they were damaged at least as badly as we."

"They could be playing possum," Montgomery pointed out, "just like us."

"How about it, D'deen?" Hancock asked the Broc in the rear. "We don't know a lot about Guck psychology. Are they that sneaky?"

I FEAR WE KNOW LITTLE ABOUT GYKR PSYCHOLOGY, GUNNERY SERGEANT, D'deen replied. WHAT LITTLE WE DO KNOW SUGGESTS THAT THEY WOULD ATTACK AUTOMATICALLY AS SOON AS THEY WERE PHYSICALLY CAPABLE OF DOING SO.

"Fight or fight," I added, nodding.

THEY APPEAR TO EXHIBIT A COLONY-TYPE RESPONSE TO EXTERNAL THREATS. THE INDIVIDUAL MATTERS NOT AT ALL. WHAT IS IMPORTANT TO THEM IS THE SECURITY OF THE ENTIRE COLONY.

"Ants," Montgomery said. "Or termites. A hive mind, maybe?"

"Not according to the EG," Ortega told her, using a towel to wipe down his seat thoroughly, then sitting down once more. "It's more complex than that."

"So what do we know about them as part of the Collective?" Montgomery asked. "D'deen?"

She was referring to the R'agch'lgh Collective, the interstellar empire that had been losing its grip on this part of the Galaxy for the past few tens of thousands of years.

VERY LITTLE, D'DEEN TOLD HER. THEY ARE NOT LISTED AS PART OF THE COLLECTIVE'S ORIGINAL MAKE-UP. THEY WERE UNKNOWN DURING THE COLLECTIVE'S APEX, AND ONLY APPEARED AS IT CRUMBLED. AS RAIDERS.

"Listen," I said. "That's all fascinating . . . but there's someone else out there we should be worrying about too."

"My God," Hancock said, startled. "Doc's right. Lloyd? Let's have the lights up a little. We won't reveal ourselves much more than we have already."

The external lights brightened, and a hazy sphere of deep blue-green illumination reached out farther into the depths.

And there, just beyond the perimeter of the glow, shadows began to take shape against the night.

Huge shadows, dozens of them, each enormous . . . like vast tentacled snakes, hovering around us on every side, watching us. Waiting . . .

Cuttlewhales . . .

Chapter Eighteen

"Motive power restored," the AI said. "Pilot has control of the vessel."

"Gunny?" Lloyd asked. "What should I do?"

"Nothing," he replied. "Nothing at all."

"They haven't made any hostile moves," Montgomery pointed out. "It's like they're just watching us."

"They may be confused about us," I suggested. "Or curious. I've been wondering if they know the difference between us and the Gykr. The fact that we were fighting may have startled them."

If something the size of a small starship could be said to be *startled*.

"C'mon, Doc," Hancock said. "You're telling us they can't tell the difference between a human and an overgrown flea?"

"Well . . . think about it," I said. "The cuttlewhales we saw on the ice were . . . what? Maybe two hundred meters long?"

"About that," Montgomery said.

"So if we and the Gykr are both one percent of a cuttlewhale's length . . . if we were the cuttlewhale, to us the human and the Gykr both would be just this tall." I held up my thumb and forefinger a centimeter apart. "We don't know how good their eyes are. Maybe at that scale, we both look the same."

"I don't buy it," Hancock told me. "Gucks have six or

eight legs, depending on how you count appendages, *and* they stand on their heads."

"When you look at a bug, do you bother to count the legs?" Montgomery asked. "I think Doc's right. And if their eyes see at infrared wavelengths, they wouldn't see the same level of fine detail we do."

"Besides," I said, "what they're looking at now are two deep submersibles, and they're not all that different from one another—an egg shape and a cigar. I—"

A high-pitched squeal sounded through the compartment, and all of us looked up at the overhead, our hearts suddenly hammering. "Jesus!" Lloyd said.

The sound continued, growing slowly deeper, rougher . . . punctuated by a loud, sharp pop.

"Is the hull failing?" I asked.

"N-no," Lloyd said after a moment. "No. We're okay, I think. The sound . . . it's coming from the Guck sub. We're hearing the sound transmitted through the water."

We all stared at the other submarine.

The implosion came with startling suddenness. In one instant, the Gykr vessel was egg-shaped. In the next, it was a perfect sphere, and the noise of its collapse was like a cannon's shot. *Walsh* rocked heavily as the surrounding water rebounded.

Swiftly, the Gykr vessel, what was left of it, began to outpace us, falling into the depths.

"No air bubbles?" Ortega said. "I would have thought—"

"The pressure probably pushed all the air into solution in the water," I said. "Like nitrogen in the blood when a diver is under enough pressure."

"I wonder how many Gykrs were on board," Lloyd said.

"We saw eight or ten scramble on board when *Haldane* came in overhead," Hancock said. "Must have been a damned tight fit, though. I wouldn't have thought the habitable space on board was much more than what we have here on the *Walsh*."

"They have a communal, gregarious culture," Ortega observed. "They might not mind being packed in like sardines."

"No reaction from our friends out there," Hancock observed. "Bring the light up a little more, would you, Lloyd?"

As the light intensified, we could see more details in the surrounding titans.

It was hard to tell how far away they were. They were so big that scale was tough to judge. We could switch on the sonar, of course, but we all remembered the apparent reaction of the cuttlewhales when we'd put sonar transponders into the ocean earlier.

They were quiescent at the moment, but we really, *really* didn't want to make them angry.

"Hey," I said, noticing something odd. "Look at that close one to port. Look at its mouth."

"I see it," Montgomery said. "Dr. Murdock's reports suggested chromataphore communications. That's why they named them after terrestrial cuttlefish."

When the creature closed its mouth and stretched its eyestalks and the forest of tentacles around the outside of its head wide, it revealed a ring of flat, pale skin encircling the puckered central opening. The skin there was stretched taut and had a complex, mottled look to it—gray-green markings against a paler gray. And those markings were . . . changing, creating a writhing, shifting series of patterns, one flowing into the next in pulsing waves.

"Do you think it's trying to communicate with us?" Lloyd asked.

"More likely it's talking with the others," Hancock said. He grimaced. "Something along the lines of, 'Hey, fellas . . . is it good to eat?'"

"Can you make anything of it, D'deen?" Ortega asked.

No. We have never visited this world, nor encountered these creatures before, remember. However, we do know of numerous sapient species that use sim-

ILAR METHODS FOR COMMUNICATING AMONG THEMSELVES. SOME OF THESE METHODS ARE QUITE SOPHISTICATED, AND CAPABLE OF TRANSMITTING A GREAT DEAL OF DATA IN A SHORT PERIOD OF TIME.

"Do you think you could figure out what they're saying?"

HOW? WE HAVE NO STARTING POINT, NO COMMON UNDERSTANDING.

"It's not like we can point to a chair and have them tell us their name for it," I pointed out.

"If they're intelligent," Ortega said, "they would know that."

"Hey, Gina?" I said.

"Yes?"

"Could you set up the lights on the outside of our hull to kind of . . . I don't know, repeat back those patterns?"

"Why?" Hancock asked. "We won't know what we're saying."

"It might be interesting to see what they do," I suggested.

"Yeah . . . like poking one with a stick." Hancock considered the idea for a moment. "Okay. Can you do it, Lloyd?"

"Sure, Gunny. I'm turning over all light control on the port side of the *Walsh* to the AI. It can analyze the patterns and reflect them back."

"Do it."

It took a few moments to set the system up, but after a moment, the AI said, "We are displaying the patterns of color on the hull now, with a one-tenth second delay."

Essentially, each square centimeter of *Walsh*'s surface contained a layer of solid-state nanobots that could generate varying amounts of light, and the AI, using quantum electric effects through the compressed-matter hull, could control them like individual pixels on a display screen. Other external nano registered incoming light and transmitted data to the AI, effectively giving it all-round vision. Our AI could see the pattern shifts in the encircling cuttlewhales, and return the sentiments.

The response was instantaneous. All of the cuttlewhales

became agitated, their tentacles and eyestalks lashing about in apparent reaction to our message, and several drew back into the shadows.

"It would appear," Montgomery said, "that we have established communications. They certainly seem to have gotten the message."

"A message, at any rate," Ortega added. "I wonder what the hell we just said?"

The nearest cuttlewhale was signaling again, but its message was different now, a slow and rhythmic pulse beginning at the center and spreading outward. Very slowly, the patterns became more complex, interweaving twists and turns of moving color.

"Maybe we could send pictures," Hancock suggested. "You know . . . animated images."

"Maybe eventually," Montgomery said. "But we're not just separated from them by language. Doc is right. Things that we know well—a chair, for instance—would be meaningless to them. We show them an animation of a man walking, along with the word . . . but that wouldn't mean a thing to creatures that swim or crawl."

"So we use it to convey the word *go*," Ortega said.

Montgomery sighed. "Learning a completely alien language is *never* as easy as the entertainment vids say it is," she said. She glanced aft at D'deen. "It took us two years to learn how to communicate with the M'nangat, remember. And *they* were learning *our* languages, had access to our computer Net, had some very powerful AIs of their own on-line, and have had a few thousand years of experience in learning to communicate with aliens. Not only that, we share a lot in common with the M'nangat—like environment, biochemistry, and emotional content. We're not going to learn how to discuss physics with cuttlewhales in an afternoon."

Nevertheless, the language lessons continued throughout the rest of that afternoon as *Walsh* continued its slow descent into the Abyss. We had control of the vessel now, and one by one all of the other ship's systems came back on-line. We could have stopped the descent, or begun a return to the surface, but Gunny Hancock decided we were best off leaving things exactly as they were. There was no telling what the response from our giant escorts would be if we abruptly powered up and took off.

We appeared to be at the center of a titanic conclave of the beasts. We could make out the vast and sinuous shadows coming and going out at the farthest limits of our sphere of light, and our AI estimated that there were more than a hundred cuttlewhales in fairly close proximity to the *Walsh*.

"What are the pressure limits on the *Walsh*?" Ortega wanted to know some hours later. "We must be pretty deep by now."

"Four hundred sixteen kilometers," Lloyd said.

"That's over thirty-nine tons per square centimeter," I said.

"How much more can we stand?"

"I don't think anyone knows," Hancock said. "Compressed matter is damned tough stuff. The more you squeeze it, the stronger it gets, but without internal spaces caving in."

"That doesn't seem to have helped the Gykr sub," Lloyd said. "*They* must have had a compressed matter hull, too, just to go as deep as they did."

"Ahh, there are just too many variables to draw any conclusions," I said. "We can't assess an alien technology, not from in here, anyway. And we don't know how badly they were damaged, or what their pressure indices are, or even whether they use the same type of CM that we do."

I wasn't a materials engineer, and didn't know the details. But I did know that, just as with exotic ices, there were lots of different ways to squeeze atoms together.

The question now was not so much why the Gykr sub's hull had failed, as how much deeper we could go before ours failed as well.

Still, the original idea had been to go into Abyssworld's extreme depths . . . a voyage of thirty hours to reach Sierra Five, or better than twelve days to go all the way to the bottom of Abyssworld's ocean, eleven thousand kilometers down. *Walsh*'s engineering specs must have allowed us pretty good odds of reaching those depths for the idea even to have been considered.

But then, the Gykrs must have had the same engineering assurances before they'd put their egg-shaped boat in the water.

It was not a very encouraging thought.

As more hours passed, I got to know Gina better. We were about the same age and the same rank—second class—and she seemed increasingly worried about her spur-of-the-moment brainstorm that led her to ram the Gykr sub. We regrew a portion of the deck to create a seat big enough for the two of us, side by side, and ended up talking about . . . stuff. Our careers and Navy experiences . . . our families . . . where we'd been and ships to which we'd been assigned . . . *anything*, in short, except her decision of hours before. I learned that she'd been born and raised in California, that she'd been a military brat with a father in the Navy, a mother in the Marines, and a brother in the High Guard, that she'd been engaged to a guy in a line marriage in Iowa, but broken it off when she'd learned that one of her new husbands was a religious neo-Ludd and something of a fanatic.

"That's the thing," she told me. "If God gave us hands and minds, why would She give us the capability of changing our environment to suit us, and then turn around and forbid us from doing it?"

"I don't think She cares one way or another," I said. My arm was comfortably around her shoulders now, and I wondered if Doob would have approved of my enjoying the physical proximity of his current love like this.

Well, hell. It wasn't like we could do anything about it.

Walsh's crew compartment was far too cramped to permit anything even approaching privacy. Right now, Ortega and Montgomery were two meters behind us, deep in a technical conversation about depth, temperature, and pressure on worlds like this one or Europa, while Hancock was wrapped up in a private in-head exchange with D'deen.

I played back the conversation of a moment before, and blinked. Gina had referred to God as *She*.

I commented on this, and she shrugged. "We were Trad-Gard. Pretty much old school, Goddess *and* God . . . though the male aspect was usually downplayed to the role of divine consort. The emphasis was on the Divine Feminine."

"Traditional Gardnerian?" I nodded. "My family was on the other side of the Great Split," I admitted. "Reformed Gardnerian. I never really believed, though. Not all of it. Some of the myths were pretty silly. . . ."

"Myths are just expressions of human psychology given story bodies," she said. "They're not supposed to be what we think of as 'real.' "

"Nine million women burned, hung, or tortured to death as witches during the Middle Ages? No, that's not real. It's anti-church propaganda. The actual number was probably in the tens of thousands, though we'll never know for sure."

"Tens of thousands was still ghastly."

"Of course it was. But some modern Wiccans felt the need to compete with the Holocaust of the twentieth century. As if inflating the numbers makes it worse."

"So what *do* you believe?"

"Well . . . I don't believe in the Christian hell . . . a loving father who tortures His creations for eternity because they chose to believe the wrong things."

"I thought that was the devil."

"If God is God, He's the one responsible, right? Unless you're into dualism with *two* gods. And I don't believe that there's only one way to salvation . . . or even that we *need* salvation. We're responsible for our own shit, our own decisions. That's the only way that makes any sense at all of a nonsensical universe. . . ."

Our conversation wandered on. Both of us were inclined toward the reincarnation taught by both of our respective religions, neither of us cared at all for the more organized aspects of those religions. It was interesting, I thought, that Gardenerian Wicca, which had begun centuries ago as a kind of protest against the strictures of organized religion, against the you-*must*-believe-this-to-be-saved nonsense of the Church, had itself devolved into *thou shalts* and *thou shalt nots*.

Or maybe it had always been that way, even for the Wiccans. Maybe *thou shalt not* was the central essence of all human religion, and a reflection of human nature. The Ten Commandments were a splendid expression of the social contract—of how to behave in civilized society—but they left something to be desired when they were enforced by fear of burning for all eternity. The Witches' Rede of the Gardnerians and others was gentler: "So long as it harms no one, including yourself, do what you will."

But humans being humans, even that simple statement had wandered into debate and schism. The truth of it was, so far as I could tell . . . *nothing* mattered beyond taking responsibility for your own actions, treating others with respect and kindness, and being the best possible human being you could be, because the gods know that bad human beings have brought more than their fair share of misery, death, and horror down upon our species.

My thoughts, I realized, had been growing darker and more despondent the deeper we drifted into Abyssworld's deeps. The one thing you can say about organized religion is that, if you believe what they tell you, there's a certainty to the promise of an afterlife. A paradise with halos and harps . . . the charms of seventy-two willing virgins . . . the Summerlands of the Wiccans and Spiritualists . . . all of them promise to keep believers in line, made by people who didn't *know*, not really. If some vital aspect of self or personality *did* survive death, I suspected that the reality would be very, very different from the myths told to us by our religions.

This was also, I realized, a piss-poor time to be thinking about stuff like that. We'd survived this long, but the chances were damned good that the situation was going to change, and soon.

What in the names of all the gods were the damned cuttlewhales waiting for, anyway? They continued to hover just beyond our hull, following our leisurely descent, watching, as the pressures outside grew greater . . . and greater . . . and inexorably greater. . . .

The language lesson was continuing, one of the cuttlewhales projecting those weirdly shifting patterns of color and even texture across the empty area around its mouth, our AI responding, repeating the message—whatever it was— right back at them. Some of the other cuttlewhales, we could see, were projecting animated patterns across other parts of their bodies as well. Was that part of the same conversation? Or were they engaged in the cuttlewhale equivalent of whispered cross-conversations in the background?

We couldn't possibly know.

"Any progress, AI?" I asked, using my in-head link with the sub.

"I am not certain that you would call it progress," the AI replied. "However, we do seem to have found common ground with the cuttlewhales in mathematics, which has led to a further commonality within physics. I am proceeding along lines of inquiry suggested by these aspects of shared worldview."

Well, one plus two equals three whether you're a surface dweller or hundreds of kilometers underwater . . . at least for certain values of three. But how useful is that, really, in a conversation? It's all well and good to claim that mathematics is the one, true universal language, but how the hell can you take $a^2 + b^2 = c^2$ and use it to get across the concept of "Good morning," or, more to the point in this situation perhaps, "Please don't eat me"?

Gina was staring at those monstrous shapes hovering outside. "Are they really made of *ice*, Doc?"

"They sure are. Turns out you can crystallize water in a lot of different ways. It just takes a lot of pressure . . . and sometimes a lot of cold."

"Only sometimes?"

"Yeah. Ice VI forms at just three below zero, Celsius. But you need 1.1 giga-Pascals of pressure to do it. That's over ten tons per square centimeter." I glanced at the dark water outside. "That's about what we're experiencing now."

"So why isn't there ice out there now?"

"Probably too warm. AI? What's the ambient water temperature?"

"Outside temperature is at two degrees Celsius."

"Thank you," I said. "See? It's still too warm. This planet's ocean gets warmed from two directions. The middle of dayside, at the surface, is close to boiling. And way down deep, a lot of heat must come up from the rocky core, either through volcanic vents, or else heat is generated by radiation emitted by uranium inside the rock. There may be some tide-flexing, too, just like in Europa, as Abyssworld goes around its sun."

"How were they surviving up on the ice, then? Without exploding, I mean?"

I chuckled. "Some of us have already discussed that. They certainly don't live very long up there. And . . . we've been discussing the possibility that they were . . . *manufactured* somehow. Maybe as probes to explore the surface."

"Like machines?"

"Organic machines." I thought about the phrase, and amended it. *Organic* in chemistry meant carbon-based, which the cuttlewhales decidedly were not. "Non-carbon-based organic machines. Damn, we don't have the right language to describe this. Call them not-life-as-we-know it, and let it go at that. *Artificial* not-life-as-we-know-it."

"Artificial?" Lloyd shivered. "Made by what?"

"I don't know. But there's an awfully big world down here. Plenty of room for all sorts of surprises."

"Maybe. It's an awfully empty world from what I've seen so far."

"Really?" I looked at the looming monstrosities outside. "Looks kind of crowded to me."

She punched me in the arm. "*You* know what I mean!"

"Sure. On Earth, you know, the deep oceanic abyss is like a desert. Unless you happen to find a hot oceanic vent on the seafloor—those can have astounding ecologies growing up around them—there's very little food . . . nothing but a thin drizzle of organics sifting down from the surface and the occasional carcass of a whale or some other sea creature too big to get devoured on the way down. When the *Trieste* made the first dive to the Challenger Deep, Piccard and Walsh saw a new species of shrimp . . . and what they thought was a small flounder. Scientists are still arguing over whether they saw a fish or a sea cucumber."

"Walsh . . . as in the guy our sub is named for?"

"The same. Lieutenant Don Walsh, U.S. Navy . . . and a Swiss scientist and engineer, Jacques Piccard. They reached the deepest point in Earth's ocean in January of 1960."

"They must have been brave men."

"Yeah. Big-time. They made that dive just to prove it could be done. At around nine thousand meters, they heard a loud crack inside their pressure chamber, like a gunshot, but nothing appeared to be wrong so they continued their descent. Turned out a viewing window had cracked, which they didn't know until they'd been on the bottom for twenty minutes. They . . . ah . . . decided to cut their visit sort at that point. They were *that* close to being killed."

"One hard bump . . ."

"Exactly."

She sat up suddenly, and pointed. "Elliot . . . is that one getting closer?"

I looked in the indicated direction. One of the monsters was slowly edging closer, approaching us directly from the bow.

"I think—" I started to say.

"Out of my way, damn it!" As I stood up, the twin seat dwindled to her single pilot's chair once again. I stepped behind her and called up my chair, slipping into it.

"Everybody take your seats!" I called. "We may have to maneuver!"

Montgomery stared at the approaching mass of tentacles and puckered mouth. "God in heaven . . ."

I didn't think God had very much to do with this thing. That mouth was opening, the tentacles spreading wide as six weirdly stalked eyes twisted inward to keep us in sight.

I again wondered about those eyes. What wavelengths did they see? Were they, in fact, capable of infrared vision? Infrared radiation was absorbed by seawater almost immediately—after a few centimeters, in fact, and IR wouldn't do the creature that much good.

But if it saw into the visible spectrum . . . why? If the things had evolved—or been created—down here in these lightless depths, what could possibly explain the fact of eyes that would be blind in all but the top hundred meters or so of the ocean?

Babbling. I was babbling in my mind, a kind of stream-of-consciousness monologue as I tried to control my rising terror. The mouth was wide open now, and only a few tens of meters distant. With a lurch, the *Walsh* jerked backward away from that yawning maw, then twisted hard to port, fighting for altitude and speed. Her flanks flared out, creating lift. We were rising, flying through the water and gaining height!

The pursuing cuttlewhale was now directly astern and

below us . . . but so close that I could see eyes and tentacles extending out to all sides, reaching past us . . . enveloping us . . .

"Give it full throttle!" Hancock ordered.

"It's sucking down water!" Lloyd cried. "We're caught in the current!"

And then a shadow passed across the *Walsh*, and things grew very, very dark indeed. . . .

Chapter Nineteen

THERE WAS A SAVAGE JOLT, AND THE INTERIOR LIGHTS CAME UP. I was expecting to see the interior of the cuttlewhale's gullet, but the interior surface of its mouth or throat or whatever it was that was enclosing us was pressed so closely around our vessel that no light at all was escaping from the external nano, and no images were being returned. Outside the *Walsh*, once again, there was nothing to be seen but a complete and utterly impenetrable blackness.

It had happened so quickly that no one had been able to respond. Ortega gave a low, quavering moan. Montgomery sobbed. Hancock swore.

"Holy fucking Christ!"

NOT CHRIST, D'deen wrote. BUT JONAH.

"What the hell do you guys know about Jonah?" I asked.

HE IS A CHARACTER, AS WELL AS THE NAME OF A BOOK, WITHIN THE COLLECTION YOU CALL THE BIBLE, the M'nangat said. A STORY SPEAKING OF THE NECESSITY OF OBEYING GOD'S WILL, AND POSSIBLY, TOO, ACCORDING TO LATER WRITINGS, IT IS AN ALLEGORY FOR A MESSIAH WHO RISES FROM THE DEAD AFTER THREE DAYS.

"No, I mean how do you know about all of that?"

HUMAN RELIGION DEFINES THE PSYCHOLOGY OF YOUR SPECIES, ELLIOT. HOW COULD WE HOPE TO LEARN ABOUT

HUMANKIND WITHOUT CLOSELY STUDYING YOUR MYRIAD
RELIGIOUS BELIEFS?

That brought me up short. Human religion isn't exactly
something that might inspire confidence in an extraterrestrial observer. Thousands of years of wars, murders, massa-
cres, torture, persecutions, forced conversions, witch hunts,
even the doctrine of hell itself, promising torture throughout all eternity for any who did not believe . . . and all in
the name of a loving God Who wants the very best for His
people. Surely there was a better representative of Humanity
than our *religion*?

"Not . . . not everyone believes all that stuff," I said.
I hadn't meant it to be so defensive, but that was what it
sounded like to my ears.

OF COURSE NOT. IT IS THE VERY DIVERSITY OF HUMAN
RELIGIOUS THOUGHT AND BELIEF THAT MAKES YOUR SPECIES
SO INTERESTING.

Great. Fucking *great*. They were studying us because our
religious tendencies were *interesting*.

"None of that helps us at the moment," Hancock said.
"Lloyd . . . can you goose the sub a bit? Move us? Maybe we
can give our friend out there a case of indigestion."

"I've tried, Gunny," she said. She shook her head. "We're
being held in a non-fluid medium with a pressure exceed-
ing forty tons per square centimeter. Trust me . . . we're not
going *anywhere*!"

"Except where it wants to take us," Montgomery said.
"The deck is tilting. I think we're going—"

She shrieked, and Hancock swore again. The deck had
suddenly tilted toward the bow until we were hanging in our
seats, facing almost directly down. I could feel that stomach-
twisting lightness again, too, stronger now, the feeling of a
very rapid descent.

"Is the pressure increasing?" I asked.

Lloyd nodded. "Going up at a steady rate. We must be
just past the five-hundred-kilometer mark now."

Hanging like that was hideously uncomfortable, with the safety arm of the seat across my stomach tightly enough that I was having trouble breathing. I toyed with the idea of reprogramming the nanomatrix to rotate my seat 180 degrees, but decided to see if I could tough it out. If the sub changed attitude again while I was trying to scramble from one configuration to another, I might end up slamming into a bulkhead.

And then the deck began to level off again, though we were still going down at a steep angle.

"God," Hancock said. "Is the damned thing deliberately taking us somewhere? Or is it just looking for a quiet place to digest us?"

"If it is," I said, "it's taking us down deep." I was linked in with the AI, watching the pressure readings increase. Six hundred kilometers . . .

The cuttlewhale was moving at an astonishing speed. It had just dived an additional hundred kilometers in something just under ten minutes . . . which worked out to six hundred kilometers per hour. I'd *never* heard of anything traveling at that kind of speed underwater.

And *still* we were going down.

I think all of us had our ears cocked for the warning creak or pop that might tell us that our CM hull was about to fail. I was afraid, sure . . . but the earlier, babbling panic I'd felt was gone. I think that was because some part of my brain knew and accepted the fact that no matter what happened in the next few moments, it was completely out of my control.

Not only that, but the cuttlewhales had been attempting to communicate! Gods, but that was big! That alone suggested that they were intelligent, at least on some level, and, perhaps most important, they were not acting randomly, but according to some sort of plan. The cuttlewhale that had swallowed us *could* have crushed us—I was sure of that, even with our CM hull—but it had not. Instead, it was carrying us into the deeps.

Carrying us down, perhaps, to meet its maker.

The thought struck me funny, enough to make me chuckle out loud.

"Enjoying yourself, Doc?" Hancock asked. He didn't sound amused.

"Sorry, Gunny," I said. "I just realized we were being taken to meet whatever it was that created the cuttlewhales. Their *God* . . ."

"Do you seriously think these things were *manufactured*?" Ortega asked.

"It's the only hypothesis that makes sense," I replied. "Otherwise . . . why do they have eyes?"

"Maybe down where they evolved, most life forms make their own light," Montgomery suggested. "Like in Europa."

"Or maybe they feed at the surface," Ortega added. "Or they evolved at the surface, and gradually migrated to the deeps."

"Maybe." But I wasn't at all convinced. I didn't bother arguing the point, though, because I was willing to bet that, in a short time—a few hours at most—we would learn the truth firsthand.

"Well *I* think Doc's right," Lloyd insisted. "Why else would they be taking us this deep?" She hesitated. "Past the seven-hundred-kilometer mark, now."

"They're *alien*," Ortega said. "Damn it, they're going to do inexplicable things!"

I remembered my conversation with Wiseman . . . and with others. There would still be, I was certain, points of common rationality even between species as mutually alien as humans and cuttlewhales. There *had* to be. Hunger . . . a need to reproduce . . . curiosity. . . . We must share *some* things in common, even when we live in worlds as far apart as the surface of Earth and the Abyssworld deeps.

I was well aware that I was grasping at a rather slender hope. If cuttlewhales were created, maybe they didn't have reproductive urges. Maybe they didn't feel anything like hunger *or* curiosity if they were designed as tools and manufactured for a specific purpose. Maybe . . .

I could speculate about it all day, I knew, and never get anywhere. All I could say with any certainty was that we were getting closer to an answer, one way or another, with every passing minute, with every passing kilometer.

Eight hundred kilometers.

We were aware now of a gentle rocking motion from side to side . . . as if the titanic beast enclosing us was weaving slightly back and forth, propelling itself with vast and powerful sinuous weavings of its body. The speed had picked up too. We no longer were going straight down . . . but we were descending now at a rate of about 120 kilometers per hour. The outside pressure continued to increase. I forced myself not to think about that; *Walsh*'s designers had been confident enough that the little submersible could go considerably deeper than this.

I *did* hope that those engineers hadn't dropped a decimal or two along the way, though.

Nine hundred kilometers.

Would cuttlewhale motives be any harder to understand than, say, human religious belief? If we got out of this, I was determined to have a talk with D'deen or the other M'nangat. What did they really think of us and our—what had the Broc called it?—our *interesting* religious thought and belief.

And what *did* I believe? That I would be physically reborn some day, in a new life, like my parents had taught me? Or did life simply . . . end?

Well, if it was the latter, I would never know anything. If the former—

Static crashed and howled inside my head.

I screamed, my hands going up to my ears. Dimly, I saw the others making the same, instinctive protective gesture, clapping their hands over their ears as their faces contorted. Then the static spread from my in-head windows to my normal vision. For a terrifying moment, I was blind and deaf, assaulted by the raw shriek of white noise at way too high a volume.

The pain grew worse . . . and I thought I saw something on my in-head.

At first I couldn't tell what it was, what I was seeing. It looked like . . . a planet? A smooth, featureless white sphere against the blackness of space?

I only had a glimpse of the thing, whatever it was . . . and then the static was gone.

"Jesus, Mary, and Joseph!" Ortega gasped. "What the fuck was *that*?"

"A hack," Hancock said, still rubbing his ears. "Something just hacked our in-heads! God knows how!"

Gina Lloyd was unconscious. I released myself from my chair, leaning against the back of her seat in order to reach around and check the pulse at her throat. It was running at about eighty, strong and a bit fast. I patted her cheek. "Gina! Gina! Snap out of it!"

Her eyes opened. "Gods!" she said. "What happened?"

"I think something tapped into our in-head circuitry. I don't know how."

"That's not supposed to be possible!" Montgomery said. "Shit! D'deen is out too!"

Lloyd seemed to be okay, if a bit shaken. I left her and pulled my way up across the steeply slanted deck to reach D'deen's bucket. I tried using my in-head to reach him, but I couldn't pick up anything. "D'deen? D'deen! Are you okay? Write something to me!"

No response. The M'nangat's skin felt clammy and cold . . . but they were always a bit on the chilly side, despite having a body temperature only a degree or so lower than human. The thick, outer integument tended to insulate their body, and felt cool to the touch. The clamminess might just be from the high humidity inside the *Walsh*. The boat's environmental controls appeared to be having some trouble catching up with the moisture from our breathing after having been shut down for a while.

The truth was, I just didn't know enough about Broc

physiology to tell what might be wrong. The data Net running inside the *Walsh* had only the bare-bones essentials; I would need a link with Ludwig and the full medical AI complement on board *Haldane* before I could even make some decent guesses.

"Leave it, Doc," Hancock told me. "We have other things to worry about right now."

"At least let me know he's stable," I replied. I took out my N-prog and an injector, shooting a dose of medical nanobots into D'deen's system. Moments later, I could see something of the Broc's internal functions—both hearts beating steadily in a back-and-forth rhythm, circulatory fluid circulating . . . everything looked fine. I ordered my fleet of 'bots to highlight D'deen's brain. The problem we'd experienced, all of us, had been a sudden burst of energy going through our cerebral prosthesis, the nano-chelated electronics grown inside our brains.

I could see the artificial structures inside D'deen's brain now . . . a complex web of bright metal threads, like a spider's web, running through the equivalent of the M'nangat's cerebral cortex. I magnified the image as much as I could, until my in-head was actually showing me strands of what looked like gold rope stretched across masses of living cells, with sub-micron filaments actually connecting the rope with the branching dendrites of alien neurons.

Then I pulled back and had the 'bots do a simple electrical activity scan. I hoped that M'nangat brains operated on the same sort of biochemical-electrical interaction as human neurons. The chemistry, I noted, *was* different, but there were still exchanges of ions across synaptic gaps, creating what amounted to a very low-voltage current.

I would need a full brain-function scan back in *Haldane*'s sick bay to be sure, but it looked to me like D'deen's brain was working okay . . . but quiescent.

In other words, he was unconscious.

"I don't see any cellular damage in D'deen's brain," I told

the others. "Nothing burned out, or bleeding, or anything like that. He's just been knocked unconscious."

I just hoped that what I was seeing wasn't the Broc equivalent of deep coma, or that there was some other serious medical issue that I simply didn't recognize because I didn't know what the hell I was doing.

I made certain that D'deen's seat was holding him securely. "Did anyone else . . . see anything?" I asked. "During that blast of static?"

"I did," Montgomery said. "A white ball against a black background."

"I thought it might be the planet, the planet's nightside, seen from space," Hancock said.

"It looked uniformly lit to me," Ortega said. "And there was no local sun, no stars. I don't know what it was."

"I think I . . . heard something," Lloyd said, hesitant.

"Oh?" Hancock said. "What?"

"It was hard to make out . . . but something like the words . . . 'help us'?"

"Interesting," Hancock said, frowning. "Does anyone have any idea, any idea at all, what happened just then?"

"I'm not sure, Gunny," I said, "but I think maybe somebody was trying to talk to us."

"Who?"

"Whoever . . . *what*ever is running things down here."

"The cuttlewhale gods?" Ortega said. He laughed, a sharp, almost barking laugh that felt uncomfortably close to hysteria. "And they want *us* to help *them*?"

"But how did they do that?" Hancock wanted to know.

"You know, Gunny," I said slowly, thinking it out carefully with each word that I spoke, "if you have something big enough, intelligent enough, powerful enough to create a pseudo life form as impressive as the cuttlewhales . . ."

"Yes?"

"I just wonder if there's anything they *can't* do."

"Explain that," Hancock said.

I shook my head. "I can't. But . . . okay. Somehow, some-one interfered with our in-head circuits, right? That would have to be either a very powerful radio signal, or possibly a focused magnetic induction of some kind."

"You lost me there, Doc," Montgomery said.

"That's because I really don't know what I'm talk-ing about," I replied. "But maybe a cuttlewhale carrying us inside its throat can somehow sense us, and the wiring inside our brains. Or maybe it's . . . someone, something, working through the cuttlewhale, using it like a teleoperated probe or a remote explorer."

"Through a CM hull?" Ortega said. "I don't think so."

I shrugged. "Why not? We use wave induction to send signals through our hull . . . for the outside lights, and to pick up vid images."

"Point," Ortega said. "But this 'someone' of yours would have to be very, very sophisticated technologically."

"So, it sends us a signal. A message. Maybe it's learned enough through our AI's communications attempts to make a guess about how our electronics work."

"Somehow, Doc," Montgomery said, "I find it very hard to imagine an underwater species understanding electronics!"

"Why? Electricity conducts through saltwater."

"They would have had to develop a lot of science first," she said. "Starting with metallurgy . . . smelting metals, de-veloping ways to make wires, electromagnets, radio trans-mission in a medium that absorbs radio waves . . . uh-uh. No fire, no metalworking."

"The way we did things on Earth, you're right. But maybe this someone didn't do things the same way we did. Maybe it learned to smelt metals at hot, undersea volcanic vents. Maybe it learned tricks with exotic ice shot through with metallic impurities. Maybe—"

The *Walsh* gave another lurch, and the deck suddenly lev-eled off.

"I think we've arrived," Lloyd told us. "*Look!*"

Directly ahead, the light still shining off the *Walsh*'s outer hull was now illuminating a widening tunnel or passage. We felt a kind of surge through the deck as the submarine lurched forward . . . and then . . . *my gods*. . . .

We'd emerged within a vast, clear, empty volume lit blue-green by the *Walsh*'s external lights. For hundreds of meters in all directions, the water was sparklingly transparent, fading to translucence in the distance.

"*Out of the belly of the beast . . .*" Ortega said, his voice almost reverently hushed.

"My God," Hancock said. "What *is* that?"

It was difficult to know exactly what we were looking at, and impossible to determine a scale of what we were seeing. Above us, the blue-green glow faded rapidly into the blackness of the Abyss, but below, the water appeared to be . . . *thick*. Gelatinous, perhaps, something not quite water, but not solid either, something spreading out in motionless waves and folds and hills and gently rolling valleys extending into the distance in all directions as far as we could see. It reflected our light in odd ways, creating a shimmering, diffuse effect that was indescribably beautiful. Was it ice? Or . . . something like thick water? I couldn't tell.

"Do you think we could have a sonar ping sent down into that translucent stuff?" I asked.

"I advise against it," Ortega said. "Remember what happened when we used sonar from the surface."

"That was at extremely high power and low frequency," I said. "The cuttlewhales weren't reacting to low-power scans."

"Try it," Hancock said.

"Pinging . . ." Lloyd said. "Low power."

Sonar targets appeared on the viewalls, overlaying the shimmering panorama of light and water.

"We're getting odd reflections off that jelly stuff," she said. She paused, then added, "it's more like refractions . . . and the sound waves are moving a lot faster through it."

"Sonar indicates the water beneath us is unusually dense,"

the AI added. "It appears to be fluid, and may represent an extremely diffuse form of amorphous ice VIII."

I didn't remember offhand the characteristics of ice VIII, except for one. All of the exotic ices from ice III on were denser than water . . . which meant that they would sink rather than float like normal ice I_h. Quite possibly, most of the Abyssworld ocean was a fluid form of ice, solid or semi-solid, but dense enough to sink to the seafloor thousands of kilometers below. It was even possible that what we were looking at was not on the list of fifteen known phases of ice, that it was something *really* exotic—ice XVI, perhaps.

And in this environment . . . why not? I checked with the AI and noted that we were at a depth of close to a thousand kilometers, and that the pressure on our hull was now in excess of ninety tons per square centimeter. At such pressures, the exotic would be commonplace—ice that acted like fluid, perhaps, or water that acted like thick, glassy gelatin.

"What the hell," Hancock said, leaning forward, "is *that*?"

He was staring at a sonar target forward and slightly below us.

"Can you magnify the image?" Ortega asked.

"Here you go . . ."

The image expanded, centered on the object we'd earlier tagged as target Sierra Five. Lloyd gasped, and I nearly shouted.

Sierra Five was a perfect sphere floating within the glassy-water zone right at the border between ocean and amorphous ice.

A white sphere identical to the thing I'd glimpsed during that burst of in-head static earlier.

"Curiouser and curiouser," Montgomery said, thoughtful. "Miss Lloyd . . . can you perhaps probe that sphere with the sonar? A very tight beam?"

"To get an idea of what it's made of?" she said. "Maybe. Just a sec. . . ."

"Whatever it is," Ortega said, "it *must* be artificial. You don't get perfect spheres in nature."

"You might," I said. "Remember, sir, down here the absolute best shape to resist pressure is a sphere. The pressure would be evenly distributed over the entire surface that way."

"As near as I can tell," Lloyd informed us, "that thing is ice."

"Ordinary water ice?" I asked. "Or something exotic?"

"Ordinary ice . . . I *think*. It's under a lot of pressure."

I pulled up the data on exotic ices I'd downloaded earlier. Several ice phases, I saw, could be formed by applying insane pressure to ordinary ice, and it was likely that this had happened here. But there was no way to tell without moving in close and taking a sample.

"That's odd . . ." Lloyd said after a few moments. We were moving slowly toward Sierra Five, which was now only a few kilometers distant.

"What?" Hancock asked her.

"I'm getting . . . I think it's a signal!"

"What kind of signal?"

She put the sound on the cabin speakers. The surrounding water, it seemed, was filled with noise—a kind of low-grade rushing sound, punctuated by creaks, groans, clicks, and whistles. It was possible, *more* than possible, that we were hearing life out there in those normally lightless depths.

"I don't hear any—" Ortega started to say.

"Shh!" Lloyd hissed. "Wait . . . there!"

I heard it. We all did. A *clank*—the unmistakable sound of metal striking metal. And again . . . and again. The noise was muffled, and so faint that it almost wasn't there at all.

Clank-clank-clank . . . clank . . . clank . . . clank . . . clank-clank-clank . . .

"The cuttlewhales?" Montgomery asked.

"Shit, no," Hancock said, shaking his head. "That's someone banging on a bulkhead with a wrench!"

"Or a piece of pipe," Lloyd agreed.

"Another Gykr sub?" Ortega suggested.

"If it was, they'd have jumped us by now," I said. "That sound is *close*. I think it's coming from Sierra Five."

Clank-clank-clank . . . clank . . . clank . . . clank . . . clank-clank-clank . . .

"*Christ on a crutch!*" Hancock shouted. "That's *Morse!*"

"What is Morse?" Montgomery asked.

"A kind of code. From centuries ago, before radio. People sent dots and dashes representing letters over wires, and later with primitive radio, wireless transmission."

"So . . . do you know this code?" Ortega asked.

"Don't need to! They're sending SOS!"

"That used to be some kind of a distress call, didn't it?" I asked.

"Not *a* distress call. *The* distress call . . . the international signal for help. It means 'save our ship.' "

I was amazed that Hancock knew this bit of historical trivia. We'd had voice radio and in-head transmissions for so long now that this Morse Code he was talking about must by now be of interest only to historians.

"The first use of 'SOS' in an emergency radio broadcast was the HMS *Titanic*, when she sank in 1912," he went on. "Before that, they'd used a different code group . . . 'CQD.'"

"How the hell do you know this stuff?" Ortega asked.

Hancock shrugged. "I've always been a nut on maritime history," he said.

That made sense. I knew that Gunny Hancock cared passionately for his Marines, and that passion obviously extended to arcane tidbits of Marine history or ancient military technology. When he went in for rejuvenation some year, he'd have his hands full deciding what memories to cull.

"There's something else," I said.

"What's that, son?" Ortega asked.

"'Save our ship,'" I said. "And when we got blasted by that static a while ago, Gina heard the words 'help us.' "

"Are you sure of what you heard, Lloyd?" Hancock asked her.

"As sure as I can be, Gunny. It was faint . . . *real* faint, almost not there at all."

"I'd say that this code we're hearing validates what she thinks she heard," Montgomery pointed out. "You know what that means, don't you?"

"What?" Hancock asked her.

"That white sphere out there is what's left of Murdock Base . . . and there are still survivors on board."

"My God!" Hancock said.

"She's right," I said. "It makes sense. The wreckage of the base would sink to the point where it was the same specific gravity as the water around it. Or maybe it sank until it's floating on that gelatinous liquid ice."

"But the base wasn't a sphere!" Ortega said.

"No . . . but they would have had an external nanomatrix, same as we do," I said. "Suppose they programmed their external nano to grab water molecules and reassemble them into hexagonal crystals."

"Freeze them, you mean," Hancock said.

"Freeze enough of them to make a giant ice ball," I said, nodding. "To withstand the increasing pressure as it sank."

"That's . . . crazy . . ." Hancock said.

"I don't know how else they would have survived the pressure this deep," I said. "If they were sinking slowly enough, they might have been able to keep adding on more and more ice, and letting the ice get squeezed until it was essentially incompressible. If their original dome was CM, it might work."

"'Save us,'" Montgomery said. "A call for help. . . ."

Save us . . .

At dead-slow speed, we continued our approach to Sierra Five.

Chapter Twenty

"THERE'S SOMETHING ELSE," MONTGOMERY SAID AS WE AP-
proached the huge dull-white sphere adrift in the eerie light.
"The cuttlewhales . . . they deliberately brought us down
here. They want to help!"

"Looks that way," Ortega replied. "Still, we're best off if
we don't jump to wild conclusions."

"What else are we supposed to think?" I said. "It would
have taken us over a day to get down here at a steady descent rate of ten meters per second. That cuttlewhale swallowed us, brought us here, and let us go, bang on target."

"Where is that cuttlewhale, anyway?" Hancock asked.

"Astern," Lloyd said. "And drawing off. I'm picking up a
lot of them in the area . . . over two hundred. They seem to
be keeping their distance."

"They dropped us off, then withdrew to a discreet distance," Montgomery said. "To observe? To appear non-
threatening?"

"Maybe just to watch what we do," Hancock said. "And
speaking of which . . . what *can* we do? If Dr. Montgomery is
right and that's our base . . . we're going to have a hard time
just getting in there. And the *Walsh* is way too small to take
more than a handful of survivors to the surface at a time."

"How many people were stationed at the base?" Lloyd
wanted to know.

"Eighty-five humans," Hancock told her. He glanced over his shoulder at D'deen, still unconscious in his bowl, before adding, "And twelve Brocs."

"Ninety-seven," I said, "would make things a bit crowded in here."

"How thick is that ice?" Ortega asked.

"The original central dome of the station was about thirty meters across," Hancock said. "That sphere is . . . what? A hundred meters wide?"

"Almost that," Lloyd confirmed. "Sonar readings give a diameter ninety-eight point one meters."

"Close enough. So assuming the base itself is at the exact center of all that, it's underneath a minimum of thirty-five meters of super-compressed ice."

"It might not be that bad," Lloyd said. "We have a see-through."

One of the bulkhead viewalls brought up a translucent image of the sphere. "Sound waves travel through solid structure," Lloyd told us, "and their backscatter can give us an idea of what's inside."

"Sonograms," Montgomery said. "So where's the baby?"

"We can see a kind of hollow area inside," Lloyd said. On the image, the dome inside the ice, given a yellow color by the computer, had a broken, crumpled look, but a deep purple blob at the center suggested an internal void. A slender purple shaft ran from the interior space to within a few meters of the outside surface.

"What's that?" I asked. "An access shaft?"

"I think so," Hancock said, studying the image closely. "I'm not sure how it's holding up under the pressure, though."

"The borders of that shaft are CM," Lloyd said. "I think they must have built it by cannibalizing other parts of the dome itself with construction nano."

"It certainly looks like the way in," Hancock said. "Let's get in close."

The *Walsh* slowly moved to within twenty meters of

the sphere and carefully circled it, probing with her sonar. Lloyd was using a lower-frequency pinging now, the better to penetrate ice and CM metal, but there seemed to be no response from the distant, watching cuttlewhales. Perhaps they'd thought of the earlier, extremely loud sonar pulses as a hostile act, but now knew that we were using them to feel our way through the depths.

At close range, we were able to get a bit more detail on the sunken base's interior, but not much. Sound imaging is wretchedly imprecise for fine detail, compared to electromagnetic radiation. We couldn't tell if there were people moving around inside or not. It was all blobs and fuzziness inside.

"The survivors have stopped banging," Hancock observed.

"They probably heard our sonar," Lloyd told him. "They stopped to listen."

"Give them one ping . . . then two more."

A moment later, an answer came back. *Clank . . . clank . . . clank.*

"I'd say we've established communications," Montgomery said.

"Great," Ortega said. "So what do we do about it?"

"We see about getting inside," Hancock replied. "Lloyd? Take us in close. Put us up next to where that long passageway is."

"Aye, aye, sir."

The *Walsh* was completely coated by a thin layer of nanobots—the source of our external light and our vid imaging from the outside. In addition, large portions of the hull were titanoplas nanomatrix, meaning the individual particles of matter could rearrange themselves in order to, for instance, change the submarine's shape to give more or less lift as she flew through the water. It was the matter of a few moments to program most of the external 'bots, directing them to migrate to the port side and begin building a docking collar. Doing this cost us most of our external vid. We kept a few nanobots in place as image receivers and transmitters, as well as some light along our port side. To starboard, above, and below, the ocean deeps returned to a primordial blackness punctuated, surprisingly, by flashes and ripples of pastel-colored light in the distance. Evidently, life within this ocean world, as on Earth and as within Europa, had learned the trick of generating organic phosphorescence.

Slowly, a squat cylinder began to grow out from the *Walsh*'s port side, burrowing into the wall of ice alongside.

The toughest part of the process was working against that incredible pressure outside. One advantage of working at nano scales, however, is the obvious one that a nanobot has much less surface area against which the weight of the water can press. One square micron is one ten-thousandth of a square centimeter; each individual 'bot was experiencing something like ten kilos of pressure, a hell of a lot on a device a fifth the size of a human red blood cell, but not impossible. Each individual device, working with molecular motors and minute electrical and magnetic fields, was incredibly strong. The speed of each device was considerably reduced; under these pressures it would have taken days, perhaps *weeks* to erect the dome instead of a couple of hours. A docking collar was a lot simpler than a habitation dome; our AI predicted that the construction time would be about eight hours.

We had *Walsh*'s small on-board nanufactory put together dinner for us. Then we slept in our seats, with Hancock, Lloyd, and myself sharing the watch, staying awake to make sure everything continued to proceed as planned.

Eventually, the docking collar was complete, creating a solid connection between the newly grown airlock in *Walsh*'s port side and the end of the purple void buried about ten meters back within the ice. Much more difficult than growing the thing, though, was depressurizing the collar once it had been extended out from our hull nanomatrix. Our fleet of microscopic construction engines had burrowed away into the ice, hollowing out the space inside the collar by decoupling the oxygen and hydrogen from each other, breaking water ice into gasses that promptly vanished into solution. Once the ice was gone, however, it had been replaced by liquid water.

Fortunately, that water was not at the outside ambient pressure. Water is not compressible . . . meaning that if the docking collar carried the weight of the water outside, the water inside remained at a more sane pressure. So long as there was no break in the seals or any opening to the outside, the interior of the collar was as safe as an Earthside swimming pool.

We still faced a problem in getting the water out of the collar. The traditional means—using air pressure to force the water out—wouldn't work here, not unless we had a pump that could deliver more than one hundred tons per square centimeter.

The answer was to grow a reservoir alongside the collar and pump the excess water into that. Eventually—another couple of meals—the water was gone from the collar, replaced now with air from *Walsh*'s reserves at standard temperature and pressure.

Meanwhile, we had other external 'bots working outside the sub and the docking collar, creating layer upon layer of compressed ice to build up a strong pressure shell. *Walsh*, by this time, was firmly bonded to the ice sphere enclosing the base, nearly lost within the much larger mass of ice.

Oddly, though, we'd stopped hearing any of the banging communications from inside. We tried both radio and sound, but there was no reply, an ominous silence that had Hancock worried.

"I don't like it," he said, staring at the inner hatch of *Walsh*'s new airlock. "What happened to them?"

"Maybe their arms got tired," I suggested.

"Very funny."

"Look, are we sure that collar is going to hold the pressure?" Ortega asked. "If that collapses after we open our hatch . . ."

"It's as solid as we can make it, Dr. Ortega," Lloyd told him. "The collar is holding the pressure now just fine. That won't change when we crack the hatch."

"Then let's get on over there," Hancock said. He looked at Gina, then at me. "Doc? You with me?"

"Let me get my M-7, Gunny."

We'd discussed procedure exhaustively during the past day, going over the situation and searching for anything we might have missed. Hancock would go first . . . just in case, because he was our only Marine. I would go with him because I was the Doc, and there might be—probably were—people in there who needed medical attention. We'd considered donning our Marine armor, but eventually decided against it. The long, narrow passageway into the interior of the ice-shrouded base was only a meter and a half high and wide. Mk. 10 suits were just too cumbersome and bulky to allow for easy maneuvering in such a cramped space.

The only reason to wear armor would be if the air in the long access tunnel wasn't good, but nanoprobes had already reported that the atmosphere beyond the docking collar was breathable, a standard oxygen-nitrogen mix, at one standard atmosphere. It would be a bit chilly over there, and the humidity was near 100 percent . . . but we wouldn't need to carry our own air.

Gunny Hancock produced a weapon—a holstered 12 mm Republic service pistol—which he holstered on his hip. I'd not even known he'd brought one along . . . but then, the idea of a Marine going anywhere without at least a sidearm when the tactical situation was unknown was . . . unthinkable.

Besides, the survivors in the sunken base had been here for weeks now, presumably. We might need at least the threat of firepower to maintain control.

I hoped that would not be the case.

I stood with Gunny as he opened the *Walsh*'s inner lock.

"Doc?" Gina said. "You be careful over there, okay? Make sure you come back."

"Always," I told her, grinning. "Careful is what I do best."

At first I was touched that she seemed concerned for my safety. Then I realized that a likely reason for that concern was the fact that if anything happened to us, it would happen to the people left on board *Walsh* as well. It was easy to forget just how unforgivingly deadly this environment truly was. And the wrecked dome inside its ice ball *would* be dangerous, if the shell was already partially collapsed.

We moved through *Walsh*'s airlock, and opened the hatch between the collar and the airlock. The air inside was thick with moisture, steamy hot, and with water dripping down the bulkheads and collecting on the deck. Both ice and CM are excellent insulators, and the interior was still hot after driving off most of the water.

Good.

Hancock opened the collar's outer hatch, revealing yet another doorway beyond. This one looked . . . strange, not like a typical base airlock access at all. It was solid dark-gray metal, with no obvious way of opening it.

It gave us both pause. "What the fuck?" Hancock said, looking the barrier up and down. "You know, Doc, I think—"

The barrier opened of its own accord, the metal puckering at the middle and then rippling open in all directions, creating a circular opening, a doorway leading into near total darkness. And beyond, within that darkness just a couple of meters away, loomed a shadowy, monstrous figure . . . an armored Gykr.

"Get down, Doc!" Hancock screamed, drawing his weapon. The Gykr already had a weapon in one of its forward appendages, a complicated-looking tube with a massive grip designed for its manipulatory claspers.

It fired, and I heard a sharp crack and smelled the tinny

stink of ozone as a bolt of energy snapped above our heads and slammed into the docking collar's outer hatch behind us. Hancock brought his pistol up and got off two shots. The Republic 12mm was an old-style slug-thrower, but had the considerable advantage of not requiring a heavy battery or other power supply. Both rounds, however, appeared to shatter against the Gucker's carapace without effect. Hancock must have loaded the seven-round magazine with frangibles . . . a good idea if you were planning for a firefight within an enclosed environment where putting a round through a bulkhead was not recommended, but useless when it came to penetrating armor.

Hancock cursed, came up off his hands and knees, and collided with the Gykr soldier. The only light was coming from a few nanolights in a circle around the outside of the docking collar behind us; inside the long access tunnel beyond, it was completely dark, so much so that I couldn't see if there were more Gykrs waiting for us farther along.

For a moment, Hancock and the Gykr struggled, and all I could see was a confusion of spidery limbs around the black, central mass of the alien; then the Gykr fired its weapon again . . . and again . . . sending one bolt into the overhead. The second burned through Gunny Hancock's left arm.

He screamed and sagged to one side. I'd been looking for an opening, but the passageway was too narrow for the two of us to engage the Gucker at once. Now I was able to crowd past Hancock and grapple with the Gykr hand-to-hand . . . or maybe, in this case, it was more hand-to-hand-to-hand-to-hand. The Gykr had several limbs that could serve as legs or arms, and several small arms that were useless for heavy lifting, but which could grasp and claw at me.

"Get him up!" Hancock screamed at my side. *"Get him up!"*

I saw what he wanted. Normally, Gykrs went about like giant insects, heads low to the ground, their rounded backs well protected by bands of artificial armor grafted on over bands of natural calcareous armor or chitin. Their undersides were less well protected, especially around the face and mouth parts.

Grappling with two of the Gykr's longer arms, including the one wielding the alien weapon, I dug in and pushed, hard, lifting the creature up and back. I was aided by the gravity, 9 percent less than Earth's, and doubt that I could have lifted it in a full G or without a personal exoskeleton suit.

I managed to push it up and back, however, its legs flailing as it tried to get a grip on my body. Hancock's pistol went off right beside my ear, a painful, thundering *crack-crack-crack* that left my ears ringing, but the rounds slammed into the thinner armor covering the Gykr's face, ripping open its suit above its breathing flaps.

From the autopsy Chief Garner and I had performed, I knew that there were six breathing slits along its head, three to either side of the being's face behind and below the bulge of its compound eyes. Gykrs breathed oxygen, though they needed a lower partial pressure than did we—about 10 percent.

But they also appeared to need a higher level of carbon dioxide—over 33 percent—a level that would have been fatal to humans without breathing gear, and they required an ambient atmospheric pressure a third lower than ours.

As I wrestled there in the dark with that armored horror, I could hear a hissing, rasping gurgle as it struggled with the tunnel's gas mix forcing its way into its suit. I freed one hand, stuck two fingers into a gaping hole opened by one of Hancock's bullets, and yanked as hard as I could, peeling open a layer of artificial outer armor as thin as paper.

The Gucker broke free from me, staggering backward, its arms flailing wildly, its weapon landing with a splash in a shallow pool of water a meter in front of me. Ducking down, I scooped up the weapon, wondering how to fire it . . . and then finding the trigger recessed into the grip. The bolt slammed into the Gykr's chest, burning open a ragged crater the size of my head and dropping the struggling creature onto its back.

I immediately turned to check on Hancock. The bolt, I saw, had burned clean through his left arm about at the level of his elbow. His lower arm and hand were lying on the deck, grotesque and steaming.

The stump of his arm appeared to have been cauterized, the flesh charred and blackened halfway to his shoulder. There was no bleeding, but when I held my small flash to his eyes, they looked glassy and unfocused.

"Did . . . we get 'im?"

"You got him, Gunny. Good shooting!"

"We—"

And then another bolt of hot plasma seared down the tunnel, striking one bulkhead a few meters away in a blue-white flare of light.

I spun around, raising the alien weapon again. There was another Gykr down that black passageway, perhaps forty meters away at the far end of the passage, and I couldn't see it. A second shot, this one hitting the puckered, alien door just behind us. Steadying the captured weapon in both hands, I tried to guess where the bolts had come from and began squeezing off shots one after another.

The weapon appeared to be a compact plasma weapon— probably using either water or the local atmosphere, super-heating it to an electrified plasma, and hurling the bolt down range with a magnetic accelerator.

After five or six shots, though, the weapon suddenly became hot, hot enough to burn my unprotected hands. I dropped it, and heard the sizzle as it splashed in water. Picking it up again, I hesitated a moment, then fired again.

There were no more shots returning from down range, however. I couldn't see. Had my wild fusillade hit the plasma gunner?

I returned my attention to Gunny Hancock, though I kept

one eye out for movement in the darkness. I gave him a jolt
of medical nano programmed to kill the pain and counteract
the shock.

"That's . . . that's doing the trick, Doc," he said. "Thanks."

"Think you can make it back to the *Walsh*?"

"Yeah."

"C'mon. I'll help you."

I half carried him back through the airlock, where Ortega
and Lloyd helped pull him inside. "He should be okay, at
least for now," I told them. "We'll need to get him back on
board the *Haldane* to grow him a new arm, but he's not hurting much right now, and there's no bleeding."

I put skinseal over the end of the stump, though, just to
make sure he didn't start bleeding again . . . and the artificial
skin would also start treating the burned tissue, getting it
ready for regen.

"Okay," I said when I was done. "I'm going back out
there, and see what's at the far end of that tunnel."

"You can't go out there alone!" Montgomery said.

"Why not? We need to make contact with the base personnel in there."

"Suppose there are more Gucks?" Lloyd said.

"I'll go with him," Ortega said.

"I'll be fine on my—"

"Stop being a fucking hero," Hancock said from his
couch. Hell, I'd thought he was unconscious. He had enough
'bots both inside his skull and in what was left of his arm,
all turning off pain receptors with enthusiasm enough to
send him off to floaty-floaty land. "The two of you go across
and try to make contact. If you even smell another Gucker,
hightail it back to the *Walsh*, we'll decouple, and head for
the surface. We might need to come back down with a real
military force."

And so, a few minutes later, I walked into the dark accessway with Ortega right behind me. I held the captured
alien plasma gun, while he had Hancock's Republic-12. We

took a few moments to make sure he understood how the pistol worked, and then Gunny provided us with fresh mags loaded with AP rounds—armor piercers, which would do a better job on Guckers than would frangibles. "I *think* the bulkheads will stand up to those," Hancock said as we prepared to head off. "But don't test it, okay? If a round went through the accessway bulkhead, it might crack the ice on the other side, and that would likely ruin your whole day."

Not to mention ruined days for those we were leaving behind on the *Walsh*, and the survivors inside the station. One failure, one cascade of incoming water at over a hundred tons per square centimeter, and bulkheads, airlock hatches, and the docking collar doors wouldn't be able to stop the final, complete, and absolute collapse.

Just beyond the docking-collar door, I stooped to check on the wounded Gykr. It had curled up into a kind of fetal position, like an armadillo, so that only its segmented dorsal armor was exposed.

"Is it dead?" Ortega asked.

"I think so," I replied. "I wish I knew more about its respiratory metabolism."

Chief Garner and I had pulled a lot of samples from the Gucker we'd dissected, and lab tests should tell us a lot more about them.

The EG did tell us that the atmosphere they breathed was . . . unusual, with oxygen, which they appeared to use in a metabolic process similar to that of humans, but also apparently requiring a high concentration of carbon dioxide. There were ecosystems, I knew, that used carbon dioxide instead of oxygen—not to support combustion, obviously, but through a carbolic acid cycle that did much the same thing.

But a life form that used *both* was something new.

Or . . . possibly the CO_2 was nothing more for the Gykrs than a background gas, like nitrogen is for us, unreactive and uninvolved in their metabolic processes. That seemed unlikely, because carbon dioxide is rather reactive when put into solution in water . . . though it tends to be unreactive as a gas.

Damn, we had so much to learn. . . .

Ten steps from the docking collar, and we were in pitch-blackness. We could see the wan circle of hull lights behind us, but they didn't shed much illumination farther into the shaft. I was tempted—very tempted—to haul out my light so I could at least see where I was putting my feet, but if there were any more Gucks up ahead, hidden in the darkness, a light would make us perfect targets.

It was bad enough that we were partially blocking the hull lights at our backs. We must be clearly silhouetted against them for anyone waiting up ahead.

My steps slowed the farther in I got. Ortega bumped up against me. "Sorry . . ."

"S'okay," I whispered. "But hang back a little, okay?"

Where the docking collar had still been steamy and hot, that forty-five-meter tunnel, low and narrow, was bone-chillingly cold. Water dripped constantly from the walls, and in places it was freezing into sheets of ice. I felt it as I put my hand out to steady myself once. The deck underfoot was treacherous, and the curving tunnel wall was glazed over.

And then I tripped over something large and hard in the darkness.

I was sure I must be close to the end of that seemingly endless passageway, and we'd not yet been challenged. Stepping back, cautioning Ortega to stop, I decided to take a chance. I pulled my penflash out of my M-7 and directed it at the deck ahead.

It was another Gykr, curled into that same, familiar fetal position, and quite dead. I picked up the plasma weapon lying beside it. "You want this?" I asked, offering it to Ortega.

"Hell, no," he said. He gestured with the Republic-12. "I barely know which end is the business end of this thing."

"Fair enough." At least I *had* fired one of these things before. It wasn't hard to operate—hold *this* and press *that*—but it was clumsy for a human hand. Gykr manipulators are combinations of one long claw and six spidery, double-jointed fingers, and the grip is damned awkward for a human hand. I felt a bit foolish facing that last door at the end of the long tunnel with an alien plasma weapon in each hand, but I wasn't about to leave the second weapon lying on the deck.

I was staring at the door, wondering how to make it work, when it puckered suddenly and flowed open. According to our sonar scans, that door should open into the sunken base at an airlock.

Four Guckers were waiting on the other side of that door, weapons raised and pointing straight at my head. "Drop weapons!" a harsh voice clattered in my head. "Drop now!"

There was nothing Ortega or I could do but comply. . . .

Chapter Twenty-One

THE GYKRS CROUCHED IN A SEMICIRCLE IN FRONT OF US, HEADS LOW to the deck, threatening us with their plasma weapons. Behind them, in the near darkness of a ruined lab, I could see several humans, dirty, ragged, and unshaven . . . about what you would expect of people cut off from most technological amenities for several weeks.

"Do what they tell you, *please*," one of the humans said. He was an older man . . . and I thought he looked familiar. It took me a moment to place him, though—Dr. James Eric Murdock, the commander of the first Abyssworld research base.

"Dr. Murdock?" I said. "Are you and your people okay?"

"Do . . . do I know you, sir?"

"Your virtual avatar was my guide in a docuinteractive, sir," I said.

"No speech!" the Gykr growled. The words were coming through my in-head circuitry, which meant that the Gykrs had their own cerebral implants, along with the software that let them translate their thoughts into Gal3, which in turn could be translated into English by my own implants. That, I thought, was a considerable relief. Dealing with hostile aliens when you don't share a common language can leave you with no options at all except gunfire.

I opened a second channel back to the *Walsh*. "Trouble!"

I snapped. "We have a number of human survivors, but they've been captured by Gykr—"

"*No speech!*" The Gykr reared up on its splayed, long hind legs, its shorter forelegs weaving in an agitated manner. Apparently, it was linked in closely enough with the local communications Net that it could pick up any back-channel chatter that might be going on in the area. Secret conversations would be impossible.

I was able to drop the security interlock on my cerebral hardware. I wouldn't be able to get a direct signal out without being detected, apparently, but perhaps the others could listen in over the local Net.

I hoped.

"Take it easy," I thought at him. "We are not a threat to you. . . ."

It was the only approach that occurred to me. From the little we new of Gykr psychology, they were easily triggered by the perception of a threat, and their response tended to be immediate and violent.

It was easy to think of them as hostile alien monstrosities . . . or as somewhat dim-witted sociopaths who would kill you as soon as look at you . . . but the truth, I knew, had to be considerably different. They had developed a technological civilization sophisticated enough to give them starflight . . . after evolving deep within a solitary rogue planet light years from any other world. *How had they managed to pull that off?*

If what we thought we knew of their origins was accurate, they'd evolved from marine organisms deep within a lightless ocean . . . or possibly inside lightless caves warmed by upwelling magma within their dark and isolated world's crust. How long had it taken them to develop even simple tools, smelting, their equivalent of an industrial revolution, electronics? . . .

How long before Gykr explorers first tunneled up to the frozen surface of their world, wearing artificial armor to protect them from the airlessness and cold?

With eyes evolved to see the near infrared, the heat within their caverns . . . how long before they even became aware of the stars?

Humankind had gone from primitive experiments with electricity to putting men on Earth's moon in two centuries, more or less . . . and to sending ships to the nearer stars in three and a half. It might have taken the Gykr a million years to reach the stars . . . 10 million . . . or more. . . .

The fact that they had done so, to my mind, was an astonishing statement of the sheer persistent determination of life over adversity, of *intelligence* over darkness. After such a journey, I thought, they might be excused for a certain lack of social graces.

The upright Gykr appeared to be considering my words and, slowly, it dropped the forward part of its body back to the deck. That odd, golden, compound eye-ring that encircled both the ventral and dorsal surfaces of its head gave it all-round vision, and I knew it was still watching me closely.

But just how closely was that? According to the information I remembered from Gykr entry in the Encyclopedia Galactica, their visual range overlapped ours only slightly. They could see red and orange light, possibly the way we see blue or violet, but their visual range was actually centered down in the near infrared. That compound eye-ring would be best for seeing movement, not sharp detail . . . and the large, dark simple eyes extending from either side of that blunt excuse for a head probably saw only heat, fuzzy and less than precise. Gykr eyes obviously were evolved for seeing in the dark or near darkness, by the wan and ruddy glow of subsurface volcanic vents, perhaps, and not in the levels of light taken for granted by humans.

Was there *anything* there I could use? I didn't see anything obvious. They would still see if I stooped for one of the plasma weapons lying on the deck at my feet.

"Your . . . underwater vessel . . . is mine . . . now," the voice rasped.

"Mine," not "ours." That might be an artifact of the Gykr tendency toward a hive mentality. Did the four beings in front of us really share a hive mind? Could they even be thought of as individuals? Or did the word merely identify the speaker as the leader of this group? I didn't know.

"You're trapped down here, aren't you?" I said, looking for a way to turn a Gykr monologue into a conversation. "Just like us. . . ."

"My vessel . . . did not . . . return."

No, I thought, it damned well hadn't. The Gykr sub must have dropped some of them off here, then returned toward the surface where it had encountered the *Walsh* coming down. These Gykr were marooned, and the only way back to the surface was on board the *Walsh*.

"We're here to rescue you," I said. "*All* of you."

"You are . . . here . . . to rescue you."

"We are *not* your enemy," I said. "We're not at war, you and I. We can help you."

I could almost see the Gykr struggling with alien concepts. Xenosophontologists back on Earth had speculated that the Gykr had no concept for "war," in the same way that a fish might not understand the concept of "water." And yet they *had* accepted the treaty of Tanis, at least more or less.

Damn it, was there something *there* I could use? The Battle of Tanis had been a one-sided affair, with the Fifth Fleet catching a much smaller Gykr squadron and supply base by surprise. And . . . when we'd arrived in the GJ 1214 system, that lone Gykr starship had run for it, rather than putting up a fight.

I would need access to a history database—something I didn't have right now, a thousand kilometers underwater—but I thought I remembered that in the forty-some years since the Battle of Tanis, there'd been numerous Gykr raids and skirmishes with the bastards, but nothing like a stand-up war. Maybe that idea of "fight-or-fight," suggesting that they always attacked no matter what the tactical situation, wasn't entirely true.

Could it be true, even, for any species worthy of the term *intelligent*? There would always be situations that were simply too dire, too unbalanced in number, too hopeless to permit an attack-at-any-odds response. Creatures that always attacked and never ran away when the odds were against them were unlikely to survive in the long haul. Evolution was damned efficient at culling those who were reckless.

It could be that Tanis had taught the Gykr a measure of caution.

"You would have to take our vessel by force," I told them. "I don't think you have the numbers to do that."

It was pure bluff. The people still back on board the *Walsh* were completely unarmed.

"How many . . . of you . . . on vessel?"

"Twenty," I said. "Heavily armed."

"You are . . . twenty?"

"Twenty-two," I replied. "Dr. Ortega and I didn't know there were more of you here when we left our vessel." I wondered if I should mention it, then pushed ahead. "We killed the two Gykr we met in the passageway. They tried to kill us, so we felt . . . justified."

The Gykr appeared to be uncertain. I couldn't read their body language, but that was okay because I was willing to bet that they couldn't read ours, either.

"The deaths . . . of two units . . . is of no consequence."

"I repeat," I said, "we are *not* at war. We can cooperate to get out of this."

"You will . . . leave the vessel," the Gykr said after a moment, as though it had just seen the perfect solution. "All but . . . the vessel's guide. You will . . . remain here with . . . the rest of you."

The vessel's guide . . . they meant our pilot, Gina Lloyd. And the rest of us would be trapped on this ice-bound derelict a thousand kilometers beneath the surface. That wasn't quite what I had in mind by *cooperate.*

As it spoke, I was trying to assess the Gykr's worldview, the way it saw the world around it and interacted with it. Thanks, perhaps, to an e-entertainment industry favoring simple plots and exciting action sequences, most people see aliens as *people* . . . funny-looking, perhaps, and with some odd ideas now and again, but beings essentially the same as them, with the same values and the same ways of responding to stimuli, with reactions as varied as anger, love, hatred, or fascination. And, of course, nothing could be further from the truth.

We'd assumed the Gykrs to be a hive mentality. Their entry in the Encyclopedia Galactica had got us thinking along those lines. That did *not* mean that all Gykrs everywhere were a single vast and complex individual—which was what most people thought when they considered termite mounds or bee swarms. No, what it seemed to mean in this case was that Gykrs had leaders within any given group, and those leaders did most of the thinking and communicating for the whole. I noticed that all four of the Gykrs in front of me appeared identical. Nothing marked one off as distinct or different from the others . . . but one was doing all of the talking while the others just . . . crouched there.

Well, you could say the same thing about the U.S. Marines, or of any well-disciplined but non-democratic organization of humans. The difference, perhaps, was that Marines had to be carefully trained to be both able and willing to set aside their personal urges and reactions—like fear—and accept what was necessary for the entire group. Charging an enemy plasma-gun nest—or, say, a space station occupied by dangerous terrorists—was lunacy for any individual. Lunacy, however, might be necessary to prevent those terrorists from dropping a small planetoid onto a densely populated Earth.

The Gykr had evolved within an environment utterly hostile and alien to human sensibilities, and to do so they would have evolved a native sense of discipline as thorough and as rigorous as that of any human Marine. They *had* to have done so.

Marines are the way they are because of training, and that gives them a certain amount of flexibility. The Gykr are the way they are because of breeding, the way their brains are hardwired from birth or hatching or whatever it is they do.

And *that* was the tactical advantage I was looking for.

"I'm not the leader of this group," I told the Gykr. "I'm not in charge, I don't give the orders. I *can't* order everyone off our vessel. The others would never agree."

All of the Gykr stirred uneasily. " 'Leader'?" the one said. "We are having . . . trouble . . . understanding this."

Well, of course that would be true. The concept was so deeply rooted in their evolutionary design they might not even be aware of it . . . like a fish unaware of the water within which it swam.

"Do you have a word," I asked, treading carefully, "for the one of you who makes decisions for the group? Who speaks for the group?"

I heard a harsh *clack* in my in-head, evidently the Gykr word itself, untranslated. "It means . . . 'chosen.' "

"I see." That made sense. Not "chosen" as in democrati-cally elected or anything so cerebral as determining who was best to lead. "Chosen" as in chosen by circumstances, or by an uncaring universe. A group of Gykr finds itself isolated, and one among them becomes the leader, making decisions for the entire group, which automatically rallies around the flag. Perhaps there were subtle biochemical cues that nudged the process along; the selection process prob-ably wasn't due to chance.

I remembered reading of certain species of fish in Earth's oceans. Clownfish schools have a female fish at the top of the hierarchy; when she dies, the most dominant male in the school will change into a female and take over. Among wrasses, the largest female will turn into a male and take over the harem if the school's male leader dies. The choosing of a Gykr leader might be similar, although apparently the condition was temporary. A leader is needed, and one appears, with all others falling into line and following orders.

As a survival tool, the process would neatly avoid the dangers of warring tribes or egoistic posturings or the idiocy of power for power's sake alone within a deadly and unforgiving environment.

"Among humans," I told the Gykr, "we're *all* chosen. We agree to cooperate to achieve certain goals, and we'll agree to accept orders from one trained or experienced individual . . . but if I give orders that the others disagree with, like leaving the submarine, they will not do what I say."

"But . . . if the Akr strikes, you would be devoured!"

I could actually hear the emotion shaking behind the Gykr's words. Human individuality must be sheer insanity from the Gykr point of view.

"You've been a Galaxy-faring species for a long time," I said. "You must have encountered other species who think . . . who behave the way we do."

"Not . . . we, personally. We have heard . . . stories . . ."

I remembered that the Gykr had something like 10 percent fewer synaptic connections within their brains. Knowledge might circulate within the entire species as hearsay or legend or be accessed, as with us, through a download from the local Net, but in general they would respond more to habit, to tradition, or to biochemical tides within their neural makeups than they did to education.

It was tempting to think of them as *stupid*, but I resisted the thought. Their system worked well enough for them, as proven by the fact that they'd not only survived the night-shrouded world of their birth, but freed themselves from it.

The distinction was bogus in any case. One version of

the IQ scale designated *normal* as anything between 85 and 115, so an average species IQ of 90 certainly qualified as human-normal.

"Your ship abandoned you here, didn't it?" I said in what I hoped was a light and conversational tone. "You need to get back to the surface, so your ship can return and pick you up?"

"My submersible . . . has not returned . . . as expected. The . . . Akr . . . might have attacked. . . ."

That was the second time the being had used that untranslatable term. In context, I assumed that it was the Gykr name for some sort of sea monster in the ancient ocean of their world. It took me a moment longer to realize that the Gykr must be referring to the cuttlewhales.

And *that* was an entirely different piece of the puzzle. We'd battled cuttlewhales on the surface ice—and I'd watched a Gykr devoured by one. And yet, a cuttlewhale had . . . *helped* us, if that was the word, by swallowing the *Walsh* and transporting us hundreds of kilometers deeper into the ocean, to bring us *here*.

"Then let me offer you this: Our vessel can't take all of you back to the surface at once. We can provide transport for you to the surface . . . one at a time. Each trip our submersible makes will carry one of you, plus several of the humans trapped here, to safety. Our pilot will then return for another load . . . and another, until all of us have reached safety."

It was a monstrous gamble on several levels. By limiting each trip to one Gykr, I knew we could maintain control over them—Gunny Hancock or Dr. Montgomery watching it with a plasma weapon in his good hand. It would also avoid letting the Gykr remaining below know that I'd exaggerated the number of armed humans on board the *Walsh*.

But each trip would take a hell of a long time unless one of the cuttlewhales decided again to intervene and shorten the passages for us. Would a lone Gykr assume the role of leader during the long voyage to the surface, and perhaps make its own decisions about whether or not to go along with the process?

I was reminded of an ancient riddle. A man reaches a ferry on a river with two chickens and a fox. The ferry will carry two at a time; if the fox is left alone with a chicken, the chicken will be killed. So how does the man get across with his livestock intact?

Obviously, you took the fox across first, went back for one chicken, carried it across, then brought the fox back with you to the near bank and left it there when you picked up the second chicken. You could then make a third crossing to retrieve the fox.

This situation wasn't quite that simple, but there were ways to guarantee the safety of the human chickens.

"You and I will remain here," I added, "until the very last trip. So that you can trust me."

"We do not . . . understand . . . the term . . . 'trust.' "

Well, that stood to reason, didn't it? "You *trust* your *chosen* to make the appropriate decisions in a group," I suggested.

"No. We accept that . . . necessary decisions . . . are made."

"Close enough." The Gykr appeared to be far more passive in their relationships with one another, again, the result, I guessed, of the biochemical imperatives that had arisen through their evolutionary history. "If we're going to get out of this trap, humans and Gykr together, we're going to have to cooperate. That is a necessary decision, agreed?"

"A decision might be made . . . to kill . . . all of you here," the Gykr replied, impassive, "and take your vessel . . . for my own use. Or . . . you all remain here . . . while we and your vessel's guide . . . make the ascent."

The Gykr's curious, broken mode of conversation was fast becoming annoying. It was as though the being had to stop and think about each phrase before speaking it.

"We won't agree to that," I said. "We don't *trust* you. But we have a means of working together, so that all of us can get out of this."

I wondered, though, about that Gykr starship. On board the *Haldane*, we'd assumed that they'd be back, probably with a larger fleet. There was the distinct possibility that we would return to the surface and find *Haldane* fled, with a Gykr fleet in complete possession of the surface of GJ 1214 I.

"We could . . . kill all of you."

"Can you?" I said. "All of us in here, yes. You have the weapons. But can you attack our submarine, and everyone on board? Without damaging the vessel so badly that it can't undock? And I promise you . . . if you kill the humans on this station, the humans on board our submarine will *never* trust you, *never* work with you, *never* agree to cooperate with you. You will be trapped down here in the darkness, at the mercy of the . . . of the *Akr*, forever. . . ."

The Gykr stirred, again uneasy. They were definitely on new and uncertain ground. The question was, Were they flexible enough to overcome hardwired evolutionary conditions and try something as alien to them as interspecies cooperation?

"Tell you what," I added. "If your ship is waiting for us when we reach the surface, we can agree to turn control of the transfer over to one of them . . . a new chosen, one of yours."

"Doc!" Ortega said, startled. "What are you saying?"

I shrugged. "It's a foregone conclusion, isn't it?" I asked him. "If the Gykr are in control up there, they'll take command of the *Walsh* anyway, no matter what we do. We'll be forced to trust them to come get the rest of us."

"I don't like it . . ."

"Neither do I. You have another suggestion?"

"What you offer . . . is acceptable," the Gykr chosen said after another long moment's pause. "I see no . . . reasonable alternative."

"You will permit us full contact with our vessel."

"Yes."

"You will put down your weapons. As have we."

"Yes."

"And we will work together in order to survive."

"Yes."

As an interstellar treaty, it had a few shortcomings, but it was the best we could hope for at the moment. I exchanged thoughts with Hancock, back on board the *Walsh*. As it happened, they'd been able to follow most of the exchange, having picked up on the fact that both Ortega and I had killed our privacy interlocks.

"You done good, Doc," Hancock said. "We'll make a Marine of you yet."

"Thanks, Gunny. There are still twenty of you over there, heavily armed, right?"

"Right."

That, I knew, was the weakest part of the plan. It seemed unlikely that we'd be able to get one of our weapons over to the *Walsh* without the Gykr knowing about it. Once the first Gykr came on board the *Walsh*, he would realize that things were not as I'd represented them. If he was in communication with the other three Gykr, the whole situation could change in an instant.

As it would if a landing party from the Gykr starship was waiting for us topside.

"Tell 'em, Doc," Hancock said, "that we've removed all weapons from the *Walsh*'s bridge, and that there's just four of us here, okay? And the Gykr and the base survivors can ride up with us. The armed Marines are in the main compartment aft."

"Did you hear that, Chosen?" I asked the temporary Gykr leader.

"We . . . did."

How long could we carry off the bluff? Well . . . once the *Walsh* decoupled from the docking collar, submarine and base would be cut off from each other. It would be up to Hancock to continue the deception on the *Walsh*. Maybe he had a means of cobbling together something that looked like a weapon. Or maybe he actually had a holdout somewhere on board; Marines often did.

The idea was to keep the Gykr *here* calm and reasonably satisfied as we transferred them, one by one, to the surface.

One of the uncommunicative Gykrs went through the airlock into the access tunnel, along with eight human survivors and one M'nangat. I braced myself for some sort of protest or scene . . . but eventually we heard some muffled, metallic sounds and felt a distant tremor through the deck. *Walsh* had just cast off from the station and was on her way to the surface.

Unfortunately, the base did not have any outside nano to provide us with vid images of what was going on. Whatever had been out there had been encased in the ice shell deliberately woven around what was left of the base, so we were blind to everything outside the base's crumpled interior.

I would have liked to see if one of the cuttlewhales had moved in to give us another assist.

"So . . . Dr. Murdock," I said. "What the hell happened here?"

His eyes shifted to the remaining Gykr. "We were . . . attacked," he said. "A bombardment from orbit. The ice around and under us melted enough that the weight of the main base caused us to break through and sink."

"But how did you end up *here*?" Ortega asked. "Floating . . . but a thousand kilometers down!"

"Our specific gravity," Murdock said with a wan smile, "the ratio of CM hull to internal air space, was . . . low enough that we sank fairly slowly. It was a near thing, though. The pressure was seriously beginning to deform the hull before we could reprogram the external hull nano to begin adding layers of ice . . . a jury-rigged pressure hull."

I'd not closely examined the base interior, not with all of the back-and-forth with the aliens . . . but I could see now what he meant. The main lab occupied perhaps a quarter of the original dome, but the bulkheads had been crumpled inward under tremendous force, buckling and folding to give the compartment the feel of something more like a natural cavern than an architectural structure. I estimated that well over half of the original internal space had been taken over by collapsing CM hull structure.

"As for why we're motionless here," Murdock continued, "we couldn't see out, didn't know what was happening. Before we were attacked, we'd probed as deeply as we could with sonar, and discovered what we think is a layer of exotic ice at this depth. Maybe we're aground on that."

"That is the case," Ortega told him. "We're hypothesizing a kind of soft slush of exotic ice in an amorphous state . . . maybe ice VII or ice VIII . . . maybe something even stranger."

"We've learned that the cuttlewhales are made of ice VII," I added. "Certain metals and other exotic ices mixed in . . . but it's organic ice VII. I think it likely that what the base is resting on is a layer of organic ice VII."

"Wait-wait," Ortega said, startled. "*Organic* ice? Like the cuttlewhales?"

"The cuttlewhales evolved somewhere," I said, "and some*how*. The entire substrate of compressed amorphous ice VII might actually be alive."

"I don't think I can accept *that*," the environmental planetologist said.

I shrugged. "It may not matter. I've just been wondering about how something as unlikely as the cuttlewhales could have come about. Dr. Murdock . . . how about your people? How many are there, anyway?"

He looked stricken. "Thirty-five," he said, "plus four of our M'nangat. "Most of the others were caught in compartments that flooded in the first few moments of the attack."

"Are there injured?" I patted my M-7 kit. "I'm a combat medic."

He nodded. "Six serious ones. We put them in a berthing compartment, through here."

"We should have evaced them first," I said, "with the first load."

He sighed. "We're not sure any of them are going to make it," he said. "I thought it more important that the *living* escape this trap. . . ."

And he had a perfectly valid point. Triage—determining who lives and who dies based on available supplies and seriousness of wounds—can be a heartbreaking aspect of field first aid. I learned that three of the four medical doctors assigned to the base had been killed, and the fourth was one of the unconscious injured. I checked all six of them, four men, two women, and found there was little I could do for them. Automated systems had pumped them full of nano to control the pain and keep them unconscious. Three were hooked up to full life-support units that were doing their breathing for them. Skinseal and injected nano had controlled bleeding and stabilized them all . . . for now. I could use my N-prog to further tweak the nanobots to facilitate healing, but more than anything I could do, they all needed extensive surgical intervention . . . and that meant a sick bay at least as good as *Haldane*'s, and someone with surgical training at least as good as Kirchner's, but without the insanity.

In the meantime . . .

I'd just emerged from the improvised sick bay. I wanted to discuss with the chosen Gykr the possibility of moving the wounded as soon as the *Walsh* returned for a second load, when the burst of static in my head came out of nowhere, as suddenly as the last one, and much sharper, more wrackingly painful. I couldn't help myself; I dropped to my knees, my hands uselessly over my ears.

Through the pain, I could see, barely, that three remaining Gykrs were being affected as well. All were on the deck, curled up tightly, as if their armor could block out the thundering blast of white noise. The human survivors too, all of them, were down.

And through the noise I could still hear the Gykr's electronic voice. *"The Akr! The Akr! It is the Akr . . . !"*

Chapter Twenty-Two

IF ANYTHING, THE STATIC BECAME WORSE, LOUDER AND MORE INTRU-
sive, searing down into the very core of my being, drowning thought, burning reason. And this time, I could hear the
voice as well.

I wondered if it had made a difference, my switching off my
privacy filters earlier. The . . . Voice, a booming but muffled
thunder, was deeply imbedded within my in-head circuitry.
Someone, I knew, had figured out how to interface with my
cerebral implants, had learned at least the *shape* of my language, and was now trying to insert words . . . phrases . . . alien
concepts from my hardware directly into my left parietal lobe.

I felt . . . adrift, as if in a vast and achingly empty abyss.
That was my right parietal lobe, a part of me thought, trying
to make sense of spacial relations.

My left parietal lobe was just trying to make sense of the
words. What I was hearing was . . . something very like a
schizophrenic's word salad, but as isolated sounds that were
almost words, achingly *close* to words . . . somehow just
beyond the boundaries of the intelligible.

*We . . . kam . . . off . . . in . . . try . . . shan . . . no . . . kray
. . . shem . . .*

The boom of nonsense syllables filled a cosmos. I had
the impression that each syllable was a burst of sound, filled
with content.

"Can you . . . turn it down a bit?" I cried out in my mind. "Dial back the damned signal strength!"

And astonishingly, the thunder receded.

Theseagullstrengthisseasonofdiscontentbutgoodcontent-dialsonetwothreeseeme . . .

"Almost there," I hazarded. It *was* word salad. I could very nearly understand now. . . . "Slower, please! It's coming through too fast."

It'scomingthroughslowernow . . .

"Still slower. Please!"

It is coming through slower now . . .

"Perfect! Perfect! Hold it right there!"

I expected more words, intelligible at last.

What I got instead knocked me flat on the deck. I'm not sure even now if I was conscious, or lost in a mind-twisting dream, an intensely vivid hallucination unlike anything I'd ever experienced.

I was still hearing conversation, like far-off voices, myriads of them, and still just on the edge of comprehension.

What I was seeing, however, appeared to be a vast, red-violet mist-filled void.

And I was falling through it.

"Where am I?"

Where am I? boomed back in reply. *I am where? Am I where? I where am? . . .*

The red-and-purple-mist-filled Creation, but overhead it shaded to black, and beneath me, in the ultimate Deep, lay Night Absolute.

And then that Night exploded with billions of stars, stars of every brightness, every color, swirling and sparkling and streaming along in vast, surging currents . . . closely packed blood cells rushing along invisible arteries and veins, streams of stars following gravitational currents across and around the shoals and deeps of galactic space, a scintillating, pulsing, *living* dynamic of light and matter on a truly titanic scale. . . .

I seemed to merge with the flow, joining a current of fast-moving specks of light, only the individual specks, I now saw, were organisms, *huge* organisms. They must have been huge if the cuttlewhales I saw moving along those enormous arteries were, like their counterparts on the surface, each hundreds of meters long.

"Where am I?" I thought. I had the distinct impression that *some*one, or some*thing*, was listening in on my thoughts. Unless, of course, I was in the middle of a psychotic break and hallucinating my little heart out. One possible symptom in paranoid schizophrenia is the sensation, the feeling that someone is listening to your thoughts, eavesdropping on your innermost self.

I shut *that* train of thought off in a hurry.

But I did hear an answer.

This is the universe.

I seemed to be hurtling deeper into the streaming network of stars, billions upon billions of them. I tried to understand what I was seeing, tried to see it in my terms, not the terms of whatever was feeding me the vision.

It didn't work. "Do you mean your universe? Your *experience* of the universe? Or something else?"

The mathematical centers of my brain were being directly stimulated, I knew. In general, the right parietal region handles basic quantity processing, like figuring out which is more, three or five, while the left parietal takes on more precise calculations, like addition and subtraction. I wasn't seeing anything, not imaging it visually, but it felt as though numbers shifted and flashed and built upon themselves everywhere I looked. The math, it seemed, was as much an integral part of this picture as the image of moving currents and myriad gleaming stars. Some of it was connected to the images; there were, I realized without knowing how, more than 12 billion cuttlewhales moving with me through just this one stream. Other functions were far more complex and intricately interconnected, but had nothing to do with what I was seeing.

Or . . . did they? I'm not that hot in math; I let my in-head processors do the rough stuff, which for me is just about anything more complicated than two times three. But I knew, without knowing *how* I knew, that there was a process called *Gödel encoding*, that it was possible to assign a unique number to each and every item of information in the cosmos—items that were as diverse as the number two and the quantum wave-form equation describing every object in a solar system—with numbers derived from factored primes.

These Gödel numbers could be staggeringly large. But once you had such a number, you could manipulate it, extract information such as true or false logical values from it, and eventually retrieve the original information from it, *if* you had enough computing power.

The numbers need not be unique. Only the numbering systems of distinct sets were unique, with one set, say, for numbering cuttlewhales, and another for describing minute creatures entering the Intelligence's awareness.

And one set for encoding the language and the thoughts of one dust-mote creature that identified itself as Elliot Carlyle, with data sets nested within data sets nested within data sets, stacked to dizzying levels of complexity and subtle meaning.

I knew, without knowing *how* I knew, that Kurt Gödel had used Gödel encoding to prove his Incompleteness Theorems in 1931 . . . that even with the advent of the computer, most problems had required years of calculation time until the advent of quantum computing, that even now the system was limited in its scope simply because of the complexity of the more advanced calculations.

How was I *knowing* this stuff?

Ah. That was it. My own in-head AI, the artificial intelligence riding within my cerebral implant that's served as personal secretary and digital avatar and e-link facilitator was a part of the moving stream, a part of the implacable and cosmic awareness filling me and surrounding me and guiding me through that maze of light and shifting numbers. It was accessing data, lots of data, from my personal RAM.

And the intelligence carrying me was reading it.

This is the universe. . . .

Each individual sound of that phrase—or rather, the individual electrical signals moving through my brain that were interpreted as that sound—could be described as two numbers, frequency and wavelength. Those could be multiplied together, and become the factor for a prime number—two, say—and then all of those factored primes could be multiplied together. . . .

I watched it happen, felt the numbers opening, *blossoming* like flowers. . . .

The universe is all I experience.

"But . . . there are parts of the universe that are outside of your experience."

Where had that insight come from? It felt like I was being swept along with the river of mathematical understanding.

Truth . . .

Fear . . .

Save us!

"Save you from what?"

From . . . ending. . . .

And I saw in my mind's eye a new scene, a *familiar* scene overlying the red-violet and the streaming stars . . . Kari and me standing side by side on Haldane's mess deck, a few other Marines in the background, lost in the spectacular viewwall image of GJ 1214 as we hurtled in past the mottled red star. Ahead, we saw Abyssworld, half ice, half boiling, red-illumined sea and hemisphere-sized storm, and streaming out behind it into the blackness of space, the faint, hazy wisp of cometary tail as the star blasted water vapor off from the planet's atmosphere.

And that image connected with an inner, nested set of data, an older set of data, and I relived in vivid detail a scene experienced and saved weeks earlier.

It was a memory . . . a memory of the docuinteractive. . . .

THE MODEL OF ABYSS DEEP *FLOATING ABOVE* MURDOCK'S *HAND DEveloped a faint, ghostly tail streaming away from the daylight side. "In many ways," he continued, "Abyssworld is similar to a comet . . . a very large comet with a tail of hot gasses blowing away from the local star."*

"That can't be a stable configuration," I said. "It's losing so much mass that the whole planet is going to boil away."

"Correct. We believe Abyssworld formed much farther out in the planetary system, then migrated inward as a result of gravitational interactions with the two outer gas giants. We don't have a solid dating system with which to work, but it's possible that the planet began losing significant mass as much as five billion years ago, when it would have been perhaps six times the diameter it is now.

"Abyssworld is now losing mass, which has the advantage of bleeding away excess heat. Within another billion years, though, this ongoing loss of mass will significantly reduce the planet's size, until the entire world ocean has boiled away. At that point, Abyssworld will be dead."

I SAW ABYSSWORLD HANGING IN SPACE, ITS TAIL STREAMING AWAY into darkness, its star boiling its oceans.

A dying world.

A cry for help.

Save us.

Overlying the images drawn from my own memory were other images, other sensations, and an impression that I was this world, the Deep of this world, far below in chill and unending Night. Increasingly, powerfully, I was aware of the world below, a world I experienced through the senses of myriad swarming entities hundreds of meters long.

Cuttlewhales, *everywhere* cuttlewhales, sinuous and ropy and as minute as teeming bacteria compared to the sheer bulk and volume that was *me*. The cuttlewhales, I realized, were literally parts of myself born from frigid, gelatinous ice, deliberately teased from the organic ice to serve as senses allowing me to access the cosmos, the totality of my underwater existence. I saw . . . mountains, smoothly rounded, compressed under vast pressure, translucent, glowing, layer upon mist-veiled layer, like an impossibly beautiful nebula hanging in the Void. I saw the streams of shining stars, sensed again the sheer depth and vastness of that scale . . . a mountain, a *world* of moving light, and realized that what I was seeing was not a hallucination born of stress or fear or lack of sleep or incipient schizophrenia, but the heart of the world, *this* world, itself alive and vibrant.

My perception rose from the translucent mountains of light and inner stars, accelerating, rushing up into blackness.

And eventually, blackness gave way to red-violet light, to unfamiliar hues and an intense, almost painful glare of sky. I emerged, and found myself surrounded by a distorted image that could only be the surface of GJ 1214 I as seen through the weird eyes of a cuttlewhale, a world of red water and orange mist and mountains of cracked and broken ice calving into the sea. A scene divided into six overlapping segments in a circle, and which seemed to show me the seascape ahead and the icescape behind and the sky above and the water below all at the same time.

My head ached trying to grasp it all.

I *was* the cuttlewhale, moving in sinuous ripples across a wind-lashed sea, moving out into open water farther and farther from the ice, as the wind grew stronger and the water grew hotter, as the bloated red sun with its spot-mottled face and magnetically twisted prominences rose higher and yet higher into the sky, searing the surface with unendurable heat.

The cuttlewhales rose in vast numbers from the safe, cool comfort of their genesis in the Deep, emerged into a fury of heat and near-vacuum, and *observed* as their bodies gradually scaled and crumbled away. And as the first melted, more came . . . and more.

And then the others came, a ship of strange, hard ice hovering in the sky, and creatures, other intelligences, moving on the ice.

I felt *pain* as the beings used weapons of directed energy against the cuttlewhales.

And the cuttlewhales responded in kind . . . and I realized that from their scale, the cuttlewhales literally could not tell the difference between Gykr and human.

IMAGINE A WORLD.

The world is 34,160 kilometers in diameter, or 2.678 times the width of the Earth. At the center of this world is a solid core 12,000 kilometers—give or take a few hundred—across, very close to the size of the Earth. Likely, the structure is similar—a hot, innermost sphere of molten iron enveloped in a plastic mantle, the whole sheathed over by a thin crust of solid rock.

And above that crust, a liquid ocean 11,000 kilometers deep.

The top thousand kilometers of that ocean is liquid water. Below that depth, though, between liquid and rock, those insane pressures keep piling up and up and *up*, one full atmosphere every ten meters, and the water is compressed and congealed into something like slush, an amorphous exotic ice exhibiting Debye relaxation and odd electrical effects, a matrix of gelatinous fluid shot through with other forms of exotic ice, and veins and streaks and currents of heavy metals upwelling from the solid, hot planetary crust far, far below.

An *organic* exotic ice, amorphous and shot through with contaminants, a dirty ice that has evolved and developed over the eons to become . . . a brain.

A very, very *large* brain.

The adult human brain has a volume, very roughly and on average, of 1,200 cubic centimeters. Twelve hundred ccs of neurons and glia and distinct organs like the amygdala, the thalamus, and the hippocampus, of cortex and neocortex, of tectum and tegmentum, of dendrites and synapses. Twelve hundred ccs of quivering jelly containing, roughly, 100 trillion—that's 10^{14}—neural connections.

The brain of the Abyss Deep had a volume of over 900,000 cubic kilometers. Make that 10^{23} cubic centimeters . . . or about 700 quintillion times larger than the brain of a mere human like myself. *A single brain* . . .

If its NCE, its Neural Connection Equivalence, was on anything like a human scale in terms of packaging, it contained 10^{20} more synapses than a human, something like 10^{34} neural connections in all . . .

What the hell did that mean in terms of relative intelligence? If humans had 10 percent or so more synaptic connections than the Gykr, which made them a bit slower on the uptake than we were, what did that say for a comparison between my intelligence, say, and that of the Abyss Deep?

In my mind, the word *Deep* had just shifted in meaning, from a general term for the extreme depths of the Abyssworld to the living being itself that by volume made up 76 percent of that entire planet.

Vast . . . mysterious . . . unimaginably ancient. And unimaginably *smart*, a truly superhuman intelligence that embraced an entire world.

And it was terrified of dying.

I am the Abyssworld Deep. . . .

Is Dr. Murdock correct? The Voice thundered in my mind. *Is my world doomed, the ocean within which I exist to boil away so soon?*

"Well, your world will dry up eventually," I said. "But that will still take a billion years, at least. Probably more." I couldn't be sure of the exact figure, and it might be considerably less—a few hundred million years? But still, geological ages . . . *eons*. . . .

I could feel it rummaging through my in-head RAM, possibly trying to judge what I meant by the term *years*.

I have existed for a billion years already. . . .

I felt . . . dizzy. In shock. As though my brain was muzz-ily firing on only a fraction of its usual go-juice. A being—a potentially *immortal* being—a billion years old, and as far beyond me in terms of neural processing power as I am above a single specimen of *Staphylococcus aureus*.

Was communication even possible, I wondered, with a being, with an *intellect* that vast and that powerful? Most of the intelligent species we've encountered so far—plus most of those explored through the agency of the Encyclo-pedia Galactica—are, like the Gykr and the M'nangat and the Qesh and the Durga, all at very roughly the same level of intelligence, of consciousness, and of innate mental abil-ity. There were a few oddballs out there that were tough to evaluate—the Durga were a great example, with such an alien worldview that we hadn't learned how to really com-municate with them in almost a century.

An ant runs across the bare toe of a human being, and causes the toe to twitch. Can that ant be said to be in com-munication with the human?

The Deep represented, I knew, an entirely different order of intelligence than the merely human. Could I truly be said to be in communication with it now? Or was I in contact with some minute subset of that near infinitely vaster brain . . . as the ant might be in communication with the nerve impulses that cause the skin of the human's toe to flutter in response to its touch?

I found myself thinking of god.

Of course, I wasn't entirely sure what I meant by that word. For me, the word *god* had always been a place marker for a rather vague, cultural concept, for something much larger, more powerful, more intelligent than me.

Well, the Deep qualified on that count, didn't it?

Okay . . . try this instead. There was the traditional, mono-theistic Creator, the capital-G God, believed in by so many humans still as a kind of old, bearded father figure in the sky, all-seeing, omnipotent, omniscient, ruler of His cosmos . . . and yet according to human thought, straightjacketed by a peculiarly narrow mind, a *human* mind concerned with concepts like prayer and worship and the salvation or pun-ishment of those humans who one way or another fail to meet His standards.

I had never been able to wrap my head around such a limited, *pathetic* notion of what a divine creator-being might truly be. Surely, that image of God had more in common with the Zeus of the ancient Greeks than with any purely spiritual reality.

In contrast, there were the multiple deities of Neo-pagans like my own family, of Wiccans and Dianics and the religious reconstructionists of Norse or Saxon or Greek traditions—idealized deities that were human, easygoing and undemanding, Earth-centered representations of fertil-ity, sometimes contentious, often humorous, and perhaps best understood as the expressions or projections or facets of purely human psychologies. A popular theme in Neo-pagan religious thought was that we humans were evolving, through a succession of lifetimes, into gods ourselves.

And now I was facing within my own mind the physical reality of a deity utterly unlike either of those concepts, a physical being so far beyond me in mental scope and power that I would never, *ever* be able to fully grasp or compre-hend it.

I felt . . . very small. Very slow. Very stupid. And very, very inconsequential.

Save us.

And it wanted my—*our*—help.

What, I wondered, did a brain 700 quintillion times larger than a human brain think about? How did it pass the eons?

What did it experience . . . especially when it evolved as a motionless layer ten thousand kilometers thick embracing the core of a world? The depths of the world Abyss didn't exactly offer intellectual stimulation, did they? Very cold and very dark and eternally unchanging, save for upwelling currents carrying warmth from the core, and drifting flecks of life, and nothing, *nothing* more for age upon age upon measureless age.

What had stimulated that sentience?

Perhaps the Deep began as an . . . an *awareness* of change. Of plumes of heat bubbling up from cracks in the solid crust beneath it. Of the seep and flow of sulfur and metallic compounds emerging from volcanic vents and keeping the water above liquid.

Perhaps it had evolved ways to affect this leakage somehow. Like predators developing intelligence in order to better hunt their prey, the Deep had developed intelligence to manipulate its deepest surroundings, finding new sources of heat and developing them, expanding them, making use of them. Without being told, I was aware that the Deep must be a true thermovore, deriving sustenance directly from heat.

And after that . . .

Had the unending boredom of existence generated within the Deep an interest in, even a fascination for, mathematics? Surely, though, there had to be intelligence *before* the boredom, for the boredom to be realized. A non-sentient lump of ice could not be *bored*.

Why was the Deep super-intelligent?

Did there have to be a reason? I felt that I was on the right track about controlling its environment—that, after all, was a large part of what had led to human sentience. Perhaps, eons past, intelligence, sentience had appeared here on a very small scale . . . a simple curiosity about its surroundings, an awareness of cold and dark, and of plumes or currents of heat rising through its inner substance.

And that had led to trying to control those currents . . . the gods alone know how. Had the Deep learned to change, to *control*, those incredible pressures within itself? Or to use those pressures to redirect warm currents to where they needed to be?

Eventually, with the passage of enough time, perhaps that Mind had developed mathematics, simply as a means of measuring what it knew . . . depth, pressure, hot and cold, flow rate, distance.

How it might have progressed from there to Gödel encoding was utterly beyond me. Its understanding of mathematics would have started with counting, and counting would have led to arithmetical manipulations . . . and that to prime numbers, and that to factoring primes.

Could intelligence bootstrap itself from simple awareness of physical events to higher mathematics, simply through introspection, through self-aware *mindfulness*?

Given the slow passage of enough millennia, perhaps . . .

But now the universe of the Deep had suddenly expanded with the arrival of other intelligences from off world. It had for the first time seen the planet it inhabited from outside, heard the discussion of some of those alien intelligences, and realized that it was doomed.

The sheer injustice had me on the verge of sobbing . . . or was I picking up some sort of emotional leakage from the Deep? It was hard to tell, so closely entwined at that moment were its thoughts with mine. But a life form as intellectually capable, as *smart* as the Deep was completely helpless in the face of its world's inevitable doomsday.

What could be done to help?

Not evacuation, certainly. There was no way to load the Deep from GJ 1214 I into a spaceship and carry it to some other world. You might as well think about moving the entire planet. . . .

And with that thought, I began to emerge from the dream.

"Doc? Hey, Doc? You okay?"

I opened my eyes. I was in one of the racks in the sunken

base's makeshift sick bay, staring at a dark and pressure-crumpled overhead. "W-what . . . ?"

It was Staff Sergeant Thomason . . . but he'd been left up on the surface, hadn't he? What was he doing down here?

I sat up with a gasp. Gods . . . had that been *real*?

"Whoa, easy there, Doc. You've been out of it for the better part of a day!"

A day! "What . . . what happened? The brain . . . the Gykr . . ."

I knew I wasn't making any sense. I swung my legs off the bunk and leaned forward. I started to sag, dizzy, and Thomason caught me. "You stay put for a moment, Doc. Everything is okay. Everything is *very* okay."

"No it's not," I told him, still muzzy. "We've got to save the whole fucking planet. . . ."

Chapter Twenty-Three

OKAY, SO I WASN'T THINKING STRAIGHT JUST THEN. BUT I *MEANT* well.

A few hours later, I was back on the surface, entering our dome and receiving rounds of congratulations from Marines and scientists alike. They seemed to be of the impression that I had somehow saved the expedition.

All four of the Gykr had reached the surface already. It turns out that the cuttlewhales had gotten involved—the cuttlewhale express, we were calling it. The *Walsh* would move out into open water, a cuttlewhale would move up behind it and swallow it down, and a short time later the sub would be released at its destination, alongside the sunken base or beside the new base at the surface. Over the course of an afternoon, the *Walsh* had transported all four Gykr, the four M'nangat, and twenty-some of the other survivors to the surface, and was now making her final trip.

But the big news was that when the *Walsh* surfaced with that very first Gykr, it was to the discovery that the Gykr starship had returned during our absence . . . and, as expected, had brought along some friends. Space around GJ 1214 I was now occupied by eight orbiting alien starships, and they'd come loaded for bear.

Or, in this case, human.

The base we'd nanufactured on the ice had been well

hidden and remained undiscovered. But when *Walsh* had surfaced, the Gykr aboard had immediately contacted his friends. He'd been released at the edge of the ice, and a ship had arrived shortly afterward to pick him up.

That Gykr, though, had become a Chosen during the ascent; he'd been the only Gykr aboard, after all, and apparently it was being *alone* that triggered the greater sense of independence, the ability to give orders, among Gykr individuals. And apparently that Gykr Chosen had been impressed enough with the agreement I'd hammered out with them that he'd told his friends . . . and they'd been impressed as well. They'd not even demanded—as our informal treaty had stated—that they take over control of the rescue. They simply constructed a surface base of their own, and then watched closely as *Walsh* continued to shuttle personnel up and down.

Exactly how the Gykr fleet was choosing to interpret that treaty, or our activities, was unknown as yet. Captain Summerlee felt, however, that anything other than an immediate attack counted as a positive step. She'd ordered the *Haldane* to land on the ice near the dome, and for several hours now, the two sides, human and Gykr, had been warily watching each other.

Yes, the Skipper was back in command. Chief Garner had used the ship's medical 3D printer to run off a batch of hESC—human Embryonic Stem Cells—and injected them into her brain to repair the damage there. Her in-head implants were still down, and she would need to have partial replacements regrown when she got back to Earth. There was nothing to stop her from resuming command, however. After all, she had plenty of people on her command staff who could access AIs, navigational and engineering data, and ship's departmental reports and handle them for her . . . and she could call up paperwork on her office viewall rather than within open mental windows. Her toughest problem would be remembering manual overrides for things like shipboard elevators and coffeemakers.

She was waiting for me at the entrance to the *Haldane*'s mess deck when I walked in. "Captain Summerlee! Ma'am!"

"Welcome back, Carlyle. I'm told that you've been busy."

"Busy enough, Captain. I'm afraid I may have committed Humankind to a new long-term project."

"Well, it'll have to be ratified by the Commonwealth Senate. They normally take a dim view of enlisted personnel forging diplomatic agreements with aliens. In this case, though, I think they'll be willing to overlook the embarrassing details, in exchange for a solid peace treaty with the Gucks."

I blinked at her for a moment, not quite comprehending. "Actually, ma'am," I managed after a slack-jawed moment, "I wasn't talking about the Gykr."

She gave me a Look. "Don't tell me you've gone and established diplomatic relations with someone else! First the Qesh . . . then the Gykr. *Now* who?"

"The Abyss Deep," I told her.

"The what?"

So I explained.

It was actually a bit embarrassing, because once I actually started describing my exchange with the Deep, I realized that I didn't have any actual proof that what I'd seen was . . . *real*. The whole exchange could so easily have been a hallucination, something I'd imagined in vivid detail, perhaps, while unconscious.

"He's right," Gina Lloyd said, at least partially validating my wild story. "I could hear parts of the conversation in the *Walsh*. I couldn't see anything, though."

"You were halfway back to the surface," I told her.

"*And* inside a cuttlewhale," she agreed. "But I think we were . . . on the same wavelength? Like when it was asking about Dr. Murdock. And . . . when it said it was a billion years old, I had shivers going down my spine. I think maybe it has some kind of channel open in us, y'know?"

"That's as good a theory as anything else I've heard,"

Summerlee said. "Come on. We're going to have an emergency pow-wow."

"Emergency?"

"The Gykr have asked us to leave the system," the captain said. "They *did* ask nicely . . . for them. But they want us out of here in one orbit of Abyssworld around its sun. That's one day, fourteen hours, or thereabouts. And we have to decide how we're going to respond."

The mess deck was crowded. Garner was there, and Doob and McKean. Gunny Hancock was there, looking wan and pinched, his stump wrapped in a surgical sealer that told me they'd already started working on growing him a new left arm. Kemmerer was present, and most of the other Marine officers, too, as were *Haldane*'s department heads. All seven Brocs—our three, plus the four rescued from the sunken base, were occupying a far corner like a thick clump of small trees. It was a full crowd, and apparently no one cared to telecommute this time.

"Thank you all for coming," Summerlee said, taking her spot at the head of the longest mess table. "Before we get started, I know you'll all join me in welcoming HM2 Carlyle back from the Murdock base. While there, Mr. Carlyle was instrumental in defusing what was potentially a *very* nasty situation with the Gykr, and got them to accept a scheme that allowed both our people and them to leave the sunken base."

There was applause from the audience, and a few shouts of "Go, Doc!" and similar sentiments.

Summerlee held up her hands, motioning for silence. "In addition," she said as the ruckus quieted, "I'm given to understand that Mr. Carlyle also, while inside the Murdock facility, made contact with an alien life form, an extremely large and extremely intelligent life form, native to this world. Mr. Carlyle has provisionally named this organism 'the Deep.' Mr. Carlyle? Perhaps you'd tell us all about this . . . this extraordinary being."

I stood, awkward and unsure of myself, and began talking. I described the Deep, my hallucinogenic impressions of it, and what I thought it actually was . . . an immense, sessile thermovore evolved from dirty exotic ice under inconceivable pressure.

"The creatures we call cuttlewhales," I concluded, "appear to be artificially fabricated somehow by the Deep inside the exotic ice mass. For probably some millions of years, it has been using the cuttlewhales as a kind of sensory system, letting it see itself from the inside. More recently, it has learned that there is an outside as well, and begun sending the cuttlewhales up to Abyssworld's surface, as remote probes.

"As a result—and partly because of the Deep's, ah, unexpected interface with me—it has learned that this world is tidally locked in close orbit around its star . . . and that in a short time, cosmically speaking, the heat from that star is going to strip this planet of its ocean. When that happens, the Deep, which depends on both water and on intense pressures, will be killed."

"You say this Deep thing is *immortal*?" Ortega said.

"Except for the fact that its environment is going to go away soon, yes, sir."

"Does it reproduce?" Montgomery asked. "*Can* it reproduce?"

"Where? It makes up three-quarters of the volume of this planet!"

"I don't know. I was wondering about being able to transfer germ cells to a new home, somehow."

"As far as I could tell, ma'am, no. It . . . developed awareness, sentience, a long time ago as a result of various ebbs and flows of heat, minerals, and so on deep inside its substance, its body, if you will. I imagine parts of that body replace themselves over the centuries . . . although, really, there doesn't appear to be anything like a genome with a built-in timer or destruct sequence, like human DNA."

"We should probably think of it," Lieutenant Ishihara said, "not as a life form, but as a kind of natural AI . . . an enormous computer, in fact."

"It takes in nutrients and energy, sir," I told the engineering officer, "and it generates order out of chaos. I would say it's *alive.*"

"So does a computer, young man," Ishihara told me, "if by *order* you mean accumulating and storing useful information. Oh, I'm not saying this thing isn't worth saving! The mathematical information it has stored within its matrix alone must be staggering!"

I didn't reply to that. Ishihara hadn't *been* there, hadn't felt himself wired in to the Deep's emotional processes. It was alive . . . and it was self-aware. Computer AIs were neither. They could simply *act* as though they were self-aware with the appropriate programming, and we humans were too slow to tell the difference.

Or . . . did he have a point? Was that what was going on in the Deep, a system that mimicked what we thought of as sentient self-awareness?

Well for that matter, what proof did we have for *human* self-awareness? We thought we were, sure, but there was no way to prove that it wasn't a kind of all-embracing illusion, like the old philosophical chestnut that said we only *thought* we had free will in a fixed, predestined timeline.

"Well, whether it's alive or not, how the hell are we supposed to rescue it?" Chief Garner asked.

"That," I told them, "is the easy part. The hard part will be waiting it out."

I'd given the problem a lot of thought, and checked in with the *Walsh*'s AI during our ascent to the surface. *Haldane*'s larger and more powerful AI agreed with me. We *could* save the Deep.

It would just take some time.

The concept of the "gravity tractor" has been with us for a long time. Back in the early twenty-first century, as humans became aware of the terrifying threat posed to civilization, even to all life on Earth, by asteroids like the one that wiped out the dinosaurs 65 million years ago, we examined a lot of schemes for changing the orbit of an incoming cosmic missile. You couldn't just blow the thing up with nukes; the individual fragments would continue on the original trajectory, and might even end up doing more damage than the original intact flying mountain.

One promising mechanism was the idea of parking a spacecraft near the asteroid and keeping it there, possibly with solar sails, possibly with a steady, low-thrust ion drive, and letting the gravity of the spacecraft deflect, ever so slightly, the path of the asteroid.

Oh, it would take a long time, of course . . . centuries, perhaps. The thrust provided by that tiny gravitational impulse would be microscopic, but over year upon year upon year, the effect would add up. Catch the killer asteroid early enough, and you would be able, eventually, to deflect its course *just* enough to miss Target Earth.

We also, back then, were beginning to learn just how chaotic early solar systems were. As accreting worlds formed around their parent star, planetary bodies interfered with one another, collided with one another, nudged one another gravitationally into entirely new orbits. We now know that in our own Solar System, four and a half billion years ago, Jupiter and Saturn had developed a one to two resonance with each other, Jupiter circling the sun once for every two orbits of Saturn. As a result, Jupiter had been nudged closer to the sun while Saturn had been pushed farther out, and that dual migration had generated the cascade of orbital changes leading to the late heavy bombardment of the inner system 600 million years after its birth.

Orbital resonance could remake or destroy a planetary system, could move gas giants from the remote outer portions of the star system in to tight, close orbits—the "hot Jupiters" discovered in such numbers in the early days of exoplanet discoveries a couple of centuries ago, because they *were* so massive and had such short periods.

And in the same manner, worlds could be summarily ejected from their home star systems entirely. The Gykr Steppenwolf homeworld, a rogue and sunless planet adrift in interstellar space, was an example.

So what did that have to do with saving the Deep?

Everything, really.

There were several outer gas giants orbiting GJ 1214, together with GJ 1214 II, a Mars-sized world 10 million kilometers out from the star, and with an orbital period of just over sixteen days. What if we could change Planet II's orbit, actually nudge it into a period of, say, *precisely* half that of Abyssworld—to nineteen hours or so? Properly calculated and executed, the two-to-one resonance would bump Planet II in closer to the star, and shove Abyssworld farther out. By working out the numbers to enough decimal places, we could plop Abyssworld down in just about any orbit we pleased . . . one where the dayside was pleasantly habitable . . . or even one far enough out that the entire world-ocean froze over. That wouldn't bother the Deep one bit.

It would take a hell of a long time of course, but so what? A million years? Ten million? Hell, even if readjusting Abyssworld's orbit took a hundred million years, *the Deep had time*. A million centuries is a mere 10 percent of the billion years it would take the planet's ocean to finally boil away.

And there was the additional promise that human technology would rapidly advance to the point where slinging planets around a star system was child's play. What would we be capable of in just a few thousand years? Generating artificial black holes, perhaps, and using directed gravitational singularities to change planetary orbits? Or perhaps we would command even more advanced and magical technologies as yet undreamed of.

A billion years was *plenty* of time. . . .

The downside was that we humans have a pathetically brief attention span, and a political will that rarely extended past the next elections. What if we simply never got around to doing something about it? After all, there *was* lots of time left. I reflected that what constituted lots of time for humans was something else entirely for an all-but-immortal being that had been a couple of hundreds of millions of years old back when sex had first been invented on Earth.

"An . . . audacious idea, Carlyle," Ortega said. "Moving planets around to order . . ."

"We've known as a species that we were going to have to do stuff like that someday," I replied. "In another few hundred million or a billion years, our own sun will be getting hotter and brighter. Unless we decide to abandon Earth entirely, we'll need to figure out how to move the planet to a cooler orbit."

Of course, a few billion years after that, the sun would expand into a red giant, engulfing the inner planets of the Solar System, then dwindle to a white dwarf barely larger than Earth herself. Unless we *were* real quick on the uptake, able to move Earth farther out on short notice, then move her much closer in, our homeworld would likely die.

By then, of course, if Humankind still existed in anything like a recognizable organic form, we would be firmly out among the stars, reshaping the entire *Galaxy* to order. Perhaps we would by that time be independent of planetary surfaces entirely.

"But you question . . . what did you say?" Kemmerer said. "Our political will?"

"Compared to the Deep," I said, "humans are mayflies. Ephemera. While we're waiting for the technology to move whole planets to come along, we could forget all about this place."

I wasn't claiming that humans were either callous or forgetful, or anything like that. But civilizations do not last forever, no more than do worlds, and each time a civilization falls, so much information is lost. That might be less of a problem now that we had colonies on other worlds, but humanity wasn't solidly established as a multiworld species yet. A bad interplanetary war with the Gykr or the Qesh, and Humankind could easily find itself back to chipping flints among the crumbling ruins of New York or Singapore or, looking out-system, Hope, out on Tau Ceti IV.

"Well, our problem at the moment," Summerlee said, "is *these* folks. Mr. Walthers, if you please?"

A vid image came up on the viewall behind her, called up by her exec. A squat, angular, flat-topped structure, startlingly black against the surrounding icescape, appeared in the middle distance. A Gykr ship hovered above the building—ugly, complicated, looking something like a tailless stingray with the wings cocked downward at a sharp angle. A column of air beneath the ship shimmered with unknown energies as the vessel held its position against gusting westerly winds.

"The Gykr commander has given us one local year to pack up and move out," Summerlee said. "Any agreement we have with HM2 Carlyle's Deep will be entirely contingent on whether we can maintain a presence on this world . . . or whether the Gykr will be taking over from us completely."

"That may be a problem for the Deep," Montgomery pointed out. "The Gykr aren't exactly on good terms with the locals."

"Carlyle?" Summerlee said. "Do you have any observations on that?"

"From the Deep's perspective? Nothing hard and fast. I did have the impression that the cuttlewhales have a lot of trouble telling the difference between humans and Gykr. And . . . I gathered that the first Gykr to land opened fire on some cuttlewhales more or less without provocation. That's why the cuttlewhales attacked *us*, later."

"They can't tell the difference?" Lieutenant Walthers said, chuckling. "Humans, two legs, Guckers, eight or ten or twelve, depending. Can't the damned cuttlewhales count?"

"If you saw something this big," I said, holding up my thumb and forefinger a few millimeters apart, "wiggling and multilegged and squishy looking . . . would you stop to count the legs?"

"Well, I wouldn't just step on it."

"Some people would," Kemmerer said. "And if it was shooting lasers or plasma bolts at you, you might not want to stop and try to have a conversation."

"We know the Gykr have a . . . a tendency to shoot first if they feel threatened," Montgomery observed. "But what do they think about the cuttlewhales now?"

"Right," Ortega said. "Maybe we could pass the Deep and its problems off to them."

"I don't think that would be a good idea," I said. "At least, not from the Deep's point of view."

"Surely a species that evolved in a similar environment—in an under-ice ocean—would be best for dealing with something like the Deep," Ortega said.

"Would the Gykr do anything to help?" Montgomery asked.

"That may not be our problem," Walthers said.

"Well if it's not our problem," I asked, "whose problem is it?" I looked at the skipper. "Ma'am . . . it's in our best interests to help the Deep. Whether it's a life form or some kind of planet-sized organic computer, it has information that spans a billion years! It may have mathematical insights that we can't even dream of, yet! We can't just . . . just turn it over to the Gucks!"

It was a dirty trick, I know, throwing in the human self-interest angle, but it felt like I was losing the group. Some of them were perfectly okay with abandoning the Deep to the tender mercies of the Gucks, and I didn't want to do that. I hadn't exactly promised the Deep that we would help it—at the time, I'd not seen how we could—but now that I knew it was possible, I wanted to see it through.

And there *were* advantages for the Commonwealth and for Humankind as a whole. I have to admit that in at least a small way I was thinking about my father—a senior vice president of research and development for General Nano-dynamics. He'd encouraged me to join the Navy Hospital Corps in the first place because of the chance of my stumbling across something a civilian corporation like General Nan could use . . . something, as he liked to say, that would make us all *rich*.

I wasn't particularly proud of that thought, though, and I pushed it to the back of my mind. Truthfully, I wanted to help the Deep because doing so was *right*.

"You had the impression, you said, that the Gykr were afraid of the cuttlewhales?" Summerlee asked.

"They seemed to be associating them with something they called the 'Akr,' " I replied. "I don't know what that is, though. I haven't had time to track that down. But it sounded like the Akr might be something the Gucks *really* didn't like . . . or something they feared."

"Which was it?" Summerlee asked.

"I'm not sure, ma'am. Maybe both." I frowned. "It's tough reading non-human emotions, y'know?"

"So what the hell is an Akr, anyway?" Ortega wanted to know.

WE HAVE BEEN IN COMMUNICATION WITH THE GYKR ON A MORE OR LESS CONTINUOUS BASIS SINCE THEY ARRIVED, D'deen told us, the words writing themselves across our in-heads. I glanced at the skipper; Walthers had coded the tabletop to repeat his own in-head, so that she could read the M'nangat's words there. APPARENTLY, THEY THINK OF THE AKR IN MUCH THE SAME WAY THAT YOU HUMANS THINK OF 'GOD.'

"Akr is the Guck god?" I said. "Yeah, that makes sense. It sounded like that when we got blasted by the static down there!"

BUT WITH A SINGULAR DIFFERENCE, a different M'nangat, D'dnah, added.

"What difference?" Montgomery wanted to know.

ALTHOUGH WE HAVE ONLY HEARSAY TO GO ON, D'dnah continued, AND ALIEN HEARSAY AT THAT, IT IS LIKELY THAT THE ORIGINAL AKR WAS A VERY LARGE, VERY DANGEROUS SEA CREATURE THAT THREATENED THE GYKR EARLY IN THEIR EVOLUTIONARY HISTORY. IT IS POSSIBLE THAT THEY LEFT THE WATERS OF THEIR PRIMORDIAL SEA, AND TOOK UP RESIDENCE ON LAND—IN DEEP, SUBSURFACE CAVERNS WITHIN THEIR WORLD—IN ORDER TO ESCAPE AKR PREDATIONS.

"They got chased out of the ocean by a *fish*?" Ortega said.

"If the fish was anything like a cuttlewhale?" I said, grinning. "Two hundred meters long, for a baby one, and hungry? Yeah, I could see that happening."

"These Akr must have made one hell of an impression on the Guckers," Hancock said.

FOR THE GYKR, D'dnah said, THE AKR IS AN ADVERSARIAL GOD . . . A SUPREME BEING TO BE FEARED, A DEITY THAT MADE THEM EVOLVE INTO WHAT THEY ARE BY SEEKING TO DEVOUR THEM.

"Sounds like the vengeful God of some human religions I know," Hancock said. "All fire, brimstone, and holy judgment."

IT IS SIMPLY A DIFFERENT WAY FOR . . . DIFFERENCE FOR . . . DIFF . . .

I waited for D'dnah to complete the thought.

YGHA JSI GDEHG VTFITYFVERT . . .

Word salad, as served by the M'nangat.

"D'dnah?" Summerlee said, looking toward the small group of M'nangat in the far corner, concern on her face. "Are you okay?"

One of the Brocs swayed, suddenly, and collapsed to the deck.

I was already out of my chair and pushing past the other people at the table. The standing Brocs were agitated, their tentacles probing and caressing their fallen compatriot. IT IS HERM'S TIME, D'drevah said. PLEASE! HELP HERM!

I glanced up at the skipper. "You might want to let the Gucks know we have a medical emergency over here," I told her.

"What's wrong?"

"D'dnah is having a baby."

Chapter Twenty-Four

So why do things like this always happen at the *worst* possible time?

The hours were trickling away, and in another thirty or so hours we would have to leave Abyssworld . . . or fight for the privilege of staying. At odds of eight to one, this last did not sound like a particularly good choice.

But the alternative—abandoning a billion-year-old super-intelligence to the Gykr—didn't sound all that hot either.

We got D'dnah onto a floater pallet and got herm down to sick bay. On the scanner table, I could see herm's buds . . . three miniature M'nangat that until recently had been growing from the inside wall of the body cavity—literal buds. Apparently, among the M'nangat, the male fertilized the female, and the female passed the zygotes, usually three of them, one of each sex, on to the life carrier, in this case D'dnah. The zygotes attach themselves to the body cavity wall and begin growing, and the life carrier carries the fetus-buds to term.

D'dnah was bleeding internally. I suspect that the emotional stress of the meeting had caused a bud to break free, and maybe that explained why it was happening *now*, of all possible moments.

Chief Garner had joined me in the sick bay to assist, but I was the doc of the hour, since the M'nangat had requested *me*, personally, as the attending medic. It was still an honor I would like to have avoided. You see, all the male and female are concerned about is the survival of the newborns. The life carrier is expected to die.

"Does she *have* to die?" Garner asked.

"Herm," I said, correcting him. "Not she."

I double-checked to make sure that D'dnah had been taken off-line. I didn't want herm hearing the discussion.

A REQUIREMENT? D'deen replied. NO, NOT AS SUCH. THERE ARE LIFE CARRIERS WHO SURVIVE. BUT . . . WHAT WOULD BE THE POINT? THEY CAN NEVER CARRY ANOTHER CLUTCH OF BUDS.

"The point?" I said, angry. "How about the fact that D'dnah is a smart, interesting, rational, intelligent being with a right to life?"

WE DO NOT UNDERSTAND . . . 'RIGHT TO LIFE.'

M'nangat attitudes, I was beginning to think, could be compared to those of salmon on Earth. You go through hell to get back to the pond where you were born, you have sex, the female lays her eggs . . . and then there's no reason left to live, so you die. Nature is full of similar examples; after all, what's important is continuing the species, not your quality of life after you give birth. Look at humans . . . as they came in the package, not what we got after we started tinkering with life extension. Like all Earthly animals, they grow up, they reproduce . . . and a few years later, the telomeric time bombs built into human DNA go off, and both the man and woman die.

"We hold these truths to be self-evident," I grumbled, "that the M'nangat are endowed by their creator with certain inalienable rights, and that among these rights are life, liberty, and the pursuit of happiness . . ."

While I worked, I was injecting a stream of medical nanobots into D'nah's abdomen. I'd done a lot of research on M'nangat anatomy and physiology since that incident in the mining station in low Earth orbit. Their immune system, especially, would tolerate the nanobots okay. Using the table's N-prog link, I programmed them to move in on the bleeders and seal them off. I dispatched another fleet of 'bots to herm's brain. M'nangat pain receptors are different for their nervous system than they are for ours, but my research had suggested that I could cut off the pain signals from herm's body if I could deaden a particular nerve bundle just at the base of the brain. My biggest worry was that in shutting down one set of nerves, I would turn off something really important, like the autonomous neural connections required to keep both of the Broc's hearts beating in synch.

The one bit of good news here was that the M'nangat actually had deoxyribonucleic acid—good old DNA—as a means of expressing genomic characteristics and for controlling cell growth and reproduction. This wasn't as unlikely as it might seem at first glance. We've only encountered a handful of ways of passing on genes or gene equivalents among the extraterrestrial species we've encountered. The Gykr use glycol nucleic acid for the purpose–GNA. The Qesh use threose nucleic acid, or TNA, and there are five or six others. A very few, like the Deep, appear not to need genes at all.

But the Brocs use DNA, which crops up a lot as the result of parallel evolution. Because it's flexible and efficient at what it does and comes together naturally and easily from RNA and from nucleotides, its organic precursors. That doesn't mean the Brocs are related to terrestrial life in any way; they just use the same biochemical building blocks as we do.

But the similarity allowed me to fine-tune the nanobots to begin manipulating cells to encourage healing. It also gave me a fair chance of at least dulling the pain D'dnah was feeling right now. I checked the Broc's hearts-beat, and yanked on one tentacle, looking for a response. D'dnah appeared to be unconscious, now, though herm's bodily functions continued to work.

The babies, meanwhile, all three of them, appeared to have latched onto D'dnah's internal organs and were beginning to feed.

I looked up at the two M'nangat hovering nearby. "I'm going to open herm up to get the babies out," I said. "Is there a problem with that?"

D'deen's tentacles writhed helplessly. I DO NOT KNOW. . . .

DO WHAT MUST BE DONE, D'drevah said.

Typical . . . the female in the delivery room cool and calm, the male a helpless wreck.

"I am *not* going to let D'dnah die," I told them. At least—though I didn't add this out loud—not if I could help it, but I didn't feel that I was on real solid ground, here. I'd had training in human obstetrics—a little, anyway, enough to manage an emergency delivery—but this was a whole new world for me.

SOMETIMES THE LIFE-BEARER LIVES. She said it as if saying that sometimes humans had two heads.

"You just be ready to take the babies when I pull them out. If there's anything you need to do with it to make sure they're healthy, you take care of that. Right?" I certainly wasn't going to give the things a slap to the things' bottoms to get them breathing . . . but if there were other, peculiarly M'nangat rituals to ensure a healthy birth, they would have to do them, not me.

WE ARE READY.

"Is herm ready?"

I BELIEVE THE INJECTION YOU GAVE HERM HAS MADE HERM UNCONSCIOUS.

"That's the idea." I glanced at Chief Garner. "Scalpel . . ."

Chief Garner handed me a laser cutter the size of a pen. Holding it against D'dnah's midsection, I pressed the pressure switch and made a careful slice along the gray-green integument, watching for a physical response. Getting none, I extended the slice, going deeper. We had the sterile field switched on over the table, just to be sure. Despite the similarities in genetics, M'nangat biology is different enough from ours that our bugs shouldn't hurt them and theirs wouldn't hurt us. That's why I was now confident that the nano I was putting into D'dnah wouldn't hurt herm. Still, there would be M'nangat bacteria or other microorganisms on the *Haldane* simply because they'd been aboard her so the sterile field would protect D'dnah from *their* bugs now that I had herm opened up.

Black-green liquid welled up out of the incision, copper-based M'nangat blood plus various internal fluids. Garner used a handful of gauze pads to mop the stuff away, but it kept coming. I ordered the nanobots to redistribute themselves, to begin sealing off the new bleeders.

And at that moment, the *Haldane* lurched violently, there was a crack of thunder, and the sick bay lights winked out.

"*What the fuck?*" I yelled, pulling back the scalpel. The laser, I noted, no longer had power.

A siren whooped in the darkness, though I wasn't sure what it meant since we already were on full red alert. Then the compartment lights and the laser cutter both came back on. "I'll check," Garner said, closing his eyes. I kept working, opening the incision further. It would have to be large enough for me to get both hands inside. The trouble was the cartilaginous latticework that served as an internal skeleton. I would have to cut through that, or I wouldn't have room to work.

His eyes snapped open. "The Gucks are attacking," he said. "It looks like just warning shots, but I gather that the skipper told them we weren't moving until our medical emergency was over. And the Gykr captain is expressing his displeasure at that idea."

Haldane lurched again. What were they doing, trying to shoot up the ice underneath us? "This would go a *lot* easier if they wouldn't do that," I said.

There . . . *that* should be enough. I switched off the scalpel, drew a deep breath, and then reached into the incision with both hands. The cartilage closed in on my wrists. "Retractors," I told Garner.

He used a pair of manual retractors to pull the incision open a bit. I could watch the table's screen, then, watch my hands slip deep inside D'dnah's body and began working their way in toward the first of those damned parasitic babies.

The damned *slippery* parasitic baby. I could feel it wiggling, but it didn't feel like there was anything convenient to grab and hang on to.

I heard a shrill screech from somewhere overhead, and assumed Captain Summerlee had just returned fire from *Haldane*'s dorsal turret. We were in a bad position, tactically . . . outnumbered eight to one, and we were parked on the ice while the Gykr ships were either in orbit or free to move through the atmosphere at will.

"Uh-oh," Garner said.

"What? Ah! *Damn* it!" The baby slithered away from my grasp again, tucking its way up behind D'dnah's lower heart. It *liked* it in there. . . .

"Gykr ground troops. I'm linked in through the ship's outside cameras. I can see a line of those walker tank-things of theirs moving toward us."

There! I had the baby by a handful of tentacles! Holding on with my right hand, I slipped my left farther in, trying to gently untangle the squirming creature from D'dnah's lower heart. I could feel the hearts-rate increasing through my arms. Was herm feeling pain? Or simply reacting to the stress? I didn't know, and couldn't tell.

A sharp, searing pain jolted my right hand and shot up my arm, and I lost hold of the creature. "*Fuck!*"

"What's wrong?"

"The little bastard *bit* me!"

From my research, I knew that the baby M'nangat began feeding on the life carrier, drawing blood directly from the interior body wall while they were buds, then breaking free and literally gnawing their way out with a kind of parrot's beak arrangement located among the caudal tentacles. More often than not, they began by feeding on the carrier's internal organs. Usually, the life carrier was dead by the time all three had chewed their way to freedom.

I knew there were some spider species on Earth that exhibited matriphagy—the young eating the mother. Aristotle had written about this charming behavior a couple of thousand years ago, but I'd never expected to see it manifested by sapient species. Nature, however, doesn't much care who gets hurt, so long as the survival of the genes is ensured. And in the case of the M'nangat, of course, it wasn't the mother that was devoured, but the living incubator.

The living, intelligent, *self-aware* incubator. I shuddered.

I almost pulled out to tend my hand—I was sure I was bleeding—but I was so damned close. I thought I had the knack of it now, and grabbed the writhing bundle of tentacles at the infant's bottom, gently held D'dnah's beating lower heart aside, and *pulled. . . .*

Again, the *Haldane* shuddered and the power went down. "They hit the dorsal turret," Garner told me. "We're helpless, now. . . ."

But I maintained my grip, holding the Broc baby's tentacle-legs in the wet dark, and continued a slow, steady pull. The lights came back up, and with a sharp sucking sound, then, the infant came free, emerging from the incision covered in black and green glop and hissing.

"Here you go, Mom," I said, handing the squirming infant to D'drevah, who was waiting with a towel in outstretched tentacles. "I do hope you know what to do, because I sure don't."

THANK YOU, DOC CARLYLE. . . .

She took the squirming, snapping infant from me, dried it carefully, and then pressed its tentacles against her torso. She keened, suddenly, as the infant bit down.

Human infants are suckled with milk from the mother's

breasts. Among the M'nangat, newborns are suckled with mother's blood for several months. Eventually, the new-born's beak falls off, and it begins eating regurgitated food.

And human mothers thought *they* had it rough!

I couldn't watch her—fortunately—because I still had two more of those little monsters inside my patient. Of somewhat less concern at the moment was the fact that I'd left some protein inside D'dnah's body cavity; my right index finger was bleeding freely where the little monster had bitten me. Alien proteins could be a problem . . . though I suspected that human and M'nangat biologies were too dif-ferent for my blood to trigger an allergic anaphylaxis.

I would worry about that later.

The next one was nestled in among the coils of D'dnah's intestine, and I needed to get it out before it chewed its way through and flooded herm's body with toxins.

"*All hands, all hands,*" sounded from a loudspeaker in the sick bay, as words wrote themselves across my in-head repeating the message. "*Stand by to repel boarders. Marine fireteams to the airlocks.*"

The Gykr must be closing in. If Garner was right, and they'd managed to take out our dorsal turret, the ship was pretty much defenseless. I briefly wondered why Summerlee hadn't lifted the ship up off the ice . . . then realized that that was a really dumb question. Once we were in space, or even while we were moving up through the atmosphere, we'd be easy prey for the circling Gykr starships. We were easy prey on the ice, too, for shots from orbit or the sky, but evidently the Gykr were more interested in capturing the *Haldane* than in reducing it to radioactive fragments.

But I had absolutely no doubt that they would vaporize us if it looked like we were getting away.

Or . . . would they? Maybe they were just ensuring that we left. Unfortunately, there were still human personnel in the dome outside on the ice . . . and the *Walsh* might still be underwater, making a final trip up from Base Murdock. Summerlee certainly wasn't going to abandon them to the Gykr . . . and there was still the question about abandoning the Deep.

The Deep. Was there a possible answer there?

I grabbed the second Broc infant by the tentacles, carefully disentangled it from several meters of ropy intestine, and pulled it free. I handed it to Mom, who dried it off with Dad's help, then parked it on what might pass for a Broccoli's hip next to the first one.

I looked at the table image. The third and final Broc baby appeared to have attached itself to the body cavity wall. There was a lot of blood . . . but at least it wasn't about to take a bite out of D'dnah's heart or intestine.

"Relax a sec," I told Garner, and he let the incision close.

"You okay, Elliot?" he asked.

I nodded. "I'm fine. Just give me a moment, here."

I rested a moment, leaning against the side of the table. Gods, there was so much alien blood. I was soaked in the stuff almost up to my armpits.

I closed my eyes. . . .

How do you make contact with a super-intelligent planetary mind? In the past, the Deep had been the one to initiate contact . . . we thought by manipulating electrical fields either through its ice VII substance, or through the body of a cuttlewhale. Was it possible for me to reach out and talk to it? Might a channel of some sort been opened when it had taken me into its thoughts?

I reached out . . . questing . . . *pushing* . . .

Nothing.

Okay, let's try something else. I opened a new channel, this one to the bridge. "Captain Summerlee?"

"This is the XO," Walthers' voice came back. "Clear the channel! We're *busy* right now, damn it!"

I could actually hear some of the chaos in the background of Walthers' mind, leakage from what he was seeing and hearing at the moment. Someone was shouting that there was a breach at Airlock One.

Damn, I'd forgotten that the skipper was off-line.

"Look . . . we might have a chance if we can get in touch with the Deep!" I said. "We could ask it to help!"

A pause. "I'm listening. . . ."

"If you can patch a comm signal through to the sonar transmitters . . . are they up and running?"

There was another brief pause. "Affirmative. What do you want to transmit?"

I thought for a moment. "Okay," I said. "Try *this*. . . ."

IT WORKED, OF COURSE.

I didn't get to see what happened, damn it, though I was able to watch recordings of the battle's conclusion later, at my leisure. As soon as I told Lieutenant Walthers what to try, I went back to work on D'dnah . . . *in* D'dnah, rather, fishing around for the third and last bud.

That one took me almost ten minutes. It had reattached itself to herm's body wall and was chewing away happily. In another hour, or two, it might have eaten its way all the way out.

I wanted to save D'dnah that physical trauma, though. I had Chief Garner pull *way* back on the retractors, giving me as much room to work as possible, and I extended the incision a bit farther, opening the body cavity more toward where the infant was latched on. I reached in with my left hand then, and did my best to gather up all of those tentacles, pulling them aside and out of my way, until I had a good view on the table display of that chewing beak imbedded inside D'dnah's muscle wall. Carefully, I moved my right hand in, holding the laser scalpel. The trick was getting the emitter head right up against muscle tissue before I pressed the trigger, because otherwise the dark green and black ichor of D'dnah's blood and internal fluids would absorb the beam and begin to boil, cooking my patient from the inside out.

I did wish I could have brought ROBERT in on the operation, but I did feel a responsibility to the M'nangat, who, after all, had requested that I do this. Maybe I could have convinced them that ROBERT was under my supervision, and so that would count . . . but on the other hand, there was something wonderful, something exhilarating about bringing these new lives into the light, and in saving the carrier's life at the same time.

To tell the truth, I'm not sure how much I trust robotic surgery in any case. Sometimes—with brain or eye surgery, the precision is absolutely vital, especially with microsurgeries . . . but usually it's better, I think, if you can actually feel what you're doing through your own hands and senses.

Carefully, watching the table projection the whole time, I sliced away a three-centimeter circle of muscle tissue around the infant's beak, cauterizing the wound as I cut. I slipped once; the infant gave a sudden twist and lost one of its tentacles. It almost let go then, I think, but then it dug in harder and tighter. I finished cutting it free and then carefully pulled it out, black and glistening in the overhead lights of the sick bay.

In another moment, Mom had the third infant attached to her other side, and she had three gray-green blobs attached in a band of writhing tentacles around what technically would have been her hips if she'd been human.

"Are you okay, D'drevah?" I asked. When I didn't hear a reply, I looked at D'deen. "Is she okay?"

SHE IS FINE, D'deen wrote. I could see the relief as the words printed themselves across my in-head. SHE IS FINE. . . .

"It looks like the battle outside is all over but for the shouting," Garner told me. "*Very* well done."

I'D ACTUALLY SUGGESTED THREE DIFFERENT APPROACHES TO LIEUTENant Walthers. We knew that the sonar transmitters we'd buried in the ice would reach all the way down to the Deep.

We also knew that too strong a signal had been interpreted as an attack. I don't know; maybe the chirp had hurt the Deep's equivalent of ears. Or maybe the cuttlewhales closer to the surface had felt like they were being attacked, and since they'd already experienced an attack by the Gykr, they'd surfaced to stop what they perceived as a threat.

So as a first attempt, I'd suggested that they transmit the words *help us* into the depths. The problem, of course, was that Gina had heard the words *help us* in her head, not out loud. The Deep had certainly been accessing my personal RAM storage in English, and learning the language as it did so, but I couldn't be certain that it would interpret the sound of "help us" and realize it was the same as the collection of zeros and ones stored in my in-head hardware.

Okay, so then try a second approach. Run "help us" through *Haldane*'s AI, and have it convert that audio signal into an electrical signal. Wavelengths and frequencies, after all, are wavelengths and frequencies, whether they occur as sound waves in water or as electromagnetic waves in a radio transmission. Make the conversion, and transmit that as sonar waves into the depths.

And, while you're doing all of that, have the AI run one final set of calculations. Take the wavelength and frequency of the initial "h" sound in "help us," and raise the number one to *that* power. Take the wavelength and frequency of the short "e" sound and raise the number two to that power. Then do three to the "l" and five to the "p," and go on to the numbers seven and eleven for the "m" and the "e." Now multiply those together to get one very large number.

And transmit *that*: the phrase "help us" encoded as a Gödel expression.

As it turned out, we didn't actually do the Gödel number thing. It would have taken a long time for *Haldane*'s AI to do the necessary calculations, too long for our survival, at any rate . . . and in any case the Deep had responded to either the first or the second attempt. We still don't know which.

But respond it did. . . .

I was on the mess deck, which was crowded with Marines and *Haldane* crew members and the other Corpsmen. Even Captain Summerlee was there, grinning ear to ear as Lieutenant Walthers called up the recordings of the battle from different camera vantage points. Chief Garner was there. . . . and Gunny Hancock . . . and Dr. Murdock and a number of his people as well.

So was Gina Lloyd, sitting next to me with her arm around me. I was a bit concerned at first about Doob . . . but he was on the other side of me, and didn't seem concerned.

"Here it is! Here it is!" the skipper said, excited, pointing at the viewall. "Watch this!"

It was *only* the third or fourth time we'd seen it.

The deck-to-overhead scene showed the unrelenting ice outside. *Haldane* had grounded about five kilometers from the edge of the ice pack, and perhaps three from the nanoflaged base. Drawn out in a long line about a kilometer from the ship we could see a line of black dots—the four-meter-tall, six-legged walking tanks used as heavy mobile armor by the Gykr.

Closer—*much* closer—crossing *Haldane*'s shadow on the ice, a dozen individual Gykr were sprinting toward the Number One airlock.

About halfway between the two, the ice began to buckle, heaving up . . . and up . . . and up, then shattering in sparkling shards of crystal as the massive, shaggy, and impossibly huge front end of a cuttlewhale emerged from beneath the surface, heaving itself into the red-violet sky, tentacles questing, and then the sound reached us: a low, throbbing, pounding thunder that went on and on.

A few hundred meters away, a second cuttlewhale breached the ice, exploding into the open air in a geyser of ice fragments and spray and churning steam.

The third emerged farther off, almost on top of the advancing line of walkers.

Walthers shifted to other cameras, giving us an all-around view. Altogether, sixty-five of the monstrous cuttle-whale shapes broke through the ice, emerging around both the *Haldane* and the dome of our base.

There was the small problem that cuttlewhales had trouble telling the difference between humans and Gucks, but that was handily solved by the fact that we didn't have anyone out on the ice . . . not at first, anyway. In a few seconds, the air was so filled with ice crystals whipped along by the incessant wind that we couldn't see what was happening in any case. We could still see the Gykr who'd reached *Haldane*, of course. The appearance of the cuttlewhales between them and their main force seemed to have utterly paralyzed them, however. Several were on the ice, twitching, while others were wandering around in vague circles, as though lost. I wondered which one was Chosen. . . .

Then the Marines appeared, spilling out of the airlock, firing into the confused Gykr, which immediately began dropping their weapons.

Gykrs, *surrendering*. We'd not known if that was even possible with their take-no-prisoners psychology.

But the final act still had to play itself out.

The camera angle shifted, looking up at a Gykr star-ship as it drifted in closer, black, ominous, its down-canted wings shuddering as it fought the wind. We couldn't see the beam, of course, but below, a cuttlewhale exploded into hur-tling chunks of exotic ice, steam, and slush. The enemy ship drifted closer, coming lower. Another cuttlewhale exploded under that onslaught, and it appeared to be lining itself up for a shot at the *Haldane*.

The Deep and its cuttlewhale creations understand pres-sure. We still don't know how they do it, but it is clear that they manipulate pressure in various ways . . . and we watched in jaw-hanging awe as they manipulated it here, on the surface.

A cuttlewhale reared high, tentacles spread open. Something glinted in the weak, red sunlight as it squirted from gaping mouth to hovering starship too quickly to see. And the starship . . . came apart.

Somehow, muscles of exotic ice-jelly powerful enough to resist pressures of hundreds of tons per square centimeter had closed within the cuttlewhale's gut, forcing a stream of water out the mouth and across several hundred meters of open air. We have cutting tools that use high pressure to expel streams of water at several times the speed of sound, pressure enough to slice through solid titanium or plasteel like a hot knife through butter. This was like that . . . a thin stream of water traveling at an estimated Mach 40 . . . a living squirt gun that could shred a starship like paper.

Other cuttlewhales were looking up into the heavens now, and radar indicated that they were opening up on Gykr starships in orbit.

In orbit. But I worked out the numbers later. Abyssworld has an escape velocity of a bit less than eleven kilometers per second. The speed of sound is roughly a kilometer per three seconds . . . a bit less in Abyssworld's thinner atmosphere, or call it a thousand kilometers per hour. Forty times that is a bit more than eleven kilometers per second.

Cuttlewhales could spit at escape velocity, and with careful aim could hit a starship in low orbit. I don't know if what hit those ships was solid ice, liquid water, or gaseous steam, but whatever it was carried enough kinetic energy to do some serious damage, even after transiting a couple of hundred kilometers of atmosphere. We found out later that one Gykr starship had been destroyed, and two others damaged. The others pulled back in a considerable hurry.

And Walthers was able to open a Gal3 dialog with them a few minutes later.

The entire engagement, from the moment when the first cuttlewhale had broken through the ice to the Gykr ships' retreat, had taken two minutes and five seconds.

"All I can say," Summerlee said, grinning, "is that I'm sure as hell glad those things are on *our* side!"

"Having a super-intelligent planet on your side doesn't hurt either," I said. I don't think she heard me, though. There was too much wild cheering and thunderous applause going on in the background.

Some hours later, *Haldane*'s AI worked out the Gödel algorithms for another set of transmissions into the Deep. The message was pretty simple, though it took a long time to work out the math.

"Thank you," it said. "We will help."

If it took Humankind a million years, we would help. . . .

Epilogue

Two weeks later, I was back on Earth . . . well, at the Commonwealth's Starport, anyway, up-El. *Haldane* had pulled into port alongside the *Clymer*. Liberty had been granted, and most of the Marines were elsewhere now, down on Earth, or enjoying the entertainment facilities at Geosynch.

Me . . . well, I wasn't up for partying much.

The message from Personnel had been waiting for me when we pulled into port. It told me that Sergeant Joy Leighton had deployed with Marine 1/1 to Dushanbe a week after *Haldane*'s departure. Her Cutlass had grounded just outside of Dushanbe, where she'd participated in a ground assault against a heavily fortified missile base.

She'd been killed, one of fifteen Marines caught in the open by a pocket nuke. Not even Mk. 10 MMCA combat armor can stand up to a one-kiloton warhead going off a couple of hundred meters away.

They'd recovered her body. They'd flown her back to NNMC Bethesda.

And they'd brought her back with CAPTR technology: Cerebral Access PolyTomographic Reconstruction.

The trouble was that her brain had been badly damaged in the blast; parts of it had been fried by the radiation pulse. What was left had not been enough to take the implant download.

"*Treatment is continuing,*" the message told me, "*and massive infusions of stem cells may yet restore Sergeant Leighton's cerebral activity in full. Partial success has been achieved in personality reconstruction. However, Sergeant Leighton as yet has no memory of her life more recently than approximately ten years ago. She does not remember her time with the Marines, and cannot remember acquaintances and relationships developed since that time. We request that you not attempt to contact her directly, as such contact would be disturbing or upsetting, and might possibly interfere with her recovery. . . .*"

Apparently, that message had gone out to a number of her friends in the service. Our personnel records keep track of the friends we make while we're in—and those who are more than friends—just in case this sort of thing happens.

Of course, what the records didn't show, *couldn't* show, was that desperate battle to save Joy's life during the fight on Bloodworld, or her intense, desperate gratitude later, when she'd thanked me for bringing her back *without* turning her into a zombie.

And here she'd become a zombie after all, her life saved by CAPTR, but her mind a recording downloaded into her brain . . . and an incomplete recording at that.

I'd prayed for CAPTR technology when Paula had her stroke. I'd not been able to get her help in time, and she had died.

And now Joy *had* been CAPTRed . . . but it seemed that I'd lost her as well.

Gods!

Dr. Kirchner, it turned out, was doing just fine, thank you. He'd been shipped down to SAMMC, where the cause of his psychosis had finally been diagnosed. It turned out that there'd been a problem during his last rejuvenation treatment. Certain types of schizophrenia—and autism, too—can be caused when for some reason new proteins in the brain don't fold quite right. One bad fold can actually trigger a cascade of identical mistakes, and the result can be a serious imbalance in brain chemistry. They were using nanobots and stem-cell injections to repair his brain's physical problems, and CAPTR technology to fill in the holes. He was going to be fine.

And Kari Harris? She'd been shipped down to Bethesda in her S-tube. The official word was that she would live, though an awful lot of her body would need to be grown from scratch. There'd been enough brain damage that they'd used her CAPTR backup as well. Apparently, that had gone okay, but they wouldn't know for sure for a few weeks yet.

Gunny Hancock was well on the way to having a whole new lower left arm. I was happy for him, at least. D'dnah was doing well, too, as were all three baby Broccolets.

Everyone was doing great, apparently . . . except for Joy.

Damn it, and *she'd* been worried about *me* when I'd shipped out!

Yeah, I was feeling thoroughly sorry for myself. Survivor guilt, I guess. Why had *she* been killed, and not me?

For that matter, why had they been able to bring Kirchner back, but not Joy?

That was a disgustingly unworthy thought . . . but I savored it anyway. It hurt. Damn it, I *wanted* to hurt. . . .

"How's the hero?" Gina Lloyd asked.

I was in my old quarters on board the Clymer. I'd not been aware of the door opening; maybe she'd used an override. But now she was there, wearing civilian clothes . . . though her garment appeared to be more light than anything else, a shimmering, rainbow sheath of radiance hugging her form.

"What do *you* want?" I asked. Okay, I was being less than welcoming, probably even less than civilized . . . but I really didn't want to see anyone right now.

"Doob and McKean and Chief Garner and a few others are headed down-El," she told me, ignoring my poor manners. "We're celebrating!"

"Celebrating what?"

She shrugged, the movement doing delightful things to the light hugging her skin. "Getting back from Abyssworld? That new treaty with the Gucks? A formal long-term mutual-assistance protocol with the Deep? I'll bet *that* makes your dad happy!"

"I suppose." I'd shot off a file to him while we were still inbound, with as many details as I was allowed to share. The military would be looking for civilian corporations to follow up our contact with the Deep. General Nanodynamics stood to make a lot of money with the work out there . . . especially when full communication was established with the Deep and it began to share with us everything it had been thinking about for the past billion years.

There was also talk of using Gödel encoding with the Medusae at Europa.

"Damn it, Elliot, you've made a real difference on this voyage."

"I suppose. But Joy . . ."

"You couldn't have helped her, even if you'd been there with her, okay? And she knew the risks when she raised her hand and swore in as a Marine."

"But I'm alive, and Joy . . . the real Joy, the Joy I knew . . . she's—"

"*Fuck* you, Carlyle!" The profanity on her lips startled me. "Get a grip, okay?"

"What . . . ?"

"You lost your friend. I'm sorry about that, I really am! But you have *other* friends who love you and care for you and want to help! Damn it, you've pulled off the coup of the century and saved all of our lives in the bargain, and we're going to celebrate with you if it kills you! You hear me?"

I knew what she was doing, of course—trying to shock me out of the doldrums. Maybe distract me from myself. Maybe even remind me that life was still worth living.

I didn't want to be jollied along, no . . . but she wasn't

jollying me. She was metaphorically giving me a swift, hard kick in the ass.

I sighed. "Okay, okay. Let put on some civvies."

She watched while I dissolved my utilities and then slapped on a conservative black skinsuit. I wondered what Doob would say about his girlfriend watching me dress, then decided it didn't matter. He . . . they . . . we were friends, with a bond forged in blood.

"Ready?" she said. She reached out, grabbed my hand, and yanked me toward the door. "You've been healing so many *other* people, E-Car, it's about time you had some for yourself! Let's go!"

I went. And . . . she was right.

I felt myself starting to heal.

Printed by RR Donnelley at Glasgow, UK

TRANSPERSONAL BOOKS

James Fadiman, *General Editor*

Transpersonal Books explore the psychology of consciousness
and possibilities for transcendence
through altered states of consciousness,
paranormal phenomena, spiritual disciplines,
and other modes of extended awareness

GAY HENDRICKS is an assistant professor in the School of Education,
University of Colorado, Colorado Springs.
He is the author, with Russel Wills,
of *The Centering Book* (Prentice-Hall).

JAMES FADIMAN is a lecturer
in the Department of Mechanical Engineering,
Stanford University,
and former president
of the Association for Transpersonal Psychology.
H̶e̶ h̶a̶s̶ ̶w̶ritten and edited several books
̶i̶n̶ ̶t̶r̶a̶n̶s̶p̶ersonal psychology.

TRANSPERSONAL EDUCATION

A Curriculum for Feeling and Being

Edited by

GAY HENDRICKS

JAMES FADIMAN

A SPECTRUM BOOK

PRENTICE-HALL, INC., ENGLEWOOD CLIFFS, NEW JERSEY

Library of Congress Cataloging in Publication Data
MAIN ENTRY UNDER TITLE:

Transpersonal education.

   (Transpersonal books)   (A Spectrum Book)
   Bibliography: p.
   1. Creative thinking (Education)   2. Imagination.
3. Psychical research and children.   I. Hendricks, Gay.
II. Fadiman, James, (date)
LB1062.T72   370.15′3   76-15235
ISBN 0-13-930479-7
ISBN 0-13-930461-4 pbk.

*For Amanda, Susan, Stephen,
and the children of the future.*   G.H.

*For my daughters Renee and Maria,
who remind me that learning is joy*

For my wife Dorothy, who understands.   J.F.

The figures on pages 125 and 147 were adapted from *Bioenergetics* by Alexander Lowen, M.D. Copyright © 1975 by Alexander Lowen, M.D. They are used by permission of Coward, McCann & Geoghegan, Inc. and the author.

10   9   8   7   6   5   4   3   2   1

PRENTICE-HALL INTERNATIONAL, INC. (*London*)
PRENTICE-HALL OF AUSTRALIA PTY. LTD. (*Sydney*)
PRENTICE-HALL OF CANADA LTD. (*Toronto*)
PRENTICE-HALL OF INDIA PRIVATE LIMITED (*New Delhi*)
PRENTICE-HALL OF JAPAN, INC. (*Tokyo*)
PRENTICE-HALL OF SOUTHEAST ASIA PTE. LTD. (*Singapore*)

Contents

Preface

Are you one of those teachers who is always on the lookout for something new to bring to the classroom? If so, read on.

Are you a parent, a principal, or a professor who thinks it is still possible to generate real excitement in school? If so, this may be your book.

We believe that learning is the natural state in children and that when children are learning things of interest to them, there is ease and delight in the process. Unfortunately, the ease and delight of learning begin to decline when the child enters a school setting where the whole person is not developed. Human beings are whole beings, with cognitive, social, emotional, and spiritual potentials. Transpersonal education *is* education for the whole person, and views the school as a place where this wholeness can be supported and encouraged.

It is the primary task of the teacher to maintain and strengthen the child's basic urge toward further learning. Although many people embrace this position philosophically, most schools continue to be places where the natural urge for learning is stunted, places where learning becomes a chore. Such schools have shown that it is possible to dampen children's spontaneous enthusiasm for any area of the curriculum.

There is a saying from the Middle East: "He who tastes knows." This book is about ways to help students get more of the taste of their own education, to make the classroom experience more alive. Transpersonal education helps students gain more control of their capacity to learn, so that they can expand the ways in which they understand and appreciate the objective content which is still the core of the curriculum. In addition, transpersonal education suggests a new set of activities for the classroom, activities aimed at the development of the whole person.

The papers assembled here are part of an emerging point of view which is beginning to allow greater freedom and flexibility in education. Many of the writers are practical, determined educators who, in their quest for new approaches, are incorporating practices from a dozen fields into the teaching/learning situation. Insights gained from the upsurge of interest in meditation, biofeedback, martial arts, Eastern thought, and altered states of consciousness are finding their ways into the classroom. Stripped of their jargon, these fields of study are accelerating and improving conventional learning, as well as bringing new and more personal areas of learning into the classroom.

Transpersonal education is not revolutionary (we've had enough "revolutions" in education), and it is not the ultimate solution to all our educational problems. But because it is a source of powerful new tools and possibilities for the classroom, teachers like it, and students are excited when they find that the ideas of transpersonal education are not limited to subject matter but have extensive transfer into their personal lives.

Part I of the book is an introduction to the scope of the transpersonal point of view. The content of the papers range from the practical (Roberts and Clark, Hendricks) to the visionary (Huxley, Krishnamurti). Upon close reading, however, the reader may find a wealth of practical information in the "visionary" papers, and more than a touch of the visionary in the "practical" papers. This seemingly odd posture—head in the clouds but feet firmly planted in the ground—is a common characteristic of transpersonal educators.

Part II is the how-to-do-it section of the book. Here the reader will find articles on classroom use of dreams, fantasy, biofeedback, psychic abilities, meditation, and other techniques. This section also contains reports from teachers who have used transpersonal techniques successfully in their classrooms.

Part III offers readings which the editors feel capture the essence of transpersonal education at its best. Rather than risk devitalizing these readings through summarization, the editors leave it to the reader to discover the common threads which are woven through these selections.

Finally, there is a list of materials you may eventually want to track down if you continue to expand in these areas.

Charles Darwin was once approached by two small boys, children of a family with whom he was visiting. The boys had caught a butterfly, a centipede, a beetle, and a grasshopper. Taking the centipede's body, the butterfly's wings, the beetle's head, and the grasshopper's legs, they had fashioned an alarming and original insect.

"We caught this bug in the field," they said innocently. "What kind of a bug is it, Mr. Darwin?"

Darwin examined it solemnly. "Did you notice whether it hummed when you caught it, boys?" he asked gravely.

"Yes, sir," they answered, trying to conceal their mirth.

"Just as I thought," said Darwin. "It is a humbug."

A great deal of what goes on in education under the name of "new, exciting solutions" turns out to be humbug. However, many people *are* genuinely excited about the potentials of transpersonal education. We would be pleased if you would try some of the ideas contained herein, filter out the useful from the humbug, and let us know your results.

INTRODUCTION TO TRANSPERSONAL EDUCATION

What is transpersonal education? Although no one has yet successfully defined the term transpersonal, *the authors in this section cover various facets by approaching it from very different angles.*

In his book The Psychology of Consciousness, *Robert Ornstein provides evidence from current brain research that there are two modes of consciousness at work in human beings: one, a rational, logical, and active mode, is associated with the left side of the brain, while the other, a mystical, intuitive, and receptive mode, seems to be the function of the right side of the brain. In a sense, this information is not new, since poets and philosophers have been hinting at this phenomenon for thousands of years; what is remarkable is that science is finding a physical basis for the existence of the two modes.*

These findings have profound implications for education, for it seems clear that our current educational efforts are aimed primarily at the left side of the brain, thereby leaving an entire model of consciousness to chance development. Although their approaches are widely diverse, the authors in this first section agree on one point: transpersonal education is an approach that aims at the concurrent development of the logical and the mystical, the analytical and the intuitive.

Tom Roberts and Frances Clark, in the first article, provide a concise but comprehensive statement of the domain of transpersonal education. Although focusing on the day-to-day use of transpersonal psychology in education, the authors explore the philosophical implications of the transpersonal approach. The second selection, by Aldous Huxley, contains a description of a transpersonal education curriculum that is nearly as radical today as it was when it was written twenty years ago.

The third selection, drawn from the works of the Indian teacher Krishnamurti, speaks for itself, simply and beautifully, and needs no comment from us. The last reading in the section, written by one of the editors, is a practical guide to personalizing and transpersonalizing the classroom.

We hope that through your reading of the following selections you will form your own definition of transpersonal education, and perhaps begin to formulate your own ways of using it.

Transpersonal Psychology in Education

Thomas B. Roberts
Frances V. Clark

What is the scope of transpersonal education? What are its origins? Thomas Roberts and Frances Clark, two pioneering transpersonal educators, provide cogent answers to these and other important questions.

TRANSPERSONAL PSYCHOLOGY

The development of a comprehensive educational psychology requires a theoretical framework which includes all the phenomena related to human learning, and must therefore include areas of human experience which previously have been ignored by traditional academic psychology. Freudian, behavioral, and humanistic psychologies are seen as useful, but incomplete psychologies. Transpersonal psychology offers a more inclusive vision of human potential, suggesting both a new image of man

"Transpersonal Psychology in Education." From Thomas G. Roberts and Frances V. Clark, *Transpersonal Psychology in Education,* Fastback Pamphlet Series, #53 (Bloomington, Indiana: Phi Delta Kappa Educational Foundation, 1975), pp. 7-33. Reprinted by permission of the publisher.

and a new world view. Using transpersonal psychology in education does not require a complete rejection of established educational psychologies, but may be used in conjunction with them. Conflicts occur at some points, and agreement occurs at others.

An underlying assumption of transpersonal psychology is that physical, emotional, intellectual, and spiritual growth are interrelated, and the optimal educational environment simulates and nurtures the intuitive as well as the rational, the imaginative as well as the practical, and the creative as well as the receptive functions of each individual. Transpersonal psychology has focused attention on the human capacity for self-transcendence as well as self-realization, and is concerned with the optimum development of consciousness.

Most topics being investigated by transpersonal psychologists consist of the psychological aspects of at least one of the following: a new image of man and a new world view, altered states of consciousness (including meditation, dreams, etc.), impulses toward higher states (such as peak experiences), self-realization and self-transcendence, subjective experience and inner states, spiritual growth, parapsychology and psychic phenomena, other cultures and their psychologies (especially Eastern psychologies), newly discovered forms of energy, recent physiological research (such as voluntary control of internal states), and evolving consciousness.

Many psychologists judge that we use less than 10 percent of our capacities. Transpersonal psychologists are seeking to increase our understanding of human abilities in order to unlock some of our latent potentials. How can we learn to use some of the abilities which may be hidden in our own minds? A partial answer may be found in studying people who have unusual abilities, and in the cultural, social, and psychological factors affecting their development.

Transpersonal psychology gives us a new perspective on the old Delphic precept, "Know thyself." In turning our attention to the inner world of man, we are indeed discovering a wealth of unsuspected resources. Many of the transpersonal techniques for using inner imagery in the process of self-discovery are well suited to classroom use, and may easily be introduced in the existing educational system. As the universal language of human experience, inner imagery finds expression in all forms of creativity, be it artistic, scientific, or philosophical. As a student becomes familiar with his own inner resources, he develops a new awareness of his individual uniqueness and his relationship to others and the environment. Research in transpersonal psychology has indicated that working with imagery can have a beneficial effect on physical, emotional, mental, and spiritual well-being. It is important that we begin to give students access to these tools that can be used for continuing growth and awareness throughout their lives. In applying transpersonal psychology to education, both students and teachers can assume responsibility for making choices, and develop a sense of inner direction in their lives.

CURRENT CLASSROOM APPLICATIONS

The first step in applying transpersonal psychology to education usually involves shifting the focus from external to internal awareness. As students become aware of their own inner states, they can begin to recognize important conditions which affect their learning ability.

Relaxation and Concentration

Can you remember a time when you were concentrating so intently on something, perhaps a hobby, a sport, or some creative endeavor, that you lost all sense of time and were able to think and act super-efficiently? Or can you remember a time when you were so clearheaded you learned a complex task easily? This state of mind, which occurs spontaneously at random, can also be consciously developed. Although a person's state of mind is a major variable in how well he performs, we seldom teach people to move into an appropriate state of mind before undertaking a task. Investigating such states of mind has been the focus of transpersonal psychologists who are interested in self-induced altered states of consciousness evidenced in psychic healing, parapsychological phenomena, yoga, biofeedback, and meditation. Teaching the voluntary control of internal states is one area of transpersonal psychology which is easily applied to education, and the first step is the introduction of relaxation training. Relaxation training is important both for everyday functioning as a beginning step to more advanced training in meditation and concentration. The immediate effects of relaxation can be experienced both by teachers and students, and many who have tried it find short periods of intensive relaxation to be of considerable benefit.

For example, a German teacher had a class in which the students seemed too keyed up for their own good. "Whenever we would have a Unit Test, always a biggie in their minds, no matter how much I would try to play it down, the tenseness would permeate the classroom." In one unit test, his ten students scored 5 A's, 3 B's, and 2 C's. The following unit test had proved to be more difficult in previous years, so he tried to improve their recall and ability, not by pushing and drilling them harder, but by relaxing them at the time of the test. Here is his report:

Well, I chanced the great experiment. My only worry was the time element. The 48-minute class period was cut to 38 minutes as I darkened the room and played a commercial relaxation tape received from a friend. The students sat in their seats, heads down on their forearms, legs uncrossed; then I took them on and through an original fantasy journey in the German language. This particular part had to be condensed into 8 minutes, because of the time element. With about 28 minutes of time left, the students proceeded to work on the test which usually takes at least 30 to 35 minutes to complete. Observing the students while they were writing and thinking, I detected the total absence of nail-chewing and the usual pencil tapping on the desktops and nervous, quick glances at the clock. Everybody finished the test on time. Grading the test was fun; 7 A's and 3 B's was the obvious result. The quality of writing in some of the usually more sloppy papers improved markedly. The students just could not believe this. It was only after I explained to them that a lot of their learned knowledge was not able to surface because of their nervousness and fear and the tension, and once they were relaxed, the learned storehouse of information was able to be tapped.

Other teachers who have taught their students to relax find similar results. Some students who catch on to the techniques use them to reduce tension in other classes as well as in up-tight social situations when they want to feel more at ease.

These exploratory applications of relaxation training need not be taken as proof that relaxation will automatically improve test scores, but these intriguing findings keep reappearing, and indicate an area where further investigation and experimentation may lead to the development of transpersonal teaching methods. The fact that students are able to improve their recall by controlling their breathing, relaxing their muscles, and learning to direct their own attention exemplifies two important principles: First, our behavior is influenced by *internal* states, and these states can be controlled voluntarily. Second, the mind and body are inextricably connected. When we control one, the other is inevitably affected.

Effective methods of mind/body control have been practiced in yoga for thousands of years, yet we are only beginning to explore the possibilities of mind/body learning. Training in deep relaxation has immediate physical benefits, since it can help people fall asleep quickly and gives the body a chance to revitalize itself in brief periods of time. Some coaches say they have found that it allows their athletes not to waste their energy in pregame nervousness, but to consciously direct their own levels of activity by selecting the right amount of energy for the task at hand. Relaxation is a prime mental/physical ability that people can use daily throughout their lives. As such it certainly deserves a place in the physical education curriculum alongside the rules of badminton and the techniques of wrestling take-downs.

In schools, relaxation is easily combined with concentration. After the students are relaxed, then they can direct their attention toward academic content, or they can let their minds idle in creative association. Aldous Huxley could select his degree of relaxation and breadth of concentration when he worked. If his wife were home, he would not hear the doorbell or telephone, but if she went out, he would hear them. In his "deep reflection," as he called it, he had almost perfect recall. Probably everybody has had instances of becoming so involved in reading or working that he temporarily forgets himself, and then is able to remember or accomplish much more than usual. Perhaps we would all learn to do this at will, maybe not as well as Aldous Huxley, maybe better. The challenge to education is: Can we learn to do this so that we can do it whenever we want? Can we teach others to do it too?

Guided Fantasy

One method of facilitating concentration and directing attention is guided fantasy. Specifically, directed fantasy trips are useful for learning specific content, while open-ended fantasies evoke creativity and aid self-discovery. The following example illustrates the use of guided fantasy as an aid to learning content in an electronics class.

I took my beginning electronics class on a fantasy trip into that mysterious land of invisible magnetic and electric fields surrounding the windings and core of a transformer. The procedure was as follows. The room was darkened and everyone put their heads down on the desks and were told to relax and empty their minds. Prior to beginning the journey a relaxation exercise was performed. Everyone was told to imagine themselves as an electron and to concentrate on what it might feel like to be such an incredibly small piece of (negatively charged) matter. They were to encounter two very large coils of wire, and around the wire there was a huge and rapidly changing force field. They were to enter the force field and feel the effects of it. They were then told to enter the wire of the coil and experience the movement of the rest of the electrons within the coil of wire as they were affected by the rapidly changing force field, which is the electromagnetic field. I told the students that another coil of equal size and strength was coming toward them. The two fields were interacting, and the interaction became very violent the closer the coils came to each other. The students were told that the increase in strength of one coil caused an increase in the strength of the other coil. This produced a super-strong force which moved the electrons (students) very fast.

(After a waking period, the teacher turned on a small light and discussed the experience with them.)

The next day the students read the chapter in the book dealing with inductive coils. The students said they had no trouble visualizing the forces described in the book, and other qualitative work in the lab seemed to bear this out. It is quite evident to me that the trip was worth taking since I have taught this subject matter before but not with this much success.

Teachers who have used the fantasy journeys hold a key to improved instruction: less stimulation, not more, and temporary escape from the stimulus overload of a hectic, rushing world of school halls and ringing bells.

Why do fantasy journeys work? This is a good question for educational researchers. Recent speculations of neurophysiologists studying the brain suggest that the left hemisphere of the brain thinks in words and clearly defined symbols such as chemical and mathematical symbols. It is active, calculating, reasoning, and is predominantly sequential and analytic in its functioning. The right hemisphere, on the other hand, is spatially oriented, thinks in pictures, perceives patterns as a whole, and operates in an intuitive, emotional, and receptive mode.

Although the "sideness" of mental functions is highly speculative because it is based on split-brain research, Robert Ornstein's metaphorical use of "right-function" and "left-function" is relevant to educators. According to researcher Ornstein:

> It is the polarity and the integration of these two modes of consciousness, the complementary workings of the intellect and the intuitive, which underlie our highest achievements.

Most of our education, which emphasizes verbal knowledge and reasoning, is predominantly left-brain education. Guided fantasy offers the possibility of engaging the right half of the brain in the learning process. We know that experience is the best teacher and that teaching is easier when students have had relevant experiences. Some things, however, are difficult or impossible to experience directly. The use of fantasy, however, can give students an imaginary experience which they can relate to the verbal, logical material which is usually presented in class. In this way, material geared to left-brain learning can be connected to the more diffuse, intuitive knowing of the right side. Providing students with experiences to match the usual didactic instruction may also be a key to unlocking creative insight and intuitive understanding. Perhaps when something suddenly "makes sense" or "rings true," it is an instance of making a connection between the two modes of knowing. Becoming aware in the left side of the brain of what the right side had intuitively known but had not been able to verbalize may be experienced as a flash of insight.

Philosophers and psychologists of education, as well as teachers, curriculum planners, textbook writers, and material makers can learn from Ornstein's brain research that the linear, verbal-intellectual mode of knowing is clearly not the only mode available to man. What are other ways of teaching for other modes of learning? The field is open for reconceptualizing what it means to teach and to be educated, for creative classroom innovations, for research on new teaching styles, and for the development of new topics of study and supporting educational materials.

Learning to understand and control one's own consciousness includes learning to pay attention to what one wants when one wants to, instead of being at the mercy of a roaming, untrained mind. Learning how to relax, concentrate, and freely associate are skills which we seldom teach, but which give evidence of improving current instruction. They are also basic skills for developing further transpersonal potentials, in school, outside of school, and later in life. . . .

ALTERED STATES OF CONSCIOUSNESS

Western psychology has traditionally recognized only three states of consciousness, namely waking, dreaming, and dreamless sleep. Meditation, daydreaming, hypnosis, etc., have been considered variations of the waking state. In contrast, Buddhist psychology identifies well over a hundred different states of mind. Eastern psychologies apparently are more conceptually and theoretically sophisticated than Western psychologies in matters of subjective experience and altered states of consciousness.

The importance of altered states of consciousness for psychology was first recognized by William James, who stated:

Our normal waking consciousness, rational consciousness, as we call it, is but one special type of consciousness, whilst all about it, parted from it by the filmiest of screens, there lie potential forms of consciousness entirely different. No account of the universe in its totality can be final which leaves these other forms of consciousness quite discarded.

Some altered states are currently off limits for use in schools but may nevertheless be discussed. Hypnosis, for example, should be practiced only by a qualified hypnotherapist, but it is a fascinating topic for class discussion. Popular misconceptions regarding hypnosis can be cleared up easily in discussion with a well-informed teacher. Self-hypnosis deserves attention as a tool for accelerating learning as well as a method of gaining voluntary control over physiological functions.

Psychoactive drugs, including alcohol, coffee, and marijuana are on many students' minds. Andrew Weil, author of *The Natural Mind,* says people have an innate desire to alter consciousness. Forcing this topic underground, like forcing the topic of sex underground, results in misinformation, rumors, and unfortunate experiences. Open discussion of altered states of consciousness can throw some light on this mysterious topic and inform students that there are effective non-drug ways of exploring and controlling consciousness. A complete drug education program should recognize the natural human desire for exploring consciousness and should provide acceptable alternative routes.

Dreams

What is important for education is the fact that altered states of consciousness, particularly the dream state, are eagerly picked up by students at all levels of education as a topic of study. Dreaming is an altered state that is being used successfully by teachers both as technique and as content. From a transpersonal point of view, dreams are important because they give us messages from the unconscious, and they afford easy access to a different reality. Dreaming is one door to our inner selves. Furthermore, there is a considerable body of research on dreams, and dreaming is a state readily available to almost everyone.

Questions of how to interpret dreams will inevitably be a part of any classroom discussion. It is advisable for the teacher to point out that there are many different approaches to dream interpretation, and that each person can get more out of his dreams by exploring his own feelings and associations to the dream than out of a standard interpretation of symbols occurring in the dream. Interpretations often lead to blocking and forgetting of dreams, as well as being potentially destructive or misleading. When using dreams as a source of creativity or as a beginning of self-exploration, it is therefore advisable not to interpret the dreams, but to accept them as messages, or stories, one is telling oneself.

If some students have difficulty remembering dreams they can be reassured by a suggestion that if they do not remember one, they can make one up. Allowing a few minutes of quiet time before working with dreams can help the recall process and allow time for anybody who wants to make one up to do so. Initially, it is not important whether the dream is an actual dream or a made-up dream. Either way the student has a chance to explore and express his creative imagination.

Some methods which can help people remember dreams include lying quietly for a few minutes after waking up and reviewing dreams or dream fragments; setting an alarm in order to wake up at different times during the night to catch a dream in process; keeping a tape recorder or a paper and pencil next to the bed to record dreams immediately. Dreams which can be easily recalled immediately after waking may be forgotten in a short time, so it is a good idea to record them as soon as possible. Sharing dreams can often be a way of remembering more dreams, and listening to others may also remind a person of dreams he has forgotten. . . .

Keeping a dream diary can help even young children see recurring dreams and recurring themes from different dreams. Often the feeling that different dreams are related is a more reliable indicator of their relationship than reasoned comparison of their content. Asking students to retell their dreams in a dimmed classroom following relaxation helps the sharing process. One teacher completed her instructions this way: "After we have discussed one person's dreams and have given our own visualizations as well as emotions during that time, we will move to someone else. It is also important for you to know that you are invited to share your dreams which are, in effect, your inner life, only to the degree that you feel comfortable doing so."

The chairman of a high school English department used dreams this way:

I told them that I wanted them to be very quiet and try to crawl back inside their dream for about five minutes to "see" the way it was and to recapture the feeling the dream gave them. Then, they were to write just as fast as they could without worrying about literary style or mechanics. Their purpose was to get as much of their dream as possible down on paper in vivid, sharp, detailed language.

We turned out the lights and pulled the drapes. The room became semi-dark and very, very still.

I had expected some resistance or at least some embarrassed uneasiness; there was none. Some students leaned back and stretched their legs out in front of them; others put their heads on their desks; some just sat with their eyes closed. After about five minutes, one or two began to write. One by one in the next few minutes, they all began. No one broke the silence until a few seconds before the bell rang when I asked them to bring their papers (many of which were finished by this time) with them the next day.

At the beginning of the period the following day I asked them to go through what they had written and to select the most vital parts of their dream and the most vivid wording. Using what they selected, they were to write a poem. (We had only begun poetry, having spent two days of individual browsing/reading in poetry collections.) My only instructions to the students were that they should not try to use rhyme and they should "squeeze out" every excess word. . . .

The assignment, I felt, was a success for a number of reasons: 1. Everyone had something to write about. 2. The students were fascinated by dreams and uninhibited about sharing them. 3. The vivid quality of dreams lends itself to poetic expression.

It was, I think, the best first experience in poetry that I have ever tried.

Working with dreams carries the implicit message that the dream state is useful and worth studying. It gives students practice in using an altered state of consciousness and may encourage the exploration of other altered states which contain further resources that can be made available. An educational corollary to William James' statement is: No education of man can be complete which leaves these potential forms of consciousness undeveloped.

Meditation and Centering

Meditation has already received some coverage in educational journals. Studies of the transcendental type of meditation show improved self-control, improved social relations with fellow students, teachers, and parents, decreased drug abuse, improved grades, and increased self-actualization. The Illinois House of Representatives resolved, ". . . that all educational institutions, especially those under State of Illinois Jurisdiction, be strongly encouraged to study the feasibility of courses in Transcendental Meditation. . . ." Counselors trained in Zen meditation improved their scores on self-actualization and on empathy measurement scales. Meditation has also been found helpful to athletes and effective in other forms of physiological control. Hatha yoga, which has already been introduced in some departments of physical education, is one way of teaching mind/body relationships. Various kinds of meditation are forms of altered states of consciousness which have many different uses in education. . . .

Centering exercises provide a good introduction to meditation, and are also helpful in quieting down. The process of centering can begin by focusing attention on the physical center of gravity in the body, feeling the relationship of the body to the earth and the space surrounding it. Experiencing the sense of balance and support provided by the floor or the chair helps to focus attention on physical sensations. Attention may be directed to the surface of the skin, body boundaries, and the flow of energy associated with the circulatory system. In many Eastern traditions, including the Japanese martial arts, the center of physical energy is located in the belly, about two inches below the navel, and two inches in front of the spine. Focusing attention on this center while noticing the movements of breathing in and out is an easy and widely used method of centering. Centering has a calming effect which makes concentration easier and helps students let go of distracting anxieties by focusing on being here and now. A good question to ask after giving instructions for relaxation or centering is "How does it feel to be you at this moment?" Do not expect a verbal answer. Allowing an experience of feeling without having to explain or name it is an important step in learning about oneself.

Another way of introducing meditation in a classroom is simply to suggest that students spend five minutes sitting in silence, with eyes closed. Additional instructions may be given, such as counting breaths from one to ten, and then starting at number one again, or visualizing a symbol such as a circle, cross, or triangle. Such additional instructions may make it easier for beginners to remain quiet and still, but are not essential. The instructions may be equally effective when students are asked to just sit. As the practice becomes more familiar, the period of time can be increased to twenty or thirty minutes, depending on the circumstances. Images which often emerge spontaneously during a period of meditation may also be a source of subject matter for discussion. Such imagery may be treated in the same way as dreams. A popular form of meditation among those who have not tried it before is observation meditation, where the students are instructed to simply observe themselves, and whatever is present on the physical (sensations), emotional (feelings), and mental (thoughts) levels. This process often facilitates awareness of inner imagery. . . .

Biofeedback

Biofeedback has been widely reported in the professional and popular press, and there is little need to go into detail here except as it applies to transpersonal educational interests. By amplifying activities inside the human body so that we can listen to internal processes such as heartbeat, blood pressure, brain activity, skin resistance, and many more, much of the autonomic nervous system can be brought under voluntary control. These previously hidden abilities of self-control open up whole new ranges for teaching physical education, health, and/or biology.

After seeing the film *Involuntary Control* at Sycamore High School in rural Illinois, some of the students tried some inexpensive biofeedback equipment borrowed from Northern Illinois University. One adolescent boy showed remarkable ability to raise and lower his galvanic skin response, a measure of general emotional excitability. "You can sure tell the girls I like," he said, as he looked from one to another around the room. By listening to the tone of the machine and by correlating it with his internal feelings, he was able to combine awareness of his own feelings with biofeedback knowledge from the galvanic skin response machine. If physical education means learning to control our bodies for optimum health and physical fitness, biofeedback has an important place coming in the curriculum of the late 1970s.

If every young student *knew* by the time he finished his first biology class, in grade school, that the body responds to self-generated psychological inputs, that blood flow and heart behavior, as well as a host of other body processes, can be influenced at will, it would change prevailing ideas about both physical and mental health. It would then be quite clear and understandable that we are individually responsible to a large extent for our state of health or disease. Perhaps then people would begin to realize that it is not life that kills us, but rather it is our reaction to it, and this reaction can be to a significant extent self-chosen. (E. Green, A. Green, D. Walters, "Biofeedback for Mind-Body Self-Regulation: Healing and Creativity." Menninger Foundation)

Biofeedback training also provides an interesting link between transpersonal psychology and behavioral psychology. The way a person learns to control these previously automatic functions is simply by being rewarded for doing the right thing to achieve his purpose, whether it be to cure a migraine headache, slow down his heart, or increase blood flow to injured organs. Even though he usually cannot explain what he is doing or how he is doing it, the feedback that he is accomplishing it is enough reward to improve his performance.

An even more exciting link is being explored between the biofeedback conditioning of brain waves and parapsychology. The biochemical activities of the brain produce electrical current that pulses at different speeds:

delta	0–4 times a second
theta	5–7 times a second
alpha	8–14 times a second
beta	15–30 times a second

Different frequencies predominate as a person goes into different kinds of awareness. For adults, beta is the normal waking state; alpha is a relaxed state bordering sleep; theta is associated with dreams; and delta is very deep sleep or coma. These frequencies are also associated with various altered states of consciousness. Some provocative research conducted by the Greens at the Menninger Foundation, and by Stanley Krippner and Montague Ullman at Maimonides Hospital in Brooklyn, indicates that both creativity and telepathy may be enhanced by alpha and theta conditioning. Yogic Masters develop complicated and precise control of their physiology, including brain waves. Could this partially account for the paranormal power attributed to advanced yogis? Could this physiological control also account for some instances of psychic healing?

Parapsychology

Parapsychological topics make excellent class reports. Students enjoy learning about parapsychology and doing their own experiments. The readings may be newspaper articles, inexpensive paperbacks, or highly statistical journal articles. Subjects which were formerly taboo for "respectable" psychologists are opening up, and they provide an excellent example of how fields of knowledge change with the times. One of the hardest ideas to get across to students is that things are not always true or false. With scientific controversy surrounding parapsychology, it provides a natural topic for teaching how science expands to include new observations and how our ideas of acceptability adjust from time to time.

Since many people see parapsychology in the gray area between belief and disbelief, a good teacher can capitalize on this to teach students that it is perfectly respectable intellectually to be undecided about conflicting information and that knowledge progresses by exploring these gray areas. One way to teach about parapsychology and other transpersonal topics is to treat them similarly to the way the theory of evolution was taught earlier in this century. They can be presented as ideas which some people believe and others don't, without necessarily having been proven true or false. A teacher can simply say, "Here is what some psychologists are saying . . . and here is the reasoning that disbelievers use. . . ." The confrontation is taking place between people who cite empirical evidence and want to change ways of thinking, and those who side with accepted ways of thinking and criticize the evidence: a classic battle between observation and reason.

Parapsychology is the scientific study of facts which do not fit in with the established theories of man which assume that he knows the world only through his senses. Selections from books such as *Psychic Discoveries Behind the Iron Curtain, ESP: A Curriculum Guide,* and *Dream Telepathy* can guide teachers. Investigation into parapsychology leads into other transpersonal areas too, as parapsychology is often linked with dreaming, relaxed receptivity, and other altered states. For example, states of consciousness associated with the alpha and theta brain-wave patterns are frequently associated with parapsychological events in which ordinary limitations of time and space are apparently transcended. Movies on parapsychology are also informative and provocative, and are primarily oriented toward high school and college audiences.

Stanley Krippner, president of the Association for Humanistic Psychology, and Gardner Murphy, past-president of the American Psychological Association, suggest links between successful teaching and student-teacher ESP. There is also some evidence that parapsychological abilities are not just "gifts" or inherent traits, but that they can be learned.

Spirituality

Investigation of the phenomena of transcendence and peak experiences has also reawakened interest in spiritual experiences associated with higher states of consciousness, sometimes called cosmic consciousness, mystical union, or enlightenment. Barry McWaters has indicated:

Within the past five years there has been a resurgence of both personal and empirical exploration of altered states of consciousness in which the individual experiences himself as having transcended the limitations of his ordinary waking consciousness. Physical phenomena, such as clairvoyance and astral projection, and religious phenomena, such as speaking in tongues and mystical union, are examples of transpersonal experiences. (Barry McWaters, "An Outline of Transpersonal Psychology: Its Meaning and Relevance for Education")

Some transpersonal psychologists are attempting a systematic study of spiritual experiences. Mystics, psychics, physicists, and other scientists often report their perceptions of the universe in almost identical terms. Furthermore, if adjustments are made to account for cultural differences, mystics from all over the world agree on the phenomenology of mystic experiences. Research on psychic healers at the Menninger Foundation indicates that some healers describe a "field of mind" that surrounds the earth just as the magnetic, radiation, and gravitational fields surround it. Healers seem to be able to tune in to this force, suggesting the possibility that other people can learn to do this, perhaps through biofeedback training or developing other self-controlled altered states of consciousness.

Interest in man's spiritual aspirations forms one of the historical and conceptual links between transpersonal psychology and humanistic psychology.* A.H. Maslow, one of the founders of humanistic psychology, proposed a five-stage theory of human motivation. In his studies of self-actualizers he discovered that this group reported peak experiences more frequently than other groups. Following this lead brought him to the study of transcendent experiences. In some of his later work he describes two kinds of self-actualizers, and seemed on the verge of adding a sixth stage of motivation: self-transcendence, or a motivation for cosmic consciousness. Humanistic psychologists have used the first five stages in counseling, teaching, and planning curricula. Perhaps a sixth, transcendent, stage would be helpful in considering student motivation.

Assuming such motivation helps explain why students like certain kinds of drug highs, and it simultaneously suggests that schools can help reduce drug abuse by teaching alternate means of achieving higher states of consciousness. Peak experiences and altered states occurring in poetry and prose are readily available for exploration. They are useful concepts in the literature of self-actualization and can serve as a focus for developing language skills. In social studies or other classes which consider why people do things, the desire for spiritual or transcendent experiences

---

*The transpersonal psychology movement was initiated largely by humanistic psychologists who wanted to expand beyond the humanistic movement's primary concern with interpersonal interaction. Transpersonal psychologists and educators, while recognizing the importance of interpersonal dynamics, tend to focus more on intrapersonal and transpersonal experience, the latter being that inner set which all persons share.—Ed.

helps explain human behavior. For example, much religious and cultural conflict stems from disagreement over what mystical experiences are and who has the best way of achieving them, leading to religious wars, persecution, and other intercultural conflicts. The interpretation of transcendent experiences is central to the religions and world views of different cultures. Transpersonal psychology is useful in its acceptance and study of transcendent, or spiritual, experiences as an important aspect of human nature and a legitimate field for psychological investigation. The scientific interest in transcendent experiences should not be confused with teaching religion. From a psychological standpoint, experiences are considered empirically, without resorting to metaphysical interpretation or dogmatic assumptions. As in working with dreams and fantasy, interpretations are likely to inhibit sharing of experience, and a student's subjective interpretation of his own experience should be respected.

Growth Potential

After visiting a growth center and reading some articles on transpersonal psychology, an eighth-grade teacher developed a unit called "Growth Potential." The main theme was that all human beings have vast potentials that are seldom used. He included unusual cases of physical prowess and athletic records, new inventions and medicines, suggestibility, parapsychology, fantasy, and other neglected human skills. "Everyone seemed to enjoy the experience," he reported. "The only problem for me was the insistence on doing it again. Imagination, creativity, frank and open discussion were all results of what we had tried."

Teachers are often surprised at how eagerly students respond to transpersonal teaching techniques. Some of these approaches seem to awaken the natural desire in each of us to explore our inner selves:

I have been overwhelmed by the willingness and ability of the children to remain completely still, without a motion, for 30 minutes. Six months ago I would have laughed at the idea. Julio Sanchez, an extremely active child, seems calmed down considerably. He also gets down to work much more quickly. . . . We talked about the directed dreams of Malayan children and the different ways in which dreams could better be remembered or evoked. During all of our talks the class (6th grade) was in a state which only elementary teachers really understand. All eyes on whoever the speaker was, no outside interruptions, mouths open. Once started it was amazing how eagerly children want to look inward and learn about themselves.

The teacher's experience is typical. The first time an unusual teaching technique is tried, there may be some resistance or silliness, but it almost always disappears the second time. Is this because we all have a natural desire to explore inner potentials? Perhaps dreams are successful as content because it is content that each person experiences, not just learning about something "out there," that seems to have no personal relevance.

Further development of classroom exercises is possible in the adaptation of adult-oriented exercises to schools, with a focus on developing skills which would enable students to continue personal and transpersonal growth on their own time or after they graduate. Such books as *Mind Games, Awareness,* and *Passages* provide adult learning exercises. Educators can use these to continue their own growth and as sources for classroom adaptions. Under a grant from the Quebec Ministry of Education, the Canadian Institute of Psychosynthesis has developed classroom techniques for humanistic and transpersonal growth. In the United States, psychosynthesis groups in New York City and Redwood City, California, are adapting other growth techniques developed by Roberto Assagioli to the classroom and to counseling.

FUTURE TRENDS AND IMPLICATIONS

Research

Research in transpersonal educational psychology is currently at the exploratory and descriptive stages. However, some rough-hewn applications of transpersonal ideas show considerable promise. Whenever new practices come along, the door is open to common research, which compares and evaluates new methods. Descriptive and exploratory research by teachers indicates increased content learned, student enthusiasm, student self-control, excitement in self-exploration, and investigation of topics usually shunted to the side in traditional as well as innovative schools. Relaxation, focusing, meditation, and other transpersonal practices are open fields for traditional educational research.

The importance of subjective empiricism as a method of investigation should not be overlooked, nor should the experimenter imagine himself neutral during research.

A discipline comes of age and a student of that discipline reaches maturity when it becomes possible to recognize, estimate, and allow for the errors of their tools. . . . Yet there is one instrument which every discipline uses without checking its errors, tacitly assuming that the instrument is error-free. This, of course, is the human psychological apparatus. As a result of the failure to consider the sources of error in the human being himself, when our academic disciplines assemble together in our great educational institutions, they re-enforce the tacit, fallacious assumption that man can understand the world that lies outside of himself without concurrently understanding himself. Actually, each man is his own microscope with his own idiosyncracies, to which he alone can penetrate. (Lawrence S. Kubie, "The Forgotten Man of Education")

Considering the state of consciousness as a major variable of all behavior is filled with implications. This is a previously disregarded variable in every experiment and during all teaching. If we erroneously assume there is only one state of consciousness or that all awake people are in the same state, we are neglecting this important variable. Various states of consciousness, their intensities or optimal combinations, may be a major set of variables for a new generation of educational researchers to study. Instead of changing the external stimuli given to a student, can we effect greater changes by teaching him to control his own state of consciousness?

Perhaps relaxation, receptivity, focusing, concentration, holistic perception, linear perception, reasoning, analysis, brain-wave patterns, and left-brain and right-brain activity are some of the basic mental variables. Just as reading and arithmetic are foundation skills for the intellectual, left-brain activities, there may also be primary-level skills such as fantasy, dreaming, concentration, and other skills that will allow us to develop and use the intuitive, right sides of our brains.

Teacher Education

During inservice education, teachers frequently go through three stages when they are introduced to transpersonal psychology. At first they are puzzled, put off, or simply confused. Since a transpersonal approach to education required them to look at their work in a different light, this is not surprising. The next step is accepting one or two ideas for applying a transpersonal technique in their classrooms, or introducing some transpersonal content into their lessons. This is usually dreams, some form of ESP such as a classroom experiment, discussion of psychic phenomena, or a combination of relaxation and fantasy.

Finally, having tried a transpersonal innovation, they are enthusiastic and eager to do more. I have found undergraduates generally more willing to accept transpersonal content such as ESP, psychic phenomena, and altered states of consciousness, while inservice teachers are more willing to believe that developing right-brain potentials is worth doing and that it can be done.

Here is a new realm for teacher education. Along with the cognitive, affective, and psychomotor domains, we now have the transpersonal domain. Each subject area has its transpersonal content tool. Work needs to be done on a basic information level for teachers, objective writers, textbook publishers, testing services, and others in the educational support services who prepare materials. Much of the original transpersonal research needs to be rewritten so that school students can understand it. Some existing materials can be enlarged, while entirely new lines of transpersonal materials remain to be created.

How do we prepare teachers for their roles as transpersonal educators? A new kind of teacher education and a new breed of teacher-educators are needed too. Here is a wide-open opportunity for colleges of education. If we look back at the rise and fall of educational psychologies and the rise and fall of various colleges of education, we see that frequently certain schools staked out a new educational psychology and built much of their reputation on developing it. A good part of the reputation of Teacher's College at Columbia Unversity was due to faculty members who were influential in the application of Freudian psychology to education. Stanford, Kansas, and other universities are making themselves well known in teacher education by applying behaviorism to education. Humanistic psychology applied to education is important at the colleges of education at the University of Massachusetts and at the University of California at Santa Barbara. While several institutions of higher education are flirting with transpersonal educational psychology, none has yet staked a claim and consciously built a reputation for transpersonal teacher education. Here too, there are more tantalizing possibilities than tested programs.

Philosophy

Our focus here has been primarily on those applications of transpersonal psychology which can be adapted to education immediately. However, the underlying philosophical assumptions have implications which go far beyond new teaching techniques, and which present new problems for educational philosophers to work on.

A transpersonal approach involves new, open concepts which are still being developed and clarified. For example, the concept of *consciousness* carries a new meaning in this context. It has expanded to include many different subjective and physiological states of consciousness, and should not be confused with terms such as political consciousness or social consiousness. Currently there is considerable interest in theoretically conceptualizing, or "mapping," inner states, in exploring methods for altering consciousness, and in evaluating the importance of altered states.

The mind/body problem is central to transpersonal education. It is clear that mental and emotional states affect the body, and that physical states affect the mind and emotions. The implication here is that the relationship between body and mind is far more complex and important than was previously believed. Transpersonal psychology is concerned with the integration of physical, emotional, mental, and spiritual development. It also assumes that man as a living organism is continually evolving, and capable of developing many capacities which have hitherto been neglected. Since we are concerned with the growing edge of human development, we are continually expanding the range of topics and finding new ways of learning. The meaning of the word "knowledge" itself is changing and expanding. Knowledge is no longer limited to objective subject matter or content. Awareness of inner states, experimental learning, ESP, and control of various autonomic functions are forms of knowledge which are not being incorporated in education. Since inner states cannot be observed by anyone other than the experiencing subject, subjective empiricism has become an important method of investigation.

New cross-cultural values are also emerging. The study of peak experiences and human potentials has led to a new appreciation of Eastern philosophies, and new definitions of "the good." As communication with other cultures has expanded, we now have the opportunity to learn more about alternate methods of training the mind and body. Interestingly, contemporary physicists are now describing reality in terms which coincide with the traditional views of mystics from many different religious traditions. This view affirms the essential unity of all life. This basic unity of man with his fellow men, with the environment, and with the cosmos is also affirmed in parapsychology, and is an underlying assumption in psychic healing and other psychic phenomena such as clairvoyance and telepathy. Researchers at the Menninger Foundation are investigating the speculation that there is a "field of mind" similar to the earth's magnetic field. Thoughts and ideas may exist in this field, and some people may even be able to tune in to it.

The emerging philosophy of education based on transpersonal psychology may be described as a combination of rational-analytic and intuitive-synthetic modes of knowing. With its origins in analytic philosophy, much educational thought has mistakenly equated "thinking" with "reasoning." Rational thinking, associated with the left hemisphere of the brain, is characteristically verbal, logical, analytic, and linear. Intuitive thinking, associated with the right hemisphere, is creative, holistic, visual, and pattern-oriented. Its strength is in seeing similarities, patterns, and agreements among ideas rather than analyzing differences and conflicts. Intuitive perception frequently appears to transcend or anticipate reason. Philosophies of education which do not recognize the importance of developing right-brain hemisphere potentials are seriously underestimating the human capacity for learning.

A man, having looted a city, was trying to sell an exquisite rug, one of the spoils. "Who will give 100 pieces of gold for this rug?" he cried throughout the town.

After the sale was completed, a comrade approached the seller and asked, "Why did you not ask more for that priceless rug?" "Is there any number higher than 100?" asked the seller. (Folk Tale from Central Asia, quoted from *The Psychology of Consciousness,* Robert Ornstein)

A newly opened image of man assumes that we are capable of knowing, being, and doing far more than we thought possible even a decade ago. As we continue to learn more about transpersonal dimensions of human experience, our vision of the future and the development of human potentials is constantly expanding. It is important to recognize the necessity for educating the whole person if we are to improve the human condition. Explorations in the study of consciousness hold considerable promise for education in the future.

From *Island*

Aldous Huxley

Aldous Huxley was the author of dozens of fiction and nonfiction books. Many of his works explore the farther reaches of the human potential.

The main character of Island, *Will Farnaby, is a journalist who comes to the utopian island with cynicism and doubt, but gradually sees the new heights in human potential being reached there. In this selection we are introduced to the island's educational system through a conversation between Will and Mr. Menon, the Under-Secretary of Education.*

"And the way to the Way of Disinterested Action is what I was looking at yesterday," said Will. "The way that leads through woodchopping and rock climbing—is that it?"

"Wood chopping and rock climbing," said Mr. Menon, "are special cases. Let's generalize and say that the way to *all* the Ways leads through the redirection of power."

"What's that?"

From *Island* by Aldous Huxley (New York: Harper & Row, 1962), pp. 212–32. Reprinted by permission of Mrs. Laura Huxley, Harper & Row, Publishers, Inc., and Chatto and Windus Ltd.

"The principle is very simple. You take the power generated by fear or envy or too much noradrenalin, or else by some built-in urge that happens, at the moment, to be out of place—you take it and, instead of using it to do something unpleasant to someone else, instead of repressing it and so doing something unpleasant to yourself, you consciously direct it along a channel where it can do something useful, or, if not useful, at least harmless."

"Here's a simple case," said the Principal. "An angry or frustrated child has worked up enough power for a burst of crying, or bad language, or a fight. If the power generated is sufficient for any of those things, it's significant for running, or dancing, more than sufficient for five deep breaths. I'll show you some dancing later on. For the moment, let's confine ourselves to breathing. Any irritated person who takes five deep breaths releases a lot of tension and so makes it easier for himself to behave rationally. So we teach our children all kinds of breathing games, to be played whenever they're angry or upset. Some of the games are competitive. Which of two antagonists can inhale most deeply and say 'om' on the outgoing breath for the longest time? It's a duel that ends, almost without fail, in reconciliation. But of course there are many occasions when competitive breathing is out of place. So here's a little game that an exasperated child can play on his own, a game that's based on the local folklore. Every Palanese child has been brought up on Buddhist legends, and in most of these pious fairy stories somebody has a vision of a celestial being. A Bodhisattva, say, in an explosion of lights, jewels and rainbows. And along with the glorious vision there's always an equally glorious olfaction; the fireworks are accompanied by an unutterably delicious perfume. Well, we take these traditional phantasies —which are all based, needless to say, on actual visionary experiences of the kind induced by fasting, sensory deprivation or mushrooms—and we set them to work. Violent feelings, we tell the children, are like earthquakes. They shake us so hard that cracks appear in the wall that separates our private selves from the shared, universal Buddha Nature. You get cross, something inside of you cracks and, through the crack, out comes a whiff of the heavenly smell of enlightenment. Like champak, like ylang-ylang, like gardenias—only infinitely more wonderful. So don't miss this heavenliness that you've accidentally released. It's there every time you get cross. Inhale it, breathe it in, fill your lungs with it. Again and again."

"And they actually do it?"

"After a few weeks of teaching, most of them do it as a matter of course. And, what's more, a lot of them really smell that perfume. The old repressive 'Thou shalt not' has been translated into a new expressive and rewarding 'Thou shalt.' Potentially harmful power has been redirected into channels where it's not merely harmless, but may actually do some good. And meanwhile, of course, we've been giving the children systematic and carefully graduated training in perception and the proper use of language. They're taught to pay attention to what they see and hear, and at the same time they're asked to notice how their feelings and desires affect what they experience of the outer world, and how their language habits affect not only their feelings and desires but even their sensations. What my ears and my eyes record is one thing; what the words I use and the mood I'm in and the purposes I'm pursuing allow me to perceive, make sense of and act upon is something quite different. So you see it's all brought together into a single educational process. What we give the children is simultaneously a training in perceiving and imagining, a training in applied physiology and psychology, a training in practical ethics and practical religion, a training in the proper use of language, and a training in self-knowledge. In a word, a training of the whole mind-body in all its aspects."

"What's the relevance," Will asked, "of all this elaborate training of the mind-body to formal education? Does it help a child to do sums, or write grammatically, or understand elementary physics?"

"It helps a lot," said Mr. Menon. "A trained mind-body learns more quickly and more thoroughly than an untrained one. It's also more capable of relating facts to ideas, and both of them to its own ongoing life." Suddenly and surprisingly—for that long melancholy face gave one the impression of being incompatible with any expression of mirth more emphatic than a rather weary smile—he broke into a loud long peal of laughter.

"What's the joke?"

"I was thinking of two people I met last time I was in England. At Cambridge. One of them was an atomic physicist, the other was a philosopher. Both extremely eminent. But one had a mental age, outside the laboratory, of about eleven and the other was a compulsive eater with a weight problem that he refused to face. Two extreme examples of what happens when you take a clever boy, give him fifteen years of the most intensive formal education and totally neglect to do anything for the mind-body which has to do the learning and the living."

"And your system, I take it, doesn't produce that kind of academic monster?"

The Under-Secretary shook his head. "Until I went to Europe, I'd never seen anything of the kind. They're grotesquely funny," he added. "But, goodness, how pathetic. And, poor things, how curiously repulsive!"

"Being pathetically and curiously repulsive—that's the price we pay for specilization."

"For specialization," Mr. Menon agreed, "but not in the sense you people ordinarily use the word. Specialization in that sense is necessary and inevitable. No specialization, no civilization. And if one educates the whole mind-body along with the symbol-using intellect, that kind of necessary specialization won't do much harm. But you people don't educate the mind-body. Your cure for too much scientific specialization is a few more courses in the humanities. Excellent! Every education ought to include courses in the humanities. But don't let's be fooled by the name. By themselves, the humanities don't humanize. They're simply another form of specialization on the symbolic level. Reading Plato or listening to a lecture on T.S. Eliot doesn't educate the whole human being; like courses in physics or chemistry, it merely educates the symbol manipulator and leaves the rest of the living mind-body in its pristine state of ignorance and ineptitude. Hence all those pathetic and repulsive creatures that so astonished me on my first trip abroad."

"What about formal education?" Will now asked. "What about indispensable information and the necessary intellectual skills? Do you teach the way we do?"

"We teach the way you're probably going to teach in another ten or fifteen years. Take mathematics, for example. Historically mathematics began with the elaboration of useful tricks, soared up into metaphysics and finally explained itself in terms of structure and logical transformations. In our schools we reverse the historical process. We begin with structure and logic; then, skipping the metaphysics, we go on from general principles to particular applications."

"And the children understand?"

"Far better than they understand when one starts with utilitarian tricks. From about five onwards practically any intelligent child can learn practically anything, provided always that you present it to him in the right way. Logic and structure in the form of games and puzzles. The children play and, incredibly quickly, they catch the point. After which you can go on to practical applications. Taught in this way, most children can learn at least three times as much, four times as thoroughly, in half the time. Or consider another field where one can use games to implant an understanding of basic principles. All scientific thinking is in terms of probability. The old eternal verities are merely a high degree of likeliness; the immutable laws of nature are just statistical averages. How does one get these profoundly unobvious notions into children's heads? By playing roulette with them, by spinning coins and drawing lots. By teaching them all kinds of games with cards and boards and dice."

"Evolutionary Snakes and Ladders—that's the most popular game with the little ones," said Mrs. Narayan. "Another great favorite is Mendelian Happy Families."

"And a little later," Mr. Menon added, "we introduce them to a rather complicated game played by four people with a pack of sixty specially designed cards divided into three suits. Psychological bridge, we call it. Chance deals you your hand, but the way you play it is a matter of skill, bluff and co-operation with your partner."

"Psychology, Mendelism, Evolution—your education seems to be heavily biological," said Will.

"It *is*," Mr. Menon agreed. "Our primary emphasis isn't on physics and chemistry; it's on the sciences of life."

"Is that a matter of principle?" . . .

"Mathematics," said the Principal as she opened a door. "And this is the Upper Fifth. Under Mrs. Anand."

Will bowed as he was introduced. The white-haired teacher gave a welcoming smile and whispered, "We're deep, as you see, in a problem."

He looked about him. At their desks a score of boys and girls were frowning, in a concentrated, pencil-biting silence, over their notebooks. The bent heads were sleek and dark. Above the white or khaki shorts, above the long gaily colored skirts, the golden bodies glistened in the heat. Boys' bodies that showed the cage of the ribs beneath the skin, girls' bodies, fuller, smoother, with the swell of small breasts, firm, high-set, elegant as the inventions of a rococo sculptor of nymphs. And everyone took them completely for granted. What a comfort, Will reflected, to be in a place where the Fall was an exploded doctrine!

Meanwhile, Mrs. Anand was explaining—*sotto voce* so as not to distract the problem solvers from their task—that she always divided her classes into two groups. The group of the visualizers, who thought in geometrical terms, like the ancient Greeks, and the group of the nonvisualizers who preferred algebra and imageless abstractions. Somewhat reluctantly Will withdrew his attention from the beautiful unfallen world of young bodies and resigned himself to taking an intelligent interest in human diversity and the teaching of mathematics.

They took their leave at last. Next door, in a pale-blue classroom decorated with paintings of tropical animals, Bodhisattvas and their bosomy Shaktis, the Lower Fifth were having their biweekly lesson in Elementary Applied Philosophy. Breasts here were smaller, arms thinner and less muscular. These philosophers were only a year away from childhood.

"Symbols are public," the young man at the blackboard was saying as Will and Mrs. Narayan entered the room. He drew a row of little circles, numbered them 1, 2, 3, 4, and *n*. "These are people," he explained. Then from each of the little circles he drew a line that connected it with a square at the left of the board. S he wrote in the center of the square. "S is the system of symbols that the people use when they want to talk to one another. They all speak the same language—English, Palanese, Eskimo, it depends where they happen to live. Words are public; they belong to all the speakers of a given language; they're listed in dictionaries. And now let's look at the things that happen out there." He pointed through the open window. Gaudy against a white cloud, half a dozen parrots came sailing into view, passed behind a tree and were gone. The teacher drew a second square at the opposite side of the board, labeled it E for "events" and connected it by lines to the circles. "What happens out there is public —or at least fairly public," he qualified. "And what happens when somebody speaks or writes words—that's also public. But the things that go on inside these little circles are private. Private." He laid a hand on his chest. "Private." He rubbed his forehead. "Private." He touched his eyelids and the tip of his nose with a brown forefinger. "Now let's make a simple experiment. Say the word 'pinch.' "

"Pinch," said the class in ragged unison, "Pinch . . ."

"P-I-N-C-H—pinch. That's public, that's something you can look up in the dictionary. But now pinch yourselves. Hard! Harder!"

To an accompaniment of giggles, of *aies* and *ows*, the children did as they were told.

"Can anybody feel what the person sitting next to him is feeling?"

There was a chorus of noes.

"So it looks," said the young man, "as though there were—let's see, how many are we?" He ran his eyes over the desks before him. "It looks as though there were twenty-three distinct and separate pains. Twenty-three in this one room. Nearly three thousand million of them in the whole world. Plus the pains of all the animals. And each of these pains from one center of pain to another center of pain. No communication except indirectly through S.'' He pointed to the square at the left of the board, then to the circles at the center. "Private pains here in 1, 2, 3, 4, and *n*. News about private pains out here at S, where you can say 'pinch,' which is a public word listed in a dictionary. And notice this: there's only one public word, 'pain,' for three thousand million private experiences, each of which is probably about as different from all the others as my nose is different from your noses and your noses are different from one another. A word only stands for the ways in which things or happenings of the same general kind are like one another. That's why the word is public. And, being public, it can't possibly stand for the ways in which happenings of the same general kind are unlike one another.''

There was a silence. Then the teacher looked up and asked a question.

"Does anyone here know about Mahakasyapa?''

Several hands were raised. He pointed his finger at a little girl in a blue skirt and a necklace of shells sitting in the front row.

"You tell us, Amiya.''

Breathlessly and with a lisp, Amiya began.

"Mahakathyapa,'' she said, "wath the only one of the dithipleth that underthtood what the Buddha wath talking about.''

"And what was he talking about?''

"He wathn't talking. That'th why they didn't underthand.''

"But Mahakasyapa understood what he was talking about even though he wasn't talking—is that it?''

The little girl nodded. That was it exactly. "They thought he wath going to preath a thermon,'' she said, "but he didn't. He jutht picked a flower and held it up for everybody to look at.''

"And that was the sermon,'' shouted a small boy in a yellow loincloth, who had been wriggling in his seat, hardly able to contain his desire to impart what he knew. "But nobody could underthand that kind of a thermon. Nobody but Mahakathyapa.''

"So what did Mahakasyapa say when the Buddha held up that flower?''

"Nothing!'' the yellow loincloth shouted triumphantly.

"He jutht thmiled,'' Amiya elaborated. "And that thowed the Buddha that he underthtood what it wath all about. So he thmiled back, and they jutht that there, thmiling and thmiling.''

"Very good," sid the teacher. "And now," he turned to the yellow loincloth, "let's hear what you think it was that Mahakasyapa understood."

There was a silence. Then, crestfallen, the child shook his head. "I don't know," he mumbled.

"Does anyone else know?"

There were several conjectures. Perhaps he'd understood that people get bored with sermons—even the Buddha's sermons. Perhaps he liked flowers as much as the Compassionate One did. Perhaps it was a white flower, and that made him think of the Clear Light. Or perhaps it was blue, and that was Shiva's color.

"Good answers," said the teacher. "Especially the first one. Sermons *are* pretty boring—especially for the preacher. But here's a question. If any of your answers had been what Mahakasyapa understood when Buddha held up the flower, why didn't he come out with it in so many words?"

"Perhaps he wathn't a good thpeaker."

"He was an excellent speaker."

"Maybe he had a sore throat."

"If he'd had a sore throat, he wouldn't have smiled so happily."

"*You* tell us," called a shrill voice from the back of the room.

"Yes, *you* tell us," a dozen other voices chimed in.

The teacher shook his head. "If Mahakasyapa and the Compassionate One couldn't put it into words, how can I? Meanwhile let's take another look at these diagrams on the blackboard. Public words, more or less public events, and then people, completely private centers of pain and pleasure. "*Completely* private?" he questioned. "But perhaps that isn't quite true. Perhaps, after all, there is some kind of communication between the circles—not in the way I'm communicating with you now; through words, but directly. And maybe that was what the Buddha was talking about when his wordless flower-sermon was over. 'I have the treasure of the unmistakable teachings,' he said to his disciples, 'the wonderful Mind of Nirvana, the true form without form, beyond all words, the teaching to be given and received outside of all doctrines. This I have now handed to Mahakasyapa.' " Picking up the chalk again, he traced a rough ellipse that enclosed within its boundaries all the other diagrams on the board—the little circles representing human beings, the square that stood for events, and the other square that stood for words and symbols. "All separate," he said, "and yet all one. People, events, words—they're all manifestations of Mind, of Suchness, of the Void.

What Buddha was implying and what Mahakasyapa understood was that one can't speak these teachings, one can only *be* them. Which is something you'll all discover when the moment comes for your initiation."

"Time to move on," the Principal whispered. And when the door had closed behind them, and they were standing again in the corridor, "We use this same kind of approach," she said to Will, "in our science teaching, beginning with botany."

"Why with botany?"

"Because it can be related so easily to what was being talked about just now—the Mahakasyapa story."

"Is that your starting point?"

"No, we start prosaically with the textbook. The children are given all the obvious, elementary facts, tidily arranged in the standard pigeonholes. Undiluted botany—that's the first stage. Six or seven weeks of it. After which they get a whole morning of what we call bridge building. Two and a half hours during which we try to make them relate everything they've learned in the previous lessons to art, language, religion, self-knowledge."

"Botany and self-knowledge—how do you build *that* bridge?"

"It's really quite simple," Mrs. Narayan assured him. "Each of the children is given a common flower—a hibiscus, for example, or better still (because the hibiscus has no scent) a gardenia. Scientifically speaking, what is a gardenia? What does it consist of? Petals, stamens, pistil, ovary, and all the rest of it. The children are asked to write a full analytical description of the flower, illustrated by an accurate drawing. When that's done there's a short rest period, at the close of which the Mahakasyapa story is read to them and they're asked to think about it. Was Buddha giving a lesson in botany? Or was he teaching his disciples something else? And, if so, what?"

"What indeed?"

"And of course, as the story makes clear, there's no answer that can be put into words. So we tell the boys and girls to stop thinking and just look. 'But don't look analytically,' we tell them, 'don't look as scientists, even as gardeners. Liberate yourselves from everything you know and look with complete innocence at this infinitely improbable thing before you. Look at it as though you'd never seen anything of the kind before, as though it had no name and belonged to no recognizable class. Look at it alertly but passively, receptively, without labeling or judging or comparing. And as you look at it, inhale its mystery, breathe in the spirit of sense, the smell of the wisdom of the Other Shore.' "

"All this," Will commented, "sounds very like what Dr. Robert was saying at the initiation ceremony."

"Of course it does," said Mrs. Narayan. "Learning to take the Mahakasyapa's-eye view of things is the best preparation for the *moksha*-medicine experience. Every child who comes to initiation comes to it after a long education in the art of being receptive. First the gardenia as a botanical specimen. Then the same gardenia in its uniqueness, the gardenia as the artist sees it, the even more miraculous gardenia seen by the Buddha and Mahakasyapa. And it goes without saying," she added, "that we don't confine ourselves to flowers. Every course the children take is punctuated by periodical bridge-building sessions. Everything from dissected frogs to the spiral nebulae, it all gets looked at receptively as well as conceptually, as a fact of aesthetic or spiritual experience as well as in terms of science or history or economics. Training in receptivity is the complement and antidote to training in analysis and symbol manipulation. Both kinds of training are absolutely indispensable. If you neglect either of them you'll never grow into a fully human being."

. . .

They crossed a tree-shaded courtyard and, pushing through a swing door, passed out of silence into the rhythmic beat of a drum and the screech of fifes repeating over and over again a short pentatonic tune that to Will's ears sounded vaguely Scotch.

"Live music or canned?" he asked.

"Japanese tape," Mrs. Narayan answered laconically. She opened a second door that gave access to a large gymnasium where two bearded young men and an amazingly agile little old lady in black satin slacks were teaching some twenty to thirty little boys and girls the steps of a lively dance.

"What's this?" Will asked. "Fun or education?"

"Both," said the Principal. "And it's also applied ethics. Like these breathing exercises we were talking about just now—only more effective because so much more violent."

"So stamp it out," the children were chanting in unison. And they stamped their small sandaled feet with all their might. "So stamp it out!" A final furious stamp and they were off again, jigging and turning, into another movement of the dance.

"This is called the Rakshasi Hornpipe," said Mrs. Narayan.

"Rakshasi?" Will questioned. "What's that?"

"A Rakshasi is a species of demon. Very large, and exceedingly unpleasant. All the ugliest passions personified. The Rakshasi Hornpipe is a device for letting off those dangerous heads of steam raised by anger and frustration."

"So stamp it out!" The music had come round again to the choral refrain. "So stamp it out!"

"Stamp again," cried the little old lady setting a furious example. "Harder! Harder!"

"Which did more," Will speculated, "for morality and rational behavior—the Bacchic orgies or the *Republic*? the *Nichomachean Ethics* or corybantic dancing?"

"The Greeks," said Mrs. Narayan, "were much too sensible to think in terms of either-or. For them, it was always not-only-but-also. Not only Plato and Aristotle, but also the maenads. Without those tension-reducing hornpipes, the moral philosophy would have been impotent, and without the moral philosophy the hornpipers wouldn't have known where to go next. All we've done is to take a leaf out of the old Greek book."

"Very good!" said Will approvingly. Then remembering (as sooner or later, however keen his pleasure and however genuine his enthusiasm, he always did remember) that he was the man who wouldn't take yes for an answer, he suddenly broke into laughter. "Not that it makes any difference in the long run," he said. "Corybantism couldn't stop the Greeks from cutting one another's throats. And when Colonel Dipa decides to move, what will your Rakshasi Hornpipes do for you? Help you to reconcile yourselves to your fate, perhaps—that's all."

"Yes, that's all," said Mrs. Narayan. "But being reconciled to one's fate—that's already a great achievement."

"You seem to take it all very calmly."

"What would be the point of taking it hysterically? It wouldn't make our political situation any better; it would merely make our personal situation a good deal worse."

"So stamp it out," the children shouted again in unison, and the boards trembled under their pounding feet. "So stamp it out."

"Don't imagine," Mrs. Narayan resumed, "that this is the only kind of dancing we teach. Redirecting the power generated by bad feelings is important. But equally important is directing good feelings and right knowledge into expression. Expressive movements, in this case, expressive gesture. If you had come yesterday, when our visiting master was here, I could have shown you how we teach that kind of dancing. Not today unfortunately. He won't be here again before Tuesday."

"What sort of dancing does he teach?"

Mrs. Narayan tried to describe it. No leaps, or high kicks, no running. The feet always firmly on the ground. Just bending and sideways motions of the knees and hips. All expression confined to the arms, wrists and hands, to the neck and head, the face and, above all, the eyes. Movement from the shoulders upwards and outwards—movement intrinsically beautiful and at the same time charged with symbolic meaning. Thought taking shape in ritual and stylized gesture. The whole body transformed into a hieroglyph, a succession of hieroglyphs, or attitudes modulating from significance to significance like a poem or a piece of music. Movements of the muscles representing movements of Consciousness, the passage of Suchness into the many, of the many into the immanent and ever-present One.

"It's meditation in action," she concluded. "It's the metaphysics of the Mahayana expressed, not in words, but through symbolic movements and gestures."

They left the gymnasium by a different door from that through which they had entered and turned left along a short corridor.

"What's the next item?" Will asked.

"The Lower Fourth," Mrs. Narayan answered, "and they're working on Elementary Practical Psychology."

She opened a green door.

"Well, now you know," Will heard a familiar voice saying. "Nobody *has* to feel pain. You told yourselves that the pin wouldn't hurt—and it didn't hurt."

They stepped into the room and there, very tall in the midst of a score of plump or skinny little brown bodies, was Susila MacPhail. She smiled at them, pointed to a couple of chairs in a corner of the room, and turned back to the children. "Nobody *has* to feel pain," she repeated. "But never forget: pain always means that something is wrong. You've learned to shut pain off, but don't do it thoughtlessly, don't do it without asking yourselves the question: What's the reason for this pain? And if it's bad, or if there's no obvious reason for it, tell your mother about it, or your teacher, or any grown-up in your Mutual Adoption Club. *Then* shut off the pain. Shut it off knowing that, if anything needs to be done, it will be done. Do you understand? . . . And now,'' she went on, after all the questions had been asked and answered. "Now let's play some pretending games. Shut your eyes and pretend you're looking at that poor old mynah bird with one leg that comes to school every day to be fed. Can you see him?''

Of course they could see him. The one-legged mynah was evidently an old friend.

"See him just as clearly as you saw him today at lunchtime. And don't stare at him, don't make any effort. Just see what comes to you, and let your eyes shift—from his beak to his tail, from his bright little round eye to his one orange leg.''

"I can hear him too,'' a little girl volunteered. "He's saying *'Karuna, Karuna!'* ''

"That's not true,'' another child said indignantly. "He's saying 'Attention!' ''

"He's saying both those things,'' Susila assured them. "And probably a lot of other words besides. But now we're going to do some real pretending. Pretend that there are two one-legged mynah birds. Three one-legged mynah birds. Four one-legged mynah birds. Can you see all four of them?''

They could.

"Four one-legged mynah birds at the four corners of a square, and a fifth one in the middle. And now let's make them change their color. They're white now. Five white mynah birds with yellow heads and one orange leg. And now the heads are blue. Bright blue—and the rest of the bird is pink. Five pink birds with blue heads. And they keep changing. They're purple now. Five purple birds with white heads and each of them has one pale-green leg. Goodness, what's happening! There aren't five of them; there are ten. No, twenty, fifty, a hundred. Hundreds and hundreds. Can you see them?'' Some of them could—without the slightest difficulty; and for those who couldn't go the whole hog, Susila proposed more modest goals.

"Just make twelve of them,'' she said. "Or if twelve is too many, make ten, make eight. That's still an awful lot of mynahs. And now,'' she went on, when all the children had conjured up all the purple birds that each was capable of creating, "now they're gone.'' She clapped her hands. "Gone! Every single one of them. There's nothing there. And now you're not going to see mynahs, you're going to see *me*. One me in yellow. Two mes in green. Three mes in blue with pink spots. Four mes in the brightest red you ever saw.'' She clapped her hands again. "All gone. And this time it's Mrs. Narayan and that funny-looking man with a stiff leg who came in with her. Four of each of them. Standing in a big circle in the gymnasium. And now they're dancing the Rakshasi Horn-pipe. 'So stamp it out, so stamp it out.' "

There was a general giggle. The dancing Wills and Principals must have looked richly comical.

Susila snapped her fingers.

"Away with them! Vanish! And now each of you sees three of your mothers and three of your fathers running round the playground. Faster, faster, faster! And suddenly they're not there any more. And then they *are* there. But next moment they aren't. They are there, they aren't. They are, they aren't . . ."

The giggles swelled into squeals of laughter and at the height of the laughter a bell rang. The lesson in Elementary Practical Psychology was over.

"What's the point of it all?" Will asked when the children had run off to play and Mrs. Narayan had returned to her office.

"The point," Susila answered, "is to get people to understand that we're not *completely* at the mercy of our memory and our phantasies. If we're disturbed by what's going on inside our heads, we can do something about it. It's all a question of being shown what to do and then practicing, the way one learns to write or play the flute. What those children you saw here were being taught is a very simple technique—a technique that we'll develop later on into a method of liberation. Not complete liberation, of course. But half a loaf is a great deal better than no bread. This technique won't lead you to the discovery of your Buddha-Nature: but it may help you to prepare for that discovery—help you by liberating you from the hauntings of your own painful memories, your remorses, your causeless anxieties about the future."

" 'Hauntings,' " Will agreed, "is the word."

From *Education and the Significance of Life*

J. Krishnamurti

For the last fifty years, Krishnamurti has been speaking to audiences around the world, calling for a radical change in our approach to life. This Indian religious teacher has maintained a lifelong interest in the education of young people; here he presents a compelling statement of what education should be.

Only love can bring about the understanding of another. Where there is love there is instantaneous communion with the other, on the same level and at the same time. It is because we ourselves are so dry, empty and without love that we have allowed governments and systems to take over the education of our children and the direction of our lives; but governments want efficient technicians, not human beings, because human beings become dangerous to governments—and to organized religions as well. That is why governments and religious organizations seek to control education.

Life cannot be made to conform to a system, it cannot be forced into a framework, however nobly conceived; and a mind that has merely been trained in factual knowledge is incapable of meeting life with its variety, its subtlety, its depths and great heights. When we train our children according to a system of thought or a particular discipline, when we teach them to think within departmental divisions, we prevent them from growing into integrated men and women, and therefore they are incapable of thinking intelligently, which is to meet life as a whole.

The highest function of education is to bring about an integrated individual who is capable of dealing with life as a whole. The idealist, like the specialist, is not concerned with the whole, but only with a part. There can be no integration as long as one is pursuing an ideal pattern of action; and most teachers who are idealists have put away love, they have dry minds and hard hearts. To study a child, one has to be alert, watchful, self-aware, and this demands far greater intelligence and affection than to encourage him to follow an ideal.

Another function of education is to create new values. Merely to implant existing values in the mind of the child, to make him conform to ideals, is to condition him without awakening his intelligence. Education is intimately related to the present world crisis, and the educator who sees the causes of this universal chaos should ask himself how to awaken intelligence in the student, thus helping the coming generation not to bring about further conflict and disaster. He must give all his thought, all his care and affection to the creation of right environment and to the development of understanding, so that when the child grows into maturity he will be capable of dealing intelligently with the human problems that confront him. But in order to do this, the educator must understand himself instead of relying on ideologies, systems and beliefs.

Let us not think in terms of principles and ideals, but be concerned with things as they are; for it is the consideration of what *is* that awakens intelligence, and the intelligence of the educator is far more important than his knowledge of a new method of education. When one follows a method, even if it has been worked out by a thoughtful and intelligent person, the method becomes very important, and the children are important only as they fit into it. One measures and classifies the child, and then proceeds to educate him according to some chart. This process of education may be convenient for the teacher, but neither the practice of a system nor the tyranny of opinion and learning can bring about an integrated human being.

The right kind of education consists in understanding the child as he is without imposing upon him an ideal of what we think he should be. To enclose him in the framework of an ideal is to encourage him to conform, which breeds fear and produces in him a constant conflict between what he is and what he should be; and all inward conflicts have their outward manifestations in society. Ideals are an actual hindrance to our understanding of the child and to the child's understanding of himself.

A parent who really desires to understand his child does not look at him through the screen of an ideal. If he loves the child, he observes him, he studies his tendencies, his moods and peculiarities. It is only when one feels no love for the child that one imposes upon him an ideal, for then one's ambitions are trying to fulfill themselves in him, wanting him to become this or that. If one loves, not the ideal, but the child, then there is a possibility of helping him to understand himself as he is.

If a child tells lies, for example, of what value is it to put before him the ideal of truth? One has to find out why he is telling lies. To help the child, one has to take time to study and observe him, which demands patience, love and care; but when one has no love, no understanding, then one forces the child into a pattern of action which we call an ideal.

Ideals are a convenient escape, and the teacher who follows them is incapable of understanding his students and dealing with them intelligently; for him, the future ideal, the what should be, is far more important than the present child. The pursuit of an ideal excludes love, and without love no human problem can be solved.

If the teacher is of the right kind, he will not depend on a method, but will study each individual pupil. In our relationship with children and young people, we are not dealing with mechanical devices that can be quickly repaired, but with living beings who are impressionable, volatile, sensitive, afraid, affectionate; and to deal with them, we have to have great understanding, the strength of patience and love. When we lack these, we look to quick and easy remedies and hope for marvellous and automatic results. If we are unaware, mechanical in our attitudes and actions, we fight shy of any demand upon us that is disturbing and that cannot be met by an automatic response, and this is one of our major difficulties in education.

The child is the result of both the past and the present and is therefore already conditioned. If we transmit our background to the child, we perpetuate both his and our own conditioning. There is radical transformation only when we understand our own conditioning and are free of it. To discuss what should be the right kind of education while we ourselves are conditioned is utterly futile.

While the children are young, we must of course protect them from physical harm and prevent them from feeling physically insecure. But unfortunately we do not stop there; we want to shape their ways of thinking and feeling, we want to mould them in accordance with our own cravings and intentions. We seek to fulfill ourselves in our children, to perpetuate ourselves through them. We build walls around them, condition them by our beliefs and ideologies, fears and hopes—and then we cry and pray when they are killed or maimed in wars, or otherwise made to suffer by the experiences of life.

Such experiences do not bring about freedom; on the contrary, they strengthen the will of the self. The self is made up of a series of defensive and expansive reactions, and its fulfillment is always in its own projections and gratifying identifications. As long as we translate experience in terms of the self, the "me" and the "mine," as long as the "I," the ego, maintains itself through its reactions, experience cannot be freed from conflict, confusion and pain. Freedom comes only when one understands the ways of the self, the experiencer. It is only when the self, with its accumulated reactions, is not the experiencer, that experience takes on an entirely different significance and becomes creation.

If we would help the child to be free from the ways of the self, which cause so much suffering, then each one of us should set about altering deeply his attitude and relationship to the child. Parents and educators, by their own thought and conduct, can help the child to be free and to flower in love and goodness.

Education as it is at present in no way encourages the understanding of the inherited tendencies and environmental influences which condition the mind and heart and sustain fear, and therefore it does not help us to break through these conditionings and bring about an integrated human being. Any form of education that concerns itself with a part and not with the whole of man inevitably leads to increasing conflict and suffering.

It is only in individual freedom that love and goodness can flower; and the right kind of education alone can offer this freedom. Neither conformity to the present society nor the promise of a future Utopia can ever give to the individual that insight without which he is constantly creating problems.

The right kind of educator, seeing the inward nature of freedom, helps each individual student to observe and understand his own self-projected values and impositions; he helps him to become aware of the conditioning influences about him, and of his own desires, both of which limit his mind and breed fear; he helps him, as he grows to manhood, to observe and understand himself in relation to all things, for it is the craving for self-fulfillment that bring endless conflict and sorrow.

Surely, it is possible to help the individual to perceive the enduring values of life, without conditioning. Some may say that this full development of the individual will lead to chaos; but will it? There is already confusion in the world, and it has arisen because the individual has not been educated to understand himself. While he has been given some superficial freedom, he has also been taught to conform, to accept the existing values.

Against this regimentation, many are revolting; but unfortunately their revolt is a mere self-seeking reaction, which only further darkens our existence. The right kind of educator, aware of the mind's tendency to reaction, helps the student to alter present values, not out of reaction against them, but through understanding the total process of life. Full co-operation between man and man is not possible without the integration which right education can help to awaken in the individual.

Educators' Checklist:

Questions to Ask Ourselves about Schooling

Gay Hendricks

Sometimes the process of education seems to illustrate the classic example of not seeing the forest for the trees; we get so busy teaching the required curriculum that we forget to ask what education should really be. Here one of the editors presents a series of questions designed to stimulate a fundamental evaluation of the purpose of schooling.

1. *Am I teaching students what they most want to know?*

A survey conducted by the author asked students to rank ten subjects in order of interest. The results, ranked from most interesting (1) to least interesting (10), were as follows:

1. Sex and your sexuality
2. Getting high without drugs (meditation, body awareness, etc.)
3. Communication skills (how to talk and listen to each other)
4. Keeping yourself healthy (self-healing, physical fitness, etc.)
5. Death and dying

   6. Art
   7. Social studies (history, civics, political science)
   8. Biology
   9. Geography (natural resources, etc.)
 10. Mathematics

As can be seen, the areas of greatest importance to students are rarely found in the school curriculum, while those areas in which students are relatively uninterested comprise the larger part of the curriculum. In other words, customers are being forced to go to the store to buy something they don't want. Other businesses have failed for less fundamental reasons.

Interestingly, when adults are asked to rank the same subjects, the results come out nearly identical to the students' rating. Thus, the argument that schools are teaching something that will be important later in life does not seem to be supported.

  2. *Am I teaching the whole person?*

Some facets of the whole person that deserves study are:

> feelings
> fantasy
> dreams
> personal problem solving (how to dissolve arguments, etc.)
> psychic phenomena
> decision-making

There is a substantial body of knowledge available for each of the above subjects, but little use of this knowledge is being made in schools.

Poets and scientists alike have pointed out that intellect is only part of the human potential, yet the intellect continues to get the major share of attention in schools.

  3. *Am I teaching processes?*

Take, for example, the memory process. Rather than having students memorize lists of things (state capitals, periodical table of elements), it might be more beneficial to teach them the process of memorization. We are always wanting to remember things like names and telephone numbers, and there are many excellent techniques available for building memory skills.

Memory is but one process; there are many others as important. In general, though, schools should be teaching *how* instead of *what*.

4. *Am I giving students information that is useful only in terms of future schooling?*

Schools teach many subjects (e.g., geometry) simply because they are prerequisites for another (e.g., trigonometry).

5. *Am I teaching students how to decondition themselves?*

Most of the things that cause people to be unhappy are due to conditioned ways of thinking, feeling, acting, and moving. Since schools, along with parents, are the major source of conditioning, some time should be spent teaching students how to get beyond their conditioning.

6. *Am I teaching students how to solve personal and interpersonal problems?*

Most problems can be solved with the following formula: feelings + wants = solution. In most problem situations an individual can ask, "How am I feeling?" (Sad? Angry? Scared?) and "What do I want to feel better?" (I want Jimmy to stop making fun of me.)

Here are a few examples:

Feeling	*Wants*
I'm angry	I want more attention from Dad.
I'm scared	I want to know that people aren't going to laugh when I read my oral report.

When one or more people have a problem, clear statements of feelings and wants can often lead to a solution.

7. *Am I teaching students how to learn?*

How do we go about finding out what we want to know? The *process* of learning can be useful to students throughout their lives.

8. *Am I teaching cultural relativity?*

Kurt Vonnegut writes, "A first-grader should understand that his or her culture isn't a rational invention; that there are thousands of other cultures and they all work pretty well; that all cultures function on faith rather than truth; that there are lots of alternatives to our own society. Cultural relativity is defensible and attractive. It's also a source of hope. It means we don't have to continue this way if we don't like it."

9. *Am I teaching students how to learn about themselves?*

How do I feel? What do I want? Who am I? How did I get the way I am?

We are the most important subject of all.

PRACTICING TRANSPERSONAL EDUCATION

Stimulated by visionaries like Krishnamurti, Aldous Huxley, and others, innovative educators began looking for ways in which transpersonal education could be implemented in the classroom. Theories are often fascinating to read, but the practicing educator needs activities that students can do today. In this section we present a wide variety of ideas and exercises which can provide the basis for a transpersonal curriculum for any classroom, K-12.

Among the areas covered in this section are dreamwork, fantasy, biofeedback, body awareness, psychic abilities, and meditation. It is our conviction that the quest for transpersonal experience must begin with a penetrating look into oneself. In the following section we present a number of tools meant to facilitate that exploration.

Dreams have poetic integrity and truth. This limbo and dust-hole of thought is presided over by a certain reason, too. Their extravagance from nature is yet within a higher nature. They seem to suggest to us an abundance and fluency of thought not familiar to waking experience.

—Emerson

What Would Happen to the American Psyche If, along with Homerooms, Flag Saluting and I.Q. Testing, Schools Had Daily Dream Sharing?

Patricia Pirmantgen

This article explores the fascinating world of dreams. Educators who have tried dream work in the classroom know that there is no quicker way to capture the interest of a group of students than to start them talking about their dreams. For other approaches to dreamwork, see Ann Faraday's The Dream Game, *and* The Centering Book *by Hendricks and Wills*

Patricia Pirmantgen edits a newsletter Dreams and Inner Spaces, *which offers some of the freshest ideas currently available in the field of dream work.*

We dream every night, which is analogous to having our own personal movie studio or repertory company in full-time operation. Fantastic and true, so what keeps most of us from using to advantage such fabulous facilities? Unfortunately, the snag is that we carry our culture's bias and conditioning toward the so-called irrational, so we fail to enjoy or recognize the significance of these "movies" or "dramas" that are provided, night after night, for our private viewing. Erich Fromm says it all when he calls dreams, along with myths and fairy tales, the forgotten language.[1]

While research shows that dreaming is a regular activity or state experienced by virtually all of us during sleep,[2] many people, once awake, rarely recall or work with their own dreams. When dream content does stick in the mind, the average, conditioned response is to make a vague association with Freudian psychology and/or sex; emotionally upsetting dreams (nightmares) are blamed on daytime problems or malfunction of the digestive tract.

Those dreams vivid enough to make a lasting impression still leave us at a loss for what to do with them; so dreams are shoved in the mind's unsolved mystery file, rather than being used for the direct channel they provide to one's creativity and inner space. People in our culture with some notion of how to work with their own dream content are probably met about as often as speakers of Basque or other equally exotic minorities. Even in a fairly sophisticated group, where the mention of dreams might not immediately call up that superstitious mixture of fear and fascination that things "occult" hold for Western man, a person actively involved with his own dreams would still be considered eccentric unless he could give the rationale of psychoanalysis.

Six years ago, being such a biased and conditioned American myself, I casually suggested to sixty students in creative writing that their dreams were a possible source of ideas; I mentioned dreams simply because they are vivid experiences common to everyone. That suggestion sparked an explosion of interest that led to research, experimentation and, eventually, made dream work an integral part of the teaching and curriculum writing that I do.

[1]Erich Fromm, *The Forgotten Language* (New York: Holt, Rinehart and Winston, 1951), p. 8. Fromm says, "Dreams fared even worse in the judgment of modern enlightenment. They were considered to be plain senseless, and unworthy of the attention of grown-up men, who were busy with such important matters as building machines and considered themselves 'realistic' because they saw nothing but the reality of things they could conquer and manipulate; realists who have a special word for each type of automobile, but only the one word 'love' to express the most varied kinds of affective experience."

[2]Scientists have been studying states during sleep through electrical recordings of brain and body activity. The findings show dreaming can and does happen in everyone's sleep. Even people who claim they do not dream, when awakened in the lab during REM (Rapid Eye Movement sleep) report dreams. See Related Reading for some references.

About the time my growing awareness of the significance of dreams had brought me to the point of whimsically speculating about what marvelous transformations might be made in the American psyche and culture if schools were to substitute dream sharing for I.Q. testing, I came across an article. It described a culture where dream work does play a significant and major role in the educative process and the life of a culture. The Senoi, 12,000 people living in the mountains of Malay, were visited in 1935 by a scientific expedition. The Senoi people claimed in the past two to three hundred years to have had no violent crime or intercommunal conflict. Kilton Stewart, who was in the expedition, wrote about their dream work. ". . .the absence of violent crime, armed conflict, and mental and physical diseases. . .can only be explained on the basis of. . .a high state of psychological integration and emotional maturity, along with social skills and attitudes which promote creative. . . interpersonal relations. . .Breakfast in the Senoi house is like a dream clinic, with listening to and analyzing the dreams of all the children. At the end of the family clinic the male population gathers in the council, at which the dreams. . .are reported, discussed and analyzed."[3]

Work with dreams had also led me to look again and differently at the matter of myth; here was another question to be asked, another relationship to be explored, because as two authors, Kluckhohn and Leighton, pointed out, "Folklore must be presumed to originate in the dreams and fantasies of individuals."[4] Could it be that our culture's folklore and myth are cut off from a primary source—the people's dream experiences, which express, as no think-tank or academic perspective can, what we presently term the cosmic meanings underlying human life—those same meanings that inspire art and literature? J. R. R. Tolkien once explained that he created the *Ring* series because today's English people were poor in myth. Americans suffer the same poverty; or maybe it's not that we have few myths, but that the myths we have are so bad, lacking the juices of life. Think of the myth of being male so successfully marketed by *Playboy,* or the various inane images held up as ideals in advertising or

---

[3]Stewart's article on the Senoi has been reprinted in various places; the Related Reading Section gives several sources. Stewart concludes, "In the West the thinking we do while asleep usually remains on a muddled, childish or psychotic level because we do not respond to dreams as socially important and include dreaming in the educative process."

[4]Clyde Kluckhohn and Dorothea Leighton, *The Navaho* (Cambridge: Harvard University Press, 1951), p. 136.

TV broadcasting. It seems to me we should explore whether or not our culture's exclusion of dreams from serious and creative work affects the quality of our dominant myths. It's worth pondering what kind of leaders Kennedy, Johnson and Nixon would have aspired to be if they had had the influence of different myths. We should ask whether or not there exists a relationship between dream work, our culture's dominant myths and such phenomena as drug addiction and alcoholism; conspicuous, compulsive consumption; the psychic and physical violence that is part of our culture; the rape of the ecological environment; or the prominent place we give to a kind of religion which, generally speaking, in some ways varies little from denomination to denomination and is essentially gutless, bland and devoid of qualities that uplift and inspire.

As Joseph Cambell points out, "The rise and fall of civilizations in the long, broad course of history can be seen to have been largely a function of the integrity and cogency of their supporting canons of myth; for not authority but aspiration is the motivator, builder and transformer of civilization. A mythological canon is an organization of symbols, ineffable in import, by which the energies of aspiration are evoked and gathered toward a focus."[5]

MAKING A BEGINNING

> *Beginnings are not precision. Beginnings are not confusion. They are darkness drawn to a minute point of nondarkness, and silence gathered into a small sound.*
> —*Sheila Moon*

The best place to begin is with yourself. Before trying to involve adolescents in their dreams, take time to involve yourself. For the space of two or three months, pay close attention to your own dreaming. Nightly, before going to sleep, empty your mind of the concerns of the day; clear yourself, so to speak, for dream activity. Immediately after waking, note down your dream content; if you postpone this, the dream (s) will recede from consciousness and be lost. Suggestion: record

[5]Joseph Campbell, *The Masks of God: Creative Mythology* (New York: The Viking Press, 1968), p. 5.

dreams on separate sheets, date them, keep in a file folder. Occasionally skim the collection and think about the dreams, trying to relive one or more of them. Try out some of the activities suggested later in this article for use with students. If others, teachers, friends, are interested in something of this nature, meet occasionally in a small group and share dreams.

You will notice various phenomena. For example, dreams, like movies, come in black and white or color.[6] They cover a wide range of subject matter and could be compared to the sequence of rough drafts or preliminary sketches that artists and writers go through as they clarify and refine what they are seeking to express.

At first, one's dream flow can seem without pattern, structure or coherence, but over a period of time, perhaps weeks, months or years, one finds that certain themes and motifs emerge, although from night to night they can be intermingled and mixed-up. It seems that the psyche works on several themes simultaneously, like a movie studio with many productions in process; in terms of a night's or a week's dreams, we may be seeing rushes from all the productions. Persistence in recording and working with one's dreams eventually makes it possible to tentatively group one's dreams in series on the basis of theme, setting, story or feeling values.

As a series of dreams pertaining to a theme continues, an image in it can evolve, showing itself in different ways or bringing changes in feeling in the dream self's reaction to the image. For example, a frightening dream image, such as a large, powerful dog chasing one, can go through a series of transformations from dream to dream until, while still a symbol of power, the dog image has become friendly.

It also seems that we can enter into a dream and affect its flow, so that in the case of a student who dreamed of being out in a depressing rain, not of water, but of iron balls, he could decide when next in that dream state to do something creative about the iron balls; he might catch them and build a shelter of them; he could draw a line and instruct them to fall on only one side of the line; he could call up the image of someone he trusted and ask the person for an umbrella; he could ask the sun to come out.

[6]As I've become more aware of and worked with my own dreams, the dreams themselves have become more sophisticated in their use of color. The inner dream director now uses color as a cinematographer would to create a mood, enhance a theme or convey some quality or emphasis. For visually oriented people the dream world is a rich experience.

Other phenomena you may notice: Symbols from one's religious training show up even in the dreams of those people who, consciously at least, would no longer consider themselves believers. Certain settings, people or happenings can return in dreams again and again. Extraordinarily strong feelings like terror, pain, joy and rapture can be experienced in the dream state. One's dream self may be a surprise, acting in an unexpected fashion or manifesting qualities not generally associated with oneself. Sometimes problems or matters that have consciously occupied the mind for a long time find a solution in the dream state. Much dream literature mentions the chemist Kekule, who was searching for the molecular structure of benzene; his dream of a snake with its tail in its mouth, an ancient symbol called the oroboros, was the clue leading him to the discovery that the benzene structure was a closed carbon ring.

It seems that once we show this inner dream director or filmmaker that we are serious about responding to and integrating his perspective into our conscious attitudes and judgments, a channel opens up in us. When we then refer matters like personal relationships or creative problems connected with our work to the dream director, we receive feedback that is often very much to the point, extremely helpful and sometimes something that much conscious effort and thought has not yet been able to show us.

Dreams will include what we know we know and what we know we do not know. For instance, someone who has not read ancient mythology and has no way of knowing symbols or motifs from it may find such symbols appearing in his dreams.[7] The inner dream director is also quick to incorporate recent events, experiences and discoveries into his dream continuity. Most of us, of course, are familiar with the person who is dreaming of thunder and wakes up to find a severe storm in progress.

Teachers often tell about dreams of disruptive groups, of being defied by their students. It would be interesting to write a book or article about the teaching experience which is a collection of teachers' dreams and examines them for what they imply about the contemporary educative process. In terms of helping teachers, especially in so vital an area as student-teacher relationships, dream content might be a good and basic starting point.

[7] Jungian psychology includes the concept of the collective unconscious, a level of the individual's psyche that does *not* derive from his personal experience but from which contents can manifest themselves.

DREAM WORK IN THE CLASSROOM CONTEXT

> *A solution which solves a problem intellectually, moral-*
> *ly or aesthetically but not in all three modes is a false*
> *solution. The theoretical foundation for such a view is*
> *abstruse and controversial and pedagogically the task of*
> *blending in the pupil what is separated out in the culture*
> *is difficult but the need for such unification is not*
> *controversial.*
>
> *—Harry S. Broudy*

The process covers three areas:

1. Developing a group's awareness, recognition and memory of dream states and content.
2. Creative work with their own dream material.
3. Drawing parallels between dream content and the English curriculum.

Work on dreams usually has to be a peripheral part of a curriculum, but it's not hard, I find, even with limited time to build a group's involvement. People generally are fascinated by anything pertaining to themselves and the occasional sharing of dreams and some creative work with them has been sufficient to hold interest and provide momentum for a group process to evolve.

Developing Awareness[8]

Begin by sharing an interesting dream of your own; make its images come alive as you retell it and try to communicate something of the emotional impact that it had on you. This will usually be enough to remind the group of dreams of their own that they want to talk about. Even those who retain little or no memory of dream activity at night will have had at least one dream make a lasting impression. The dream sharing stimulates memories and the session isn't long enough to include everything students are reminded of, so they leave, reluctantly, still talking.

[8]In my experience today's students are intensely interested in whatever pertains to their inner space. *"Star Trek"* re-runs, science fiction, the drug culture, meditation techniques like TM, etc., have made them curious about altered states of consciousness; they are genuinely interested in working with their dreams.

This first mention of dreams usually calls up two sets of reactions: [some students] are immediately interested or at least curious and [some students] say they do not dream. The following steps help people with either reaction grow more aware of their own dream activity, especially carrying some memory of it over into waking consciousness.

A.   Before going to sleep, think of the mind as a chalkboard. Wipe it clear of daytime stuff; let sleep come. Or think of the mind as a TV or movie screen where nothing is now being projected; the screen is empty, waiting for the dream images to be projected on it.

B.   In the morning, immediately after waking up, take five minutes to write or tape whatever details of dreams are still on the screen, i.e., remembered. Don't give up because there is nothing there the first few mornings. Persistence, eventually, will bring results.

Once a week or every other week set aside a regular time to share something from recent dreams. Tell one or more of your own that are appropriate; someone who has had a frightening dream may be relieved . . . if he sees that others also have them. At first, some will be shy, but if there is an accepting/enjoying tone to the sessions, reticences gradually dissolve and in time everyone is vying for a turn. Within weeks (three to seven in my experience), the "non-dreamers" discover themselves dreaming. Several side effects of the process eventually become noticeable: those who thought themselves uncreative and lacking in imagination begin to feel they do have creative talents. The group process and exchange grow closer to true democracy with differences such as race, social class and verbal ability no longer such barriers or the sole basis of their response to each other. They also begin to find more meaning in the traditional content of English and composition work.

After the process is on-going and there is real interest in dreams, I mingle the dream-sharing with simple activities like the following:

The group goes through the letters of the alphabet giving words that begin with each letter (abacus, butter, calluses, etc.). Then each one, using this word list, makes up a story; everyone reads his or her stories aloud. Or we take a group of typical images that come in dreams (flower, mountain, house, mysterious stranger, road) and with them create a story or an outline for a film.[9]

The point of these activities is to give the group experience in creating where the conscious, planning part of themselves works along with the

---

[9]These stories can sometimes be surprisingly coherent and interesting; for the student who thinks writing impossible they can be a breakthrough.

unknown part of themselves, that mysterious aspect of the self from which dreams may also flow. As we discuss the stories and the method by which they were created, several questions are explored:

* Did I know this story was in me before I wrote it?
* Where did it come from?
* Could I have written it without the list of words?
* Could we speculate that something akin to this happens in dreaming—a presently unknown source or power within ourselves creates "movies" that consciously we don't know are in us?
* Is the key to creative writing in a combination of conscious work, materials and finding a way to open the flow from that unknown source or power in one-self?

At this point in the process, I might plan a creative writing project which will draw on their own dreams for content. I am careful, however, not to give creative work related to dreams until I see that they are really interested and involved.

The first time doing dream work with a group, it's well to limit the activity to the simple and regular sharing of dreams. If teachers go slowly, gradually coming to an intuitive grasp of the process rather than trying too much too soon, they will be able to nuture the process and bring it to a fruit-bearing stage. But if we get all excited and involved ourselves with dreams, it's tempting to flood students with our newly acquired information and enthusiasm. That can be harmful because it may block the way to the students' own discovery of meaning in dream work; it's best not to share a lot, initially, of what we know about dreams, but to wait until questions come that show a readiness, a context for taking in what we have to give.

One more caution: In group work of this sort the content is being generated by teacher and students, which implies the need for a healthy group dynamic, a real relationship between the teacher and the group. For the kind of sharing that's involved here, people have to be to a degree open, trusting, enjoying and accepting of themselves and others. However, it should be noted that the very process of dream sharing seems to help create the kind of atmosphere that is needed.

Creative Work

There are many ways of proceeding here. Create your own or select from the following on the basis of inclination, group interest, need.

ACTIVITIES:

A.   *Keep a dream diary or journal. Record dreams in it, dating them, putting down the details that are remembered or the feelings they held. Occasionally, review the dream diary; look for images or themes that repeat themselves, that are evolving and changing. Work with and amplify such images; see H. for the process.*

B.   *Dreams can be re-created as short stories, as films or filmstrips or as continuity for short, experimental dramas. A group might select from their dreams several to weave together in dramatic form. Groups could present their plays to each other.*

C.   *Some dream images make striking posters. Combine efforts with the art and/or photography departments.*

D.   *Role-play, using the dream material as a starting point for a character or a situation. Ask the student whose dream it is to select group members to act it out with him. This is a beginning way of probing dream content for meaning, of interpreting the dream.*

E.   *Create a dialogue between one's waking self and one of the dream characters.*

F.   *In writing or in cartooned sequences continue the dream from its last remembered scene. Or create variations of it.*

G.   *Write descriptions of unusual dream characters or dream settings.*

H.   *Work with some of the dream images, amplifying their meaning by building up a web of related associations. For example, in one group after several students had had houses in their dreams, we took down everything we could think of concerning houses—openings such as doors and windows; many rooms with different purposes such as a kitchen where things were cooked, closets with things hidden in them, the bathroom, halls linking rooms to each other. We noted that houses could have levels from underground basements to dusty, seldom entered attics. There were places in houses that were little used; there were rooms or furnishings that received much use. A house itself was a container in which more than one life process was happening—birth, growth, conflict, love. A child living in a house would not know everything that went on within its walls. A grown-up might have forgotten much that had gone on within it; he might be ignorant of its past, unable to predict its future. We recalled literary associations such as the house of Usher. We remembered different houses from our dreams and experiences that we had had with houses. Then we made the transition from a house as a house to a house as a symbol of image for one's own self or being, paralleling all the items we had noted for houses with possible equivalents in the human life or psyche.*

Such brainstorming sessions in which everyone shares associations with a symbol or image are helpful in several ways. They show how to begin to extract meaning from a dream and they develop the students' intellectual and emotional comprehension of images and symbols, no matter what the context-film, poetry, novels or dreams.

After the group just mentioned had worked with the images of house, dog, cat and tree, a girl came one day, excited and curious about a dream of washing machines. The group went to work on the image and in five minutes the chalkboard was filled with associations related to washing machines.

While a dictionary of symbols is helpful for the teacher, it is best not to bring it into the classroom for several reasons. Although there is a universal meaning that attaches to or is communicated by symbols, the person who has had a dream is the one best suited to know what its images mean for him. But for students and for most of us, so far as meaning goes, our dreams are puzzles, seemingly beyond figuring out. Carl Jung says a dream is a hint and to unlock its meaning we have to fill out the implications of the hint. The work the group did with the images of the house and the washing machines was that kind of filling out. When a group amplifies enough dream images together, they learn how to exercise the skill for themselves; if they look up symbols in a dictionary, they will miss out on valuable practice and experience. Also, when they work with a dream image, they are grappling with the dream content; if they go to a dictionary, they may come away with information but they will not necessarily have acquired a personal understanding of their own dream content.

Drawing Parallels Between Dream Content and the English Curriculum

It should not be necessary to modify much whatever is one's present curriculum; there is such a wealth of possibilities in the area of English and the humanities. Much poetry; a novel like *Moby Dick,* the work of Shakespeare; themes such as hero, conflict, courage; authors like Faulkner, Conrad, Frost, Blake; the world of myth; many contemporary films—all begin to take on new significance for a group when dream work is integrated with their reading, writing and discussion. The students see themselves in dreams experiencing the same mythic, weird, mysterious, emotionally charged worlds and situations that are the stuff of fiction and poetry. In becoming more conscious of their own dreams, they have found a reason to identify. They have also discovered how difficult it is to communicate these complex states and experiences. Since social recognition is more or less denied inner states, we presently lack a commonly accepted nomenclature or working concepts to readily make our dream states intelligible to each other. But often in lyric poetry, in some section of a novel or play, or in a scene from a film, we can catch a glimpse of something that reminds us of a dream experience.

I would also speculate that the level of the psyche where dreams originate is akin to the level of stratum of the psyche where creative works are initiated.[10] The students, in making conscious contact with that level in themselves, are sensitized, are put in touch through empathy with the creative experience and emotional states expressed in literature and film. An awareness of this adds to the intellectual study of literature a feeling dimension that helps students grasp the texture or flavor of a particular piece. Students begin to catch the shimmer of significant meaning in literature; they learn to feel respect and appreciation for a literary heritage that previously may have seemed to them little more than irrelevant deadwood.

It seems to me that, properly handled, dream work in the context of the English class is an area, a place, a way to achieve a real integration of the affective and the cognitive domains in the educative process.

CLOSING THOUGHTS

No one should make the mistake of assuming this article covers the full range of potential and possibility that is implied by dream states and their content. There are many aspects of the dream experience and questions concerning what really does happen in the state of dreaming that are not touched upon here.

It should be mentioned that much of today's literature on dreams comes, of course, from various schools of psychiatric thought; while the English teacher will have to rely on this for help, it is necessary to keep in mind that dreaming is an activity of the healthy psyche as well as the disturbed psyche; the psychoanalytic perspective suffers inevitable distortion because it is one that thinks primarily in terms of disturbance, unhealth and disease; it is wise, therefore, not to make blanket applications of psychoanalytic insights or to take them for infallible and universal truths. The various schools of thought do not yet themselves agree upon such basics as the origin of dream activity and the interpretation of dream content.

---

[10]R.L. Stevenson, Blake, Poe, Coleridge, Mozart and Saint-Saens are a few to consciously draw on dream activity for creative work.

We are just at the start of systematic study of the various aspects of dream activity, but some interesting and provocative physiological data has already emerged. For example, in his book, *Dreams and the Growth of Personality,* growth therapist Ernest Rossi summarizes data that give support to the view, he says, that new protein structures are actually being synthesized in the brain during the dream state. Dr. Rossi says, "These new organic structures are the forerunners of creative change in our view of ourselves and the world. They are the biological foundation of a naturally occurring process of constructive change in our personalities and behavior."[11]

Dr. Rossi, like many others writing on dreams, has had training in the Jungian perspective on the human psyche. It is my experience that an English, humanities or media teacher beginning dream work will find more help in the writings of people trained in the Jungian school than in the works of people from the Freudian school.[12]

Dream work in the classroom does not call for elaborate materials or textbooks; it's little more than the age-old teaching process of the log with the master at one end and the student at the other. Dream work can be easily and creatively integrated into most English or humanities curriculum. It ties in particularly well, of course, with film; so well that I sometimes ask myself whether or not the development of film is an outward projection of certain inner psychic processes and space/time relationships that operate at some level within us but that we are presently not cognizant of.

The goal in the classroom is to build a conscious, responsible and accepting attitude toward one's dreams and to try to use them as a channel to one's creativity. The work with dreams in the classroom context will not be able to reduce the dream experience to a verbalized kernel that makes a definitive statement about the meaning or message of a dream; nevertheless, some feeling and intuitive understanding of dream content will develop as students work with and re-create their own dreams. The students also find in the experience a valuable freedom to

[11]Ernest Rossi, *Dreams and the Growth of Personality* (New York: Pergamon Press, Inc., 1972).

[12]George Steiner said, in an interview printed in *Psychology Today* (February, 1975), about Jung: "The more I try to structure a model for translation for the way we move from language to language via images and symbols, the more I find in Jung suggestions of extraordinary interest. It looks as if Jung, more deeply than Freud, understood the whole problem of the nature of universality—not in the Chomskian sense, but in the way that language creates fictions, creates life lies, creates complex symbols. . . . I believe that Jung is going to loom larger and larger in the tradition."

take seriously this aspect of themselves. It could even be that such explorations of their own inner space as take place when working with dreams may be a factor to help students decide against trying to alter consciousness through the use of drugs. Dream states themselves can be so rich and varied that a student might say of drugs, "Who needs them?"

There are depths hinted at and mysteries about the nature of space, time and being in dreams which centuries of thought and effort have still not answered, or perhaps the answers were once known and later lost. Apparently, judging from Biblical passages and other ancient literature such as the Greek myths and healing rites connected to the god Asklepius, dreams were considered significant by more than one society and used in healing, in religious rites and in decision-making. Remember the Pharaoh who stored grain against a famine predicted in a dream. It may well be that in taking an interest in dreams, as groups and individuals are, today, we are working our way back to a lost wisdom or art.[13]

No occasional and peripheral work such as that suggested in this article is going to completely unravel the meanings, both individual and collective, that dreams hint at, but work such as this is of much importance because it helps people open themselves to an area of their own being which is rich in meaning and probably closely allied to one's creative talents. The work gives respect to rather than ignoring a vital area of activity, for almost one-third of man's life is spent in sleep. To re-apply Shakespeare, ". . . who knows what dreams may come?" Could the American psyche be transformed if, along with homerooms and I.Q. tests, American schools were to have daily dream work?

RELATED READING

CIRLOT, J.E., *A Dictionary of Symbols.* New York: Philosophical Library, 1962. (Also available in paperback. Thus far the only symbol dictionary in one volume that I have found to be worth having.)

FARADAY, DR. ANN, *Dream Power.* New York: Berkley Medallion, 1972. (Paperback. The author's personal experience with various schools of dream analysis; the eclectic approach she worked out for herself.)

FROMM, ERICH, *The Forgotten Language.* New York: Holt, Rinehart and Winston, 1951. (On myth, dreams and fairy tales.)

[13]Stanley Krippner, head of the Maimonides Dream Laboratory in New York, was reported to be on the West Coast in 1973 to help set up a dream curriculum for the college level.

HALL, CALVIN S. and NORDBY, VERNON J., *The Individual and His Dreams.* New York: Signet, 1972. (Paperback. A how-to-analyze-your-own-dreams book. Hall and Nordby have studied more than 50,000 dreams and move beyond the approach of traditional psychoanalysis in their treatment of dream content, but they occasionally betray the usual biases of the American scientist.)

JUNG, CARL G., ed., *Man and His Symbols.* New York: Dell Publishing Co., Inc. 1964. (Paperback; also available in hard cover but it's considerably more expensive. Jung's works are generally not easy to read but this one has been designed for the general public. Jung's dream insights are especially helpful for anyone beginning to take the dream world seriously.)

KRIPPNER, STANLEY and HUGHES, WILLIAM, "Genius at Work," in *Psychology Today* (June 1970), pp. 40-43. (A brief article on the relationship between dreams and creativity. Also other articles on dreaming in this issue of PT.)

MAHONEY, MARIA F., *The Meaning in Dreams and Dreaming.* New York, Citadel Press, 1966. (Paperback. A Jungian approach to dreams for use by an individual working on his own; a helpful book with which to make a beginning.)

PIRMANTGEN, PATRICIA, *Dreams and Inner Spaces,* Edendale P.O., Box 26556, Los Angeles, Calif. 90026. (A recently formed non-commercial publishing company which is developing inexpensive materials related to: dreams, altered states of consciousness, mystical states, creativity, intuitive modes. Sample copy of the *Dreams and Inner Spaces* newsletter available at no charge; please send SASE, #10 size.)

ROBERTS, JANE, *The Education of Oversoul Seven.* Englewood Cliffs, N.J.: Prentice-Hall, 1972. (A science-fiction novel which revolves around manifestations in the dream world and the concept of simultaneous reincarnation. The insights regarding dreams in this book go much further than Jung, Hall, Faraday, Fromm, etc.)

ROSSI, ERNEST LAWRENCE, *Dreams and the Growth of Personality.* New York: Pergamon Press, Inc., 1972. (A fascinating book to read in that it contains the odyssey, largely expressed in dreams and visions, of a young woman in analysis with Dr. Rossi.)

TART, CHARLES T., ed. *Altered States of Consciousness.* Garden City, New York: Doubleday Anchor, 1969. (Paperback. The section on dream consciousness contains five articles. Tart's introduction to the section briefly surveys the published literature on studies and experiments related to dream states.)

WALCOTT, WILLIAM, ed., *Psychological Perspectives,* Volume 3, Number 2 (Fall 1972). (A periodical publication of the C. G. Jung Institute of Los Angeles. This issue contains a special section of four articles on dreams and dreaming. One of the four is an article on the Senoi Tribe and their use of dreams, by Kilton Stewart. The same article also appears in Tart's book. Single issues available for $2.75. Address: 595 E. Colorado Blvd., Pasadena, Calif. 91101).

Ways of Teaching

John Blofeld

John Blofeld traveled in the interior of China in the decades before the 1949 Communist revolution. These remarks were made to him by a Taoist monk who had been a prominent banker before retiring to a small, quite obscure monastery in the country.

The younger recluses here and the three young boys receive teaching from us elders. Good, but we do not set about it by laying down what they, as Taoists, must study. Instead, we start by observing our pupils, leading them on to reveal what is in their minds and to display what talents and bents belong to them naturally. Then, by whatever means come to hand, we guide each along the lines he is best fitted to follow, often learning more than we impart. What wonders would be wrought and what tragic failures avoided if schoolmasters did the same! Sooner or later, our pupils come to study the works of such sages as Laotzu, Chuangtzu and Lichtzu—not because they must, but because they grow

"Ways of Teaching." From John Blofeld, *Beyond the Gods: Buddhist and Taoist Mysticism* (New York: E. P. Dutton & Co., Inc., 1974), p. 58.

curious about the sources of our ideas. If they had no tendency that way, the young recluses would not have come here in the first place. Even so, just *how* we teach them depends not on our own preferences but on the pupils' natural aptitudes and inclinations.

Learning through Fantasy

Frances Vaughan Clark

Guided fantasy is a useful learning tool and it has another appeal: it's fun. With a combination like that, it is amazing that educators have only recently discovered the use of fantasy techniques. Frances Vaughan Clark, a pioneer in the use of fantasy in the classroom, provides a helpful introduction to this area of transpersonal education.

Fantasy is the use of imagination in the creation of mental images. Fantasy may be either voluntary or involuntary. It can be used as a tool for creativity, for piecing together unrelated facts, for overcoming obstacles, and for experimenting with new ways of being in the world. The young child needs no instruction in the uses of fantasy. It arises spontaneously as a means of integrating the vast amount of learning which takes place during the early years. The importance of fantasy in the development of the human mind and spirit is readily accepted by artists, writers, and others who contribute to the make-believe world of childhood. When a child goes to school, however, he is expected to begin to learn about the real world, and put away the rich imaginings of his early years. Nevertheless, fantasy remains an important part of play and creativity at every age. When we reminisce, daydream, or imagine anything real or unreal, we are using fantasy. We experience fantasy journeys spontaneously every day whenever we speculate about "What if . . ." The fantasy journeys we will be discussing are not so spontaneous. They are planned, triggered by a stimulus for a particular purpose, and provide for the integration of the experience into everyday life. The ability to use fantasy and imagination is an essential part of any creative endeavor, whether it be in artistic expression or scientific discovery. Everyone is called on to solve problems in life, and no matter what the person's vocation, the ability to find imaginative alternatives and creative solutions is an asset. A student who has experienced his own creative ability will have an asset that he can call upon in any future endeavor.

Teachers, parents, or counselors who are interested in opening up the world of fantasy for exploration by children should not overlook the fact that they too may benefit personally from the experience. Adults need not remain detached observers. On the contrary, they can be better guides if they themselves have experienced the power and excitement of participating fully in a fantasy journey. Fantasy is a tool for human growth and development which is effective and rewarding at any age. Its value has long been recognized in psychotherapy, but more recently techniques derived from Jung's active imagination, DeSoilles' guided daydream, and Assagioli's psychosynthesis have been introduced into education with very positive results. Here we are not concerned with therapy, but with the development and growth of the healthy personality. Many adults need psychotherapy because their education failed to give them a sense of self-worth and the ability to take responsibility for their lives. Education which does not teach students how to use their inner resources is incomplete. Education of the whole person needs to recognize the importance of subjective as well as objective learning and to integrate inner experience with the outer reality of the environment. Learning through fantasy is one way in which this integration can take place.

Recent physiological findings indicate that our brains function in two ways. The function of the left hemisphere of the brain is predominantly linear, rational, and verbal. The function of the right hemisphere is predominantly holistic, intuitive, and metaphoric. Most of our educational process is geared to the development of left-hemisphere functions, even though we know that the greatest achievements of the human mind require the integrated functioning of both hemispheres. The ability of the right cerebral hemisphere to perceive patterns and possibilities, meaning and relationship, and to create symbolic images is essential both to the creative process and the development of the healthy personality. Yet we are only beginning to recognize the importance of validating these functions within our educational system.

What Jerome Bruner called left-handed knowing in 1962 (Bruner, J., *On Knowing: Essays For the Left Hand.* New York: Atheneum, 1962) is what we now refer to as right-hemisphere knowing, since the right hemisphere of the brain controls the left side of the body, while the left hemisphere of the brain controls the right side of the body. Although the importance of both modes of knowing has been affirmed in learning theory, the primary focus of learning theorists such as Piaget and Bruner has been on the cognitive functions of the left cerebral hemisphere.

One way of including the development of right-hemisphere functions in the educational process is through the introduction of fantasy as a valid and exciting way of learning. Recent evidence indicates that children who do not daydream are more likely to become emotionally disturbed than children who do daydream. Night dreams are also important for the maintenance of mental health, and often serve as a source of creative inspiration. By encouraging the development of fantasy thinking we can help students learn to value those subjective, visual, and artistic processes which are so important in the development of full human potential.

The kind of learning provided by altered states of consciousness such as dreams, meditation, and guided fantasy is an essential part of education for the whole person. Moreover, this type of experimental learning gives us direct access to right-cerebral functioning. By giving students the opportunity to explore their inner resources of inventiveness and creativity, affirming the importance of divergent as well as convergent thinking, we are also encouraging initiative and self-reliance. In *The Crack in the Cosmic Egg,* Joseph Pierce points out how we create our reality by the way we structure our perceptions of the world. We are now beginning to understand how a limited imagination structures reality in such a way as to prevent discovery of personal power and the assumption of responsibility for change and growth in one's own life. Learning to create a subjective reality in fantasy can also lead to a new appreciation of our capacity to change and restructure our perceptions of reality in order to allow a broader perspective on human experience and human potentials.

The use of fantasy also allows students to learn by using a variety of modalities in addition to the rational, verbal, literary approach to learning. Some students learn more quickly when visual images are evoked. Others respond more readily to such modalities as touch, texture, or kinesthetic imagery. In fantasy all the sensory modalities may be brought to bear on the experience. Sights, sounds, sensations, emotions, and thought processes are all called into play as an integral part of the process. Sometimes a teacher or guide may wish to introduce movement into the fantasy by, for instance, asking children to curl up small while imagining that they are a seed, and to stretch up as they begin to imagine themselves as a growing plant.

The importance of training the imagination as a specific psychological function has been discussed by Roberto Assagioli in *Psychosynthesis*. It is easy to see that as a person learns to take responsibility for overcoming obstacles in fantasy, where anything is possible, he is actually learning about his capacity for solving problems, overcoming obstacles, and making decisions in his life. He is also learning that he can voluntarily choose to control his own thoughts, or to relinquish control and allow spontaneous imagery to emerge. Improved self-image, increased sense of responsibility for oneself, improved ability to concentrate, and a greater appreciation and acceptance of individual differences are some of the changes which tend to be associated with learning through fantasy.

In order to create optimum conditions for increasing self-reliance and self-esteem through the experiential appreciation of inner resources, it is necessary to establish an environment of trust. Fantasies should therefore not be evaluated, interpreted, or rewarded in any way. In fantasy each individual is expanding the frontiers of his awareness and exploring the unknown by creating and combining objects, situations, and occurrences which have never existed before. Such exploration is intrinsically satisfying, and needs no secondary reinforcement. In fact, secondary reinforcement only tends to diminish interest and genuine spontaneity.

In the world of fantasy we are truly limited only by a lack of imagination. Unfortunately, the development of imagination is frequently stunted early in life when it is referred to derogatorily as "only imagination." Sometimes a good deal of practice and encouragement is needed, particularly with adults and older children, before self-imposed limitations can be discarded and the inner wellsprings of creativity can be unblocked. As a person learns to transcend the boundaries of a limited imagination the process becomes more and more enjoyable and rewarding. With increased practice, the participant may be willing to risk more in his fantasies and begin to experiment with changing self-image. For example, if he always sees himself as a heroic figure in his fantasies, and this stance is neither praised nor criticized, he may also be able to explore in fantasy his feelings of being timid or scared. Exploring alternate roles and ways of being in the world through fantasy is another aspect of learning which can have lasting effects on the individual by making him more aware of alternatives and his capacity for making choices.

By allowing participants to respond in any way they want, and make their own observations about the process, the teacher can create an atmosphere of trust and acceptance which is essential for this type of learning experience. By maintaining a non-judgmental attitude the teacher is also modeling behavior for other students who may not, at first, know how to respond. In sharing a fantasy a person always reveals something about how he feels about himself and his creations. If he becomes deeply involved, he may experience the fantasy as something which shapes itself of its own accord. The process of allowing imagery to unfold involves what we call passive volition. By this we mean simply maintaining an attitude of willing receptivity to the fantasy experience. Excessive attempts at control and conscious formulation frequently interfere with the emergence of imagery, and it is therefore recommended that fantasy journeys be preceded by a period of physical and mental relaxation. Each and every participant gets to be the director, producer, star, and audience at every show, and there is always something new to be discovered. Right now, use your fantasy: imagine how you want to guide your first fantasy journey.

How Three Teachers Use Fantasy Journeys

Richard Meznarich,
Robert Habes,
Claudia Binter

Readers who want to explore the use of fantasy for fun and personal growth are encouraged to turn to DeMille's delightful Put Your Mother on the Ceiling *and to* The Centering Book *by Hendricks and Wills.*

Here, however, three creative teachers show how fantasy can be used in several different areas of the traditional academic curriculum.

RICHARD MEZNARICH:
TEACHING ELECTRONICS
THEORY THROUGH FANTASY

I took my beginning electronics class on a [fantasy] trip into that mysterious land of invisible magnetic and electric fields surrounding the windings and core of a transformer. The procedure was as follows.

"How Three Teachers Use Fantasy Journeys" by Richard Meznarich, Robert Habes, and Claudia Binter. Used by permission of the authors. This article appears for the first time in this volume. It was edited by Thomas Roberts.

The room was darkened and the students put their heads down on the desks and were told to relax and empty their minds. They were told they were going on a trip into an electromagnetic field. Prior to beginning the journey a relaxation exercise was performed to get everyone into a totally relaxed state. Unfortunately, with dirty tile floors we could not lie down so we had to settle for sitting at the desks. Everyone was told to imagine himself or herself as an electron and to concentrate on what it might feel like to be such an incredibly small piece of negative matter. They were told to consider the world around them and to imagine what it looked like. Most of the students said they felt like planet earth compared to the universe in size relationships and they visualized everything in very rapid motion. Huge swirls of gas were constantly battering them from side to side as they traveled throughout the universe.

The students were then told they were to encounter two very large coils of wire and around the wire there was a huge and rapidly changing force field. They were to enter the force field and feel the effects of it. They were then the electrons within the coil of wire as they were affected by the rapidly changing force field which is the electromagnetic field. After allowing them to spend time adrift within the field, I told the students that another coil of equal size and strength was coming toward them, that the two fields were interacting, and that the interaction would become very violent the closer the coils came to each other. The students were told that the increase in strength of one coil caused an increase in the strength of the other coil. This produced a super-strong force which moved the electrons (the students) very fast until the electromagnetic interacting forces ceased to interact.

When the fields no longer were in existence the students felt calm and then we went into a waking period. At the end of the waking period a small light was turned on and the experience was discussed. Surprisingly, most students agreed upon what they had felt. For example, when they were told to enter the coil, they all said they felt confined despite their size. When the second coil came to interact with the first coil, most of the students felt as if a tropical storm was occurring, except that it didn't rain. They said it was more like a huge violent multicolored stream of gas clouds swirling around them, something like being on a strange planet. Only one student did not want to enter the force field and he said he just stayed in space where it was calm. One other student fell asleep and we had to awaken him.

The time for the entire trip was thirty minutes. Most students did not feel that it was that short. They felt the trip had been at least an hour long.

Since the purpose of the trip was to gain understanding of an electromagnetic field and interaction of two fields, it remained to see how well we had done. The next day the students read the chapter in the book dealing with the inductive coils. The students said they had no trouble visualizing the forces described in the book and their qualitative work in the lab seemed to bear this out. It is quite evident to me that the trip was worth taking since I have taught this subject matter before but not with this much success. What remains to be done now, of course, is to teach the material again to two different sections of the class, using both methods, and then compare the results. At any rate, it was and is interesting, for there must be a better way to teach than the centuries-old lecture method.

ROBERT HABES:
USING FANTASY IN THE
ELEMENTARY CLASSROOM

Because of the supply of methods presented in transpersonal psychology, I was able to assemble a little unit in the area. I was able to teach subject areas also. The following is an outline of each method along with some evaluations or conclusions. With few exceptions all projects were done in my sixth-grade class.

The first idea I tried was using a candle for meditation. We were challenged to create images or let the mind roam as we concentrated upon the flame of a candle. From this point we quickly jotted down what we came up with. Then the most "powerful" phrases were circled, edited, and written in poetic form; this idea was adapted from "Do You Have a Dream for English?" Although I was skeptical about such a large class trying this, I had few problems, and enthusiasm for other projects was generated. Two important points were worth observing. First, the creative images which were produced surprised even the students in retrospect. No individual had an "intellectual" advantage. Second, it may be that there is great creative capacity within all of us; only the ability to fetch it up and give it meaning differs from individual to individual. The ability to give meaning to creativity may be easier to learn than we might imagine.

The students were dramatically proud of their efforts, and we concluded with a display of their work. A reinforcement for poetry may finally be at hand.

My next endeavor was that of a fantasy journey. I made a relaxation tape recording, then taped a journey similar to the "mountain" journey.* As I made the tape I tried to include as many non-specifics as possible. Examples include: "See what you can see . . . something glowing . . . get rid of it [I didn't say how]. . .enter the opening [some did not see caves]. . .figure of *someone* [a large variety of answers]. . .how do you feel?" The class was excited at the differences in experiences, and many were quite proud of the uniqueness of a particular image. The results of such an experience are intangible and difficult to measure. One can only observe and draw conclusions, hoping to be as objective as possible. It seemed almost immediately that the class was better able to get themselves into a frame of mind suitable for thought or work. There is one reality which I cannot deny, however. Any teacher will attest to the rigors of Fridays. Following the first Thursday fantasy we had the best Friday I have ever experienced.

During the next fantasy journey I discovered that unspecific sounds create wonderful images. An airplane passed overhead while I was tape recording the journey in preparation for class. Since it seemed to fit the dialog, I increased the volume to pick it up. When the students listened to the tape in class, they saw waves, trains, planes, and planets. During this second fantasy my goal was to evoke physical and emotional feelings. Those included: "You are disappearing . . . only a thought remains . . . drift around . . . feel better than you ever felt before in your life . . . running faster . . . leaving the ground . . . flying over treetops . . . faster . . . earth disappears . . . you are becoming light itself . . . filling up your body. . .full circle. . .coming back."

I have been overwhelmed by the willingness and ability of the children to remain completely still, without a motion, for thirty minutes. Six months ago I would have laughed at the idea. Peter S———, an extremely active child, seems calmed down considerably. He also gets down to work much more quickly.

---

*A fantasy journey in which the students are led (imaginatively) up a mountain to a cave, then instructed to go inside for an adventure.

We had a discussion about dreams and what possible bearing they have on our lives. We talked about the directed dreams of Malayan children and the different ways in which dreams could be better remembered or evoked.* During all of our talks the class was in a state which only elementary teachers really understand: all eyes on whomever the speaker was, no outside interruptions, mouths open. Once started, it is amazing how eagerly children want to look inward and learn about themselves.

In an effort to make these efforts coincide with our district curriculum, I grasped at ways to include certain subject matter in the fantasy journey. Finally I hit upon taking a fantasy journey over the geographic regions of the Soviet Union. Actually, this journey lends itself to some really fascinating imagery including: "Feel the cold of the earth . . . frozen just below the surface of the earth (tundra) . . . soaring over the forests from coast to coast . . . a green wave . . . feel dry warmth of the desert . . . sand between your feet . . . soar above the snow-capped mountains." Four days after this journey I put four objective questions about the regions on a quiz. Nearly all students got these questions right even though I had not reinforced this trip or any of the concepts. Obviously, the students had a visual picture.

CLAUDIA BINTER:
FANTASY IN THE FIRST GRADE

Whenever I ask the children to write a story, I always hear "I don't know what to write." I feel that all of us are creative, but it is a matter of knowing how to get at our creativity and use it. Fantasy trips are an experience which teachers can use to help solve this problem. I asked the children to find a space on the floor, lie down, and we went through a relaxation period of about seven minutes. Their reaction to this was one of giggling. Only about four of the children were seriously taking part. I guided them along a beach, walking along, feeling the water and sand. They then found an object on the beach, picked it up, looked at it and felt it. Afterwards we discussed their experiences. What they did, how the sand and water felt, what they found in the sand, and what they did with their object were all questions I asked.

*See the section on Senoi dream work in *The Centering Book*.

The second time I tried a fantasy trip with the class, the children were much more responsive. There was not the silliness during the relaxation period that I had observed previously. I asked them to stand at the bottom of a mountain looking up. They were to climb the path which led up the mountain. I asked them to stop suddenly before a cave and then go in. They were to see something in the cave, then climb back down the mountain. This time I asked them to write about their experience. One child exclaimed, "I'm going to need about three pages to tell everything I did!" This type of preparation before a creative writing session is very beneficial. Their story is something they have just experienced, and the image is fresh in their minds. Through the use of visual imagery, creative writing is much more successful, and it also avoids the frustration of not knowing what to say.

To try a slightly different approach to the fantasy trip, I asked the children to find a space on the floor and proceeded with a short relaxation period. After the session they were asked to remain in the same position while listening to the record *Peter and the Wolf*. The record tells the story but leaves time for the children to use their imaginations and visualize the scenes during the interval of music. The children were relaxed and quietly listened to the music and story. Afterwards, I asked them to show me what they had seen and felt during the record through the medium of fingerpaints. I told them that if they had been thinking about something other than the story, to show that. I also played the record over again while they were fingerpainting. Most of the children worked quietly: if they spoke, it was in a whisper. The children are always in a rush when doing any art project, but they were much more relaxed during this project and took their time. They seemed to enjoy it more. Afterwards I discussed the picture with the individual child. Most of them drew pictures which were related to the story. However, one child pictured the duck eating the wolf instead of the wolf eating the duck. There were a few children who painted pictures that were not related to the story.

Many of the ways in which transpersonal psychology can be used are not applicable to a first-grade classroom. However, there are transpersonal experiences which would be very profitable for the young, such as dreams and the use of fantasy trips. If personal awareness is to be fully achieved by an individual, it should begin at an early age in order that the individual may function at a higher level by the time he reaches adulthood.

From *Psychic Development*

Jean Porter

The area of psychic phenomena seems to be universally interesting. In this article, Jean Porter dispels the notion that this is a mysterious faculty possessed by only a few, arguing, instead, that all of us possess untapped potential for what she calls NSP—normal sense perception. Jean, who had her psychic abilities awakened through techniques like those in this article, now teaches classes on psychic development in Berkeley.

There are several reasons why I have written this as well as why I teach classes in psychic development. One is to dispel the mystique of the psychic and remove superstitious and spooky interpretations of its function in our lives. The other is to encourage you to explore and develop your own NSP, or *Normal Sense Perception.* Such an exploration will remove the incredulity which so often surrounds the prospect of considering and experiencing your own psychic abilities. Everyone has psychic abilities. Not everyone has explored some of the ways to develop them. . . .

NOW TO BEGIN . . .

The first step involves going inward to find a place which for you is experienced as an inner sanctuary, a retreat, or a place of inner peace. This is a real place in the inner environment of your mind and is to be explored with care, delight, and a sense of discovery. You will use the psychic abilities of seeing, hearing, and sensing as well as telepathic communication.

There is a distinction I want to make regarding your experience of *mental pictures.* These occur in two different modes which are important to understand. The two modes are *active imaging and receptive visualizing. Active imaging,* often called active imagination, is an intentionally created product of the conscious mind. This mode of expression has an electric or "moving-out quality" of energy which is aggressive in its nature and is very dynamic when intensely focused. Most cultures value the active, creative imagination because it helps one to be productive in the world. There is a doingness about it which we active Westerners like. Through active imaging we create buildings, transportation systems, educational processes, diagnostic techniques, and so on. Children as well as adults are usually highly praised for the fruits of their creative imaging.

Receptive visualizing, however, is a different experience which you have of the capacity to make mental pictures. It is the psychic ability called clairvoyance, in which pictures are *received* by the perceptual, subconscious part of the mind. There is a change in the quality of your mental energy in that it becomes magnetic or "drawing-in." This quality of receptive visualization occurs often in meditation when you have stilled the active part of your mind. I want to emphasize that this is not a passive state, as it may appear to be outwardly. Rather, it is a state of awareness which is *receptive* to whatever impressions, thoughts, pictures, or feelings may pass through it.

You probably have experiences with this receptive state of conscious without realizing it. When you were staring off into space without conscious thoughts, suddenly the picture of someone's face flashed before you. Perhaps in the wee hours of the morning when you have been in that half-waking, half-sleeping state you may have heard a voice say something to you, or heard some music coming from what seemed to be nowhere. You may have experienced a strong feeling that something was not going well for someone you were very close to. As an example of this later, or clairsentience experience, I will share with you something which recently happened to me.

A very close friend of mine had left for Europe for several months on business. One particular characteristic of this man which relates to this experience is the way he handles himself when he either is weary from a lot of traveling or confronted with a lot of chaotic disturbances around him. He withdraws into himself and just sort of disappears emotionally until he has sorted things out and is centered within himself again. For about two weeks after he had left I had not been in communication with him by mail. I awoke one morning with the strong feeling that he had totally disappeared from the face of the earth! I don't mean that he had died, just that he had withdrawn. So I opened my receptive channel and waited for impressions to come which would clarify the situation for me. I received pictures of him traveling a great deal, working hard, being surrounded by strangers most of the time and just simply becoming exhausted so that he had to withdraw to replenish his own energies. This withdrawal and my reception of it lasted for three and a half days. My experience was that I, too, was feeling weary, low on energy, and sensing chaos in my surroundings. However, when I looked at my own schedule, it simply did not warrant such a feeling. About the fourth day, my sense of withdrawnness totally lifted and, again, there was nothing within my daily events to explain what I had experienced. As it happened, a few days later I talked with my friend on the telephone and asked him what had been going on with him the previous week. He described exactly what I had seen and felt. It coincided with the days I had experienced it. We both laughed at this discovery and decided to use this openness to one another to explore some more areas psychically, inasmuch as there were some eight thousand miles of land between us. Over the next few weeks we each discovered many delightful new things and learned a great deal about our inner processes.

What I have just described was a personal psychic experience. To demonstrate that similar experiences are possible for you, I want to give you a very simple process to do. You can read the instructions and experience the visualization at the same time. Pause at the dots to clearly experience what is there with each step. If you like, you can have a friend read this process to you while you experience it. This is more effective because you can close your eyes and shut out all that your physical eyes usually observe.

Close your eyes and relax . . . See a familiar room which you are not now physically occupying . . . Be aware of all the textures, colors, and shapes . . . See each object within the room . . . Notice the placement of decorative items . . . Be aware of fragrances and odors . . . Listen to sounds inside or outside the room . . . When you have seen, heard, smelled, sensed all that you want to, return to your present location by opening your eyes or refocusing on the words on this page.

The experience you just had will give you an idea of how the mind receives a mental picture and all that is related to it. I didn't specify the room. Your mind received it. You were not physically in the room. You were mentally there.

Here is another process for you to do:

Close your eyes and relax . . . See, in your mind's eye, a supermarket . . . Enter it and go to the produce section . . . See a large bin of fresh, juicy oranges . . . Go over to it and select an orange which meets all of your qualifications . . . Pick it up and hold it in your hands . . . Feel the weight of it . . . Experience the texture of the rind . . . Smell the fragrance . . . Now, with your thumb break into the center of it and begin to peel the skin . . . Be aware of the effect of the citrus fragrance within your nose . . . When the skin is removed, feel the difference in texture of the orange . . . Again, with your thumb, break open the segments . . . Place a segment into your mouth and bite into it . . . Sense the juice flowing around in your mouth as it mixes with the saliva . . . Chew on the pulp . . . Feel the cool, refreshing juice slide down your throat . . . One by one, consume each of the sections, being aware of all of the sensations you experience . . . When the orange is gone go to the bin where there are some fresh lemons . . . Select one and take time to examine it as you did the orange . . . When you are ready, pick up a small knife nearby and cut the lemon open . . . Place a slice in your mouth and suck the juice from it . . . Be aware of the experience your mouth is having . . . Smell the lemon rind . . . Feel the juice slip down your throat . . . When you have had all that you want of the lemon, return from the experience simply by opening your eyes.

Again, this is a simple process whereby the mind enables you to experience many different things which are not in your actual physical environment. I have given you these two simple processes in order to prepare you for a more extensive inward journey. To fully realize this inner experience will require that you first use the active, creative part of your mind to follow my instructions. Then you will move to the receptive visualizing part of your mind and allow to come to you whatever is there to be received. Once you have received new information in this way you can move back into the active mode and evaluate whether or not and how you want to use the information. Become aware, as you undertake this journey, of the rhythm that is right for you in moving from one of the modes of your mind to the other. If I were sitting there with you, guiding your inward journey, I would sense the rhythm of your unfolding visions and go with it. For instance, when I take people through this process in my class, some go through it completely in about ten minutes while others take fifteen or twenty minutes. Since I am not sitting with you, the reader of this book, you will have to find your own sense of timing.

When you are ready to begin your journey, have someone read these instructions to you or read them and pause at each step to allow the visualization to present itself to you.

Close your eyes and relax . . . In your mind's eye see or sense yourself projected into a natural scene . . . See a place unfold before you, as if on a screen, a place which gives you a strong feeling of warm, uncomfortable, peaceful, relaxed safety . . . It might be a setting at the seashore, in the mountains, by a lake, in a meadow, etc. . . . Just get a sense of what the general area is like . . . Keep your eyes closed and take time to allow the details of this scene to pass through your mind . . . Allow your awareness to encompass the colors, textures, shapes, spaces, forms, sounds, and general ambience of your place . . . When you have noted the details of this inner sanctuary of the mind, get a sense of or begin to see a pathway emerging near where you are standing. Notice that off in the distance it blends with the scenery . . . Sense yourself walking along this path . . . As you look down the path or off in the distance you become aware of a radiant, blue-white glow which is moving slowly toward you . . . As you approach it, it gradually becomes transparent . . . Now the outline of a human form takes shape, although light continues to emanate from it . . . Slowly you see some garments covering the figure of this human-like form . . . As you and this figure come closer to each other, the details of the face, hair, eyes, bone structure and stature of this being become clearer . . . You now are aware as to whether this being is masculine in appearance and energy or feminine . . . In a warm, friendly manner this being approaches you . . . When you are quite close, you reach over and swiftly peel off the face as if it were a mask . . . Observe what is there . . . If, under the mask, there is a face which is frightening to you, step back and demand that the being leave your sanctuary, then mentally let go of it . . . Return to the path, walk along it and again see the radiant, blue-white glow beyond you. Slowly move toward it, repeating this part of the process . . . If, after the mask is peeled off, the face remains essentially the same, this being is your guide who now approaches you and placing an arm around your shoulder, leans close to your ear and whispers softly, "I am _____" . . . Now hear the name being spoken . . . Receive the first one that comes.

I would like to stop your inward journey here a moment and talk about what you may have experienced. I specifically did not do this to begin with as I didn't want you to have any expectations concerning what might happen. I wanted you to receive naturally whatever came. Now, let's look at what that may have been. First of all, if the sanctuary in which you found yourself seemed dark and formidable or even hostile, that could hardly be considered a place of peace, tranquility, and safety.

Go back and do the whole process again some other time when you are in a mood that is more positive and receptive. It's sort of like spooky places are out and safe, peaceful places are in. Okay? Now, what about the being or essence or personality or entity (whichever term you choose) who appeared out of the radiant glow? Well, if it seemed to be someone living whom you know, greet them as you would at any time and then let them go. This is not your spirit guide, which is the designation I give to that energy force field which you perceived on the path. If the being is in the physical body of a friend, they have all the limitations of the physical body, as do you, and so will be limited to their guidance, also. A true spirit guide has no such limitation.

What has happened is that this spirit guide, a nonphysical part of yourself but not a product of your imagination, is perceived by your receptive visualization as a form to which you can relate as you would to a friend. It is the expression of your higher consciousness, perceived as a form by the subconscious, psychic mind.

A Few Well-Chosen Words

O. M. Burke

Some people focus on an interest in psychic phenomena to the neglect of a more holistic approach to growth. A broader view of psychic matters sees them as events that may occur while on a deeper search for personal growth, but which can impede development if unduly emphasized. Patanjali, for example, who codified Indian yoga practices 1,500 years ago, listed a number of psychic phenomena (among them walking on water, clairvoyance) which occasionally emerged during the practice of yoga. At the end of this presentation of enticing potential powers, Patanjali says: "These are all barriers to spiritual growth."

In the selection that follows, a Sufi master addresses a group of persons who have sought his advice concerning psychic phenomena. The Sufis, a spiritual brotherhood whose members are largely in the Mideast and Asia, are known for their ability to develop psychic powers in a holistic framework.

Standing in the middle of his audience, the teacher immediately started to speak:

"Welcome. For as far back as there is any recorded history, people have been interested in two things: whether they would survive death,

"A Few Well-Chosen Words" (editors' title). From O. M. Burke, *Among the Dervishes* (The Octagon Press, Ltd., 1972), pp. 144–45. Copyright © 1973 and reproduced by permission.

and seemingly occult phenomena. Students of humanity in every branch of science and scholastic discipline have tried to account for this interest. The method which most people seem to adopt in their search for the answers to the questions implicit in the two forms of interest to which I have referred has usually been the same. This method is to seek out things which seem to indicate the supernatural. Then the phenomena are studied and attempts are made to create or duplicate these phenomena. Alternatively, people who seem to control or to be controlled by their phenomena, to whatever degree, are sought and followed. One moment's thought, which few people will spare in their eagerness to find something out, would show the weakness of this method of approaching the supernatural phenomenon. I therefore invite you to ask yourselves, individually and collectively, what method you have established that you are competent to judge either theories or so-called proofs.

"This has never been established. The method which you are using is to try to understand something by means of something which is not objective: your ordinary, or even abnormal, mind.

"The Sufis in general will not discuss these matters with people who are not Sufis. The reason is that if they did, the non-Sufis would consider that they were mad; and the Sufis would be able to make no progress. Few people in their right minds would attempt to discuss, or evaluate, nuclear physics without preparation for the task. Yet almost every human being feels that he can have a reasonable opinion about the supernatural. He asks for information, it is true, for phenomena, for tales and demonstrations. But he does not ask for basic training to enable him to understand. This is like the child who goes to a school for the first time and expects to be taught a foreign language at an advanced level, without having any basic knowledge about that language, and what makes it up.

"The child is, not unnaturally, impatient. This is a characteristic of children. He sees people talking in a foreign language, and wants to know one, too. He sees the wonder, but not the mechanism. He asks questions which have no answers which he would understand, like: 'Who is the Moon?' or 'Why are two and two not three?' The child, however, can be told by the teacher or parent that 'It is so because it is so'; or 'This does not matter at the moment—eat up your food.' The 'raw' seeker after supernatural truth *can,* of course, be told these things by a teacher. But, unlike the ordinary infant, he will drift away from the stern 'parent' who talks like this. You can imagine the plight of the tiny infant who, instead of allowing the parent to discount his questionings, slips away and tries to live on his own: or seeks, every few days, another parent who will teach him the things he wants to know: not the things which he should be taught.''

The *Chutzpah* Factor in the Psychophysiology of Altered States of Consciousness

Kenneth Pelletier and Erik Peper

Biofeedback has been called the yoga of the West, because it combines Western hardware with Eastern techniques for altering states of consciousness. Pelletier and Peper, both young biofeedback researchers, present an account of remarkable phenomena and point to ways in which children might be trained to be masters of their bodies.

Biofeedback has been heralded as a quick path to the attainment of the higher states of consciousness exhibited by yogis and advanced meditators. In addition to this popular interest, meditation and biofeedback have emerged as a prominent area of research and clinical application in neurology, psychophysiology, and medicine, as well as the study of consciousness. Sophisticated instrumentation and computer analysis have enabled modern researchers to probe the nature of human consciousness with unprecedented accuracy.

Although the phenomenon of a marked degree of autonomic control has received much recent attention and has been recounted in anecdotes for hundreds of years, it also has been empirically verified since 1935

"The Chutzpah Factor in the Psychophysiology of Altered States of Consciousness" by Kenneth Pelletier and Erik Peper. Used with permission of the authors and the *Journal of Humanistic Psychology*.

when the French cardiologist Thérèse Brosse first recorded a marked degree of heart-rate control in yogis (Brosse, 1946). Since that time, there have been several major research projects which have reported marked degrees of brain wave, heart rate, and blood flow control. One of the most productive approaches to the study of altered states of consciousness and to the interaction between mind and body has been the intensive study of adept individuals.

Beginning in May 1971, Erik Peper heard about a visiting South American, a man who practiced unusual control over pain and bleeding, who walked on fire, had himself hoisted by hooks in the back, and regularly punctured his flesh without damage with sharpened bicycle spokes. We hoped that by taking physiological recordings from people who do these feats, we could convert this information to help the average person gain control over pain, bleeding, and other purportedly involuntary body functions.

Our intention has been to formulate a model of biofeedback and altered state phenomena which is comprehensive enough to encompass both subjective and physiological states. First, we approached the task of verifying whether or not these reported marked degrees of autonomic control were true. If true, the next issue was to have these adepts demonstrate their abilities under laboratory conditions in order to determine how they achieved this control. From this research, we hoped to create a biofeedback paradigm to teach others to attain comparable levels of autonomic control and psychological tranquility. It is important to note that each of these adepts maintains that they have no special ability and that anyone can attain an equal degree of autonomic autoregulation through concerted practice and meditation.

This first subject, a young Ecuadorian (R.C.T.), agreed on June 2, 1971, to spend a day and a half demonstrating his controls in a New York University laboratory. In an overcrowded EEG laboratory in the psychology department, while people churned around to gawk, Peper recorded the subject's EEG, heart rate, and GSR (galvanic skin response). R.C.T. proceeded to: chew and swallow pieces of an electric light bulb; to push sharpened bicycle spokes through one cheek, through the center of his mouth, and out through the other cheek . . . and push these spokes through the sides of his body while physiological parameters were measured. When R.C.T. pushed the unsterilized sharpened spokes through the skin, the presence of occipital alpha activity increased to 100% time in his EEG and the amplitude increased 73% over the eyes-closed baseline. This is unusual since normally we would expect alpha to block, which would indicate a stress response. Even though he has performed such punctures many times, he has few scars on his body.

According to such adepts, anyone can learn to control the pain and bleeding by quickly relaxing and then detaching their awareness (consciousness) away from the insertion point, since "pain is mainly the fear of pain and one's attention to pain." In R.C.T.'s case, he entered his meditative state rapidly and upon command, and this resulted in a rapid, unfocusing relaxation, and dissociation from any stimuli.

This experiment suggested that it may be possible to control pain by increasing alpha EEG. Based upon the research with R.C.T., a pilot study was conducted with two subjects who learned to increase their alpha with feedback as a means of pain control. One went to the dentist and kept her alpha on and therefore did not need novacain, while the other subject stuck safety pins through the back of his hand. The model would suggest that pain control seems to work if there is no alpha blockage.

Later in July 1972, with Marjorie and Herschel Toomim, Peper studied a 31-year-old karate expert, J.S.L., who placed a sharpened spoke through a fold in the skin of his forearm and suspended a 25-pound bucket of water from it.

The karate expert's occipital EEG consisted mainly of beta activity with some low-amplitude alpha; although the frontal leads showed some slowing, the main physiological change was an increase of the EKG from 81 to 100 beats when he stressed himself. He reported that instead of passively detaching his attention from his body, he focused upon a small point of energy which he subjectively moved upward from the bottom of his abdomen to a point where he inserted the needle. "Once you concentrate on that square, you can allow the energy to flow into any part of the body. The concentrated mind can be applied to anything it does, and when it is applied, it no longer feels. The concentrated mind is the activity itself; it does not exist in the world." Rather than a detachment of the experience, there was a total focus on sensation. This focus was associated with the absence of alpha, since alpha usually blocks when a person responds to stimulation. The common factor in the case of R.C.T. and the karate expert was the ability to maintain a fixed focus of attention. Whether the attention was focused away from or directly upon the puncture, the ability to control the pain remained the same.

Most recently, during August 1973, J.S. was tested by K. Pelletier in Dr. Joe Kamiya's Psychophysiology Laboratory at the Langley Porter

Neuropsychiatric Institute. In a week-long period of intensive research, J.S. pushed an unsterilized, sharpened knitting needle through his left bicep on three occasions while under the observation of an attending physician. . . . While he performed these punctures, he was being monitored on twelve psychophysiological channels which indicated [that he had] no response to the pain, and that he remained in a state of high alpha meditation before, during, and after the puncture. Previous bleeding: time tests had indicated that J.S. bled and responded to pain normally while out of his meditation state. J.S. was able to control completely the bleeding from those punctures and to heal the wounds within twenty-four hours without infection. (Similar findings have been reported about J.S. when he was tested in 1971 at the Menninger Foundation in Topeka, Kansas, and also with R.C.T.) When asked how he accomplished this control, he responded, "It's very simple. I do it by changing a single word. I don't stick a needle in *my* arm, I stick a needle through *an* arm. I move outside my body and look at the arm from a distance; with that detachment, it becomes an object. It is as though I am sticking the needle into the arm of a chair." This paradoxical degree of meditative awareness and detachment, often called "passive attention," has been observed to be a consistent characteristic of all of these adepts who are able to achieve a marked degree of autonomic control. Based upon this research, a clinical pilot study was performed with a patient suffering from pain due to multiple reconstructive surgeries on his face. Through alpha feedback the patient learned to progressively dissociate himself from the pain of a pin stuck in the back of his hand, and no alpha blocking was evidenced. This dissociation was successfully carried over into surgery. In many cases research with these adepts changed our belief structure of what is possible in self-control and self-healing and has helped to extend the parameters and possibilities of biofeedback training.

These demonstrations of autonomic control are important and impressive because they indicate that anyone can assert control over the healing process. The deeper meaning resides in the psychological state which permits such control to occur. All of these individuals have trained themselves to assume a particular transpersonal view of themselves which was summarized by Swami Rama as "all of the body is in the mind, but not all of the mind is in the body." This statement suggests that these individuals are able to enter into a meditative state of focused attention in which they are aware of but detached from their physical bodies. While such a concept appears alien to Western psychology, it has been an accepted aspect and goal of all Eastern meditative systems for centuries.

Implications of these meditative systems and our research indicates that individuals could be taught to control bleeding and pain in accidents, while undergoing surgery, or in a dentist's office. Also, this highly specific degree of control may be of use in such instances as cutting off blood flow to an inoperable tumor, correcting essential hypertension, or in the self-control over a migraine attack, headaches, epileptic seizures, or ulcers.

Based upon our research with adept individuals, both authors worked from the assumption that a very marked degree of autonomic control is possible. We have trained a number of subjects to attain voluntary control over electromyographic tension, peripheral temperature, galvanic skin response, and EEG with biofeedback.

An implicit assumption of our research is that any physiological function which can be monitored, amplified, and made visible or audible to the person can be brought under voluntary control. For example, some of our subjects have been able to increase their hand temperature as much as 18 °F, which means that there is a highly significant change in local blood blow. Similarly, subjects can be trained with feedback to control *single motor units.* This implies that with practice we can have voluntary control over single neuron firing. Thereby we have the ability to control our bodies to the micro level, again reinforcing our notion that we could heal ourselves through voluntary control. Possibly the localized control may explain the phenomenon of stigmata.

While some promising clinical work with biofeedback has been conducted with several of the disorders cited above, our research with individuals such as J.S., R.C.T., and J.S.L. has indicated that an even greater degree of self-initiated healing and personal growth is possible.

In studying these adepts, we have noted that physiological recording has been inadequate to assess some of the most important attributes of these remarkable individuals. Although the psychophysiological recordings, especially the EEG, have been of considerable importance in formulating biofeedback training paradigms, we feel that a considerable amount of information is deleted by focusing exclusively on the psychophysiology. In our experience, multivariate analytic techniques are necessary but not sufficient for explaining these phenomena. One of the most important factors excluded from a purely physiological analysis is how the control was initially developed and maintained. By studying the self-training procedure and the inner dynamics of these adepts, we hope to improve the range and technique of biofeedback training by focusing on the learning process. Without formal instruction, these adepts have learned to master their own fear. Often during childhood and early adolescence they created challenging situations for themselves with an attendant audience so that they had to perform or be seen as a "fool," since sticking needles in yourself is "obviously" a foolish act, but failing to do it after claiming it is even more foolish. By experiencing success in the mastery of these "foolish deeds," the adept learned "that the limit of their experience was the limit of their belief." This is the lesson which is taught by many meditative systems.

There are many disciplines, such as yoga, Zen, Tai Chi, judo, karate, which instruct individuals to overcome their own fear and obtain psychological and physiological mastery. In these various disciplines, the initiates are brought to the point where they must go beyond the teaching and incorporate the training in their own manner. Some individuals continue as perpetual students, others drop out, and a few succeed in true mastery.

Initial attainment of true mastery means going beyond what the individual initially thought was possible. Instead of looking at the precipice and retreating, the initiate must take the leap into the unknown. In many systems, the teacher pushes and allows no retreat by the student. This ability to transcend fear and enter into the unknown we have called the *"chutzpah* factor."* This *chutzpah* quality is most readily seen in our two subjects J.S. and R.C.T., since they developed themselves without the initial help of teachers or systems.

This process of self-discipline endowed them with an unusual degree of self-confidence and daring. Psychophysiological training and meditation were not the initial means by which they achieved voluntary control. These men taught themselves to achieve a remarkable degree of control and that ability was induced and sustained by this psychological quality of chutzpah. In our interviews, we noted that both of these men shared some common personality characteristics which appear to be elements of the chutzpah factor. One aspect of this factor is that they were rewarded in childhood for performing unusual feats such as R.C.T. hypnotizing his friends and then painlessly sewing buttons on their arms, or J.S.

---

*The *chutzpah* factor is a multidimensional parameter which has many interrelated factors and is best illustrated in the following example: At trial for murdering both his mother and father, the defendant pleaded for the mercy of the court because he was an orphan.

learning to lie upon a bed of nails with someone standing on his stomach. Under most conditions, such acts would be considered foolish or even destructive, but they are indicative of a unique state of self-awareness rather than simple antisocial acts.

Another important psychological factor which we have observed in these adepts is a willingness to accept what appears to be an impossible task or challenge. In fact, they appear to place themselves deliberately in demanding situations which will force them to perform a difficult task which they have never previously attempted. Most individuals avoid situations where failure may lead to physical or psychological injury. However, these adepts respond to challenges in a counter-phobic manner in the sense that they create situations in which the expectation of the people around them is sufficiently high that they are able to overcome their own fears and reservations. Hence, when R.C.T. claimed he could walk through fire (a wall of flames six feet wide and seven feet high) he did it before a live audience of 100 people and was shown on Channel 6 TV in Montreal on February 10, 1969. . . .

Lastly, another important psychological factor is the ability of these adepts to transcend social limitations and constraints. In terms of the Jungian types, the adepts appear to be extraverted intuitives who respond well to innovative and challenging situations. According to Jung, these individuals do not adhere to the socially accepted values and have a capacity to inspire and kindle enthusiasm for innovative views of social reality. Essentially, they are visionaries, and tend to express their vision in a convincing and charismatic manner. Since they have little patience for social convention or restraint, they may be unjustly condemned as insensitive or sensationalist, but this is mainly due to the fact that they value their conviction and unique view of reality above all else. They do not allow themselves to be constrained by the accepted limitations of social, physiological, or psychological standards, and thus they do not convince themselves that something is impossible before they have tried the task themselves. In essence, this quality of dramatic self-reliance accompanied by their own experience of themselves as capable of unusual tasks comprises the essence of the chutzpah factor. It is ironic that the educational system and childhood upbringing inhibits and punishes us for daring and chutzpah-inducing behavior, so that when a child has become an adult he has become afraid to try or afraid to "buck the system." Yet it is precisely these qualities, if maintained, which allow these adepts to achieve their self-mastery, a mastery which we now attempt to relearn by meditation and other forms of self-discipline.

Perhaps we could look at children and reward them for their daring, fearlessness, and for their "trouble making" instead of punishing them for the sake of conformity. In this manner we might reinforce the spirit of inquiry and self-assertiveness so that as adults they may not become helpless, hopeless victims, but responsible and competent for their own healing and growth process. It is our observation that patients who are trained (re-educated) with biofeedback not only learn control but also subtly change their attitudes and concepts which initially enhanced the disease process and take increased responsibility for their health.

Since this chutzpah factor has been developed to a pronounced degree in these adepts, there is a great deal which can be learned from their example. Their willingness to maintain an open mind concerning their fullest potential enables them to develop abilities which have been considered unlikely or impossible. An important factor in all systems of self-development and self-healing is the degree to which any individual believes in his ability to overcome obstacles of ill health or psychological distress. In research this is often dismissed or actively eliminated as experimental expectance, or placebo effects in clinical practice. All of the individuals discussed here, both adepts and patients, lend evidence to the power of volition and belief in the development of an individual's fullest potential. Today we are witnessing a remarkable convergence of ancient Eastern meditative systems and the most modern and sophisticated electronic instrumentations. Perhaps out of this interface there will emerge a Western yoga which will fulfill the arcane dictum of "know thyself." Above all else, the most striking aspect of this Western yoga is that it demonstrates that man has limited his growth through his own beliefs rather than through necessity. By daring to dream, imagine, and challenge these self-imposed limitations, man can learn to fulfill his human potential.

RELATED READING

T. BARBER et al., eds., *Biofeedback and Self-Control Reader,* 1970, 1971, 1972, Chicago: Aldine-Atherton, 1971, 1972, 1973.

BROSSE, THERESE, "A Psycho-Physiological Study," *Main Currents in Modern Thought,* 1946: 4, 77–84.

GREEN, E. E., A. M. GREEN, E. D. WALTERS, *A Demonstration of Voluntary Control of Bleeding and Pain.* Unpublished report, The Menninger Foundation, March 9, 1972.

KAMIYA, J., "Conscious Control of Brain Waves," *Psychology Today,* 1968:1, 57-60.

MULHOLLAND, T. B., "Biofeedback: It's Time to Try Hardware in the Classroom," *Psychology Today,* December 1973, 103-104.

PELLETIER, K. R., *Neurological, Psychophysiological, and Clinical Differentiation of the Alpha and Theta Altered States of Consciousness.* Unpublished Ph.D. dissertation, Psychology Clinic, University of California, Berkely, 1974.

PEPER, E., "Voluntary Pain Control: Physiological and Psychological Correlates," in *Alterations in Awareness and Human Potentialities,* ed. T. X. Barber. New York: Psychological Dimensions, Inc., 1974 (in press).

PEPER, E., *Biofeedback as a Core Technique in Clinical Therapies.* Paper presented at the American Psychological Association convention, Montreal, 1973.

Transpersonal Graduate Education

Robert Frager

Robert Frager is the director of the California Institute of Transpersonal Psychology, based in Palo Alto. It is probably the first program in the transpersonal domain to grant graduate degrees. The following brief selection is taken from the institute's brochure.

CURRICULUM

A graduate career devoted to purely intellectual development is no longer an adequate preparation for growth and research in psychology. The core of our program is the *balanced* development of the individual—the integration of the physical, emotional, intellectual, and spiritual aspects of the personality. Our goal is to explore and experience behavior in an environment that provides opportunities for intensive personal growth and integration.

"Transpersonal Graduate Education" by Robert Frager. From the brochure of the California Institute of Transpersonal Psychology that sets forth course offerings, faculty, etc. Used by permission of the author.

Five areas of study are emphasized. Each area involves intensive personal participation, academic study, and an emphasis on professional training related to therapy, counseling, teaching, and research. Tools for communication will be taught in each area.

1. Body Work

Students are expected to develop competence sufficient to teach a physical growth discipline or to practice professionally a body-oriented therapy. Body disciplines that will be available include:

Hatha Yoga	Alexander technique	Bioenergetics
T'ai-Chi	Feldenkrais method	Reichian therapy
Aikido	Dance and movement therapy	

Academic study includes course work in anatomy, physiology, nutrition, and kinesics. In addition to individual intensive training in a specific discipline, we provide basic familiarity with centering, relaxation, movement techniques, sexual therapy, and massage. We stress new ways of integrating various body disciplines and exploring how they complement one another.

2. Group Work

Extensive use of group techniques will allow students to work on communication skills and to develop a transpersonal orientation to group work, facilitating honesty, trust, and love. Instead of competition and grade-orientation we strongly emphasize the building of a sense of family, developing a supportive group community within the program. Specific systems include:

Gestalt Therapy	Rogerian group work
T.A.	Problem-oriented group work
Psychodrama	

3. Individual Work

Exposure to various techniques and systems of individual therapy and counseling will be available in order to facilitate personal development and clarification of individual goals, as well as for professional training. Systems offered include:

Psychoanalysis
Jungian analysis

Psychosynthesis
Client-centered therapy

4. Intellectual Work

At the core of the academic program is an in-depth study of a single system of philosophy or a single theorist in psychology, chosen by each student. General skills such as speed reading and memory training are offered. Students read what they are most interested in, teach each other what they have learned, and evaluate each other's work.

5. Spiritual Work

Emphasis is placed on a personal commitment to a specific path which will help to actualize each student's individual goals. We stress integration of one's spiritual discipline and perspective in daily life, along with periods of intensive retreat. The academic aspect will involve study of the Buddhist, Yogic, Jewish, and Christian traditions. Group meditation is a central part of the curriculum. Chanting, concentration exercises, and biofeedback training are also offered. We are working toward incorporating spiritual, transpersonal perspectives into all aspects of the program.

On Meditation

Wilson Van Dusen

Meditation is one of the foundations of transpersonal education. There are many ways to meditate—some easy, some more difficult. For example, most Zen masters advocate the cross-legged lotus position, which Westerners often find uncomfortable; on the other hand, Transcendental Meditation as taught by Maharishi Mahesh Yogi suggests that its practicioners sit in a comfortable chair. No matter what type of meditation is practiced, there are a number of observations that are commonly made as practice continues. Wilson Van Dusen, a psychologist who has been exploring inner spaces for many years, presents a concise summary of events that are likely to occur as persons explore their inner worlds through meditation.

Those who haven't spent hours meditating may well wonder why people bother. Those who have spent even twenty minutes a day meditating over a period of months are visibly different. They seem calmer, integrated, all together. It is as though they collected themselves and they remain collected. Their bodily movements are smoother, less hasty, more

"On Meditation (editors' title)." From Wilson Van Dusen, *The Natural Depth in Man* (New York: Harper & Row, 1972), pp. 75-79. Copyright © 1972 by Wilson Van Dusen. Reprinted with permission of Harper & Row Publishers, Inc.

balanced. On inquiry they show considerable sensitivity, both inward and outward. Their knowledge of inner experience is noticeably beyond the average. Practice at stilling the mind lends peace to the individual. It also intensifies inner processes so that the individual can embark on a free self-analysis. It is a very intimate kind of learning because one isn't verbally talking about experiences but is working within experience itself. Also, stilling the mind gives one a refuge that can always be entered. I remember in one bitter life experience I was also meditating on the beauty of flames in the fireplace. Much of psychic disorder seems to stem from the psyche feeling it has no real alternatives. It must work out *this* problem, whatever it is. Meditation opens up alternate worlds as valid as that of one's painful problems.

Meditation is quite closely related to dealing with feeling-images. While heading in the same general direction as when working with feeling, it involves a greater focusing and limiting of the attention with a consequent increase in spontaneous inner processes. Meditation exposes more of the underlying nature of human experience itself.

The possible discoveries from meditation can be arranged in a rough series. Your first experiences are likely to illustrate how unruly the mind is. When you try to fix on a spot, all kinds of ideas may go through your head. You will find yourself asking, "Why am I doing this? When can I quit? I should be doing some work, etc." You will also discover a host of itches and intruding sensations. If you identify with the statements that call you away from meditation, you soon quit. Or you can let them go by like the comments of some impatient stranger. You don't have to identify with everything said in your head! The itches are a more fundamental resistance. If you don't scratch them, your first meditation can focus around the agonies of itching. Scratch the worst of them, but don't let the stubborn animal within get away with too much.

As you get into meditation, the mind, finding itself bereft of the usual garbage that occupies it, begins playing like a child. Your attention wanders from this to that aspect of the spot you are focused on. Gradually meanings are suggested. At this level you are close to what is experienced in feeling-images. For a long while the mind will skip around from an extraneous sound, to an itch, to implied meanings in the spot, to tiring of the eyes, etc. You may wrestle with the issues in this skipping around. You may wonder if you make the skipping. Generally the answer is no. As the restless mind tires of one aspect it lights on anything else handy. It is almost like an animal desperate to be occupied. If you look closely you may find it is almost impossible to trace the fading of interest in one thing before another replaces it. In fact, you may find you just went through a blankness only after you suddenly realize you are focused on a new aspect. There is a pattern: noticing one thing, fading interest, blankness, new interest emerging, sudden realization you lost the old focus. You may also flash back and forth between sensory or inward awareness and rediscovery of the spot. This is the beginning of a number of discoveries that suggest the operations of mind are much more spontaneous than we normally suspect.

There are a number of sensory changes that can emerge. You notice different aspects of the spot: it can move, become something not seen before, change color, and even disappear. This goes along with a success-ful focusing on a visual stimulus. Then it will vary the stimulus itself. These variations take on more and more dramatic meaning as though the spot were beginning to perform. It should take relatively little effort at this point to understand how the performance is related to your own life, for, after all, the performance is made out of your nature. If the perfor-mance gets lively enough you can even inwardly ask the spot questions and have it enact answers. At this point the results of meditation are rich enough to hold the attention to the spot.

Along the way a long battle may develop over how all this is controlled. You may wish to adopt one attitude and find its opposite reigning. You may want to keep the mind focused, yet it wanders so cleverly. You may even want to divest yourself of willfulness only to find you are being so willful about it. This is perhaps the most difficult rock and shoal of meditation. Things go much easier if you learn early that the inner processes have a will of their own and simply follow that will to learn from its direction. There are several alternatives in meditation if you have the problem of unwilling will. Don't identify with acts of will. For instance, if you find yourself saying, "I don't want to control this," don't identify with this willful statement. Even the effort not to will is willful. Willing, choosing, deciding, can be split away as autonomous processes that happen and drift by. Another way out is to exhaust the will. If willfulness can't be let go of, then use it ruthlessly until it is worn out. Some sail by the rocks of willfulness easily because they enjoy watching the inner drift of mind and never particularly want to control it.

There are also several pleasant plateaus of experience you can stumble upon. There is the discovery that meditation is a world of its own and that it can be returned to any time not only as a refuge, but to gain perspective on the outer world. In this state you may enjoy long periods of just feeling pleasant and peaceful. From this perspective thoughts of the outer world may seem rather distant and unreal. It is possible to review your behavior in that outer world and feel it was unnecessarily frantic or foolish. At this point the mind has become tame to the centering process itself. It no longer balks at focusing as it did at first. Related to this plateau are pleasant discoveries about time itself. The formerly inexorable clock-ticking time may languidly spread out and discover its own peace. Hours can become moments or moments hours. Time becomes stretchable and quite relative. Time itself may disappear as a useless issue.

After the mind is tamed to focus, it then playfully lays out a number of possibilities that gradually knit into a general understanding. Here the power of the inner message begins to carry over into your life. Life experience is not just another harsher world now; it is one of the components of meditation, the component in which you try out new insights.

The above experiences are sufficient reason for meditation. Yet within meditation it is possible to achieve a much higher state that has become the main goal for some. This has variously been called enlightenment, satori, moksha, and other terms. It comes at first as a very brief experience of seeing into the nature of things. At higher levels there are periods of a loss of self-identity and a sudden awareness of the total nature of creation. The higher levels of this experience are relatively rare. It would be well not to bend all one's efforts to attain this kind of breakthrough because effort certainly does delay its appearance. It would be wiser to enjoy and master all the lower levels of meditation first. Satori is more likely to occur where the individual has come to understand himself in depth. And this understanding of the self in depth is sufficient reason in itself for meditation.

A Basic Meditation

C. G. Hendricks
Russel Wills

Here is an easily learned form of meditation that can be used with students of all ages. This technique uses the natural ability of the mind to observe itself.

THOUGHT WATCHING

One of the most interesting worlds to explore is the world inside our heads. Something is always going on there, even when we're sleeping.

Although it is essential that we learn to observe our thought processes in our quest for self-understanding, we do not learn as much as we could for at least two reasons. First, it takes practice to learn to observe accurately, and we do not receive much encouragement for engaging in this type of activity. Second, we are too evaluative in our observations. No sooner do we see a thought of feeling than we rush to label it *good* or *bad, right,* or *wrong.*

"A Basic Meditation" (editors' title). From Gay Hendricks and Russel Wills, The *Centering Book: Awareness Activities for Children, Parents, and Teachers* (Englewood Cliffs, N.J.: Prentice-Hall, Inc., 1975), pp. 29-31. © 1975 by Prentice-Hall, Inc. Reprinted by permission of the publisher.

One type of meditation, which originated in the Orient, involves just watching our thoughts in a nonevaluative way. The goal is to see the thoughts, images, and sounds as they are, without making judgments about them. And when we find ourselves making judgments about the thoughts, we try to observe those judgments.

This activity can be done by sitting or lying down.

Instructions

"Settle back and let your body relax, and as your body begins to quiet down and become comfortable, let your eyelids close. Relax a while in the darkness, letting your body become peaceful and comfortable. As you lie there, feel around until you find a place where you can find your pulse, and when you do, rest your fingers lightly on that place and get in touch with the quiet rhythm of your pulse as it moves the blood through your body."

Pause (thirty seconds)

"And now in the quiet, let's begin watching our thoughts and feelings that come through our minds . . . just looking and listening for the pictures and sounds in our heads. Pictures, voices, scenes, music, whatever comes in, just watch and listen . . . just observe. When you find yourself lost in thought, just return to watching and listening."

Pause (three to four minutes; work up to about ten minutes as the exercise is repeated).

"Now in the future, when you find yourself angry, sad, or bored, or in any kind of mood, happy or sad, just watch and listen to what is going on inside your head. This will help get you in touch with how you are feeling.

"Let yourself become alert at your own speed. Feel the alertness come into your body, stretching a little to feel more alert. Open your eyes and let the light in, feeling rested and calm."

Education and the Body

William C. Shutz

The body plays an important role in transpersonal education. Just as meditation, imagery, and dreamwork are ways of overcoming the conditioning placed upon the mind, there are many activities that can help the body overcome its history of negative conditioning. William Schutz, one of the pioneers of the human potential movement, presents an introduction to the role of the body.

THEORY OF PERSONALITY

Physiological aspect. The body is born with an inherited potential growth. Under optimal conditions all organs will grow to their capacity in size, function, and flexibility. Part of this growth—vegetative functions, emergency reactions, and so on—is determined by the lower centers of the brain, is primarily inherited, and only with great difficulty or

"Education and the Body" (editors' title) by William C. Shutz. From Raymond Corsini, ed., *Current Psychotherapies* (Itasca, Ill.: F. E. Peacock Publishers, Inc., 1973), pp. 408-11. Reproduced by permission of the publisher.

with esoteric methods (such as biofeedback) is subject to alteration by external factors. Another part of the growth of the body is determined by the higher brain centers, the cortex, and is subject to external factors including learning. Man differs from lower animals in the relatively small percentage of his capacity that is instinctive and the relatively large proportion that is subject to learning (Feldenkrais, 1972).

As a person develops, if his tissues and organs are all used in the various ways in which they are capable of being used, he develops to his full potential. Of course, no one does. Three factors prevent it: physical trauma, emotional trauma, and limited use.

To see how these factors inhibit growth, conceive of a person as a process rather than as a static entity. Most of the body is, in fact, in constant change. Except for the nervous system, all body cells are replaced approximately every two years. The person can be viewed as a process throughout time, starting at the moment the sperm enters the ovum. Seeing the person as a process can also be put in terms of constant transformations of energy, a concept that will prove valuable later.

As the body/person/process evolves through time, this optimal unfolding is altered by the three factors mentioned above. The distinction between natural or unimpeded evolution and optimal evolution is important. Unimpeded development, that is, development without trauma, will not lead to the body's development of all of its potential. The simple act of not impeding the child's sense of sound will not lead to his having a concert master's ear. His ear will be unflawed but not extraordinary. Similarly, growing up without being impeded does not guarantee full growth, as many classic studies of babies raised without sufficient handling have shown (Goldfarb, 1943).

As we view the body/person/process evolving through time, trauma and limits begin to affect body form, just as strong winds, fires, overcrowding, and periodic lack of nourishment affect the growth of a tree. And as with the tree the effect of these external factors can be read by observing the physical structure.

Physical trauma can interfere with the natural growth process (Rolf, 1972) just as constant external interference (pruning) reduces a fullgrown tree to a midget bonsai. Suppose that a boy breaks an ankle early in life. During the healing process he feels unsteady on his feet and throws his weight forward onto his toes. This imbalance must be compensated for or else he will fall forward. The compensation may be accomplished by tightening the muscles in the small of the back. If these muscles become too strong, the body will fall backward so another compensation is made by thrusting the head forward. The resulting posture thus restores the feeling of body balance though at the cost of muscle tensions in the legs, back, and neck.

If this posture is adopted, through time, the muscle tensions become chronic and the muscle and connective tissue grow to hold these muscles in a rigid position. The muscles lose their ability to flex and relax as appropriate. Also, related structures are affected. The tight muscle, for example, may constrict a local blood vessel, partially closing it and restricting the blood supply to neighboring areas. Or the lungs may be prevented from inflating fully, thus cutting down on the oxygen supply. Or the spinal nerves issuing from the aberrated spine may be impinged upon and nerve impulses to the corresponding organs impaired. This can lead to a heightened susceptibility to disease of the affected organ. The area of impingement of nerves through misalignment of vertebrae (subluxations) is the subject matter of the field of chiropractic (Gallert, 1966).

Emotional trauma can also alter the course of physical development as has been shown especially in psychosomatics (Simeons, 1961) and bioenergetics (Lowen, 1971; W. Reich, 1949). The flow of the body/person/process is impeded by emotional trauma. Whenever a person has a feeling he wants to express and a conflicting feeling inhibits this expression, he is left with a tension in his body. This is particularly true if he is not aware of this conflict. If the same out-of-awareness conflict occurs frequently, the tense muscle will become chronic with the same result as described above. Take, for example, a person who when he was a child was never allowed to express his anger. When he got angry he wanted to bite, his eyes narrowed, his fists clenched, his shoulders drew back, his stomach tightened to prepare to strike, his stance widened to prepare for a counterblow. But his parents forbade the completion of these incipient actions. Soon the parents' prohibitions were internalized and whenever he felt anger he would inhibit himself. If this was a frequent occurrence, very likely his jaw muscle would become chronically tense, his eyes would form a permanent narrowing, his forearms would form a permanent narrowing, his forearms would be chronically tight, his shoulders held back, his stomach muscles would be very tense, and his stance would be a permanent straddle. The interdependence of the body organs is such that digestion, excretion, breathing, and so on are affected by these body changes. Certain illnesses, such as stomach trouble, now become more probable because of body tensions which weaken organs, making them more vulnerable to disease (Selye, 1950).

Limited use. The third limitation on the optimal unfolding of man is not as pathological as emotional trauma and may stem from social and psychological origins as well as from physical causes. Although our bodies are capable of moving in thousands of ways, as we grow up, a very small proportion of these ways is utilized. This applies to single movements, such as putting a leg over the head; and combinations of movements, such as the common game of rotating hand on stomach while patting the head. The number of combinations of things we can do simultaneously goes into the millions. Not using the body in all the ways it is capable of functioning leads to a restriction in movement and in intellectual, emotional, and sensation functioning (Feldenkrais, 1972). This is seen most clearly by observing people who do spend time developing an aspect of their potential to its fullest. An acrobat can move his pelvic muscles through a wide range of motion far beyond the ability of the normal person; the yogi has control of his breathing; the chess master has developed his analytical ability; the weight lifter his strength; and the piano tuner his sense of sound discrimination in ways that many normal people are capable of, but haven't done.

Lowen (1970) has stressed the intimate relationship between movement and other activities:

The functional identity of thinking and feeling stems from their common origin in body movement. Every movement of the body that is perceived by the conscious mind gives rise to both a feeling and a thought. The concept that body movements give rise to feelings and thoughts runs counter to ordinary thinking. . . . Seen from below, movement not only precedes but also provides the substance for our feelings and thoughts. We are accustomed to see movement as a result of thinking and feeling rather than the other way around. These informative movements are the involuntary bodily movements. Volitional movements, on the other hand, proceed from feeling and thought.

Lowen also makes the point similar to Feldenkrais', that movement is central to human functioning. "If thinking stems from movement, it follows that man's greater thinking capacity derives ultimately from the greater range of movements that he is capable of performing." (Lowen, 1970)

When learned movement uses a set of muscles in only one pattern it makes it more difficult for other patterns to be used with ease. An obvious example is the learning of a language. During this process the muscles of the mouth, tongue, vocal cords, neck, and the muscles used for breathing are trained in certain ways so as to make the appropriate sounds. The muscles accommodate to these positions so that making certain sounds in another language is very difficult to do since the musculature has been set. For a person with English as his native tongue this difficulty is especially evident when trying to pronounce German guttural or French nasal sounds. Thus to achieve the freedom to use alternate combinations of muscles often requires overcoming built-in resistances.

An unusually large number of simultaneous actions in a few brief seconds are performed by a professional quarterback. He must feel the football, turn it to the proper position for throwing, place his hand on it to throw, look for one or more receivers, step behind his blockers, move so as to avoid onrushing tacklers, fake a pass to one side of the field, look to the other, judge how hard and where to throw, decide whether to throw or run. Thus he must coordinate sight, sound, judgment, movement, effort, all at once. In ordinary life this kind of demand is rarely made.

In a series of ingenious exercises, Feldenkrais (1972) demonstrates how limited our body motions are and how restricted our capacities. At the same time he feels that these exercises demonstrate that by practicing unusual movements we send new messages to the nervous system that allow the nervous system to send new messages to the body to release some of the built-in restrictions and allow the body more freedom and mobility. Along with the new body freedom many subjects report a feeling of psychological loosening.

Here is an example of a Feldenkrais exercise (enormously condensed). Stand with your right arm extended straight out in front of you at shoulder level. Look at your hand and turn your arm, head, and eyes together to the right as far as they will go without strain. Note a point on the wall corresponding to that distance. Now come to the front position. Let your arm down. Relax. Put it up again to the front position. Move your arm to the right as before but simultaneously move your head to the left. Move both head and arm as far as you can go without strain. Do this five times, returning to the center position between trials. Be aware of the feelings in your neck, shoulders, and waist during these five movements. Put your arm down and relax. Now once again try the original motion of looking at your hand and moving your arm, head, and eyes to the right as far as they can go without strain. Compare it with the original point on the wall. Come back to the center position. Put your arm down and relax. Again put your arm in the front position. Now move your arm to the right and your head and hips (pelvis) to the left, all as far as they can go without strain. Do this five times, returning to the center position between trials. Again be very aware of all your body movements. Put your arm down and relax. Again try the original movement, moving to the right as far as you can go without strain. Compare this with the original points. It is probable that your arm now turns noticeably farther to the right than it did originally.

Now hold your left arm straight out to the front, look at your hand and turn your head, trunk, and arm to the left as far as you can without strain and note the point on the wall. Come back to the front. Put your arm down. Relax. Put it up again in the front position. Now *only in imagination* repeat the movement made for the right arm, three times each; that is, imagine your arm going left, and head going right, three times. Then imagine your arm going left and your head and hips going right three times. While you do this concentrate on the muscle feelings. After imagined movement open your eyes, and put your arm down and relax. Now put your left arm out in front as before, look at your hand, and move your arm, trunk, and head to the left and note the difference in the point on the wall. There will probably be about as large an increment as with the right side, although it was all done without movement.

Recent work on the Involuntary Nervous System provides an explanation for this ideational part of this exercise and for the body/mind view generally. Miller (1969) says:

> Cellular electric current can be made to occur in protoplasm *by the very act of thinking. Thought alone* can therefore, in and of itself, be the *stimulus* to induce an electric current to flow down any nerve to the affected tissue—demonstrating that *thought is a source of energy.* . . . The Involuntary Nervous System is not necessarily involuntary . . . it is more under our conscious control than previously believed. (Italics in original.)

REFERENCES

FELDENKRAIS, M., *Awareness Through Movement.* New York: Harper & Row, 1972.

GOLDFARB, W., The Effects of Early Institutional Care on Adolescent Personality, *Journal of Experimental Education,* 1943, 12, 106-29.

GALLERT, M., *New Light on Therapeutic Energies.* London: Clark, 1966.

LOWEN, A., *Pleasure.* New York: Coward-McCann, 1970.

LOWEN, A., *The Language of the Body.* New York: Collier, 1971.

MILLER, H. B., "Emotions and Malignancy (hypnosis-psychiatry and organic tissue changes)." Paper presented at American Society of Clinical Hypnosis Convention, San Francisco, 1969.

REICH, W., *Character Analysis.* New York: Orgone Press, 1949.

ROLF, I., *Structural Integration*, in preparation.

SELYE, H., "Adaptive Responses to Stress," *Life Stress Bodily Diseases,* Association for Research of Nervous and Mental Disease, 1950, 29, 4.

SIMEONS, A. T. W., *Man's Presumptuous Brain.* New York: E. P. Dutton, 1961.

Why Johnny Can't Run

And Other Gym Class Scandals

George Leonard

George Leonard, author of Education and Ecstasy *and* The Ultimate Athlete, *is a sports fan of a very special sort. In this selection he explores some of the potentials of a new approach to physical education.*

One perfect spring morning in a small Virginia town, a group of thirty-five or forty boys and girls in their early teens were sitting on a grassy bank, attending to the instructions of a taut-muscled young man with gym shoes, gym pants, a white T-shirt, a crew cut, a whistle, and a clipboard. Next to the young man, like a guillotine in the sunlight, stood a chinning bar.

The man looked at his clipboard. "Babcock," he called.

There was a stir among the boys and girls. One of them rose and made his way to the chinning bar: Babcock, the classic fat boy.

Shoulders slumped, he stood beneath the bar. "I can't," he said.

"You can try," the man with the clipboard said.

"Why Johnny Can't Run" as it appeared in the August 1975 issue of *Atlantic Monthly*, pp. 54-60. From George Leonard, *The Ultimate Athlete* (New York: The Viking Press, Inc., 1975). Copyright© 1974, 1975 by George Leonard. All rights reserved. Reprinted by permission of The Viking Press, Inc. and The Sterling Lord Agency, Inc.

Babcock reached up with both hands, touched the bar limply—just that—and walked away, his eyes downcast, as all the boys and girls watched, seeming to share his shame and resignation.

This scene, which I happened upon a couple of years ago, contains no particularly noteworthy information. Yet it does evoke painful memories of an aspect of American schooling which many of us have managed to forget and which educational reformers have chosen, for the most part, to ignore. In an age when sports have become a major American spectacle, physical education in our schools remains mostly in the shadows. No significant national study has been conducted on the subject, which is considered a "frill" by some educational policy-makers, and even the most rudimentary facts and figures on the education of the body in this country are hard to come by.

In the elementary schools, where children are likely to form their basic physical self-image, offerings in physical education are very meager. The subject is typically taught, if it is taught at all, by classroom teachers who may or may not have had a course in "games and relays" during their teacher training. An especially enlightened school district might have one elementary physical education specialist shared among five to ten schools. Physical education in the formal sense is traditionally left to the secondary schools, and it is there that most of the painful memories accumulate. Indeed, a description of a traditional "P.E.," or "gym," class—the kind that still prevails in perhaps well over half of our junior high and high schools—tends to read like a caricature.

The class period begins with students scrambling to change into gym clothes, then standing for a quasi-military dress inspection. The military sensibility continues to hold sway through five or ten minutes of calisthenics—push-ups, sit-ups, jumping jacks, toe touches, knee bends. Students may then be ordered to run a lap around the track, though running laps is in some cases reserved by the instructor for use as a punishment. After this, discipline goes rather rapidly downhill as students move on to the game of the day—softball, volleyball, flag football, field hockey, basketball. Play is sometimes preceded by a brief status-confirmation ritual known as "choosing sides." What with all of this, there is little time for the game itself.

Students have yet one more ritual ahead of them: the shower. So much attention is devoted to this activity, in fact, that it might be seen by an anthropologist as the raison d'être of traditional physical education; in some schools students are inspected as they leave the shower room, ostensibly to make sure they are wet all over. Needless to say, boys' classes are separate from girls'.

Obviously this mode of instruction fails in its own proclaimed goal of significantly increasing physical fitness and skill. It offers too little sustained physical activity to increase heart-lung capacity. (This "training effect" is best achieved when an accelerated heart rate is maintained over an extended period—as in distance running, swimming, or cycling—while most team sports in gym classes are played in spurts.) It offers too little exercise, and often not the right kind, to build strength, flexibility, and agility. It offers too little individualized instruction to improve physical skills—balance, hand-eye coordination, fine muscle control—to any appreciable extent. And the activities it does offer are precisely those competitive team sports that the average person is least likely to play after school and college.

A few students in each class, already good at sports, excel in traditional P.E. and go on to a lifetime of rewarding physical activity. But many of the boys and a clear majority of the girls are simply confirmed in their ineptitude. Turned away from the potentialities of their own bodies, they smile approvingly at the familiar statement made by Dr. Robert Hutchins, among others: "Whenever I feel the urge to exercise coming on, I lie down until it passes over." A national survey by the President's Council on Physical Fitness and Sport in 1973 indicates that those who took physical education in school are more likely to exercise later in life than those who did not. But such "education" has hardly turned us into a physically aware nation. According to the survey (directed at adult physical fitness, not physical education in the schools), only 55 percent of adults report that they do any exercise at all. Of those who do, the majority name "walking" as their exercise. The favorite participatory sport of American adults is bowling, but nearly one half of the bowlers participate in their sport "less than once a month."

It is against this background that a major reform movement has at last begun to challenge the practices familiar to generations of P.E. students. "The New Physical Education," as it is called by the American Alliance for Health, Physical Education and Recreation (AAHPER), has by no means swept the field. It prevails in only one fourth of the nation's schools, according to the most optimistic estimate. It has not yet been examined by the national media. Many ranking educators have never heard of it, but it represents the viewpoint of most young teachers entering the field and is supported by such professional organizations as AAHPER, an affiliate of the National Education Association.

How can you recognize The New Physical Education? Literature distributed by AAPHER has characterized the reform in terms of "Lifetime Sports" rather than the usual team sports in secondary schools; "Movement Education" in elementary schools; and, in addition, individualized instruction and the inculcation of a "strong self-concept" all along the way. These general characterizations translate into changes that are fairly easy to spot. In junior high, high school, and even college classes, you might look first of all for a de-emphasis on dress code and showers and anything else that gets in the way of actual instruction and play. Then you will begin to notice the presence of such "recreational sports" as tennis, golf, and archery, along with sports that have not previously graced gymnasium floors. Students at San Rafael (California) High School, for example, can choose from an offering of forty-two sports, only a half-dozen of which could be called traditional team sports. Among the more exotic offerings are T'ai Chi Chuan, Body Conditioning, Yoga, Scuba Diving, and Rock Climbing.

"Some of these activities are very, very appealing to people who've been turned off by team sports," William H. Monti, a physical education reform leader at San Rafael High, explained. "A number of students who rebelled against all forms of physical education have gravitated toward rock climbing. These were the types who said they didn't like team sports of any kind. Later, of course, they found out that rock climbing involves as much teamwork as the traditional team sports, or more. They still love it.

"You know, rock climbing teaches the kind of thing we've always claimed for physical education—the ability to operate under stress. We create situations here in which stress is compounded by time. Running creates stress, but you can always stop if it gets too bad. During a rescue practice on a climb, when you have to tie a knot very quickly to take the pressure of a rope off your body, coolness and efficiency are absolutely required. And when you're tied to other people, teamwork and responsibility can mean life or death. In this sport, boys and girls and instructors work together and really *become* a team."

San Rafael, like other high schools with reformed programs, opens its sports activities to boys and girls alike. "When we first started modernizing our program about five years ago." Monti said, "we found that our women teachers had skills that men didn't have in some of these new areas, so we ended up with some women teaching all-boy classes. That didn't make much sense, so we started opening up all our classes to both sexes. At first, we even had girls playing touch football and basketball with boys. That was too much of a mismatch, but in almost everything else, we've found the mix is very good. We've found that co-ed classes in such things as volleyball and tennis push girls to improve much more rapidly than we though possible. We even have co-ed weight lifting classes. As you know, some experts believe that the large male-female difference in physical abilities is to a great extent due to cultural expectations, and that with the proper training, women can make tremendous strides in all sports.

"The main thing we're trying to do here is to help every student develop a good self-image. Body language is very important, and I think in physical education one's personal identity is realized more than in any other area of the curriculum. Students are different, and ideally, we'd like every student to have success in *some* area of physical education, and to *keep* having success. When enough successes have been deposited in a young person's bank account, then he or she can afford to take some risks in order to gain further success."

Along with a new emphasis on individual physical differences have come new and sophisticated methods for measuring and evaluating those differences. Missouri Western State College at St. Joseph, Missouri, for example, requires a "Concepts of Physical Activity" course for all students in general education. The course introduces the latest thinking on such matters as body type, fitness, nutrition, cardiovascular conditioning, posture, stress, and relaxation. But what makes it popular among students is that they themselves are the main subjects of study. During the semester, they go through a complete battery of physical tests.

First, they perform nine varied feats to discover their overall physical fitness. Skin folds at the chest, stomach, and tricep are then measured to estimate their percentages of body fat. Their silhouettes are projected on a screen so that their body types can be established. They do a five-minute step test to find out the heart's ability to return to normal pulse rate after exercise, run a measured twelve minutes to determine the body's capacity to process oxygen, and ride a bicycle ergometer to evaluate physical work capacity. Their isometric strength is measured by means of specially designed scales, and their isotonic strength by ability to do chins, dips, and jumps. Flexibility of the joints is measured. Posture is evaluated. Agility, reaction time, and speed are determined by timed tests. Finally, there is an evaluation of swimming ability.

Students at Missouri Western are not just tested and left with the evidence of their physical pluses and minuses, as is often the case with school testing programs; they are offered programs for improvement. The flexibility test, for instance, is followed by an introduction to flexibility exercises. At the end of the Concepts of Physical Activity course, students draw up their own physical summary profiles, which are compared to national norms. The profiles show where improvement is needed and also help in the choice of physical activities. Students are required, in fact, to write up a tentative personal physical activities program for both the college years and the adult years that follow. In this, they are guided by a long list of activities, some of which (aerobics, orienteering, tap dancing) would never appear in the Olympics.

"Seventy percent of body types are not represented at the Olympics," Dr. James Terry explained. Terry, an exercise physiologist, teaches the Concepts course at Missouri Western and runs the human performance lab there. "Highly competitive sports are appropriate only for a certain number of people. But there are sports or physical activities for every body type. There are good and poor activities for everybody. Maybe the person who is naturally heavy, the pure endomorph, shouldn't be a runner. But that person can swim, and swim more easily because of the higher percentage of body fat. The important thing is to get people started in *some* physical activity."

When Terry averaged out the fitness scores of the first 1000 persons he tested, he was appalled, "Most of our students are free from disease and physically unhealthy. That is, their general state of physical fitness is below the national college norm, which is pretty low anyway. More than 54 percent of all deaths in America last year were caused by disease of the heart of circulatory system. Medical doctors suspect that the stress and tensions of our way of life might be a major factor in the development of heart and blood vessel diseases." Terry, himself an avid jogger, sees exercise as a way toward relaxation as well as conditioning, and therefore as a key to good health. "We try to educate our students to the value of that vibrant, dynamic feeling that comes from being more than just well."

We have no way of knowing how much of our current sickness and malaise could be eliminated if people of all ages were turned on to "the vibrant, dynamic feeling that comes from being more than just well."

But a number of scientists, notably Dr. Rene Dubos, have marshaled evidence to show that way of life is a major factor in the incidence of sickness. The degenerative diseases—ulcers, colitis, asthma, arteriosclerosis, hypertension, obesity, and the like—are clearly assoicated with the life-style of the technologically advanced nations, and could undoubtedly be reduced by a change in that life-style, as could the current abuse of tobacco, alcohol, and other drugs. The healthy, fully active body provides the foundation for such a change.

In terms of health and economy, The New Physical Education makes good sense. What's more, professional journals, workshop sessions, and annual conventions of physical educators are filled with words of praise for it. Why, then, isn't it put into effect in every junior high, high school, and college in the nation? There are, of course, the usual inertia, the fear of change, the presence of an Old Guard too close to retirement for new-fangled ideas. But reformers in physical education face a problem unlike those of other educational reformers. It concerns their longtime love-hate relationship with athletics.

The male athletics department, which may or may not be part of the physical education department, is occupied with the voluntary, after-school, extramural sports program. Its job is to recruit, coach, and administer teams that will compete with teams in other schools. Athletics coaches are not necessarily members of the physical education department. The track coach might be a civics teacher. The football backfield coach might teach math. But athletics and physical education share common facilities; they use the same balls, the same gyms, the same fields. And, whenever possible, it is expected that physical educators will serve their stints as after-school coaches, for which they receive stipends from the athletics budget.

Actually, it's hard to draw a line between the two activities. And the athletics program, which serves relatively few students, often overshadows the physical education program, which serves all students. The backfield coach who is also a physical education teacher might support the theory of The New Physical Education, but he doesn't have time for it. He checks his sixty first-period students for proper dress, leads them through five minutes of calisthenics, gives them four volleyballs, and hurries back to continue analyzing the films of last week's football game with Central High.

In small communities with large high schols, the situation is particularly insusceptible to reform. There the high school football and basketball teams may well provide the town's major entertainment. Residents are proud to support their local athletics program while their own children go to seed physically. And those talented youngsters who do make the team may not be getting the best preparation for a long life of healthy play. This is especially true in the case of football, a vivid sport that can be hazardous to one's health.

"I view football as an act between consenting adults," Dr. George Sheehan said. Dr. Sheehan, a cardiologist and internist in Red Bank, New Jersey, is medical editor for *Runner's World* magazine and a leading authority on sports medicine. "Actually, football and baseball players are not in very good shape. The life expectancy of football players is significantly shorter than that of their classmates, and their tendency to become obese in later years is greater than usual."

Football players are strong, quick, and fast over a distance of forty to sixty yards. At any greater distance, they risk embarrassment. There is something preposterous about a strapping linebacker lying helplessly on the artificial turf being administered oxygen after an unexpected eighty-yard interception runback. Few indeed are the pro football players who can run a mile in four minutes and forty-seven seconds, which is what George Sheehan ran at age fifty in setting the world's record for that age and over. But you don't have to go to aging world's-record holders to illustrate the poor conditioning that prevails in this sport; literally thousands of amateur runners in their forties, fifties, and even sixties could beat the average pro player over the distance of a mile or longer. The glamour of competitive sports and the traditional dominance of athletics departments tend to blind us to facts such as these.

The demand for women's rights in sports and physical education, sharply focused by the provisions of Title IX of the Education Amendments Act of 1972, cuts two ways as far as reform is concerned. Title IX withholds federal funds from any school or college that discriminates on the basis of sex in any of its programs, including physical education and athletics. One can imagine the threat this law poses to athletic scholarship programs, which now favor the male sex. The law may tend to cool off the present hot chase for male athletic stars, encourage co-ed physical education, and aid the reform movement. On the other hand, it may simply encourage women to mimic the old male model, to go all out for scholarships in female competitive sports, and to end up with cries of "Winning isn't everything. It's the only thing."

Proponents of The New Physical Education are certainly not asking the athletics be done away with. They are asking for a balance between programs for the few and for the many. One reformer in a tightly knit community with a popular high school football team explained how this balance might be achieved. "Right now, we have an opening for a physical education teacher in our high school. We also need a backfield coach for the football team. In the old days, we would have recruited for a backfield coach, period. What we're doing now is interviewing people to find someone who is a physical educator first and a backfield coach second."

Changes in physical education in secondary school are needed, and they are possible, but the roots of change go down to the early elementary grades. There one may find a form of physical education that could revolutionize the way children feel about sports and their own bodies. It generally goes under the label of "Movement Education."

In the old-model physical education, children in the lower grades are likely to be playing games and relays. This means that a great deal of the time they are just standing or sitting around. In some games (dodge ball, for instance), they stand or sit around after being eliminated. In other games (kickball and other variations of baseball), they stand or sit around waiting for their turns to strike or catch the single ball that is shared by two whole teams. In still others (capture the flag), they stand or sit around in "jail" waiting to be rescued by a teammate. Almost always, they spend time milling about while the game or relay is being organized. And under these peculiar and inefficient circumstances, they are to learn whether they are "winners" or "losers."

It's just assumed, in this games-and-relays approach, that all children know how to move efficiently, to throw, to judge others' movements, to coordinate hand and eye. Of course this is not so. Many, perhaps most, first-graders are not very good at throwing or catching or performing other basic physical skills. Some children of that age, the majority of them boys, do happen to be good at the basic skills. Though the teacher may try to give all children a chance to play, the capable and aggressive boys tend to dominate the games. They become the "winners." And when the teacher is not supervising closely, these boys may begin forcing other children out of the games, helping establish that human category known as "losers." The girls drift away, realizing more and more that that athletic world is not for them. The unsuccessful boys find other things to do. Some of them retreat into books. Some become behavior problems. In the game itself voices become louder; movements become more frantic; play becomes rather unpleasant.

And the boys who dominate the games—the "winners"—are they getting the best physical education? Far from it. Driven to win, they are likely to repeat the primitive skills that first brought victory, and to compensate with aggression and large-muscle action for possible lack of the fine perceptions and small-muscle control required for high achievement in sports.

Movement Education, on the other hand, tries to cut the win/lose knot while systematically teaching the basic movement skills that are needed in sports and life. For one accustomed to the games-and-relays approach, a large room full of young children doing Movement Education makes a striking picture. In a class devoted to ball play, for example, every child has a ball and every child is moving.

"See if you can put the ball in the air without using your hands," the teacher says. The children use their feet, knees, forearms, wrists, elbows, and chins to handle the ball.

"Now roll your balls to each other, and see how many body parts you can use to stop them." More activity and experimentation. "Now, stand and move slowly around the room. Throw the balls to each other while you're moving. Throw gently." The air is filled with balls. Surprisingly, very few are dropped. Later, the children are asked to make up their own games with their balls. Everybody is involved.

The same approach is used for teaching balance, flexibility, strength, agility, control. Since the children are in constant motion, their acrobic capacity is also increased.

"The principles of the new approach to early physical education are simple," Dr. Margie Hanson, AAHPER elementary education consultant, told me. "There's a lot of equipment—every child has a ball or a jump rope. Every child is busy. No one gets eliminated. Everyone feels successful."

The equipment needed for Movement Education is not necessarily expensive. Most of it can be salvaged or built by teachers, parents, and children. For example, townspeople in Ocilla, Georgia, a village on the southern flatlands of that state, have worked together to create a model program in The New Physical Education. Large, brightly painted tractor tires provide a tricky environment for movement exploration. "Show me how you can move without bumping into anybody," a teacher says in a thick southern accent as children scramble over the tires. Other children walk the lines of a giant map of the United States painted on pavement, solving the problem of moving from Oregon to Florida without leaving a line and without running into anyone else. Young boys and girls learn hand-eye coordination with yarn balls and bean bags sewn by volunteers. Older children climb a stairway made of telephone-pole-sized posts of varied heights. Some walk on stilts made of empty coffee cans. Others make their way across balance beams built by amateur carpenters.

Once elementary school teachers become involved in Movement Education, they are likely to become its most enthusiastic advocates. But sometimes the demand for it comes first from parents who have seen demonstrations. Jack Capon, consultant in physical education for the Alameda Unified School District in California, is one of the specialists who travel around the country introducing people to the new approach. In addition to his crusading work in his own district, Capon gives up to fifty weekend workshops in other communities during a school year.

Capon believes that better development of perception and movement skills can improve a child's ability to read and write. But he views this possible improvement as a by-product. "If it were proved that our work also helped a child read, that would be a great bonus. But our goal should be primarily efficiency of movement. After all, what more fundamental right do we have than to move with comfort and control?"

Other educators and researchers are more insistent in arguing that there is a direct connection between ability to move and ability to learn. The argument gains force in the case of those learning disabilities that seem to appear so mysteriously in many of our children today. Seeking to explain the disabilities, the behaviorists point to deficiencies in the environment, to poor "contingencies of reinforcement." The psychoanalysts tend to attribute them to dark, quasi-sexual relationships in the family. Both of these explanations, though true as far as they go, seem to leave something out: the body itself, the way of moving, the way of *being* in the world.

One of the boldest theorists now linking movement with learning disabilities is Dr. A. Jean Ayres of the University of Southern California. Dr. Ayres has observed that vestiges of certain infant muscular reflexes tend to show up in children who have trouble learning. For example, when an infant's neck is turned to the right, its right arm tends to extend and its left arm to curl up around its head—a reflex motion that is self-protective. In the normal course of development, the reflex is "integrated" by nine months or so; in other words, the neck moves independently of the arms. In some children, however, this "tonic neck reflex" lingers on, so that there is unnecessary muscular action in the arms every time the head is turned. Sometimes the child will rotate the whole body to avoid rotation at the neck. Such an unwanted reflex makes graceful, controlled movements difficult. In addition, it can interfere with thinking. The reflex is normally integrated at the brainstem, so it is controlled automatically, without conscious thought. When it is not integrated, it must be controlled consciously, in the cortex of the brain, thus getting in the way of the child's attempt to read or to do other academic tasks.

The tonic neck reflex is only one of several for which Dr. Ayres has worked out a series of remedial physical activities. The Ayres work is usually offered not under the physical education program, but under the educationally handicapped program. Its primary aim is to improve not a child's ability to throw and catch a ball, but his ability to read and write. More and more studies show that the brain has something to do with perception and movement, that reading and writing are forms of perception and movement, that ultimately there is no way you can separate academic learning from movement, feeling, sensing, and the body.

I was greatly impressed when an Ayres-trained specialist unerringly picked out children with learning problems from random groups brought to her by their teachers, and did it with a series of simple movement tests taking no longer than five minutes. The specialist, Marsha Allen, a consultant to the Marin County (California) schools, was testing children in groups of eight and generally finding one or two children with infant reflexes in each group. Then a group came in that seemed to startle her.

She pulled the teacher to one side and said in a low voice: "I hope all your children aren't like these, because all of these are showing up with dysfunctions."

"Well no," the teacher answered. "They're not all like this. On an impulse—I don't know why—I brought you all my children with learning problems first."

The connection indeed seems clear. When our children are turned away from the joys of the body in motion, they are not merely losing their chance to compete someday in the Superstars; they are being deprived of what is fundamental to all learning—coordination, perception, health. Topflight competitive teams and television sports spectaculars are well and good; they inform us on the nature of human potential. But it would be ironic if the current sports boom ended up by making us even more passive spectators.

Transpersonal Communication in the Classroom

Barry K. Weinhold

Classrooms are places where people talk and listen to each other. That being the case, it's odd that schools require students to spend many years studying grammar, spelling, and other relatively trivial aspects of language but offer them little practice in communication skills.

Barry Weinhold has taught communication skills to children, parents, teachers, business people, and mental health professionals. Here he presents a concise summary of the hows and whys of good communication and problem-solving.

WHAT IS TRANSPERSONAL COMMUNICATION?

Transpersonal communication involves the use of skills and understanding to help individuals reach and maintain a conscious experience of their essential unity and connectedness with all life energy. It is based upon the belief that unity, not separateness or aloneness, is the basic human condition.

Transpersonal communication rests upon the foundation of effective interpersonal and intrapersonal means to bring people in contact with the highest in themselves and others. Effective interpersonal communication helps build an atmosphere of trust and connectedness with other people. Effective intrapersonal communication enables people to establish contact with and utilize their inner thoughts, feelings, and experiences. When people have this inner and outer trust and contact they are free to explore their beings at the highest levels.

Figure 1. Structure of Transpersonal Communication

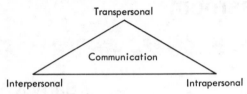

Transpersonal communication is designed to help people learn to trust the validity of their personal experiences and accept what they learn from these experiences as their best source of wisdom and truth. This includes both thinking and feeling processes. It teaches people to play hunches, use their intuition, and follow their thoughts and feelings rather than direct them in predetermined ways.

Trust in the validity of personal experiences will lead to an affirmation of the inner core of the person that transcends the cultural roles, ego defenses, muscular defenses, and emotional defenses (See Figure 2). This inner core is where unity with all life energy occurs.

All the numerous approaches to effective interpersonal and intra-personal communications can be used creatively in this inner search for truth and meaning. Many of the methods developed for humanistic education can be utilized as a means toward these ends. Maslow (1971) proposed that education should help children to look within themselves and from this self-knowledge form their own values. Many humanistic educators stop short of this goal and maintain a more interpersonal focus to self-knowledge and value formation.

In summary, the main goal of transpersonal communication is the realization and maintenance of higher states of consciousness in which intrapersonal and interpersonal actualization is subsumed, not bypassed.

Figure 2. Levels of Self-Knowledge (Adapted from Lowen, *Bioenergetics,* 1975, p. 119)

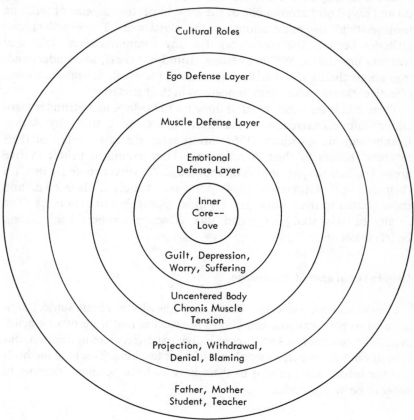

BELIEFS OF EFFECTIVE TEACHERS

Teachers who wish to develop transpersonal communication skills in themselves and their students need to examine their belief systems and attitudes toward teaching and learning. To be effective in fostering transpersonal communication in the classroom, a teacher must have faith in and commitment to the self-discovery process. This is a process whereby the teacher is able to create a learning environment that facilitates students in the development of their own self-knowledge.

Teachers teach more by *who they are* than by what they know. They model what they believe and they communicate their beliefs by what they do and say. This becomes one of the most important aspects of teaching transpersonal communications in the classroom. These beliefs and attitudes become the framework for any communication skills that teachers may learn. Without certain attitudes, beliefs, and understandings about children, the skills that teachers learn will not produce more effective transpersonal communications in their students.

There has been some research done on the beliefs and attitudes associated with effectiveness in teachers. An extensive study by Arthur Combs and his associates (1969) investigated the relationship of their teachers' beliefs to their effectiveness. They examined beliefs in five areas: (1) their subject or area of knowledge, (2) what people are like, (3) their concept of themselves, (4) purposes—society's, their own, and those related to their work, and (5) their approaches to their work. The results of this study suggested that effective teachers held certain beliefs in common.

Beliefs about area of knowledge.

Combs and his associates found that knowledge about subject area must be so personally meaningful to the teacher that it becomes a belief in itself. A teacher can *know* about individual differences in children, but if he doesn't *believe* it, he won't use it in his teaching. Teaching methods and the information related to them have to have personal meaning in order to be incorporated.

What are people like?

Here clear differences were found between effective and ineffective teachers.

Able—unable. Effective teachers perceive children as having the capacity to deal with their problems as opposed to doubting the capacity of children to solve problems.

Friendly—unfriendly. Effective teachers see children as being friendly and well-intentioned. They do not regard children as threatening and evil-intentioned.

Worthy—unworthy. Effective teachers see children as being worthy rather than unworthy. They see them as having dignity and integrity which must be respected and maintained. They do not see children as unimportant beings whose dignity and integrity may be violated or discounted.

Internally—externally motivated. Effective teachers see children's behavior as essentially coming from within rather than as a response to external stimuli, to be molded and directed. They see children as creative and dynamic rather than passive or static.

Dependable—undependable. Effective teachers see children as essentially trustworthy and dependable in the sense of behaving in predictable ways. They regard the behavior of children as understandable rather than capricious, unpredictable, or negative.

Helpful—hindering. Effective teachers see children as being basically willing to help. They regard children as important sources of satisfaction rather than as sources of frustration and suspicion.

WHAT AM I LIKE?

Effective teachers know how to use *self* as an instrument. They are willing and able to share themselves and to deal appropriately with themselves and life.

Identified—apart. Effective teachers feel identity with others rather than feeling apart from others. They see themselves as similar to others rather than removed, apart, or alienated from others.

Adequate—inadequate. Effective teachers feel basically adequate rather than inadequate, and capable of dealing with problems.

Trustworthy—untrustworthy. Effective teachers see themselves as essentially dependable and reliable. Ineffective teachers tend to have doubts about themselves in these areas.

Wanted—unwanted. Effective teachers see themselves as wanted rather than unwanted. They see themselves as essentially likeable, warm, attractive and responded to in this manner.

Worthy—unworthy.   Effective teachers see themselves as worthy rather than unworthy. They see themselves as persons of dignity and integrity, worthy of respect.

What are my purposes?

The effective teachers were found to have goals different from those of ineffective teachers. The purposes of ineffective teachers tend to inhibit their ability to teach.

Freeing—controlling.   Effective teachers see their purpose as that of freeing rather than of controlling people. They see the purpose of teaching as one of assisting, releasing, and facilitating rather than controlling, manipulating, coercing, blocking, or inhibiting behavior.

Larger issues—smaller ones.   Effective teachers tend to be more concerned with large rather than small issues. They have a broad rather than narrow perspective. They seem to have more long-range than immediate and specific views.

Self-revealing—self-concealing.   Effective teachers are more likely to be self-revealing than self-concealing. They are willing to disclose the self and can treat their feelings and shortcomings as important and be open about them. They seem willing to be persons and not roles.

Involved—alienated.   Effective teachers tend to be involved with people rather than alienated from them. Their purpose is to enter into interaction with students rather than being inert or remaining aloof or remote.

Process-oriented—goal-oriented.   Effective teachers are more interested in processes than achieving goals. They see their purpose as that of encouraging and facilitating the process of search and discovery as opposed to working toward some personal goal or preconceived solution.

Approaches to the task

Teachers' beliefs about how to approach the teaching-learning task were found to relate to their success in carrying out the task.

People—things. Effective teachers are more oriented toward people than things. They have a student rather than a subject orientation.

Subjective—objective. Effective teachers are more likely to approach students subjectively and are more concerned with the learning experience rather than teaching objective facts.

TEACHERS' MISCONCEPTIONS
ABOUT CHILDREN

Teachers often don't understand children because they see them as miniature adults and want them to behave like adults. When children behave like children instead of adults, often teachers feel angry, scared, and sad. Admittedly, it would be easier to teach if children looked at the world and behaved as adults do. However, they don't; understanding how they look at the world and why they do and say what they do helps to build the rapport needed for effective teaching (Holt, 1974). Below are some characteristics teachers tend to overlook:

1. Children are concrete and not abstract. They need concrete examples in order to understand concepts.
2. They seem happy and carefree because they use their energy and curiosity to discover new things and not to brood about old things.
3. Even though they seem happy and carefree they have as many fears as most adults.
4. They are very sensual. They are tuned into their senses and respond to what their senses tell them. They often do what feels good at the moment.
5. They are very self-absorbed and self-centered. They don't naturally see things from another person's point of view. This quality needs to be developed through interaction with other children.
6. They often appear cruel and inconsiderate. What adults fail to see is that whether they are cruel or kind depends upon an impulse rather than a plan or principle.

ELEMENTS OF EFFECTIVE
TEACHER-STUDENT RELATIONSHIPS

In order to build an effective relationship with students, a teacher must be able to see children the way they are and not the way adults would like children to be. In addition, teachers and students need the following:

1. *Openness*—Each must be willing to risk being open, direct, and honest with the other.
2. *Caring*—Each must value the relationship and care what happens to the other.
3. *Interdependence* (as opposed to dependence)—Each must view his goals as characterized by interrelatedness.
4. *Separateness*—Each must be willing to see the other as a separate person who will grow and develop in unique, creative, and individual ways.
5. *Mutual needs and wants*—Neither person's needs and wants can be met at the expense of the other's.

POWER AND AUTHORITY

Children are attracted by the natural authority of any adult who responds authentically and respectfully to them. Many teachers are confused about their power and authority and give double messages to children. Natural authority or power is based upon expertise, knowledge, experience, and a willingness to treat others who may have fewer of these qualities with respect and genuineness.

Teachers who are afraid of losing their authority or power are concerned about another kind of power: the power to give rewards and punishments. This power works only as long as those receiving the rewards and punishments are dependent on them or at least think they are. As students become more mature psychologically and adopt a more internal frame of reference, they have less need for this kind of authority.

The need to relate to other people from an authentic and respectful position does not decrease. The process whereby students can move toward an interpersonal framework requires this kind of nurturing, supportive, freeing authority.

Rollo May (1972) defines power as the ability to cause or prevent change. He sees five types of power present in every person all the time and holds that each person must learn to use the kind of power appropriate to a particular situation. The five types of power are: (1) *exploitative,* where the strong meet their needs at the expense of the weak; (2) *manipulative,* where the strong collude to get the weak to cooperate so the strong can get their needs met; (3) *competitive,* where the strong use their power to defeat another strong person (this is the only kind of power with both destructive and creative forces); (4) *nurturant,* where the strong use their power for the benefit of others; (5) *integrative,* where the strong use their power with another to benefit both.

Natural power in people is the *power to be*. The use of integrative power recognizes the *power to be* as natural and part of the transpersonal unity all people share. Teachers who utilize integrative power with their students are affirming the *power to be* necessary for effective transpersonal communication.

INTERPERSONAL COMMUNICATION

Effective interpersonal communication is a necessary part of developing a framework for transpersonal communication. Below is a list of basic concepts for effective interpersonal communication in the classroom:

1. What people behave upon is their *perception* of what others have said or done, not what really has been said or done.
2. People need skills to help them check their perceptions against reality.
3. People can think and feel at the same time and need to use both thinking and feeling in solving problems.
4. There is no such thing as a "bad feeling." Feelings are natural and important cues telling people they need and/or want something.
5. Needs are things that only one person can meet.
6. Wants are things that you can get from a number of people.

There is a healthy way of processing feelings and using energy that comes from feelings to get wants and needs met (Falzett and Maxwell, 1974).

HEALTHY BEHAVIORAL PROGRESSION

1. Person becomes aware of an unmet need/want which leads to
2. feelings (sad, scared, angry) which if the person has permission to feel them will lead to
3. thoughts about the need or want and related needs and wants and
4. how these are connected to significant persons in the environment and to this specific situation which leads to
5. the person generating options for getting the need or want met which leads to
6. a decision to act on one of the options which
7. turns the feelings of fear, sadness, or anger into excitement which, if the option leads to the person getting what he needed, turns to feelings of happiness/joy.

HEALTHY FEELING STRUCTURE

The basic structure for communicating feelings/wants is:

"I am _____
          [feeling: sad/scared/angry]

about _____
          [situation/person's behavior]

and I want from you _____
Are you willing to give me that?"

Many people need permission and support in order to deal effectively with their feelings. One of the most helpful ways to deal with feelings is to listen to them and respond in a listening manner. Example: "You seem *(feeling word)* about *(facts)*." This allows the other person to "own" his feelings and begin to use them to solve problems. Students in your classroom will need to learn effective ways to deal with and use their feelings to get needs and wants met. What follows are some definitions of some basic feelings and suggestions on how to deal effectively with students having these feelings.

HOW TO DEAL WITH HEALTHY FEELINGS IN OTHERS

Feelings	Definition	Suggestion on What to Say
1. Angry	A response to not getting a want/need met. May not have permission to express anger and is scared, too.	"Wow, you are really angry about something, do you want to talk about it?"
2. Scared	Person perceives physical or emotional danger. May not have permission to think and feel at the same time. May be covering anger.	"You look afraid of something. Do you want to talk about it with me?" "You can be scared and still think about what you want/need." "The scared feeling's telling you to think of something that would make things better."
3. Sad	About the loss of a person, thing, or relationship (real or fantasy). It is an important part of "giving up" something you are attached to. There may be some anger connected with the loss.	"You are looking sad today. Will you talk to me about it?" "It's ok to feel sad about that." "Cry about it if you need to." "It's ok to be mad, too, about losing that."

Feelings	Definition	Suggestion on What to Say
4. Excited	Anticipation of something good happening. Scared and excited are closely related. Some children don't have permission to show excitement.	"You are really excited about your <u>birthday party</u>." [situation] "It's ok to feel good about the plans you have made."
5. Happy or Joyful	Satisfaction is getting what you wanted/needed, or doing something effectively. Some people don't know it's acceptable to be effective and be happy.	"You look really pleased about the story you wrote." "It's really neat that you took care of yourself by asking for what you want."

Some people use other words as feelings and these often become ways to avoid the basic feeling or to justify behavior. Words like "frustrated," "guilty," "hurt," "annoyed," or "irritated" are usually covering anger. Words like "confused," "nervous," "uneasy," or "tense" cover scared. Sadness is often expressed as "lonely," "bored," "empty," or "low." Some words represent a combination of feelings. "Depressed," "unhappy," or "upset" can be a combination of anger, fear, and/or sadness. Suffering is usually anger and fear operating in a person who doesn't have permission to express these emotions.

HOW TO TEACH EFFECTIVE THINKING AND PROBLEM SOLVING

Many children come to school having already decided not to think effectively and not to solve problems. The way that teachers relate to them will either reinforce that decision or help them redecide. Many of the thinking problems in school-age children are the result of adaptive patterns in which they have gotten their parents or other adults to do their thinking and problem solving for them (unhealthy symbiosis). This is a natural occurrence in children before the age of two, but if parents don't begin to transfer the thinking and problem-solving responsibility, children don't learn to think and take care of themselves in appropriate ways (Schiff & Schiff, 1971). Teaching children to think and solve problems then becomes an important task of the teacher. This is part of the process of teaching responsibility (response-ability) or the ability to think and respond appropriately in a situation. Being responsible therefore means doing or saying what you already know is appropriate to do in a situation.

Children use passivity and discounting to avoid thinking and solving problems for themselves. If teachers recognize these avoidance techniques, they will be able to confront them effectively and help children decide to stop using them.

PASSIVE BEHAVIORS AND HOW TO CONFRONT THEM EFFECTIVELY

Behavior	Reasons for the Behavior	What to Say and Do
1. Does nothing. May say "I don't know" a lot when faced with a problem. Shy children may do this frequently. May not answer questions. May engage in long silences before answering simple questions.	Hopes that you will do the thinking. Learned that appearing weak and helpless got someone else to think for them.	"I know you have that information, so how about your thinking about it and letting me know when you have." "I expect you to think." "If you need information that you don't have, you can ask for it." "Think about what you need from me (or others) and ask for it."
2. Overadaptation.	People in this position don't learn reasons for things. Usually have faulty cause and effect relationships. This leaves the responsibility with another person to solve the problem.	"What are your reasons for doing that?" "People have reasons for doing what they do and I expect you to think about what you want to do and why you want to do it." Need to make sure the person sets his own goals that take into account (1) what is appropriate for the situation (2) his feelings, and (3) other people's feelings.
3. Agitation. These are nonproductive repetitive behaviors (tapping a pencil, chewing on an eraser, pacing back and forth, talking without saying anything new).	They are attempts to avoid solving a problem by waiting out someone or making them uncomfortable enough so they solve the problem instead.	"Stop that and think about what you want." "Instead of doing that, I want you to put energy into solving the problem."
4. Incapacitation or violence. These include temper tantrums—kicking, hitting, breaking something or hitting someone, or developing physical symptoms—fainting, having a seizure, etc.	This is a more desperate attempt to get someone to take responsibility. Following the discharge of energy is a good time to give them messages to think and solve problems more effectively.	Take whatever steps necessary to restore order or control. The person is out of control and at that point taking control is appropriate. Following the blowup: "It is not ok for you to solve problems that way." "Think about what you could have done instead to solve problems."

DISCOUNTING

Instead of solving problems, people often suffer about them and engage in discounts about the problem. They may pretend that there isn't a problem and block their feelings. To do that they may get giddy, depressed, or engage in repetitive behavior to avoid thinking/feeling about it. They may deny the significance of a problem and may attempt to block feelings. They may say that they are not angry/scared/sad/excited enough to do anything about their feelings. They may act as if there is nothing that can be done about the problem. Finally, they discount their ability to deal with problems. Discounts need to be confronted with caring to get people to stop suffering and get them to deal with what is bothering them.

HOW TO DEAL WITH DISCOUNTS

Discount	*Confrontation*
1. "There's nothing the matter." (Problem discount)	"How about your thinking about what you are feeling?" "I'm willing to talk to you about it if you want to." "It is not ok with me for you to discount your feelings. They are important and you can deal with your feelings or ask for help."
2. "Oh, it's not important; I'll probably feel better tomorrow." (Significance discount)	"Sounds like you are having some feelings that you are not dealing with." "Will you think about what you are feeling and talk to me about it?" "It's not ok with me for you to discount the importance of your feelings."
3. "Well, there is nothing that can be done anyway." (Solvability discount)	"Sounds like it seems hopeless to you right now." "Will you think about what you are willing to do about your problem? Only if you have tried at least ten options without success will I accept your definition that it is hopeless." "You can think effectively and solve problems."
4. "I don't know what to do, it's too much to think about." (Self-discount)	"Sounds like you are feeling helpless about solving your problem." "You can think and feel at the same time and use both to solve your problem." "How about thinking about what you can do to solve the problem."

Many students will not learn to think and solve problems unless you are willing to put energy into confronting passivity and discounting. Since the way out of passivity is for the passive person to think about what he wants or needs and how to get it, he must be willing to stop using passivity and discounting to get what he wants. You also need to make sure that you don't support any of the passive behaviors. One of the most common ways that teachers support passivity is through Rescuing. Rescuing is defined as doing something for someone else that she/he could do for himself/herself. Common forms of Rescuing involve thinking and solving problems for a passive person who could do that for himself/herself. Teachers who engage in Rescuing use it to achieve feelings of being needed and important, control over another person, and avoidance of problems in themselves.

PERMISSIONS

Another effective way to promote healthy interpersonal and intrapersonal communication is through the use of permissions. Many students at some time in their past have been given negative messages (verbal or nonverbal, direct or indirect) about their abilities or their personal worth. These children need to receive permissions or positive messages from teachers and others to replace the negative ones. The negative messages are often in the form of injunctions (Don't think, Don't be you, etc.) or attributions (Be lazy, Be a child, Be passive). Permissions are "You can" or "I expect you to" statements. If the teacher has established rapport with a student, then permissions may be an extremely helpful way to promote effective behavior. The negative messages are often tied to passivity and discounting and support "not ok" decisions the person has made. Below are listed some commonly held injunctions with the appropriate permission statement for each.

HOW TO GIVE PERMISSIONS

Negative Message	Permission
1. "Don't have needs and wants of your own."	"You can figure out what you want for yourself from this class and decide how to get it."
2. "Don't think."	"I expect you to think about what you want and take care of yourself by asking for what you want."
3. "Don't be you."	"It's ok to be you and get what you want."
4. "Don't feel (angry, sad)."	"It's ok to feel angry and decide how to express it appropriately."
5. "Don't question things, just do them."	"It's ok to question why rules are made and to think of reasons for doing things."

Since thinking, feeling, problem solving, and active meeting of one's needs and wants are necessary to breaking the unhealthy symbiosis, permissions in these areas are particularly useful. Permissions that many children need to hear are that they are expected to think, to ask for what they need and want, and that it's ok for them to grow up. An indirect way to give a child permission to think is to say to a child who asks you to solve a problem for him: "How about you figuring out what to do about that and coming to talk to me when you have figured it out." Even if the child is unable to figure it out, you have given him permission to think and then ask for information that he needs to figure it out.

THINK STRUCTURES AND PROBLEM-SOLVING STRUCTURES

There are a number of ways to teach students how to mobilize their thinking processes and how to solve problems effectively. Again, the most effective way is to model the behavioral skills that you wish your students to learn.

Levin (1973) developed a simple way for teaching effective thinking that is presented in modified form below:

I am _____ *and I think (or fantasize)*
　　　　[feeling word]
that if I _____
　　　　　[what behavior]
I will be _____
　　　　　[what others will do to you]
instead of _____
　　　　　　[what you would like others to do]
so I _____
　　　　[what you usually do: a game, passivity or discounting]

After you ask someone to diagram this negative think structure, ask him to think about what he could do to get the response he wants.

Problem solving from a position of equal power and equal responsibility is necessary to promote effective interpersonal communication in the classroom (Gordon, 1974). The process presumes that students and teachers are convinced that a win-win structure is possible and the other skills are operating at a high level.

The six steps in problem solving are listed below:

Step One—Defining the Problem. Each person has a turn stating what he thinks the problem is and how he feels about it. The other person listens and restates what he/she heard the other say and checks out whether or not that is what was meant (negotiation for meaning). Then both state and agree on a definition of the problem. State the problem in terms of unmet needs and wants and not solutions. Example: "I cannot hear the group I am working with and I'm angry about that" instead of "I want it quiet in this room" (solution).

Step Two—Brainstorming Possible Solutions.   All ideas or possible solutions are accepted without evaluation. What do you need/want and what does the other person need/want to feel good about himself or the problem?

Step Three—Evaluating the Possible Solutions.   Estimate what the probabilities of success are for each possible solution and consider what internal and external resources are necessary and available to make the solution work. Ask: "How can each of us get as much as possible of what we want?"

Step Four—Deciding Upon a Solution.   "Which solution would I feel best about?" Agree on the one that "feels best" to both of you and write down what is expected by both parties.

Step Five—Implementing the Solution.   Determine who is to do what by when. Be specific about this and write it into the contract, including a deadline for implementing the solution.

Step Six—Evaluating the Success of the Solution.   It is also important to agree that if for some reason the solution no longer is working for one of the parties, he/she can request another problem-solving session and the process will begin all over again. Therefore, the contract is always open-ended.

CONTRACTS

Contracts can be an effective tool for developing good interpersonal communication in the classroom because (1) they spell out rules and policies, (2) they make expectations clear, (3) they allow students to question and understand rules and expectations, (4) they set up a structure in which there is mutual responsibility for enforcing the conditions of the contract.

One form of contract used by some teachers is a no-discount contract. In this, two or more people have an agreement not to discount themselves or each other. This kind of contract can become the framework for effective thinking. If the student contracts to say what he doesn't like and what he wants to do instead, he really has to think about how to structure time for himself.

A no-discount contract may look like the following:

Because we work together and both have needs and wants to be successful, we agree that we will not intentionally discount ourselves, the other person, or the importance and solvability of problems. We agree to state what we don't like and what we want instead. We agree to confront any unintentional discounts that we perceive in ourselves or the other person. We agree to say what we don't like in a way that doesn't put the other person down. We agree to solve all problems that arise in the classroom (or outside, if they affect us) so we both get our needs/ wants met.

This contract is our way of agreeing to work together, cooperate, and assume equal responsibility for making this classroom a place where we both want to be and feel good.

Signed: _____

[teacher]

_____

[student or students]

Other similar contracts can be used for schoolwork. Also, cooperative rule setting for the classroom can be developed and stated in contract form.

COMMON ERRORS IN INTERPERSONAL COMMUNICATION

Below is a list of the common errors people make in communicating with other people.

1. Making a statement instead of asking for what you want or need: "I wish you were going into town."
2. Asking a question instead of making a statement: "Don't you think that. . .?"
3. Saying "I feel" to mean "I think": "I feel that you are rude."
4. Saying "one" or "people" or "you" in expressing your point of view: "People are afraid to. . ."
5. In a group, talking about a person and not to him or her: "I like her idea."
6. Using "I can't" to mean "I don't" or "I don't want to": "I can't go with you because I'm too tired."

7. Using "have to's" and "shoulds" when you mean "choose to": "I have to go to the school play tonight."
8. Not answering a question directly: "How do you feel today?" "Why do you want to know?"
9. Using words like "I guess," "I think," "maybe," when you are sure.
10. Using "try" instead of "do": "I'll try to do that today" instead of "I'll do that today."
11. Blaming your feelings on someone else: "You made me angry" instead of "I am angry."
12. Confusing inference and observation: "John is a poor sport" instead of "John hit Jimmy with the ball and [observation] I think he is a poor sport [inference]."
13. Interrupting someone when he is speaking. This usually means you aren't listening.
14. Changing the subject, or "chaining." This is listening to just enough of what someone says to change the subject to something you know more about or want to talk about. First person: "I watched the Monday night football game and it was really exciting." Response: "We have tickets to see the Colorado-Nebraska football game next week."
15. Using statements like "always" or "never" to support your point of view.

INTRAPERSONAL COMMUNICATION

The ability of a person to stay in touch with what is happening inside of him is referred to as intrapersonal communication. Another way to express this is self-awareness: how aware you are of what is going on inside of you, outside of you, and how you are relating these experiences to yourself, as opposed to relating them to others (interpersonal).

ESSENTIAL INTRAPERSONAL PROCESSES

Intrapersonal communication can be thought of in several ways:

1. Awareness of what is going on inside of you. This would include awareness of the signals your body is sending out all the time: the tensions you feel in your muscles; the physical sensations that go with feelings; and feelings themselves. It also includes awareness of the inner world of thoughts and ideas.
2. Awareness of what is happening around you. This includes what your senses tell you about what is present in the here and now.

3. Awareness of past events and how these events influence you in the present. Sometimes past events continue to influence us in ways of which we are not aware.
4. Awareness of fantasy experiences. Fantasy can be useful to discover more about ourselves. Fantasy can enable us to imagine, guess, play hunches, and try out things we are not experiencing now.

One unmistakable fact about awareness is that it is irreversible—you cannot become unaware once you are aware. You can attempt to repress or block awarenesses but they are difficult to block and it requires much energy to do so.

In the classroom, you can assist children in the process of intrapersonal communication by developing their awareness of themselves in the areas mentioned above. This process can teach children to trust in their awareness as an important tool for learning about themselves and the world around them.

Another important principle of intrapersonal communications is that of "here and now." This is a way of establishing a continuum of awareness and adding a new dimension of time and space to that continuum. Starting with what I am aware of in the present, I can then move to the future through use of fantasy awareness and move to the past from the perspective of how the past is affecting me in the present.

INTERNAL AWARENESS

Ways We Talk to Ourselves

One of the most common ways people trap themselves is by the words they use when they talk to themselves. We say "I have to," "I can't," "I should," and act as if someone else were telling us what to do and what not to do. Most people talk to themselves in very critical ways and don't know how to give themselves very many positive messages. Listen to and observe your thoughts about yourself for about ten minutes and check how many thoughts are critical and how many are nurturing.

All phrases like "have to," "should," and "ought to" imply that you have no choice. Make a list of things that you do that you think of as "have to's. "Start each one with "I have to . . ."; then, after you have completed the list, change the beginning of each one to "I choose to. . .'' This can be very useful in helping you to take responsibility for the choices you make instead of acting as if you were forced to make them.

Listening to the ways that students talk to you about themselves gives you some clues as to how they talk to themselves. Confront inappropriate critical words by saying: ''You meant to say you choose to do that, didn't you?''

Ways to Stay in Touch with Feelings

Feelings are the basic level of awareness and are necessary for effective thinking and problem solving. They provide the energy required for people to know what they need and want.

Most people are not in touch with the feelings that underlie their thoughts. According to Hendricks (1975), any unobserved feeling symbolizes into a thought that actually distorts the feeling. We then act from a thought that is not accurately reflective of the underlying feeling. If people can be taught to see their feelings as they are, they will be more centered in their actions.

One way to help students in this process is to take time during the school day and have them stop what they are doing and tune into their feelings. Ask them ''What are your feelings right now? How do you experience them?'' Example: ''I am feeling angry because I can't figure out this problem and I am experiencing the anger as tightness in my jaws.''

Once students have learned to identify their feelings and know how the feelings are experienced, they can then be taught to integrate feelings and thoughts. One way to do this is to give a person permission to fully experience the feeling in his/her body, then to let it go, and then to himself or herself give positive messages for having the feeling and letting it go (Golas, 1974). This allows a person not only to experience the feeling fully but also to accept or ''own'' that feeling in its purest form.

Ways to Listen to the Body

The body is sending out signals constantly, but most people don't know how to listen to these signals and make use of them. Much is yet to be discovered about how we can bring all bodily functions under conscious control through increased awareness and biofeedback devices. We do know, however, that the structure of the body is very malleable and can be changed through the function of increased awareness.

One important fact about the notion of control of bodily functions and sensations is that it teaches people that they are responsible for what they are experiencing. For example, if you are experiencing tension in your back it is not correct to say "My back is hurting me." Rather, you should say "I am tensing my back and hurting myself."

Muscle tension in our bodies is usually chronic and because of that often goes unnoticed. Ask students to close their eyes while lying down and pay attention to any tension they are experiencing. Then get them to exaggerate the tension so they can feel it more acutely. After this level of awareness has been reached, ask them to own the experience ("I'm tensing my arm and hurting myself"), then release the tension and focus their awareness on completely relaxing that muscle and again owning the experience ("I'm relaxing my arm and making myself feel good").

EXTERNAL AWARENESS

Most people need to be taught to listen to their surroundings and to restore contact with those things going on outside of them. One way to help students do this is to ask them to focus their awareness on objects in their environment and let each object speak to them. Example: "I am the chalkboard and you write on me sometimes but someone usually erases it."

PAST AWARENESS

Feelings associated with past experiences that haven't been integrated tend to crowd into our present awareness often at crucial times. These unintegrated feelings from our past are still pushing into our awareness in order to give us the opportunity to integrate them.

Most unintegrated feelings from our past call up images of situations involving parents, teachers, or other adults. One way to assist students in this process of integration is to ask them to imagine a dialogue with one of their parents. Say to them: "With your eyes closed, picture one of your parents sitting in front of you. Notice as many things as you can about him (clothing, facial expression). How do you feel as you look at your parent? Tell him all the things that you never told him. Express everything that is on your mind that you have held back from saying, being aware of your feelings and your body." (Take five minutes to do this.)

"Then become your parent and respond: 'How do you feel toward your child? Tell your child how you feel.'" (Five minutes).

"Switch places and become yourself again, this time telling your parent what you need and want from him. Be specific about what it is you are wanting. Reverse roles and respond to what your child has said. Then tell your child what you want from him.

"Now switch again and tell your parent what you appreciate in him. Be specific. Then become your parent and respond. Now tell your child what you appreciate in him. Continue this dialogue as long as you want, dealing with issues and feelings you are hanging on to from the past."

If your students do this, eventually they will let go of the unintegrated feelings, give up making demands that their parents be different, and forgive them for their faults. This is an extremely important process for everyone to go through in order to restore his own power and let go of the past.

FANTASY AWARENESS

Fantasy can be a way that people avoid contact with the here and now. Most of us can spend a lot of our time worrying or hoping and planning for events and things that will never happen. Fantasy can be a valuable tool in the classroom, though, as long as it is integrated into the here and now and supports or extends our present awarenesses. If fantasy is split off from the present, it becomes merely an escape from the unpleasant experiences of daily living.

Full awareness involves identification with what you are experiencing in the here and now, whether you like the experience or not. When you have achieved that level of awareness with yourself and with others, then you can utilize fantasy to extend the here and now and integrate more into your experience of the present.

Unintegrated emotions and fantasies around them interfere with being in the here and now and being open to present experiences. Children need to learn how to develop, expand, and utilize fantasy awareness in learning about themselves and the world.

One important skill that children need is to learn how to distinguish between reality and fantasy in ways that don't discourage fantasy. A child who makes up a "pretend story" needs to hear that it's ok to do that. He or she should be encouraged to look at the real parts and the fantasy parts without making fantasy bad.

One activity that a teacher can utilize almost at any time in teaching content is to ask "What would happen if . . ." questions. For instance, "What would happen if you had eyes on the back of your head instead of on the front of your head?" or "What if the letter *e* were outlawed and when you wrote something you had to leave it out?")

In doing this kind of activity with a group it is important that everyone be given a chance to express to another person what he or she fantasized. In large groups have students pair off and share their fantasies. It is also important to model ways to be open and accepting in sharing fantasies.

If children have permission to fantasize and share fantasies, you as the teacher will be in a position to help them deal with scary fantasies and unintegrated feelings. Through use of regular small-group sharing sessions you can work with fantasies and feelings that need to be integrated. One example involved a four-year-old boy whose mother worked for the Forest Service. His father had been killed in a plane crash when he was a baby. The teacher noticed that at times he would fight and be mean to other children. He reported in a sharing session that every time his mother went into the forest overnight, as she did at times as part of her work, he would get very frightened that something would happen to her and she wouldn't come back. The teacher listened to the feelings and said, "You are afraid she won't come back and you will be left all alone." Then she held the child in her lap, comforted him, and asked what he thought he could do to feel less afraid. He came up with several ideas like "Tell Mommy not to go," but finally decided to tell her he was scared and ask her to take good care of herself so she would come back. The teacher talked to the parent several days later and found out that the child had dealt with his scary feelings with her and that they had had a beautiful experience sharing their feelings. After this there was a sharp reduction in the boy's fighting behavior at school, and the teacher checked on his feelings each time his mother went away for a day or two.

INTRAPERSONAL PROBLEM-SOLVING STRAGEGIES

At time we have problems that we have to work out ourselves and not in a problem-solving session with another person. We face decisions, choices, and problems where we have to communicate with ourselves.

There are a number of strategies that are useful in this process. Consider the following structure:

The problem or decision is _____

_____

My choices seem to be _____

_____

I believe it is wrong to _____
            right to _____
My mother or father would say _____
                    and do _____
                    and feel _____
The facts that I already have are _____

_____

The facts that I need to get are _____

_____

My basic feelings about this are _____

_____

The feelings I'm supposed to have about this are _____

_____

My hunch is _____

_____

My fantasy about solving this problem is _____

_____

TRANSPERSONAL COMMUNICATION

Teachers who have developed a classroom climate where effective interpersonal and intrapersonal communication is present have established the atmosphere necessary for transpersonal communication to occur. Transpersonal communication is designed to expand all human abilities and is best represented as the whole that is greater than the sum of its parts. It includes all effective interpersonal and intrapersonal communication as means to reaching higher levels of awareness and functioning. Effective interpersonal communication and intrapersonal communication are necessary to help people make contact with and break through cultural roles, ego defenses, body defenses, and unintegrated feelings. Through these processes a person can establish and maintain contact with his inner core, where unity with all life energy occurs. Figure 3 illustrates these processes and the conditions necessary for transpersonal communication to occur.

Figure 3.
The Transpersonal
Person

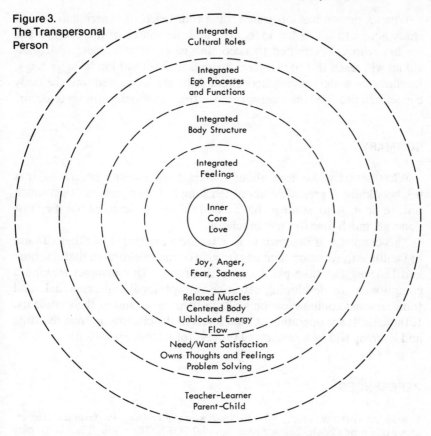

The transpersonal individual has integrated cultural roles to the extent that he or she can be both teacher and learner or both parent and child. The roles are flexible and adaptable to the situation. At the second level, the ego functions are free from the usual defenses and operate to enable the person to get needs and wants satisfied without discounting. The person who is free from ego defenses can readily "own" his or her thoughts and feelings and engage in effective problem solving.

At the third level, the body reflects the integration. Muscles are relaxed, the body maintains a centered position, and there is an unblocked energy flow throughout. At the emotional level, the person is in touch with basic feelings and is able to utilize these feelings in thinking and solving problems.

When a person has integrated these four levels of functioning he has ready access to his or her inner core and the source of life energy. The teacher who is committed to becoming more of a transpersonal individual will teach this to children through an informal modeling process. In addition, a classroom where these skills are integrated into the daily curriculum provides the atmosphere for transpersonal learnings to occur.

SUMMARY

What seems to be true about the teaching-learning process is that teachers know a great deal about teaching but they just don't get much time to do it. Also, students have a natural love of learning but they just don't get much time to use it in school.

This chapter was designed to give teachers practical tools they can use to facilitate the development of effective communication so that teaching and learning can take place in the classroom. This involves making a commitment to developing effective intrapersonal, interpersonal, and transpersonal communication skills in themselves and in their students. If these skills are operating at high levels in the classroom, then teaching and learning will be an enriching process for all those involved.

REFERENCES

COMBS, ARTHUR W. *et al., Florida Studies in the Helping Professions.* University of Florida Social Science Monograph No. 37. Gainesville, Fla.: University of Florida Press, 1969.

FALZETT, WILLIAM, and JEAN MAXWELL, *OK Childing and Parenting.* El Paso, Tex.: Transactional Analysis Insitute of El Paso, 1974.

GOLAS, THADDEUS, *The Lazy Man's Guide to Enlightenment.* Palo Alto: The Seed Center, 1972.

GORDON, THOMAS, *Teacher Effectiveness Training.* New York: Peter H. Wyden, 1974.

HENDRICKS, C. G., *Integral Therapy.* Unpublished manuscript, 1975.

HOLT, JOHN, *Escape From Childhood.* New York: Ballantine Books, 1974.

LEVIN, PAM, "A Think Structure for Feeling Fine Faster," *Transactional Analysis Journal,* January, 1973.

LOWEN, ALEXANDER, *Bioenergetics.* New York: Coward, McCann and Geoghegan, 1975.

MASLOW, ABRAHAM, *The Further Reaches of Human Nature.* New York: Viking, 1971.

MAY, ROLLO, *Power and Innocence. New York: W.W. Norton, 1972.*

SCHIFF, AARON W., and JACQUI SCHIFF, "Passivity," *Transpersonal Analysis Journal,* January, 1971.

EDUCATION AS A TRANSPERSONAL EXPERIENCE

You cannot teach transpersonal experience. You can hear about it, you can see it happening, and you can experience it. You can also get a feeling for it so that your own relationships allow it to occur more easily and more often. As a teacher, you can create an environment which facilitates it.

Throughout this book we have drawn from situations which are close to the normal school setting. Here we go farther afield. Out intention is to give you a clearer vision of the broad range of educational possibilities that open up transpersonal vistas.

These final selections are an opportunity for you to enjoy a variety of examples and points of view. All the selections are reflections or illustrations of how persons concerned with transpersonal teaching go about their business.

For learning to take root there must be the proper situation, the proper teacher, the proper tools, and the proper students. The selections here offer glimpses of moments in which all of the criteria have been met.

Please do not "learn" from reading what follows. Simply enjoy and perhaps reflect on what you read. We would appreciate it if you would share with us any other passages you have read or experiences you have had that have been meaningful in your own education.

Gurdjieff as Elementary Teacher

Fritz Peters

Georges Gurdjieff, a Russian philosopher who had a wide-ranging influence in Europe and the United States during the twenties and thirties, taught that people were "asleep," unaware of much of their daily life, routinized into creatures of habit.

Students all over the world continue to practice the principles set down by this man described as a superb and extremely difficult teacher. Fritz Peters was sent to Gurdjieff's institute by his avant-garde guardians. Here he recalls his first meeting with this most unorthodox "elementary" teacher.

I met and talked to Georges Gurdjieff for the first time in 1924, on a Saturday afternoon in June, at the Château du Prieuré in Fontainebleau-Avon, France. Although the reasons for my being there were not very clear in my mind—I was eleven at the time—my memory of that meeting is still brilliantly clear.

It was a bright, sunny day. Gurdjieff was sitting by a small marble-topped table, shaded by a striped umbrella, with his back to the château

"Gurdjieff as Elementary Teacher" (editors' title). From Fritz Peters, *Boyhood with Gurdjieff* (New York: E. P. Dutton and Co., Inc., 1964), pp. 5–8; 162–64. Reprinted by permission of the author.

proper, facing a large expanse of formal lawns and flower beds. I had to sit on the terrace of the château, behind him, for some time before I was summoned to his side for an interview. I had, actually, seen him once before, in New York the previous winter, but I did not feel that I had "met" him. My only memory of that prior time was that I had been frightened of him; partly because of the way he looked at—or through—me, and partly because of his reputation. I had been told that he was at least a "prophet"—at most, something very close to the "second coming of Christ."

Meeting any version of a "Christ" is an event, and this meeting was not one to which I looked forward. Facing the presence not only did not appeal to me—I dreaded it.

The actual meeting did not measure up to my fears. "Messiah" or not, he seemed to me a simple, straightforward man. He was not surrounded by any halo, and while his English was heavily accented, he spoke far more simply than the Bible had led me to expect. He made a vague gesture in my direction, told me to sit down, called for coffee, and then asked me why I was there. I was relieved to find that he seemed to be an ordinary human being, but I was troubled by the question. I felt sure that I was supposed to give him an *important* answer; that I should have some excellent reason. Having none, I told him the truth: That I was there because I had been brought there.

He then asked me why I wanted to be there, to study at his school. Once more I was only able to answer that it was all beyond my control—I had not been consulted, I had been, as it were, transported to that place. I remember my strong impulse to lie to him, and my equally strong feeling that I could not lie to him. I felt sure that he knew the truth in advance. The only question that I answered less than honestly was when he asked me if I wanted to stay there and to study with him. I said that I did, which was not essentially true. I said it because I knew that it was expected of me. It seems to me, now, that any child would have answered as I did. Whatever the Prieuré might represent to adults (and the literal name of the school was "The Gurdjieff Institute for the Harmonious Development of Man"), I felt that I was experiencing the equivalent of being interviewed by the principal of a high school. Children went to school, and I subscribed to the general agreement that no child would tell his teacher-to-be that he did not want to go to school. The only thing that surprised me was that I was asked the question.

Gurdjieff then asked me two more questions:

1. What do you think life is?
and
2. What do you want to know?

I answered the first question by saying: "I think life is something that is handed to you on a silver platter, and it is up to you (me) to do something with it." This answer touched off a long discussion about the phrase "on a silver platter," including a reference by Gurdjieff to the head of John the Baptist. I retreated—it felt like a retreat—and modified the phrase to the effect that life was a "gift," and this seemed to please him.

The second question (What do you want to know?) was simpler to answer. My words were: "I want to know everything."

Gurdjieff replied immediately: "You cannot know everything. Everything about what?"

I said: "Everything about man," and then added: "In English I think it is called psychology or maybe philosophy."

He sighed then, and after a short silence said: "You can stay. But your answer makes life difficult for me. I am the only one who teaches what you ask. You make more work for me."

Since my childish aims were to conform and to please, I was disconcerted by his answer. The last thing I wanted to do was to make life more difficult for anyone—it seemed to me that it was difficult enough already. I said nothing in reply to this, and he went on to tell me that in addition to learning "everything" I would also have the opportunity to study lesser subjects, such as languages, mathematics, various sciences, and so forth. He also said that I would find that his was not the usual school: "Can learn many things here that other schools not teach." He then patted my shoulder benevolently.

I use the word "benevolently" because the gesture was of great importance to me at the time. I longed for approval from some higher authority. To receive such "approval" from this man who was considered by other adults to be a "prophet," "seer," and/or a "Messiah" —and approval in such a simple, friendly gesture—was unexpected and heartwarming. I beamed.

His manner changed abruptly. He struck the table with one fist, looked at me with great intensity, and said: "Can you promise to do something for me?"

His voice and the look he had given me were frightening and also exciting. I felt both cornered and challenged. I answered him with one word, a firm "Yes."

He gestured towards the expanse of lawns before us: "You see this grass?"

"Yes."

"I give you work. You must cut this grass, with machine, every week."

I looked at the lawns, the grass spreading before us into what appeared to me infinity. It was, without any doubt, a prospect of more work in one week than I had ever contemplated in my life. Again, I said "Yes."

He struck the table with his fist for a second time. "You must promise on your God." His voice was deadly serious. "You must promise that you will do this thing no matter what happens."

I looked at him, questioning, respectful, and with considerable awe. No lawn—not even these (there were four of them)—had ever seemed important to me before. "I promise," I said earnestly.

"Not just promise," he reiterated. "Must promise you will do no matter what happens, no matter who try stop you. Many things can happen in life."

For a moment his words conjured up visions of terrifying arguments over the mowing of these lawns. I foresaw great emotional dramas taking place in the future on account of these lawns and of myself. Once again, I promised. I was as serious as he was then. I would have died, if necessary, in the act of mowing the lawns.

My feeling of dedication was obvious, and he seemed satisfied. He told me to begin work on Monday, and then dismissed me. I don't think I realized it at the time—that is, the sensation was new to me—but I left him with the feeling that I had fallen in love; whether with the man, the lawns, or myself, did not matter. My chest was expanded far beyond its normal capacity. I, a child, an unimportant cog in the world which belonged to adults, had been asked to perform something that was apparently vital.

[Later in his education, Fritz was given the job of tending the herb garden.]

What with adolescence, lack of supervision, lack of interest, and just plain laziness, I managed to do as little work as possible in the Herb

Garden. I avoided going there except when it was necessary for me to bring various herbs to the kitchen. When the quality of the herbs became noticeably poorer and when I was at times unable even to supply a small quantity of some particular herb, someone must have taken it upon themselves to investigate the garden and report their findings to Gurdjieff.

The result was that Gurdjieff made a personal inspection of the garden with me, walking up and down between all the small beds, examining every plant. When he had finished he told me that as far as he could see, I had done absolutely nothing at all there in the way of work. I had to admit that I had done very little work, but defended myself to the extent of pointing out that I had done some occasional weeding. He shook his head and said that in view of the state of the garden it would be better not to defend myself at all. He then assigned several of the children to work with me in the garden until it was in proper shape, and instructed me as to what had to be done to the various plants: hoeing between the rows, trimming certain plants, dividing and replanting others.

Although the children were very annoyed with me for having shirked my own work and thereby caused them to have to work on "my" garden, they all pitched in and we carried out Gurdjieff's orders very easily and quickly. It was a very small plot of land and it could not have taken us more than a day or two. When we had finished the work, Gurdjieff pronounced it satisfactory, complimented all the other children on their work, and said that he wanted to have a talk with me, alone.

He first told me that I could see for myself that I had not performed a task that had been assigned to me, and that it had been necessary for him to intervene in my work and take measures to repair the damage that had been caused by my neglect. He said that this was a very good example of the way in which one person's failure to accomplish his duty could affect the general welfare of everyone else and that, while I might not think of herbs as important, they were important to him and were needed in the kitchen; also that I had caused him an unnecessary, if minor, expense because various plants had had to be purchased, which would not have been necessary if I had done my job properly.

He went on to say that it was true, in one sense, that the herb garden was not important; what was important, however, was to be responsible and to do one's work, particularly when that work could affect the welfare of others. However, there was another, still more important reason for accomplishing any assigned task, which was for one's own sake.

He spoke again about the exercise of "self-observation" and said that since man was a three-centred or three-brained being, it was necessary to do exercises and perform tasks that were valuable for all three centres, not just the physical or "motor" centre; that "self-observation" as I knew it was a purely physical exercise in that it consisted in the observation of one's physical body and its movements, gestures and manifestations.

He said that there were various important exercises having to do with "self-remembering" which was a very important aspect of his work. One of them was to conscientiously and with all one's concentration, try to remember, as on a movie film, everything that one had done during each entire day. This was to be done every night before going to sleep. The most important thing in the exercise was not to let the attention wander —by association. If one's attention did wander from the focus upon the image of oneself, then it was absolutely necessary to begin all over again at the beginning each time this happened—and it would, he warned, happen.

He talked to me for a very long time that morning, and emphasized the fact that everyone had, usually, a particular, recurring problem in life. He said that these particular problems were usually a form of laziness, and that I was to think about my laziness, which took a fairly obvious physical form, as in the case of the garden: I had simply put off doing anything in the garden until someone had taken notice of that fact. He said that he wanted me to think seriously about my laziness—not the outward form, which was not important, but to find out what it was. When you see that you are lazy, necessary find out what this laziness *is*. Because in some ways you already lazy for many years, can take even many years for you to find out what it is. Must ask yourself, whenever you see your own laziness: "What is this laziness in me?" If you ask this question seriously, and with concentration, is possible someday you will find answer. This important and very difficult work I give you now."

I thanked him for what he had said and added that I was sorry that I had not done my work in the garden and that I would do it properly in the future.

He brushed aside my thanks and said that it was useless to be sorry. "Is too late for that now, and is also too late to do good work in garden. In life never have second chance, only have one chance. You had one time to do good work in garden, for self; you not do, so now even if you work all your life, in this garden, cannot be same thing for you. But also important not be 'sorry' about this; can waste all life feeling sorry. There is valuable thing sometimes, thing you call remorse. If man have real remorse for something he do that is not good, this can be valuable; but if only sorry and say will do same thing better in future is waste of time. This time is already gone forever, this part of your life is finished, you cannot live over again. Not important if you do good work in garden now, because will do for wrong reasons—to try to repair damage which cannot be repaired ever. This serious thing. But also very serious not to waste time feeling sorry or feeling regret, this only waste even more time. Must learn in life, not to make such mistakes, and must understand that once made mistake is made forever.''

An Interview with One of Gurdjieff's Teachers

Rafael Lefort

In this selection a writer tracks down one of the people responsible for Gurdjieff's own transpersonal education, Hassan Effendi, who has some surprising things to say about the "curriculum" he taught.

". . . I taught Gurdjieff to breathe. I say this and you burst into a flood of how's, why's and ifs and buts and can I teach you? The answer is, I can but I will not."

"May I ask, Sheikh, why only breathing?"

"Only! Only! Stupid question! More stupid than to have asked why or how. Do you think that to learn to breathe correctly is easy? Does your shallow panting do more than supply your blood with the minimum amount of oxygen needed to keep that portion of your brain that you use alive? One of the functions of correct breathing is to carry the baraka to the farthest recess of the deep consciousness. Undeveloped men try to use thought or random action to affect the consciousness. Neither of these

"An Interview With One of Gurdjieff's Teachers" (editor's title). From Rafael Lefort, *The Teachers of Gurdjieff* (London: Gollancz, Ltd., 1970), pp. 62–65. Reprinted by permission of the publisher.

works as the dose and the direction and the intensity are not known to them. Only to breathe! Do you know how long it takes before you can be trained to take your first *real* breath? Months, even years, and then only when you *know* what you are aiming for.

"Gurdjieff came to me with a capacity to breathe and I taught him how to do it and how to breathe with his system, his consciousness and his entire being. You breathe to sustain your level of existence. Higher man breathes to maintain the breakthrough that he has made into a superior realm of being. Your ignorance, while not surprising, terrifies me. Gurdjieff stayed with me for twenty years. Yes, twenty years! Five months in Erzurum and the remainder of the time in rapport with me wherever he was learning to use his breath. Do you know what can be carried into your consciousness by your breath? Do you know why a Sheikh will breathe on a disciple? Do you know why a Sheikh breathes into the ear of a newly born child? Of course you do not! You put it down to magic, primitive symbols representing life, but the practical reasons, the deadly serious business of nourishing the inner consciousness, passes you by. Flows over your head, bent as it is over physiology, psychology, causative phenomena, theoretic ecstasies. You blind yourself, life does not blind you. You call out in your pitiful arrogance for enlightenment, you claim your right to it as a birthright. You earn it, my friend, you earn it by dedication, toil and discipline. A hundred years must a body travel until it is seasoned. A seeker does not become a real Sufi until the very marrow of his bones has been seasoned in the oven of reality! Talk less of 'only breathing' and see how pitifully unprepared you yourself are even to approach the concept of Existence! Your capacity to profit from anything is directly proportionate to the efficiency of your system.

"This is true physiologically as well as esoterically. You cannot, and you know it, expect your body to extract and process sugar if you have no pancreas, and yet, in your arrogant, intellectual way, you expect to be able to profit from the knowledge that others have bought for you. You want to use what you call the 'process of thought or logic' to pick over the whole and eat the parts that you consider nourishing. At best your thought processes are surface reactions, at worst you cannot absorb a reaction or thought before it is fallen upon, diluted, dissected and malformed by the infernal process that you call academic reasoning. Reason, you call it! Do you call it reasonable to gulp down great pieces of wisdom and regurgitate them in the form of theory, the speech and the drivelings of a raw mind? The so-called Age of Reason in Europe produced less reason, less *real* intellectual progress, than one day's activity by a developed man.

"You aspire, you dream, but you do not do! Tenacity is replaced by hair-splitting, courage by bluster, and disciplined thought by narrow, pedantic attempts at reason. Bend what little you have left of your intellect to practical activity, realising your severe shortcomings. Cease your diabolic 'examination of self.' Who am I? How many I's do I have? You have not the capacity at all to understand the concept of true self-examination. Follow a valid philosophy or condemn yourself to join the generations who have drowned themselves in the stagnant pools of slime that they call the reservoirs of reason and intellect!

"You have no reason, no intellect, do you understand? Even less have you of the catalytic substance that would allow you to use the reason and intellect that might just have survived the conditioning you have so warmly welcomed.

"Yes, I only taught Gurdjieff to breathe! No more, no less." . . .

The Hows and Whys
of Power Points

Reshad Feild

Enlightenment can strike at the strangest times. Here, a ten-year-old boy learns an unforgettable lesson from a true transpersonal teacher.

. . . I was 10 years old and my family had an estate in the southern part of England. There was a gamekeeper on the estate who taught me all about the world of nature.

I would have to walk out with him with an unloaded gun on his rounds. and, once a week, when all the adults would assemble to slaughter whatever moved or flew, I would walk out with them, standing in line as they did, always my gun unloaded so that I could learn the discipline necessary to be a safe shot when I grew up.

Once a week the gamekeeper would take me out into the woods and teach me how to catch rabbits with my hands. To be able to do this it was essential that I could come to "think" like a rabbit, to know what instinct

Excerpted from "The Hows and Whys of Power Points," by Reshad Feild, in *East-West Journal,* IV, no. 5, June 1974, 26, 27, 35. Reprinted by permission of the *East-West Journal,* 31 Farnsworth St., Boston, Mass.

made it sit in this place or that place when it was not in its hole, how the weather affected it, and the time of the day.

Pretty soon I came to almost be able to put myself into the brain of that tiny creature.

The day came when I had to experiment with the actual catching of one of the rabbits that I had watched and loved for so long. "What you have to do," the gamekeeper said, "is to be able to know which way it is going to move before it does. . . . You have to be quicker than the rabbit, and if you are very, very aware you will be where it will be before it has moved. . . ."

I stamped my foot in the same way that the rabbit does in time of danger, and then threw myself in the direction that I knew he would move. In a time quicker than I would have thought possible, the rabbit was struggling in my arms.

"Now you must kill it as you have been taught," the keeper said to me.

How could I ever forget that moment? Through loving the animal kingdom I had come to learn about it and to understand it, and now I was confronted with a similar experience to that of Castaneda's with Don Juan, the conscious transmutation of energy. As the rabbit died it was as though I was transported into another world. Everything shone, the trees gave off a silver light, there was a sense of recognition in every leaf, every plant, and in the earth itself. I knew then that I was not inside my body, but my body was *inside me*. I was participating in the great drama of life, and for a 10-year-old boy, shot into the realization of the Oneness of all life, the experience left a mark that has never been forgotten.

The Education of
the Buddhist Child

The Reverend Jiyu Kennett, Roshi

The Reverend Kennett, who has spent much time in Japan, describes education and childrearing among contemporary Buddhists.

With young Buddhists growing up around us by the score and more and more of the members of the Society marrying and having their own children, not to mention interest in the education of the young on the part of the Sufis and other friendly religious organizations, I have been asked to discuss, or rather delineate, the usual method of education of the Buddhist child throughout the east. There are certain differences with regard to the approach to the education of Buddhists as opposed to members of other religions and I think these are basic to a Buddhist education anywhere, whether it is in the east or west. So, first and foremost, I would like to point out what is probably obvious to most of you, but which is certainly not obvious to the average parent in England, for example, where I myself was brought up; and that is that the child must

"The Education of the Buddhist Child" by The Reverend Jiyu Kennett, Roshi. From the *Journal of the Zen Mission Society,* 5, no. 12 (December 1974), 12–16. Reprinted by permission of the publisher.

be cherished—not merely looked after or even loved but cherished. However foolish its comments, however childish, however silly, however babyish, the child is trying to express itself and must never be thought of as something that is *needing* to be educated rather as that which has within itself all the knowledge that matters that ever was. And it is our duty as educators to unlock the doors of that knowledge so that the child may *experience* and *express* what it already knows.

Buddhism, unlike some other religions, does not believe in original sin. Therefore it places no guilt on the child from the moment it is conceived. Instead, it says that we are simply born and later, as a result of what we do with ourselves, of what happens to us and as a result of our going into dual thinking—right and wrong—"this is right, that is wrong; this is good, this is bad"—we educate ourselves out of our original oneness of mind into a duality which, at a later date, we have to transcend if we are to be able to do anything whatsoever to overcome the spiritual illnesses our education has generated.

The average child going to school in the west is taught from the moment it enters, "Now, you are a child and I am *the* teacher. *You* do *not* know and *I do* know." I can certainly remember, and I am sure most of my readers can remember also, the moment when something inside us was almost killed or, at least, shut off by a watertight door. We were perfectly all right until the moment when it was made quite clear to us that we did not know and that the teacher *did.* For this was the moment when doubt entered our minds—and fear entered them because we had been told that we were inadequate—and we were already in the toils of duality.

Buddhist education does not do this. The Buddhist teacher, if he is a real teacher, says. "This child knows all, as indeed I know all, but he cannot yet express it and I can only express it partially. Therefore he and I are on the same road. I have been going along it for a little longer than he has and I will try to go at the speed he is going at so that he may catch up with me and, perhaps, be able to surpass me—who knows?" So it is the duty of the Buddhist teacher to get his egocentric self out of the way to a very, very great extent so that the education of the child may be a free and beautiful thing, untrammeled by "Look at what *I* have achieved in *my* educating of this child!" It is the child that does the educating of itself by using its experiences to fall back on later; the child that makes the running; and the child that matters—we are all children in the Buddha Nature. When we say, as teachers, "*I* know and *you* do not," we are really saying, "*Our* Buddha Nature is better than *your* Buddha

Nature"; thus is set up duality, self, fear and inadequacy. If, on the other hand, we say, "Your Buddha Nature and our Buddha Nature are one but there is a difference between us because you are smaller than us and we are older than you; therefore we have run a little farther but we will come back to help you run as far," the difference in our attitude of mind, the difference in the attitude of the child to learning, is phenomenal.

I am often asked, "How do you teach meditation to children and what is the best age to start at?" In the east the average child is taught to meditate as soon as it is possible for it to sit upright; i.e., around one or two years old. No doctrine is put into the child's head. The mother and father, and the rest of the family, will sit quietly in front of the family altar; the child, without being restrained, will either sit for a few moments or roll around on the floor with the parents taking no notice. The parents thus express their knowledge of the child's latent understanding and do not treat it as less than themselves. In a very short time the child wants to sit like the parents, as do, interestingly enough, the dog and cat. I have sat down to meditate and my cat has come up, looked at the wall and then sat down to look at it with me. Thus, if the parents meditate, the child will meditate too. I have seen children at the age of two and a half doing formal meditation in the laymen's meditation hall in Sojiji— and doing a wonderful job. I have photographs of them. These children do a meditation so pure and exquisite it is unbelievable to watch; but they would not be able to discuss the Buddha Nature with you, nor would they be able to put into words the doctrine of the Trikaya—nor would they be able to explain the "all is one" and the "all is different" that their little bodies express. Their explanations are not as the world understands explanations. And yet every part of their bodies will express the "all is one" and the "all is different"—they will express the Buddha Nature for they have learned to meditate with their whole being untrammeled by duality. They are indeed *whole* creatures and can teach us much.

The education of the child starts prior to birth, on the very night of its conception. The attitude of mind of the parents—whether they are in a selfish mood, simply wishing to gratify their own pleasure, or whether they are wishing to produce a child which both of them will love—will affect the child at a later date. The Buddha Nature, which is within all of us, knows what is happening to itself, and the future child is conditioned by the attitudes of mind of the parents at conception. Therefore, education does not even begin at the first look that passes between the mother and the child; it begins with the look in the eyes of the two parents, whether they be full of lust or whether they be full of self-less love. There used to be an old saying that there was such a thing as a "love child" in existence. It is unfortunate that it became a derogatory term, pertaining to a child born out of wedlock.

From what I have said, therefore, in a very real sense, "The sins of the fathers are visited upon the children," and the children are born carrying the karmic load which the parents have put upon them; their teachers later force them to continue to carry it. This is indeed a great grief. Parents should know well what it is they do on the night of conception and make no mistakes. They should also know well why it is that a child may ask, at a later date, with genuine grief in his heart, the old Zen kōan, "Why did you beget me? Why was I born? Before my parents conceived me, what was my original face?" These kōans can be taken on many levels and can be understood by many, many means. The next step is for the parent to cherish the child, not merely love it; the parent must always be open to the child, never sneering at, or belittling its efforts, never looking down upon it, from first seeing it at birth until it becomes an adult.

Those of you who have read my diary will remember certain incidents in my own childhood: for instance when I came running home to my family, longing to tell them what I had learned, and the supercilious laughter when I explained, as best I could, what my lessons had been. "Oh, how clever you are," I was told, and something snapped shut inside me. This would never happen in a Buddhist family or school that is properly run. However childish the remarks, however silly even, the child will always be treated as if it is a serious human being. As the child gets steadily older the strictness with which it is treated by the teachers increases gradually, but it is never a strictness that is, in any way, derogatory of the child's ability. Even the stupidest child is fully accepted as having the Buddha Nature; it is embraced within the Buddha Mind and never made to feel inferior. "There are some Buddhas that are tall, some short, some fat, some thin, some bright, some stupid," say the scriptures. Unless you can see the Buddha in the little child who comes to you with his "silly" story, as we *great* grown-ups consider it; unless you can see the Buddha in the little boy with his hand in the cookie jar and unless you can see the Buddha when you spank him—and spank him with love and cherish him in your heart whilst doing it—you will not be able to educate the Buddhist child.

Formal education starts the moment the child is first held in his mother's arms. The openness within her heart and within her eyes are the beginning of that formal education. That openness must remain; the full acceptance of the oneness of the mother and child must also be the full acceptance of the oneness of the teacher and pupil. My advice to those who educate anyone is, "Remember, there is no difference between you and the pupil other than that of age. Neither of you possess more than the other; there is only the illusion of knowledge. Unless you understand that mental knowledge is an illusion in the religious sense you will never be able to impart anything whatsoever of real value."

We need to remember that age barriers are created by pride—"I am older than you, therefore I know more than you"; to which the young reply with the words, "We are younger than you and we don't care whether you know more than we do or not because we are younger and have more time to learn." So, by being proud, the old are despised, and so is their knowledge; and, by despising the old, the young are deprived of the passed-down practical wisdom of the ages. If, from the very beginning, education is understood as starting with unselfish conception and then the loving and the cherishing, not only of the child when it is your own, but when it is your pupil, there is no danger whatsoever of there ever being an age barrier and education is seen to be a means of growing together within the Spirit of the Buddhas.

From *On Having No Head*

D. E. Harding

Education is usually concerned with teaching people how to think. Douglas Harding's article suggests that perhaps we should be helping them to stop thinking.

The best day of my life—my rebirthday, so to speak—was when I found I had no head. This is not a literary gambit, a witticism designed to arouse interest at any cost. I mean it in all seriousness: *I have no head.*

It was eighteen years ago, when I was thirty-three, that I made the discovery. Though it certainly came out of the blue, it did so in response to an urgent enquiry; I had for several months been absorbed in the question: what am I? The fact that I happened to be walking in the Himalayas at the time probably had little to do with it; though in that country unusual states of mind are said to come more easily. However that may be, a very still clear day, and a view from the ridge where I stood, over misty blue valleys to the highest mountain range in the world,

From *On Having No Head: A Contribution to Zen in the West,* by D. E. Harding (New York: Harper & Row, Publishers, Inc., 1963), 5-7. Reprinted by permission of The Buddhist Society of London, England.

with Kangchenjunga and Everest unprominent among its snow-peaks, made a setting worthy of the grandest vision.

What actually happened was something absurdly simple and unspectacular: I stopped thinking. A peculiar quiet, an odd kind of alert limpness or numbness, came over me. Reason and imagination and all mental chatter died down. For once, words really failed me. Past and future dropped away. I forgot who and what I was, my name, manhood, animalhood, all that could be called mine. It was as if I had been born that instant, brand new, mindless, innocent of all memories. There existed only the Now, that present moment and what was clearly given in it. To look was enough. And what I found was khaki trouserlegs terminating downwards in a pair of brown shoes, khaki sleeves terminating sideways in a pair of pink hands, and a khaki shirtfront terminating upwards in—absolutely nothing whatever! Certainly not in a head.

It took me no time at all to notice that this nothing, this hole where a head should have been, was no ordinary vacancy, no mere nothing. On the contrary, it was very much occupied. It was a vast emptiness vastly filled, a nothing that found room for everything—room for grass, trees, shadowy distant hills, and far above them snow-peaks like a row of angular clouds riding the blue sky. I had lost a head and gained a world.

It was all, quiet literally, breathtaking. I seemed to stop breathing altogether, absorbed in the Given. Here it was, this superb scene, brightly shining in the clear air, alone and unsupported, mysteriously suspended in the void, and (and *this* was the real miracle, the wonder and delight) utterly free of "me," unstained by any observer. Its total presence was my total absence, body and soul. Lighter than air, clearer than glass, altogether released from myself, I was nowhere around.

Yet in spite of the magical and uncanny quality of this vision, it was no dream, no esoteric revelation. Quite the reverse: it felt like a sudden waking from the sleep of ordinary life, an end to dreaming. It was self-luminous reality for once swept clean of all obscuring mind. It was the revelation, at long last, of the perfectly obvious. It was a lucid moment in a confused life-history. It was a ceasing to ignore something which (since early childhood at any rate) I had always been too busy or too clever to see. It was naked, uncritical attention to what had all along been staring me in the face—my utter facelessness. In short, it was all perfectly simple and plain and straightforward, beyond argument, thought, and words. There arose no questions, no reference beyond the experience itself, but only peace and a quiet joy, and the sensation of having dropped an intolerable burden.

The Joy of Fishes

Chuang Tzu

Thomas Merton, who freely translated this selection, has written: "Chuang Tzu is not concerned with words and formulas about reality, but with the direct existential grasp of reality in itself." The original was written in China about the third or fourth century B.C. As another Taoist teacher put it, "Nothing is gained by speculation. Things are always as they are."

Merton, a Trappist contemplative, was deeply interested in the relationship between Eastern and Western mysticism.

Chuang Tzu and Hui Tzu
Were crossing Hao river
By the dam.

Chuang said:
"See how free
The fishes leap and dart:
That is their happiness."

Hui replied:
"Since you are not a fish
How do you know
What makes fishes happy?"

Chuang said:
"Since you are not I
How can you possibly know
That I do not know
What makes fishes happy?"

Hui argued:
"If I, not being you,
Cannot know what you know
It follows that you
Not being a fish
Cannot know what they know."

Chuang said:
"Wait a minute!
Let us get back
To the original question.
What you asked me was
'How do you know
What makes fishes happy?'
From the terms of your question
You evidently know I know
What makes fishes happy.

"I know the joy of fishes
In the river
Through my own joy, as I go walking
Along the same river."

How Knowledge Was Earned

Idries Shah

The teaching story, used widely as an educational tool in the East, has only recently come to be widely appreciated in the West. Stories such as these are said to speak to students on deeper than ordinary levels.

Once upon a time there was a man who decided that he needed knowledge. He set off to look for it, bending his steps towards the house of a learned man.

When he got there he said: "Sufi, you are a wise man! Let me have a portion of your knowledge, so that I may grow it and become worthwhile, for I feel that I am nothing."

The Sufi said: "I can give you knowledge in exchange for something which I myself need. Go and bring me a small carpet, for I have to give it to someone who will then be able to further our holy work."

So the man went off, looking for someone who could let him have thread. When he arrived at the hut of a spinner-woman, he said to her:

"Spinner-woman, give me thread. I have to have it for the carpet-man, who will give me a carpet which I will give to a Sufi, who will give it to a man who has to do our holy work. In exchange I will get knowledge, which I want."

The woman immediately answered: "You need thread, what about me? Away with this talk about you, and your Sufi and your carpet-man and the man who has to have the carpet. What about me? I need goat-hair to make thread. Get me some and you can have your thread."

So the man went off, until he came to a goat-herd, and he told him his needs. The goat-herd said: "What about me? You need goat-hair to buy knowledge, I need goats to provide the hair. Get me a goat and I shall help you."

So the man went off, looking for someone who sold goats. When he found such a man he told him his difficulties, and the man said: "What do I know about knowledge, or thread or carpets? All I know is that everyone seems to be looking after his own interests. Let us instead talk about my needs, and if you can satisfy them, then we will talk about goats, and you can think about knowledge all you wish."

"What are your needs?" asked the man.

"I need a pen to keep my goats in at night, because they are straying all over the place. Get me one and then talk about your having a goat or two."

So the man went off to look for a pen. His inquiries led him to a carpenter, who said: "Yes, I can make a pen for the man who needs one. As for the rest, you could have spared me the details, for I am just not interested in carpets or knowledge and the like. But I have a desire, and it is in your interests to help me gain it, otherwise I need not help you with your pen."

"And what is that desire?" asked the man.

"I want to get married and nobody will marry me, it seems. See whether you can arrange a wife for me, and then we will talk about your problems."

So the man went off, and after making exhaustive inquiries he found a woman who said: "I know a young woman who has no other desire than to marry just such a carpenter as you describe. In fact she has been thinking about him all her life. It must be some sort of miracle that he does exist and that she can hear of him through you and me. But what about me? Everyone wants what he wants, and people seem to need things, or want things, or imagine that they need help, or really want help, but nobody has yet said anything about *my* needs."

"And what are your needs?" asked the man.

"I want only one thing," said the woman," and I have wanted it all my life. Help me to get it, and you can have anything I have. The thing that I want, as I have experienced everything else, is—knowledge."

"But we cannot have knowledge without a carpet," said the man.

"I do not know what knowledge is, but I am sure that it is not a carpet," said the woman.

"No," said the man, seeing that he had to be patient, "but with the girl for the carpenter we can get the pen for the goats. With the pen for the goats we can get the goat-hair for the spinner. With the goat-hair we can get the thread. With the thread we can get the carpet. With the carpet we can get the knowledge."

"It sounds preposterous to me," said the woman, "and I for one am not going to go to those lengths."

In spite of his entreaties, she sent him away.

These difficulties and the confusion which they caused him first made him almost despair of the human race. He wondered whether he could use knowledge when he got it, and he wondered why all those people were only thinking of their own interests. And slowly he began to think only of the carpet.

One day this man was wandering through the streets of a market-town, muttering to himself.

A certain merchant heard him, and drew near to catch his words. The man was saying: "A carpet is needed to give to a man so that he may be able to do this holy work of ours."

The merchant realized that there was something exceptional about the wanderer, and addressed him:

"Wandering dervish, I do not understand your chant, but I have deep respect for one such as you, who has embarked upon the Path of Truth. Please help me, if you will, for I know that the people of the Sufi way have a special function in society."

The wanderer looked up and saw the distress on the merchant's face and said to him: "I am suffering and I have suffered. You are undoubtedly in trouble, but I have nothing. I cannot even get a piece of thread when I want it. But ask me and I will do anything that I can."

"Know, fortunate man!" said the merchant, "that I have an only and beautiful daughter. She is suffering from an illness which has caused her to languish. Come to her and perhaps you will be able to effect a cure."

Such was the man's distress and so high were his hopes that the wanderer followed him to the girl's bedside.

As soon as she saw him, she said: "I do not know who you are, but I feel you may be able to help me. In any case there is nobody else. I am in love with such-and-such a carpenter." And she named the man whom the traveller had asked to make the pen for the goats.

"Your daughter wants to marry a certain respectable carpenter whom I know," he told the merchant. The merchant was overjoyed, for he had thought that the girl's talk about the carpenter had been the symptom, not the cause, of her disease. He had, in fact, thought her mad.

The traveller went to the carpenter, who built the pen for the goats. The goat-seller presented him with some fine animals; he took them to the goat-herd, who gave him goat-hair, which he took to the spinner, who gave him thread. Then he took the thread to the carpet-seller, who gave him a small carpet.

This carpet he carried back to the Sufi. When he arrived at the house of the wise man, the latter said to him: "Now I can give you knowledge; for you could not have brought this carpet unless you had worked for the carpet, and not for yourself."

Sources and Resources

AHSEN, AHKTER, *Eidetic Behavior*. Yonkers, N.Y. Eidetic Publishing House, 1973.

———*Basic Concepts in Eidetic Psychotherapy*. New York: Branden House, 1973.

AMERICAN SOCIETY for PSYCHICAL RESEARCH, "Courses and other Study Opportunities in Parapsychology," November 1974 (revised periodically), $2.00, 5 West 73rd Street, New York, N.Y. 10023.

ANASTASIOW, NICHOLAS, "Updating Intellectual Growth in Children and Bioplasmic Forces," *Phi Delta Kappan*, 55, no. 8, (April 1974), pp. 561-62.

ANDERSON, MARGARET, and RHEA WHITE, "ESP Score Level In Relation to Students' Attitude Toward Teacher-Agents Acting Simultaneously," *Journal of Parapsychology*, 22, pp. 20–28, 1958.

ARONS, HARRY, *Hypnosis for Speeding Up the Learning Process*. Irvington, N.J.: Power Publishers, Inc., 1974.

ASSAGIOLI, ROBERTO, "The Education of Gifted and Super-Gifted Children." New York: Psychosynthesis Research Foundation, 1960.

ASTOR, MARTIN, "Learning Through Hypnosis," *Educational Forum,* May 1971, pp. 447-55.

———"Transpersonal Approaches to Counseling," *Personnel and Guidance Journal*, 50, no. 2, pp. 801–8, 1972.

———"Transpersonal Counseling as a Form of Transcendental Education," *Counseling and Values*, 19, no. 2, (February, 1975), pp. 75–82.

BARLOW, W., "Psychosomatic Problems in Postural Re-education," *The Lancet,* September 24, 1955, pp. 659–64.

BERGER, E., "Zen Buddhism, General Psychology, and Counseling Psychology," *Journal of Counseling Psychology*, 9, (1962), pp. 122–127.

BIOFEEDBACK RESEARCH SOCIETY, *Biofeedback and Self-Regulation*, $6.50, Francine Butler, Executive Secretary, BRS, University of Colorado Medical College, C-268, 4200 E. Ninth Avenue, Denver, Colorado 80220. First published in 1973, contains a 113-page paperback of 800 references representing 850 authors.

BONNY, HELEN, *Creative Listening, Vol. 1: Music and Imagination Experiences for Children* (stereo record). Baltimore, Md.: Institute for Consciousness and Music, 1973.

BONNY, HELEN, *Creative Listening, Vol. 2: Dancing Around the World and Surprise Journey*. Baltimore, Md.: Institute for Consciousness and Music, 1975.

BONNY, HELEN and LOUIS SAVARY, *Music and Your Mind: Listening With a New Consciousness*. New York: Harper & Row, 1973.

BRUNER, JEROME, *On Knowing: Essays for the Left Hand*. New York: Atheneum, 1975.

CHRISTENSEN, J. A., "Cosmic Consciousness," *Media & Methods,* 11, no. 6, (February 1975), pp. 18-21.

CLARK, FRANCES V., "Rediscovering Transpersonal Education," *Journal of Transpersonal Psychology,* 6, no. 1, (1974), pp. 1-7.

———, "Fantasy and Imagination," in *Four Psychologies Applied to Education: Freudian, Behavioral, Humanistic, Transpersonal.* ed. T. B. Roberts, Cambridge, Mass.: Schenkman Publishing Co., 1975 C.

COLLIER, R. W., "The Effect of Transcendental Meditation Upon University Academic Attainment," Proceedings of the Pacific Northwest Conference on Foreign Languages, in press.

COUNSELING and VALUES, February 1975, whole number is on transpersonal counseling.

CRAMPTON, MARTHA, "Some Applications of Psychosynthesis in the Educational Field," speech before the Psychosynthesis Seminars 1971-72 series. Published by Psychosynthesis Research Foundation, New York, 1972. Also see entry 1975 C in this list for Thomas B. Roberts.

CRISWELL, ELEANOR, "Experimental Yoga Course for College Students: A Progress Report," *Journal of Transpersonal Psychology,* 2, no. 1, (1970), pp. 71-78.

DANSKIN, D. G., and E. D. WALTERS, "Biofeedback and Voluntary Self-Regulation Counseling and Education," *Personnel and Guidance Journal,* 51, no. 9, (1973), pp. 633-638.

———, "Biofeedback Training as Counseling," *Counseling and Values,* 19, no. 2, (February 1975), pp. 116-22.

DILLEY, JOSIAH S., "Mental Imagery," *Counseling and Values,* 19, no. 2, (February 1975), pp. 110-15.

DOWNING, GEORGE, *The Massage Book.* Berkeley: Bookworks (distributed by Random House), 1972.

DOWNING, JACK, *Dreams and Nightmares.* New York: Harper & Row, 1973.

DRISCOLL, FRANCIS, "TM as a Secondary School Subject," *Phi Delta Kappan,* 54, no. 4, (December 1972), pp. 236-37. Also see entry 1975 C in this list for Thomas B. Roberts.

EGAN, RICHARD M. and WILLIAM, "The Effect of Hypnosis on Academic Performance," *The American Journal of Clinical Hypnosis,* (July 1968), pp. 31-34.

EHRENWALD, JAN, "The Occult," *Today's Education,* 60, no. 6 (September 1971), 28-30.

ELLIOT, JAMES, "ESP and Relaxation," *Personal Growth,* no. 21 (1974), pp. 13-17, P. O. Box 1254, Berkeley, Calif. 94701.

EVANS-WENTZ, W., *Tibetan Yoga and Secret Doctrines.* New York: Oxford University Press, 1935.

FARADAY, ANNE., *Dream Power.* New York: Coward, McCann & Geoghegan, 1972.

———, *The Dream Game.* New York: Coward, McCann & Geoghegan, 1975.

FELDENKRAIS, MOSHE, *Awareness Through Movement.* New York: Harper & Row, 1972.

————, *Body and Mature Behavior.* New York: International Universities Press, 1970.

FENG, GIA-FU and H. WILKERSON, *Tai-Chi: A Way of Centering.* New York: Macmillan, Collier Books, 1969.

FREYBERG, JOAN T., "Increasing Children's Fantasies: Hold High the Cardboard Sword," *Psychology Today,* 8, no. 9 (February 1975), pp. 63–64, 120.

Fundamentals of Progress: Scientific Research on Transcendental Meditation. Los Angeles: Maharishi International University, 1974.

GALLWEY, W. TIMOTHY, *The Inner Game of Tennis.* New York: Random House, 1974.

GOLAS, THADDEUS, *The Lazy Man's Guide to Enlightenment.* Palo Alto: The Seed Center, 1972.

GOVINDA, LAMA, *Way of the White Cloud.* Berkeley: Shambala Publications, 1971.

GREEN, ELMER E., ALYCE M. GREEN, E. DALE WALTERS, "Voluntary Control of Internal States: Psychological and Physiological," *The Journal of Transpersonal Psychology,* 2, no. 1, (1970), pp. 1–26.

GREEN, ELMER E., and ALYCE M, "The Ins and Outs of Mind-Body Energy," *Science Year, 1974: World Book Science Annual,* Chicago: Field Enterprises Educational Corp., 1974. Also in Roberts, 1975.

GUNTHER, BERNARD, *Sense Relaxation.* New York: Macmillan, Collier Books, 1968.

HAIGHT, M., and G. JAMPOLSKY, "An Experience with Biofeedback in a Public High School," *Journal of Bio-feedback,* (Winter 1974).

HEATON, D. P., and D. ORME-JOHNSON, "Influence of Transcendental Meditation on Grade Point Average: Initial Findings," in Orme-Johnson, D. W. L. Dumash, and J. Farrow (eds.), *Scientific Research on Transcendental Meditation: Collected Papers & Vol. I.* Los Angeles: Maharishi International University Press, 1975.

HENDRICKS, GAY, and RUSSEL WILLS, *The Centering Book: Awareness Activities for Children, Parents, and Teachers.* Englewood Cliffs, N.J.: Prentice-Hall, Inc., Spectrum Books, 1975.

HIGGINS, JAMES E., *Mystical Fancy in Children's Literature.* New York: Teacher's College Press, Columbia University, 1970.

HOLT, JOHN, *Escape from Childhood.* New York: E. P. Dutton, 1974.

HOUSTON, JEAN, "Putting the First Man on Earth," *Saturday Review,* February 22, 1975, pp. 28–32, 53.

HUANG, AL, *Embrace Tiger, Return to Mountain.* Moab, Utah: Real People Press, 1973.

HUXLEY, ALDOUS, "Education on the Nonverbal Level," *Daedalus,* Spring 1962. Also in *Contemporary Educational Psychology,* ed. Richard M. Jones. New York: Harper & Row, 1967.

————, Introduction to *The Perennial Philosophy* Cleveland: World Publishing Co., Meridan Books, pp. iv–viii, 1968.

————, *Island.* New York: Harper & Row, 1972.

IYENGAR, B. K. S., *Light on Yoga.* New York: Schocken Books, 1966.

JACOBSON, E. O., *You Must Relax.* New York: McGraw-Hill, 1957.

————, *Anxiety and Tension Control.* Philadelphia: Lippincott, 1964.

JONES, RICHARD M., "Involving Fantasies and Feelings," in *Facts and Feelings in the Classroom,* Louis J. Rubin. New York: Viking, Compass Books, 1973, pp. 171-92.

KANELLAKOS, DEMETRI P., *The Psychobiology of Transcendental Meditation: An Annotated Bibliography,* Los Angeles: Maharishi International University, Spring 1973.

KANTOR, ROBERT, "The Affective Domain and Beyond," *Journal for the Study of Consciousness,* 3, no. 1 (January–June 1970), pp. 20–42. Also in Roberts, 1975 C.

KATZ, RICHARD, "Education for Transcendence," in *Preludes for Growth,* pp. 206–24. New York: Free Press, 1973.

KELEMAN, STANLEY, *Bio-Energetic Concepts of Grounding.* San Francisco: Lodestar Press, 1970.

KENNETT, JIYU, *Selling Water by the River.* New York: Random House, Vintage Books, 1972.

KRIPPNER, STANLEY, "Parapsychology and Education," *Journal of Humanistic Psychology,* 13, no. 4 (Fall 1973), pp. 17-20. Excerpt from "Humanistic Psychology and Parapsychology," pp. 3-24. Also in Roberts, 1975 C.

KRISHNAMURTI, JIDDU, *Education and the Significance of Life.* New York: Harper & Row, 1953.

LAGERWERFF, E. B., and K. A. PERLROTH MENSENDIECK, *Your Posture and Your Pain.* Garden City, New York: Doubleday, Anchor Books, 1973.

LANGFORD, CRICKET, *Meditation for Little People.* Novato, Calif.: Inner Light Foundation, 1974.

LEONARD, GEORGE, "The Human Potential," in *Education and Ecstasy,* Chapter 2, pp. 23–50. New York: Delacorte Press, 1968.

LESH, TERRY V., "Zen Meditation and the Development of Empathy in Counselors," *Journal of Humanistic Psychology,* 10, no. 1 (Spring 1970), pp. 39-74. Also in Roberts, 1975 C.

LESHAN, LAWRENCE, *How To Meditate: A Guide to Self-Discovery.* Boston: Little, Brown, 1974.

————, *The Medium, The Mystic, and the Physicist.* New York: Random House, Ballantine Books, 1975.

LINDEN, WILLIAM, "The Relation Between the Practice of Meditation by School Children and Their Levels of Field Dependence-Independence, Text Anxiety and Reading Achievement," *Journal of Consulting and Clinical Psychology,* 41, no. 1, (August 1973), pp. 139–43.

LOWEN, ALEXANDER, *The Betrayal of the Body.* New York: Macmillan, 1967.

LUCE, GAY G., *Body Time.* New York: Pantheon, 1971.

LUK, C., *The Secrets of Chinese Meditation.* London: Rider, 1964.

MCCONNELL, R. A., "ESP and Credibility in Science" *The American Psychologist,* 24, (1969), pp. 531–38.

MCKIM, ROBERT H., *Experiences in Visual Thinking,* ERIC, ED-073-690. Monterey, Calif: Brooks/Cole, 1972.

MASLOW, ABRAHAM, "Lessons From the Peak-Experiences," *Journal of Humanistic Psychology,* 2, no. 2, (1962), pp. 9–18.

————, *The Farther Reaches of Human Nature.* New York: Viking, 1971.

MASTERS, ROBERT., and J. HOUSTON, *Mind Games.* New York: Viking, 1972.

MAUPIN, EDWARD W., "Zen Buddhism: A Psychological Review," *Journal of Counseling Psychology,* 26, (1962), pp. 362–78, No month of publication available.

MORRIS, FREIDA, *Self-Hypnosis in Two Days.* Berkeley: Intergalactic Publishing Co., 1974.

MURPHY, MICHAEL, "Education for Transcendence," *Journal of Transpersonal Psychology,* 1, no. 1, (Spring 1969), pp. 21–32. Also in Roberts, 1975.

————, *Golf in the Kingdom.* New York: Viking, 1972.

MUSES, CHARLES, "Taint Necessarily So: A New Look at Education," *Journal for the Study of Consciousness,* 4, no. 2, (1971), pp. 101–4.

NARANJO, CLAUDIO, "The Oneness of Experience in the Ways of Growth," from *The One Quest,* pp. 123–28. New York: Viking, 1973.

NARANJO, CLAUDIO, and ROBERT ORNSTEIN, *On The Psychology of Meditation.* New York: Viking, 1971.

NORDBERG, R. B., *The Teenager and the New Mysticism.* New York: Richards Rosen Press, 1973.

————, "Paths to Mysticism in the 1970's," *Counseling and Values,* 17, no. 3, (1973), pp. 167–75.

————, "Meditation: Future Vehicle for Career Exploration," *Vocational Guidance Quarterly,* 22, (June 1974), 267–71.

————, "Mysticism—Its Implications for Helping Relationships," *Counseling and Values,* 19, no. 2, (February 1975), pp. 99–109.

OGLETREE, EARL J., "Rudolf Steiner: Unknown Educator," *Elementary School Journal,* 74, no. 6, (March 1974), pp. 344–52.

ORME-JOHNSON, D. W., L. DOMASH, and J. FARROW (eds), *Scientific Research on Transcendental Meditation: Collected Papers, Vol. 1.* Los Angeles: Maharishi International University Press, 1975.

ORNSTEIN, ROBERT E., "The Education of the Intuitive Mode," in *The Psychology of Consciousness.* Chapter 7, pp. 143–79, San Francisco: W. H. Freeman, 1972.

OSTRANDER, SHIELA, and LYNN SCHROEDER, "Artificial Reincarnation," in *Psychic Discoveries Behind the Iron Curtain,* Chapter 12, pp. 146–59, New York: Bantam Books, 1971. Also in Roberts, 1975 C.

PEARCE, JOSEPH, *The Crack in the Cosmic Egg.* New York: Simon & Schuster, Pocket Books, 1973.

———, *Exploring the Crack in the Cosmic Egg,* New York: Julian Press, 1974.

PEERBOLTE, M., "Meditation for School Children," *Main Currents in Modern Thought,* 24, (1967), pp. 19–21.

PIAGET, JEAN, *The Construction of Reality in the Child.* New York: Ballantine, 1954.

PULVINO, CHARLES J., and JAMES L. LEE, "Counseling According to Don Juan," *Counseling and Values,* 19, no. 2, (February 1975), pp. 125–30.

RAPPAPORT, BERNARD S., "Carnal Knowledge: What the Wisdom of the Body Has to Offer Psychotherapy," *Journal of Humanistic Psychology,* 15, no. 1 (Winter 1975), pp. 49–70.

REPS, PAUL, *Be! New Uses for the Human Instrument.* New York: Weatherhill, 1971.

RICHARD, MICHAEL, "Attention Training: A Pilot Program in the Development of Autonomic Control," *Contemporary Education,* 43, no. 3, (January 1972), pp. 57–60.

RICHARDS, MARY C., *Centering.* Middletown, Conn.: Wesleyan University Press, 1969.

ROBERTS, THOMAS B., "Transpersonal: The New Educational Psychology," *Phi Delta Kappan,* (November 1974), pp. 191–93.

———, *Transpersonal: The New Educational Psychology,* ERIC ED-099-252, April 1975 A.

ROBERTS, THOMAS B. (ed)., "Transpersonal Psychology Applied to Education," Section IV of *Four Psychologies Applied to Education,* pp. 392–550. Cambridge, Mass.: Schenkman Publishing Co., 1975 C.

ROBERTS, THOMAS B., and FRANCES V. CLARK, *Transpersonal Psychology in Education,* Fastback Pamphlet Series #53 (April 1975). Bloomington, Ind.: Phi Delta Kappa Educational Foundation. B.

ROLF, IDA P., "Structural Integration," *Journal of the Institute for the Comparative Study of History, Philosophy and the Sciences,* 1, no. 1 (June 1963), pp. 56–57.

SAMPLES, ROBERT E., "Kari's Handicap: The Impediment of Creativity," *The Saturday Review,* July 1967, pp. 56–57.

———, *Opening: A Primer for Self-Actualization,* Menlo Park, Calif.: Addison-Wesley, 1973.

———, "Learning With the Whole Brain," *Human Behavior,* 4, (February 1975), pp. 16–23, 79.

———, "Are You Teaching Only One Side of the Brain?", *Learning,* (February 1975), pp. 25–28.

SAMUELS, MICHAEL., and HAL BENNETT, *The Well Body Book.* New York: Random House, 1973.

SATURDAY REVIEW, February 22, 1975. The entire issue is devoted to transpersonal psychology.

SCHULTZ, J. H., and W. LUTHE, *Autogenic Training: A Psychophysiological Approach to Psychotherapy.* New York: Grune & Stratton, 1959.

SEEMAN, WILLIAM, SANFORD, NIDICH, and THOMAS BANTA, "Influence of Transcendental Meditation on a Measure of Self-Actualization," *Journal of Counseling Psychology,* 19, no. 3, (1972), pp. 184–187.

SHAH, IDRIES., *Caravan of Dreams.* London: Octagon Press, 1968.

———, *The Pleasantries of the Incredible Mulla Nasrudin.* London: Jonathan Cape, 1968.

———, *The Dermis Probe.* London: Jonathan Cape, 1970.

SINGER, JEROME, *Daydreaming.* New York: Random House, 1966.

SKOVHOLT, T. M., and R. W. HOENNINGER, "Guided Fantasy in Career Counseling," *Personnel and Guidance Journal,* 52, no. 10, (1974), pp. 693–96.

SOBEL, DAVID, and F. HORNBACHER, *An Everyday Guide to Your Health.* New York: Grossman Publishers, 1973.

SPOLIN, VIOLA, *Improvisations for the Theatre.* Evanston, Ill.: Northwestern University Press, 1963.

TRUNGPA, C., *Meditation in Action.* Berkeley: Shambala Publications, 1969.

WEIL, ANDREW, *The Natural Mind: A New Way of Looking at Drugs and the Higher Consciousness,* pp. 19–25 and 30–37, Boston: Houghton Mifflin, 1972.

WHITE, JOHN (ed.), *What Is Meditation?* Garden City, N.Y.: Doubleday, Anchor Books, 1974.

WOLPE, J., and A. LAZARUS, *Behavior Therapy Techniques.* Long Island City, N.Y.: Pergamon Press, 1966.

WOODS, RALPH L., and HERBERT B. GREENHOUSE, *The New World of Dreams.* New York: Macmillan, 1974.

ZIEGENFUSS, BEATRICE W., "Hypnosis: A Tool for Education," *Education,* (April 1962), pp. 505–7.